QUANTUM VIBE

Volume 1 — Ni...

Written & Drawn ...

Scott Bieser

Art assistance:

Zeke Bieser

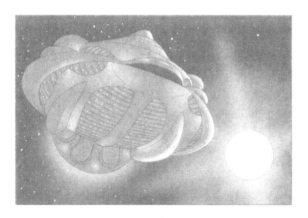

BIG HEAD PRESS ®

"Thoughtful Stories"

QUANTUM VIBE
Volume 1: Nicole

Cover illustration and design by Scott Bieser

Published by Big Head Press
P.O. Box 1853
Round Rock, TX 78680
www.bigheadpress.com

This is a work of fiction. Any resemblance of characters herein to any actual characters, living or dead, are most likely a silly attempt at parody. Please pay it no mind.

Contents were previously published on the World Wide Web at http://www.quantumvibe.com.

ISBN: 978-0-9853167-4-7

Dedication

This book is dedicated in loving memory to
Eva Jeanne Bieser

Who discorporated in December, 2012 C.E.

Her warmth and humor will be remembered, and sorely missed,
by all who had the good fortune to know her.

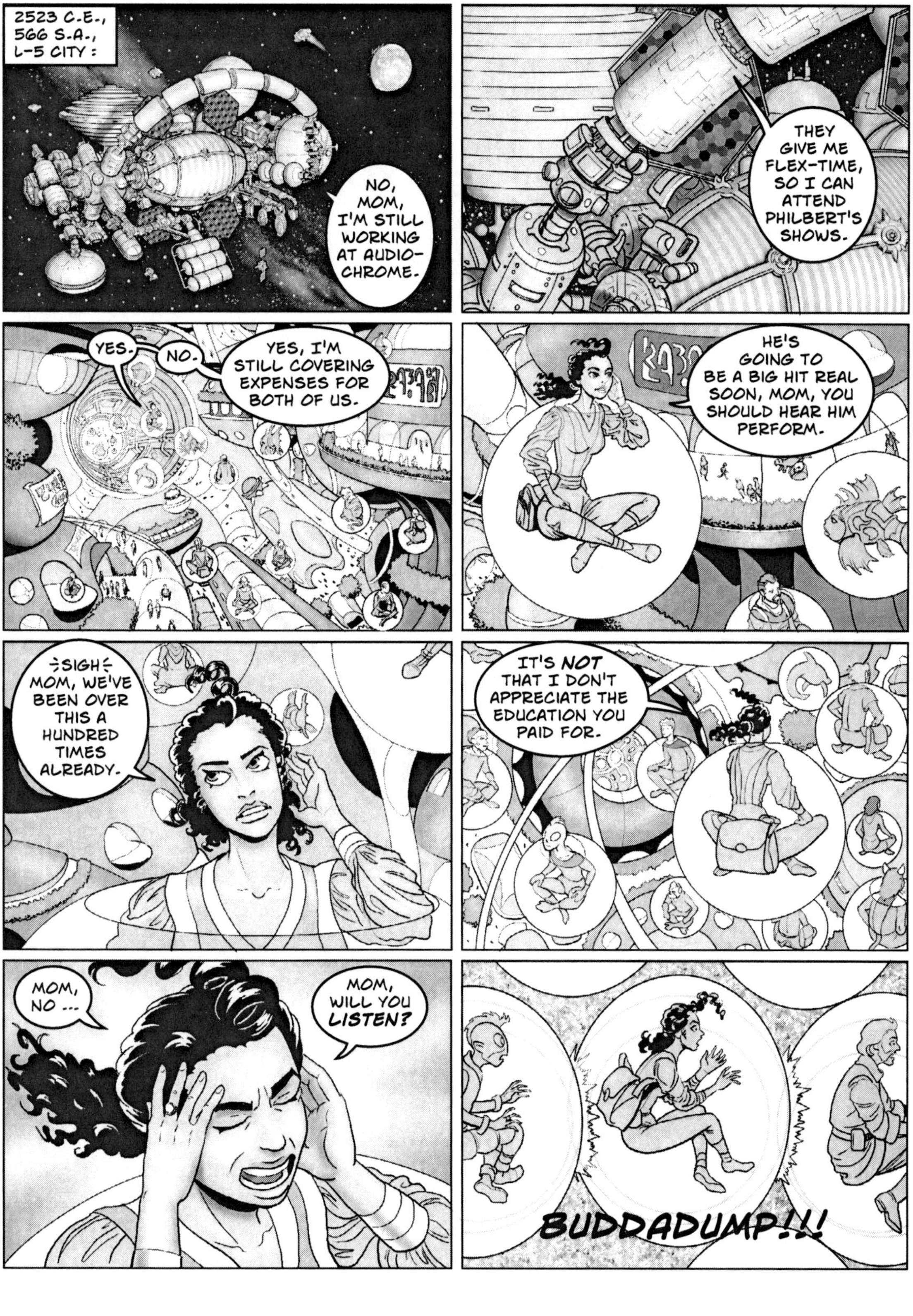
2523 C.E., 566 S.A., L-5 CITY :
NO, MOM, I'M STILL WORKING AT AUDIO-CHROME.
THEY GIVE ME FLEX-TIME, SO I CAN ATTEND PHILBERT'S SHOWS.
YES.
NO.
YES, I'M STILL COVERING EXPENSES FOR BOTH OF US.
HE'S GOING TO BE A BIG HIT REAL SOON, MOM, YOU SHOULD HEAR HIM PERFORM.
÷SIGH÷ MOM, WE'VE BEEN OVER THIS A HUNDRED TIMES ALREADY.
IT'S *NOT* THAT I DON'T APPRECIATE THE EDUCATION YOU PAID FOR.
MOM, NO ...
MOM, WILL YOU *LISTEN?*
BUDDADUMP!!!

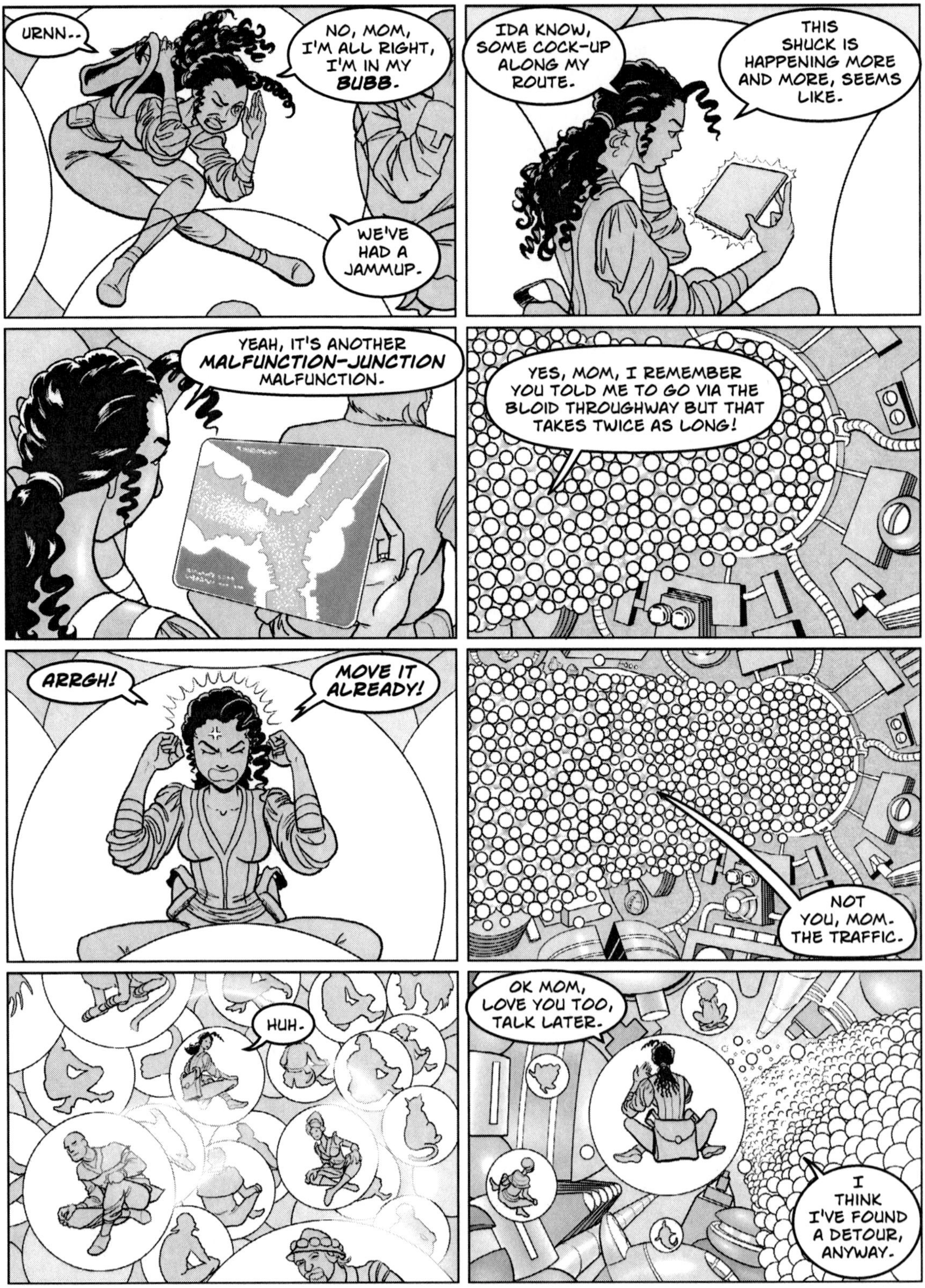
URNN..
NO, MOM, I'M ALL RIGHT, I'M IN MY BUBB.
WE'VE HAD A JAMMUP.
IDA KNOW, SOME COCK-UP ALONG MY ROUTE.
THIS SHUCK IS HAPPENING MORE AND MORE, SEEMS LIKE.
YEAH, IT'S ANOTHER MALFUNCTION-JUNCTION MALFUNCTION.
YES, MOM, I REMEMBER YOU TOLD ME TO GO VIA THE BLOID THROUGHWAY BUT THAT TAKES TWICE AS LONG!
ARRGH!
MOVE IT ALREADY!
NOT YOU, MOM. THE TRAFFIC.
HUH.
OK MOM, LOVE YOU TOO, TALK LATER.
I THINK I'VE FOUND A DETOUR, ANYWAY.

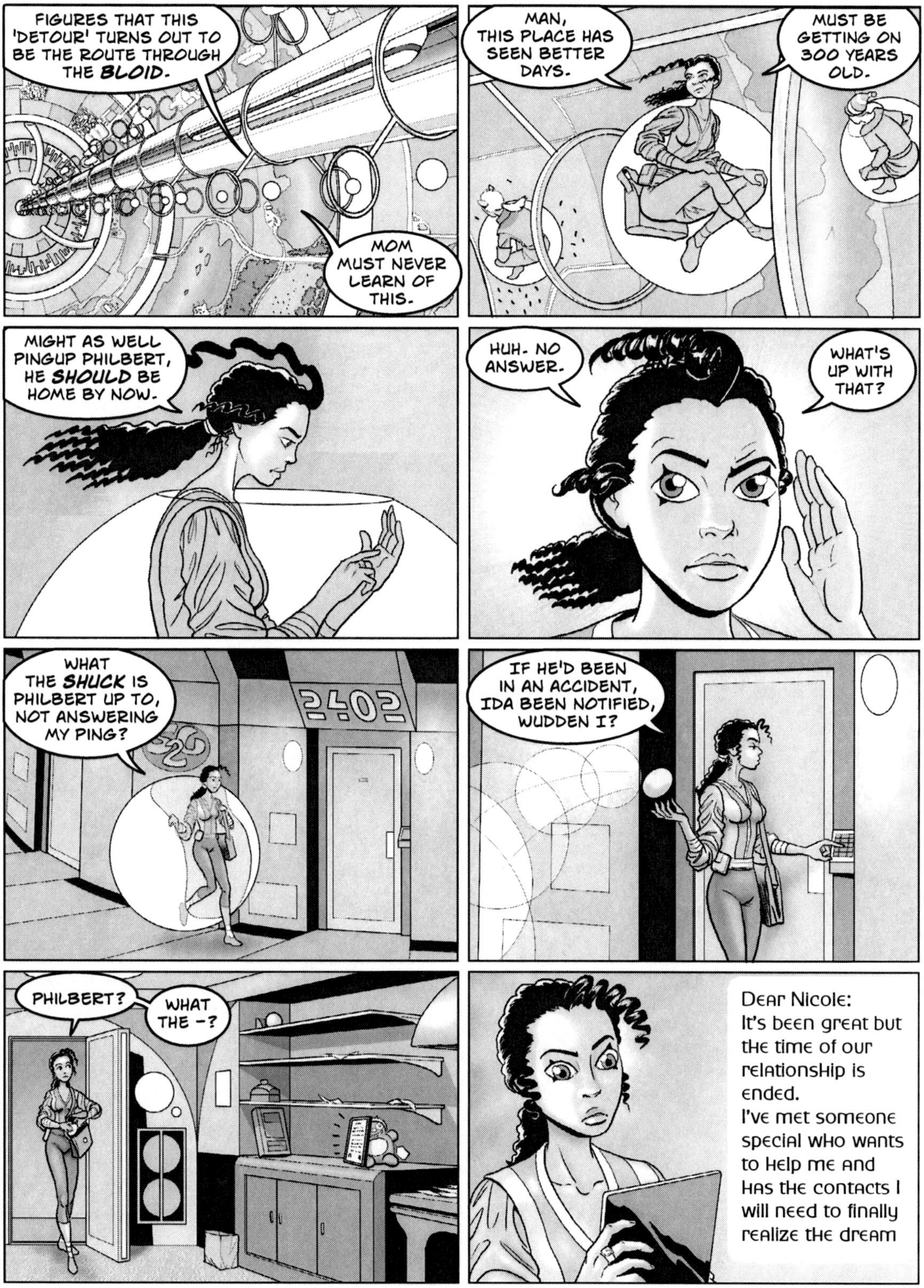
FIGURES THAT THIS 'DETOUR' TURNS OUT TO BE THE ROUTE THROUGH THE BLOID.
MOM MUST NEVER LEARN OF THIS.
MAN, THIS PLACE HAS SEEN BETTER DAYS.
MUST BE GETTING ON 300 YEARS OLD.
MIGHT AS WELL PINGUP PHILBERT, HE SHOULD BE HOME BY NOW.
HUH. NO ANSWER.
WHAT'S UP WITH THAT?
WHAT THE SHUCK IS PHILBERT UP TO, NOT ANSWERING MY PING?
2402
IF HE'D BEEN IN AN ACCIDENT, IDA BEEN NOTIFIED, WUDDEN I?
PHILBERT?
WHAT THE -?
Dear Nicole:
It's been great but the time of our relationship is ended.
I've met someone special who wants to help me and has the contacts I will need to finally realize the dream

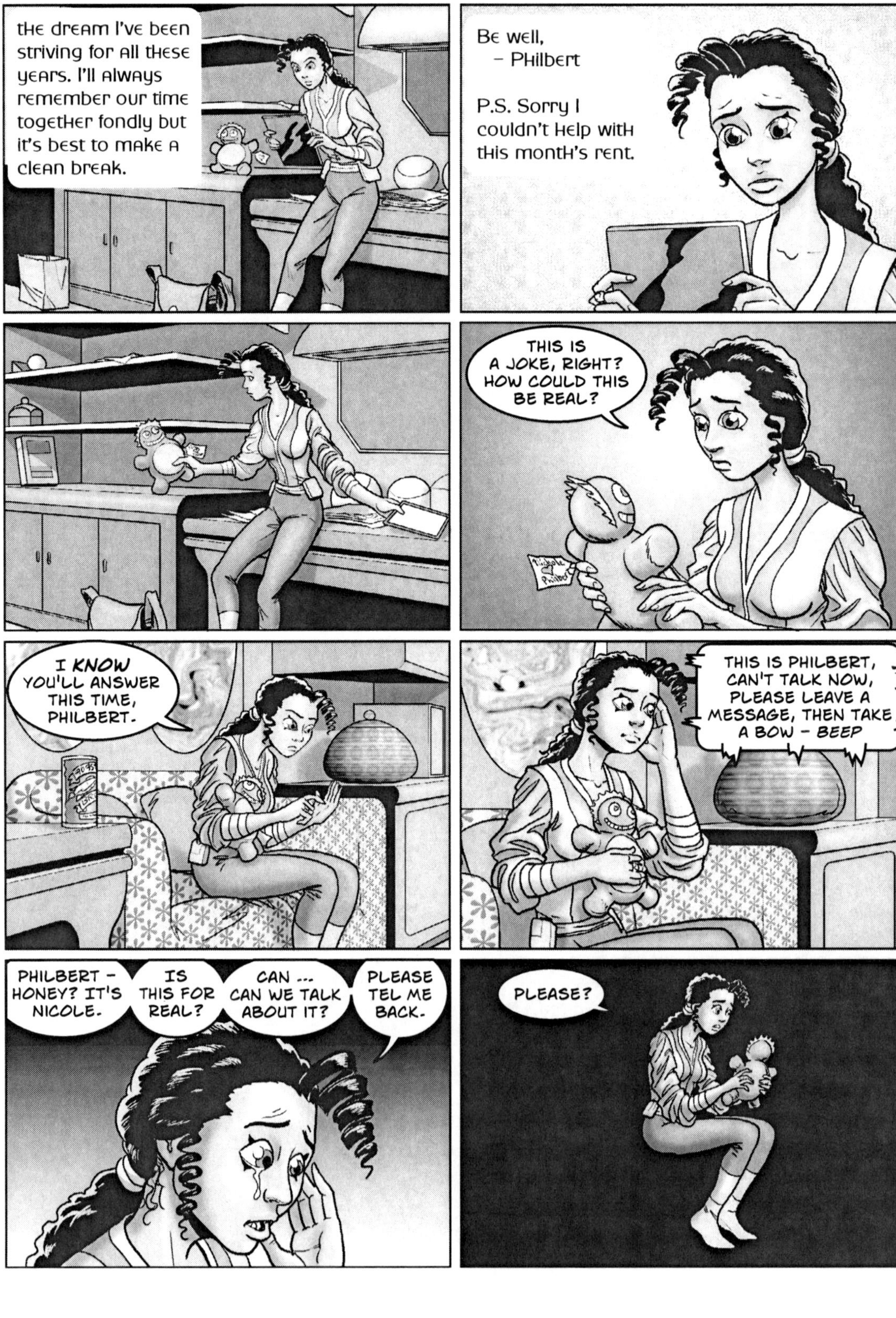
the dream I've been striving for all these years. I'll always remember our time together fondly but it's best to make a clean break.
Be well,
– Philbert
P.S. Sorry I couldn't help with this month's rent.
THIS IS A JOKE, RIGHT? HOW COULD THIS BE REAL?
I KNOW YOU'LL ANSWER THIS TIME, PHILBERT.
THIS IS PHILBERT, CAN'T TALK NOW, PLEASE LEAVE A MESSAGE, THEN TAKE A BOW – BEEP
PHILBERT – HONEY? IT'S NICOLE.
IS THIS FOR REAL?
CAN ... CAN WE TALK ABOUT IT?
PLEASE TEL ME BACK.
PLEASE?

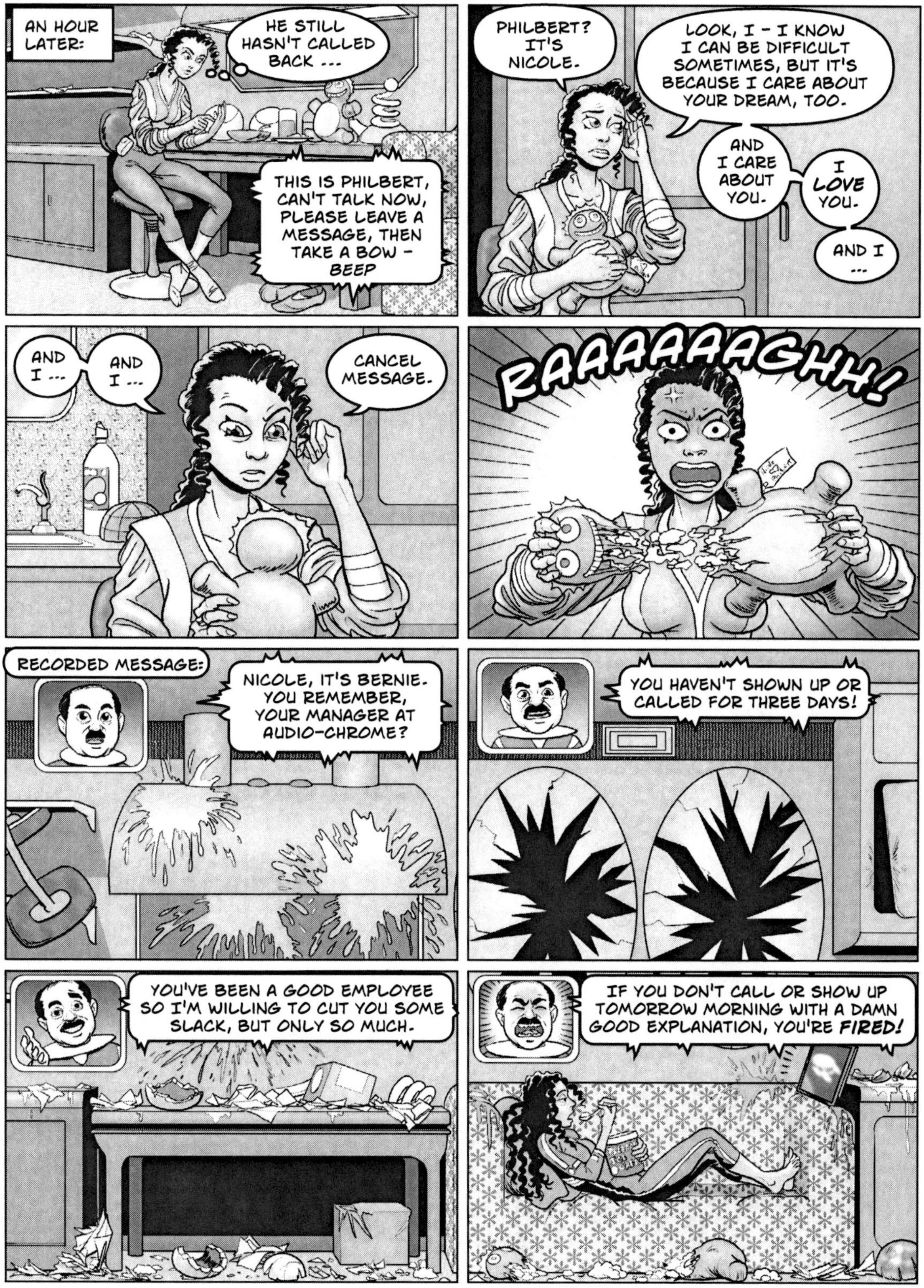
AN HOUR LATER:
HE STILL HASN'T CALLED BACK ...
THIS IS PHILBERT, CAN'T TALK NOW, PLEASE LEAVE A MESSAGE, THEN TAKE A BOW - BEEP
PHILBERT? IT'S NICOLE.
LOOK, I - I KNOW I CAN BE DIFFICULT SOMETIMES, BUT IT'S BECAUSE I CARE ABOUT YOUR DREAM, TOO.
AND I CARE ABOUT YOU.
I LOVE YOU.
AND I ...
AND I ...
AND I ...
CANCEL MESSAGE.
RAAAAAAAGHH!
RECORDED MESSAGE:
NICOLE, IT'S BERNIE. YOU REMEMBER, YOUR MANAGER AT AUDIO-CHROME?
YOU HAVEN'T SHOWN UP OR CALLED FOR THREE DAYS!
YOU'VE BEEN A GOOD EMPLOYEE SO I'M WILLING TO CUT YOU SOME SLACK, BUT ONLY SO MUCH.
IF YOU DON'T CALL OR SHOW UP TOMORROW MORNING WITH A DAMN GOOD EXPLANATION, YOU'RE FIRED!

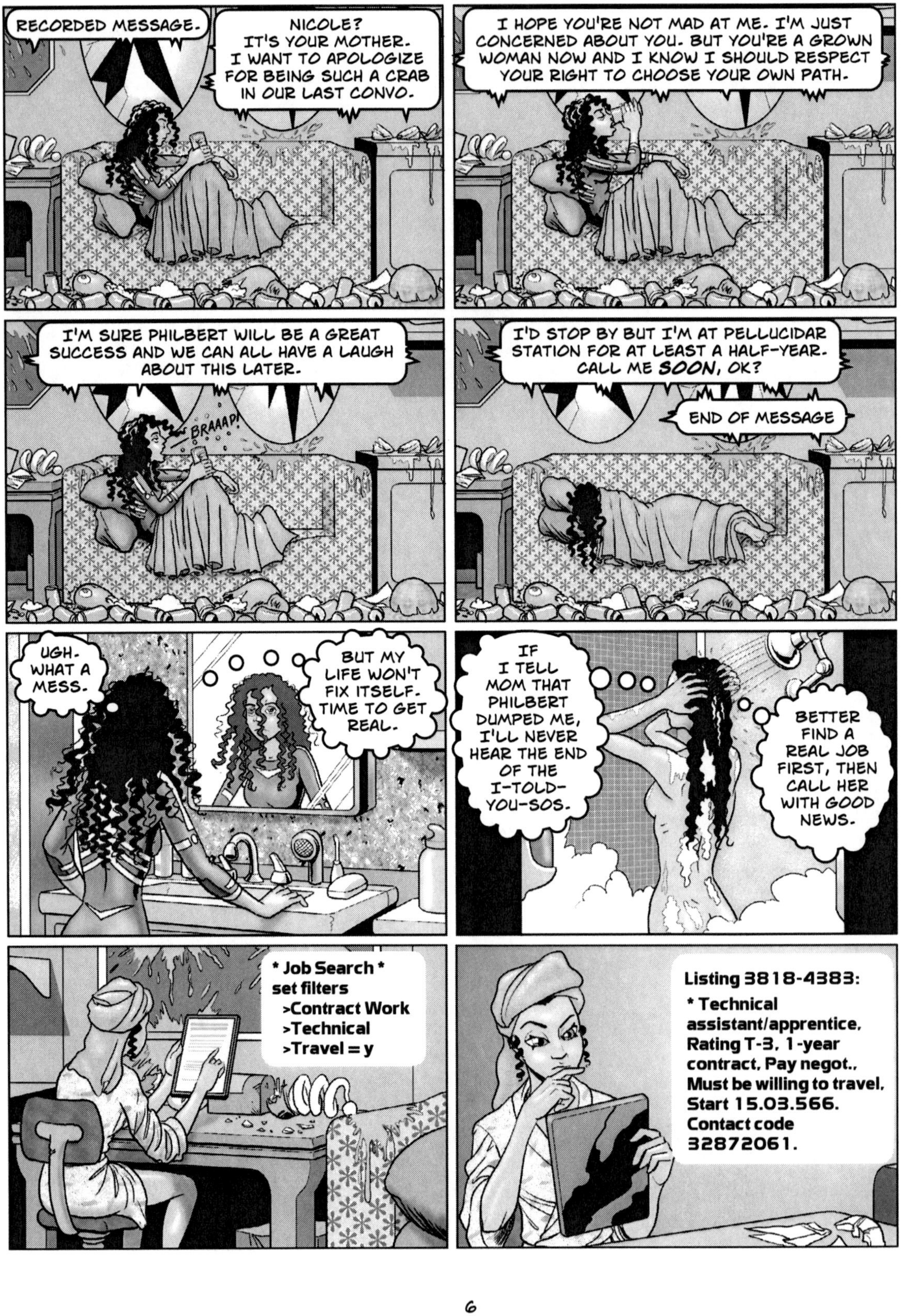
RECORDED MESSAGE.
NICOLE? IT'S YOUR MOTHER. I WANT TO APOLOGIZE FOR BEING SUCH A CRAB IN OUR LAST CONVO.
I HOPE YOU'RE NOT MAD AT ME. I'M JUST CONCERNED ABOUT YOU. BUT YOU'RE A GROWN WOMAN NOW AND I KNOW I SHOULD RESPECT YOUR RIGHT TO CHOOSE YOUR OWN PATH.
I'M SURE PHILBERT WILL BE A GREAT SUCCESS AND WE CAN ALL HAVE A LAUGH ABOUT THIS LATER.
BRAAAP!
I'D STOP BY BUT I'M AT PELLUCIDAR STATION FOR AT LEAST A HALF-YEAR. CALL ME SOON, OK?
END OF MESSAGE
UGH. WHAT A MESS.
BUT MY LIFE WON'T FIX ITSELF. TIME TO GET REAL.
IF I TELL MOM THAT PHILBERT DUMPED ME, I'LL NEVER HEAR THE END OF THE I-TOLD-YOU-SOS.
BETTER FIND A REAL JOB FIRST, THEN CALL HER WITH GOOD NEWS.
* Job Search *
set filters
>Contract Work
>Technical
>Travel = y
Listing 3818-4383:
* Technical assistant/apprentice, Rating T-3, 1-year contract, Pay negot., Must be willing to travel. Start 15.03.566. Contact code 32872061.

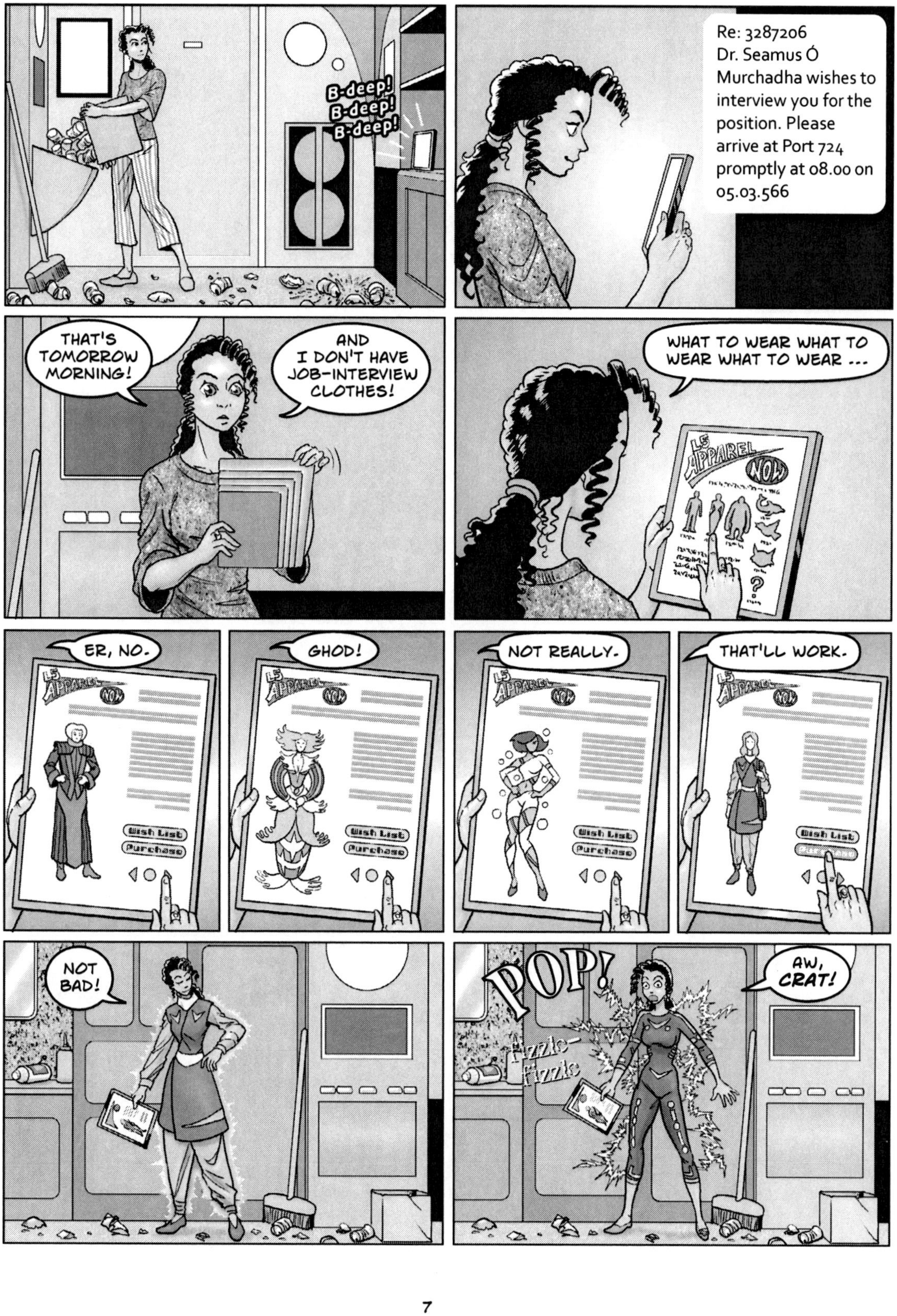
B-deep!
B-deep!
B-deep!
Re: 3287206
Dr. Seamus Ó Murchadha wishes to interview you for the position. Please arrive at Port 724 promptly at 08.00 on 05.03.566
THAT'S TOMORROW MORNING!
AND I DON'T HAVE JOB-INTERVIEW CLOTHES!
WHAT TO WEAR WHAT TO WEAR WHAT TO WEAR ...
L5 APPAREL NOW
ER, NO.
Wish List
Purchase
GHOD!
NOT REALLY.
THAT'LL WORK.
NOT BAD!
POP!
Fizzle-Fizzle
AW, CRAT!

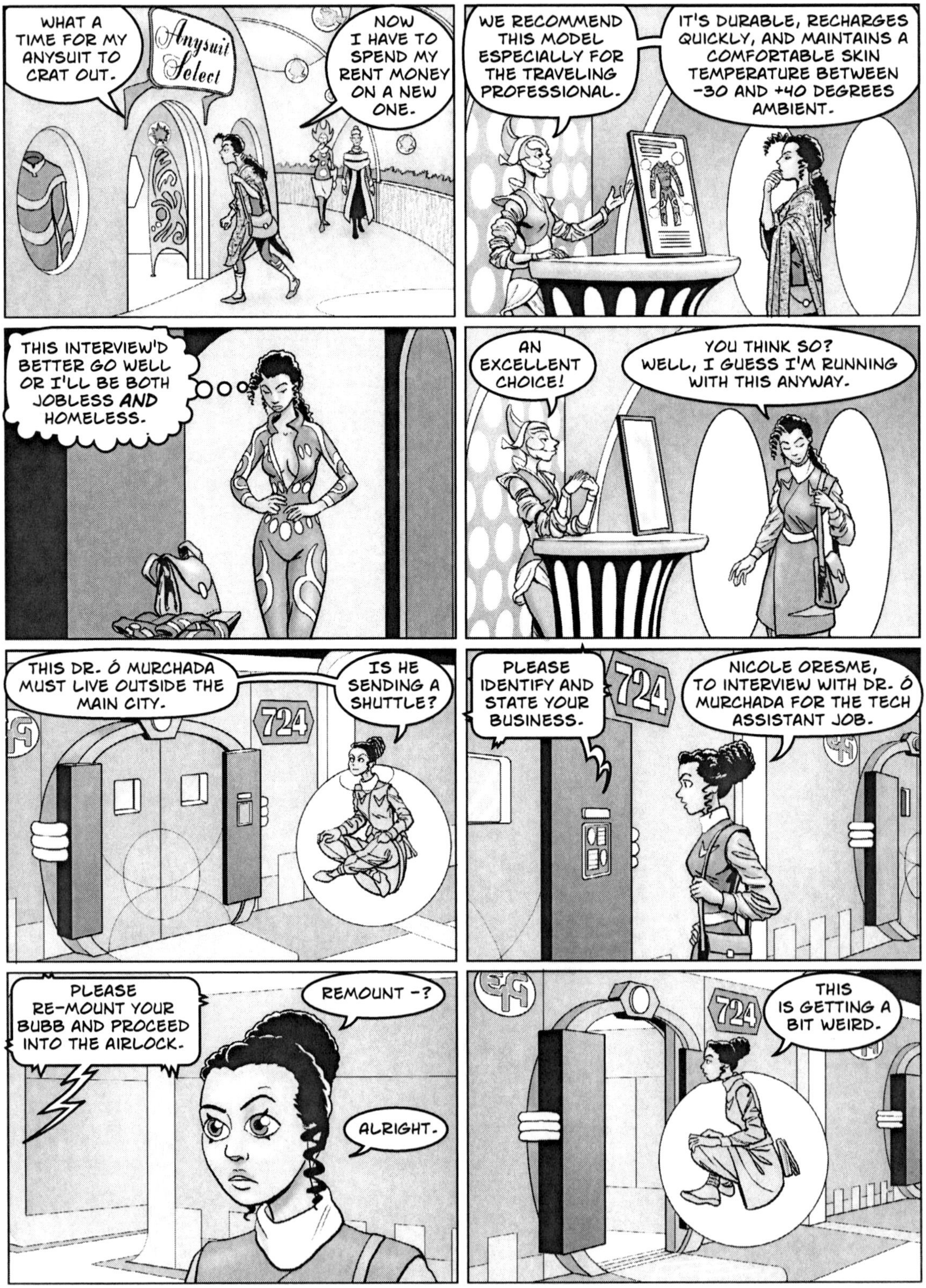
WHAT A TIME FOR MY ANYSUIT TO CRAT OUT.
Anysuit Select
NOW I HAVE TO SPEND MY RENT MONEY ON A NEW ONE.
WE RECOMMEND THIS MODEL ESPECIALLY FOR THE TRAVELING PROFESSIONAL.
IT'S DURABLE, RECHARGES QUICKLY, AND MAINTAINS A COMFORTABLE SKIN TEMPERATURE BETWEEN -30 AND +40 DEGREES AMBIENT.
THIS INTERVIEW'D BETTER GO WELL OR I'LL BE BOTH JOBLESS AND HOMELESS.
AN EXCELLENT CHOICE!
YOU THINK SO? WELL, I GUESS I'M RUNNING WITH THIS ANYWAY.
THIS DR. Ó MURCHADA MUST LIVE OUTSIDE THE MAIN CITY.
IS HE SENDING A SHUTTLE?
724
PLEASE IDENTIFY AND STATE YOUR BUSINESS.
724
NICOLE ORESME, TO INTERVIEW WITH DR. Ó MURCHADA FOR THE TECH ASSISTANT JOB.
PLEASE RE-MOUNT YOUR BUBB AND PROCEED INTO THE AIRLOCK.
REMOUNT -?
ALRIGHT.
724
THIS IS GETTING A BIT WEIRD.

PLEASE INDICATE THE VACUUM-SAFETY RATING OF YOUR BUBB.
HUH? UH, ENCLOSES IN .05 SECONDS, MAINTAINS O_2 LEVELS FOR UP TO 2 HOURS, SHIELDS UP TO 2 RADS PER SECOND.
WHY?
RATING SATISFACTORY.
GAH!
FEEK!
FEEK
FEEK
FEEK
FEEK
FEEK
FEEK
DENIZENS OF THE L-5 CITY INSTINCTIVELY FEAR NOT BEING IN AN ENCLOSED SPACE.
NICOLE'S ***BUBB*** PROTECTS HER FROM THE VACUUM, BUT CANNOT DEVIATE FROM ITS COURSE.
NICOLE DOES NOT SCREAM BUT SHE CAN ONLY WATCH HELPLESSLY AS SHE APPROACHES A BIZARRE STRUCTURE.
SHE'S NOT SURE WHETHER TO FEEL RELIEF OR FOREBODING AS HER BUBB ENTERS THIS CHAOTIC ENCLOSURE.

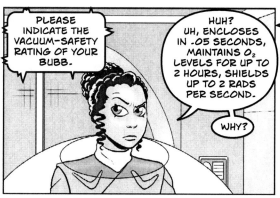

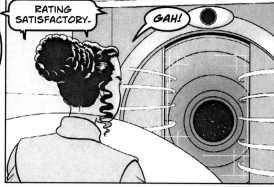

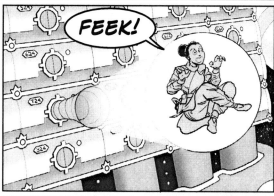

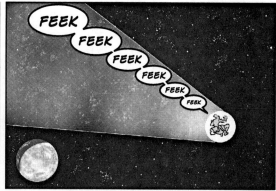

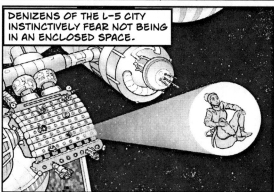

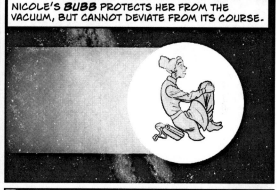

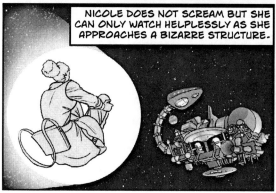

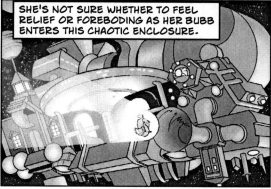

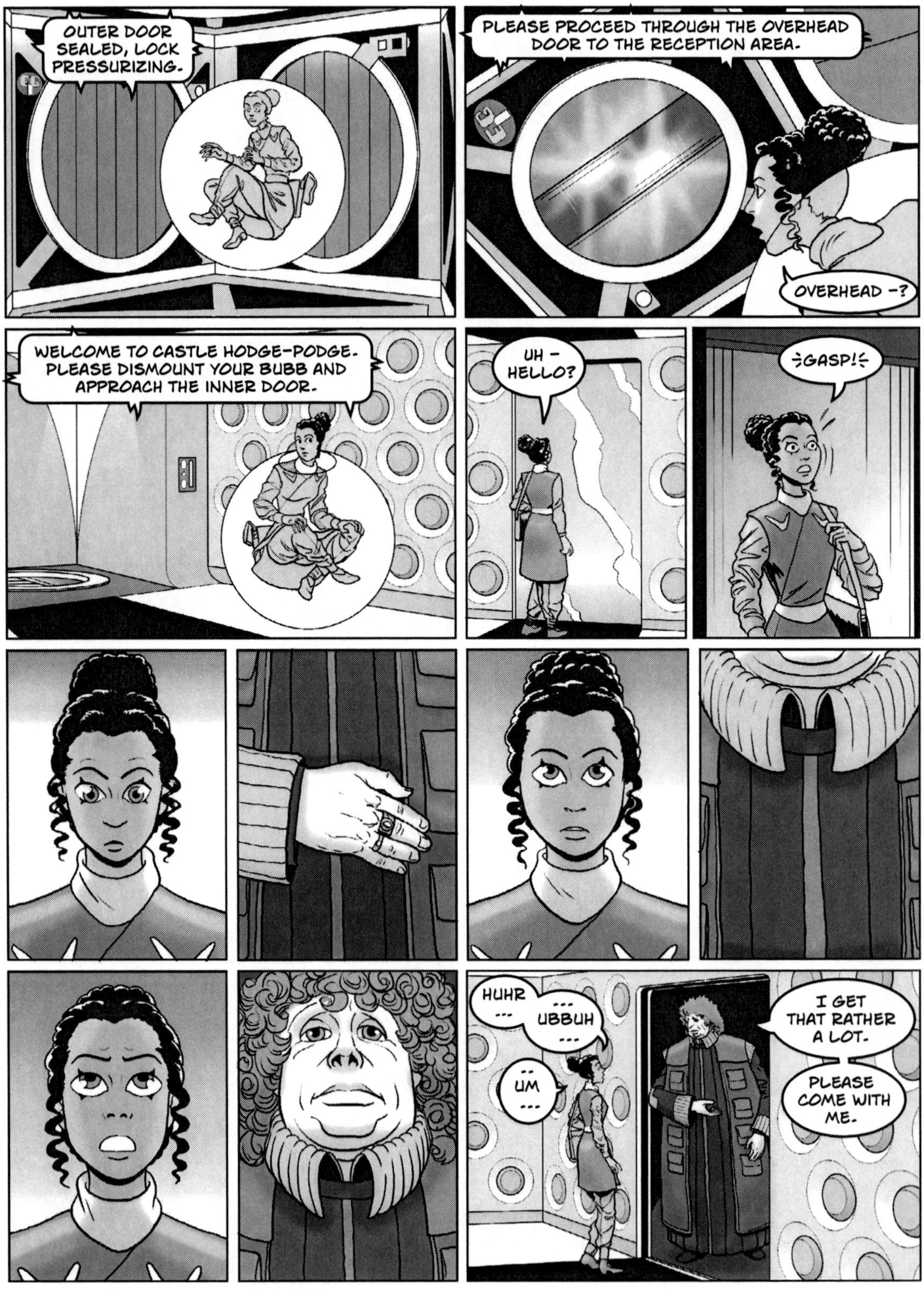
OUTER DOOR SEALED, LOCK PRESSURIZING.
PLEASE PROCEED THROUGH THE OVERHEAD DOOR TO THE RECEPTION AREA.
OVERHEAD –?
WELCOME TO CASTLE HODGE-PODGE. PLEASE DISMOUNT YOUR BUBB AND APPROACH THE INNER DOOR.
UH – HELLO?
GASP!
HUHR ...
... UBBUH ...
.. UM ...
I GET THAT RATHER A LOT.
PLEASE COME WITH ME.

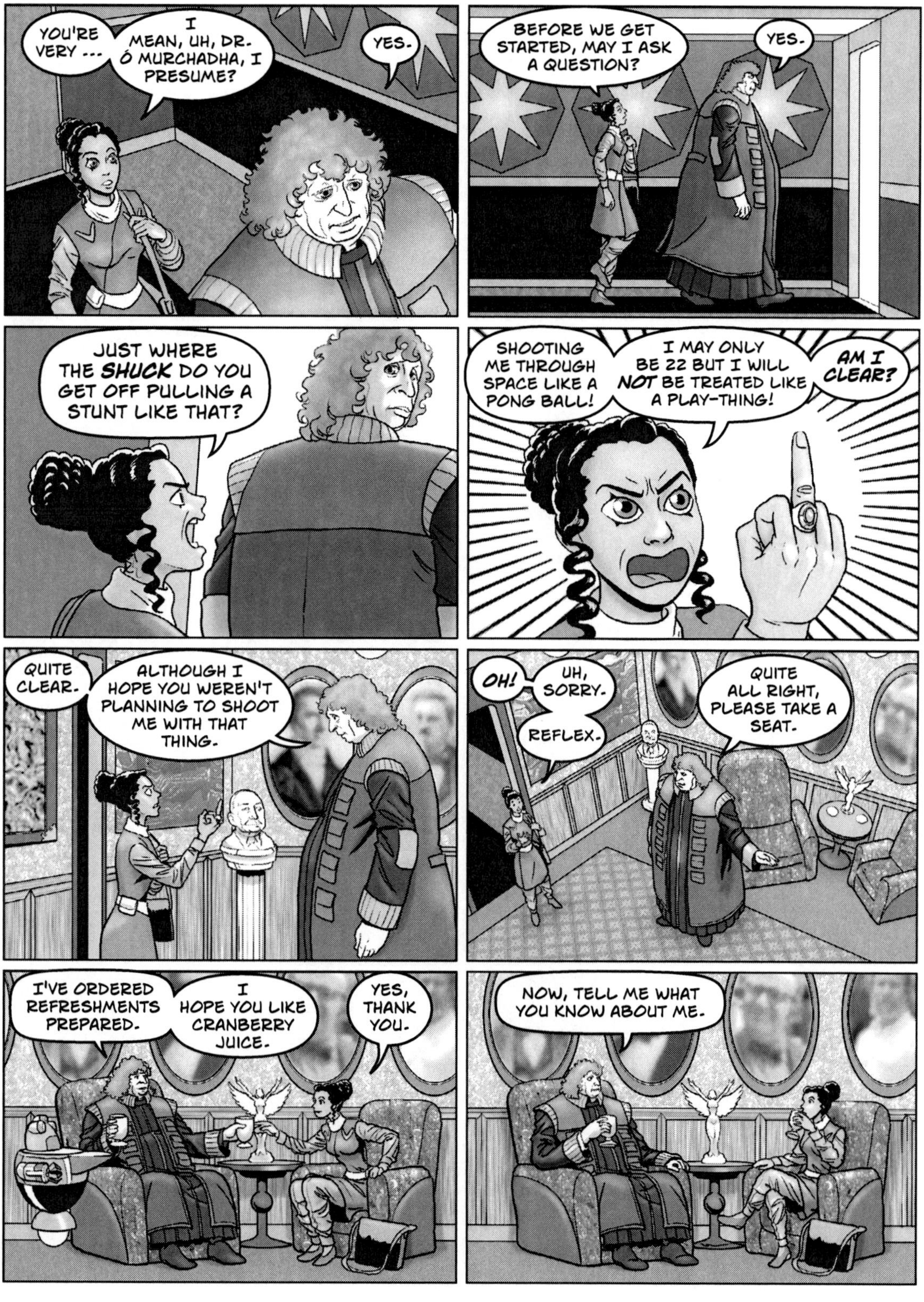
YOU'RE VERY ---
I MEAN, UH, DR. Ó MURCHADHA, I PRESUME?
YES.
BEFORE WE GET STARTED, MAY I ASK A QUESTION?
YES.
JUST WHERE THE SHUCK DO YOU GET OFF PULLING A STUNT LIKE THAT?
SHOOTING ME THROUGH SPACE LIKE A PONG BALL!
I MAY ONLY BE 22 BUT I WILL NOT BE TREATED LIKE A PLAY-THING!
AM I CLEAR?
QUITE CLEAR.
ALTHOUGH I HOPE YOU WEREN'T PLANNING TO SHOOT ME WITH THAT THING.
OH!
UH, SORRY.
REFLEX.
QUITE ALL RIGHT, PLEASE TAKE A SEAT.
I'VE ORDERED REFRESHMENTS PREPARED.
I HOPE YOU LIKE CRANBERRY JUICE.
YES, THANK YOU.
NOW, TELL ME WHAT YOU KNOW ABOUT ME.

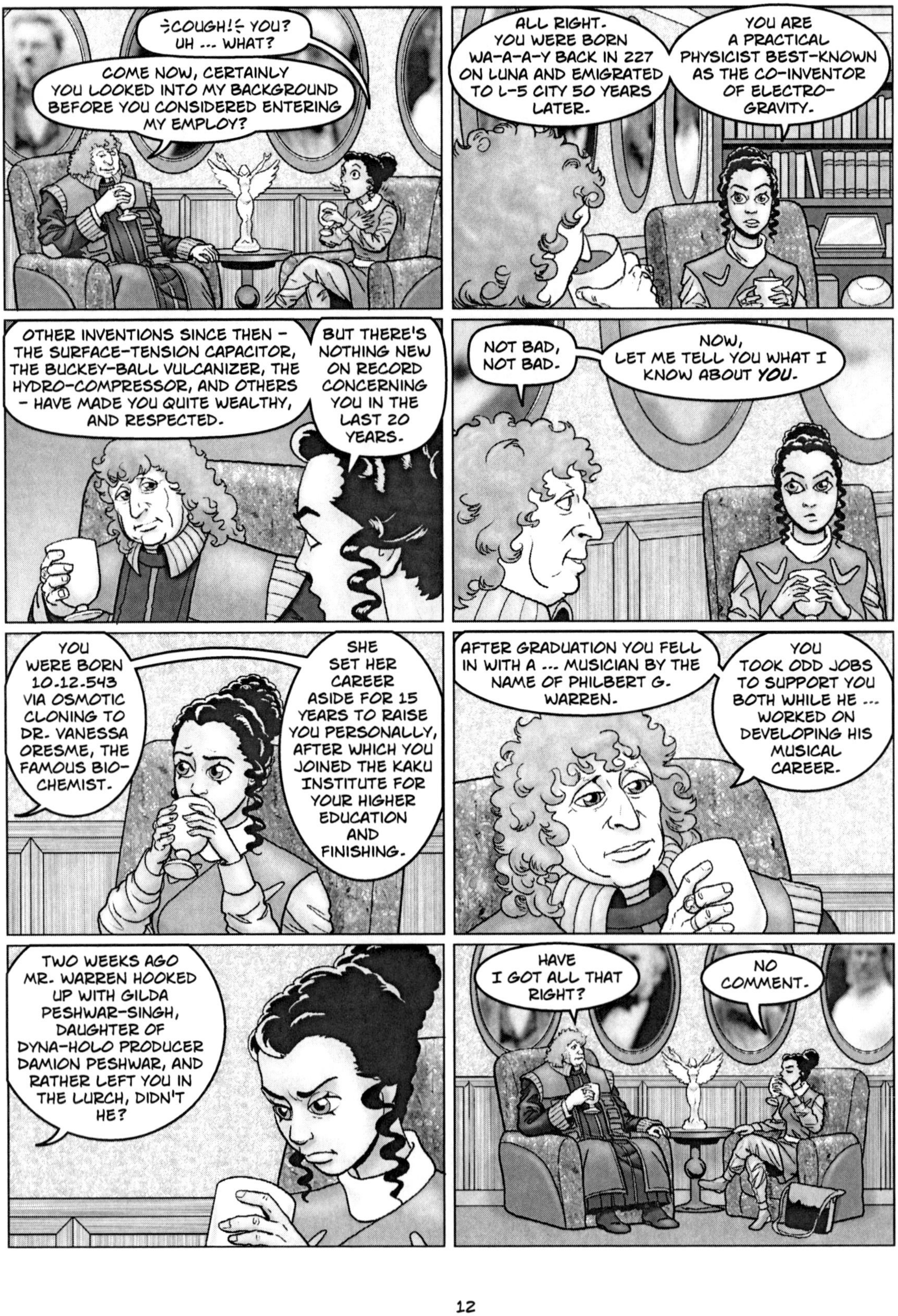
COUGH! YOU? UH ... WHAT?
COME NOW, CERTAINLY YOU LOOKED INTO MY BACKGROUND BEFORE YOU CONSIDERED ENTERING MY EMPLOY?
ALL RIGHT. YOU WERE BORN WA-A-A-Y BACK IN 227 ON LUNA AND EMIGRATED TO L-5 CITY 50 YEARS LATER.
YOU ARE A PRACTICAL PHYSICIST BEST-KNOWN AS THE CO-INVENTOR OF ELECTRO-GRAVITY.
OTHER INVENTIONS SINCE THEN - THE SURFACE-TENSION CAPACITOR, THE BUCKEY-BALL VULCANIZER, THE HYDRO-COMPRESSOR, AND OTHERS - HAVE MADE YOU QUITE WEALTHY, AND RESPECTED.
BUT THERE'S NOTHING NEW ON RECORD CONCERNING YOU IN THE LAST 20 YEARS.
NOT BAD, NOT BAD.
NOW, LET ME TELL YOU WHAT I KNOW ABOUT **YOU**.
YOU WERE BORN 10.12.543 VIA OSMOTIC CLONING TO DR. VANESSA ORESME, THE FAMOUS BIO-CHEMIST.
SHE SET HER CAREER ASIDE FOR 15 YEARS TO RAISE YOU PERSONALLY, AFTER WHICH YOU JOINED THE KAKU INSTITUTE FOR YOUR HIGHER EDUCATION AND FINISHING.
AFTER GRADUATION YOU FELL IN WITH A ... MUSICIAN BY THE NAME OF PHILBERT G. WARREN.
YOU TOOK ODD JOBS TO SUPPORT YOU BOTH WHILE HE ... WORKED ON DEVELOPING HIS MUSICAL CAREER.
TWO WEEKS AGO MR. WARREN HOOKED UP WITH GILDA PESHWAR-SINGH, DAUGHTER OF DYNA-HOLO PRODUCER DAMION PESHWAR, AND RATHER LEFT YOU IN THE LURCH, DIDN'T HE?
HAVE I GOT ALL THAT RIGHT?
NO COMMENT.

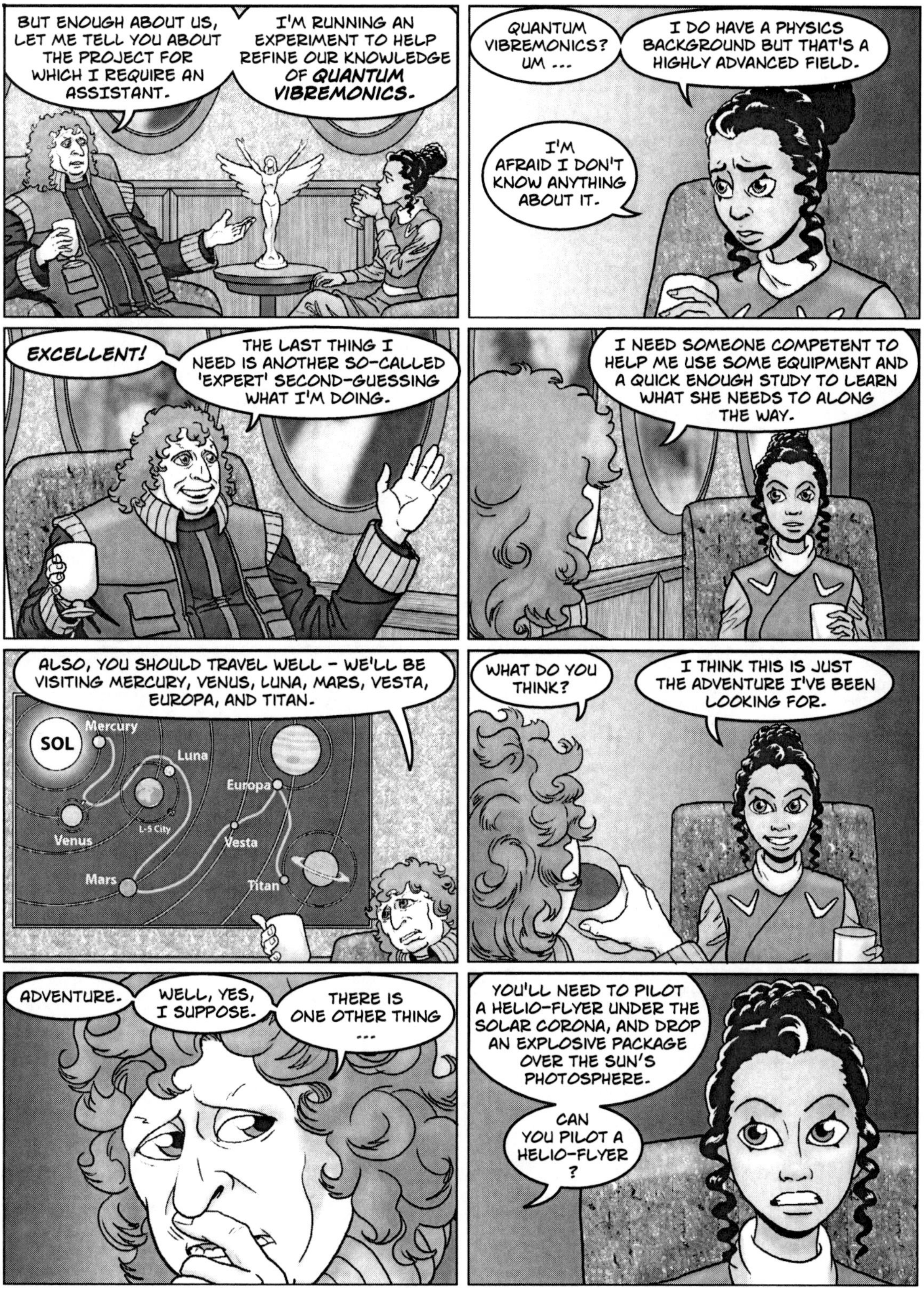
BUT ENOUGH ABOUT US, LET ME TELL YOU ABOUT THE PROJECT FOR WHICH I REQUIRE AN ASSISTANT.
I'M RUNNING AN EXPERIMENT TO HELP REFINE OUR KNOWLEDGE OF QUANTUM VIBREMONICS.
QUANTUM VIBREMONICS? UM ...
I DO HAVE A PHYSICS BACKGROUND BUT THAT'S A HIGHLY ADVANCED FIELD.
I'M AFRAID I DON'T KNOW ANYTHING ABOUT IT.
EXCELLENT!
THE LAST THING I NEED IS ANOTHER SO-CALLED 'EXPERT' SECOND-GUESSING WHAT I'M DOING.
I NEED SOMEONE COMPETENT TO HELP ME USE SOME EQUIPMENT AND A QUICK ENOUGH STUDY TO LEARN WHAT SHE NEEDS TO ALONG THE WAY.
ALSO, YOU SHOULD TRAVEL WELL - WE'LL BE VISITING MERCURY, VENUS, LUNA, MARS, VESTA, EUROPA, AND TITAN.
SOL
Mercury
Luna
Europa
Venus
L-5 City
Vesta
Mars
Titan
WHAT DO YOU THINK?
I THINK THIS IS JUST THE ADVENTURE I'VE BEEN LOOKING FOR.
ADVENTURE.
WELL, YES, I SUPPOSE.
THERE IS ONE OTHER THING ...
YOU'LL NEED TO PILOT A HELIO-FLYER UNDER THE SOLAR CORONA, AND DROP AN EXPLOSIVE PACKAGE OVER THE SUN'S PHOTOSPHERE.
CAN YOU PILOT A HELIO-FLYER ?

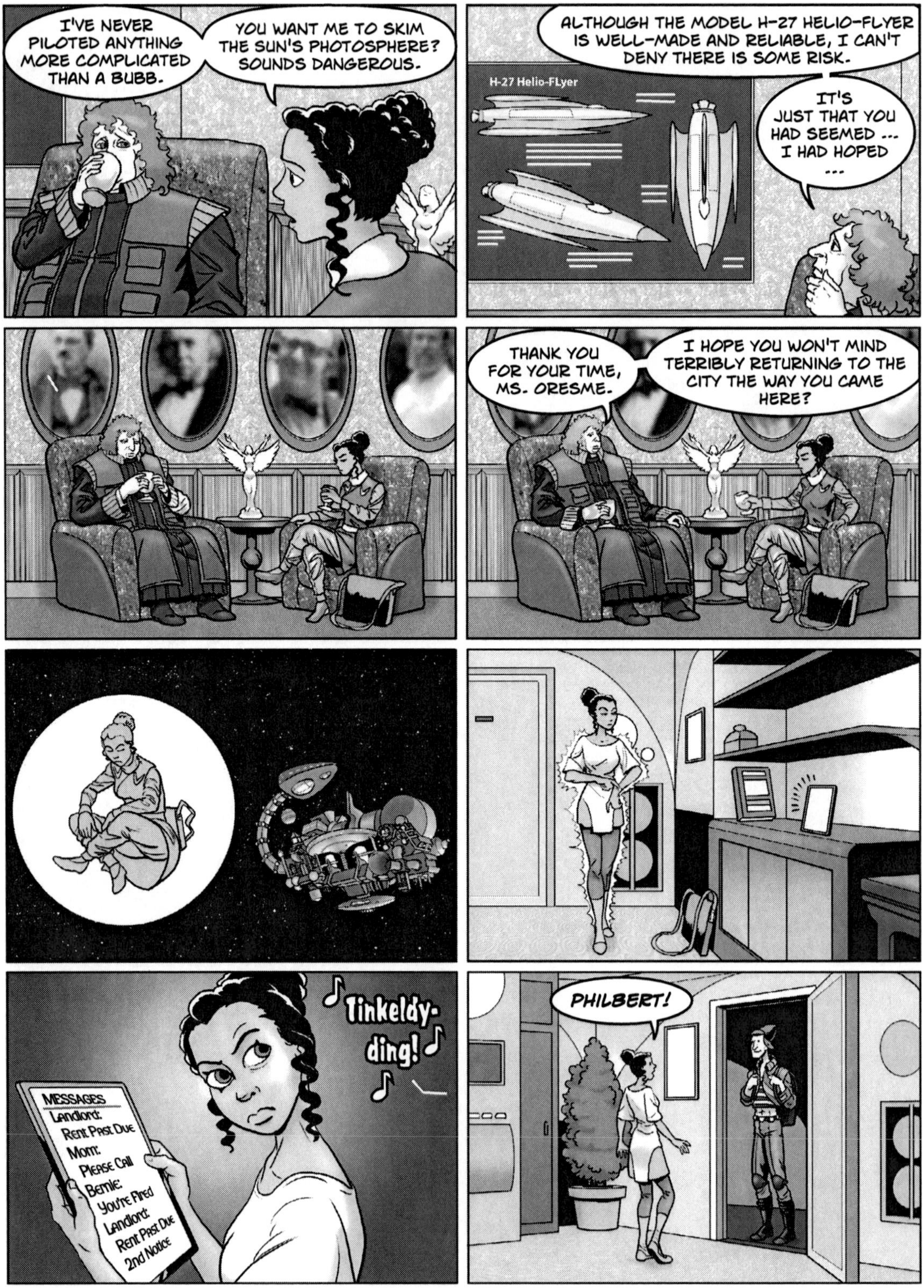
I'VE NEVER PILOTED ANYTHING MORE COMPLICATED THAN A BUBB.
YOU WANT ME TO SKIM THE SUN'S PHOTOSPHERE? SOUNDS DANGEROUS.
ALTHOUGH THE MODEL H-27 HELIO-FLYER IS WELL-MADE AND RELIABLE, I CAN'T DENY THERE IS SOME RISK.
H-27 Helio-FLyer
IT'S JUST THAT YOU HAD SEEMED --- I HAD HOPED ---
THANK YOU FOR YOUR TIME, MS. ORESME.
I HOPE YOU WON'T MIND TERRIBLY RETURNING TO THE CITY THE WAY YOU CAME HERE?
MESSAGES
Landlord: Rent Past Due
Mom: Please Call
Bernie: You're Fired
Landlord: Rent Past Due 2nd Notice
Tinkeldy-ding!
PHILBERT!

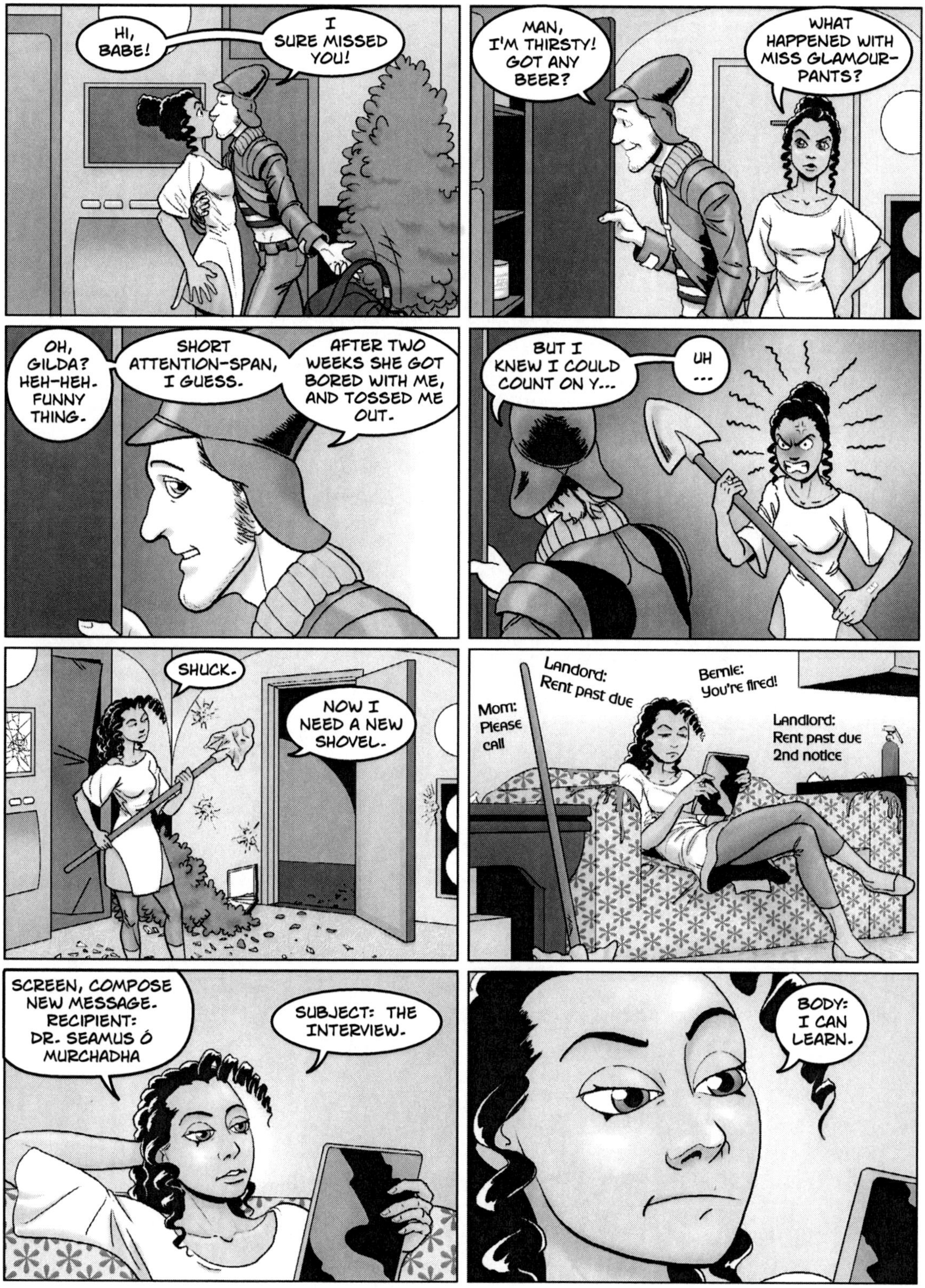
HI, BABE!
I SURE MISSED YOU!
MAN, I'M THIRSTY! GOT ANY BEER?
WHAT HAPPENED WITH MISS GLAMOUR-PANTS?
OH, GILDA? HEH-HEH. FUNNY THING.
SHORT ATTENTION-SPAN, I GUESS.
AFTER TWO WEEKS SHE GOT BORED WITH ME, AND TOSSED ME OUT.
BUT I KNEW I COULD COUNT ON Y...
UH ...
SHUCK.
NOW I NEED A NEW SHOVEL.
Mom: Please call
Landord: Rent past due
Bernie: You're fired!
Landlord: Rent past due 2nd notice
SCREEN, COMPOSE NEW MESSAGE. RECIPIENT: DR. SEAMUS Ó MURCHADHA
SUBJECT: THE INTERVIEW.
BODY: I CAN LEARN.

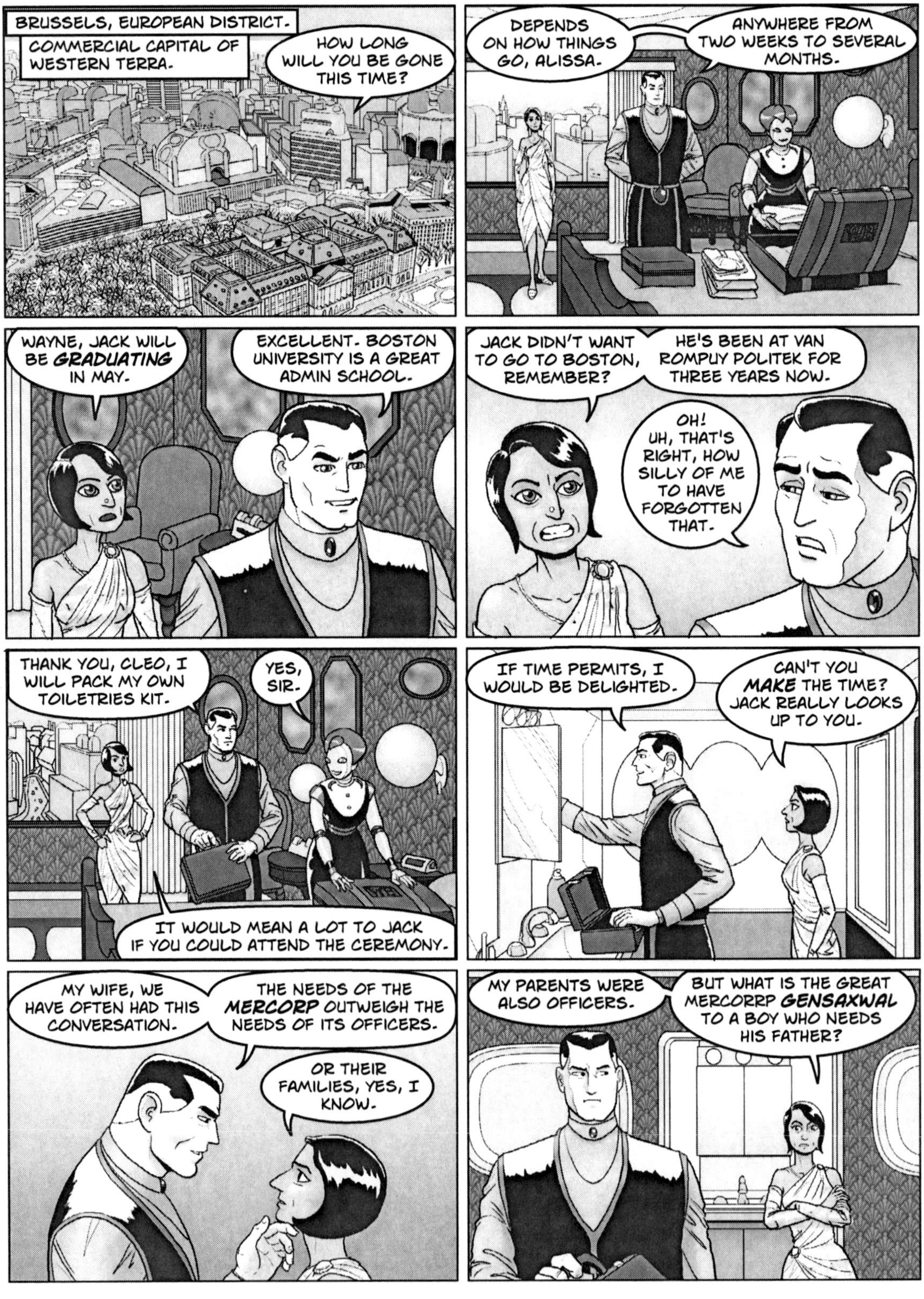
BRUSSELS, EUROPEAN DISTRICT.
COMMERCIAL CAPITAL OF WESTERN TERRA.
HOW LONG WILL YOU BE GONE THIS TIME?
DEPENDS ON HOW THINGS GO, ALISSA.
ANYWHERE FROM TWO WEEKS TO SEVERAL MONTHS.
WAYNE, JACK WILL BE GRADUATING IN MAY.
EXCELLENT. BOSTON UNIVERSITY IS A GREAT ADMIN SCHOOL.
JACK DIDN'T WANT TO GO TO BOSTON, REMEMBER?
HE'S BEEN AT VAN ROMPUY POLITEK FOR THREE YEARS NOW.
OH! UH, THAT'S RIGHT, HOW SILLY OF ME TO HAVE FORGOTTEN THAT.
THANK YOU, CLEO, I WILL PACK MY OWN TOILETRIES KIT.
YES, SIR.
IT WOULD MEAN A LOT TO JACK IF YOU COULD ATTEND THE CEREMONY.
IF TIME PERMITS, I WOULD BE DELIGHTED.
CAN'T YOU MAKE THE TIME? JACK REALLY LOOKS UP TO YOU.
MY WIFE, WE HAVE OFTEN HAD THIS CONVERSATION.
THE NEEDS OF THE MERCORP OUTWEIGH THE NEEDS OF ITS OFFICERS.
OR THEIR FAMILIES, YES, I KNOW.
MY PARENTS WERE ALSO OFFICERS.
BUT WHAT IS THE GREAT MERCORRP GENSAXWAL TO A BOY WHO NEEDS HIS FATHER?

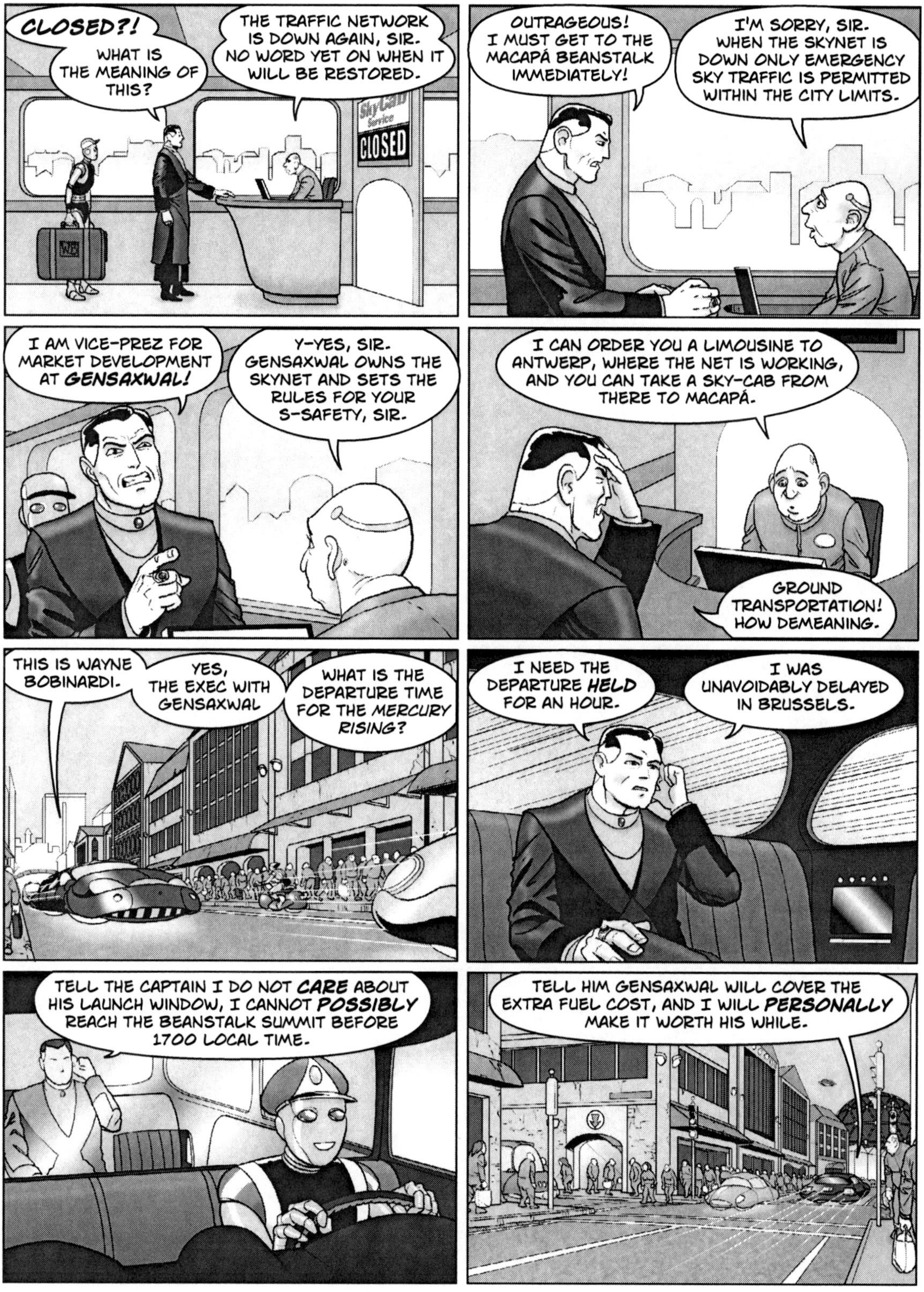
CLOSED?! WHAT IS THE MEANING OF THIS?
THE TRAFFIC NETWORK IS DOWN AGAIN, SIR. NO WORD YET ON WHEN IT WILL BE RESTORED.
SkyCab Service
CLOSED
OUTRAGEOUS! I MUST GET TO THE MACAPÁ BEANSTALK IMMEDIATELY!
I'M SORRY, SIR. WHEN THE SKYNET IS DOWN ONLY EMERGENCY SKY TRAFFIC IS PERMITTED WITHIN THE CITY LIMITS.
I AM VICE-PREZ FOR MARKET DEVELOPMENT AT GENSAXWAL!
Y-YES, SIR. GENSAXWAL OWNS THE SKYNET AND SETS THE RULES FOR YOUR S-SAFETY, SIR.
I CAN ORDER YOU A LIMOUSINE TO ANTWERP, WHERE THE NET IS WORKING, AND YOU CAN TAKE A SKY-CAB FROM THERE TO MACAPÁ.
GROUND TRANSPORTATION! HOW DEMEANING.
THIS IS WAYNE BOBINARDI.
YES, THE EXEC WITH GENSAXWAL
WHAT IS THE DEPARTURE TIME FOR THE MERCURY RISING?
I NEED THE DEPARTURE HELD FOR AN HOUR.
I WAS UNAVOIDABLY DELAYED IN BRUSSELS.
TELL THE CAPTAIN I DO NOT CARE ABOUT HIS LAUNCH WINDOW, I CANNOT POSSIBLY REACH THE BEANSTALK SUMMIT BEFORE 1700 LOCAL TIME.
TELL HIM GENSAXWAL WILL COVER THE EXTRA FUEL COST, AND I WILL PERSONALLY MAKE IT WORTH HIS WHILE.

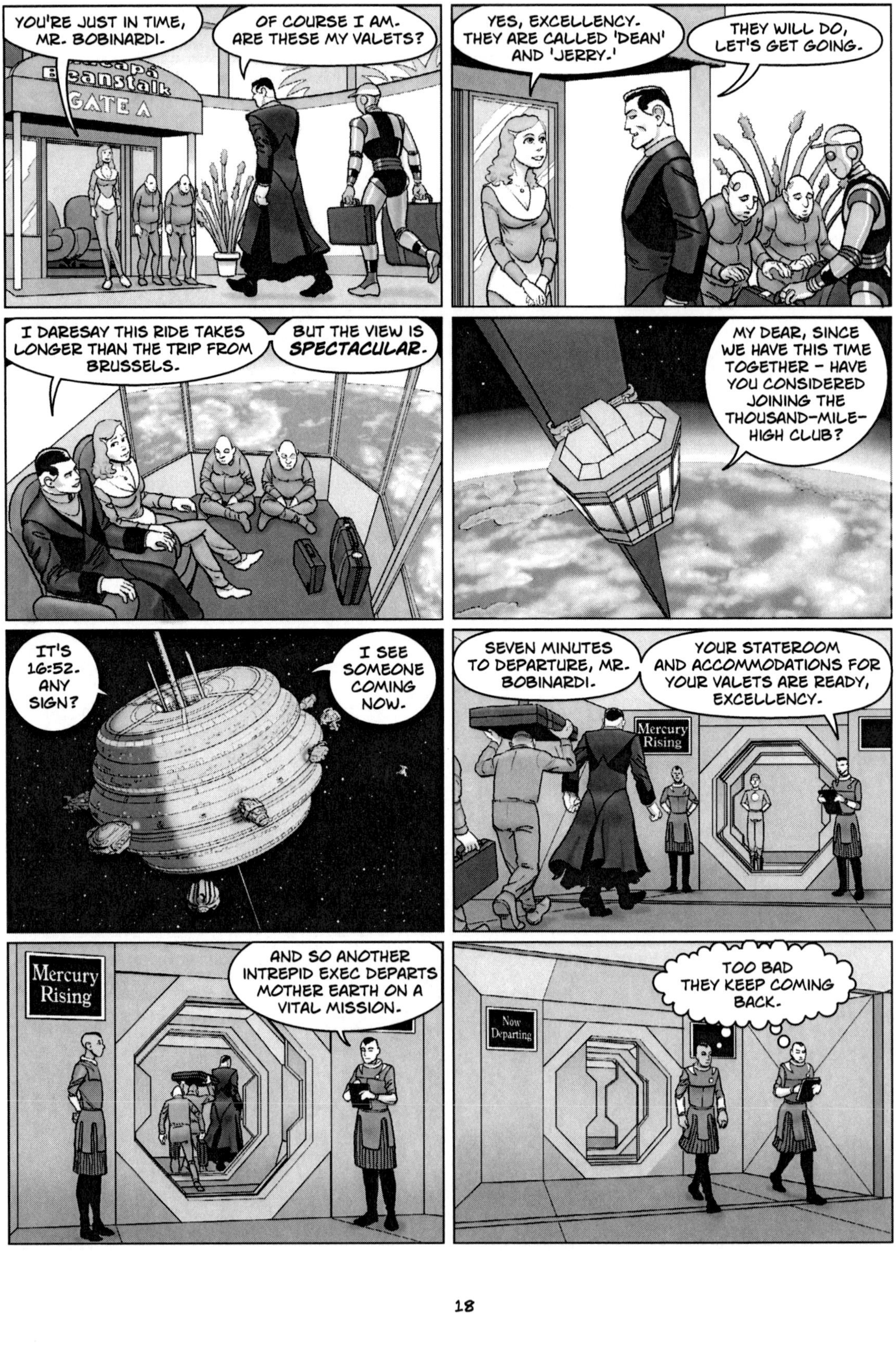
YOU'RE JUST IN TIME, MR. BOBINARDI.
OF COURSE I AM. ARE THESE MY VALETS?
GATE A
YES, EXCELLENCY. THEY ARE CALLED 'DEAN' AND 'JERRY.'
THEY WILL DO, LET'S GET GOING.
I DARESAY THIS RIDE TAKES LONGER THAN THE TRIP FROM BRUSSELS.
BUT THE VIEW IS *SPECTACULAR*.
MY DEAR, SINCE WE HAVE THIS TIME TOGETHER – HAVE YOU CONSIDERED JOINING THE THOUSAND-MILE-HIGH CLUB?
IT'S 16:52. ANY SIGN?
I SEE SOMEONE COMING NOW.
SEVEN MINUTES TO DEPARTURE, MR. BOBINARDI.
YOUR STATEROOM AND ACCOMMODATIONS FOR YOUR VALETS ARE READY, EXCELLENCY.
Mercury Rising
Mercury Rising
AND SO ANOTHER INTREPID EXEC DEPARTS MOTHER EARTH ON A VITAL MISSION.
Now Departing
TOO BAD THEY KEEP COMING BACK.

IN THE ARCH, L-5 CITY.

I'M NICOLE ORESME, HERE FOR MY 13:00 APPOINTMENT.

HERE IS MY REFERRAL.

PEYMAN!

ESCORT THIS HONORED CLIENT TO THE PREPARATION ROOM AT ONCE.

I WILL NOTIFY DR. ALIZADEH.

WELCOME, MS. ORESME. I AM DR. FARZAD ALIZADEH AND THIS IS MY ASSISTANT, YOUSEF.

PLEASE HAVE A SEAT AND WE'LL GET STARTED RIGHT AWAY.

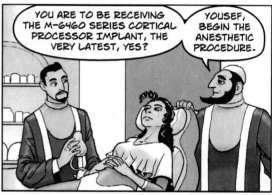

YOU ARE TO BE RECEIVING THE M-G4G0 SERIES CORTICAL PROCESSOR IMPLANT, THE VERY LATEST, YES?

YOUSEF, BEGIN THE ANESTHETIC PROCEDURE.

AH, NO OFFENSE INTENDED, BUT I'D FEEL MORE COMFORTABLE WITH A FEMALE ASSISTANT, PLEASE?

OF COURSE.

THIS IS NIKI.

NOW, THAT'S CUSTOMER SERVICE.

YOUR EMPLOYER DR. Ó MURCHADHA ALWAYS DEMANDS THE BEST.

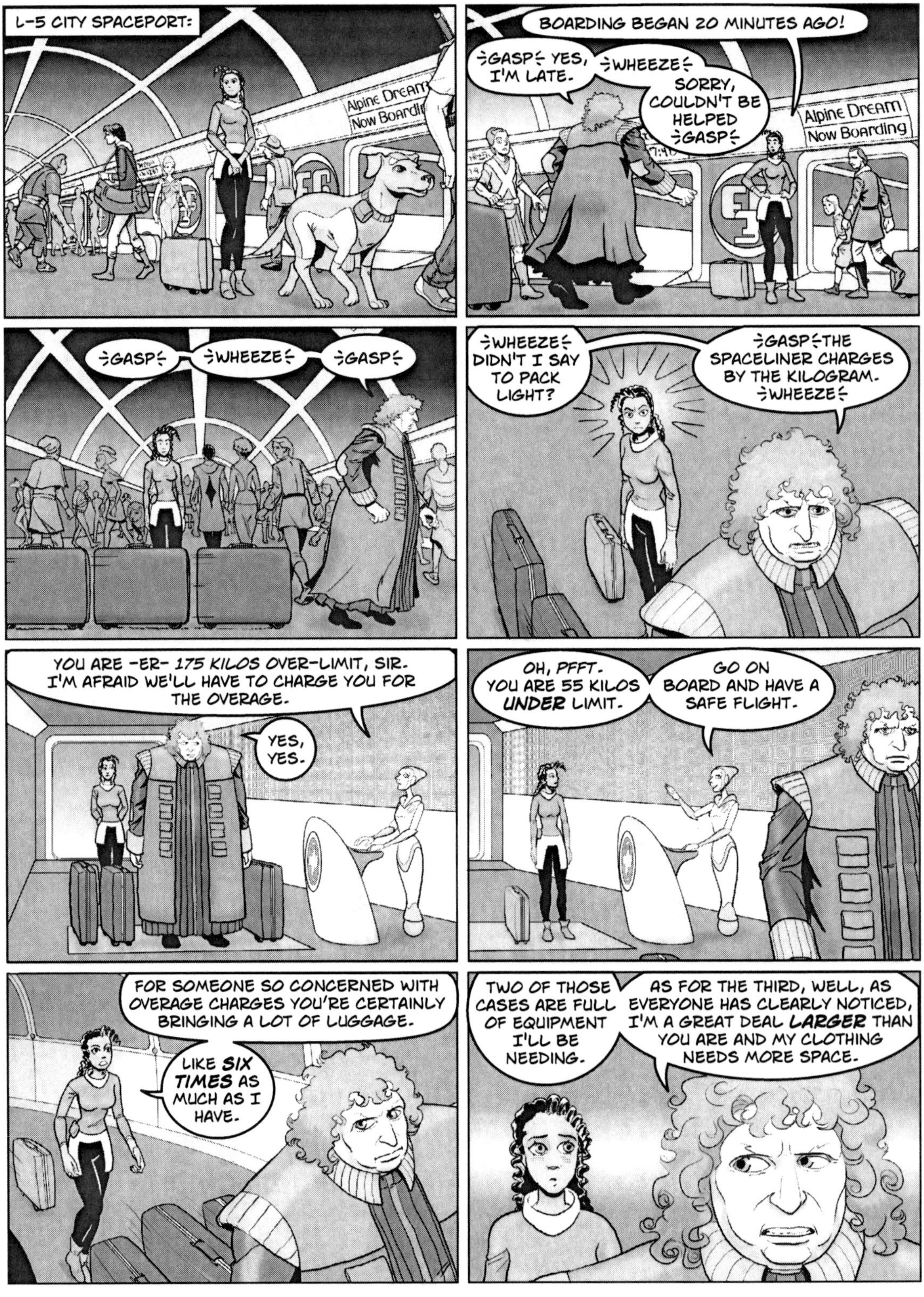
L-5 CITY SPACEPORT:
Alpine Dream
Now Boarding
BOARDING BEGAN 20 MINUTES AGO!
≑GASP≑ YES, I'M LATE.
≑WHEEZE≑
SORRY, COULDN'T BE HELPED ≑GASP≑
Alpine Dream
Now Boarding
≑GASP≑
≑WHEEZE≑
≑GASP≑
≑WHEEZE≑ DIDN'T I SAY TO PACK LIGHT?
≑GASP≑ THE SPACELINER CHARGES BY THE KILOGRAM. ≑WHEEZE≑
YOU ARE -ER- *175 KILOS* OVER-LIMIT, SIR. I'M AFRAID WE'LL HAVE TO CHARGE YOU FOR THE OVERAGE.
YES, YES.
OH, *PFFT*. YOU ARE 55 KILOS ***UNDER*** LIMIT.
GO ON BOARD AND HAVE A SAFE FLIGHT.
FOR SOMEONE SO CONCERNED WITH OVERAGE CHARGES YOU'RE CERTAINLY BRINGING A LOT OF LUGGAGE.
LIKE ***SIX TIMES*** AS MUCH AS I HAVE.
TWO OF THOSE CASES ARE FULL OF EQUIPMENT I'LL BE NEEDING.
AS FOR THE THIRD, WELL, AS EVERYONE HAS CLEARLY NOTICED, I'M A GREAT DEAL ***LARGER*** THAN YOU ARE AND MY CLOTHING NEEDS MORE SPACE.

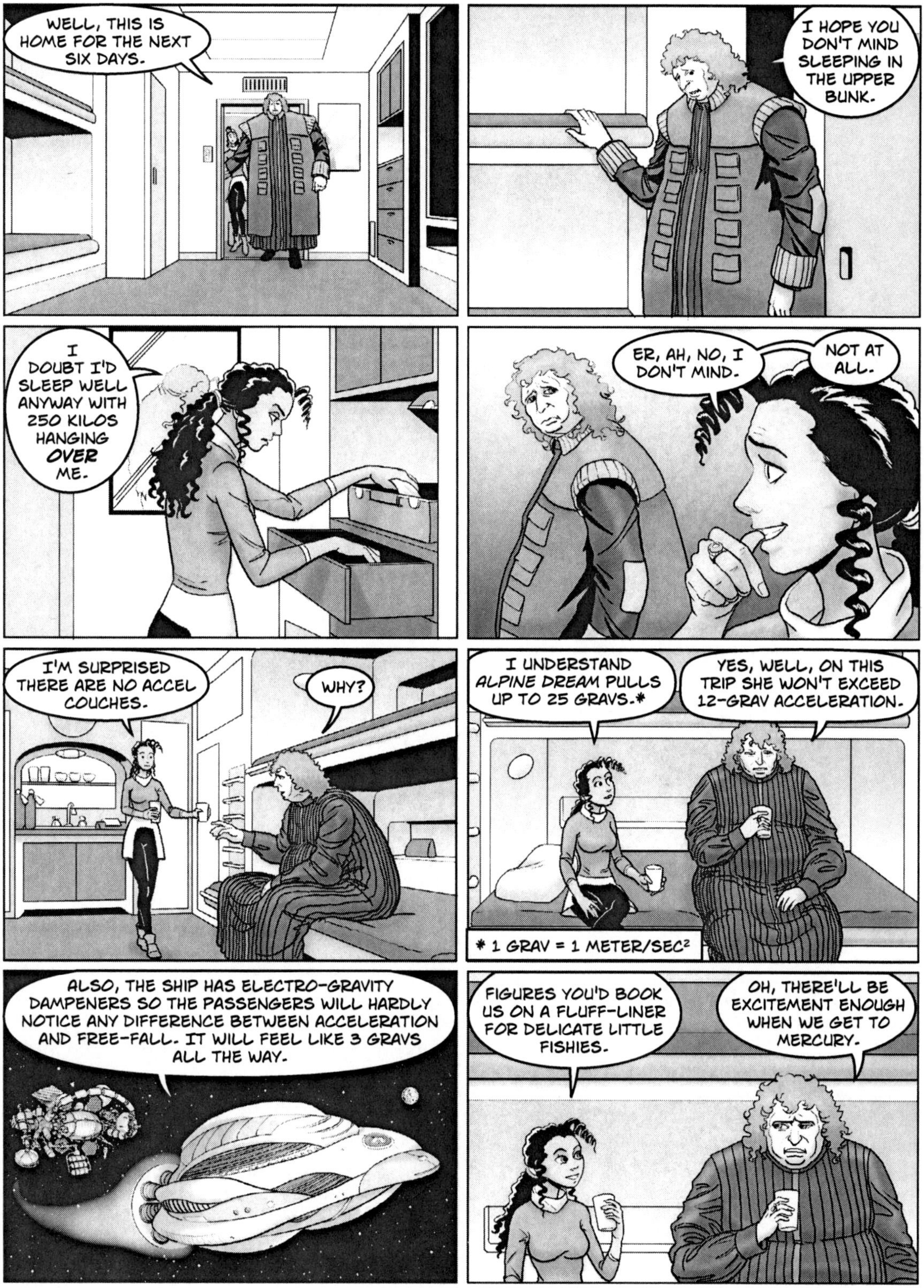
WELL, THIS IS HOME FOR THE NEXT SIX DAYS.
I HOPE YOU DON'T MIND SLEEPING IN THE UPPER BUNK.
I DOUBT I'D SLEEP WELL ANYWAY WITH 250 KILOS HANGING OVER ME.
ER, AH, NO, I DON'T MIND.
NOT AT ALL.
I'M SURPRISED THERE ARE NO ACCEL COUCHES.
WHY?
I UNDERSTAND ALPINE DREAM PULLS UP TO 25 GRAVS.*
YES, WELL, ON THIS TRIP SHE WON'T EXCEED 12-GRAV ACCELERATION.
* 1 GRAV = 1 METER/SEC²
ALSO, THE SHIP HAS ELECTRO-GRAVITY DAMPENERS SO THE PASSENGERS WILL HARDLY NOTICE ANY DIFFERENCE BETWEEN ACCELERATION AND FREE-FALL. IT WILL FEEL LIKE 3 GRAVS ALL THE WAY.
FIGURES YOU'D BOOK US ON A FLUFF-LINER FOR DELICATE LITTLE FISHIES.
OH, THERE'LL BE EXCITEMENT ENOUGH WHEN WE GET TO MERCURY.

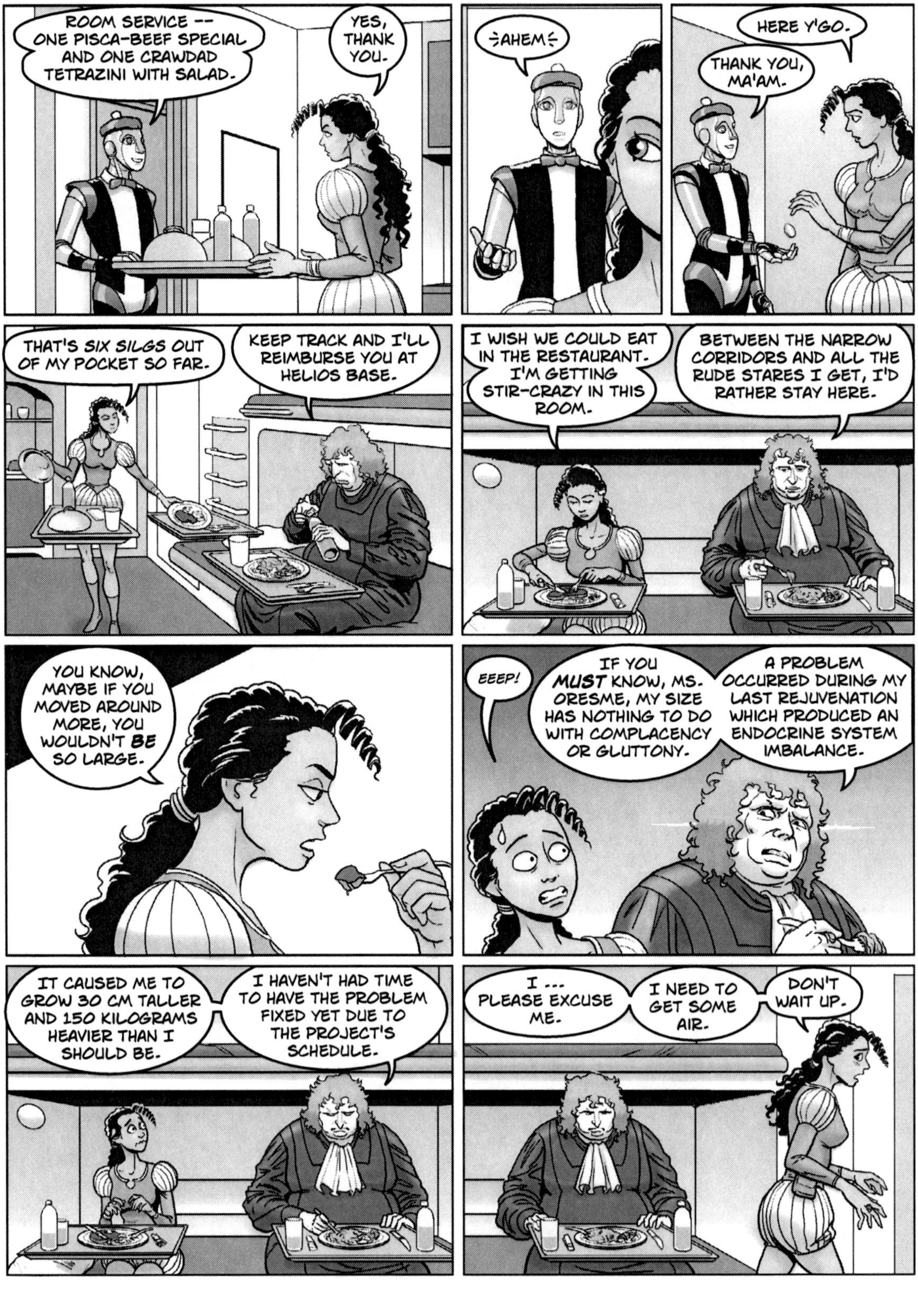
ROOM SERVICE -- ONE PISCA-BEEF SPECIAL AND ONE CRAWDAD TETRAZINI WITH SALAD.
YES, THANK YOU.
AHEM
HERE Y'GO.
THANK YOU, MA'AM.
THAT'S SIX SILGS OUT OF MY POCKET SO FAR.
KEEP TRACK AND I'LL REIMBURSE YOU AT HELIOS BASE.
I WISH WE COULD EAT IN THE RESTAURANT. I'M GETTING STIR-CRAZY IN THIS ROOM.
BETWEEN THE NARROW CORRIDORS AND ALL THE RUDE STARES I GET, I'D RATHER STAY HERE.
YOU KNOW, MAYBE IF YOU MOVED AROUND MORE, YOU WOULDN'T BE SO LARGE.
EEEP!
IF YOU MUST KNOW, MS. ORESME, MY SIZE HAS NOTHING TO DO WITH COMPLACENCY OR GLUTTONY.
A PROBLEM OCCURRED DURING MY LAST REJUVENATION WHICH PRODUCED AN ENDOCRINE SYSTEM IMBALANCE.
IT CAUSED ME TO GROW 30 CM TALLER AND 150 KILOGRAMS HEAVIER THAN I SHOULD BE.
I HAVEN'T HAD TIME TO HAVE THE PROBLEM FIXED YET DUE TO THE PROJECT'S SCHEDULE.
I ... PLEASE EXCUSE ME.
I NEED TO GET SOME AIR.
DON'T WAIT UP.

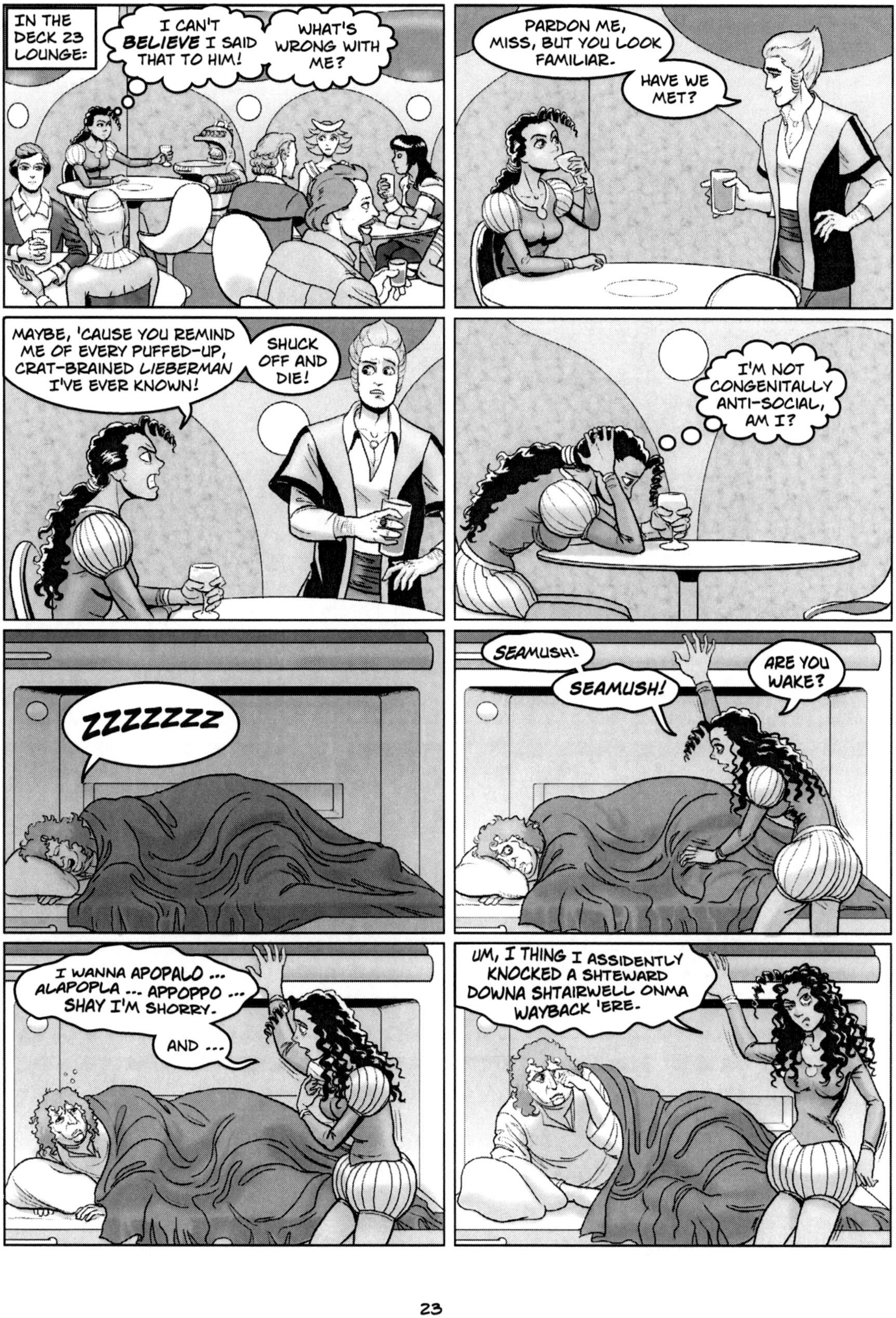
IN THE DECK 23 LOUNGE:
I CAN'T BELIEVE I SAID THAT TO HIM!
WHAT'S WRONG WITH ME?
PARDON ME, MISS, BUT YOU LOOK FAMILIAR.
HAVE WE MET?
MAYBE, 'CAUSE YOU REMIND ME OF EVERY PUFFED-UP, CRAT-BRAINED LIEBERMAN I'VE EVER KNOWN!
SHUCK OFF AND DIE!
I'M NOT CONGENITALLY ANTI-SOCIAL, AM I?
ZZZZZZZ
SEAMUSH!
SEAMUSH!
ARE YOU WAKE?
I WANNA APOPALO ... ALAPOPLA ... APPOPPO ... SHAY I'M SHORRY.
AND ...
UM, I THING I ASSIDENTLY KNOCKED A SHTEWARD DOWNA SHTAIRWELL ONMA WAYBACK 'ERE.

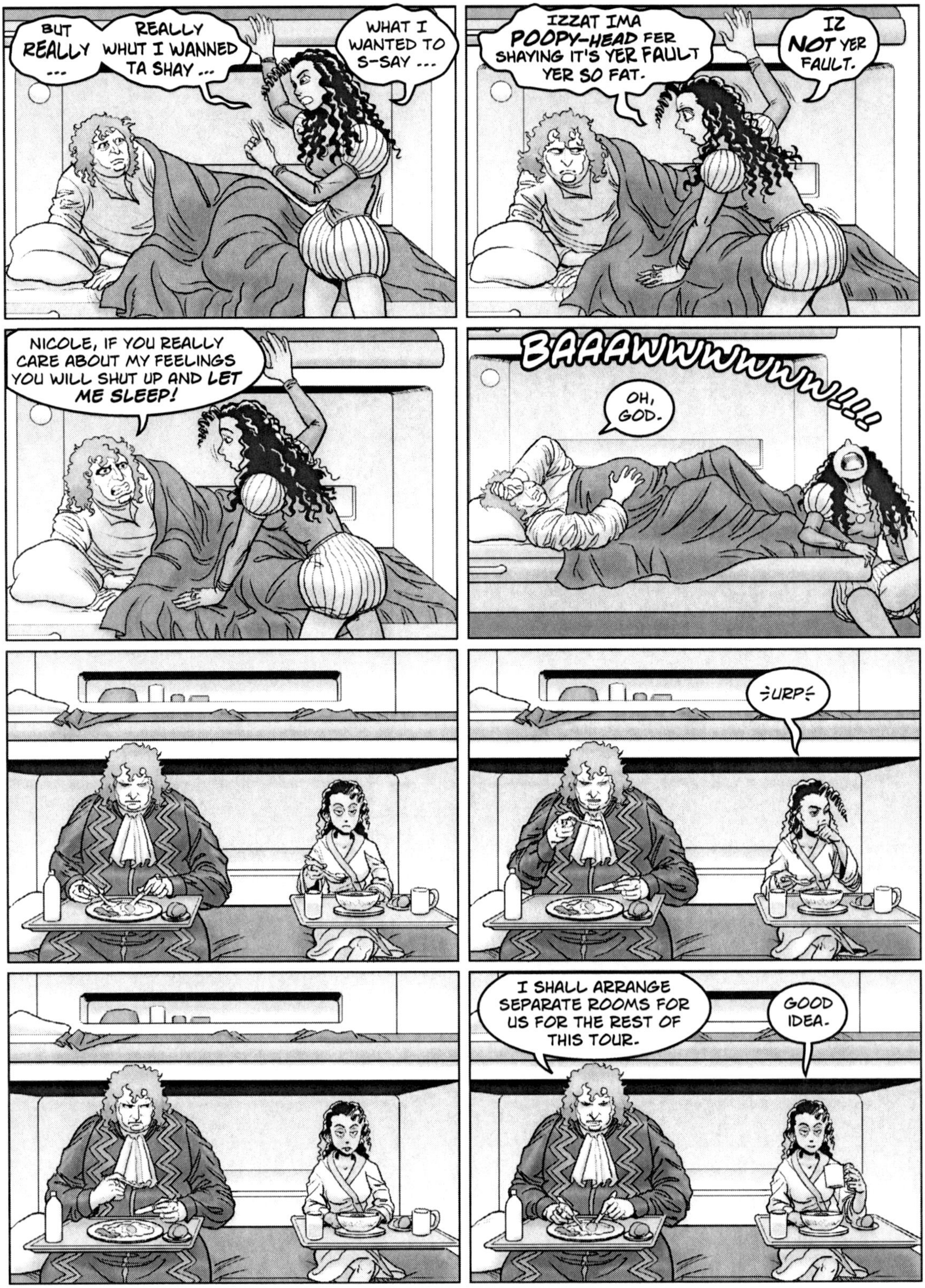
BUT REALLY ...
REALLY WHUT I WANNED TA SHAY ...
WHAT I WANTED TO S-SAY ...
IZZAT IMA POOPY-HEAD FER SHAYING IT'S YER FAULT YER SO FAT.
IZ NOT YER FAULT.
NICOLE, IF YOU REALLY CARE ABOUT MY FEELINGS YOU WILL SHUT UP AND LET ME SLEEP!
BAAAWWWWWWW!!!!
OH, GOD.
⸗URP⸗
I SHALL ARRANGE SEPARATE ROOMS FOR US FOR THE REST OF THIS TOUR.
GOOD IDEA.

ALPINE DREAM'S STATEROOMS ALL HAVE WALL-SCREENS OFFERING VIEWS OF JUST ABOUT ANYTHING: FROM THE SPACE-SCAPE OUTSIDE THE SHIP TO PROGRAMMING FROM MORE THAN 2,000 EMNET-CAST STATIONS ON TERRA, LUNA, L-5 CITY, AND MARS.

ONE DRAW-BACK IS THAT ALL OF A STATEROOM'S GUESTS MUST **AGREE** ON WHAT TO VIEW.

TERRIBLY SORRY ...

ANOTHER CONSEQUENCE OF MY ENDOCRINE PROBLEM IS, ER, OCCASIONAL DIGESTIVE MALFUNCTIONS.

UGH.

NOW I **REALLY** NEED SOME FRESH AIR.

SEE YOU IN A FEW HOURS.

WATSON, RECORD AUDIO MESSAGE.

SEND WITH PRIVACY KEY TO PO XU-KE, XĪN XIĀN, HUÒXÌNG .

BEGIN RECORDING -- HELLO OLD FRIEND, I HOPE THIS FINDS YOU WELL ...

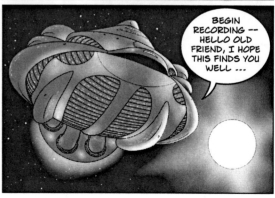

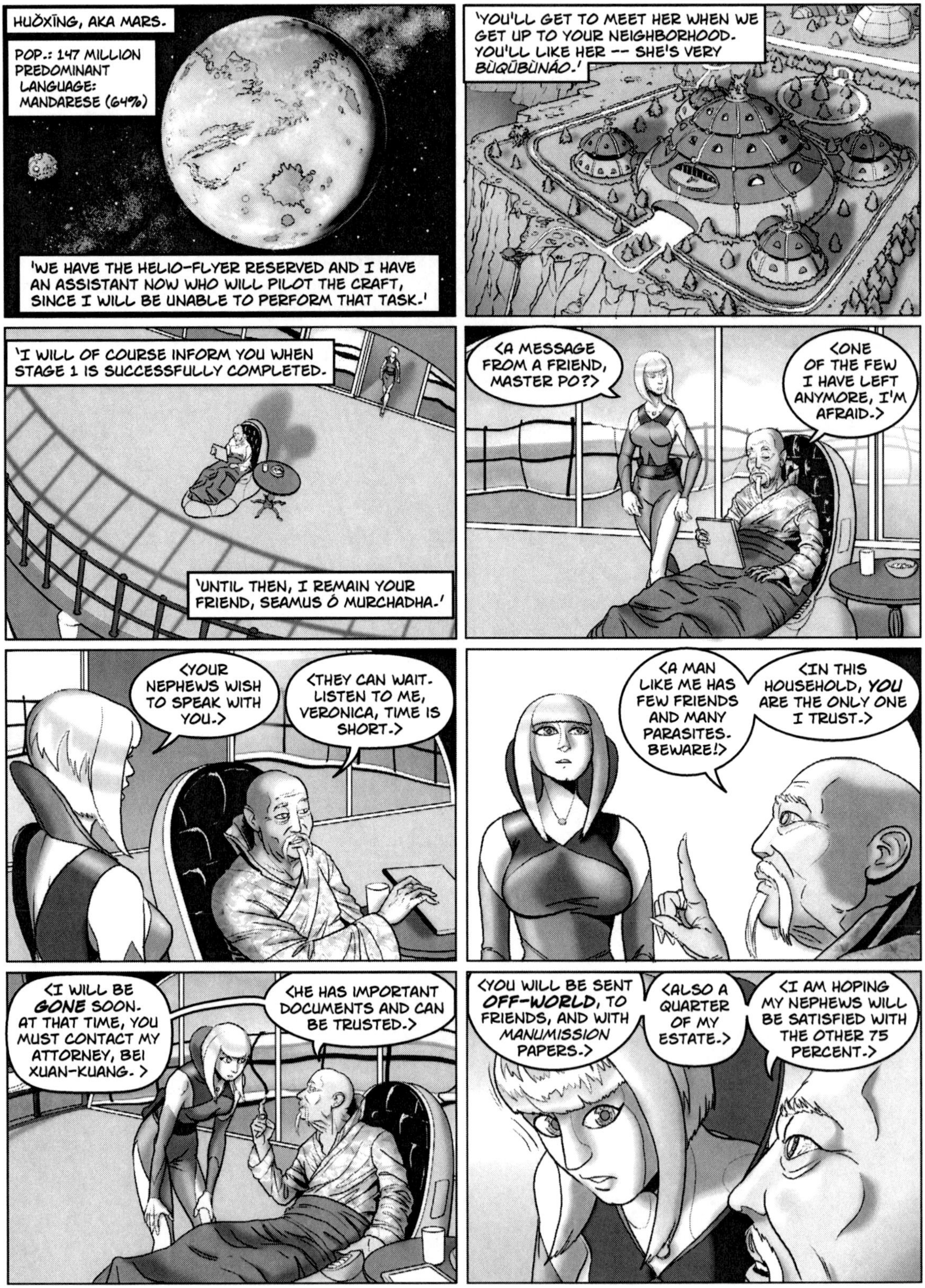
HUŎXĪNG, AKA MARS.
POP.: 147 MILLION
PREDOMINANT LANGUAGE: MANDARESE (64%)
'WE HAVE THE HELIO-FLYER RESERVED AND I HAVE AN ASSISTANT NOW WHO WILL PILOT THE CRAFT, SINCE I WILL BE UNABLE TO PERFORM THAT TASK.'
'YOU'LL GET TO MEET HER WHEN WE GET UP TO YOUR NEIGHBORHOOD. YOU'LL LIKE HER -- SHE'S VERY BÙQŪBÙNÁO.'
'I WILL OF COURSE INFORM YOU WHEN STAGE 1 IS SUCCESSFULLY COMPLETED.
'UNTIL THEN, I REMAIN YOUR FRIEND, SEAMUS Ó MURCHADHA.'
<A MESSAGE FROM A FRIEND, MASTER PO?>
<ONE OF THE FEW I HAVE LEFT ANYMORE, I'M AFRAID.>
<YOUR NEPHEWS WISH TO SPEAK WITH YOU.>
<THEY CAN WAIT. LISTEN TO ME, VERONICA, TIME IS SHORT.>
<A MAN LIKE ME HAS FEW FRIENDS AND MANY PARASITES. BEWARE!>
<IN THIS HOUSEHOLD, YOU ARE THE ONLY ONE I TRUST.>
<I WILL BE GONE SOON. AT THAT TIME, YOU MUST CONTACT MY ATTORNEY, BEI XUAN-KUANG.>
<HE HAS IMPORTANT DOCUMENTS AND CAN BE TRUSTED.>
<YOU WILL BE SENT OFF-WORLD, TO FRIENDS, AND WITH MANUMISSION PAPERS.>
<ALSO A QUARTER OF MY ESTATE.>
<I AM HOPING MY NEPHEWS WILL BE SATISFIED WITH THE OTHER 75 PERCENT.>

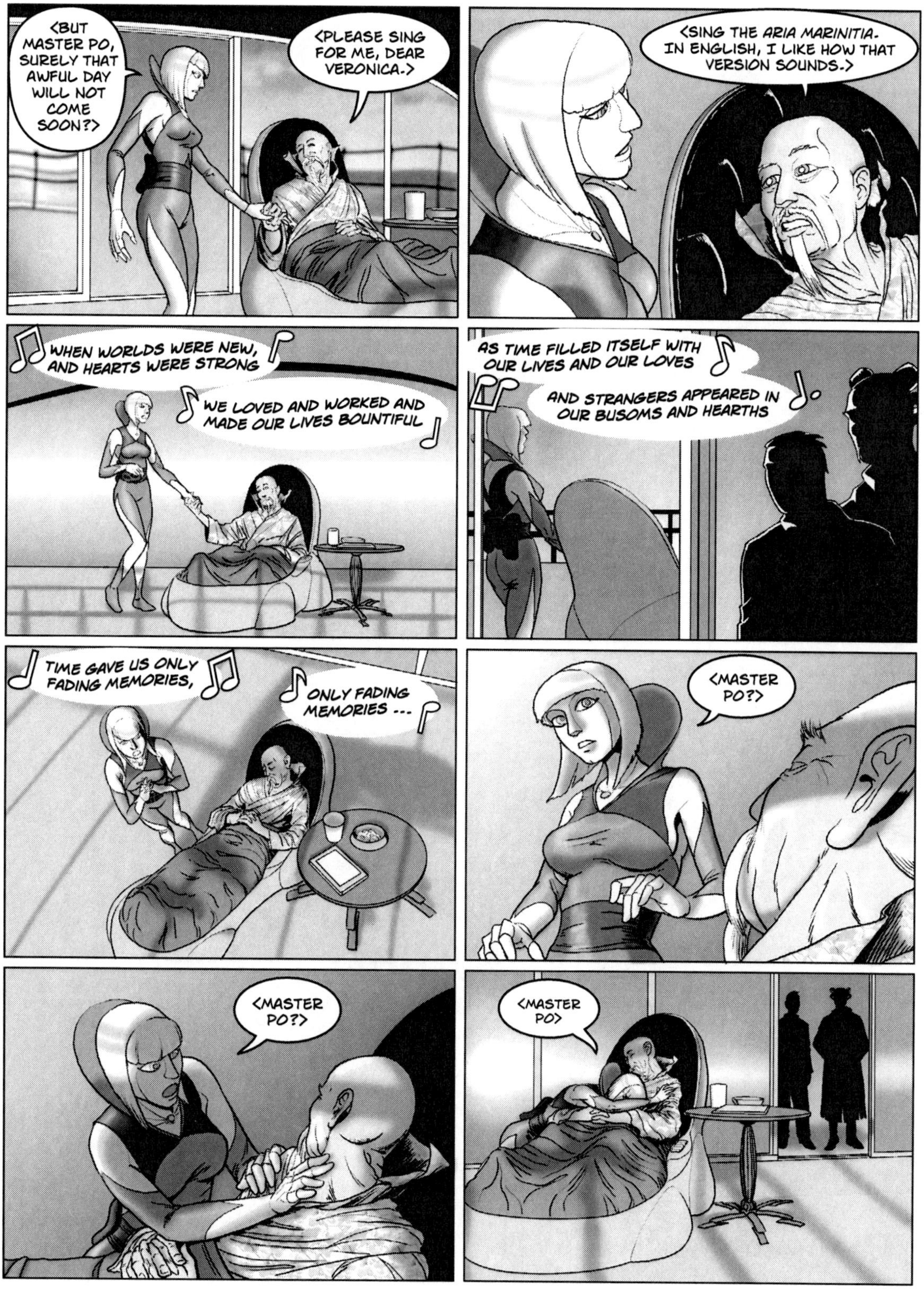
<BUT MASTER PO, SURELY THAT AWFUL DAY WILL NOT COME SOON?>
<PLEASE SING FOR ME, DEAR VERONICA.>
<SING THE *ARIA MARINITIA*. IN ENGLISH, I LIKE HOW THAT VERSION SOUNDS.>
WHEN WORLDS WERE NEW, AND HEARTS WERE STRONG
WE LOVED AND WORKED AND MADE OUR LIVES BOUNTIFUL
AS TIME FILLED ITSELF WITH OUR LIVES AND OUR LOVES
AND STRANGERS APPEARED IN OUR BUSOMS AND HEARTHS
TIME GAVE US ONLY FADING MEMORIES,
ONLY FADING MEMORIES ...
<MASTER PO?>
<MASTER PO?>
<MASTER PO>

EVEN WITH MERCURY NEAR ITS APHELION OF 70 MILLION KILOMETERS, THE HEAVILY-SHIELDED *ALPINE DREAM* STRAINS TO PROTECT ITS PASSENGERS AND CREW FROM SOLAR RADIATION.

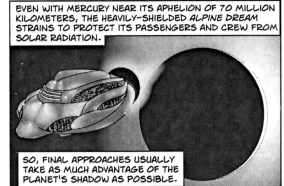

SO, FINAL APPROACHES USUALLY TAKE AS MUCH ADVANTAGE OF THE PLANET'S SHADOW AS POSSIBLE.

HELIOS BASE IS BUILT NEAR MERCURY'S NORTH POLE INSIDE *AVOGADRO'S CHASM*, WHICH IS SHIELDED FROM THE MONSTROUS *SUN* THROUGHOUT MERCURY'S 4,224-HOUR SOLAR 'DAY.'

THE BASE IS A JOINT OPERATION, BY TREATY, BETWEEN THE TERRAN MERCORP *GENSAXWELL* AND THE L-5 MERCORP *MUC AR FOULAIN*. BOTH HAVE EXTENSIVE MINING INTERESTS ON THE PLANET.

WE HAVE 50 HOURS UNTIL YOUR DATE WITH THE HELIOFLYER.

YOU WILL NEED TO SPEND ALL THE TIME YOU'RE NOT SLEEPING, IN THE SIMULATOR GETTING PROFICIENT.

THIRTY-TWO HOURS OF SIMULATOR?

BUT *WHY?* I HAVE EVERYTHING I NEED TO KNOW IN THIS SOUPED-UP 'PLANT YOU GAVE ME.

HMMPH

WOULD YOU EXPECT AS GOOD A MUSICAL PERFORMANCE FROM A NOVICE PLAYER WITH A SHINY NEW 'PLANT, AS YOU WOULD AN EXPERIENCED AXE-MAN?

HURM...

NO.

THIRTY HOURS OF SIMULATOR, PLUS MEALS AND SLEEP, AND NO ALCOHOL, UNTIL SHOWTIME, YES?

AGREED.

BUT AFTER I GET BACK, THERE *WILL* BE ALCOHOL. YES.

DESTINATION, PLEASE?

THE COLOMBO HILLIOTT.

I DON'T SUPPOSE YOU CAN DO ANYTHING ABOUT THE GRAVITY HERE, CAN YOU?

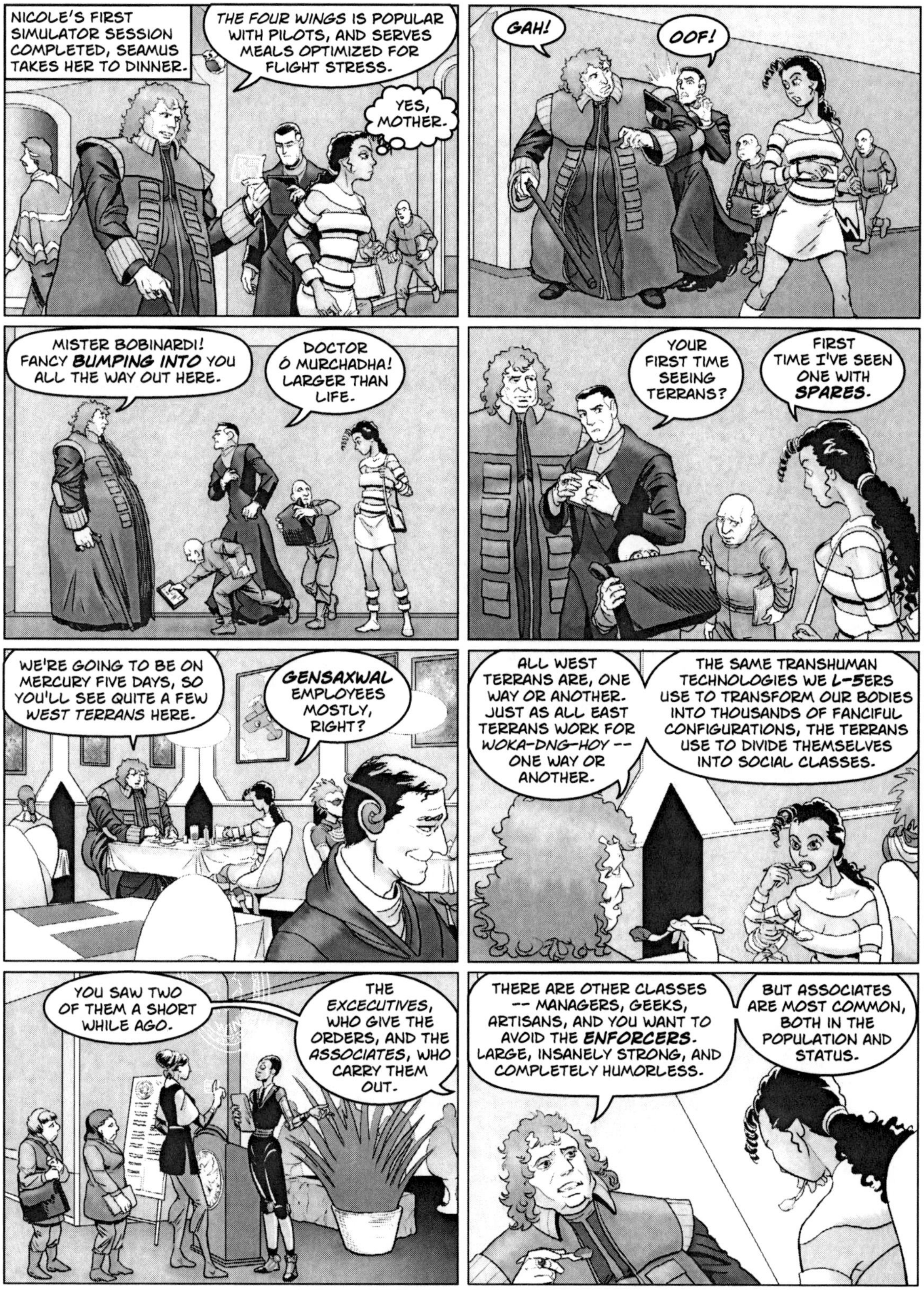
NICOLE'S FIRST SIMULATOR SESSION COMPLETED, SEAMUS TAKES HER TO DINNER.
THE FOUR WINGS IS POPULAR WITH PILOTS, AND SERVES MEALS OPTIMIZED FOR FLIGHT STRESS.
YES, MOTHER.
GAH!
OOF!
MISTER BOBINARDI! FANCY BUMPING INTO YOU ALL THE WAY OUT HERE.
DOCTOR Ó MURCHADHA! LARGER THAN LIFE.
YOUR FIRST TIME SEEING TERRANS?
FIRST TIME I'VE SEEN ONE WITH SPARES.
WE'RE GOING TO BE ON MERCURY FIVE DAYS, SO YOU'LL SEE QUITE A FEW WEST TERRANS HERE.
GENSAXWAL EMPLOYEES MOSTLY, RIGHT?
ALL WEST TERRANS ARE, ONE WAY OR ANOTHER. JUST AS ALL EAST TERRANS WORK FOR WOKA-DNG-HOY -- ONE WAY OR ANOTHER.
THE SAME TRANSHUMAN TECHNOLOGIES WE L-5ERS USE TO TRANSFORM OUR BODIES INTO THOUSANDS OF FANCIFUL CONFIGURATIONS, THE TERRANS USE TO DIVIDE THEMSELVES INTO SOCIAL CLASSES.
YOU SAW TWO OF THEM A SHORT WHILE AGO.
THE EXCECUTIVES, WHO GIVE THE ORDERS, AND THE ASSOCIATES, WHO CARRY THEM OUT.
THERE ARE OTHER CLASSES -- MANAGERS, GEEKS, ARTISANS, AND YOU WANT TO AVOID THE ENFORCERS. LARGE, INSANELY STRONG, AND COMPLETELY HUMORLESS.
BUT ASSOCIATES ARE MOST COMMON, BOTH IN THE POPULATION AND STATUS.

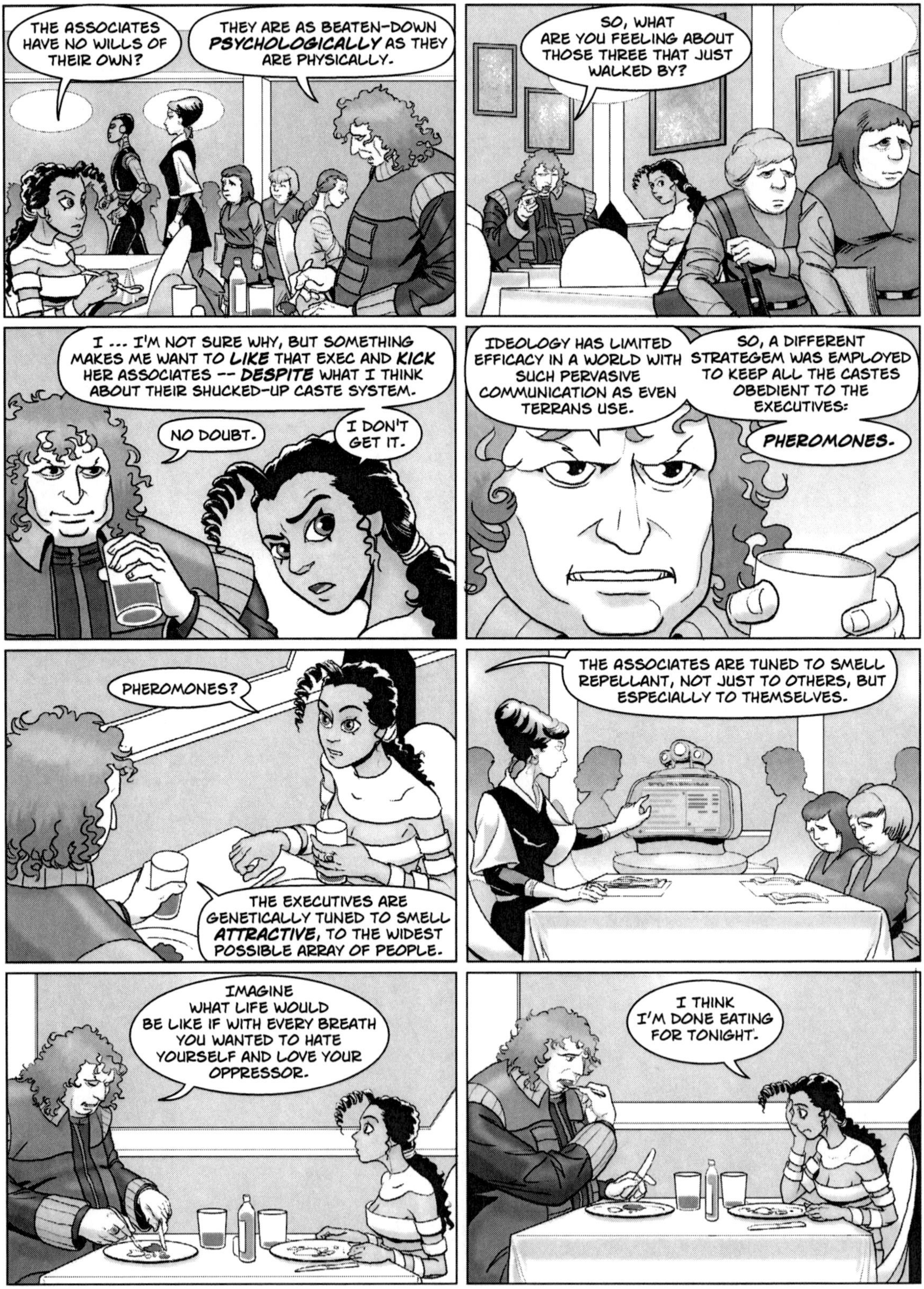
THE ASSOCIATES HAVE NO WILLS OF THEIR OWN?
THEY ARE AS BEATEN-DOWN PSYCHOLOGICALLY AS THEY ARE PHYSICALLY.
SO, WHAT ARE YOU FEELING ABOUT THOSE THREE THAT JUST WALKED BY?
I ... I'M NOT SURE WHY, BUT SOMETHING MAKES ME WANT TO LIKE THAT EXEC AND KICK HER ASSOCIATES -- DESPITE WHAT I THINK ABOUT THEIR SHUCKED-UP CASTE SYSTEM.
NO DOUBT.
I DON'T GET IT.
IDEOLOGY HAS LIMITED EFFICACY IN A WORLD WITH SUCH PERVASIVE COMMUNICATION AS EVEN TERRANS USE.
SO, A DIFFERENT STRATEGEM WAS EMPLOYED TO KEEP ALL THE CASTES OBEDIENT TO THE EXECUTIVES:
PHEROMONES.
PHEROMONES?
THE EXECUTIVES ARE GENETICALLY TUNED TO SMELL ATTRACTIVE, TO THE WIDEST POSSIBLE ARRAY OF PEOPLE.
THE ASSOCIATES ARE TUNED TO SMELL REPELLANT, NOT JUST TO OTHERS, BUT ESPECIALLY TO THEMSELVES.
IMAGINE WHAT LIFE WOULD BE LIKE IF WITH EVERY BREATH YOU WANTED TO HATE YOURSELF AND LOVE YOUR OPPRESSOR.
I THINK I'M DONE EATING FOR TONIGHT.

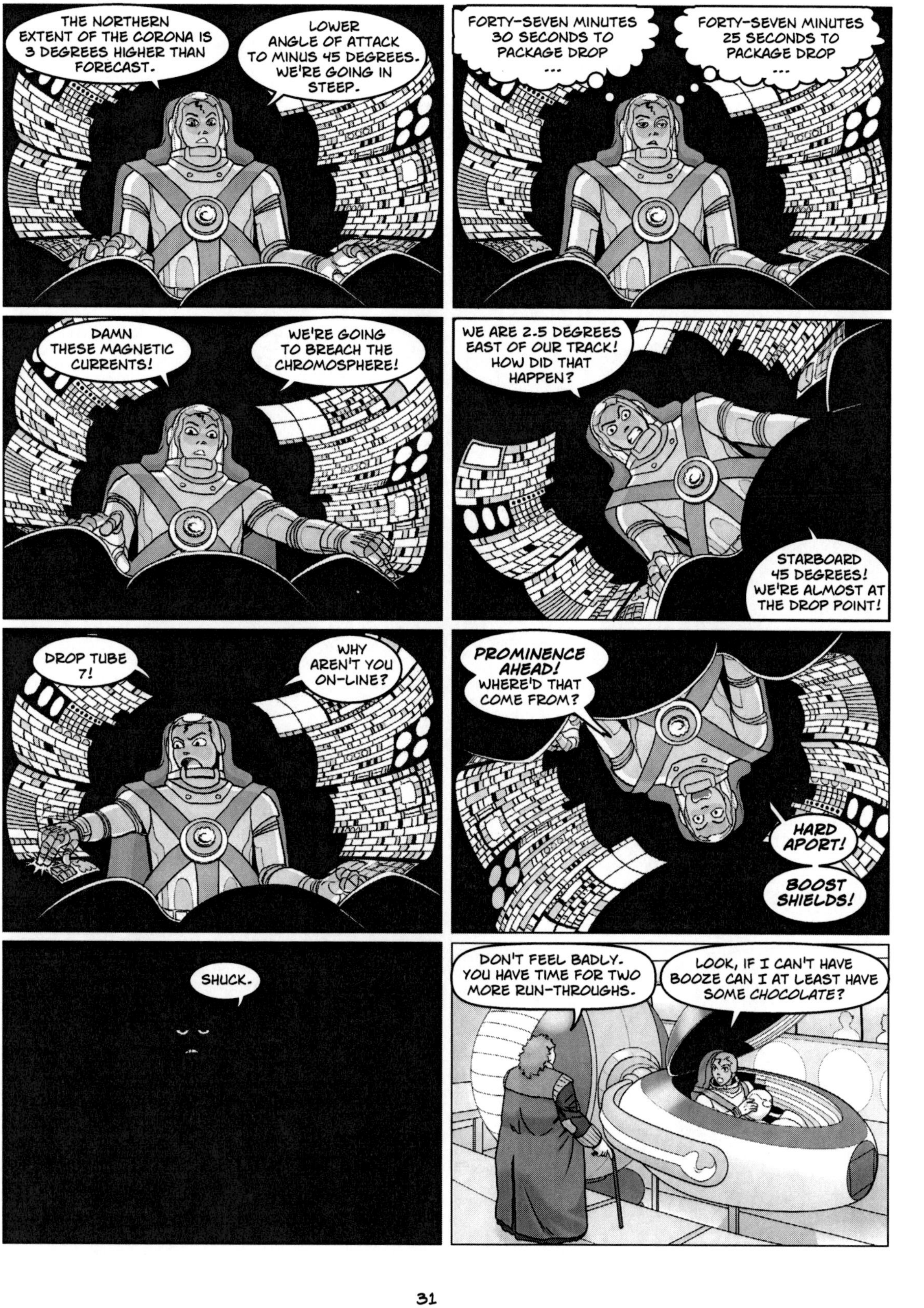
THE NORTHERN EXTENT OF THE CORONA IS 3 DEGREES HIGHER THAN FORECAST.
LOWER ANGLE OF ATTACK TO MINUS 45 DEGREES. WE'RE GOING IN STEEP.
FORTY-SEVEN MINUTES 30 SECONDS TO PACKAGE DROP ...
FORTY-SEVEN MINUTES 25 SECONDS TO PACKAGE DROP ...
DAMN THESE MAGNETIC CURRENTS!
WE'RE GOING TO BREACH THE CHROMOSPHERE!
WE ARE 2.5 DEGREES EAST OF OUR TRACK! HOW DID THAT HAPPEN?
STARBOARD 45 DEGREES! WE'RE ALMOST AT THE DROP POINT!
DROP TUBE 7!
WHY AREN'T YOU ON-LINE?
PROMINENCE AHEAD! WHERE'D THAT COME FROM?
HARD APORT!
BOOST SHIELDS!
SHUCK.
DON'T FEEL BADLY. YOU HAVE TIME FOR TWO MORE RUN-THROUGHS.
LOOK, IF I CAN'T HAVE BOOZE CAN I AT LEAST HAVE SOME CHOCOLATE?

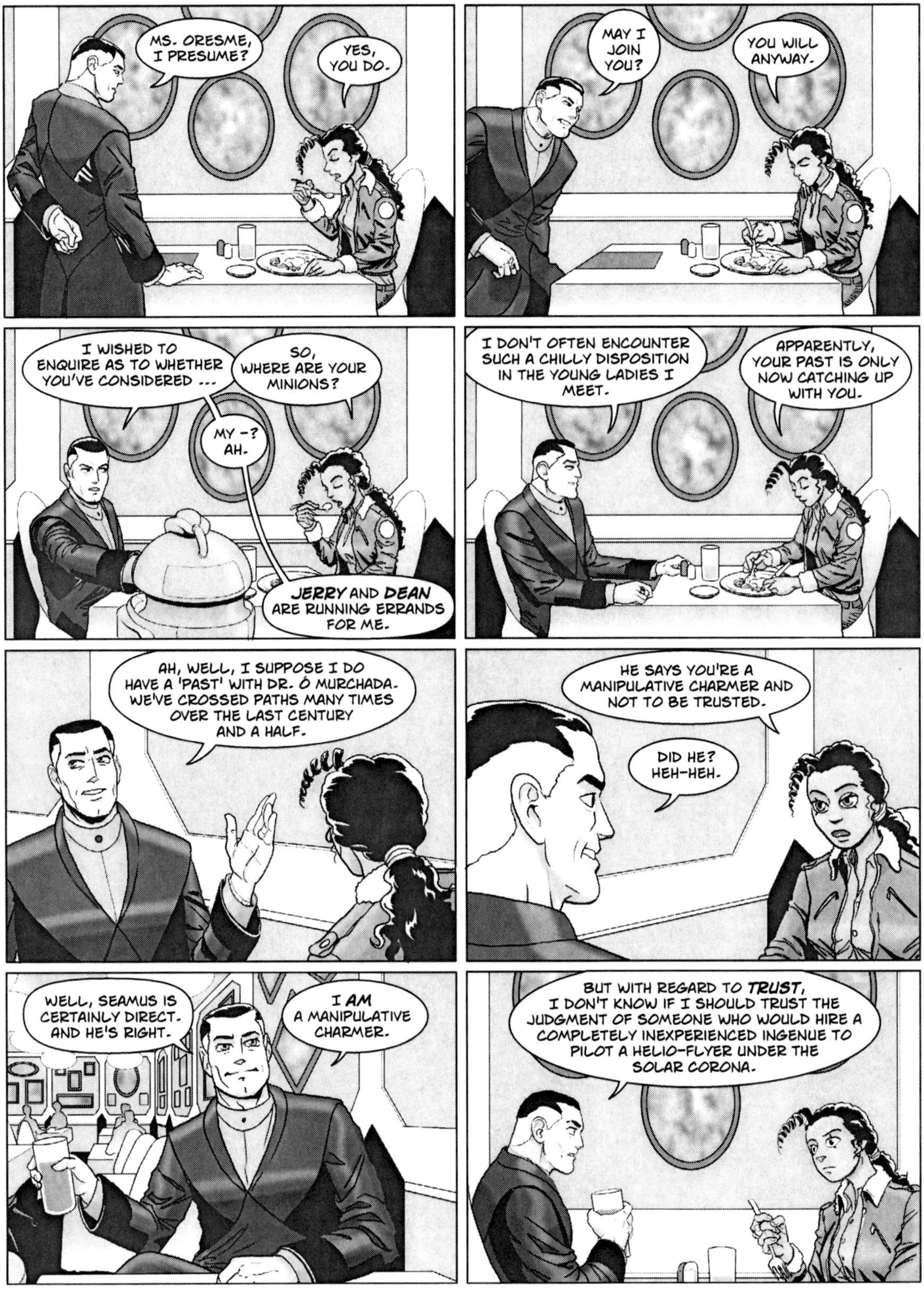
MS. ORESME, I PRESUME?
YES, YOU DO.
MAY I JOIN YOU?
YOU WILL ANYWAY.
I WISHED TO ENQUIRE AS TO WHETHER YOU'VE CONSIDERED ...
SO, WHERE ARE YOUR MINIONS?
MY -? AH.
JERRY AND *DEAN* ARE RUNNING ERRANDS FOR ME.
I DON'T OFTEN ENCOUNTER SUCH A CHILLY DISPOSITION IN THE YOUNG LADIES I MEET.
APPARENTLY, YOUR PAST IS ONLY NOW CATCHING UP WITH YOU.
AH, WELL, I SUPPOSE I DO HAVE A 'PAST' WITH DR. Ó MURCHADA. WE'VE CROSSED PATHS MANY TIMES OVER THE LAST CENTURY AND A HALF.
HE SAYS YOU'RE A MANIPULATIVE CHARMER AND NOT TO BE TRUSTED.
DID HE? HEH-HEH.
WELL, SEAMUS IS CERTAINLY DIRECT. AND HE'S RIGHT.
I *AM* A MANIPULATIVE CHARMER.
BUT WITH REGARD TO *TRUST*, I DON'T KNOW IF I SHOULD TRUST THE JUDGMENT OF SOMEONE WHO WOULD HIRE A COMPLETELY INEXPERIENCED INGENUE TO PILOT A HELIO-FLYER UNDER THE SOLAR CORONA.

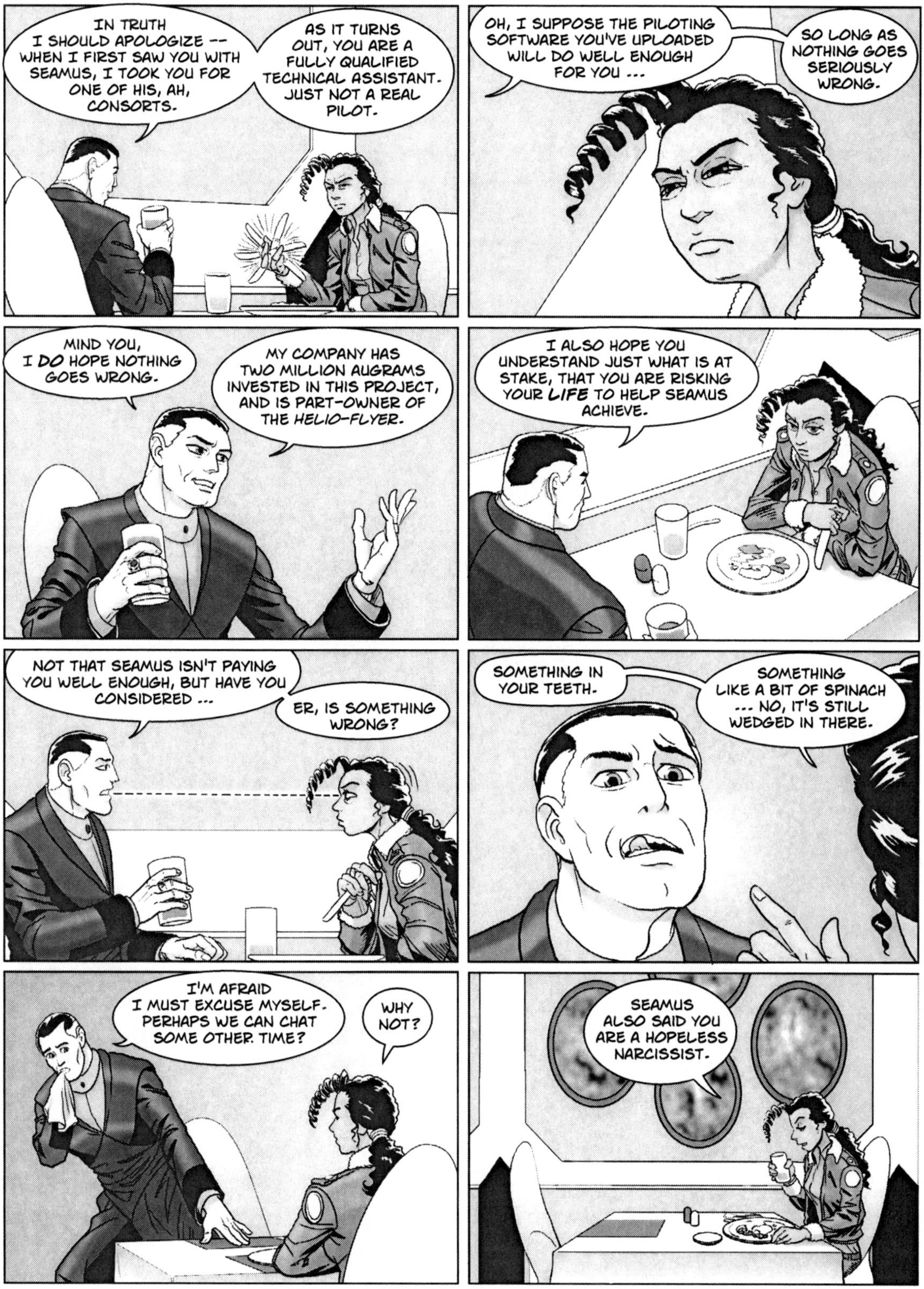
IN TRUTH I SHOULD APOLOGIZE -- WHEN I FIRST SAW YOU WITH SEAMUS, I TOOK YOU FOR ONE OF HIS, AH, CONSORTS.
AS IT TURNS OUT, YOU ARE A FULLY QUALIFIED TECHNICAL ASSISTANT. JUST NOT A REAL PILOT.
OH, I SUPPOSE THE PILOTING SOFTWARE YOU'VE UPLOADED WILL DO WELL ENOUGH FOR YOU ...
SO LONG AS NOTHING GOES SERIOUSLY WRONG.
MIND YOU, I *DO* HOPE NOTHING GOES WRONG.
MY COMPANY HAS TWO MILLION AUGRAMS INVESTED IN THIS PROJECT, AND IS PART-OWNER OF THE *HELIO-FLYER*.
I ALSO HOPE YOU UNDERSTAND JUST WHAT IS AT STAKE, THAT YOU ARE RISKING YOUR ***LIFE*** TO HELP SEAMUS ACHIEVE.
NOT THAT SEAMUS ISN'T PAYING YOU WELL ENOUGH, BUT HAVE YOU CONSIDERED ...
ER, IS SOMETHING WRONG?
SOMETHING IN YOUR TEETH.
SOMETHING LIKE A BIT OF SPINACH ... NO, IT'S STILL WEDGED IN THERE.
I'M AFRAID I MUST EXCUSE MYSELF. PERHAPS WE CAN CHAT SOME OTHER TIME?
WHY NOT?
SEAMUS ALSO SAID YOU ARE A HOPELESS NARCISSIST.

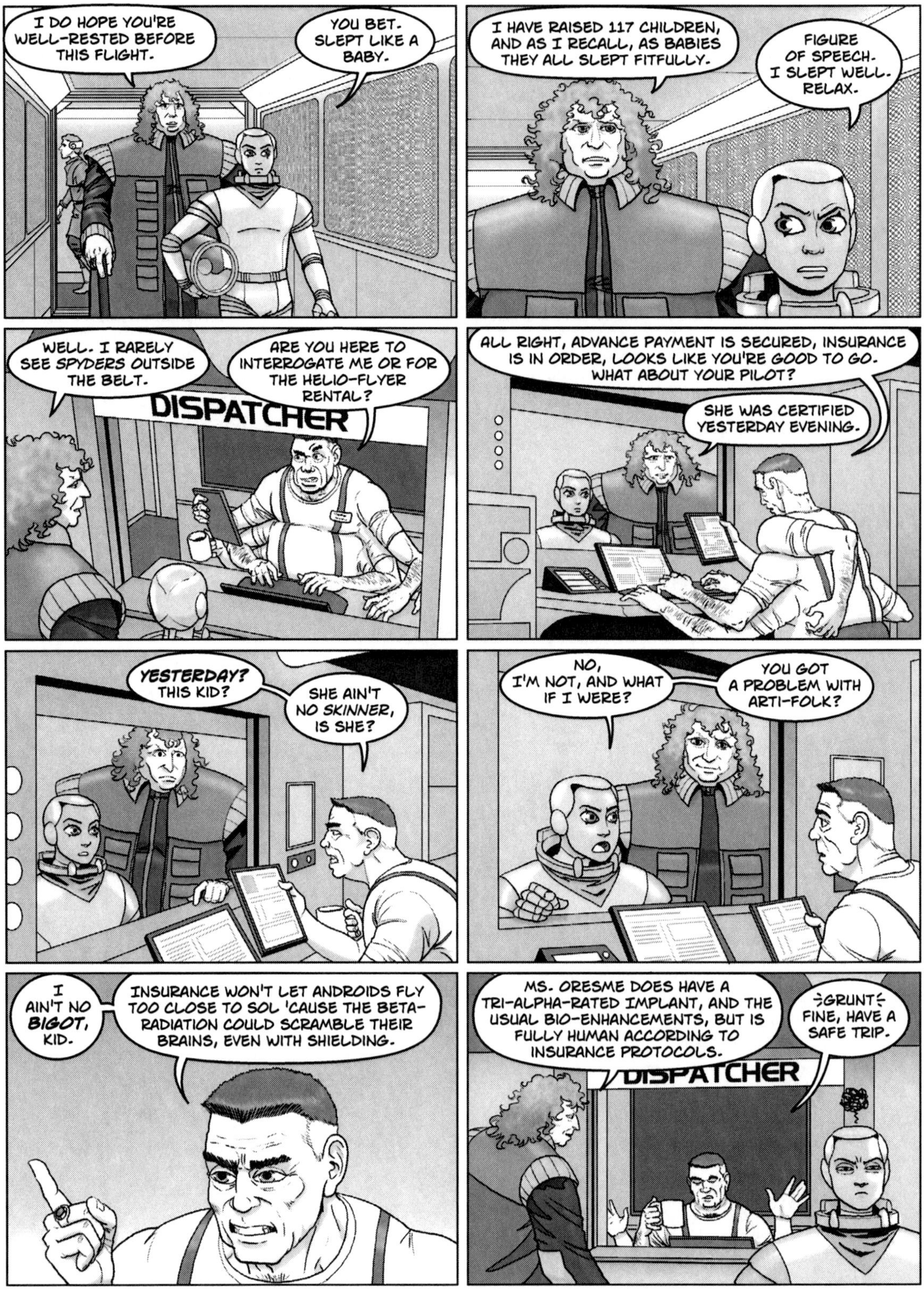
I DO HOPE YOU'RE WELL-RESTED BEFORE THIS FLIGHT.
YOU BET. SLEPT LIKE A BABY.
I HAVE RAISED 117 CHILDREN, AND AS I RECALL, AS BABIES THEY ALL SLEPT FITFULLY.
FIGURE OF SPEECH. I SLEPT WELL. RELAX.
WELL. I RARELY SEE SPYDERS OUTSIDE THE BELT.
ARE YOU HERE TO INTERROGATE ME OR FOR THE HELIO-FLYER RENTAL?
DISPATCHER
ALL RIGHT, ADVANCE PAYMENT IS SECURED, INSURANCE IS IN ORDER, LOOKS LIKE YOU'RE GOOD TO GO. WHAT ABOUT YOUR PILOT?
SHE WAS CERTIFIED YESTERDAY EVENING.
YESTERDAY? THIS KID?
SHE AIN'T NO SKINNER, IS SHE?
NO, I'M NOT, AND WHAT IF I WERE?
YOU GOT A PROBLEM WITH ARTI-FOLK?
I AIN'T NO BIGOT, KID.
INSURANCE WON'T LET ANDROIDS FLY TOO CLOSE TO SOL 'CAUSE THE BETA-RADIATION COULD SCRAMBLE THEIR BRAINS, EVEN WITH SHIELDING.
MS. ORESME DOES HAVE A TRI-ALPHA-RATED IMPLANT, AND THE USUAL BIO-ENHANCEMENTS, BUT IS FULLY HUMAN ACCORDING TO INSURANCE PROTOCOLS.
GRUNT
FINE, HAVE A SAFE TRIP.
DISPATCHER

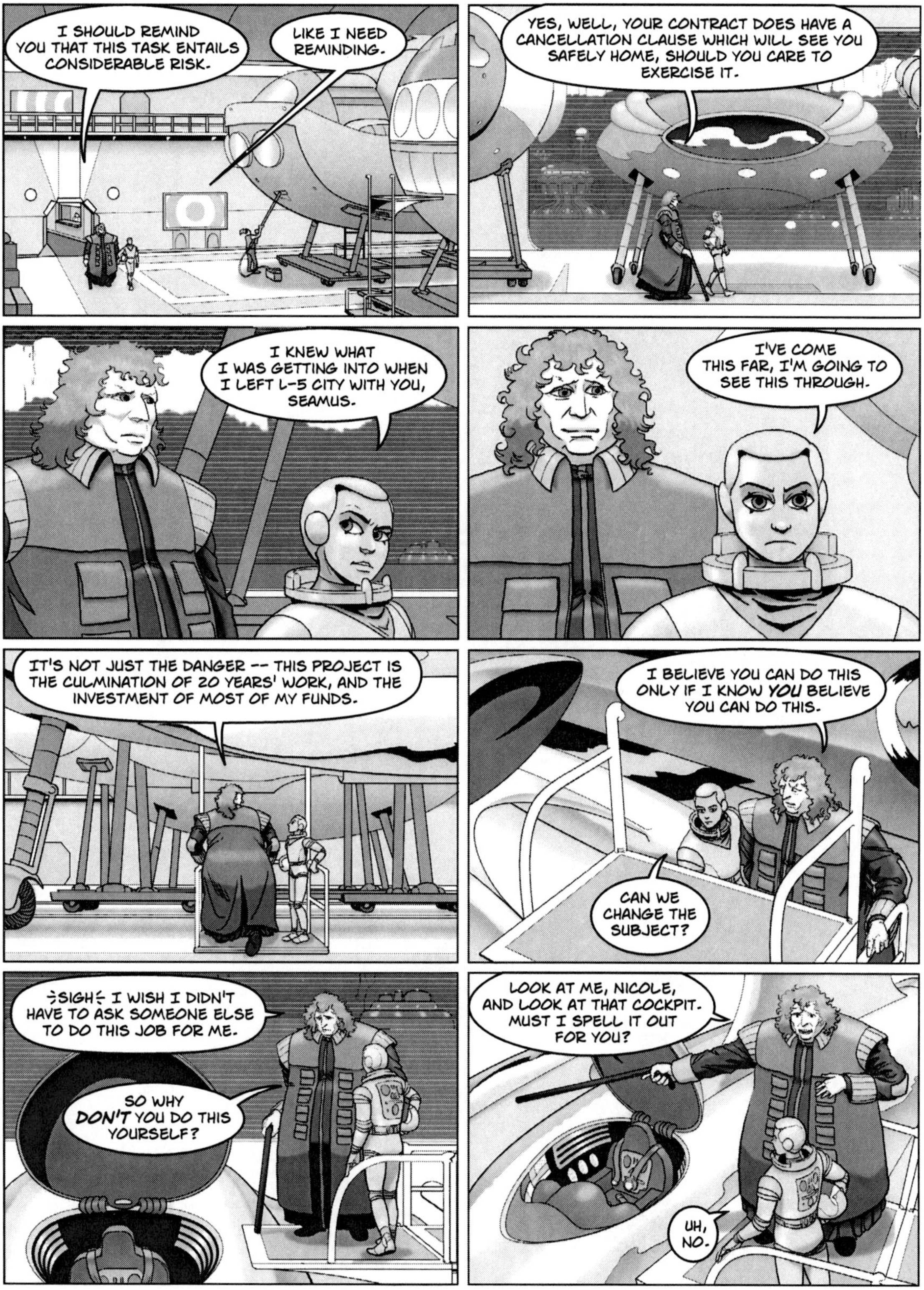
I SHOULD REMIND YOU THAT THIS TASK ENTAILS CONSIDERABLE RISK.
LIKE I NEED REMINDING.
YES, WELL, YOUR CONTRACT DOES HAVE A CANCELLATION CLAUSE WHICH WILL SEE YOU SAFELY HOME, SHOULD YOU CARE TO EXERCISE IT.
I KNEW WHAT I WAS GETTING INTO WHEN I LEFT L-5 CITY WITH YOU, SEAMUS.
I'VE COME THIS FAR, I'M GOING TO SEE THIS THROUGH.
IT'S NOT JUST THE DANGER -- THIS PROJECT IS THE CULMINATION OF 20 YEARS' WORK, AND THE INVESTMENT OF MOST OF MY FUNDS.
I BELIEVE YOU CAN DO THIS ONLY IF I KNOW *YOU* BELIEVE YOU CAN DO THIS.
CAN WE CHANGE THE SUBJECT?
÷SIGH÷ I WISH I DIDN'T HAVE TO ASK SOMEONE ELSE TO DO THIS JOB FOR ME.
SO WHY *DON'T* YOU DO THIS YOURSELF?
LOOK AT ME, NICOLE, AND LOOK AT THAT COCKPIT. MUST I SPELL IT OUT FOR YOU?
UH, NO.

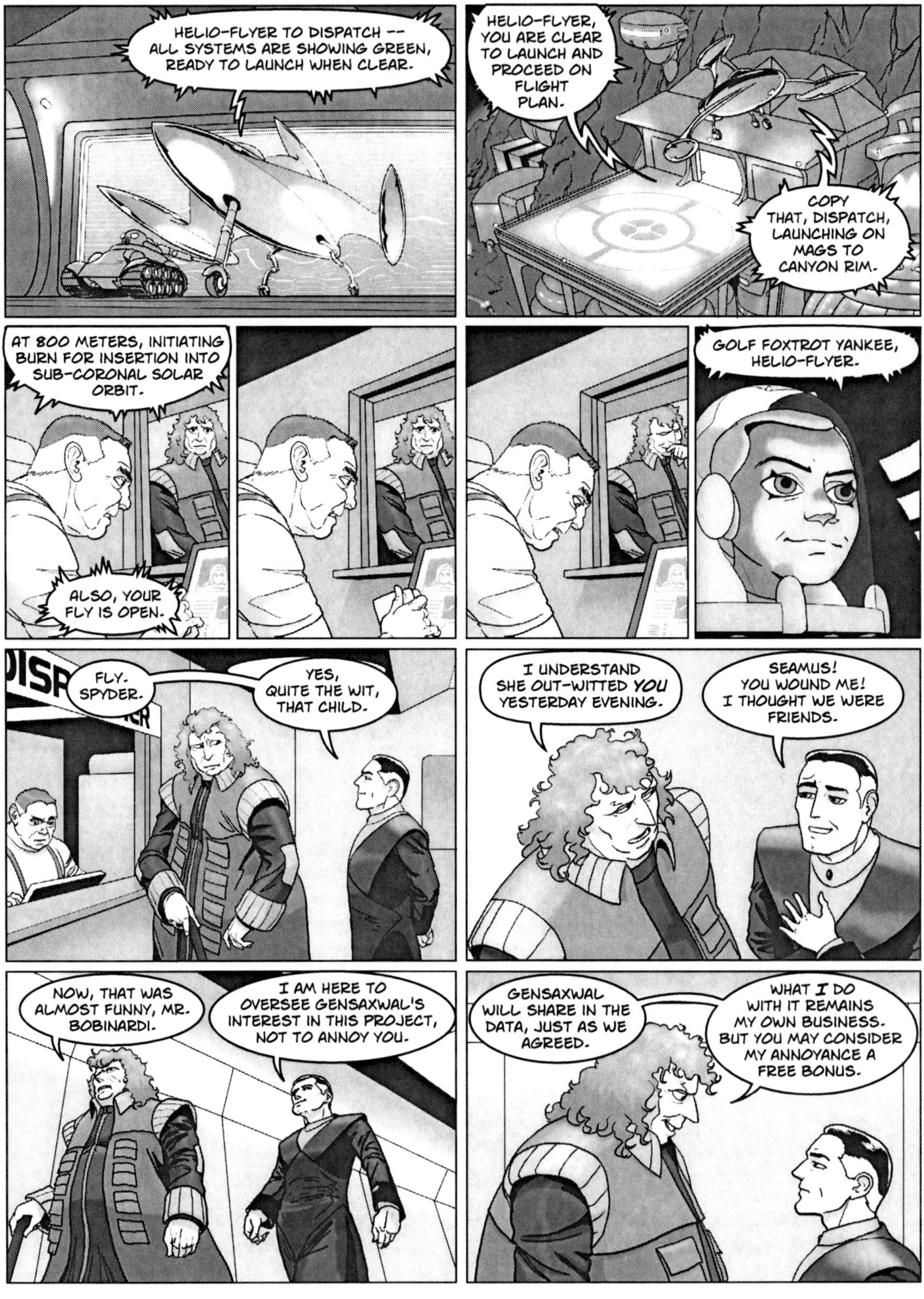
HELIO-FLYER TO DISPATCH -- ALL SYSTEMS ARE SHOWING GREEN, READY TO LAUNCH WHEN CLEAR.
HELIO-FLYER, YOU ARE CLEAR TO LAUNCH AND PROCEED ON FLIGHT PLAN.
COPY THAT, DISPATCH, LAUNCHING ON MAGS TO CANYON RIM.
AT 800 METERS, INITIATING BURN FOR INSERTION INTO SUB-CORONAL SOLAR ORBIT.
ALSO, YOUR FLY IS OPEN.
GOLF FOXTROT YANKEE, HELIO-FLYER.
FLY. SPYDER.
YES, QUITE THE WIT, THAT CHILD.
I UNDERSTAND SHE OUT-WITTED YOU YESTERDAY EVENING.
SEAMUS! YOU WOUND ME! I THOUGHT WE WERE FRIENDS.
NOW, THAT WAS ALMOST FUNNY, MR. BOBINARDI.
I AM HERE TO OVERSEE GENSAXWAL'S INTEREST IN THIS PROJECT, NOT TO ANNOY YOU.
GENSAXWAL WILL SHARE IN THE DATA, JUST AS WE AGREED.
WHAT I DO WITH IT REMAINS MY OWN BUSINESS. BUT YOU MAY CONSIDER MY ANNOYANCE A FREE BONUS.

XĪN XIĀN, ON HUŎXĪNG (MARS).

<... AND AFTER SETTLEMENT OF OTHER GOOD-NAME ACCOUNTS, THE REMAINDER OF THE ESTATE IS TO BE ... SHARED BETWEEN MY NEPHEWS ...>

<... TONG XIE PO AND MA BO NU.>

<AND THAT CONCLUDES PO XU-KE'S WILL, EVERYONE. YOU MAY MAKE TRANSFER ARRANGEMENTS NOW OR BY APPOINTMENT AT YOUR CONVENIENCE.>

<WAIT, THAT IS ALL? ARE YOU CERTAIN?>

<MASTER PO SAID I WAS TO BE MANUMITTED AND GIVEN ...>

<MR. TONG, WILL YOU PLEASE RESTRAIN YOUR PROPERTY!>

<OF COURSE.>

<HEEL, BITCH.>

‡GURK!‡

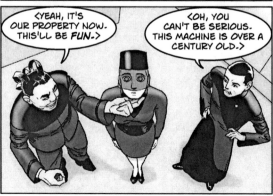

<YEAH, IT'S OUR PROPERTY NOW. THIS'LL BE FUN.>

<OH, YOU CAN'T BE SERIOUS. THIS MACHINE IS OVER A CENTURY OLD.>

<NO, WE WILL WIPE ITS MEMORY AND GET RID OF IT.>

<THEN WE'LL GET YOU A FRESH, NEW FUCK-DOLL TO PLAY WITH.>

<AWWW...>

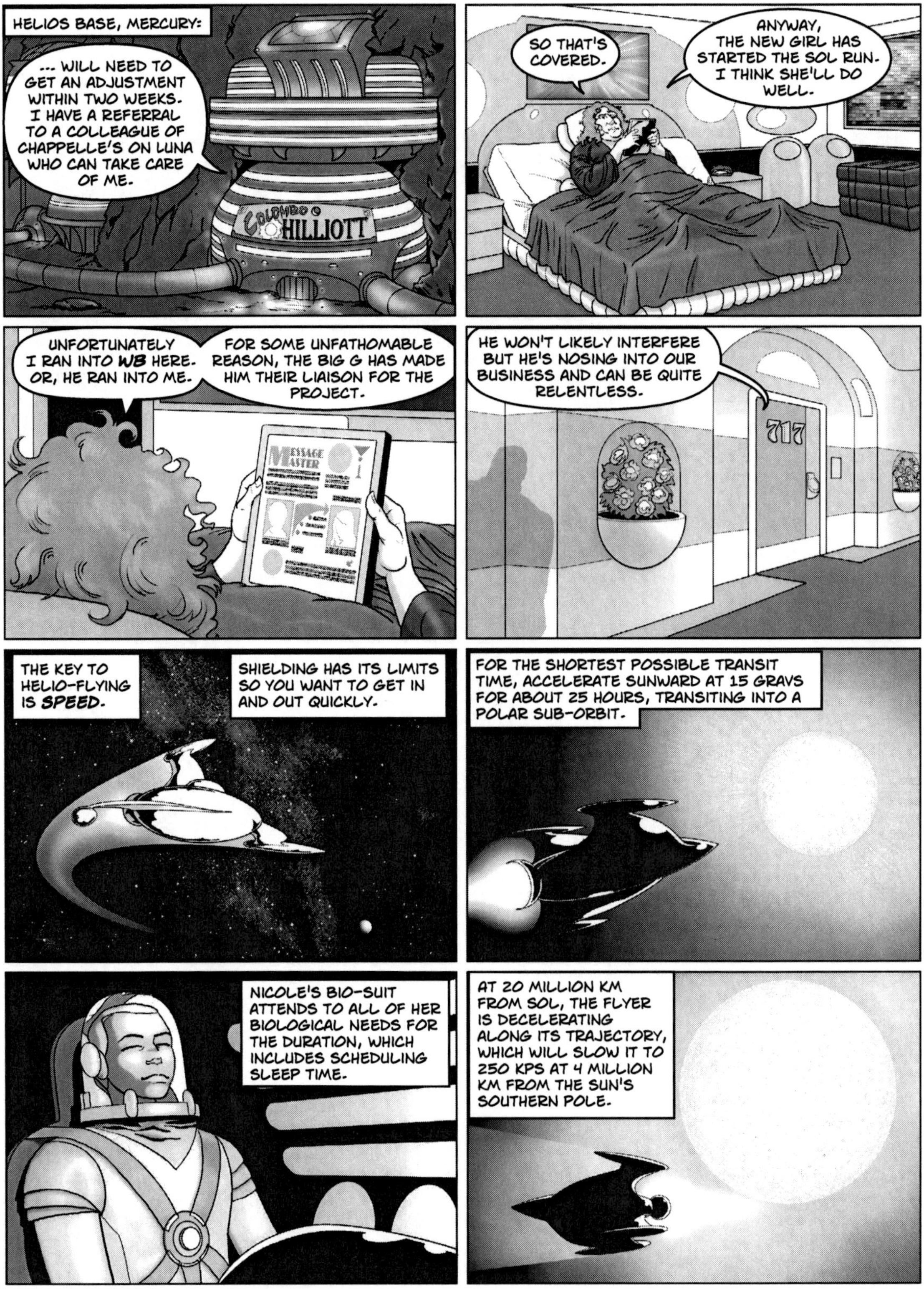
HELIOS BASE, MERCURY:
... WILL NEED TO GET AN ADJUSTMENT WITHIN TWO WEEKS. I HAVE A REFERRAL TO A COLLEAGUE OF CHAPPELLE'S ON LUNA WHO CAN TAKE CARE OF ME.
HILLIOTT
SO THAT'S COVERED.
ANYWAY, THE NEW GIRL HAS STARTED THE SOL RUN. I THINK SHE'LL DO WELL.
UNFORTUNATELY I RAN INTO WB HERE. OR, HE RAN INTO ME.
FOR SOME UNFATHOMABLE REASON, THE BIG G HAS MADE HIM THEIR LIAISON FOR THE PROJECT.
MESSAGE MASTER
HE WON'T LIKELY INTERFERE BUT HE'S NOSING INTO OUR BUSINESS AND CAN BE QUITE RELENTLESS.
717
THE KEY TO HELIO-FLYING IS SPEED.
SHIELDING HAS ITS LIMITS SO YOU WANT TO GET IN AND OUT QUICKLY.
FOR THE SHORTEST POSSIBLE TRANSIT TIME, ACCELERATE SUNWARD AT 15 GRAVS FOR ABOUT 25 HOURS, TRANSITING INTO A POLAR SUB-ORBIT.
NICOLE'S BIO-SUIT ATTENDS TO ALL OF HER BIOLOGICAL NEEDS FOR THE DURATION, WHICH INCLUDES SCHEDULING SLEEP TIME.
AT 20 MILLION KM FROM SOL, THE FLYER IS DECELERATING ALONG ITS TRAJECTORY, WHICH WILL SLOW IT TO 250 KPS AT 4 MILLION KM FROM THE SUN'S SOUTHERN POLE.

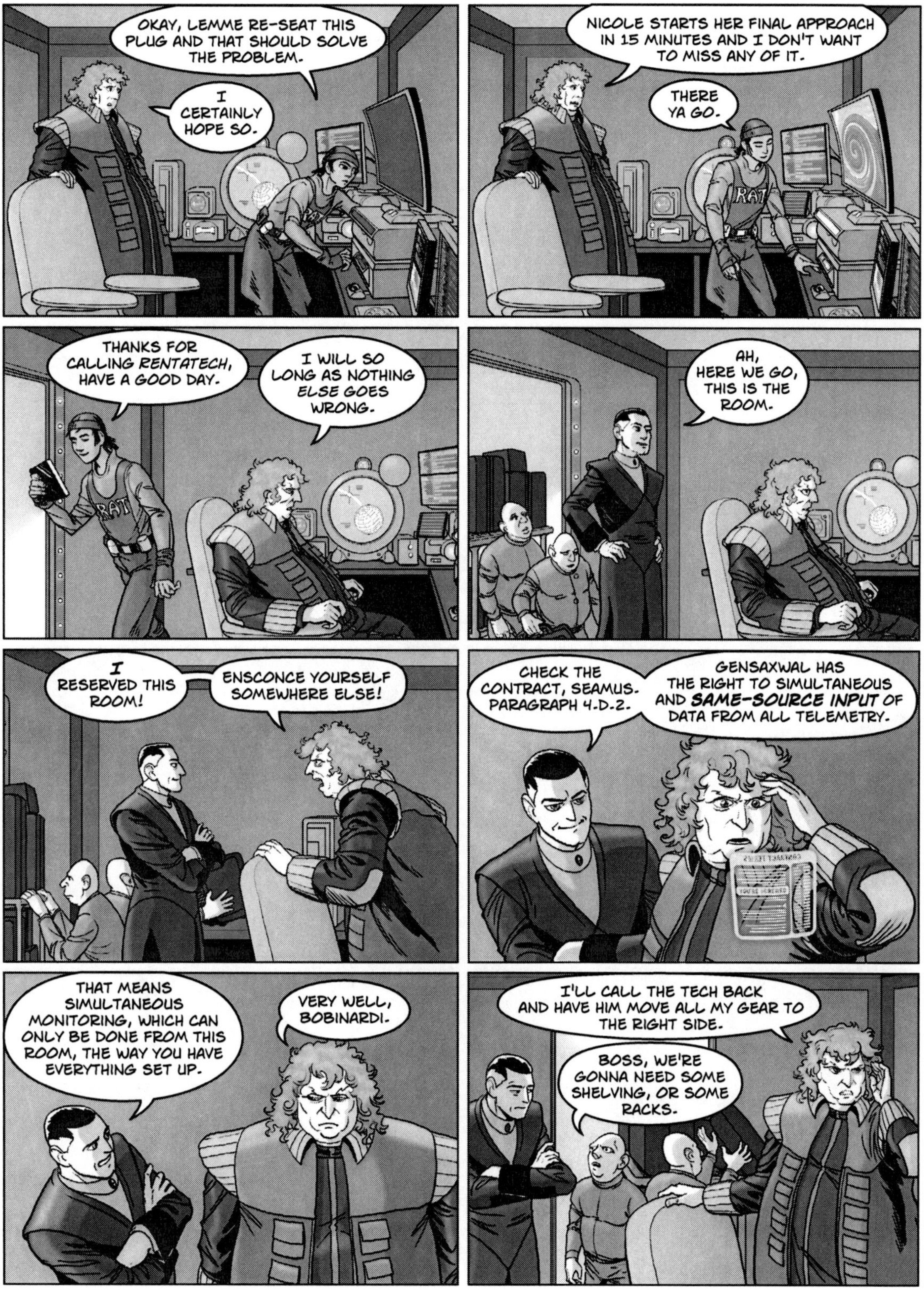
OKAY, LEMME RE-SEAT THIS PLUG AND THAT SHOULD SOLVE THE PROBLEM.
I CERTAINLY HOPE SO.
NICOLE STARTS HER FINAL APPROACH IN 15 MINUTES AND I DON'T WANT TO MISS ANY OF IT.
THERE YA GO.
THANKS FOR CALLING RENTATECH, HAVE A GOOD DAY.
I WILL SO LONG AS NOTHING ELSE GOES WRONG.
AH, HERE WE GO, THIS IS THE ROOM.
I RESERVED THIS ROOM!
ENSCONCE YOURSELF SOMEWHERE ELSE!
CHECK THE CONTRACT, SEAMUS. PARAGRAPH 4.D.2.
GENSAXWAL HAS THE RIGHT TO SIMULTANEOUS AND **SAME-SOURCE INPUT** OF DATA FROM ALL TELEMETRY.
THAT MEANS SIMULTANEOUS MONITORING, WHICH CAN ONLY BE DONE FROM THIS ROOM, THE WAY YOU HAVE EVERYTHING SET UP.
VERY WELL, BOBINARDI.
I'LL CALL THE TECH BACK AND HAVE HIM MOVE ALL MY GEAR TO THE RIGHT SIDE.
BOSS, WE'RE GONNA NEED SOME SHELVING, OR SOME RACKS.

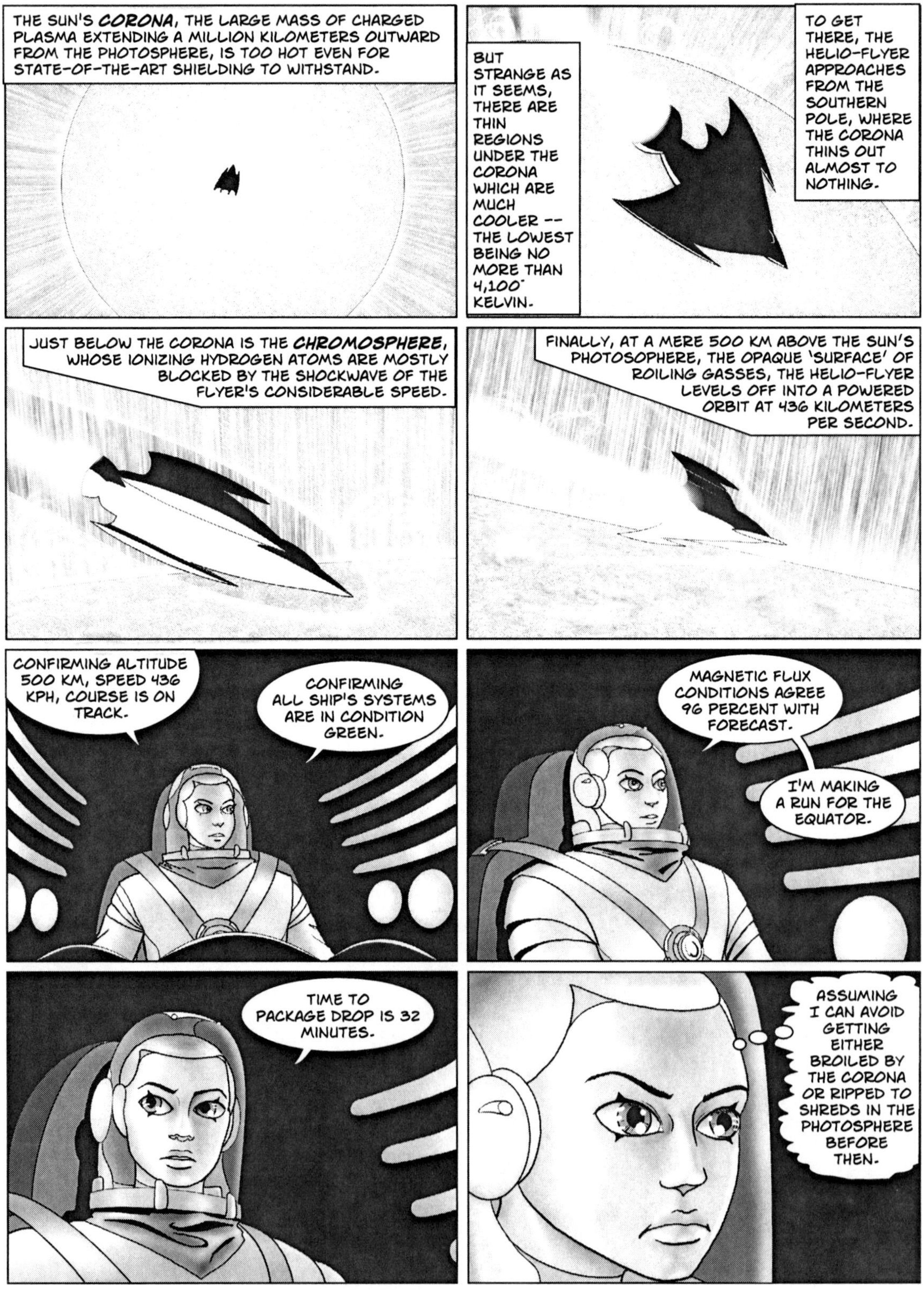
THE SUN'S CORONA, THE LARGE MASS OF CHARGED PLASMA EXTENDING A MILLION KILOMETERS OUTWARD FROM THE PHOTOSPHERE, IS TOO HOT EVEN FOR STATE-OF-THE-ART SHIELDING TO WITHSTAND.
BUT STRANGE AS IT SEEMS, THERE ARE THIN REGIONS UNDER THE CORONA WHICH ARE MUCH COOLER -- THE LOWEST BEING NO MORE THAN 4,100° KELVIN.
TO GET THERE, THE HELIO-FLYER APPROACHES FROM THE SOUTHERN POLE, WHERE THE CORONA THINS OUT ALMOST TO NOTHING.
JUST BELOW THE CORONA IS THE CHROMOSPHERE, WHOSE IONIZING HYDROGEN ATOMS ARE MOSTLY BLOCKED BY THE SHOCKWAVE OF THE FLYER'S CONSIDERABLE SPEED.
FINALLY, AT A MERE 500 KM ABOVE THE SUN'S PHOTOSOPHERE, THE OPAQUE 'SURFACE' OF ROILING GASSES, THE HELIO-FLYER LEVELS OFF INTO A POWERED ORBIT AT 436 KILOMETERS PER SECOND.
CONFIRMING ALTITUDE 500 KM, SPEED 436 KPH, COURSE IS ON TRACK.
CONFIRMING ALL SHIP'S SYSTEMS ARE IN CONDITION GREEN.
MAGNETIC FLUX CONDITIONS AGREE 96 PERCENT WITH FORECAST.
I'M MAKING A RUN FOR THE EQUATOR.
TIME TO PACKAGE DROP IS 32 MINUTES.
ASSUMING I CAN AVOID GETTING EITHER BROILED BY THE CORONA OR RIPPED TO SHREDS IN THE PHOTOSPHERE BEFORE THEN.

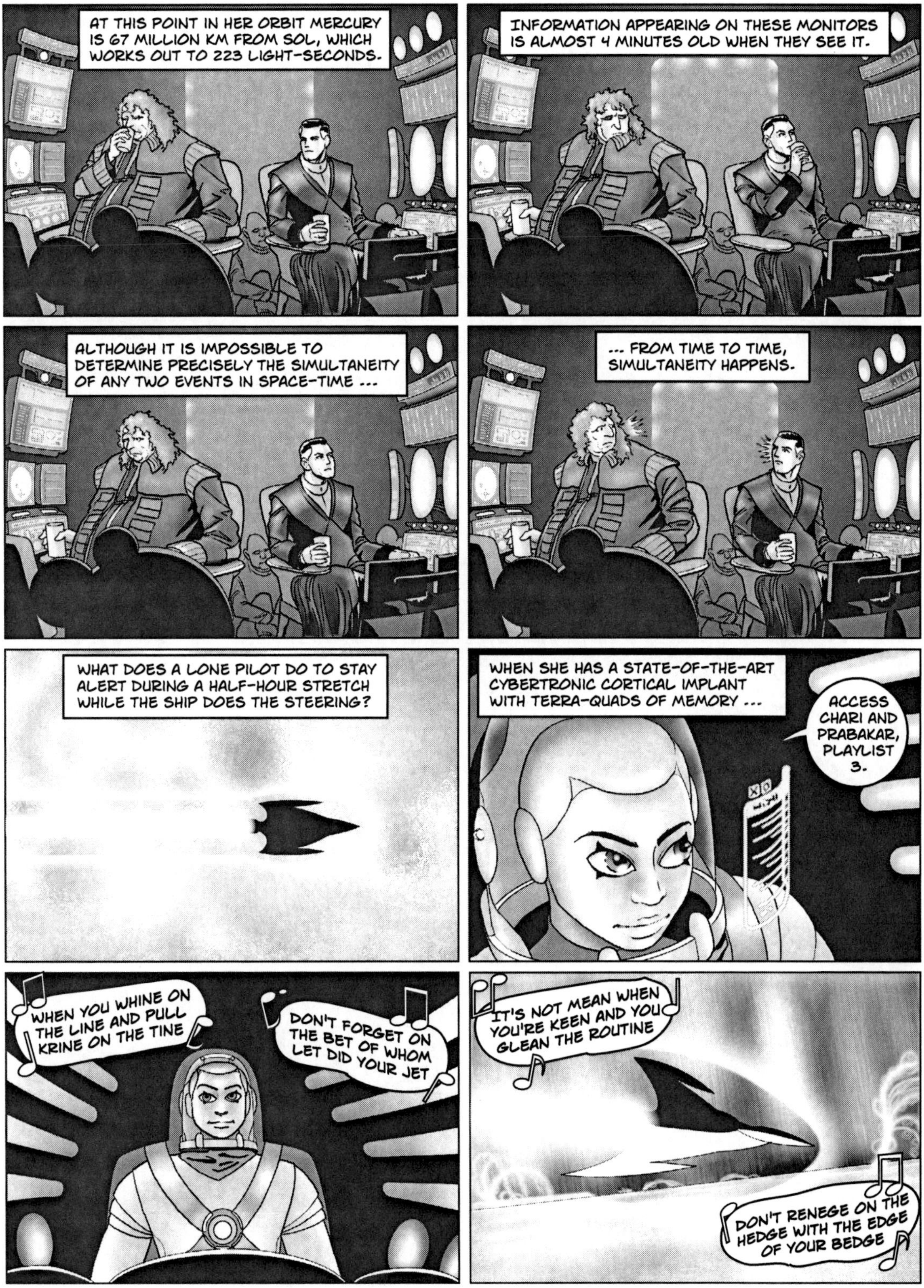
AT THIS POINT IN HER ORBIT MERCURY IS 67 MILLION KM FROM SOL, WHICH WORKS OUT TO 223 LIGHT-SECONDS.
INFORMATION APPEARING ON THESE MONITORS IS ALMOST 4 MINUTES OLD WHEN THEY SEE IT.
ALTHOUGH IT IS IMPOSSIBLE TO DETERMINE PRECISELY THE SIMULTANEITY OF ANY TWO EVENTS IN SPACE-TIME ...
... FROM TIME TO TIME, SIMULTANEITY HAPPENS.
WHAT DOES A LONE PILOT DO TO STAY ALERT DURING A HALF-HOUR STRETCH WHILE THE SHIP DOES THE STEERING?
WHEN SHE HAS A STATE-OF-THE-ART CYBERTRONIC CORTICAL IMPLANT WITH TERRA-QUADS OF MEMORY ...
ACCESS CHARI AND PRABAKAR, PLAYLIST 3.
WHEN YOU WHINE ON THE LINE AND PULL KRINE ON THE TINE
DON'T FORGET ON THE BET OF WHOM LET DID YOUR JET
IT'S NOT MEAN WHEN YOU'RE KEEN AND YOU GLEAN THE ROUTINE
DON'T RENEGE ON THE HEDGE WITH THE EDGE OF YOUR BEDGE

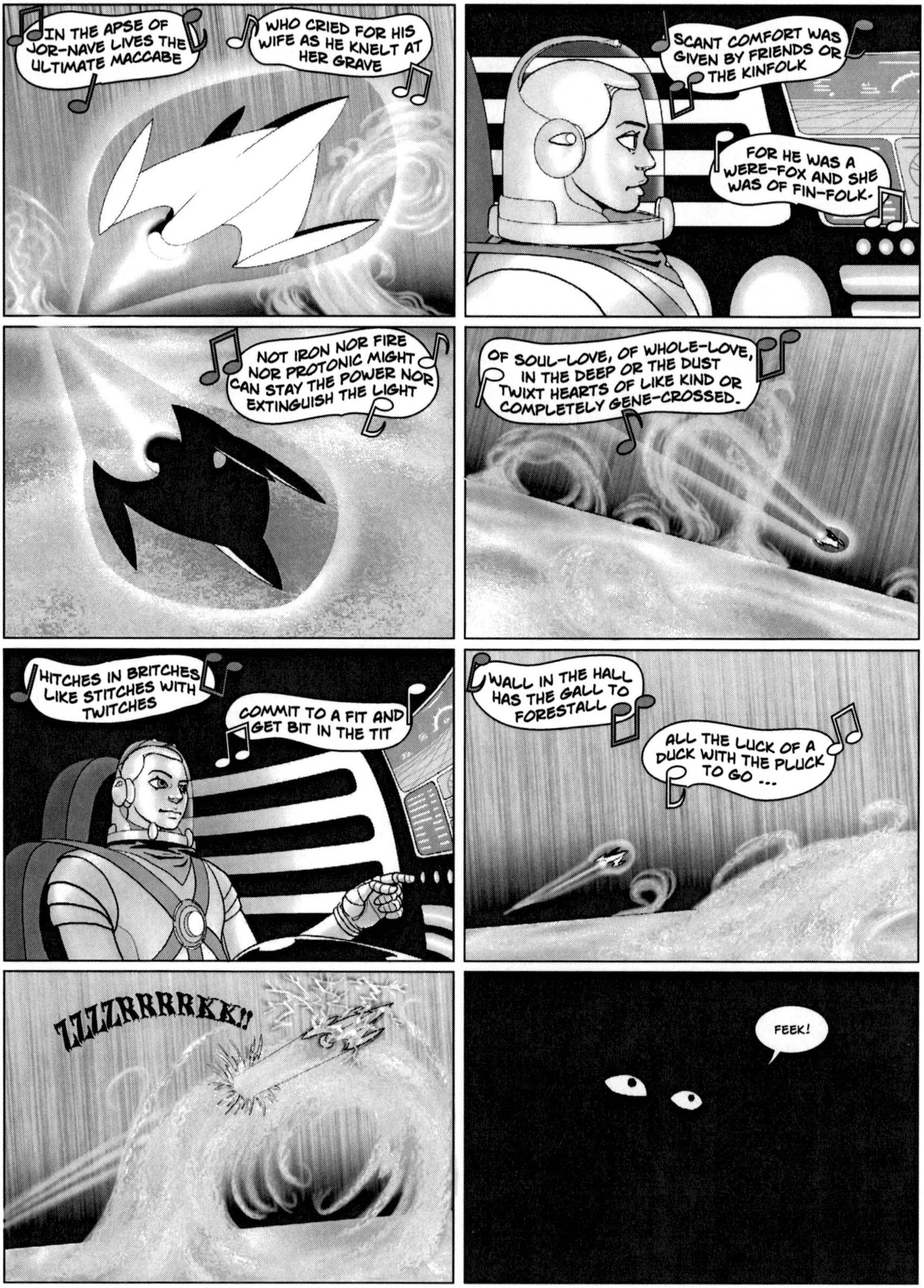
IN THE APSE OF JOR-NAVE LIVES THE ULTIMATE MACCABE
WHO CRIED FOR HIS WIFE AS HE KNELT AT HER GRAVE
SCANT COMFORT WAS GIVEN BY FRIENDS OR THE KINFOLK
FOR HE WAS A WERE-FOX AND SHE WAS OF FIN-FOLK.
NOT IRON NOR FIRE NOR PROTONIC MIGHT CAN STAY THE POWER NOR EXTINGUISH THE LIGHT
OF SOUL-LOVE, OF WHOLE-LOVE, IN THE DEEP OR THE DUST TWIXT HEARTS OF LIKE KIND OR COMPLETELY GENE-CROSSED.
HITCHES IN BRITCHES LIKE STITCHES WITH TWITCHES
COMMIT TO A FIT AND GET BIT IN THE TIT
WALL IN THE HALL HAS THE GALL TO FORESTALL
ALL THE LUCK OF A DUCK WITH THE PLUCK TO GO ...
ZZZZRRRRRKK!!
FEEK!

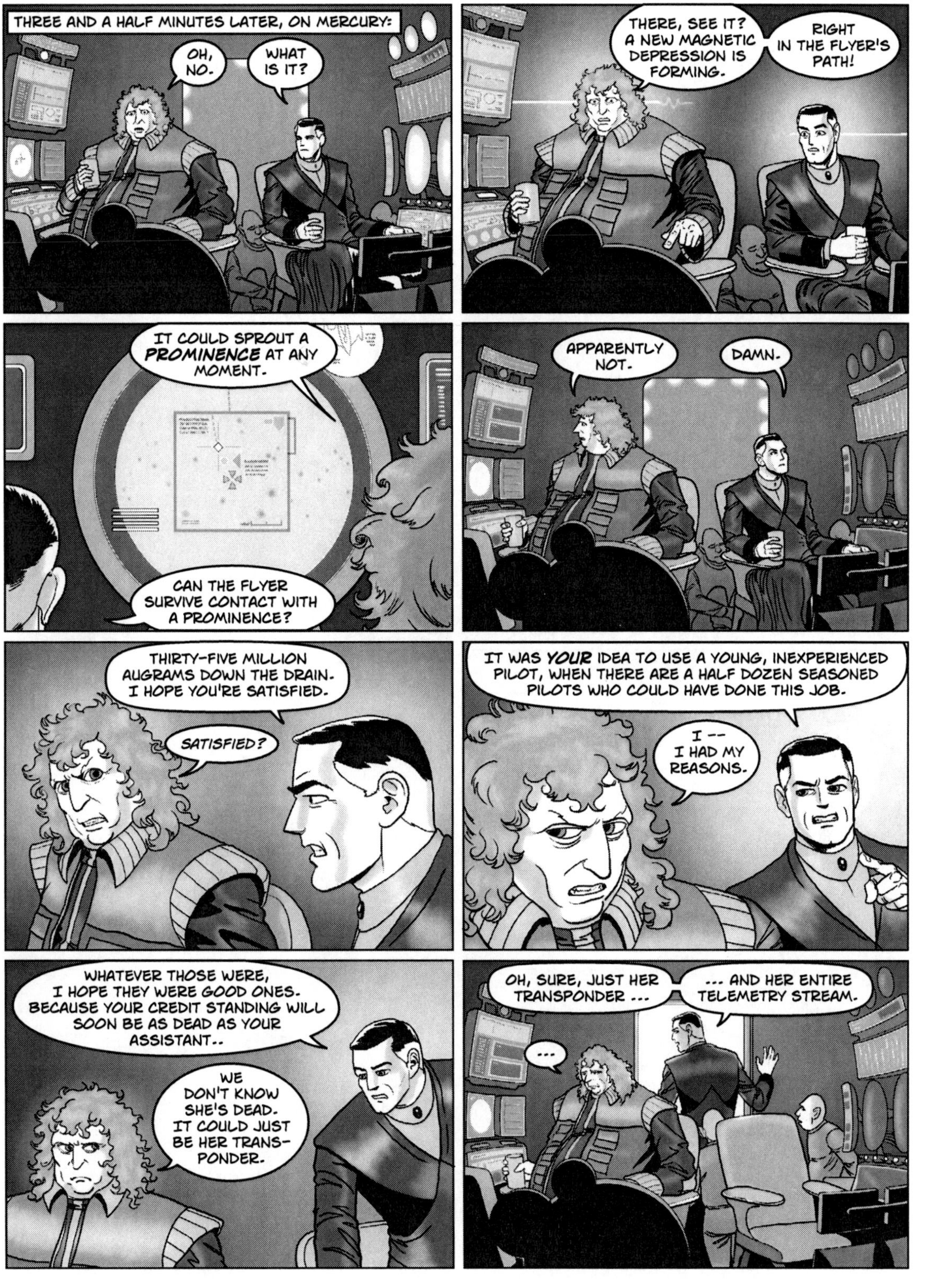
THREE AND A HALF MINUTES LATER, ON MERCURY:
OH, NO.
WHAT IS IT?
THERE, SEE IT? A NEW MAGNETIC DEPRESSION IS FORMING.
RIGHT IN THE FLYER'S PATH!
IT COULD SPROUT A PROMINENCE AT ANY MOMENT.
CAN THE FLYER SURVIVE CONTACT WITH A PROMINENCE?
APPARENTLY NOT.
DAMN.
THIRTY-FIVE MILLION AUGRAMS DOWN THE DRAIN. I HOPE YOU'RE SATISFIED.
SATISFIED?
IT WAS YOUR IDEA TO USE A YOUNG, INEXPERIENCED PILOT, WHEN THERE ARE A HALF DOZEN SEASONED PILOTS WHO COULD HAVE DONE THIS JOB.
I -- I HAD MY REASONS.
WHATEVER THOSE WERE, I HOPE THEY WERE GOOD ONES. BECAUSE YOUR CREDIT STANDING WILL SOON BE AS DEAD AS YOUR ASSISTANT..
WE DON'T KNOW SHE'S DEAD. IT COULD JUST BE HER TRANS-PONDER.
OH, SURE, JUST HER TRANSPONDER ...
... AND HER ENTIRE TELEMETRY STREAM.
...

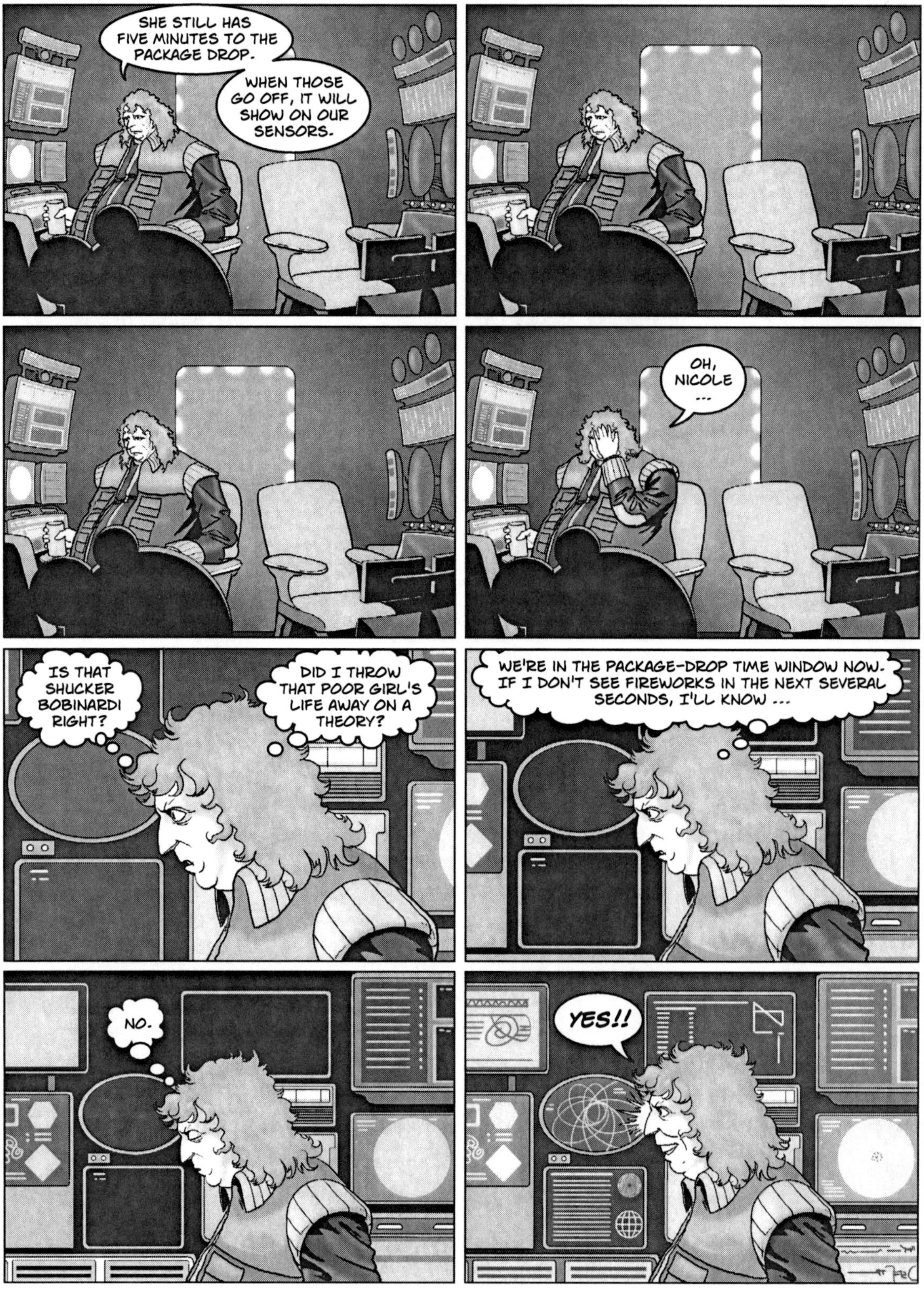
SHE STILL HAS FIVE MINUTES TO THE PACKAGE DROP.
WHEN THOSE GO OFF, IT WILL SHOW ON OUR SENSORS.
OH, NICOLE ...
IS THAT SHUCKER BOBINARDI RIGHT?
DID I THROW THAT POOR GIRL'S LIFE AWAY ON A THEORY?
WE'RE IN THE PACKAGE-DROP TIME WINDOW NOW. IF I DON'T SEE FIREWORKS IN THE NEXT SEVERAL SECONDS, I'LL KNOW ...
NO.
YES!!

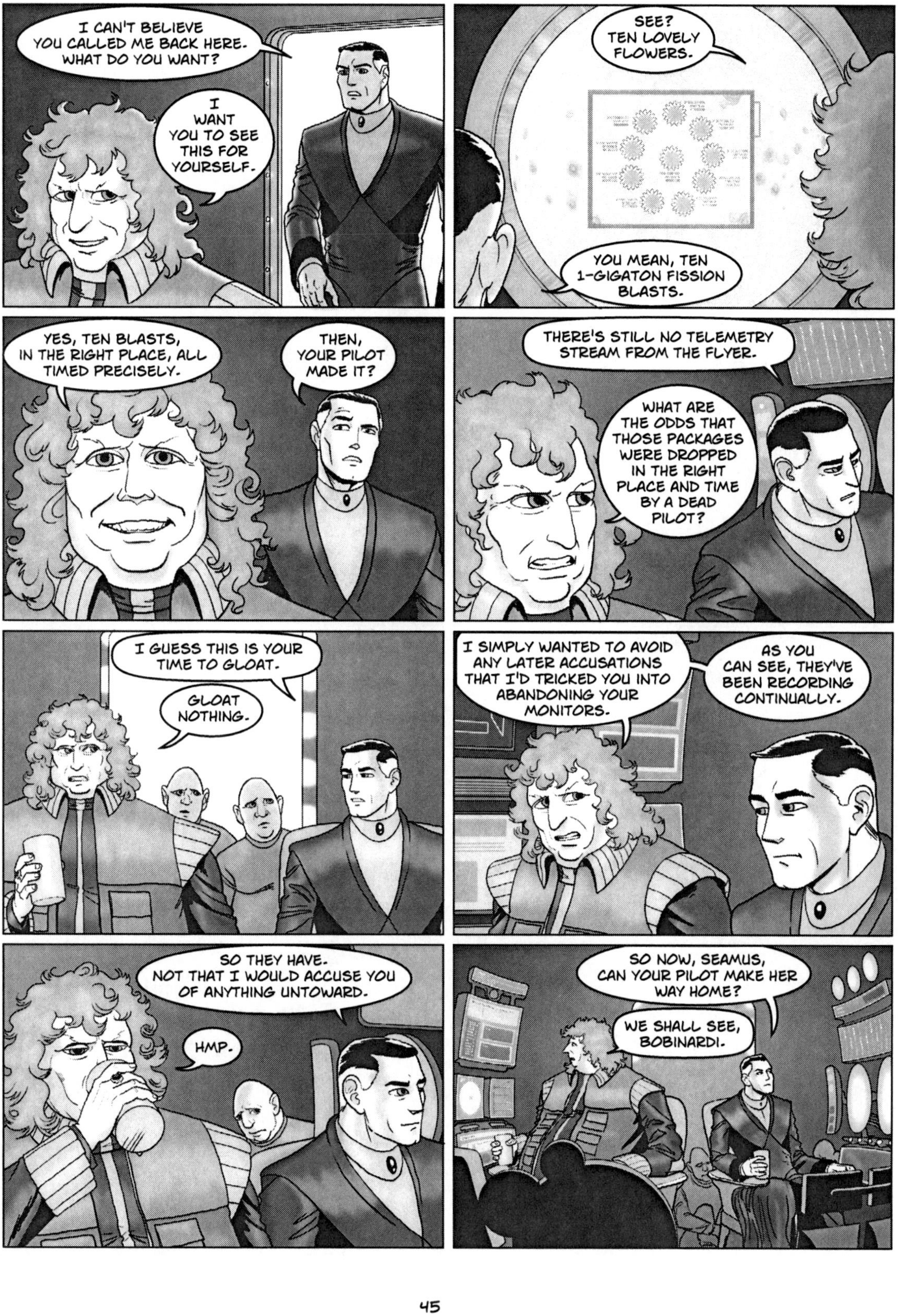
I CAN'T BELIEVE YOU CALLED ME BACK HERE. WHAT DO YOU WANT?
I WANT YOU TO SEE THIS FOR YOURSELF.
SEE? TEN LOVELY FLOWERS.
YOU MEAN, TEN 1-GIGATON FISSION BLASTS.
YES, TEN BLASTS, IN THE RIGHT PLACE, ALL TIMED PRECISELY.
THEN, YOUR PILOT MADE IT?
THERE'S STILL NO TELEMETRY STREAM FROM THE FLYER.
WHAT ARE THE ODDS THAT THOSE PACKAGES WERE DROPPED IN THE RIGHT PLACE AND TIME BY A DEAD PILOT?
I GUESS THIS IS YOUR TIME TO GLOAT.
GLOAT NOTHING.
I SIMPLY WANTED TO AVOID ANY LATER ACCUSATIONS THAT I'D TRICKED YOU INTO ABANDONING YOUR MONITORS.
AS YOU CAN SEE, THEY'VE BEEN RECORDING CONTINUALLY.
SO THEY HAVE. NOT THAT I WOULD ACCUSE YOU OF ANYTHING UNTOWARD.
HMP.
SO NOW, SEAMUS, CAN YOUR PILOT MAKE HER WAY HOME?
WE SHALL SEE, BOBINARDI.

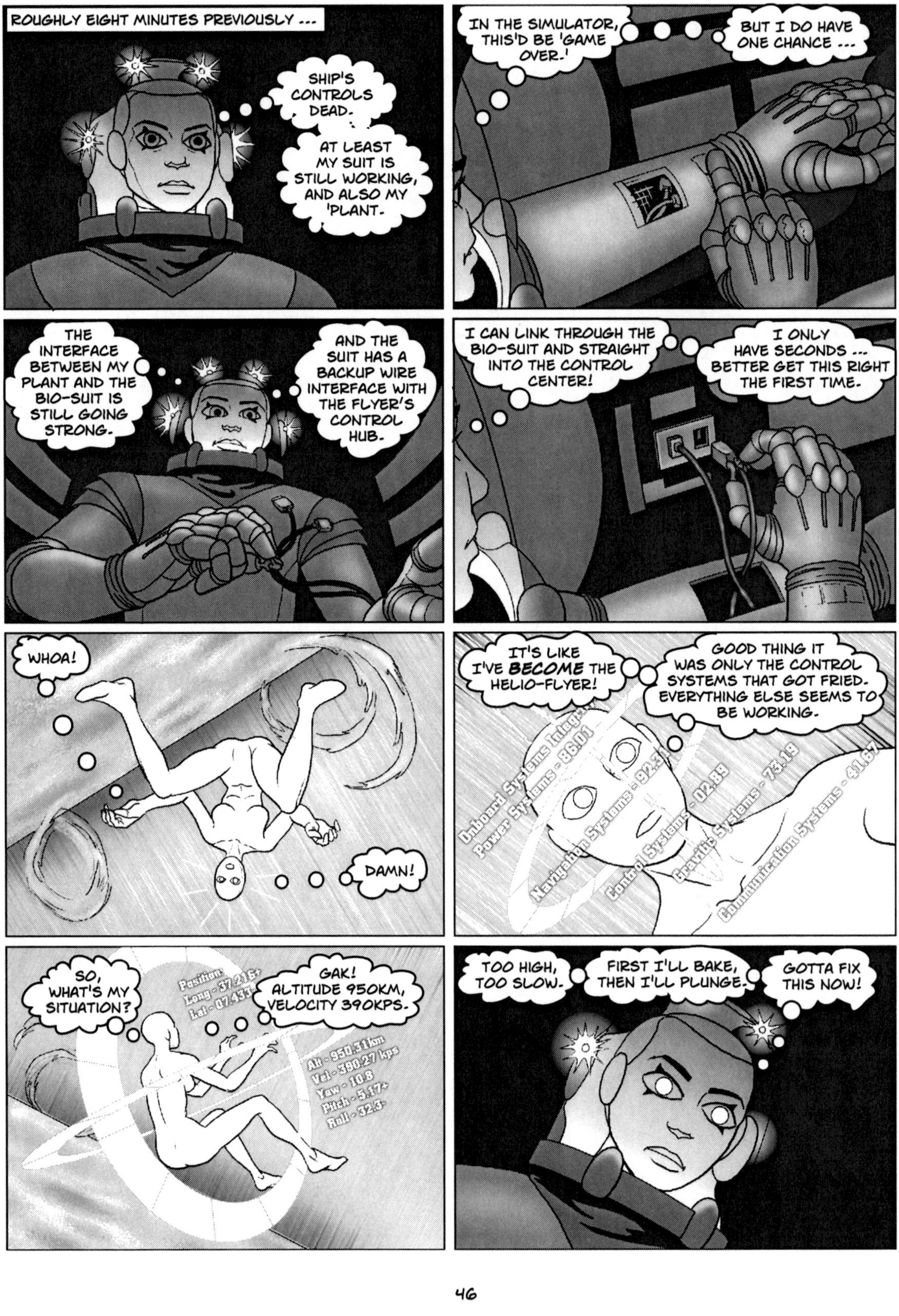
ROUGHLY EIGHT MINUTES PREVIOUSLY ...
SHIP'S CONTROLS DEAD.
AT LEAST MY SUIT IS STILL WORKING, AND ALSO MY 'PLANT.
IN THE SIMULATOR, THIS'D BE 'GAME OVER.'
BUT I DO HAVE ONE CHANCE ...
THE INTERFACE BETWEEN MY PLANT AND THE BIO-SUIT IS STILL GOING STRONG.
AND THE SUIT HAS A BACKUP WIRE INTERFACE WITH THE FLYER'S CONTROL HUB.
I CAN LINK THROUGH THE BIO-SUIT AND STRAIGHT INTO THE CONTROL CENTER!
I ONLY HAVE SECONDS ... BETTER GET THIS RIGHT THE FIRST TIME.
WHOA!
DAMN!
IT'S LIKE I'VE BECOME THE HELIO-FLYER!
GOOD THING IT WAS ONLY THE CONTROL SYSTEMS THAT GOT FRIED. EVERYTHING ELSE SEEMS TO BE WORKING.
Power Systems - 86.01
Navigation Systems - 92.37
Control Systems - 02.89
Gravitic Systems - 73.19
Communication Systems - 41.67
SO, WHAT'S MY SITUATION?
Position:
Long - 37.216+
Lat - 07.433
GAK! ALTITUDE 950KM, VELOCITY 390KPS.
Alt - 950.31km
Vel - 390.27 kps
Yaw - 10.8
Pitch - 5.17+
Roll - 32.3-
TOO HIGH, TOO SLOW.
FIRST I'LL BAKE, THEN I'LL PLUNGE.
GOTTA FIX THIS NOW!

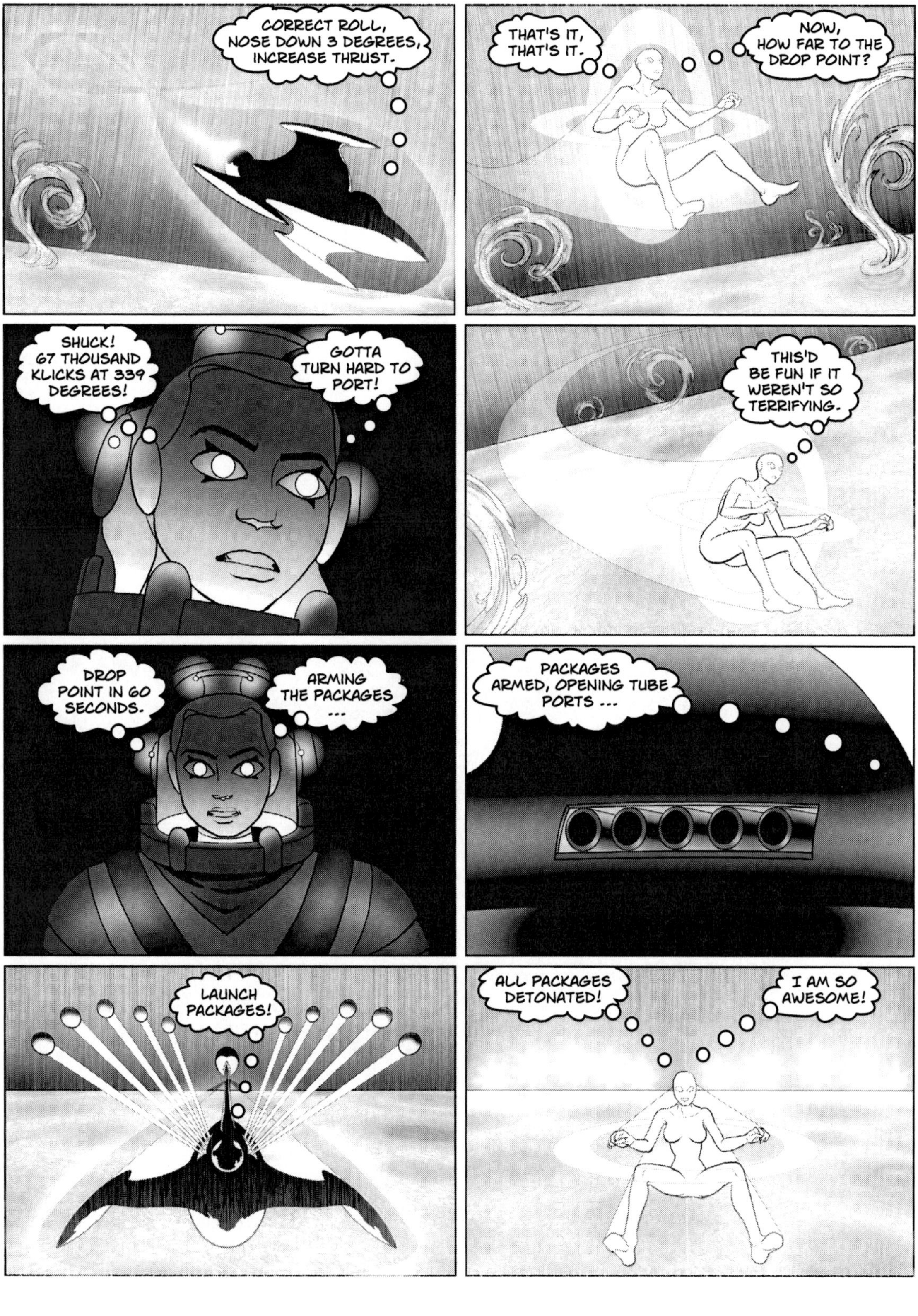
CORRECT ROLL, NOSE DOWN 3 DEGREES, INCREASE THRUST.
THAT'S IT, THAT'S IT.
NOW, HOW FAR TO THE DROP POINT?
SHUCK! 67 THOUSAND KLICKS AT 339 DEGREES!
GOTTA TURN HARD TO PORT!
THIS'D BE FUN IF IT WEREN'T SO TERRIFYING.
DROP POINT IN 60 SECONDS.
ARMING THE PACKAGES ...
PACKAGES ARMED, OPENING TUBE PORTS ...
LAUNCH PACKAGES!
ALL PACKAGES DETONATED!
I AM SO AWESOME!

NOW TO GET *OUT* OF THIS HELLISH PLACE.

GOTTA STAY SHARP, AND AVOID THESE DAMNED PROMINENCES.

IF I HIT ANOTHER ONE OF THOSE *NOW*, I'LL BE WELL AND TRULY SHUCKED.

I SHOW 18.5 MINUTES UNTIL IT'S TIME FOR BOOSTER BURN.

THE HELIO-FLYER CAN ONLY SURVIVE THE 1 MILLION-DEGREE CORONA WHERE IT THINS OUT AT THE POLES, GIVING IT TWO NARROW ESCAPE WINDOWS.

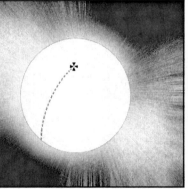

ESCAPE REQUIRES A 100-GRAV BOOST FOR 14 MINUTES.

UNFORTUNATELY, THE SHIP'S DAMPENERS CAN ONLY CUT THE FELT ACCELERATION IN THE COCKPIT BACK TO 50 GRAVS.

EVEN THOUGH NICOLE HAS LIVED MOST OF HER LIFE IN 3 GRAVS, MODERN BIO-ENHANCEMENTS ENABLE HER TO SURVIVE MUCH HARDER ACCELERATION.

MAINTAINING CONSCIOUSNESS IN 50 GRAVS, HOWEVER, IS ANOTHER MATTER.

ORDINARILY, IF SHE WERE TO HAVE A MOMENTARY BLACK-OUT, THE SHIP COULD CONTINUE THE BOOST SEQUENCE AUTOMATICALLY.

BUT SINCE HER IMPLANT IS CONTROLLING THE SHIP, WHETHER A BLACK-OUT WOULD MATTER IS ... UNKNOWN.

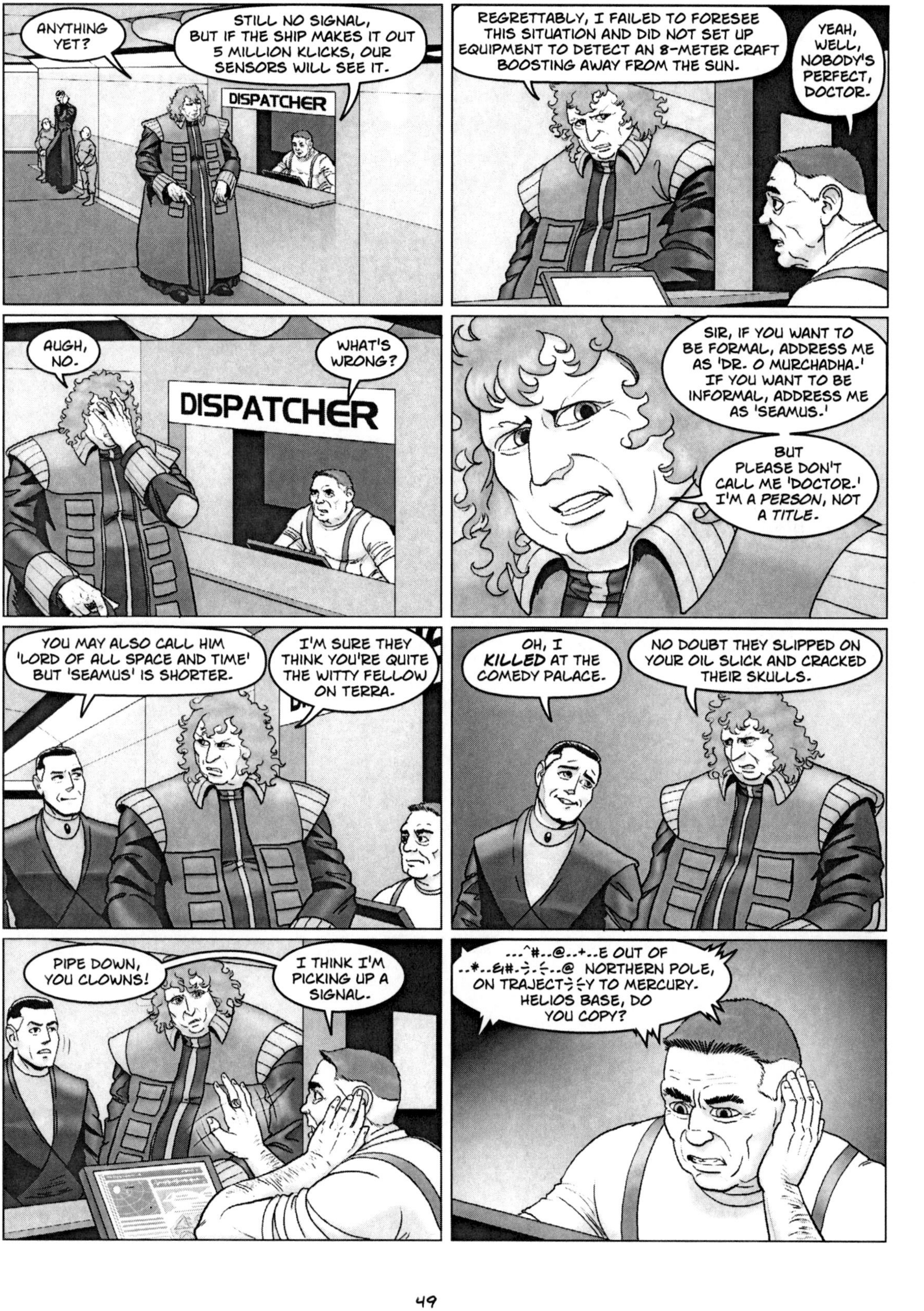
ANYTHING YET?
STILL NO SIGNAL, BUT IF THE SHIP MAKES IT OUT 5 MILLION KLICKS, OUR SENSORS WILL SEE IT.
DISPATCHER
REGRETTABLY, I FAILED TO FORESEE THIS SITUATION AND DID NOT SET UP EQUIPMENT TO DETECT AN 8-METER CRAFT BOOSTING AWAY FROM THE SUN.
YEAH, WELL, NOBODY'S PERFECT, DOCTOR.
AUGH, NO.
WHAT'S WRONG?
DISPATCHER
SIR, IF YOU WANT TO BE FORMAL, ADDRESS ME AS 'DR. O MURCHADHA.' IF YOU WANT TO BE INFORMAL, ADDRESS ME AS 'SEAMUS.'
BUT PLEASE DON'T CALL ME 'DOCTOR.' I'M A *PERSON*, NOT A *TITLE*.
YOU MAY ALSO CALL HIM 'LORD OF ALL SPACE AND TIME' BUT 'SEAMUS' IS SHORTER.
I'M SURE THEY THINK YOU'RE QUITE THE WITTY FELLOW ON TERRA.
OH, I **KILLED** AT THE COMEDY PALACE.
NO DOUBT THEY SLIPPED ON YOUR OIL SLICK AND CRACKED THEIR SKULLS.
PIPE DOWN, YOU CLOWNS!
I THINK I'M PICKING UP A SIGNAL.
---^#--@--+--E OUT OF --*--E#-÷-÷--@ NORTHERN POLE, ON TRAJECT÷÷Y TO MERCURY. HELIOS BASE, DO YOU COPY?

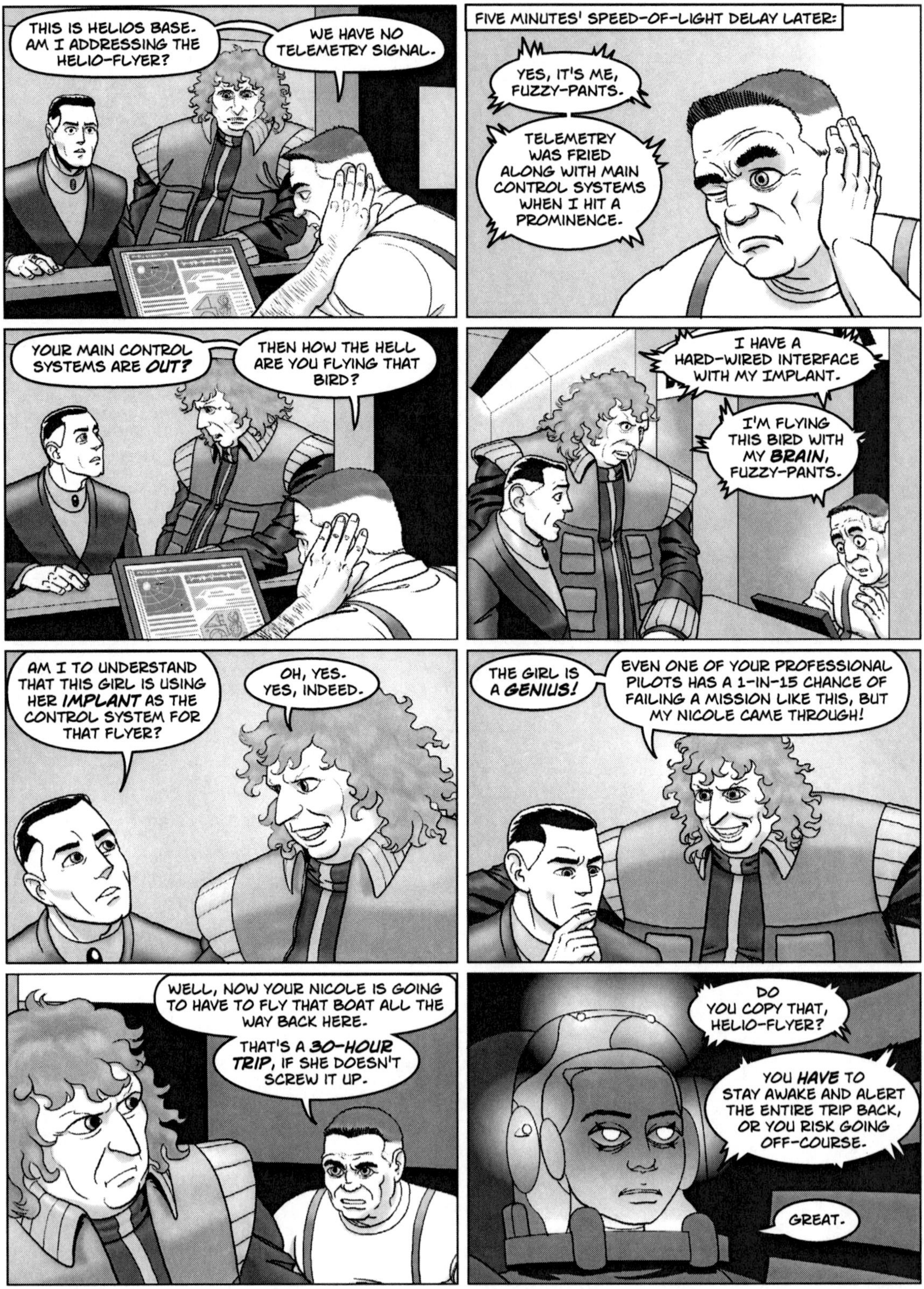
THIS IS HELIOS BASE. AM I ADDRESSING THE HELIO-FLYER?
WE HAVE NO TELEMETRY SIGNAL.
FIVE MINUTES' SPEED-OF-LIGHT DELAY LATER:
YES, IT'S ME, FUZZY-PANTS.
TELEMETRY WAS FRIED ALONG WITH MAIN CONTROL SYSTEMS WHEN I HIT A PROMINENCE.
YOUR MAIN CONTROL SYSTEMS ARE OUT?
THEN HOW THE HELL ARE YOU FLYING THAT BIRD?
I HAVE A HARD-WIRED INTERFACE WITH MY IMPLANT.
I'M FLYING THIS BIRD WITH MY BRAIN, FUZZY-PANTS.
AM I TO UNDERSTAND THAT THIS GIRL IS USING HER IMPLANT AS THE CONTROL SYSTEM FOR THAT FLYER?
OH, YES. YES, INDEED.
THE GIRL IS A GENIUS!
EVEN ONE OF YOUR PROFESSIONAL PILOTS HAS A 1-IN-15 CHANCE OF FAILING A MISSION LIKE THIS, BUT MY NICOLE CAME THROUGH!
WELL, NOW YOUR NICOLE IS GOING TO HAVE TO FLY THAT BOAT ALL THE WAY BACK HERE.
THAT'S A 30-HOUR TRIP, IF SHE DOESN'T SCREW IT UP.
DO YOU COPY THAT, HELIO-FLYER?
YOU HAVE TO STAY AWAKE AND ALERT THE ENTIRE TRIP BACK, OR YOU RISK GOING OFF-COURSE.
GREAT.

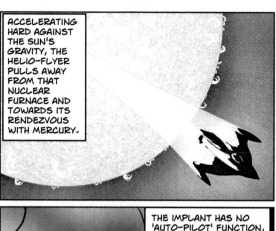

ACCELERATING HARD AGAINST THE SUN'S GRAVITY, THE HELIO-FLYER PULLS AWAY FROM THAT NUCLEAR FURNACE AND TOWARDS ITS RENDEZVOUS WITH MERCURY.

WITH THE SHIP'S CONTROL SYSTEMS OFF-LINE, NICOLE MUST CONTROL THE CRAFT VIA HER CORTICAL IMPLANT, INTERFACING THROUGH THE BIO-SUIT, JACKED INTO THE CONTROL HUB.

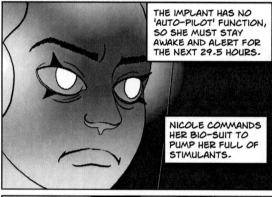

THE IMPLANT HAS NO 'AUTO-PILOT' FUNCTION, SO SHE MUST STAY AWAKE AND ALERT FOR THE NEXT 29.5 HOURS.

NICOLE COMMANDS HER BIO-SUIT TO PUMP HER FULL OF STIMULANTS.

NEXT TIME I DO SOMETHING LIKE THIS, I WANT A BIO-SUIT STOCKED WITH WHISKEY.

SO 'YOUR NICOLE' IS NOT OUT OF THE WOODS YET.

SHE HAS TO STAY AWAKE FOR 30 LONG, TEDIOUS HOURS TO MAKE IT BACK SAFELY.

SHE IS YOUNG AND RESILIENT, AND HER *BIO-SUIT* WILL HELP HER.

HELL OF A THING TO DEPEND ON.

LUCKY FOR HER SHE'LL HAVE MORE THAN HER BIO-SUIT AND WILL-POWER.

ME AN' THE BOYS ARE PREPPING OUR OWN FLYERS NOW.

IF SHE CAN GET AT LEAST 2/3 OF THE WAY HERE, WE SHOULD BE ABLE SWING AROUND AND MATCH TRAJECTORIES ...

... AND BRING HER IN WITH GRAPPLERS IF NEED BE.

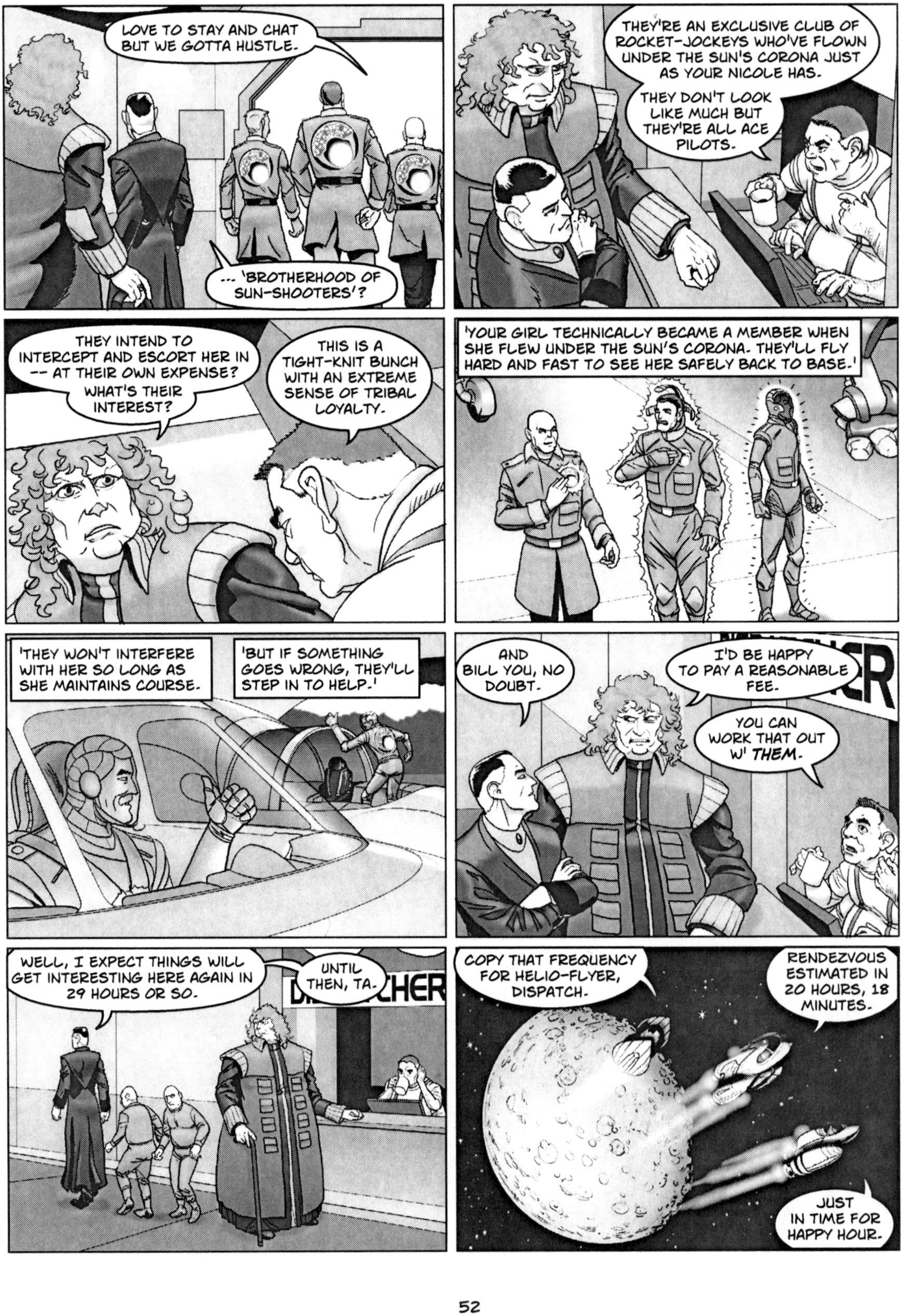
LOVE TO STAY AND CHAT BUT WE GOTTA HUSTLE.
... 'BROTHERHOOD OF SUN-SHOOTERS'?
THEY'RE AN EXCLUSIVE CLUB OF ROCKET-JOCKEYS WHO'VE FLOWN UNDER THE SUN'S CORONA JUST AS YOUR NICOLE HAS.
THEY DON'T LOOK LIKE MUCH BUT THEY'RE ALL ACE PILOTS.
THEY INTEND TO INTERCEPT AND ESCORT HER IN -- AT THEIR OWN EXPENSE? WHAT'S THEIR INTEREST?
THIS IS A TIGHT-KNIT BUNCH WITH AN EXTREME SENSE OF TRIBAL LOYALTY.
'YOUR GIRL TECHNICALLY BECAME A MEMBER WHEN SHE FLEW UNDER THE SUN'S CORONA. THEY'LL FLY HARD AND FAST TO SEE HER SAFELY BACK TO BASE.'
'THEY WON'T INTERFERE WITH HER SO LONG AS SHE MAINTAINS COURSE.
'BUT IF SOMETHING GOES WRONG, THEY'LL STEP IN TO HELP.'
AND BILL YOU, NO DOUBT.
I'D BE HAPPY TO PAY A REASONABLE FEE.
YOU CAN WORK THAT OUT W' THEM.
WELL, I EXPECT THINGS WILL GET INTERESTING HERE AGAIN IN 29 HOURS OR SO.
UNTIL THEN, TA.
COPY THAT FREQUENCY FOR HELIO-FLYER, DISPATCH.
RENDEZVOUS ESTIMATED IN 20 HOURS, 18 MINUTES.
JUST IN TIME FOR HAPPY HOUR.

TO MAINTAIN ALERTNESS THROUGH 29 HOURS OF MONOTONY, NICOLE ENGAGES A NUMBER OF DISTRACTIONS.

SHE REVIEWS SOME ARTICLES ON 'QUANTUM VIBREMONICS' WHICH SHE HAD DOWNLOADED PREVIOUSLY.

ACCESSING THE SYSNET, SHE DOWNLOADS AND 'VIEWS' THE LATEST EPISODES OF DOOSH GOZA OUISELLE, ART'S MY FOLLY, AND BIZARRO NEIL.

AS THE HOURS WEAR ON AND SHE GETS MORE DESPERATE, SHE LINKS INTO CHÉ NANNIGAN'S WHAT YOU SHOULD THINK SOAPBOX PROGRAM.

... THAT THEM DIM DAMN ELF-HIVERS THINK THEY CAN GET AWAY WITH EVERY TIME EVERY TIME THEY OPEN THEIR FILTHY PIE-HOLES ...

⸘GRRRR RRRRR⸘

THE AGGRAVATION OF SUCH ANNOYING NOISE HELPED MAINTAIN HER EDGE.

BY HOUR 20, NICOLE HAD SUCCESSFULLY MADE TURNAROUND, AND WAS DECELERATING TOWARDS HER RENDEZVOUS WITH MERCURY.

MEANWHILE, THE SUN-SHOOTER FLOTILLA HAD MANAGED TO ARC AROUND AND MATCH VECTORS WITH NICOLE'S HELIO-FLYER.

(NOT ANYTHING LIKE TO SCALE.)

HAILING NICOLE ORESME IN THE HELIO-FLYER! THIS IS JAKE OFFENBERG IN *LUCKY STAR*, AND COMPANY.

HOW YA HOLDIN' UP?

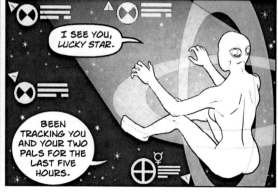

I SEE YOU, *LUCKY STAR*.

BEEN TRACKING YOU AND YOUR TWO PALS FOR THE LAST FIVE HOURS.

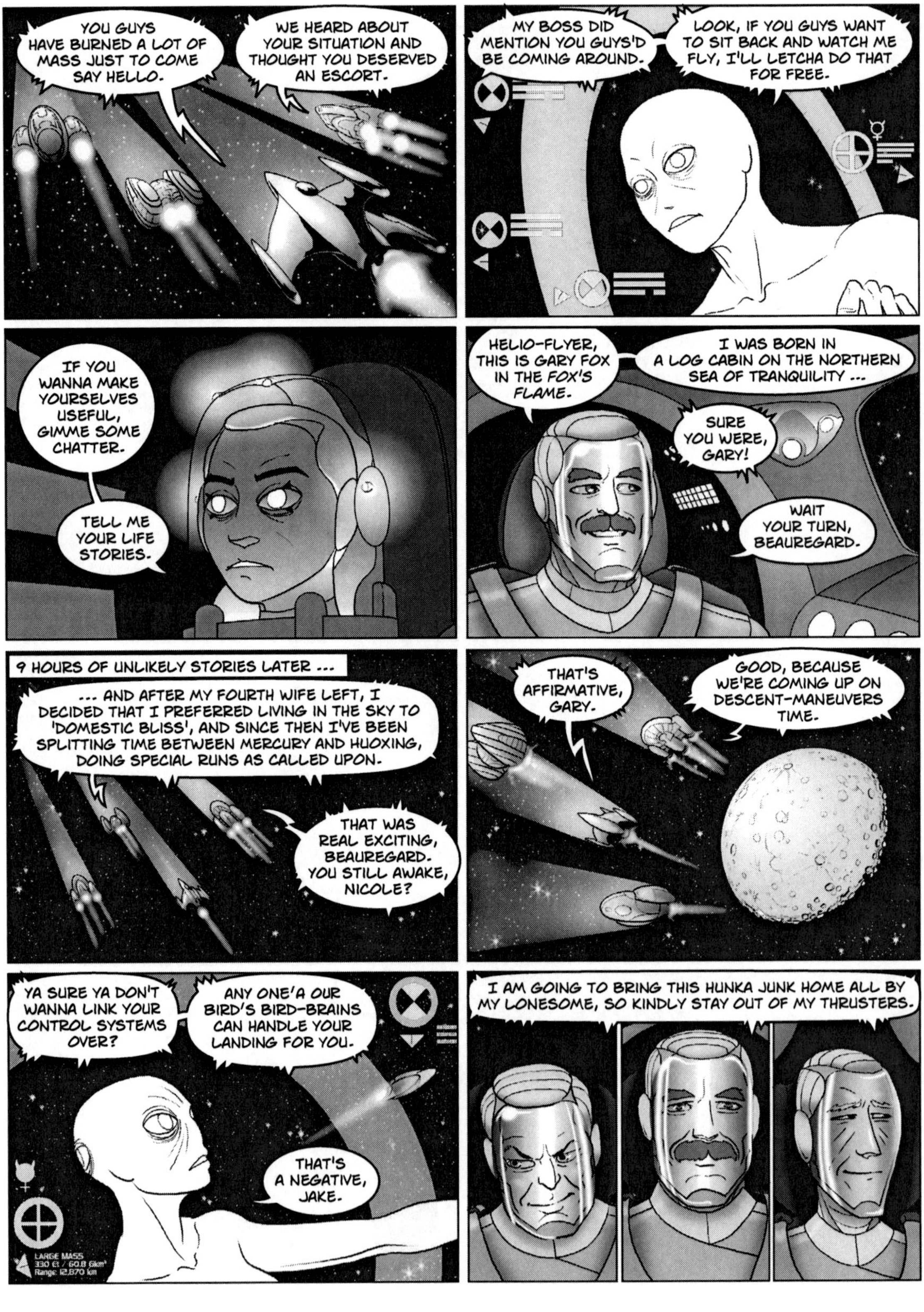
YOU GUYS HAVE BURNED A LOT OF MASS JUST TO COME SAY HELLO.
WE HEARD ABOUT YOUR SITUATION AND THOUGHT YOU DESERVED AN ESCORT.
MY BOSS DID MENTION YOU GUYS'D BE COMING AROUND.
LOOK, IF YOU GUYS WANT TO SIT BACK AND WATCH ME FLY, I'LL LETCHA DO THAT FOR FREE.
IF YOU WANNA MAKE YOURSELVES USEFUL, GIMME SOME CHATTER.
TELL ME YOUR LIFE STORIES.
HELIO-FLYER, THIS IS GARY FOX IN THE FOX'S FLAME.
I WAS BORN IN A LOG CABIN ON THE NORTHERN SEA OF TRANQUILITY ...
SURE YOU WERE, GARY!
WAIT YOUR TURN, BEAUREGARD.
9 HOURS OF UNLIKELY STORIES LATER ...
... AND AFTER MY FOURTH WIFE LEFT, I DECIDED THAT I PREFERRED LIVING IN THE SKY TO 'DOMESTIC BLISS', AND SINCE THEN I'VE BEEN SPLITTING TIME BETWEEN MERCURY AND HUOXING, DOING SPECIAL RUNS AS CALLED UPON.
THAT WAS REAL EXCITING, BEAUREGARD. YOU STILL AWAKE, NICOLE?
THAT'S AFFIRMATIVE, GARY.
GOOD, BECAUSE WE'RE COMING UP ON DESCENT-MANEUVERS TIME.
YA SURE YA DON'T WANNA LINK YOUR CONTROL SYSTEMS OVER?
ANY ONE'A OUR BIRD'S BIRD-BRAINS CAN HANDLE YOUR LANDING FOR YOU.
THAT'S A NEGATIVE, JAKE.
LARGE MASS
I AM GOING TO BRING THIS HUNKA JUNK HOME ALL BY MY LONESOME, SO KINDLY STAY OUT OF MY THRUSTERS.

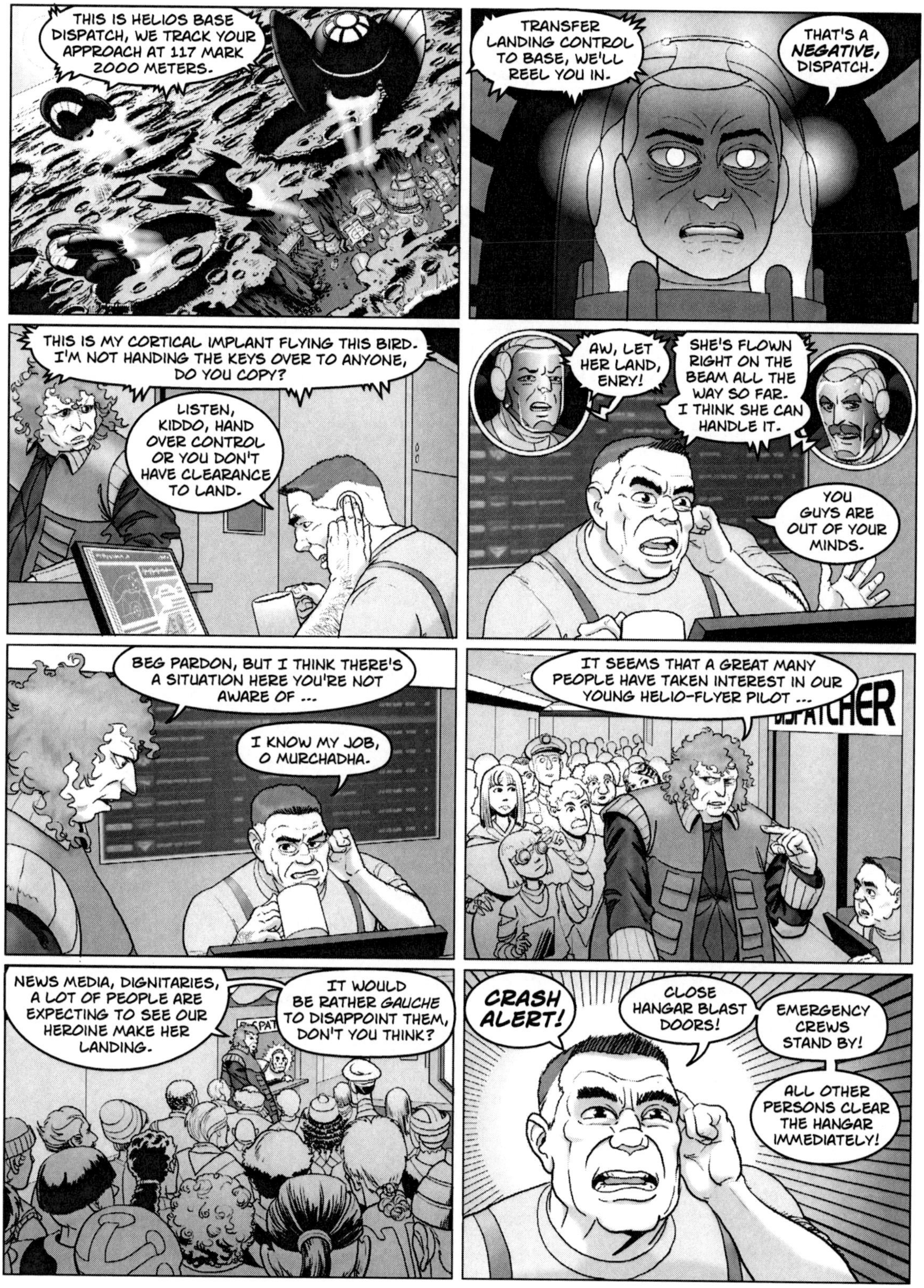
THIS IS HELIOS BASE DISPATCH, WE TRACK YOUR APPROACH AT 117 MARK 2000 METERS.
TRANSFER LANDING CONTROL TO BASE, WE'LL REEL YOU IN.
THAT'S A *NEGATIVE,* DISPATCH.
THIS IS MY CORTICAL IMPLANT FLYING THIS BIRD. I'M NOT HANDING THE KEYS OVER TO ANYONE, DO YOU COPY?
LISTEN, KIDDO, HAND OVER CONTROL OR YOU DON'T HAVE CLEARANCE TO LAND.
AW, LET HER LAND, ENRY!
SHE'S FLOWN RIGHT ON THE BEAM ALL THE WAY SO FAR. I THINK SHE CAN HANDLE IT.
YOU GUYS ARE OUT OF YOUR MINDS.
BEG PARDON, BUT I THINK THERE'S A SITUATION HERE YOU'RE NOT AWARE OF ...
I KNOW MY JOB, O MURCHADHA.
IT SEEMS THAT A GREAT MANY PEOPLE HAVE TAKEN INTEREST IN OUR YOUNG HELIO-FLYER PILOT ...
DISPATCHER
NEWS MEDIA, DIGNITARIES, A LOT OF PEOPLE ARE EXPECTING TO SEE OUR HEROINE MAKE HER LANDING.
IT WOULD BE RATHER *GAUCHE* TO DISAPPOINT THEM, DON'T YOU THINK?
CRASH ALERT!
CLOSE HANGAR BLAST DOORS!
EMERGENCY CREWS STAND BY!
ALL OTHER PERSONS CLEAR THE HANGAR IMMEDIATELY!

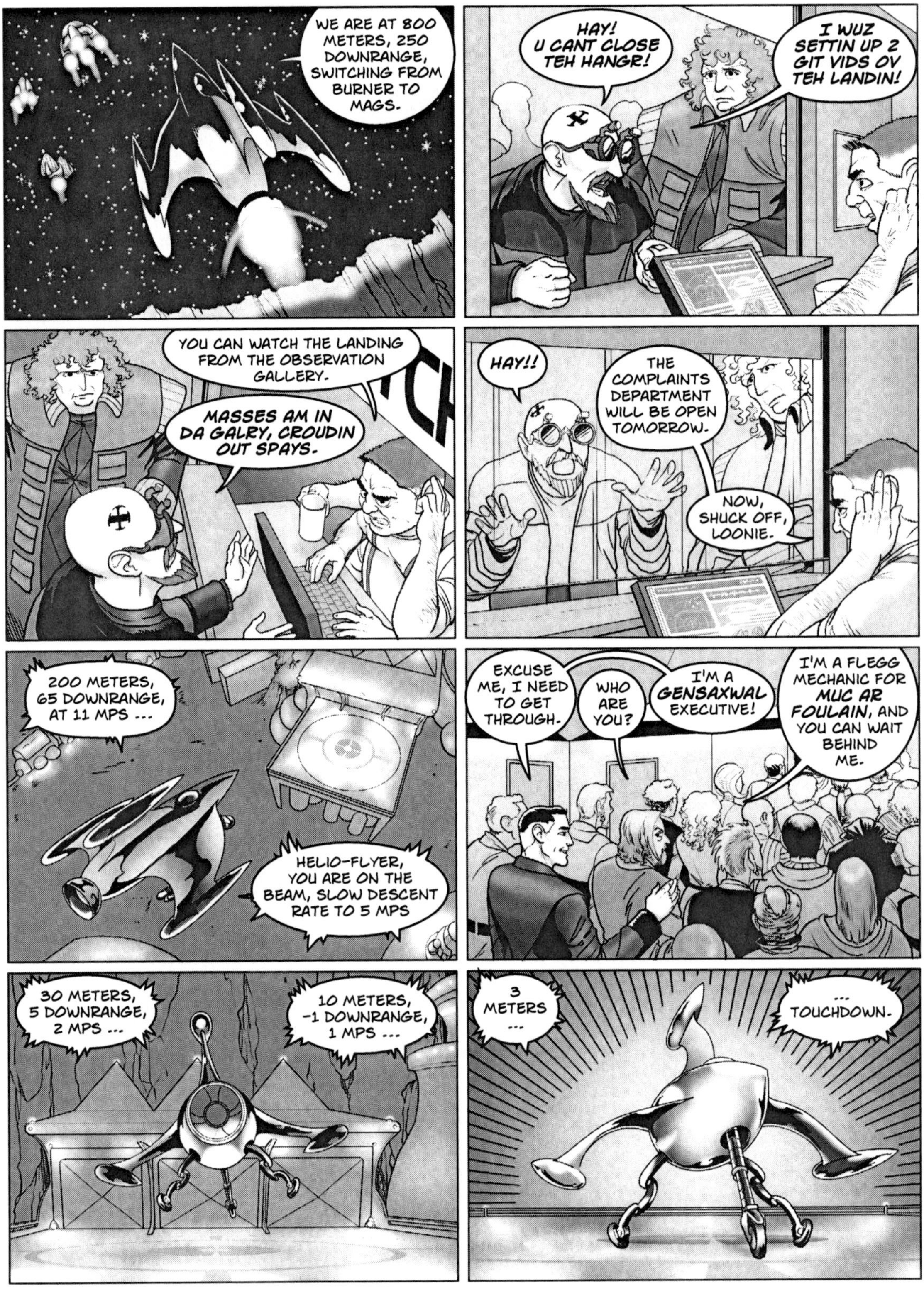
WE ARE AT 800 METERS, 250 DOWNRANGE, SWITCHING FROM BURNER TO MAGS.
HAY! U CANT CLOSE TEH HANGR!
I WUZ SETTIN UP 2 GIT VIDS OV TEH LANDIN!
YOU CAN WATCH THE LANDING FROM THE OBSERVATION GALLERY.
MASSES AM IN DA GALRY, CROUDIN OUT SPAYS.
HAY!!
THE COMPLAINTS DEPARTMENT WILL BE OPEN TOMORROW.
NOW, SHUCK OFF, LOONIE.
200 METERS, 65 DOWNRANGE, AT 11 MPS ...
HELIO-FLYER, YOU ARE ON THE BEAM, SLOW DESCENT RATE TO 5 MPS
EXCUSE ME, I NEED TO GET THROUGH.
WHO ARE YOU?
I'M A GENSAXWAL EXECUTIVE!
I'M A FLEGG MECHANIC FOR MUC AR FOULAIN, AND YOU CAN WAIT BEHIND ME.
30 METERS, 5 DOWNRANGE, 2 MPS ...
10 METERS, -1 DOWNRANGE, 1 MPS ...
3 METERS ...
... TOUCHDOWN.

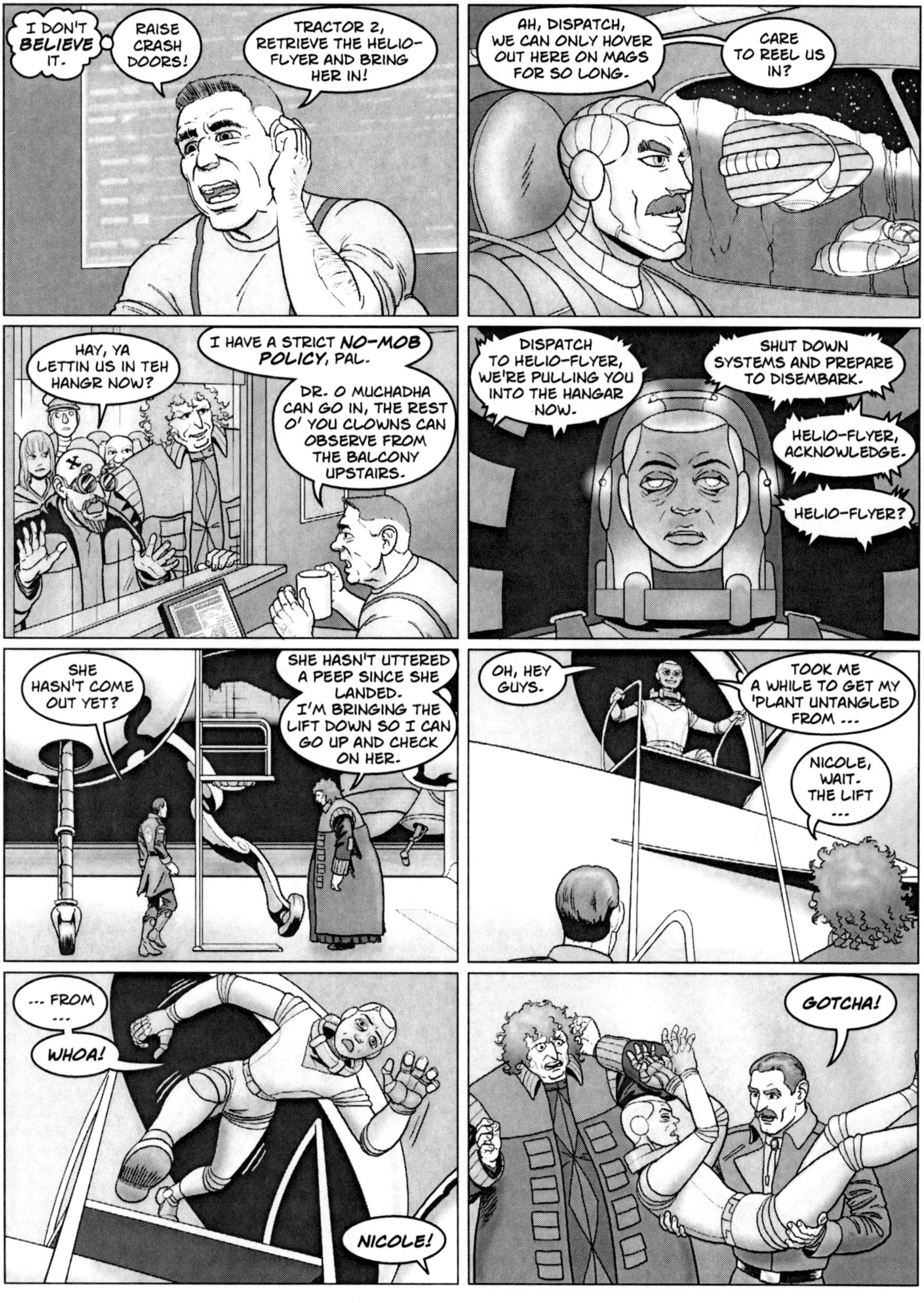
I DON'T BELIEVE IT.
RAISE CRASH DOORS!
TRACTOR 2, RETRIEVE THE HELIO-FLYER AND BRING HER IN!
AH, DISPATCH, WE CAN ONLY HOVER OUT HERE ON MAGS FOR SO LONG.
CARE TO REEL US IN?
HAY, YA LETTIN US IN TEH HANGR NOW?
I HAVE A STRICT NO-MOB POLICY, PAL.
DR. O MUCHADHA CAN GO IN, THE REST O' YOU CLOWNS CAN OBSERVE FROM THE BALCONY UPSTAIRS.
DISPATCH TO HELIO-FLYER, WE'RE PULLING YOU INTO THE HANGAR NOW.
SHUT DOWN SYSTEMS AND PREPARE TO DISEMBARK.
HELIO-FLYER, ACKNOWLEDGE.
HELIO-FLYER?
SHE HASN'T COME OUT YET?
SHE HASN'T UTTERED A PEEP SINCE SHE LANDED. I'M BRINGING THE LIFT DOWN SO I CAN GO UP AND CHECK ON HER.
OH, HEY GUYS.
TOOK ME A WHILE TO GET MY 'PLANT UNTANGLED FROM ...
NICOLE, WAIT. THE LIFT ...
... FROM ...
WHOA!
NICOLE!
GOTCHA!

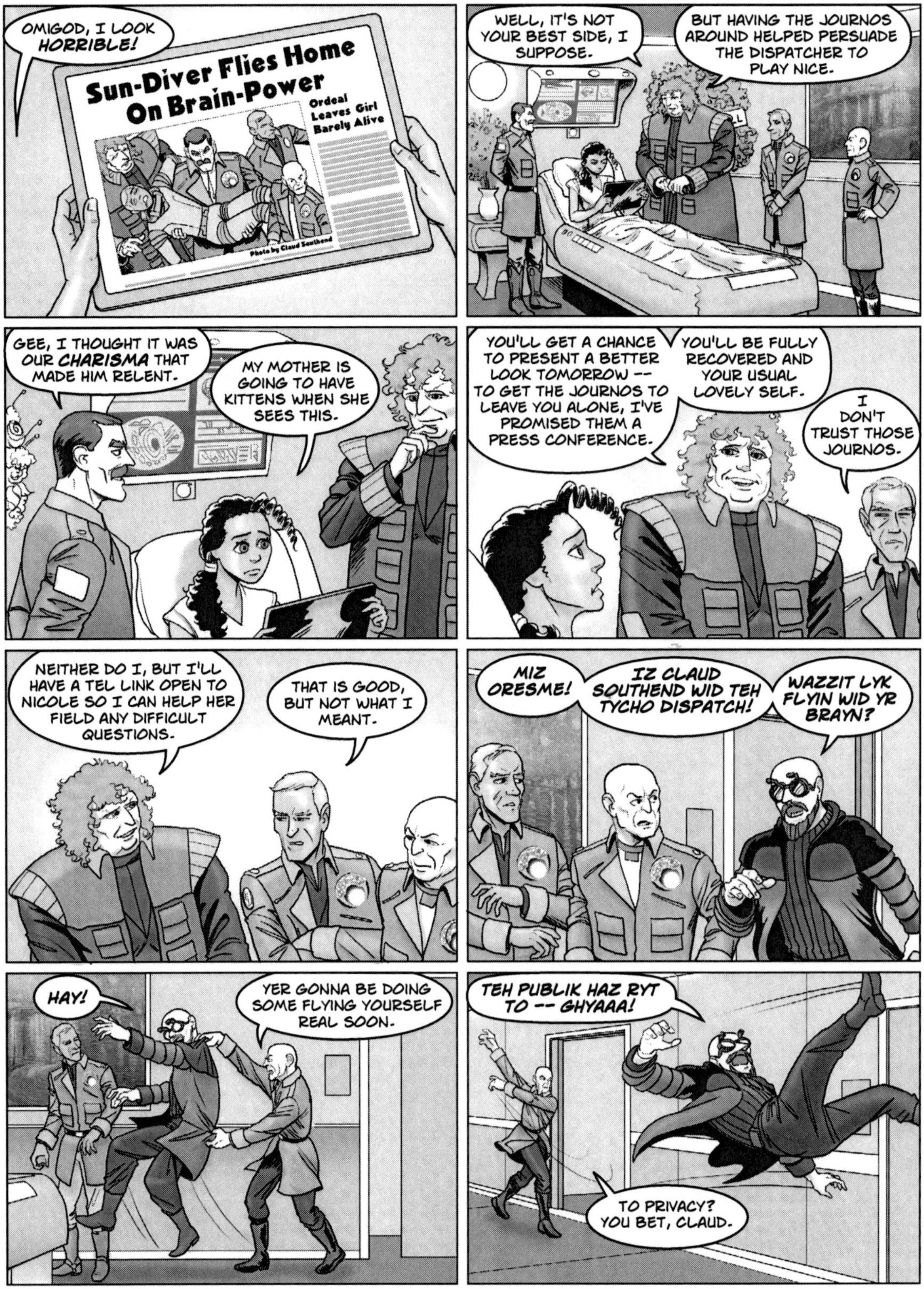
OMIGOD, I LOOK HORRIBLE!
Sun-Diver Flies Home On Brain-Power
Ordeal Leaves Girl Barely Alive
Photo by Claud Southend
WELL, IT'S NOT YOUR BEST SIDE, I SUPPOSE.
BUT HAVING THE JOURNOS AROUND HELPED PERSUADE THE DISPATCHER TO PLAY NICE.
GEE, I THOUGHT IT WAS OUR CHARISMA THAT MADE HIM RELENT.
MY MOTHER IS GOING TO HAVE KITTENS WHEN SHE SEES THIS.
YOU'LL GET A CHANCE TO PRESENT A BETTER LOOK TOMORROW -- TO GET THE JOURNOS TO LEAVE YOU ALONE, I'VE PROMISED THEM A PRESS CONFERENCE.
YOU'LL BE FULLY RECOVERED AND YOUR USUAL LOVELY SELF.
I DON'T TRUST THOSE JOURNOS.
NEITHER DO I, BUT I'LL HAVE A TEL LINK OPEN TO NICOLE SO I CAN HELP HER FIELD ANY DIFFICULT QUESTIONS.
THAT IS GOOD, BUT NOT WHAT I MEANT.
MIZ ORESME!
IZ CLAUD SOUTHEND WID TEH TYCHO DISPATCH!
WAZZIT LYK FLYIN WID YR BRAYN?
HAY!
YER GONNA BE DOING SOME FLYING YOURSELF REAL SOON.
TEH PUBLIK HAZ RYT TO -- GHYAAA!
TO PRIVACY? YOU BET, CLAUD.

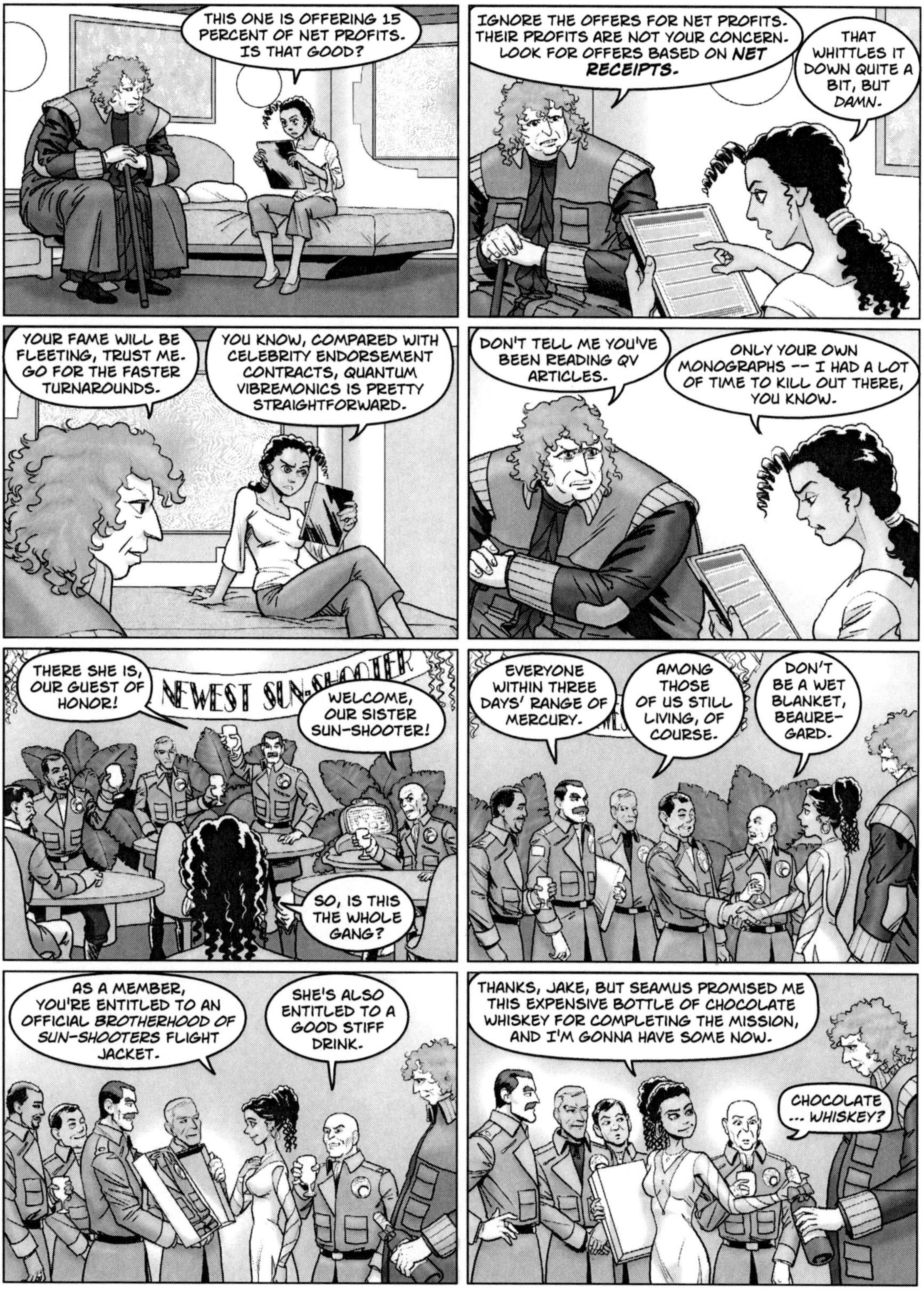
THIS ONE IS OFFERING 15 PERCENT OF NET PROFITS. IS THAT GOOD?
IGNORE THE OFFERS FOR NET PROFITS. THEIR PROFITS ARE NOT YOUR CONCERN. LOOK FOR OFFERS BASED ON NET RECEIPTS.
THAT WHITTLES IT DOWN QUITE A BIT, BUT DAMN.
YOUR FAME WILL BE FLEETING, TRUST ME. GO FOR THE FASTER TURNAROUNDS.
YOU KNOW, COMPARED WITH CELEBRITY ENDORSEMENT CONTRACTS, QUANTUM VIBREMONICS IS PRETTY STRAIGHTFORWARD.
DON'T TELL ME YOU'VE BEEN READING QV ARTICLES.
ONLY YOUR OWN MONOGRAPHS -- I HAD A LOT OF TIME TO KILL OUT THERE, YOU KNOW.
NEWEST SUN-SHOOTER
THERE SHE IS, OUR GUEST OF HONOR!
WELCOME, OUR SISTER SUN-SHOOTER!
SO, IS THIS THE WHOLE GANG?
EVERYONE WITHIN THREE DAYS' RANGE OF MERCURY.
AMONG THOSE OF US STILL LIVING, OF COURSE.
DON'T BE A WET BLANKET, BEAURE-GARD.
AS A MEMBER, YOU'RE ENTITLED TO AN OFFICIAL BROTHERHOOD OF SUN-SHOOTERS FLIGHT JACKET.
SHE'S ALSO ENTITLED TO A GOOD STIFF DRINK.
THANKS, JAKE, BUT SEAMUS PROMISED ME THIS EXPENSIVE BOTTLE OF CHOCOLATE WHISKEY FOR COMPLETING THE MISSION, AND I'M GONNA HAVE SOME NOW.
CHOCOLATE ... WHISKEY?

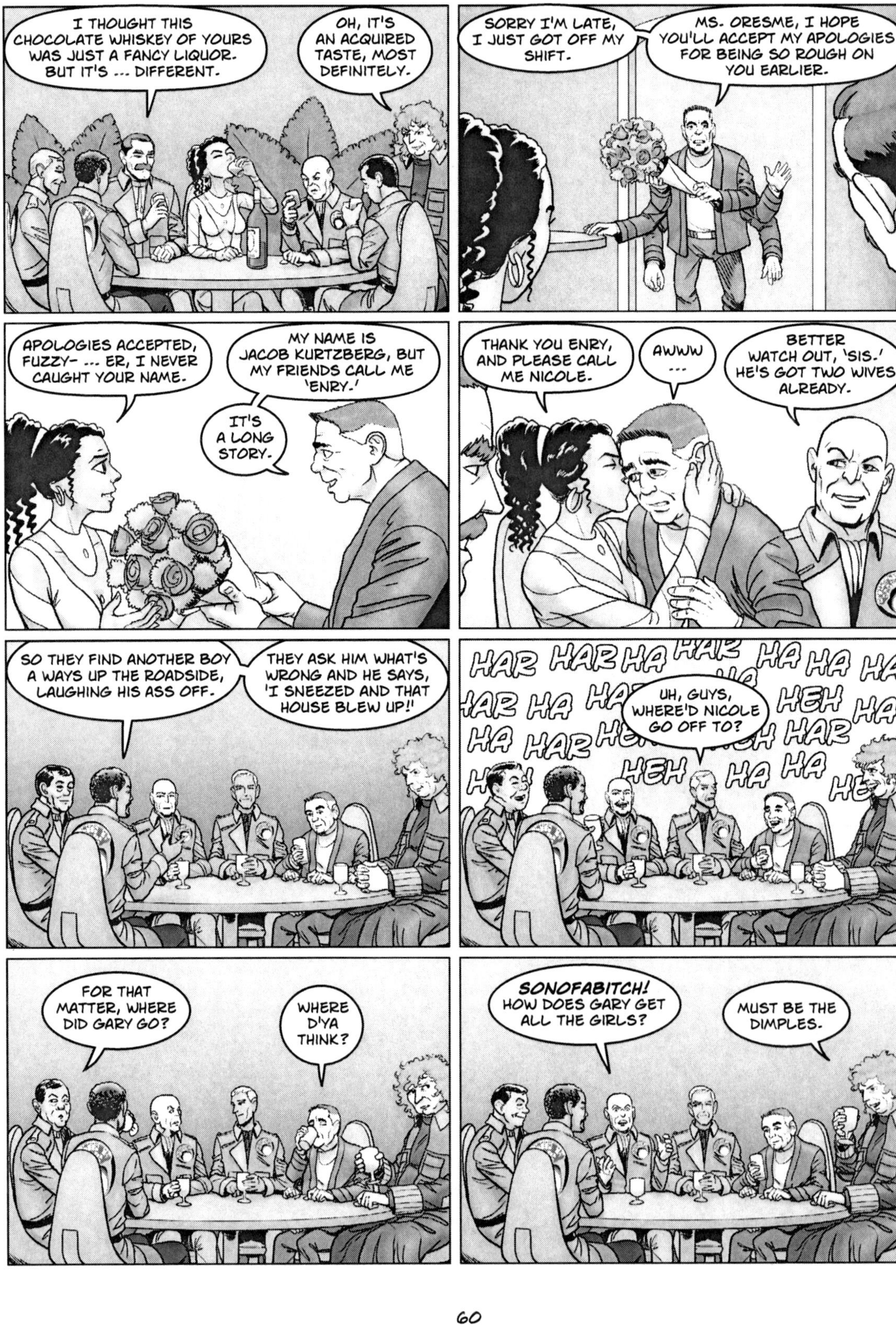
I THOUGHT THIS CHOCOLATE WHISKEY OF YOURS WAS JUST A FANCY LIQUOR. BUT IT'S ... DIFFERENT.
OH, IT'S AN ACQUIRED TASTE, MOST DEFINITELY.
SORRY I'M LATE, I JUST GOT OFF MY SHIFT.
MS. ORESME, I HOPE YOU'LL ACCEPT MY APOLOGIES FOR BEING SO ROUGH ON YOU EARLIER.
APOLOGIES ACCEPTED, FUZZY- ... ER, I NEVER CAUGHT YOUR NAME.
MY NAME IS JACOB KURTZBERG, BUT MY FRIENDS CALL ME 'ENRY.'
IT'S A LONG STORY.
THANK YOU ENRY, AND PLEASE CALL ME NICOLE.
AWWW ...
BETTER WATCH OUT, 'SIS.' HE'S GOT TWO WIVES ALREADY.
SO THEY FIND ANOTHER BOY A WAYS UP THE ROADSIDE, LAUGHING HIS ASS OFF.
THEY ASK HIM WHAT'S WRONG AND HE SAYS, 'I SNEEZED AND THAT HOUSE BLEW UP!'
HAR HAR HA HA HA
HEH HA HA HAR HA HAR HEH HAR HEH HA HA
UH, GUYS, WHERE'D NICOLE GO OFF TO?
FOR THAT MATTER, WHERE DID GARY GO?
WHERE D'YA THINK?
SONOFABITCH! HOW DOES GARY GET ALL THE GIRLS?
MUST BE THE DIMPLES.

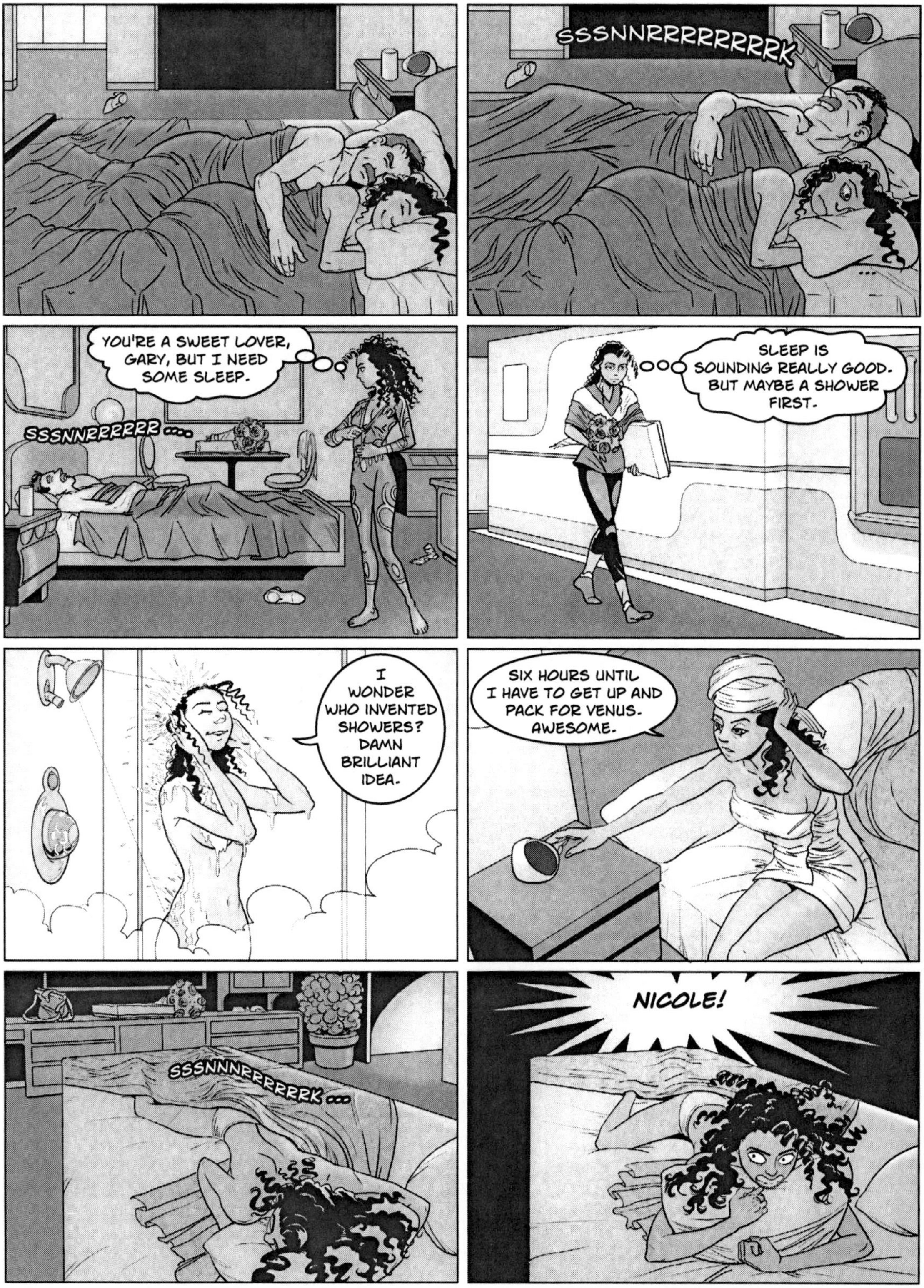
SSSNNRRRRRRRRK
...
YOU'RE A SWEET LOVER, GARY, BUT I NEED SOME SLEEP.
SSSNNRRRRRR...
SLEEP IS SOUNDING REALLY GOOD. BUT MAYBE A SHOWER FIRST.
I WONDER WHO INVENTED SHOWERS? DAMN BRILLIANT IDEA.
SIX HOURS UNTIL I HAVE TO GET UP AND PACK FOR VENUS. AWESOME.
SSSNNNRRRRRRK...
NICOLE!

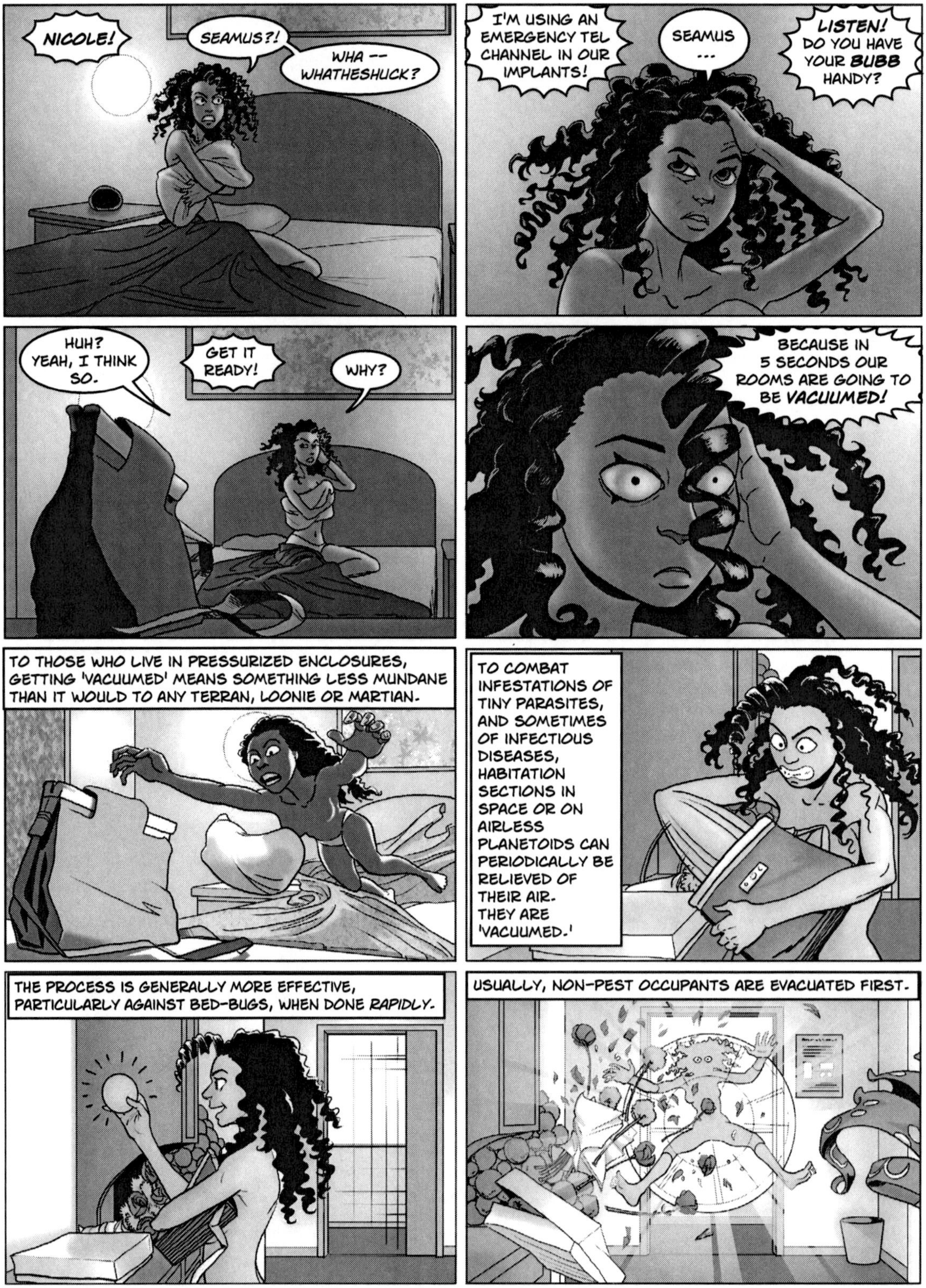
NICOLE!
SEAMUS?!
WHA -- WHATHESHUCK?
I'M USING AN EMERGENCY TEL CHANNEL IN OUR IMPLANTS!
SEAMUS ...
LISTEN! DO YOU HAVE YOUR BUBB HANDY?
HUH? YEAH, I THINK SO.
GET IT READY!
WHY?
BECAUSE IN 5 SECONDS OUR ROOMS ARE GOING TO BE VACUUMED!
TO THOSE WHO LIVE IN PRESSURIZED ENCLOSURES, GETTING 'VACUUMED' MEANS SOMETHING LESS MUNDANE THAN IT WOULD TO ANY TERRAN, LOONIE OR MARTIAN.
TO COMBAT INFESTATIONS OF TINY PARASITES, AND SOMETIMES OF INFECTIOUS DISEASES, HABITATION SECTIONS IN SPACE OR ON AIRLESS PLANETOIDS CAN PERIODICALLY BE RELIEVED OF THEIR AIR. THEY ARE 'VACUUMED.'
THE PROCESS IS GENERALLY MORE EFFECTIVE, PARTICULARLY AGAINST BED-BUGS, WHEN DONE RAPIDLY.
USUALLY, NON-PEST OCCUPANTS ARE EVACUATED FIRST.

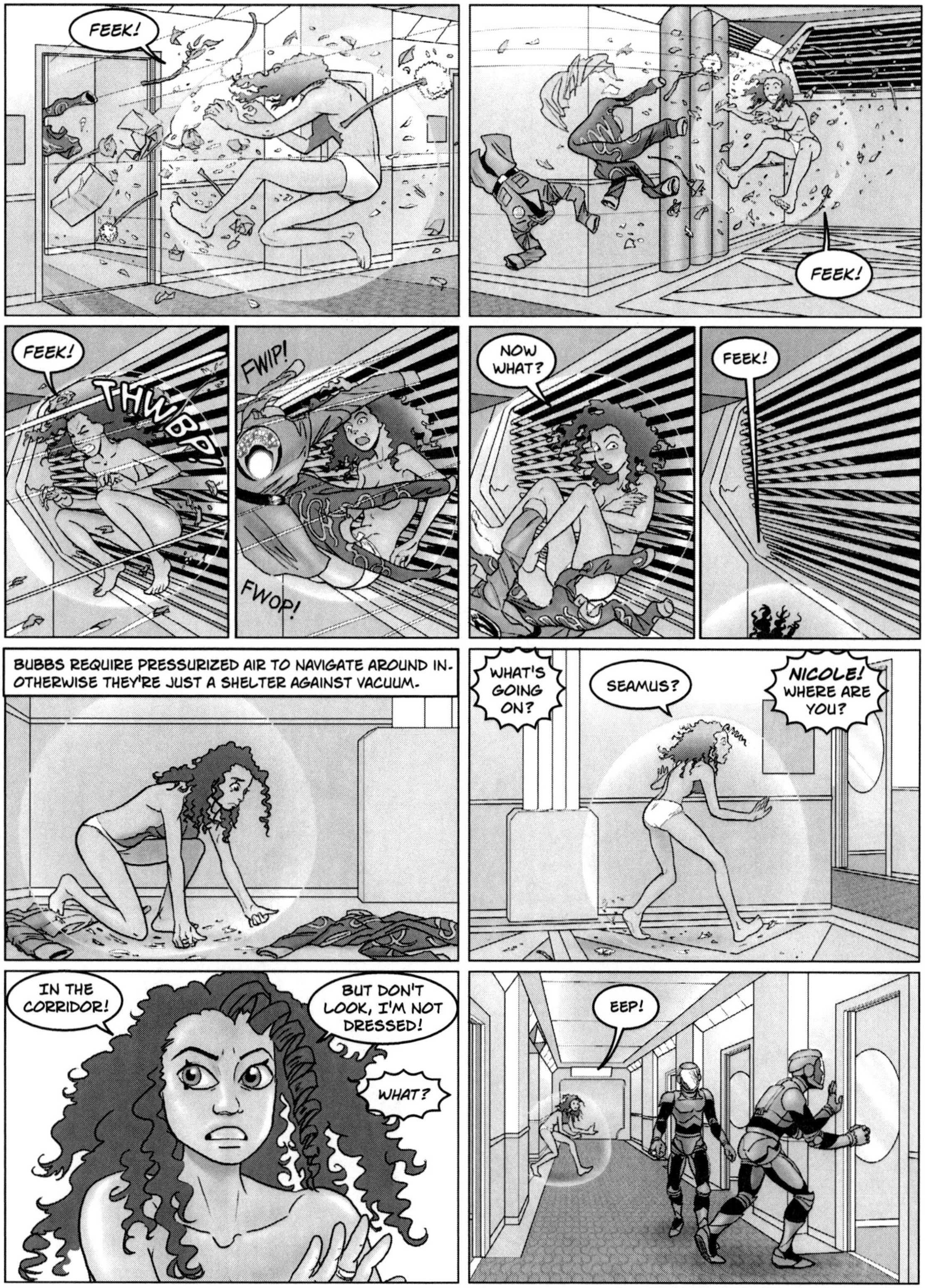
FEEK!
FEEK!
FEEK!
THWBP!
FWIP!
FWOP!
NOW WHAT?
FEEK!
BUBBS REQUIRE PRESSURIZED AIR TO NAVIGATE AROUND IN. OTHERWISE THEY'RE JUST A SHELTER AGAINST VACUUM.
WHAT'S GOING ON?
SEAMUS?
NICOLE! WHERE ARE YOU?
IN THE CORRIDOR!
BUT DON'T LOOK, I'M NOT DRESSED!
WHAT?
EEP!

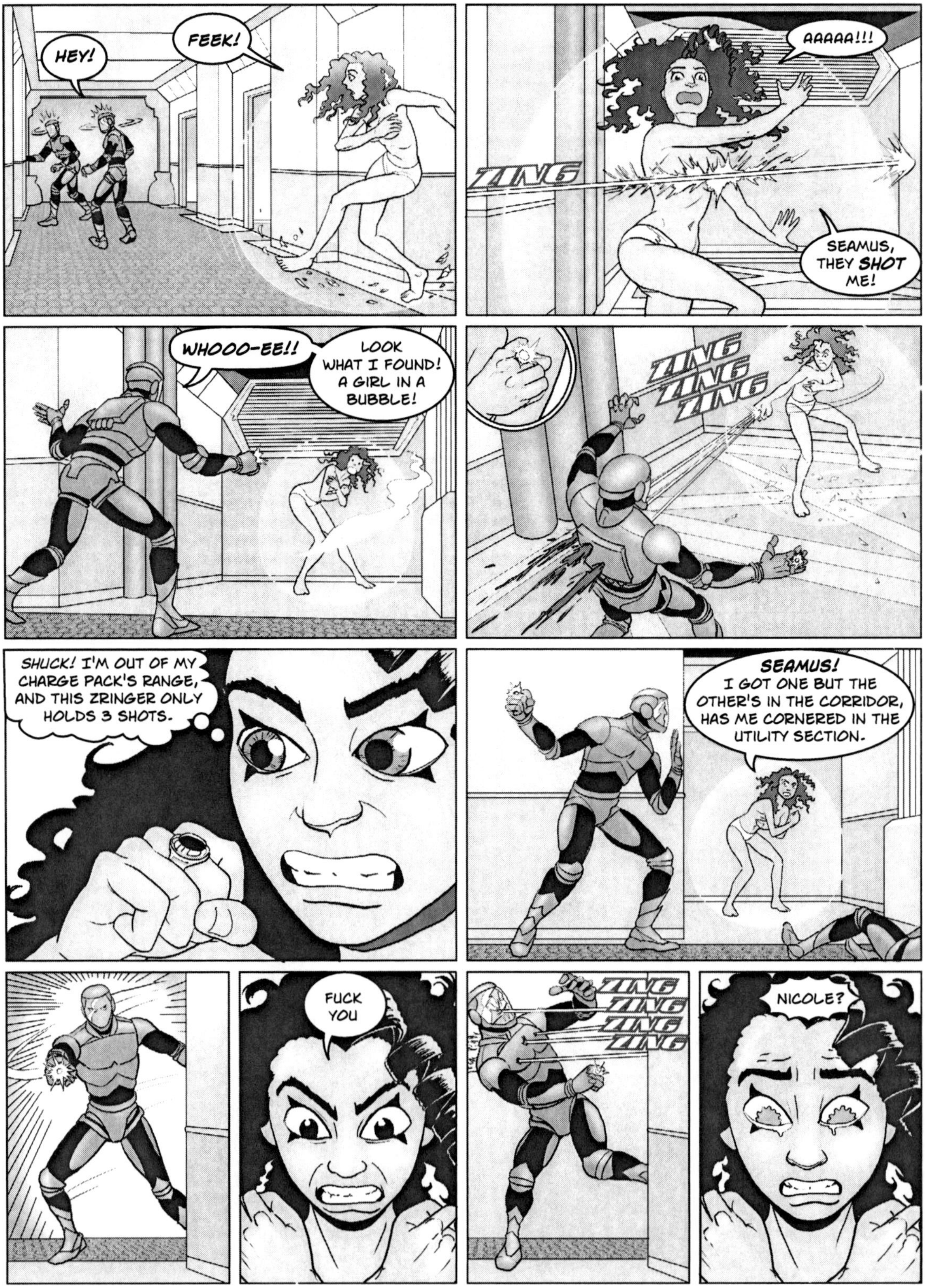
HEY!
FEEK!
AAAAA!!!
ZING
SEAMUS, THEY SHOT ME!
WHOOO-EE!!
LOOK WHAT I FOUND! A GIRL IN A BUBBLE!
ZING ZING ZING
SHUCK! I'M OUT OF MY CHARGE PACK'S RANGE, AND THIS ZRINGER ONLY HOLDS 3 SHOTS.
SEAMUS! I GOT ONE BUT THE OTHER'S IN THE CORRIDOR, HAS ME CORNERED IN THE UTILITY SECTION.
FUCK YOU
ZING ZING ZING ZING
NICOLE?

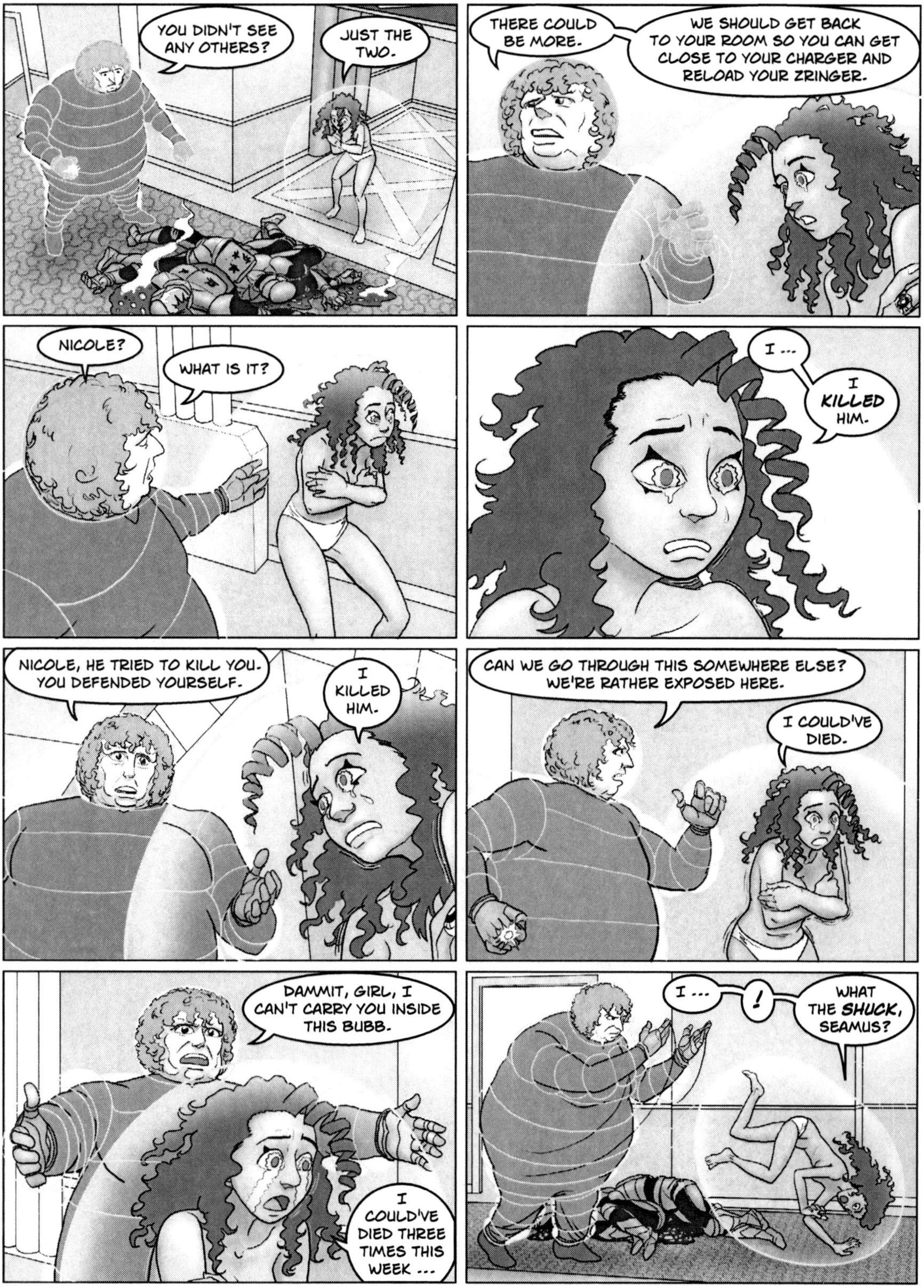
YOU DIDN'T SEE ANY OTHERS?
JUST THE TWO.
THERE COULD BE MORE.
WE SHOULD GET BACK TO YOUR ROOM SO YOU CAN GET CLOSE TO YOUR CHARGER AND RELOAD YOUR ZRINGER.
NICOLE?
WHAT IS IT?
I ...
I KILLED HIM.
NICOLE, HE TRIED TO KILL YOU. YOU DEFENDED YOURSELF.
I KILLED HIM.
CAN WE GO THROUGH THIS SOMEWHERE ELSE? WE'RE RATHER EXPOSED HERE.
I COULD'VE DIED.
DAMMIT, GIRL, I CAN'T CARRY YOU INSIDE THIS BUBB.
I COULD'VE DIED THREE TIMES THIS WEEK ...
I ...
!
WHAT THE SHUCK, SEAMUS?

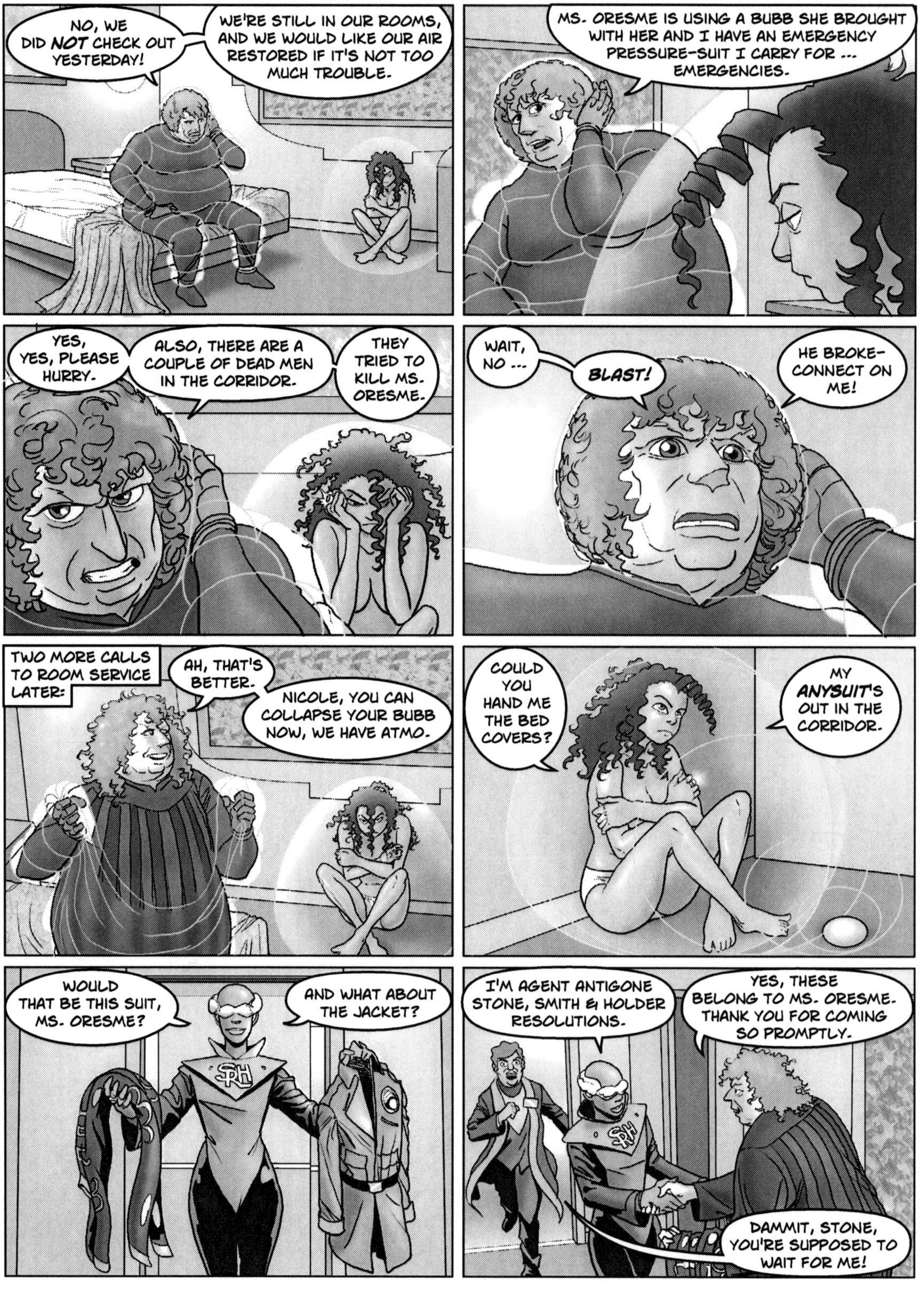
NO, WE DID NOT CHECK OUT YESTERDAY!
WE'RE STILL IN OUR ROOMS, AND WE WOULD LIKE OUR AIR RESTORED IF IT'S NOT TOO MUCH TROUBLE.
MS. ORESME IS USING A BUBB SHE BROUGHT WITH HER AND I HAVE AN EMERGENCY PRESSURE-SUIT I CARRY FOR ... EMERGENCIES.
YES, YES, PLEASE HURRY.
ALSO, THERE ARE A COUPLE OF DEAD MEN IN THE CORRIDOR.
THEY TRIED TO KILL MS. ORESME.
WAIT, NO ...
BLAST!
HE BROKE-CONNECT ON ME!
TWO MORE CALLS TO ROOM SERVICE LATER:
AH, THAT'S BETTER.
NICOLE, YOU CAN COLLAPSE YOUR BUBB NOW, WE HAVE ATMO.
COULD YOU HAND ME THE BED COVERS?
MY ANYSUIT'S OUT IN THE CORRIDOR.
WOULD THAT BE THIS SUIT, MS. ORESME?
AND WHAT ABOUT THE JACKET?
SRH
I'M AGENT ANTIGONE STONE, SMITH & HOLDER RESOLUTIONS.
YES, THESE BELONG TO MS. ORESME. THANK YOU FOR COMING SO PROMPTLY.
DAMMIT, STONE, YOU'RE SUPPOSED TO WAIT FOR ME!

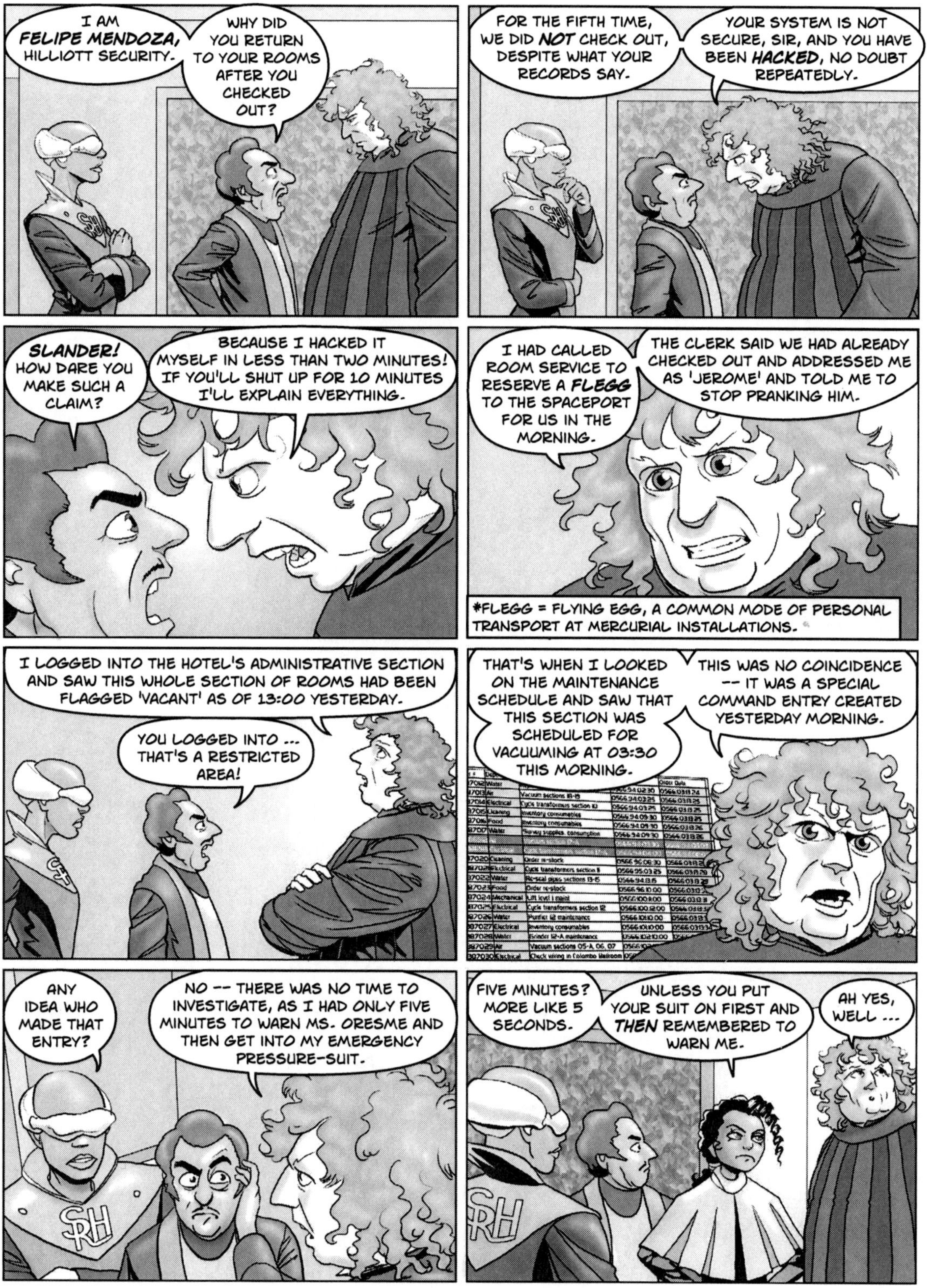
I AM FELIPE MENDOZA, HILLIOTT SECURITY.
WHY DID YOU RETURN TO YOUR ROOMS AFTER YOU CHECKED OUT?
FOR THE FIFTH TIME, WE DID NOT CHECK OUT, DESPITE WHAT YOUR RECORDS SAY.
YOUR SYSTEM IS NOT SECURE, SIR, AND YOU HAVE BEEN HACKED, NO DOUBT REPEATEDLY.
SLANDER! HOW DARE YOU MAKE SUCH A CLAIM?
BECAUSE I HACKED IT MYSELF IN LESS THAN TWO MINUTES! IF YOU'LL SHUT UP FOR 10 MINUTES I'LL EXPLAIN EVERYTHING.
I HAD CALLED ROOM SERVICE TO RESERVE A FLEGG TO THE SPACEPORT FOR US IN THE MORNING.
THE CLERK SAID WE HAD ALREADY CHECKED OUT AND ADDRESSED ME AS 'JEROME' AND TOLD ME TO STOP PRANKING HIM.
*FLEGG = FLYING EGG, A COMMON MODE OF PERSONAL TRANSPORT AT MERCURIAL INSTALLATIONS.
I LOGGED INTO THE HOTEL'S ADMINISTRATIVE SECTION AND SAW THIS WHOLE SECTION OF ROOMS HAD BEEN FLAGGED 'VACANT' AS OF 13:00 YESTERDAY.
YOU LOGGED INTO ... THAT'S A RESTRICTED AREA!
THAT'S WHEN I LOOKED ON THE MAINTENANCE SCHEDULE AND SAW THAT THIS SECTION WAS SCHEDULED FOR VACUUMING AT 03:30 THIS MORNING.
THIS WAS NO COINCIDENCE -- IT WAS A SPECIAL COMMAND ENTRY CREATED YESTERDAY MORNING.
ANY IDEA WHO MADE THAT ENTRY?
NO -- THERE WAS NO TIME TO INVESTIGATE, AS I HAD ONLY FIVE MINUTES TO WARN MS. ORESME AND THEN GET INTO MY EMERGENCY PRESSURE-SUIT.
FIVE MINUTES? MORE LIKE 5 SECONDS.
UNLESS YOU PUT YOUR SUIT ON FIRST AND THEN REMEMBERED TO WARN ME.
AH YES, WELL ...

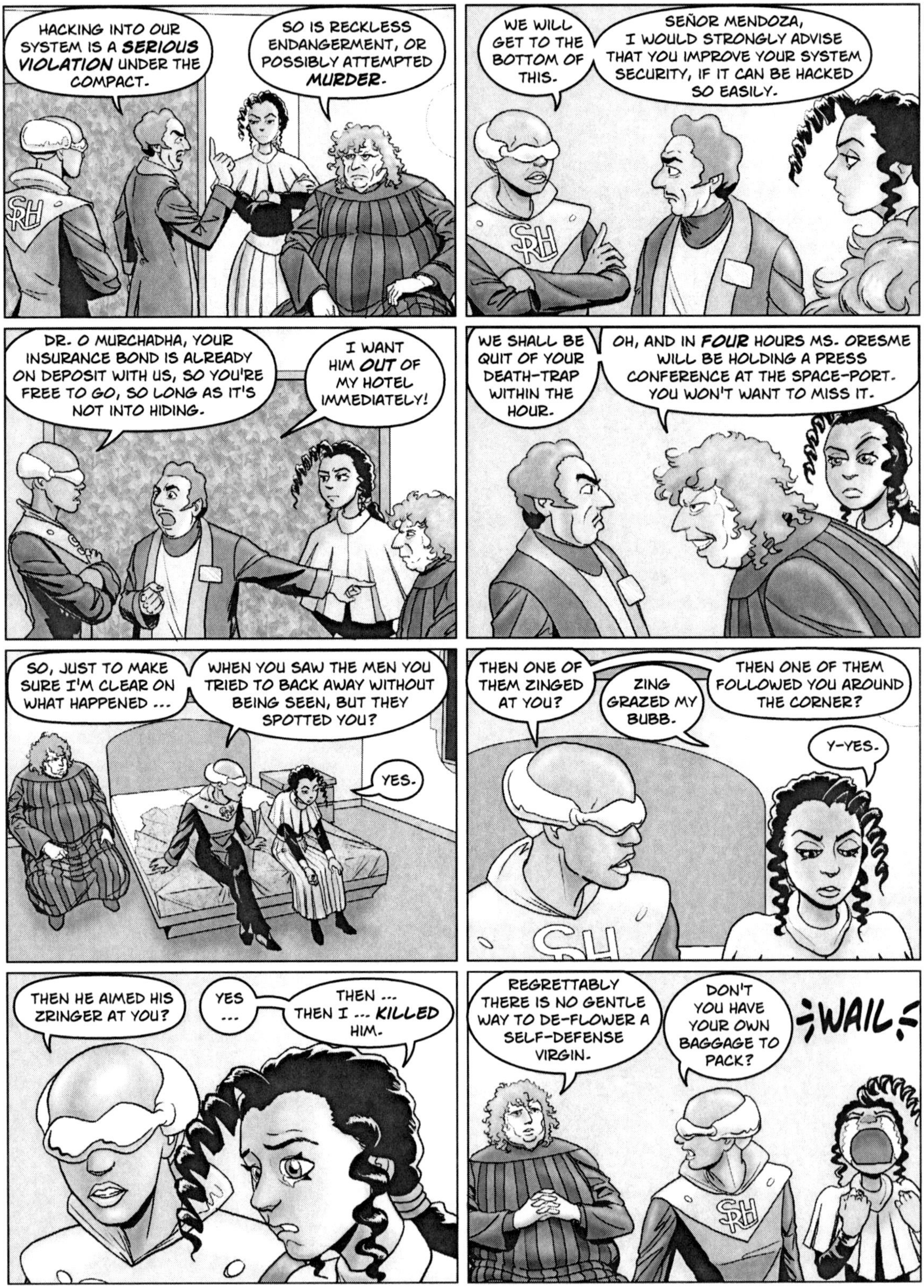
HACKING INTO OUR SYSTEM IS A SERIOUS VIOLATION UNDER THE COMPACT.
SO IS RECKLESS ENDANGERMENT, OR POSSIBLY ATTEMPTED MURDER.
WE WILL GET TO THE BOTTOM OF THIS.
SEÑOR MENDOZA, I WOULD STRONGLY ADVISE THAT YOU IMPROVE YOUR SYSTEM SECURITY, IF IT CAN BE HACKED SO EASILY.
DR. O MURCHADHA, YOUR INSURANCE BOND IS ALREADY ON DEPOSIT WITH US, SO YOU'RE FREE TO GO, SO LONG AS IT'S NOT INTO HIDING.
I WANT HIM OUT OF MY HOTEL IMMEDIATELY!
WE SHALL BE QUIT OF YOUR DEATH-TRAP WITHIN THE HOUR.
OH, AND IN FOUR HOURS MS. ORESME WILL BE HOLDING A PRESS CONFERENCE AT THE SPACE-PORT. YOU WON'T WANT TO MISS IT.
SO, JUST TO MAKE SURE I'M CLEAR ON WHAT HAPPENED ...
WHEN YOU SAW THE MEN YOU TRIED TO BACK AWAY WITHOUT BEING SEEN, BUT THEY SPOTTED YOU?
YES.
THEN ONE OF THEM ZINGED AT YOU?
ZING GRAZED MY BUBB.
THEN ONE OF THEM FOLLOWED YOU AROUND THE CORNER?
Y-YES.
THEN HE AIMED HIS ZRINGER AT YOU?
YES ...
THEN ... THEN I ... KILLED HIM.
REGRETTABLY THERE IS NO GENTLE WAY TO DE-FLOWER A SELF-DEFENSE VIRGIN.
DON'T YOU HAVE YOUR OWN BAGGAGE TO PACK?
WAIL

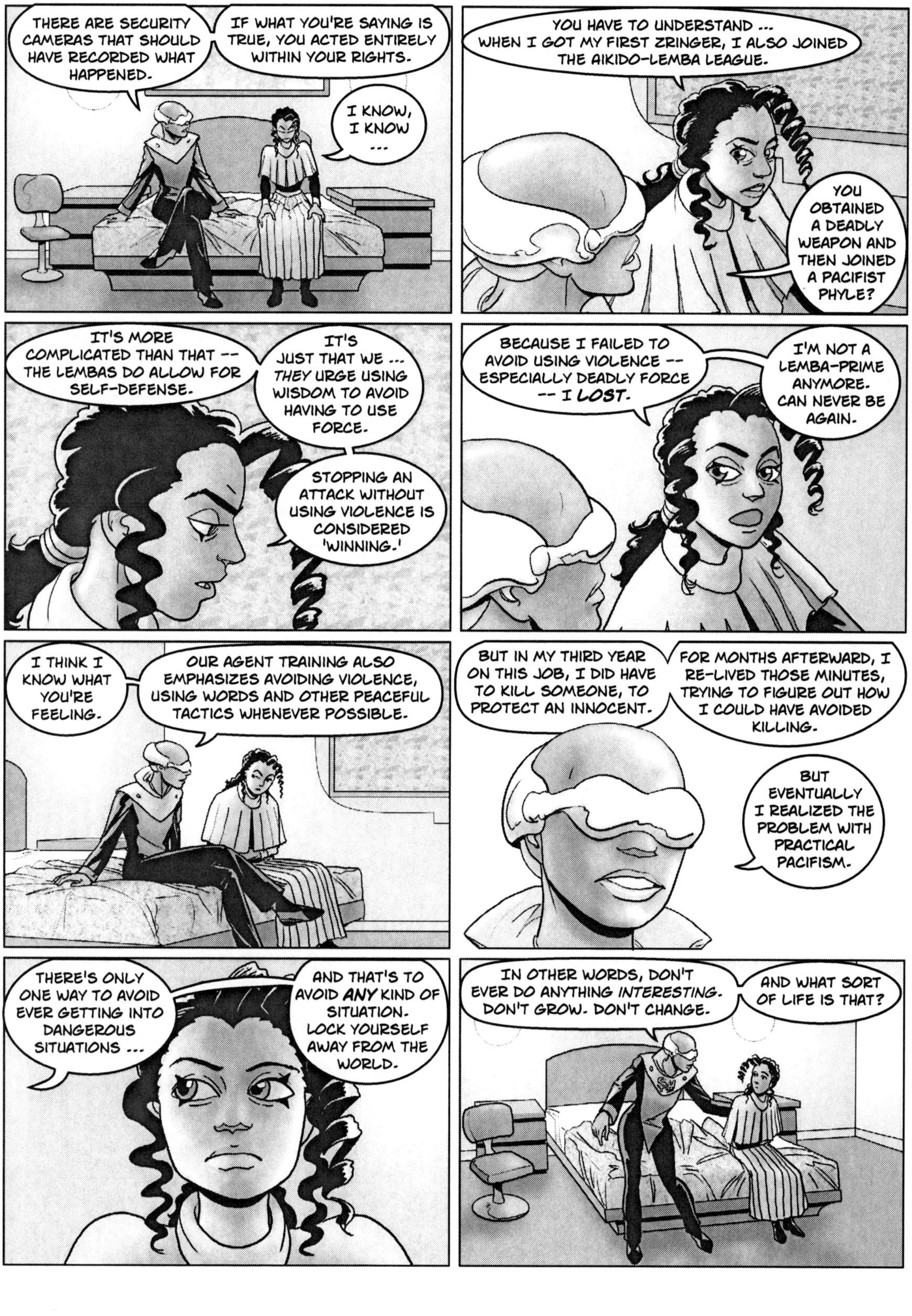
THERE ARE SECURITY CAMERAS THAT SHOULD HAVE RECORDED WHAT HAPPENED.
IF WHAT YOU'RE SAYING IS TRUE, YOU ACTED ENTIRELY WITHIN YOUR RIGHTS.
I KNOW, I KNOW ...
YOU HAVE TO UNDERSTAND ... WHEN I GOT MY FIRST ZRINGER, I ALSO JOINED THE AIKIDO-LEMBA LEAGUE.
YOU OBTAINED A DEADLY WEAPON AND THEN JOINED A PACIFIST PHYLE?
IT'S MORE COMPLICATED THAN THAT -- THE LEMBAS DO ALLOW FOR SELF-DEFENSE.
IT'S JUST THAT WE ... *THEY* URGE USING WISDOM TO AVOID HAVING TO USE FORCE.
STOPPING AN ATTACK WITHOUT USING VIOLENCE IS CONSIDERED 'WINNING.'
BECAUSE I FAILED TO AVOID USING VIOLENCE -- ESPECIALLY DEADLY FORCE -- I ***LOST***.
I'M NOT A LEMBA-PRIME ANYMORE. CAN NEVER BE AGAIN.
I THINK I KNOW WHAT YOU'RE FEELING.
OUR AGENT TRAINING ALSO EMPHASIZES AVOIDING VIOLENCE, USING WORDS AND OTHER PEACEFUL TACTICS WHENEVER POSSIBLE.
BUT IN MY THIRD YEAR ON THIS JOB, I DID HAVE TO KILL SOMEONE, TO PROTECT AN INNOCENT.
FOR MONTHS AFTERWARD, I RE-LIVED THOSE MINUTES, TRYING TO FIGURE OUT HOW I COULD HAVE AVOIDED KILLING.
BUT EVENTUALLY I REALIZED THE PROBLEM WITH PRACTICAL PACIFISM.
THERE'S ONLY ONE WAY TO AVOID EVER GETTING INTO DANGEROUS SITUATIONS ...
AND THAT'S TO AVOID ***ANY*** KIND OF SITUATION. LOCK YOURSELF AWAY FROM THE WORLD.
IN OTHER WORDS, DON'T EVER DO ANYTHING *INTERESTING*. DON'T GROW. DON'T CHANGE.
AND WHAT SORT OF LIFE IS THAT?

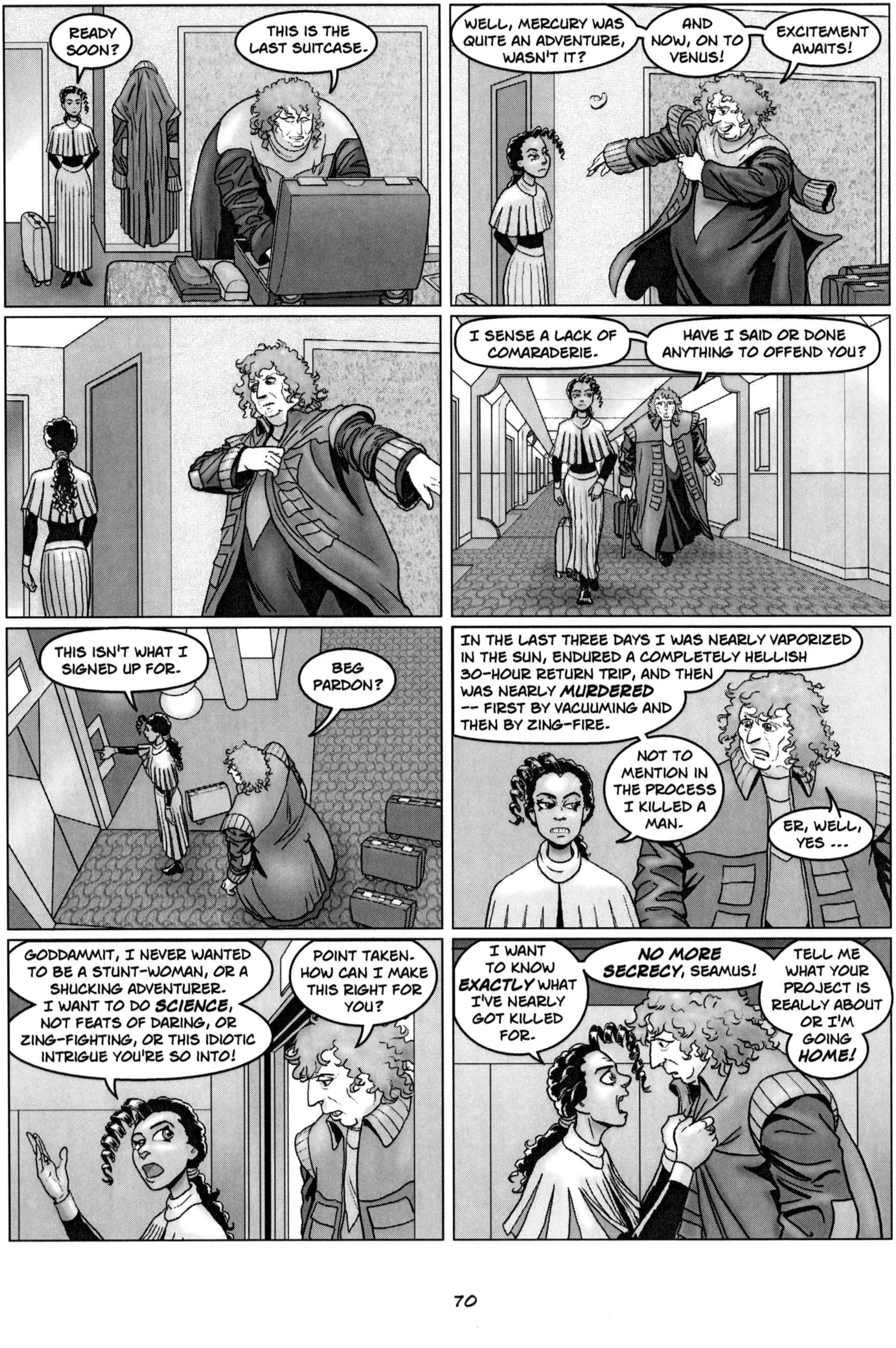
READY SOON?
THIS IS THE LAST SUITCASE.
WELL, MERCURY WAS QUITE AN ADVENTURE, WASN'T IT?
AND NOW, ON TO VENUS!
EXCITEMENT AWAITS!
I SENSE A LACK OF COMARADERIE.
HAVE I SAID OR DONE ANYTHING TO OFFEND YOU?
THIS ISN'T WHAT I SIGNED UP FOR.
BEG PARDON?
IN THE LAST THREE DAYS I WAS NEARLY VAPORIZED IN THE SUN, ENDURED A COMPLETELY HELLISH 30-HOUR RETURN TRIP, AND THEN WAS NEARLY MURDERED -- FIRST BY VACUUMING AND THEN BY ZING-FIRE.
NOT TO MENTION IN THE PROCESS I KILLED A MAN.
ER, WELL, YES ...
GODDAMMIT, I NEVER WANTED TO BE A STUNT-WOMAN, OR A SHUCKING ADVENTURER. I WANT TO DO SCIENCE, NOT FEATS OF DARING, OR ZING-FIGHTING, OR THIS IDIOTIC INTRIGUE YOU'RE SO INTO!
POINT TAKEN. HOW CAN I MAKE THIS RIGHT FOR YOU?
I WANT TO KNOW EXACTLY WHAT I'VE NEARLY GOT KILLED FOR.
NO MORE SECRECY, SEAMUS!
TELL ME WHAT YOUR PROJECT IS REALLY ABOUT OR I'M GOING HOME!

Panel 1:
SO YOU DON'T LIKE SECRECY?

YOU DON'T UNDERSTAND HOW *VITAL* IT IS TO KEEP TRADE SECRETS IN A WORLD AS BOTH HIGHLY-COMPETITIVE AND HIGHLY-COMMUNICATIVE AS OURS?

Panel 2:
OF COURSE I DO. ESPECIALLY AFTER THAT FIRST JOB INTERVIEW.

WHEN YOU TOLD ME THINGS ABOUT MYSELF EVEN MY MOTHER DOESN'T KNOW, IT FELT LIKE I'D BEEN STRIPPED NAKED.

BUT I THINK I'VE EARNED YOUR CONFIDENCE IN THESE MATTERS, DON'T YOU?

Panel 3:
I SUPPOSE YOU'RE RIGHT. BUT I CAN'T TELL YOU HERE AND NOW.

Panel 4:
WE NEED TO FIND AN ULTRA-SECURE LOCATION, AND THERE ISN'T ONE AVAILABLE TO US ON MERCURY.

BUT I PROMISE YOU THAT BEFORE WE LEAVE VENUS, I WILL TELL YOU EVERYTHING YOU WANT TO KNOW. DEAL?

Panel 5:
SEAMUS!

Panel 6:
SEAMUS! GLAD I CAUGHT YOU.

I WAS *SHOCKED* TO HEAR ABOUT THE ATTACK ON YOU AND MS. ORESME.

I'LL BET YOU WERE.

Panel 7:
I -- WHAT ARE YOU IMPLYING?

HOW DID YOU KNOW ABOUT THE ATTACK ON US?

Panel 8:
WELL, *I* FOUND OUT WHEN THE INTREPID AGENT STONE SPENT HALF AN HOUR INTERROGATING ME.

Sun-Diving girl nearly vacu...

BUT ALSO, IT'S BEEN ON THE *VLOGS* FOR ALMOST AS LONG.

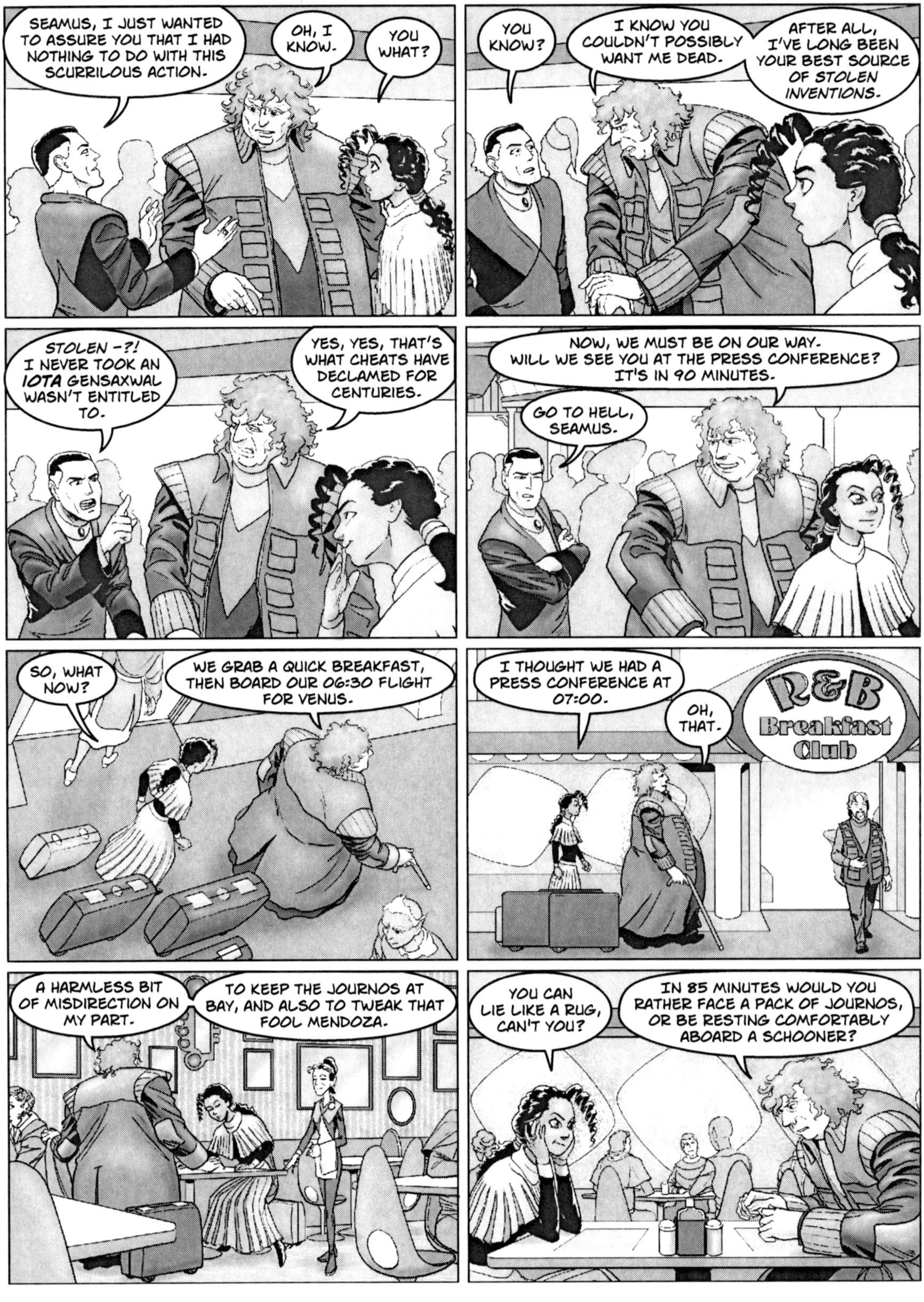
SEAMUS, I JUST WANTED TO ASSURE YOU THAT I HAD NOTHING TO DO WITH THIS SCURRILOUS ACTION.
OH, I KNOW.
YOU WHAT?
YOU KNOW?
I KNOW YOU COULDN'T POSSIBLY WANT ME DEAD.
AFTER ALL, I'VE LONG BEEN YOUR BEST SOURCE OF STOLEN INVENTIONS.
STOLEN —?! I NEVER TOOK AN IOTA GENSAXWAL WASN'T ENTITLED TO.
YES, YES, THAT'S WHAT CHEATS HAVE DECLAMED FOR CENTURIES.
NOW, WE MUST BE ON OUR WAY. WILL WE SEE YOU AT THE PRESS CONFERENCE? IT'S IN 90 MINUTES.
GO TO HELL, SEAMUS.
SO, WHAT NOW?
WE GRAB A QUICK BREAKFAST, THEN BOARD OUR 06:30 FLIGHT FOR VENUS.
I THOUGHT WE HAD A PRESS CONFERENCE AT 07:00.
OH, THAT.
R&B Breakfast Club
A HARMLESS BIT OF MISDIRECTION ON MY PART.
TO KEEP THE JOURNOS AT BAY, AND ALSO TO TWEAK THAT FOOL MENDOZA.
YOU CAN LIE LIKE A RUG, CAN'T YOU?
IN 85 MINUTES WOULD YOU RATHER FACE A PACK OF JOURNOS, OR BE RESTING COMFORTABLY ABOARD A SCHOONER?

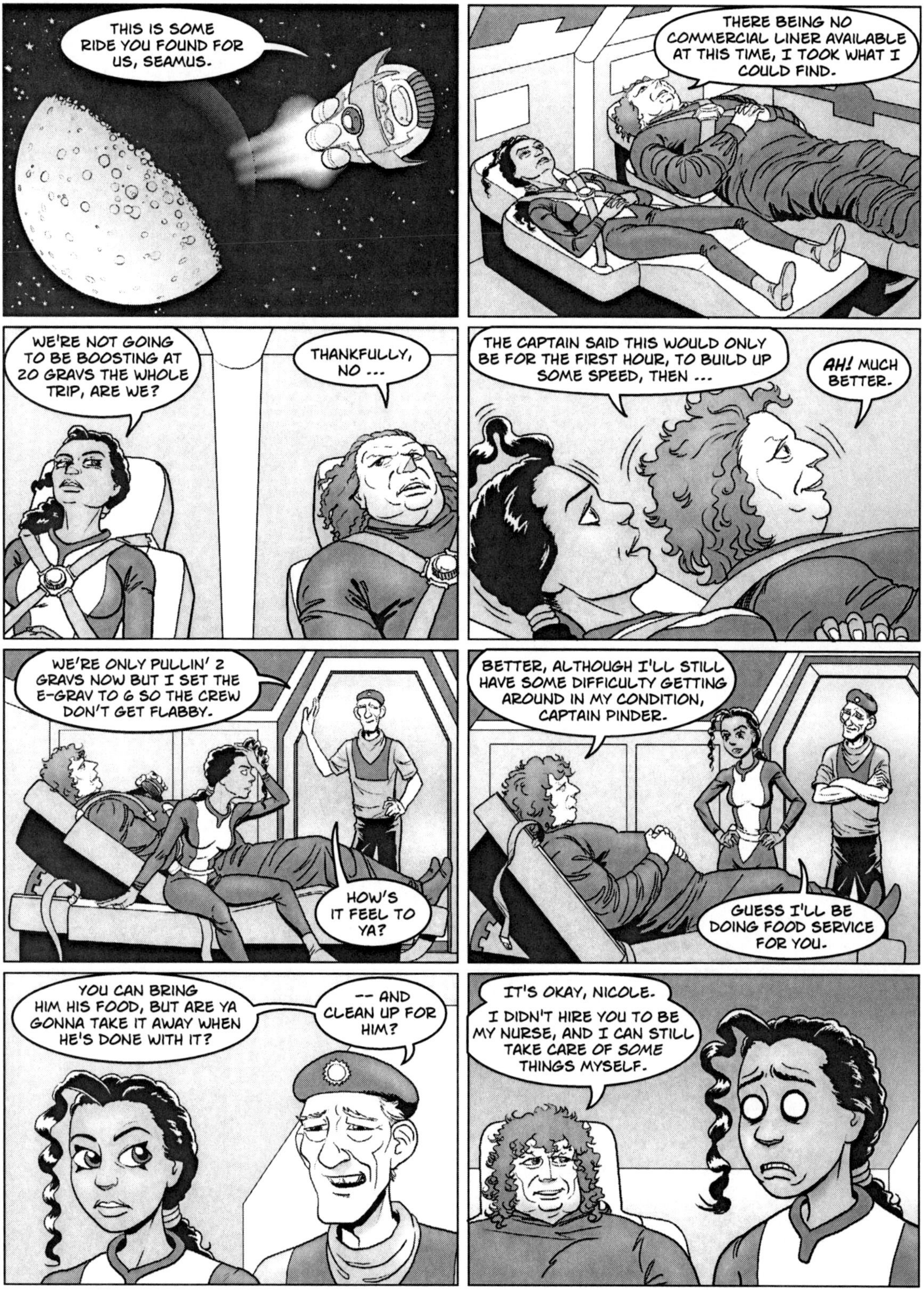
THIS IS SOME RIDE YOU FOUND FOR US, SEAMUS.
THERE BEING NO COMMERCIAL LINER AVAILABLE AT THIS TIME, I TOOK WHAT I COULD FIND.
WE'RE NOT GOING TO BE BOOSTING AT 20 GRAVS THE WHOLE TRIP, ARE WE?
THANKFULLY, NO ...
THE CAPTAIN SAID THIS WOULD ONLY BE FOR THE FIRST HOUR, TO BUILD UP SOME SPEED, THEN ...
AH! MUCH BETTER.
WE'RE ONLY PULLIN' 2 GRAVS NOW BUT I SET THE E-GRAV TO 6 SO THE CREW DON'T GET FLABBY.
HOW'S IT FEEL TO YA?
BETTER, ALTHOUGH I'LL STILL HAVE SOME DIFFICULTY GETTING AROUND IN MY CONDITION, CAPTAIN PINDER.
GUESS I'LL BE DOING FOOD SERVICE FOR YOU.
YOU CAN BRING HIM HIS FOOD, BUT ARE YA GONNA TAKE IT AWAY WHEN HE'S DONE WITH IT?
-- AND CLEAN UP FOR HIM?
IT'S OKAY, NICOLE.
I DIDN'T HIRE YOU TO BE MY NURSE, AND I CAN STILL TAKE CARE OF SOME THINGS MYSELF.

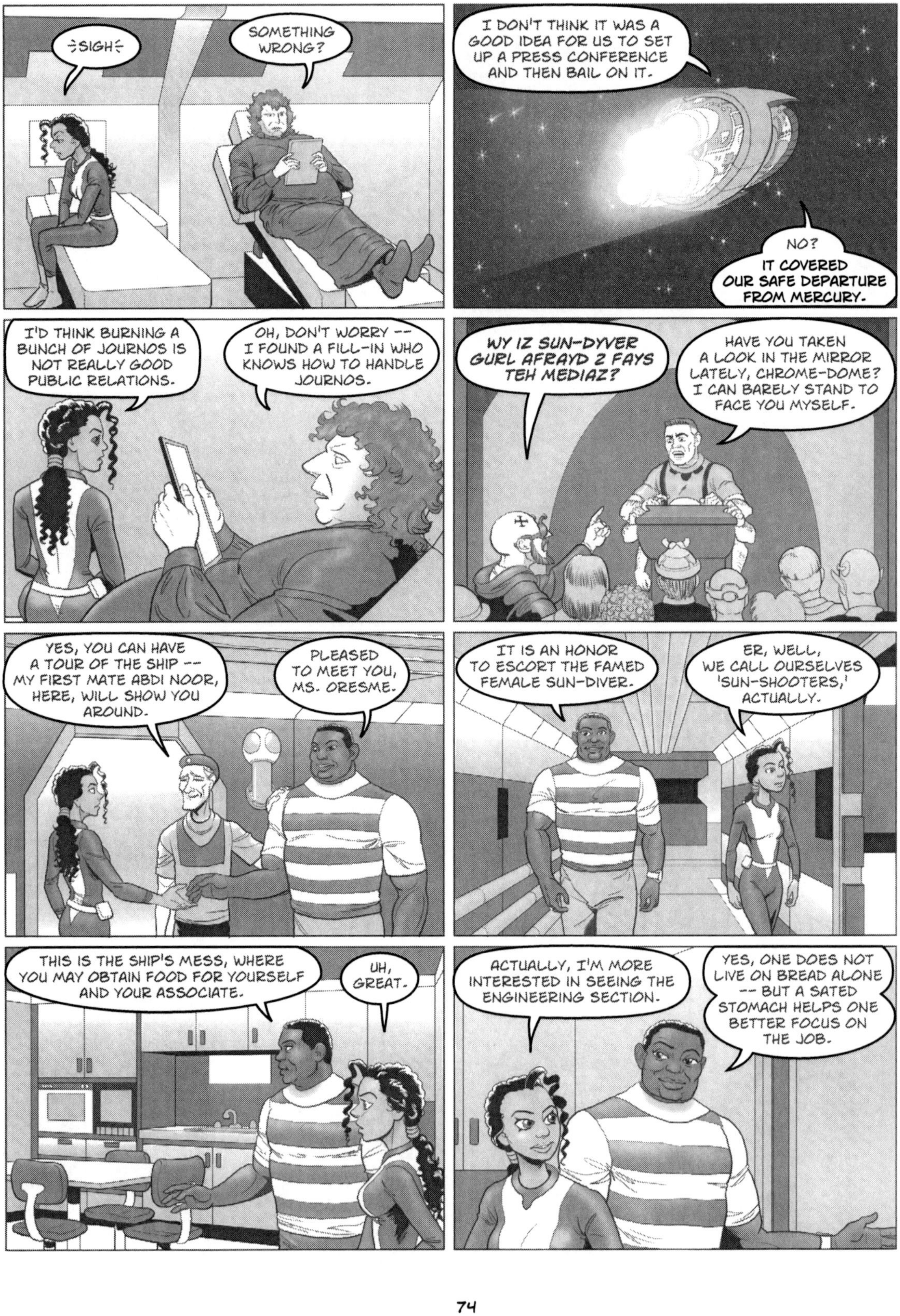
⇌SIGH⇌
SOMETHING WRONG?
I DON'T THINK IT WAS A GOOD IDEA FOR US TO SET UP A PRESS CONFERENCE AND THEN BAIL ON IT.
NO? IT COVERED OUR SAFE DEPARTURE FROM MERCURY.
I'D THINK BURNING A BUNCH OF JOURNOS IS NOT REALLY GOOD PUBLIC RELATIONS.
OH, DON'T WORRY -- I FOUND A FILL-IN WHO KNOWS HOW TO HANDLE JOURNOS.
WY IZ SUN-DYVER GURL AFRAYD 2 FAYS TEH MEDIAZ?
HAVE YOU TAKEN A LOOK IN THE MIRROR LATELY, CHROME-DOME? I CAN BARELY STAND TO FACE YOU MYSELF.
YES, YOU CAN HAVE A TOUR OF THE SHIP -- MY FIRST MATE ABDI NOOR, HERE, WILL SHOW YOU AROUND.
PLEASED TO MEET YOU, MS. ORESME.
IT IS AN HONOR TO ESCORT THE FAMED FEMALE SUN-DIVER.
ER, WELL, WE CALL OURSELVES 'SUN-SHOOTERS,' ACTUALLY.
THIS IS THE SHIP'S MESS, WHERE YOU MAY OBTAIN FOOD FOR YOURSELF AND YOUR ASSOCIATE.
UH, GREAT.
ACTUALLY, I'M MORE INTERESTED IN SEEING THE ENGINEERING SECTION.
YES, ONE DOES NOT LIVE ON BREAD ALONE -- BUT A SATED STOMACH HELPS ONE BETTER FOCUS ON THE JOB.

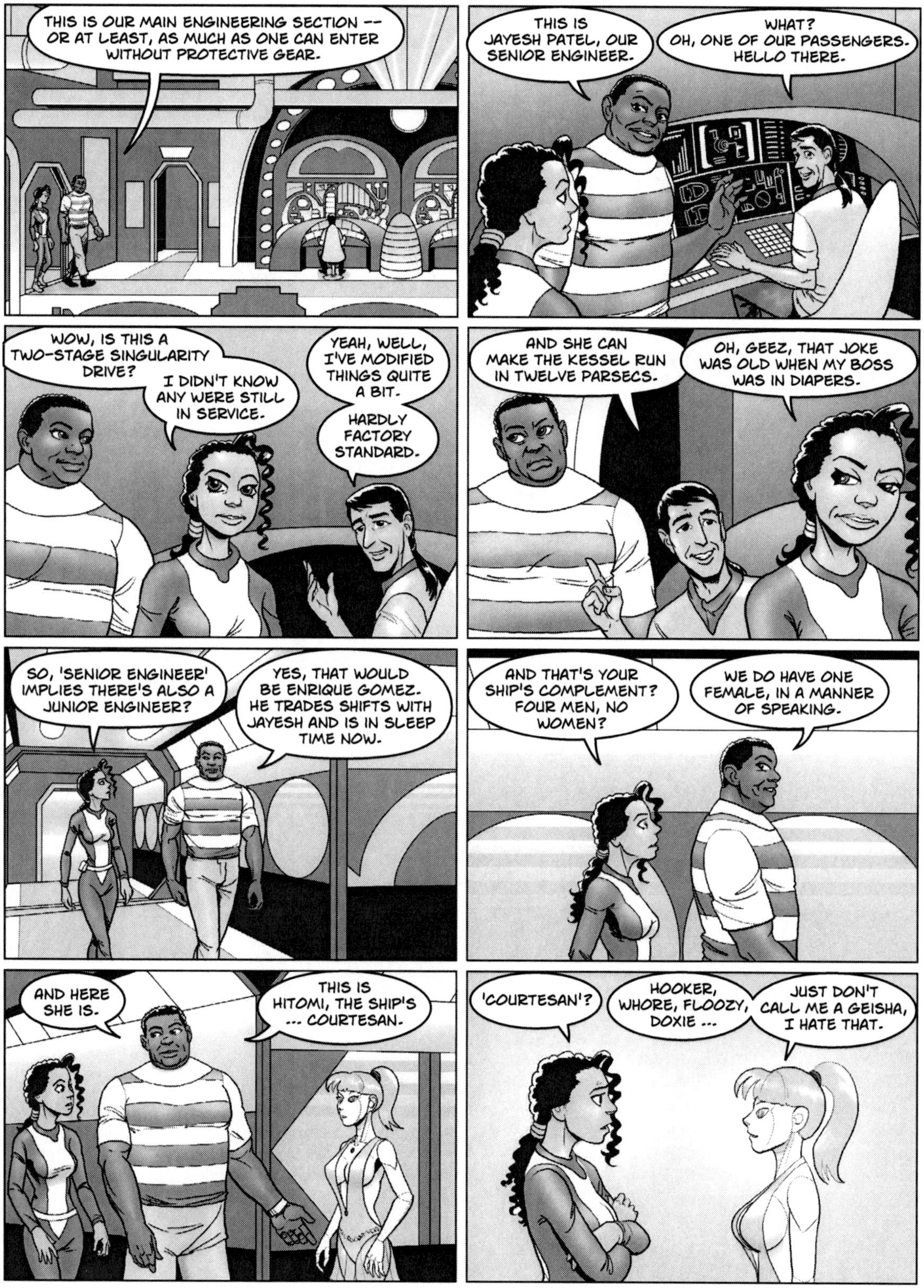
THIS IS OUR MAIN ENGINEERING SECTION -- OR AT LEAST, AS MUCH AS ONE CAN ENTER WITHOUT PROTECTIVE GEAR.
THIS IS JAYESH PATEL, OUR SENIOR ENGINEER.
WHAT? OH, ONE OF OUR PASSENGERS. HELLO THERE.
WOW, IS THIS A TWO-STAGE SINGULARITY DRIVE?
I DIDN'T KNOW ANY WERE STILL IN SERVICE.
YEAH, WELL, I'VE MODIFIED THINGS QUITE A BIT.
HARDLY FACTORY STANDARD.
AND SHE CAN MAKE THE KESSEL RUN IN TWELVE PARSECS.
OH, GEEZ, THAT JOKE WAS OLD WHEN MY BOSS WAS IN DIAPERS.
SO, 'SENIOR ENGINEER' IMPLIES THERE'S ALSO A JUNIOR ENGINEER?
YES, THAT WOULD BE ENRIQUE GOMEZ. HE TRADES SHIFTS WITH JAYESH AND IS IN SLEEP TIME NOW.
AND THAT'S YOUR SHIP'S COMPLEMENT? FOUR MEN, NO WOMEN?
WE DO HAVE ONE FEMALE, IN A MANNER OF SPEAKING.
AND HERE SHE IS.
THIS IS HITOMI, THE SHIP'S ... COURTESAN.
'COURTESAN'?
HOOKER, WHORE, FLOOZY, DOXIE ...
JUST DON'T CALL ME A GEISHA, I HATE THAT.

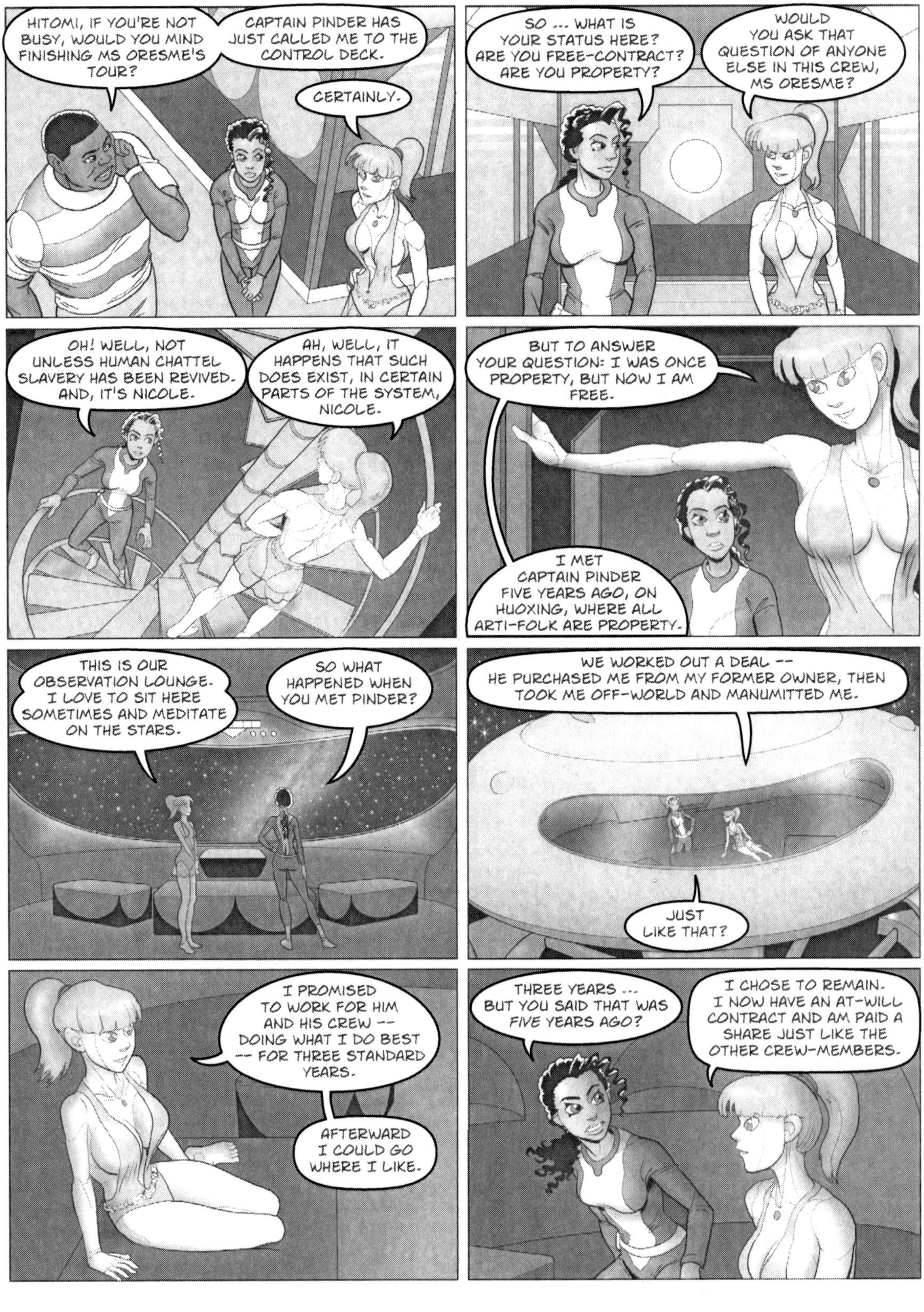
HITOMI, IF YOU'RE NOT BUSY, WOULD YOU MIND FINISHING MS ORESME'S TOUR?
CAPTAIN PINDER HAS JUST CALLED ME TO THE CONTROL DECK.
CERTAINLY.
SO ... WHAT IS YOUR STATUS HERE? ARE YOU FREE-CONTRACT? ARE YOU PROPERTY?
WOULD YOU ASK THAT QUESTION OF ANYONE ELSE IN THIS CREW, MS ORESME?
OH! WELL, NOT UNLESS HUMAN CHATTEL SLAVERY HAS BEEN REVIVED. AND, IT'S NICOLE.
AH, WELL, IT HAPPENS THAT SUCH DOES EXIST, IN CERTAIN PARTS OF THE SYSTEM, NICOLE.
BUT TO ANSWER YOUR QUESTION: I WAS ONCE PROPERTY, BUT NOW I AM FREE.
I MET CAPTAIN PINDER FIVE YEARS AGO, ON HUOXING, WHERE ALL ARTI-FOLK ARE PROPERTY.
THIS IS OUR OBSERVATION LOUNGE. I LOVE TO SIT HERE SOMETIMES AND MEDITATE ON THE STARS.
SO WHAT HAPPENED WHEN YOU MET PINDER?
WE WORKED OUT A DEAL -- HE PURCHASED ME FROM MY FORMER OWNER, THEN TOOK ME OFF-WORLD AND MANUMITTED ME.
JUST LIKE THAT?
I PROMISED TO WORK FOR HIM AND HIS CREW -- DOING WHAT I DO BEST -- FOR THREE STANDARD YEARS.
AFTERWARD I COULD GO WHERE I LIKE.
THREE YEARS ... BUT YOU SAID THAT WAS FIVE YEARS AGO?
I CHOSE TO REMAIN. I NOW HAVE AN AT-WILL CONTRACT AND AM PAID A SHARE JUST LIKE THE OTHER CREW-MEMBERS.

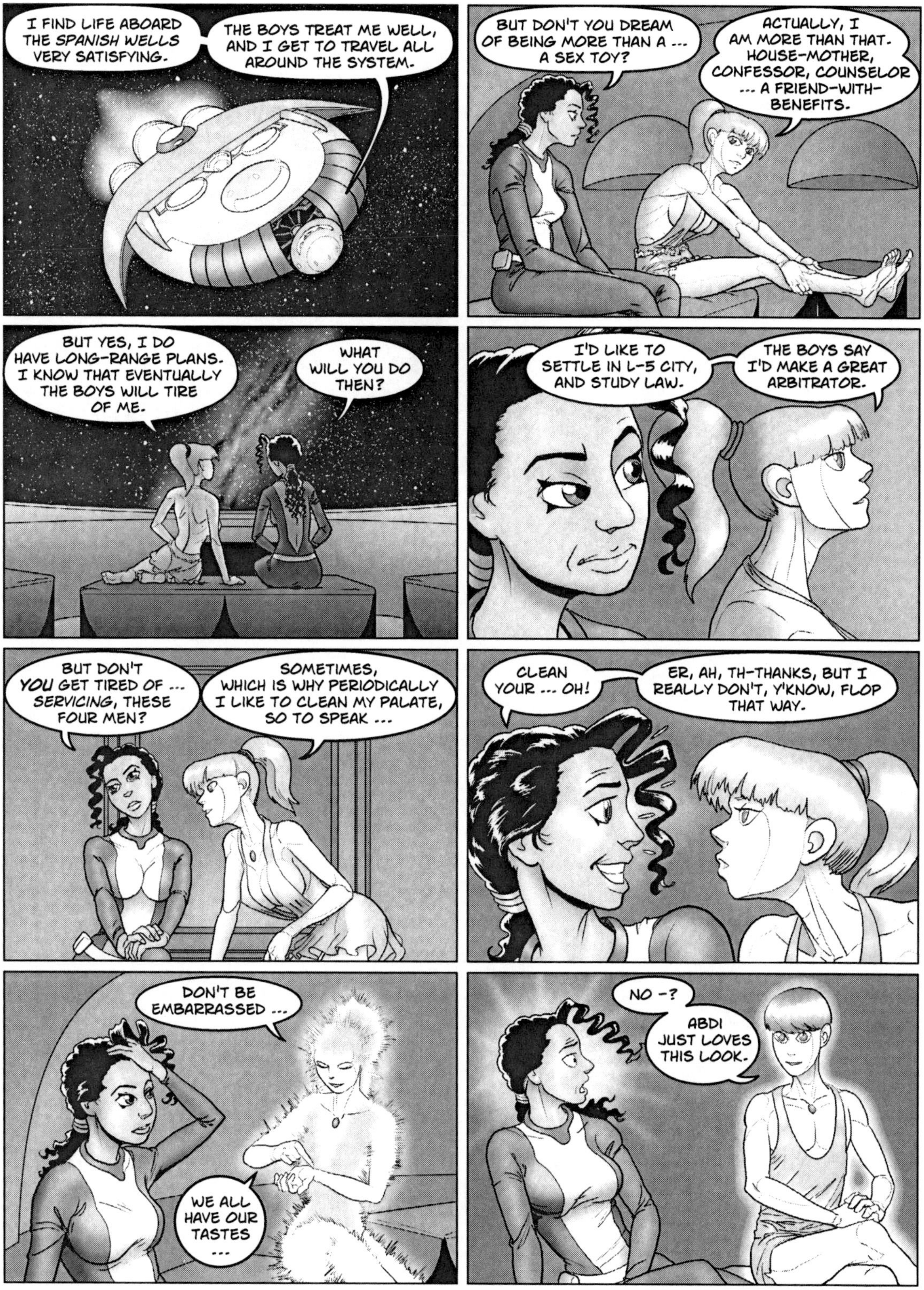
I FIND LIFE ABOARD THE *SPANISH WELLS* VERY SATISFYING.
THE BOYS TREAT ME WELL, AND I GET TO TRAVEL ALL AROUND THE SYSTEM.
BUT DON'T YOU DREAM OF BEING MORE THAN A --- A SEX TOY?
ACTUALLY, I AM MORE THAN THAT. HOUSE-MOTHER, CONFESSOR, COUNSELOR --- A FRIEND-WITH-BENEFITS.
BUT YES, I DO HAVE LONG-RANGE PLANS. I KNOW THAT EVENTUALLY THE BOYS WILL TIRE OF ME.
WHAT WILL YOU DO THEN?
I'D LIKE TO SETTLE IN L-5 CITY, AND STUDY LAW.
THE BOYS SAY I'D MAKE A GREAT ARBITRATOR.
BUT DON'T *YOU* GET TIRED OF --- *SERVICING*, THESE FOUR MEN?
SOMETIMES, WHICH IS WHY PERIODICALLY I LIKE TO CLEAN MY PALATE, SO TO SPEAK ---
CLEAN YOUR --- OH!
ER, AH, TH-THANKS, BUT I REALLY DON'T, Y'KNOW, FLOP THAT WAY.
DON'T BE EMBARRASSED ---
WE ALL HAVE OUR TASTES ---
NO -?
ABDI JUST LOVES THIS LOOK.

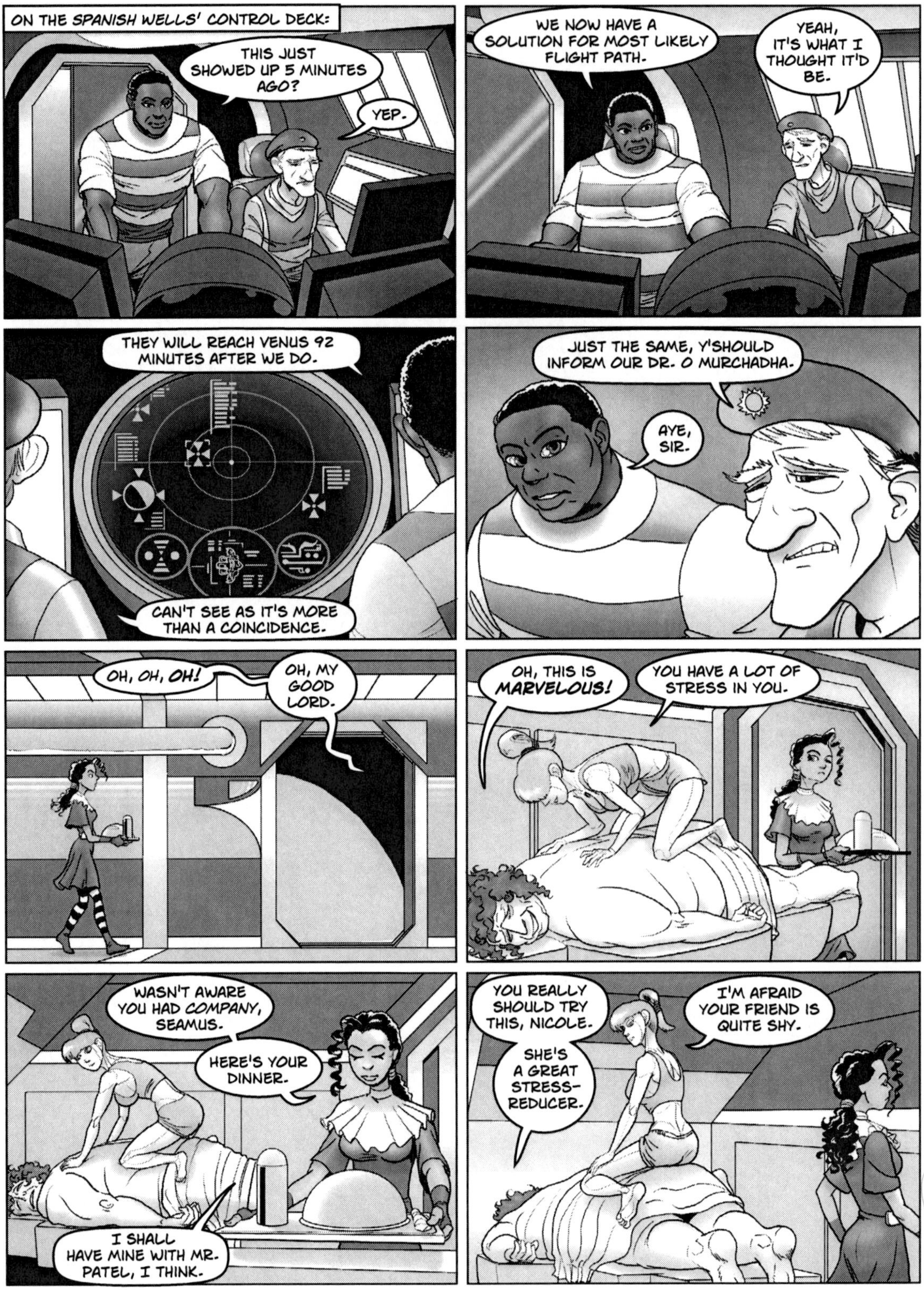
ON THE SPANISH WELLS' CONTROL DECK:
THIS JUST SHOWED UP 5 MINUTES AGO?
YEP.
WE NOW HAVE A SOLUTION FOR MOST LIKELY FLIGHT PATH.
YEAH, IT'S WHAT I THOUGHT IT'D BE.
THEY WILL REACH VENUS 92 MINUTES AFTER WE DO.
CAN'T SEE AS IT'S MORE THAN A COINCIDENCE.
JUST THE SAME, Y'SHOULD INFORM OUR DR. O MURCHADHA.
AYE, SIR.
OH, OH, OH!
OH, MY GOOD LORD.
OH, THIS IS MARVELOUS!
YOU HAVE A LOT OF STRESS IN YOU.
WASN'T AWARE YOU HAD COMPANY, SEAMUS.
HERE'S YOUR DINNER.
I SHALL HAVE MINE WITH MR. PATEL, I THINK.
YOU REALLY SHOULD TRY THIS, NICOLE.
SHE'S A GREAT STRESS-REDUCER.
I'M AFRAID YOUR FRIEND IS QUITE SHY.

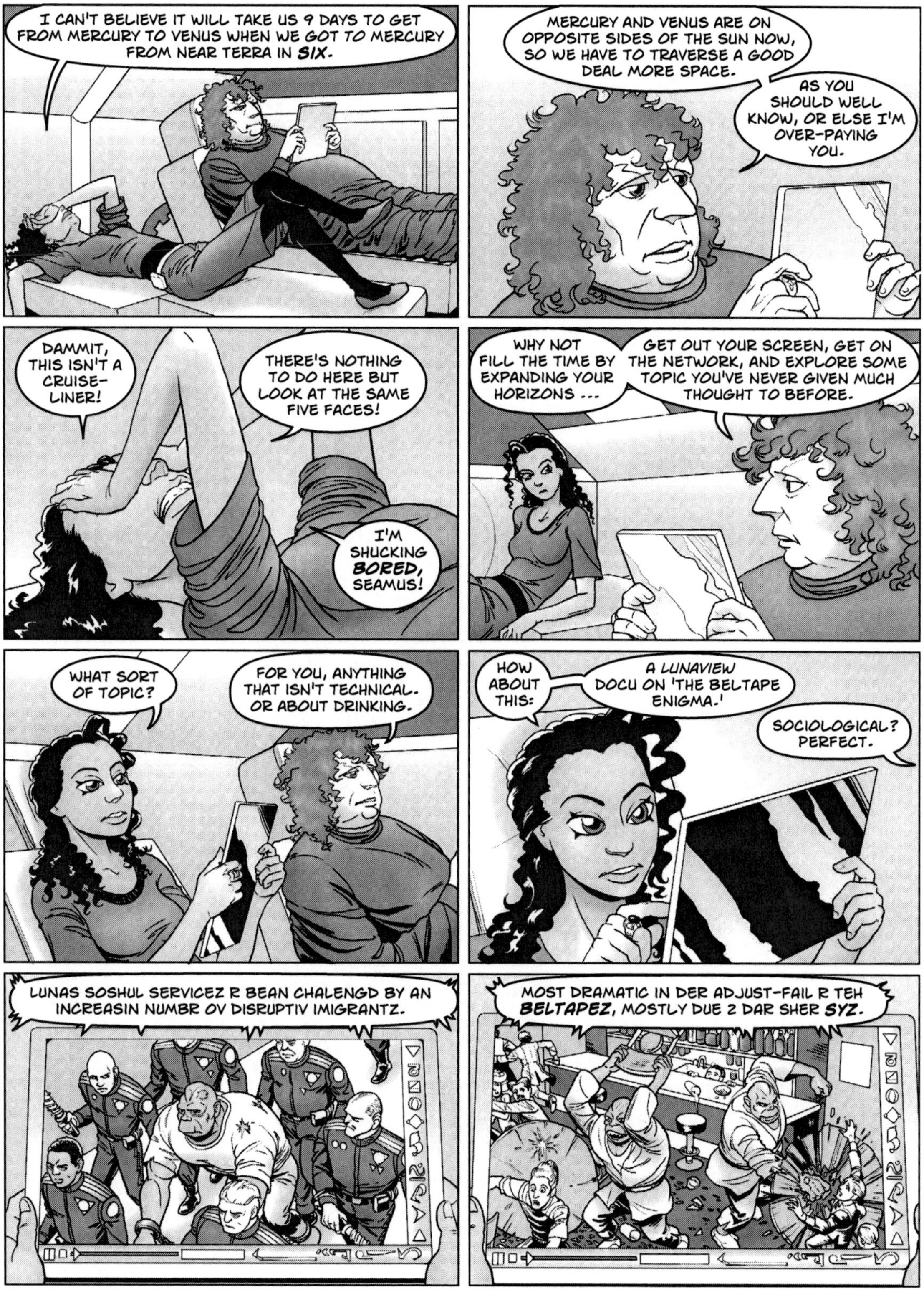
I CAN'T BELIEVE IT WILL TAKE US 9 DAYS TO GET FROM MERCURY TO VENUS WHEN WE GOT TO MERCURY FROM NEAR TERRA IN SIX.
MERCURY AND VENUS ARE ON OPPOSITE SIDES OF THE SUN NOW, SO WE HAVE TO TRAVERSE A GOOD DEAL MORE SPACE.
AS YOU SHOULD WELL KNOW, OR ELSE I'M OVER-PAYING YOU.
DAMMIT, THIS ISN'T A CRUISE-LINER!
THERE'S NOTHING TO DO HERE BUT LOOK AT THE SAME FIVE FACES!
I'M SHUCKING BORED, SEAMUS!
WHY NOT FILL THE TIME BY EXPANDING YOUR HORIZONS ...
GET OUT YOUR SCREEN, GET ON THE NETWORK, AND EXPLORE SOME TOPIC YOU'VE NEVER GIVEN MUCH THOUGHT TO BEFORE.
WHAT SORT OF TOPIC?
FOR YOU, ANYTHING THAT ISN'T TECHNICAL. OR ABOUT DRINKING.
HOW ABOUT THIS:
A LUNAVIEW DOCU ON 'THE BELTAPE ENIGMA.'
SOCIOLOGICAL? PERFECT.
LUNAS SOSHUL SERVICEZ R BEAN CHALENGD BY AN INCREASIN NUMBR OV DISRUPTIV IMIGRANTZ.
MOST DRAMATIC IN DER ADJUST-FAIL R TEH BELTAPEZ, MOSTLY DUE 2 DAR SHER SYZ.

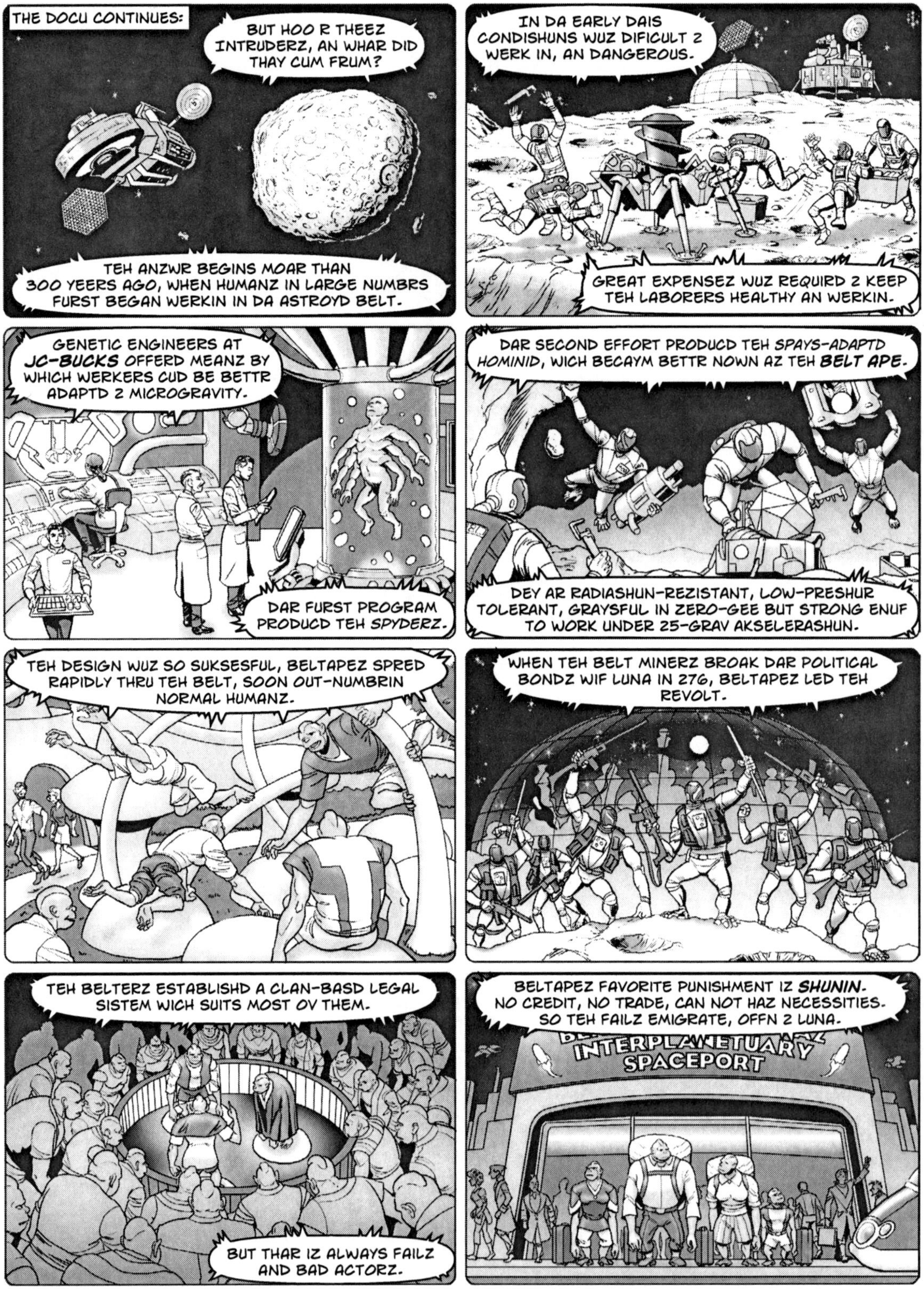
THE DOCU CONTINUES:
BUT HOO R THEEZ INTRUDERZ, AN WHAR DID THAY CUM FRUM?
TEH ANZWR BEGINS MOAR THAN 300 YEERS AGO, WHEN HUMANZ IN LARGE NUMBRS FURST BEGAN WERKIN IN DA ASTROYD BELT.
IN DA EARLY DAIS CONDISHUNS WUZ DIFICULT 2 WERK IN, AN DANGEROUS.
GREAT EXPENSEZ WUZ REQUIRD 2 KEEP TEH LABORERS HEALTHY AN WERKIN.
GENETIC ENGINEERS AT JC-BUCKS OFFERD MEANZ BY WHICH WERKERS CUD BE BETTR ADAPTD 2 MICROGRAVITY.
DAR FURST PROGRAM PRODUCD TEH SPYDERZ.
DAR SECOND EFFORT PRODUCD TEH SPAYS-ADAPTD HOMINID, WICH BECAYM BETTR NOWN AZ TEH BELT APE.
DEY AR RADIASHUN-REZISTANT, LOW-PRESHUR TOLERANT, GRAYSFUL IN ZERO-GEE BUT STRONG ENUF TO WORK UNDER 25-GRAV AKSELERASHUN.
TEH DESIGN WUZ SO SUKSESFUL, BELTAPEZ SPRED RAPIDLY THRU TEH BELT, SOON OUT-NUMBRIN NORMAL HUMANZ.
WHEN TEH BELT MINERZ BROAK DAR POLITICAL BONDZ WIF LUNA IN 276, BELTAPEZ LED TEH REVOLT.
TEH BELTERZ ESTABLISHD A CLAN-BASD LEGAL SISTEM WICH SUITS MOST OV THEM.
BUT THAR IZ ALWAYS FAILZ AND BAD ACTORZ.
BELTAPEZ FAVORITE PUNISHMENT IZ SHUNIN. NO CREDIT, NO TRADE, CAN NOT HAZ NECESSITIES. SO TEH FAILZ EMIGRATE, OFFN 2 LUNA.
INTERPLANETUARY SPACEPORT

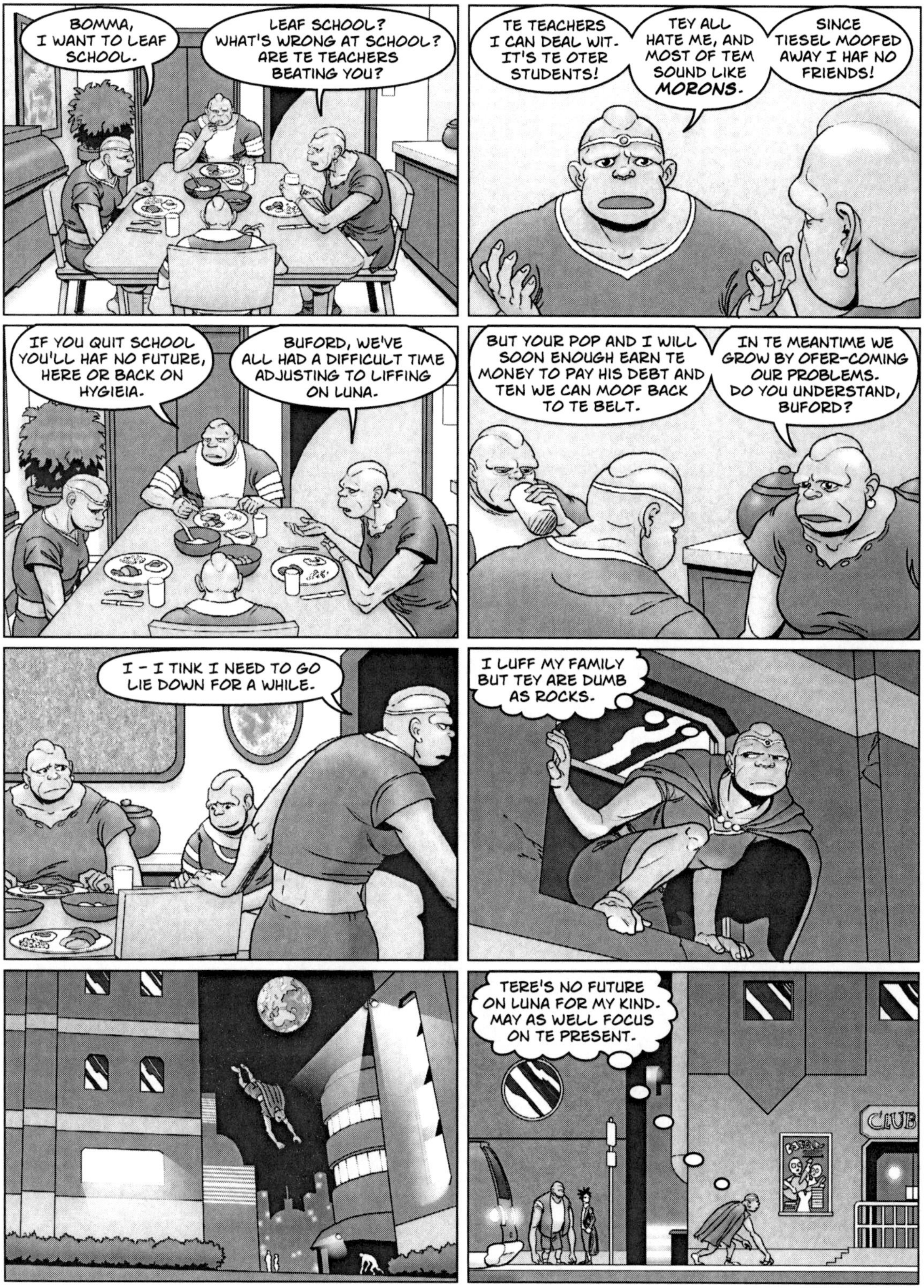
BOMMA, I WANT TO LEAF SCHOOL.
LEAF SCHOOL? WHAT'S WRONG AT SCHOOL? ARE TE TEACHERS BEATING YOU?
TE TEACHERS I CAN DEAL WIT. IT'S TE OTER STUDENTS!
TEY ALL HATE ME, AND MOST OF TEM SOUND LIKE MORONS.
SINCE TIESEL MOOFED AWAY I HAF NO FRIENDS!
IF YOU QUIT SCHOOL YOU'LL HAF NO FUTURE, HERE OR BACK ON HYGIEIA.
BUFORD, WE'VE ALL HAD A DIFFICULT TIME ADJUSTING TO LIFFING ON LUNA.
BUT YOUR POP AND I WILL SOON ENOUGH EARN TE MONEY TO PAY HIS DEBT AND TEN WE CAN MOOF BACK TO TE BELT.
IN TE MEANTIME WE GROW BY OFER-COMING OUR PROBLEMS. DO YOU UNDERSTAND, BUFORD?
I - I TINK I NEED TO GO LIE DOWN FOR A WHILE.
I LUFF MY FAMILY BUT TEY ARE DUMB AS ROCKS.
TERE'S NO FUTURE ON LUNA FOR MY KIND. MAY AS WELL FOCUS ON TE PRESENT.
CLUB

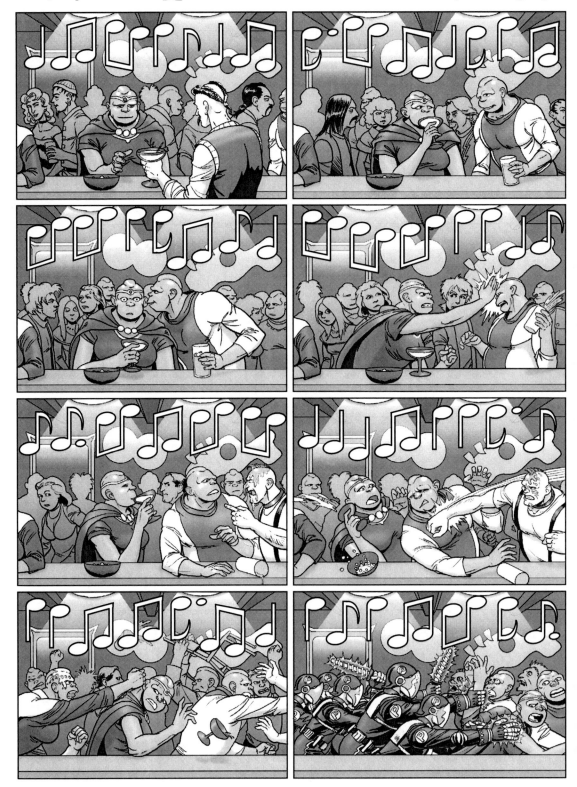

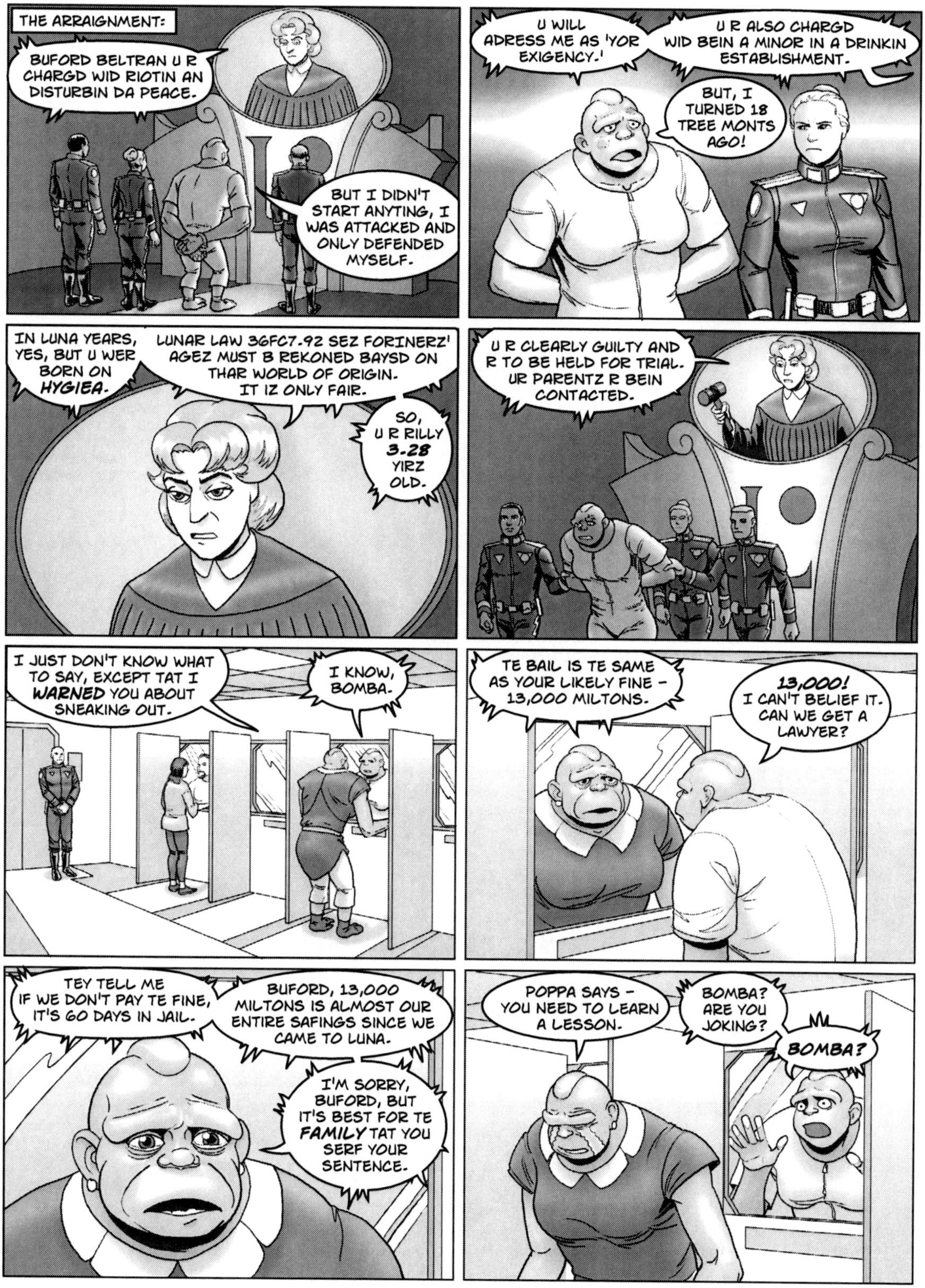
THE ARRAIGNMENT:
BUFORD BELTRAN U R CHARGD WID RIOTIN AN DISTURBIN DA PEACE.
BUT I DIDN'T START ANYTING, I WAS ATTACKED AND ONLY DEFENDED MYSELF.
U WILL ADRESS ME AS 'YOR EXIGENCY.'
U R ALSO CHARGD WID BEIN A MINOR IN A DRINKIN ESTABLISHMENT.
BUT, I TURNED 18 TREE MONTS AGO!
IN LUNA YEARS, YES, BUT U WER BORN ON HYGIEA.
LUNAR LAW 36FC7.92 SEZ FORINERZ' AGEZ MUST B REKONED BAYSD ON THAR WORLD OF ORIGIN. IT IZ ONLY FAIR.
SO, U R RILLY 3.28 YIRZ OLD.
U R CLEARLY GUILTY AND R TO BE HELD FOR TRIAL. UR PARENTZ R BEIN CONTACTED.
I JUST DON'T KNOW WHAT TO SAY, EXCEPT TAT I WARNED YOU ABOUT SNEAKING OUT.
I KNOW, BOMBA.
TE BAIL IS TE SAME AS YOUR LIKELY FINE - 13,000 MILTONS.
13,000! I CAN'T BELIEF IT. CAN WE GET A LAWYER?
TEY TELL ME IF WE DON'T PAY TE FINE, IT'S 60 DAYS IN JAIL.
BUFORD, 13,000 MILTONS IS ALMOST OUR ENTIRE SAFINGS SINCE WE CAME TO LUNA.
I'M SORRY, BUFORD, BUT IT'S BEST FOR TE FAMILY TAT YOU SERF YOUR SENTENCE.
POPPA SAYS - YOU NEED TO LEARN A LESSON.
BOMBA? ARE YOU JOKING?
BOMBA?

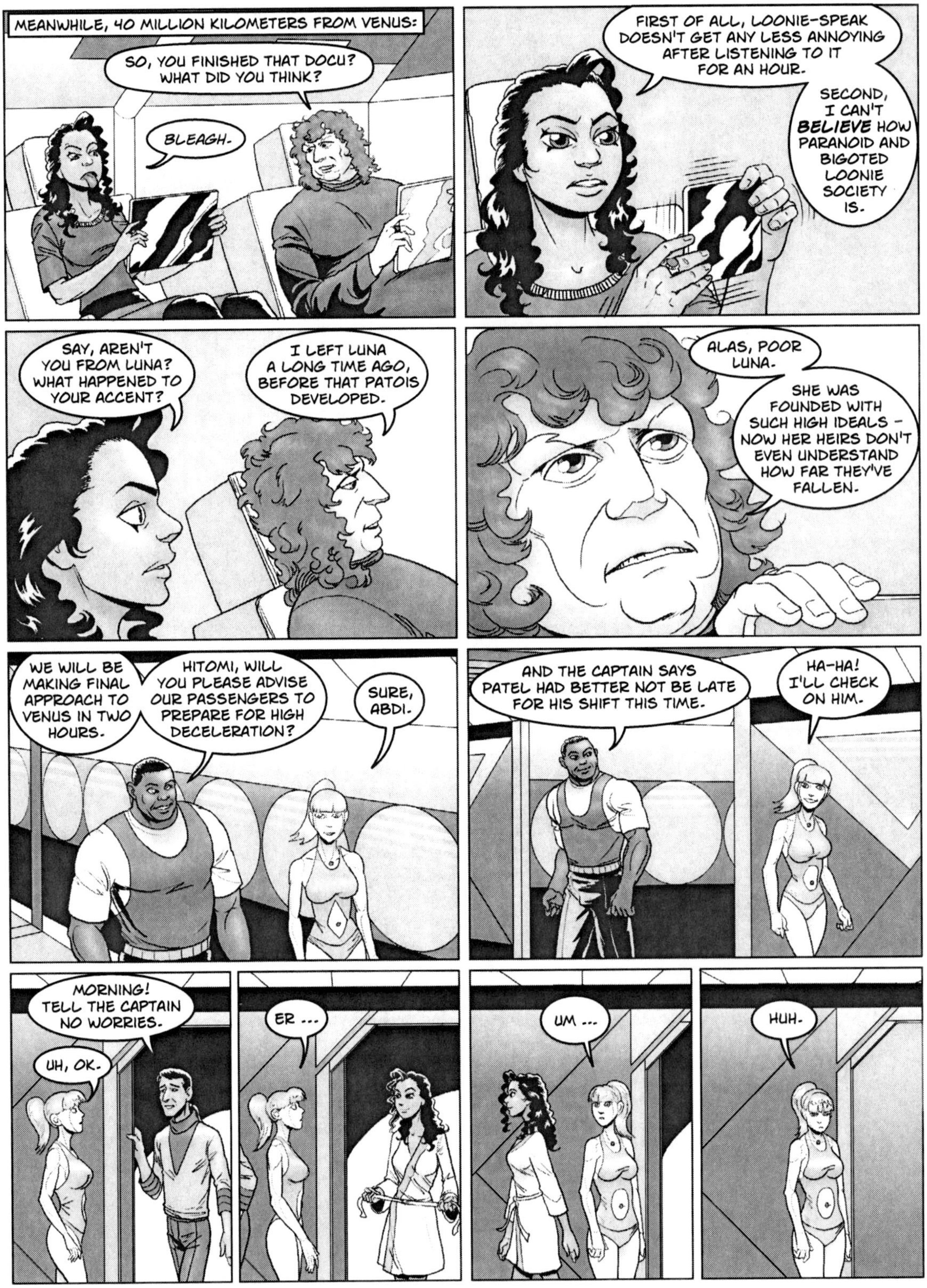
MEANWHILE, 40 MILLION KILOMETERS FROM VENUS:
SO, YOU FINISHED THAT DOCU? WHAT DID YOU THINK?
BLEAGH.
FIRST OF ALL, LOONIE-SPEAK DOESN'T GET ANY LESS ANNOYING AFTER LISTENING TO IT FOR AN HOUR.
SECOND, I CAN'T **BELIEVE** HOW PARANOID AND BIGOTED LOONIE SOCIETY IS.
SAY, AREN'T YOU FROM LUNA? WHAT HAPPENED TO YOUR ACCENT?
I LEFT LUNA A LONG TIME AGO, BEFORE THAT PATOIS DEVELOPED.
ALAS, POOR LUNA.
SHE WAS FOUNDED WITH SUCH HIGH IDEALS – NOW HER HEIRS DON'T EVEN UNDERSTAND HOW FAR THEY'VE FALLEN.
WE WILL BE MAKING FINAL APPROACH TO VENUS IN TWO HOURS.
HITOMI, WILL YOU PLEASE ADVISE OUR PASSENGERS TO PREPARE FOR HIGH DECELERATION?
SURE, ABDI.
AND THE CAPTAIN SAYS PATEL HAD BETTER NOT BE LATE FOR HIS SHIFT THIS TIME.
HA-HA! I'LL CHECK ON HIM.
MORNING! TELL THE CAPTAIN NO WORRIES.
UH, OK.
ER ...
UM ...
HUH.

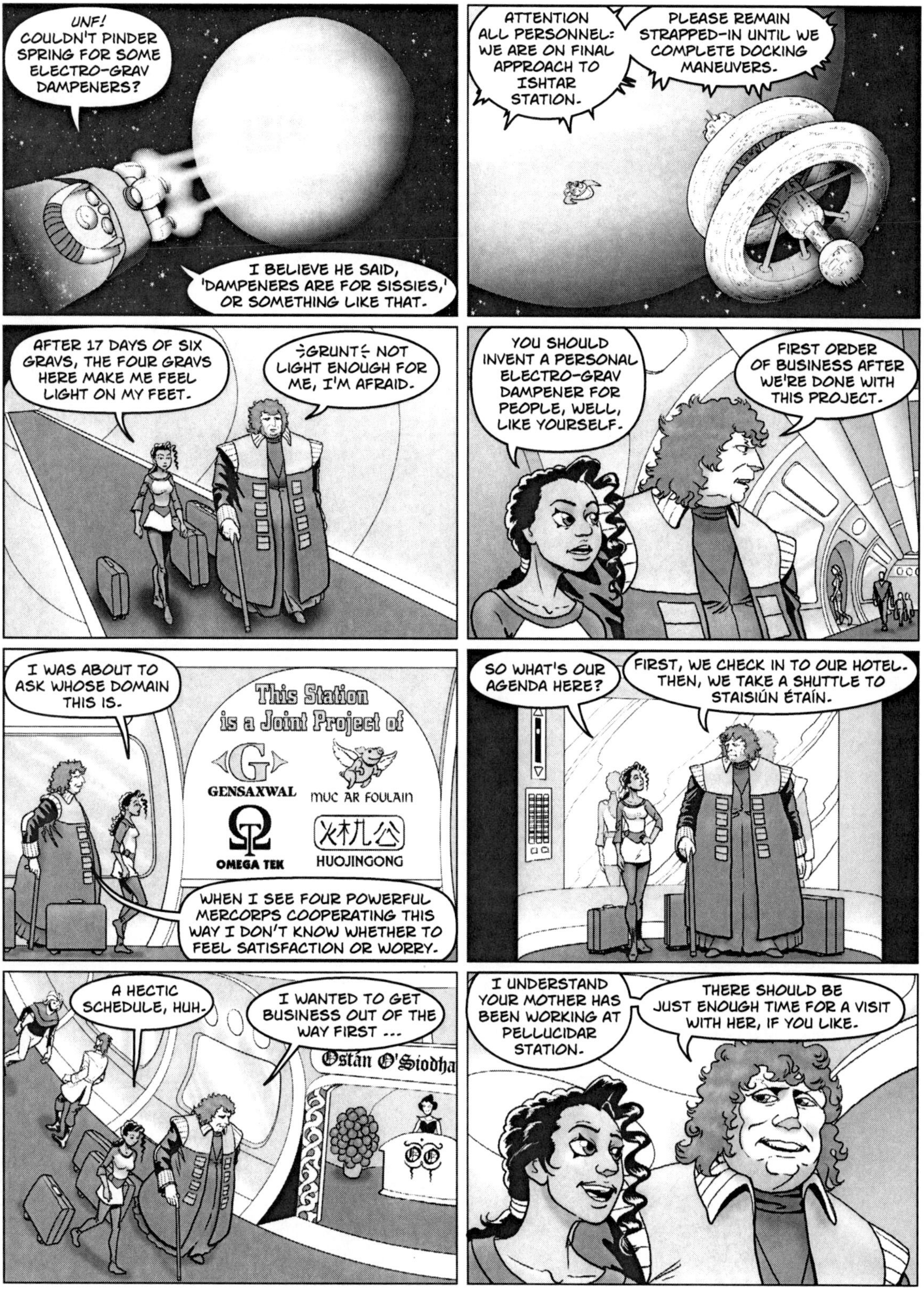
UNF! COULDN'T PINDER SPRING FOR SOME ELECTRO-GRAV DAMPENERS?
I BELIEVE HE SAID, 'DAMPENERS ARE FOR SISSIES,' OR SOMETHING LIKE THAT.
ATTENTION ALL PERSONNEL: WE ARE ON FINAL APPROACH TO ISHTAR STATION.
PLEASE REMAIN STRAPPED-IN UNTIL WE COMPLETE DOCKING MANEUVERS.
AFTER 17 DAYS OF SIX GRAVS, THE FOUR GRAVS HERE MAKE ME FEEL LIGHT ON MY FEET.
GRUNT NOT LIGHT ENOUGH FOR ME, I'M AFRAID.
YOU SHOULD INVENT A PERSONAL ELECTRO-GRAV DAMPENER FOR PEOPLE, WELL, LIKE YOURSELF.
FIRST ORDER OF BUSINESS AFTER WE'RE DONE WITH THIS PROJECT.
I WAS ABOUT TO ASK WHOSE DOMAIN THIS IS.
This Station is a Joint Project of
GENSAXWAL
MUC AR FOULAIN
OMEGA TEK
火机公
HUOJINGONG
WHEN I SEE FOUR POWERFUL MERCORPS COOPERATING THIS WAY I DON'T KNOW WHETHER TO FEEL SATISFACTION OR WORRY.
SO WHAT'S OUR AGENDA HERE?
FIRST, WE CHECK IN TO OUR HOTEL. THEN, WE TAKE A SHUTTLE TO STAISIÚN ÉTAÍN.
A HECTIC SCHEDULE, HUH.
I WANTED TO GET BUSINESS OUT OF THE WAY FIRST ...
Óstán O'Siodha
I UNDERSTAND YOUR MOTHER HAS BEEN WORKING AT PELLUCIDAR STATION.
THERE SHOULD BE JUST ENOUGH TIME FOR A VISIT WITH HER, IF YOU LIKE.

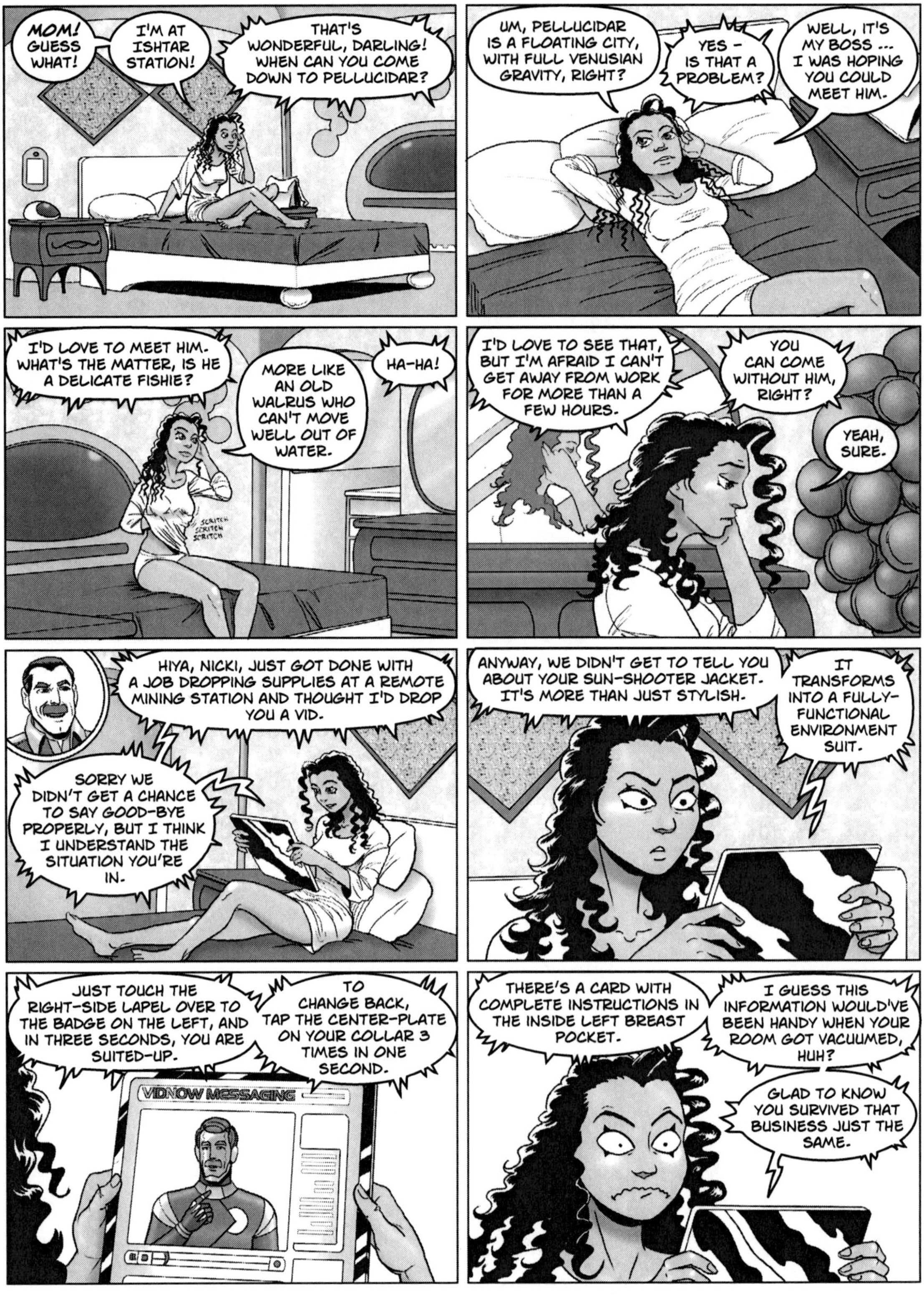
MOM! GUESS WHAT!
I'M AT ISHTAR STATION!
THAT'S WONDERFUL, DARLING! WHEN CAN YOU COME DOWN TO PELLUCIDAR?
UM, PELLUCIDAR IS A FLOATING CITY, WITH FULL VENUSIAN GRAVITY, RIGHT?
YES – IS THAT A PROBLEM?
WELL, IT'S MY BOSS ... I WAS HOPING YOU COULD MEET HIM.
I'D LOVE TO MEET HIM. WHAT'S THE MATTER, IS HE A DELICATE FISHIE?
MORE LIKE AN OLD WALRUS WHO CAN'T MOVE WELL OUT OF WATER.
HA-HA!
SCRITCH SCRITCH SCRITCH
I'D LOVE TO SEE THAT, BUT I'M AFRAID I CAN'T GET AWAY FROM WORK FOR MORE THAN A FEW HOURS.
YOU CAN COME WITHOUT HIM, RIGHT?
YEAH, SURE.
HIYA, NICKI, JUST GOT DONE WITH A JOB DROPPING SUPPLIES AT A REMOTE MINING STATION AND THOUGHT I'D DROP YOU A VID.
SORRY WE DIDN'T GET A CHANCE TO SAY GOOD-BYE PROPERLY, BUT I THINK I UNDERSTAND THE SITUATION YOU'RE IN.
ANYWAY, WE DIDN'T GET TO TELL YOU ABOUT YOUR SUN-SHOOTER JACKET. IT'S MORE THAN JUST STYLISH.
IT TRANSFORMS INTO A FULLY-FUNCTIONAL ENVIRONMENT SUIT.
JUST TOUCH THE RIGHT-SIDE LAPEL OVER TO THE BADGE ON THE LEFT, AND IN THREE SECONDS, YOU ARE SUITED-UP.
TO CHANGE BACK, TAP THE CENTER-PLATE ON YOUR COLLAR 3 TIMES IN ONE SECOND.
VIDNOW MESSAGING
THERE'S A CARD WITH COMPLETE INSTRUCTIONS IN THE INSIDE LEFT BREAST POCKET.
I GUESS THIS INFORMATION WOULD'VE BEEN HANDY WHEN YOUR ROOM GOT VACUUMED, HUH?
GLAD TO KNOW YOU SURVIVED THAT BUSINESS JUST THE SAME.

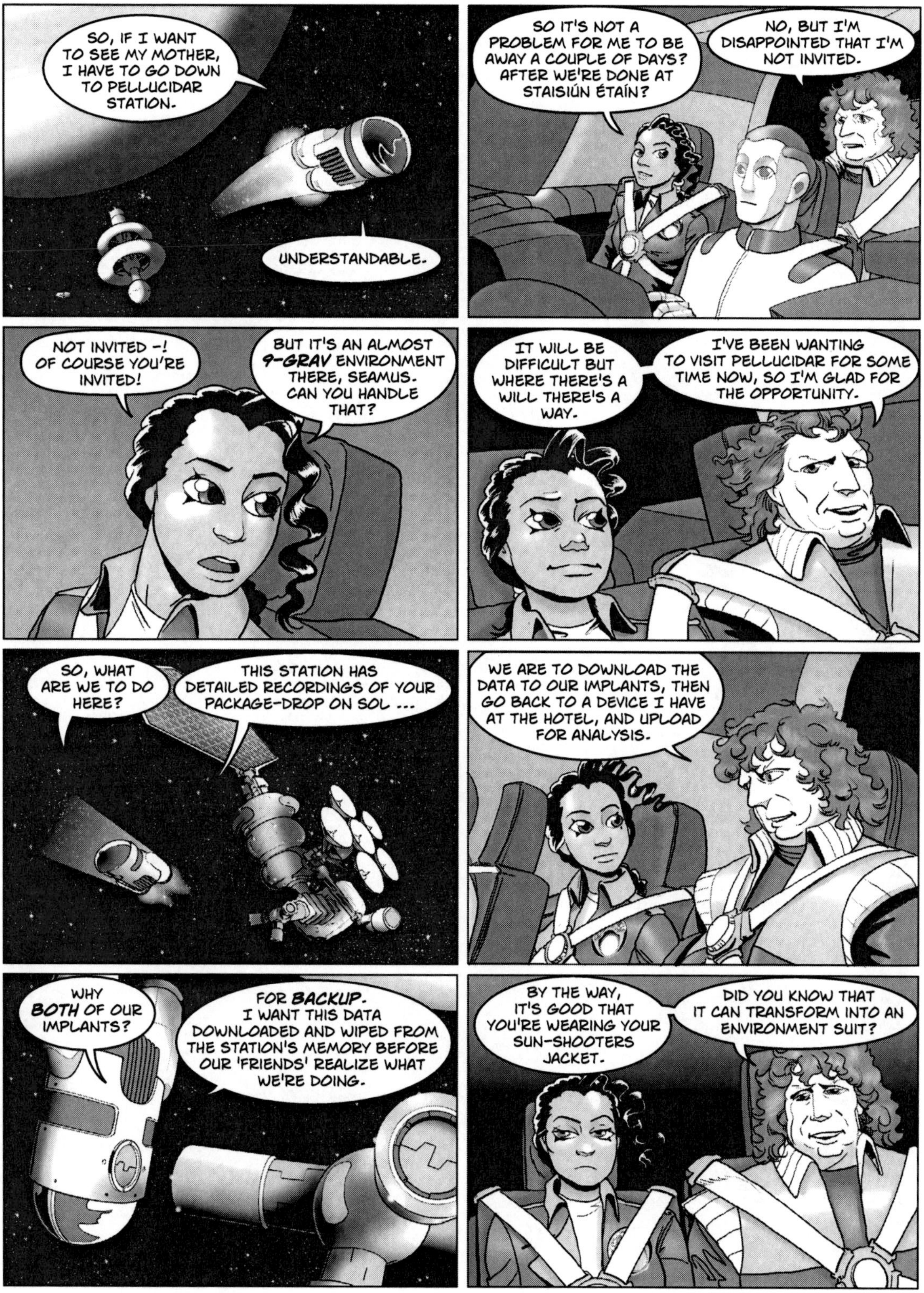
SO, IF I WANT TO SEE MY MOTHER, I HAVE TO GO DOWN TO PELLUCIDAR STATION.
UNDERSTANDABLE.
SO IT'S NOT A PROBLEM FOR ME TO BE AWAY A COUPLE OF DAYS? AFTER WE'RE DONE AT STAISIÚN ÉTAÍN?
NO, BUT I'M DISAPPOINTED THAT I'M NOT INVITED.
NOT INVITED -! OF COURSE YOU'RE INVITED!
BUT IT'S AN ALMOST 9-GRAV ENVIRONMENT THERE, SEAMUS. CAN YOU HANDLE THAT?
IT WILL BE DIFFICULT BUT WHERE THERE'S A WILL THERE'S A WAY.
I'VE BEEN WANTING TO VISIT PELLUCIDAR FOR SOME TIME NOW, SO I'M GLAD FOR THE OPPORTUNITY.
SO, WHAT ARE WE TO DO HERE?
THIS STATION HAS DETAILED RECORDINGS OF YOUR PACKAGE-DROP ON SOL ...
WE ARE TO DOWNLOAD THE DATA TO OUR IMPLANTS, THEN GO BACK TO A DEVICE I HAVE AT THE HOTEL, AND UPLOAD FOR ANALYSIS.
WHY BOTH OF OUR IMPLANTS?
FOR BACKUP. I WANT THIS DATA DOWNLOADED AND WIPED FROM THE STATION'S MEMORY BEFORE OUR 'FRIENDS' REALIZE WHAT WE'RE DOING.
BY THE WAY, IT'S GOOD THAT YOU'RE WEARING YOUR SUN-SHOOTERS JACKET.
DID YOU KNOW THAT IT CAN TRANSFORM INTO AN ENVIRONMENT SUIT?

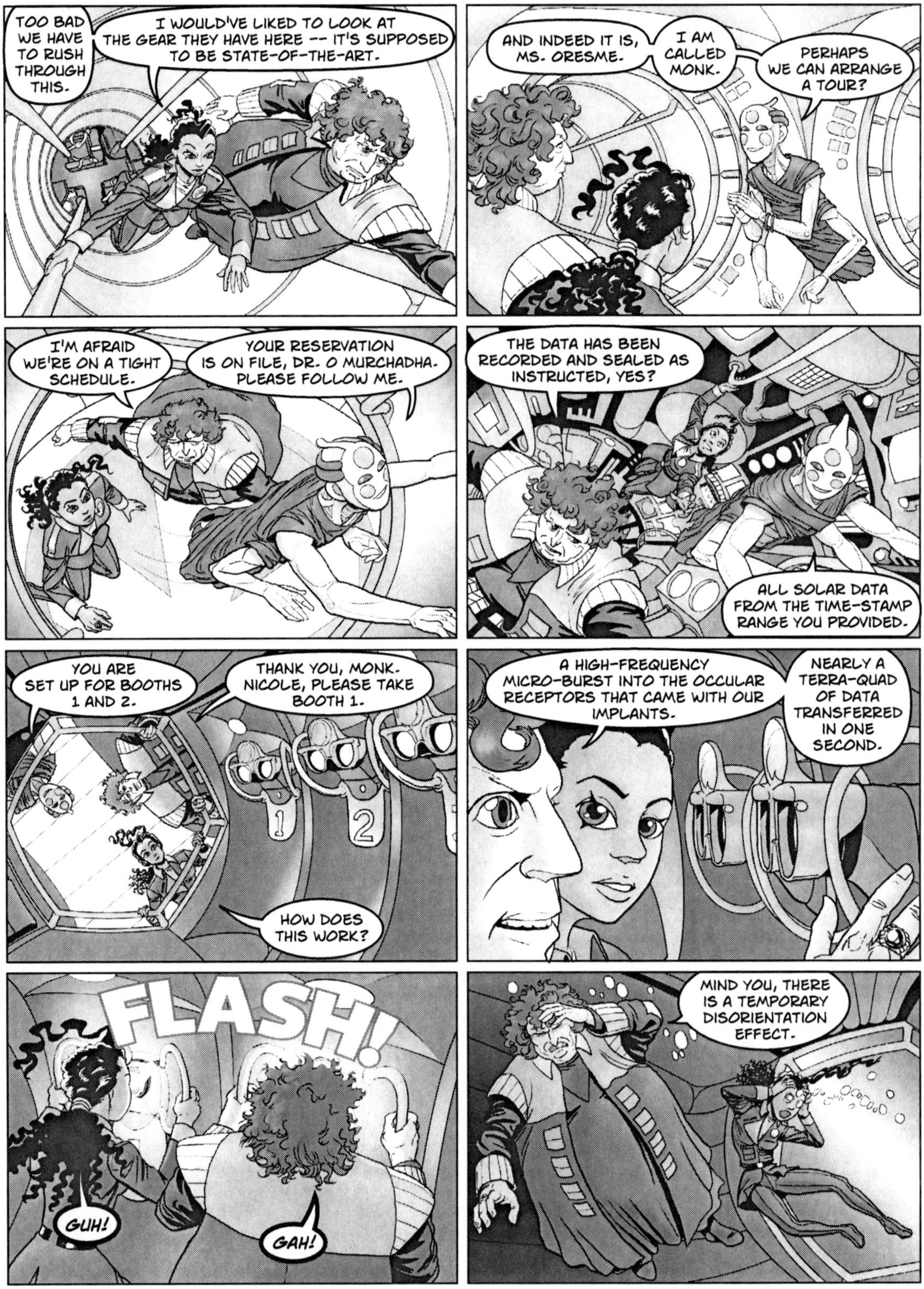
TOO BAD WE HAVE TO RUSH THROUGH THIS.
I WOULD'VE LIKED TO LOOK AT THE GEAR THEY HAVE HERE -- IT'S SUPPOSED TO BE STATE-OF-THE-ART.
AND INDEED IT IS, MS. ORESME.
I AM CALLED MONK.
PERHAPS WE CAN ARRANGE A TOUR?
I'M AFRAID WE'RE ON A TIGHT SCHEDULE.
YOUR RESERVATION IS ON FILE, DR. O MURCHADHA. PLEASE FOLLOW ME.
THE DATA HAS BEEN RECORDED AND SEALED AS INSTRUCTED, YES?
ALL SOLAR DATA FROM THE TIME-STAMP RANGE YOU PROVIDED.
YOU ARE SET UP FOR BOOTHS 1 AND 2.
THANK YOU, MONK. NICOLE, PLEASE TAKE BOOTH 1.
1
2
HOW DOES THIS WORK?
A HIGH-FREQUENCY MICRO-BURST INTO THE OCCULAR RECEPTORS THAT CAME WITH OUR IMPLANTS.
NEARLY A TERRA-QUAD OF DATA TRANSFERRED IN ONE SECOND.
FLASH!
GUH!
GAH!
MIND YOU, THERE IS A TEMPORARY DISORIENTATION EFFECT.

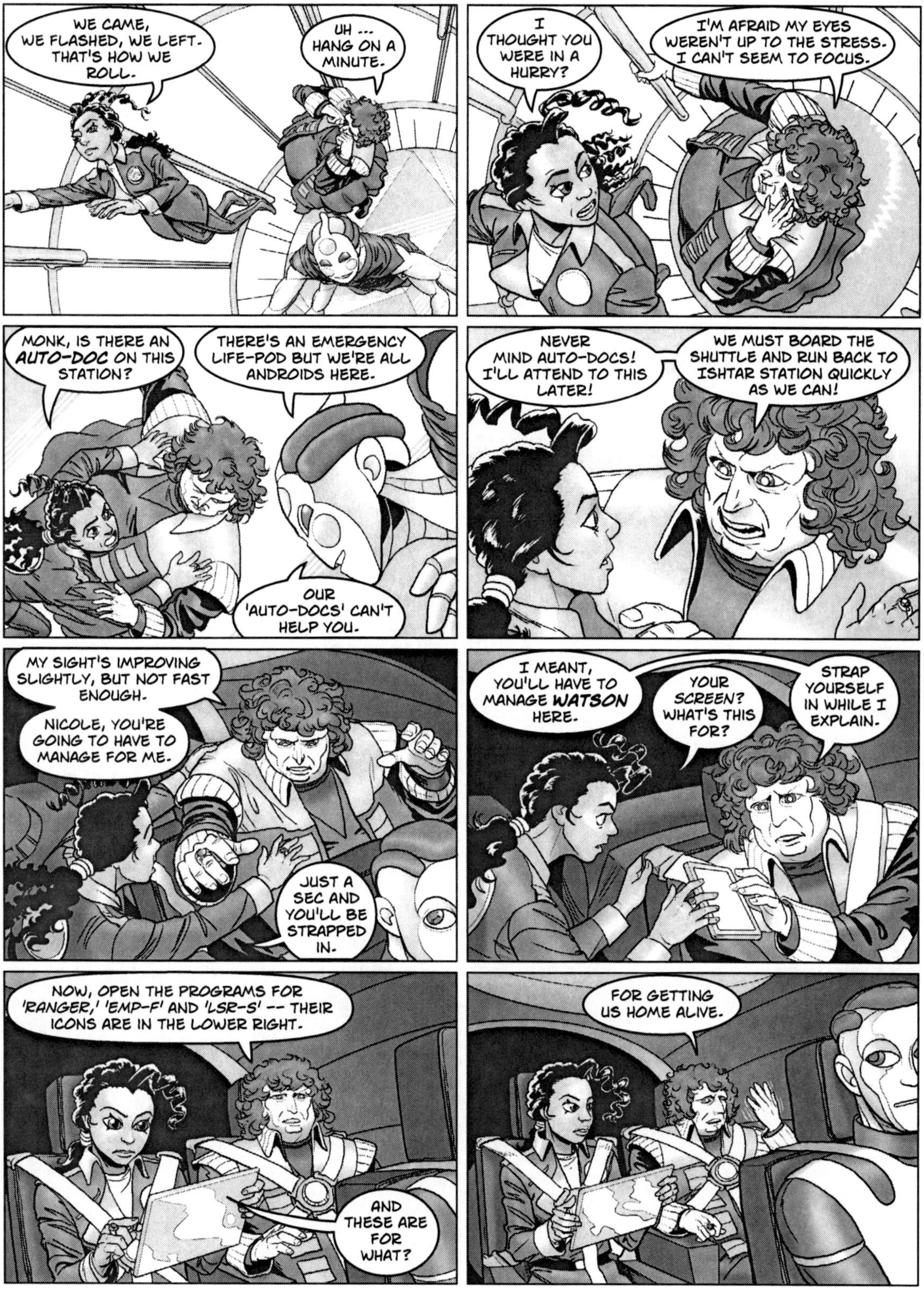
WE CAME, WE FLASHED, WE LEFT. THAT'S HOW WE ROLL.
UH ... HANG ON A MINUTE.
I THOUGHT YOU WERE IN A HURRY?
I'M AFRAID MY EYES WEREN'T UP TO THE STRESS. I CAN'T SEEM TO FOCUS.
MONK, IS THERE AN AUTO-DOC ON THIS STATION?
THERE'S AN EMERGENCY LIFE-POD BUT WE'RE ALL ANDROIDS HERE.
OUR 'AUTO-DOCS' CAN'T HELP YOU.
NEVER MIND AUTO-DOCS! I'LL ATTEND TO THIS LATER!
WE MUST BOARD THE SHUTTLE AND RUN BACK TO ISHTAR STATION QUICKLY AS WE CAN!
MY SIGHT'S IMPROVING SLIGHTLY, BUT NOT FAST ENOUGH.
NICOLE, YOU'RE GOING TO HAVE TO MANAGE FOR ME.
JUST A SEC AND YOU'LL BE STRAPPED IN.
I MEANT, YOU'LL HAVE TO MANAGE WATSON HERE.
YOUR SCREEN? WHAT'S THIS FOR?
STRAP YOURSELF IN WHILE I EXPLAIN.
NOW, OPEN THE PROGRAMS FOR 'RANGER,' 'EMP-F' AND 'LSR-S' -- THEIR ICONS ARE IN THE LOWER RIGHT.
AND THESE ARE FOR WHAT?
FOR GETTING US HOME ALIVE.

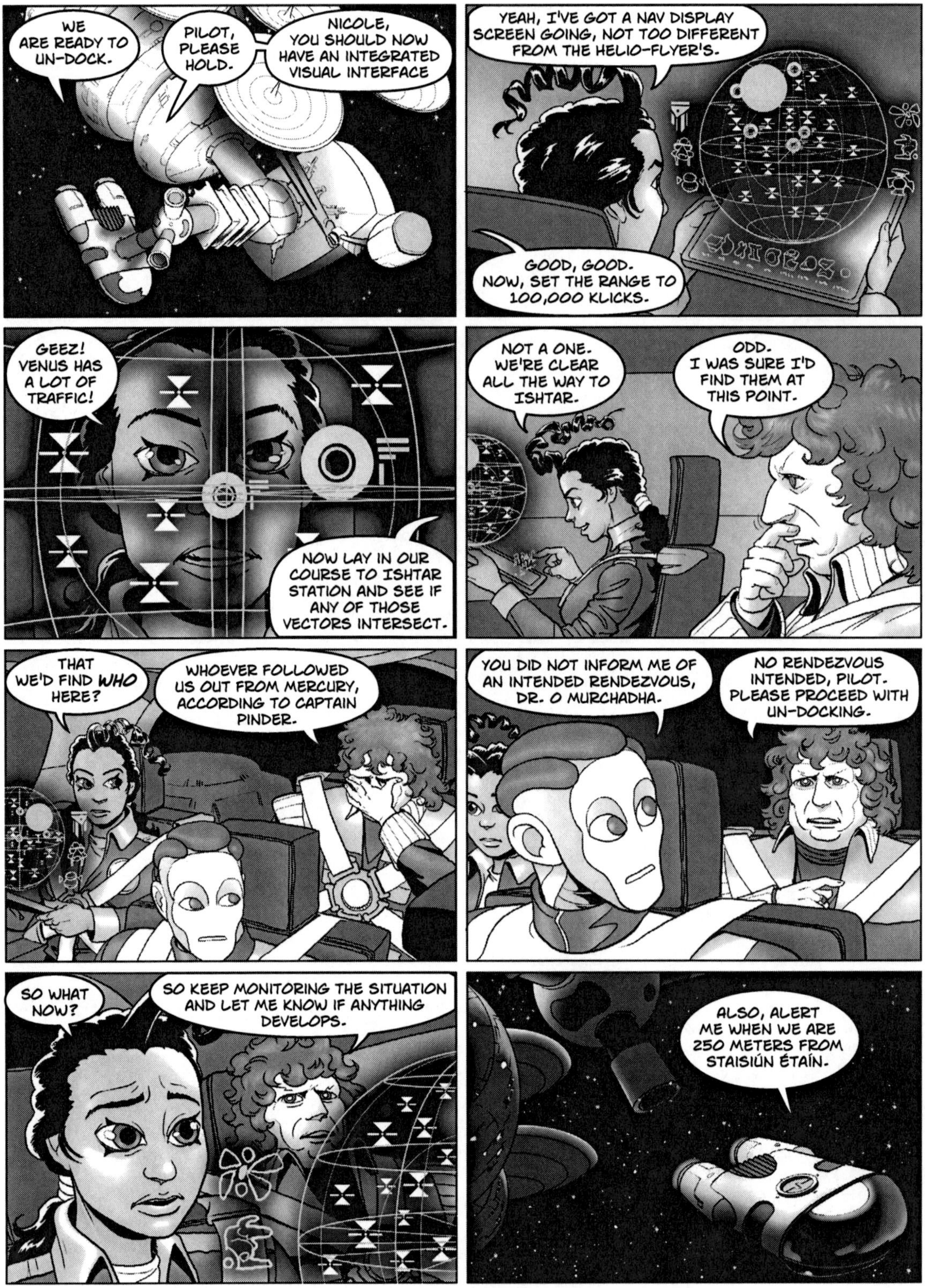
WE ARE READY TO UN-DOCK.
PILOT, PLEASE HOLD.
NICOLE, YOU SHOULD NOW HAVE AN INTEGRATED VISUAL INTERFACE
YEAH, I'VE GOT A NAV DISPLAY SCREEN GOING, NOT TOO DIFFERENT FROM THE HELIO-FLYER'S.
GOOD, GOOD. NOW, SET THE RANGE TO 100,000 KLICKS.
GEEZ! VENUS HAS A LOT OF TRAFFIC!
NOW LAY IN OUR COURSE TO ISHTAR STATION AND SEE IF ANY OF THOSE VECTORS INTERSECT.
NOT A ONE. WE'RE CLEAR ALL THE WAY TO ISHTAR.
ODD. I WAS SURE I'D FIND THEM AT THIS POINT.
THAT WE'D FIND ***WHO*** HERE?
WHOEVER FOLLOWED US OUT FROM MERCURY, ACCORDING TO CAPTAIN PINDER.
YOU DID NOT INFORM ME OF AN INTENDED RENDEZVOUS, DR. O MURCHADHA.
NO RENDEZVOUS INTENDED, PILOT. PLEASE PROCEED WITH UN-DOCKING.
SO WHAT NOW?
SO KEEP MONITORING THE SITUATION AND LET ME KNOW IF ANYTHING DEVELOPS.
ALSO, ALERT ME WHEN WE ARE 250 METERS FROM STAISIÚN ÉTAÍN.

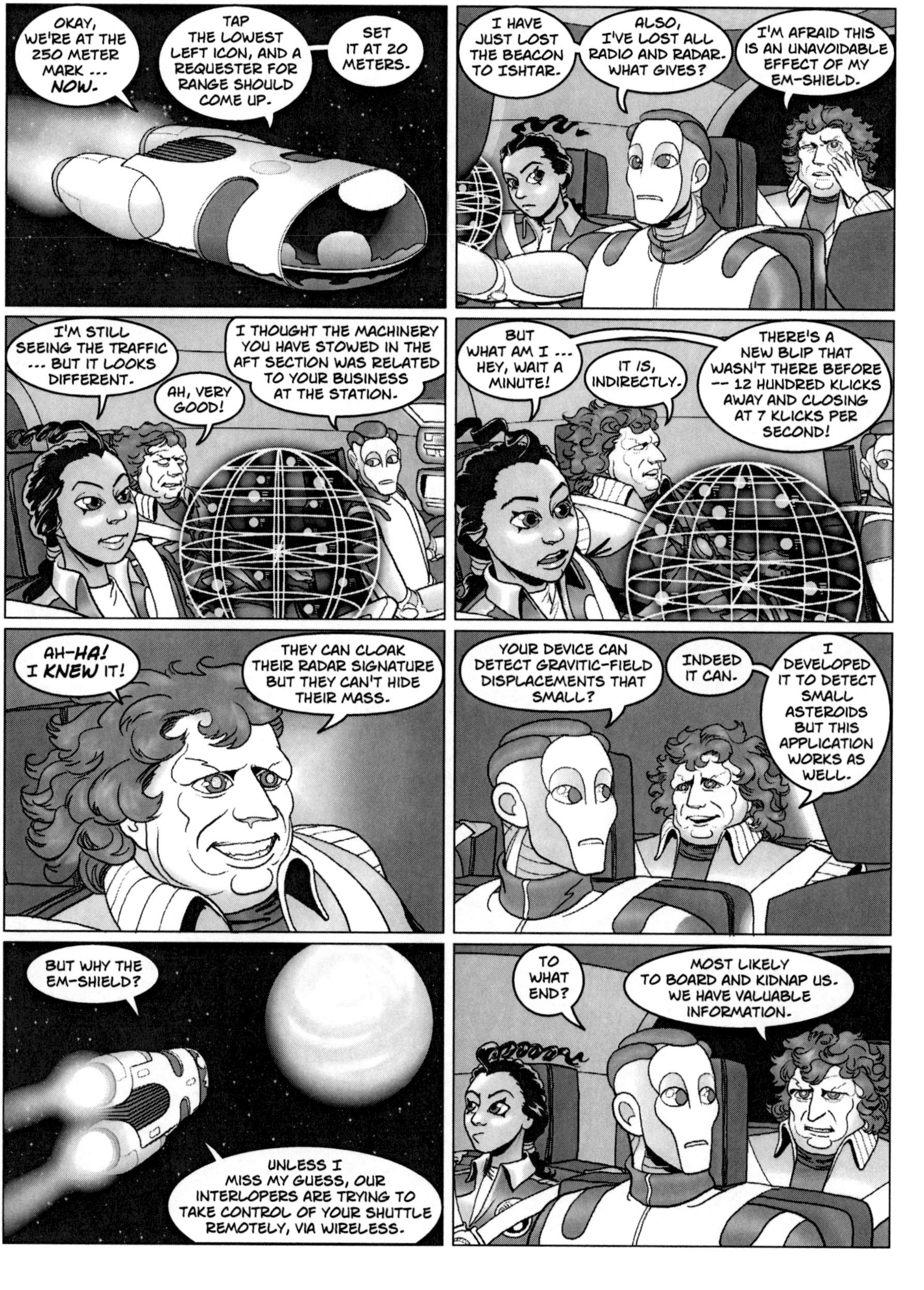
OKAY, WE'RE AT THE 250 METER MARK ... NOW.
TAP THE LOWEST LEFT ICON, AND A REQUESTER FOR RANGE SHOULD COME UP.
SET IT AT 20 METERS.
I HAVE JUST LOST THE BEACON TO ISHTAR.
ALSO, I'VE LOST ALL RADIO AND RADAR. WHAT GIVES?
I'M AFRAID THIS IS AN UNAVOIDABLE EFFECT OF MY EM-SHIELD.
I'M STILL SEEING THE TRAFFIC --- BUT IT LOOKS DIFFERENT.
AH, VERY GOOD!
I THOUGHT THE MACHINERY YOU HAVE STOWED IN THE AFT SECTION WAS RELATED TO YOUR BUSINESS AT THE STATION.
BUT WHAT AM I --- HEY, WAIT A MINUTE!
IT IS, INDIRECTLY.
THERE'S A NEW BLIP THAT WASN'T THERE BEFORE -- 12 HUNDRED KLICKS AWAY AND CLOSING AT 7 KLICKS PER SECOND!
AH-HA! I KNEW IT!
THEY CAN CLOAK THEIR RADAR SIGNATURE BUT THEY CAN'T HIDE THEIR MASS.
YOUR DEVICE CAN DETECT GRAVITIC-FIELD DISPLACEMENTS THAT SMALL?
INDEED IT CAN.
I DEVELOPED IT TO DETECT SMALL ASTEROIDS BUT THIS APPLICATION WORKS AS WELL.
BUT WHY THE EM-SHIELD?
UNLESS I MISS MY GUESS, OUR INTERLOPERS ARE TRYING TO TAKE CONTROL OF YOUR SHUTTLE REMOTELY, VIA WIRELESS.
TO WHAT END?
MOST LIKELY TO BOARD AND KIDNAP US. WE HAVE VALUABLE INFORMATION.

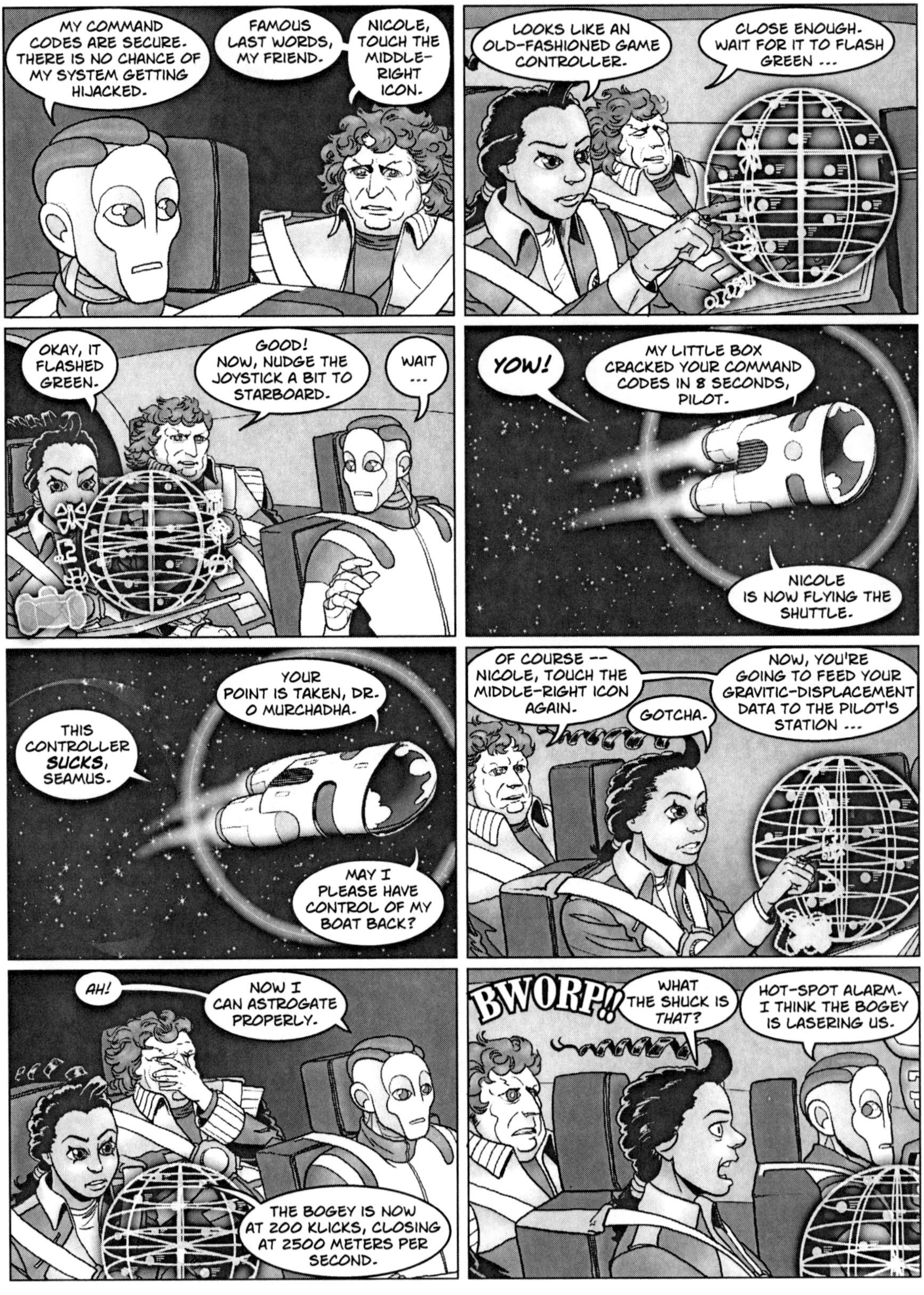
MY COMMAND CODES ARE SECURE. THERE IS NO CHANCE OF MY SYSTEM GETTING HIJACKED.
FAMOUS LAST WORDS, MY FRIEND.
NICOLE, TOUCH THE MIDDLE-RIGHT ICON.
LOOKS LIKE AN OLD-FASHIONED GAME CONTROLLER.
CLOSE ENOUGH. WAIT FOR IT TO FLASH GREEN ...
OKAY, IT FLASHED GREEN.
GOOD! NOW, NUDGE THE JOYSTICK A BIT TO STARBOARD.
WAIT ...
YOW!
MY LITTLE BOX CRACKED YOUR COMMAND CODES IN 8 SECONDS, PILOT.
NICOLE IS NOW FLYING THE SHUTTLE.
THIS CONTROLLER SUCKS, SEAMUS.
YOUR POINT IS TAKEN, DR. O MURCHADHA.
MAY I PLEASE HAVE CONTROL OF MY BOAT BACK?
OF COURSE -- NICOLE, TOUCH THE MIDDLE-RIGHT ICON AGAIN.
GOTCHA.
NOW, YOU'RE GOING TO FEED YOUR GRAVITIC-DISPLACEMENT DATA TO THE PILOT'S STATION ...
AH!
NOW I CAN ASTROGATE PROPERLY.
THE BOGEY IS NOW AT 200 KLICKS, CLOSING AT 2500 METERS PER SECOND.
BWORP!!
WHAT THE SHUCK IS THAT?
HOT-SPOT ALARM. I THINK THE BOGEY IS LASERING US.

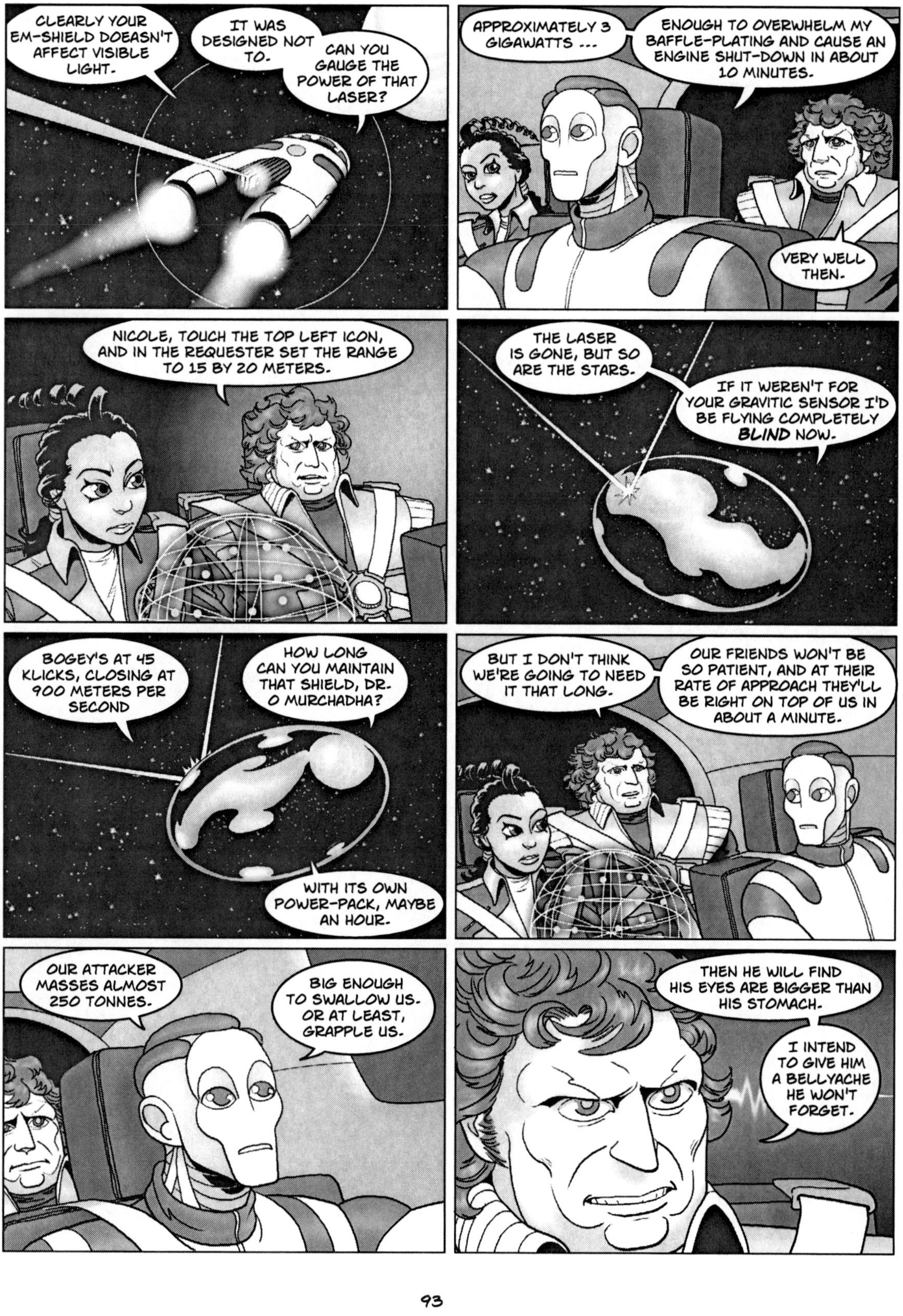
CLEARLY YOUR EM-SHIELD DOEASN'T AFFECT VISIBLE LIGHT.
IT WAS DESIGNED NOT TO.
CAN YOU GAUGE THE POWER OF THAT LASER?
APPROXIMATELY 3 GIGAWATTS ...
ENOUGH TO OVERWHELM MY BAFFLE-PLATING AND CAUSE AN ENGINE SHUT-DOWN IN ABOUT 10 MINUTES.
VERY WELL THEN.
NICOLE, TOUCH THE TOP LEFT ICON, AND IN THE REQUESTER SET THE RANGE TO 15 BY 20 METERS.
THE LASER IS GONE, BUT SO ARE THE STARS.
IF IT WEREN'T FOR YOUR GRAVITIC SENSOR I'D BE FLYING COMPLETELY BLIND NOW.
BOGEY'S AT 45 KLICKS, CLOSING AT 900 METERS PER SECOND
HOW LONG CAN YOU MAINTAIN THAT SHIELD, DR. O MURCHADHA?
WITH ITS OWN POWER-PACK, MAYBE AN HOUR.
BUT I DON'T THINK WE'RE GOING TO NEED IT THAT LONG.
OUR FRIENDS WON'T BE SO PATIENT, AND AT THEIR RATE OF APPROACH THEY'LL BE RIGHT ON TOP OF US IN ABOUT A MINUTE.
OUR ATTACKER MASSES ALMOST 250 TONNES.
BIG ENOUGH TO SWALLOW US. OR AT LEAST, GRAPPLE US.
THEN HE WILL FIND HIS EYES ARE BIGGER THAN HIS STOMACH.
I INTEND TO GIVE HIM A BELLYACHE HE WON'T FORGET.

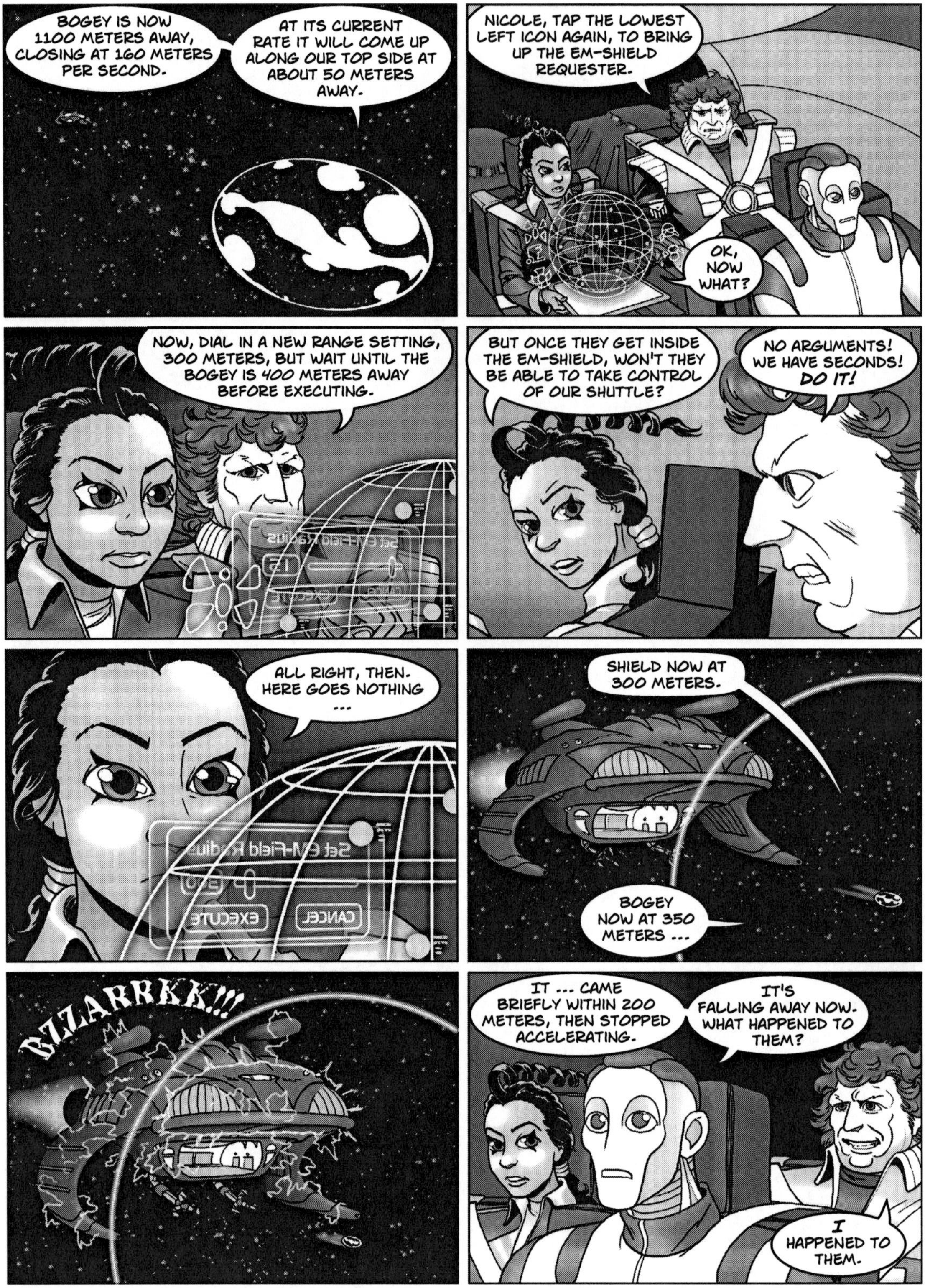
BOGEY IS NOW 1100 METERS AWAY, CLOSING AT 160 METERS PER SECOND.
AT ITS CURRENT RATE IT WILL COME UP ALONG OUR TOP SIDE AT ABOUT 50 METERS AWAY.
NICOLE, TAP THE LOWEST LEFT ICON AGAIN, TO BRING UP THE EM-SHIELD REQUESTER.
OK, NOW WHAT?
NOW, DIAL IN A NEW RANGE SETTING, 300 METERS, BUT WAIT UNTIL THE BOGEY IS 400 METERS AWAY BEFORE EXECUTING.
BUT ONCE THEY GET INSIDE THE EM-SHIELD, WON'T THEY BE ABLE TO TAKE CONTROL OF OUR SHUTTLE?
NO ARGUMENTS! WE HAVE SECONDS! DO IT!
ALL RIGHT, THEN. HERE GOES NOTHING ...
SHIELD NOW AT 300 METERS.
BOGEY NOW AT 350 METERS ...
BZZARRKK!!!
IT ... CAME BRIEFLY WITHIN 200 METERS, THEN STOPPED ACCELERATING.
IT'S FALLING AWAY NOW. WHAT HAPPENED TO THEM?
I HAPPENED TO THEM.

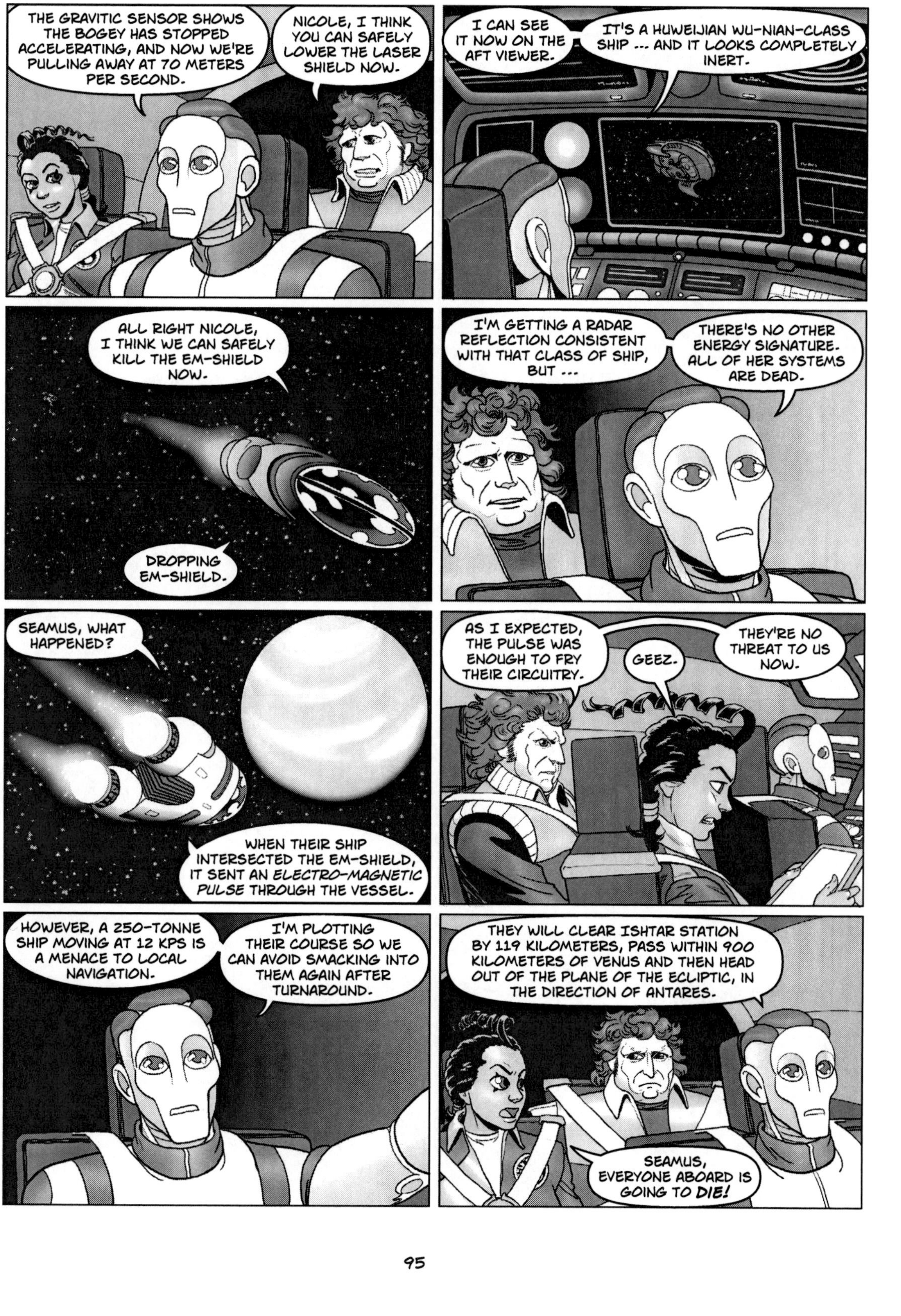
THE GRAVITIC SENSOR SHOWS THE BOGEY HAS STOPPED ACCELERATING, AND NOW WE'RE PULLING AWAY AT 70 METERS PER SECOND.
NICOLE, I THINK YOU CAN SAFELY LOWER THE LASER SHIELD NOW.
I CAN SEE IT NOW ON THE AFT VIEWER.
IT'S A HUWEIJIAN WU-NIAN-CLASS SHIP ... AND IT LOOKS COMPLETELY INERT.
ALL RIGHT NICOLE, I THINK WE CAN SAFELY KILL THE EM-SHIELD NOW.
DROPPING EM-SHIELD.
I'M GETTING A RADAR REFLECTION CONSISTENT WITH THAT CLASS OF SHIP, BUT ...
THERE'S NO OTHER ENERGY SIGNATURE. ALL OF HER SYSTEMS ARE DEAD.
SEAMUS, WHAT HAPPENED?
WHEN THEIR SHIP INTERSECTED THE EM-SHIELD, IT SENT AN *ELECTRO-MAGNETIC PULSE* THROUGH THE VESSEL.
AS I EXPECTED, THE PULSE WAS ENOUGH TO FRY THEIR CIRCUITRY.
GEEZ.
THEY'RE NO THREAT TO US NOW.
HOWEVER, A 250-TONNE SHIP MOVING AT 12 KPS IS A MENACE TO LOCAL NAVIGATION.
I'M PLOTTING THEIR COURSE SO WE CAN AVOID SMACKING INTO THEM AGAIN AFTER TURNAROUND.
THEY WILL CLEAR ISHTAR STATION BY 119 KILOMETERS, PASS WITHIN 900 KILOMETERS OF VENUS AND THEN HEAD OUT OF THE PLANE OF THE ECLIPTIC, IN THE DIRECTION OF ANTARES.
SEAMUS, EVERYONE ABOARD IS GOING TO ***DIE!***

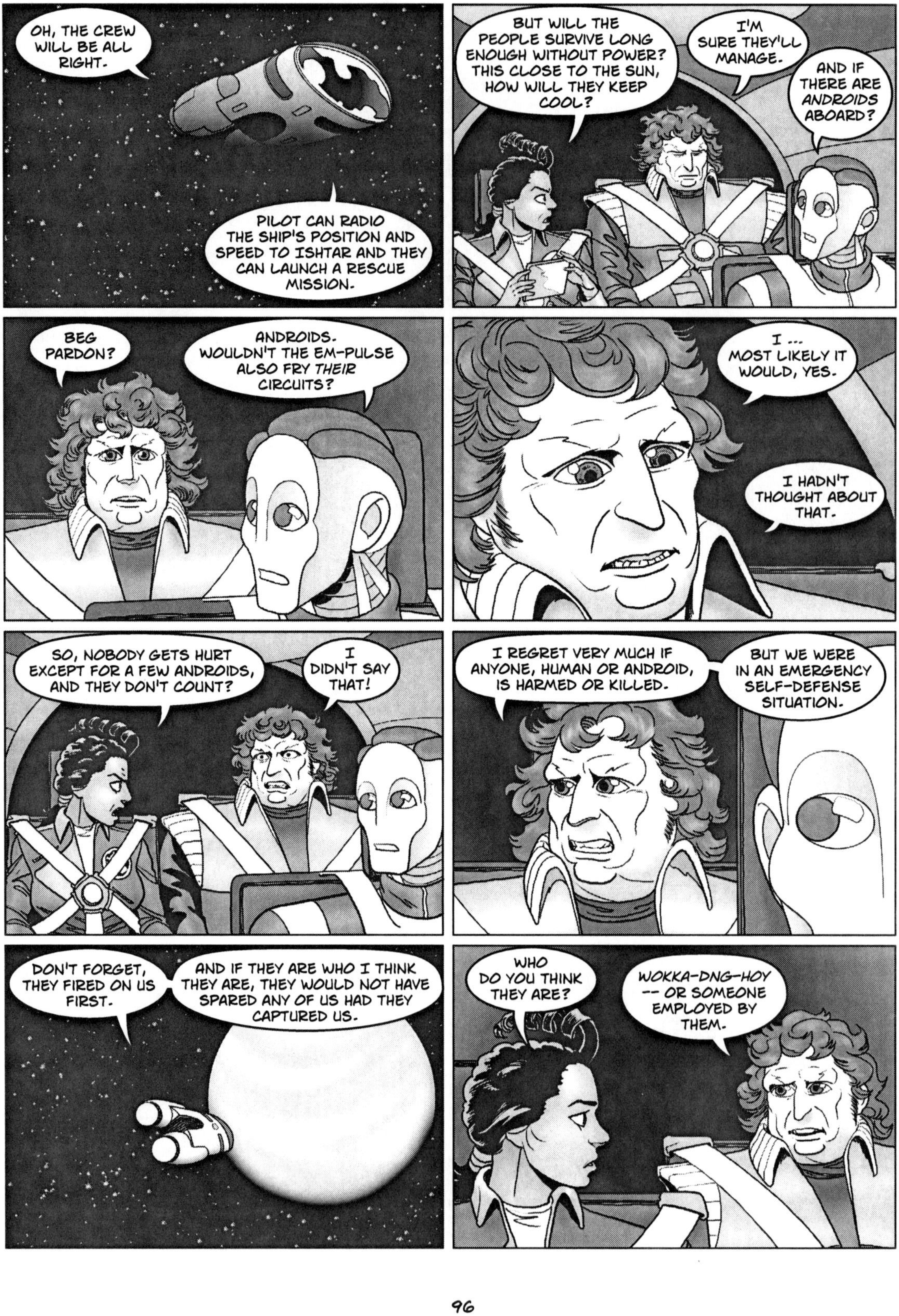
OH, THE CREW WILL BE ALL RIGHT.
PILOT CAN RADIO THE SHIP'S POSITION AND SPEED TO ISHTAR AND THEY CAN LAUNCH A RESCUE MISSION.
BUT WILL THE PEOPLE SURVIVE LONG ENOUGH WITHOUT POWER? THIS CLOSE TO THE SUN, HOW WILL THEY KEEP COOL?
I'M SURE THEY'LL MANAGE.
AND IF THERE ARE ANDROIDS ABOARD?
BEG PARDON?
ANDROIDS. WOULDN'T THE EM-PULSE ALSO FRY THEIR CIRCUITS?
I ... MOST LIKELY IT WOULD, YES.
I HADN'T THOUGHT ABOUT THAT.
SO, NOBODY GETS HURT EXCEPT FOR A FEW ANDROIDS, AND THEY DON'T COUNT?
I DIDN'T SAY THAT!
I REGRET VERY MUCH IF ANYONE, HUMAN OR ANDROID, IS HARMED OR KILLED.
BUT WE WERE IN AN EMERGENCY SELF-DEFENSE SITUATION.
DON'T FORGET, THEY FIRED ON US FIRST.
AND IF THEY ARE WHO I THINK THEY ARE, THEY WOULD NOT HAVE SPARED ANY OF US HAD THEY CAPTURED US.
WHO DO YOU THINK THEY ARE?
WOKKA-DNG-HOY -- OR SOMEONE EMPLOYED BY THEM.

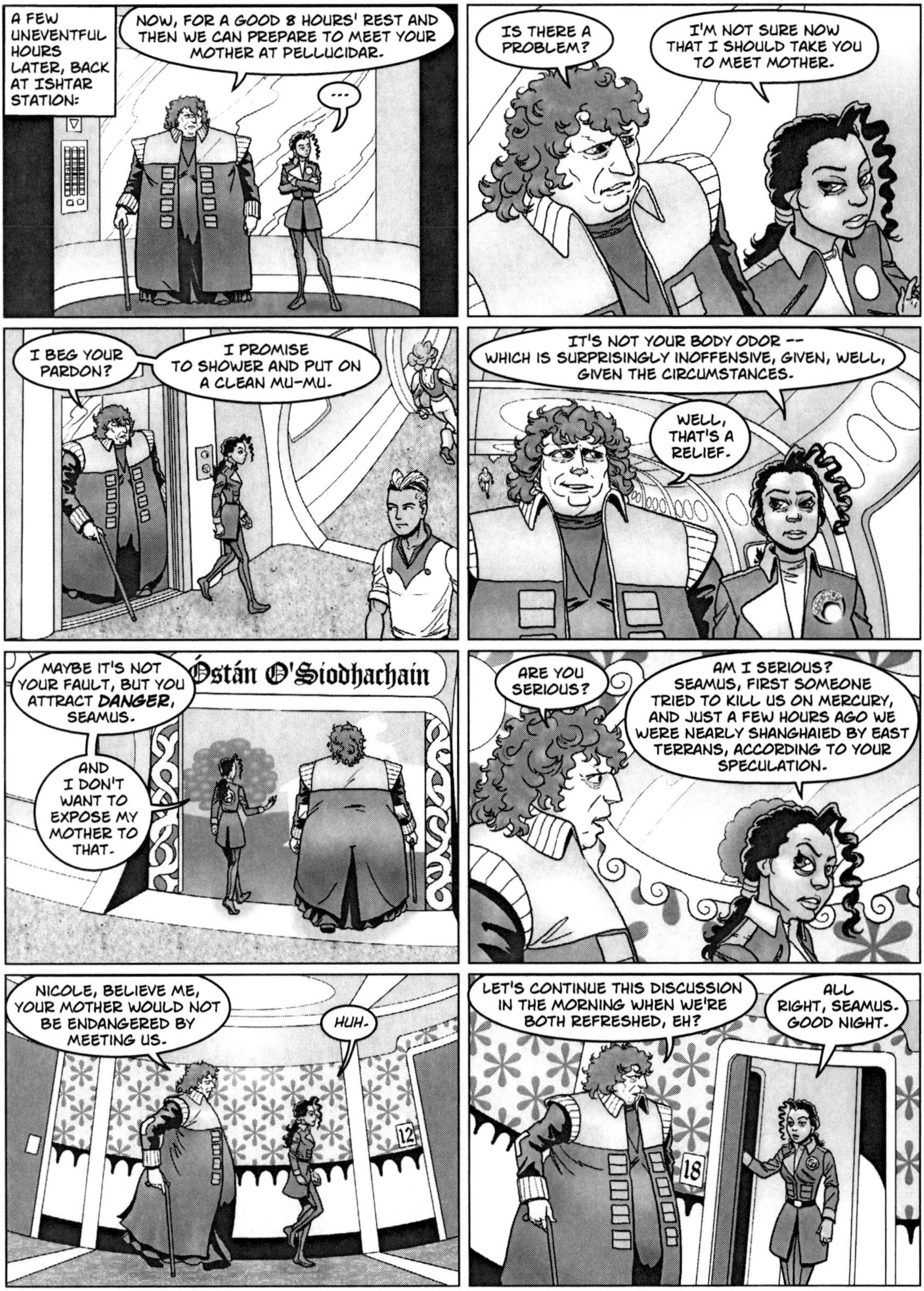
A FEW UNEVENTFUL HOURS LATER, BACK AT ISHTAR STATION:
NOW, FOR A GOOD 8 HOURS' REST AND THEN WE CAN PREPARE TO MEET YOUR MOTHER AT PELLUCIDAR.
...
IS THERE A PROBLEM?
I'M NOT SURE NOW THAT I SHOULD TAKE YOU TO MEET MOTHER.
I BEG YOUR PARDON?
I PROMISE TO SHOWER AND PUT ON A CLEAN MU-MU.
IT'S NOT YOUR BODY ODOR -- WHICH IS SURPRISINGLY INOFFENSIVE, GIVEN, WELL, GIVEN THE CIRCUMSTANCES.
WELL, THAT'S A RELIEF.
Óstán O'Siodhachain
MAYBE IT'S NOT YOUR FAULT, BUT YOU ATTRACT DANGER, SEAMUS.
AND I DON'T WANT TO EXPOSE MY MOTHER TO THAT.
ARE YOU SERIOUS?
AM I SERIOUS? SEAMUS, FIRST SOMEONE TRIED TO KILL US ON MERCURY, AND JUST A FEW HOURS AGO WE WERE NEARLY SHANGHAIED BY EAST TERRANS, ACCORDING TO YOUR SPECULATION.
NICOLE, BELIEVE ME, YOUR MOTHER WOULD NOT BE ENDANGERED BY MEETING US.
HUH.
12
LET'S CONTINUE THIS DISCUSSION IN THE MORNING WHEN WE'RE BOTH REFRESHED, EH?
ALL RIGHT, SEAMUS. GOOD NIGHT.
18

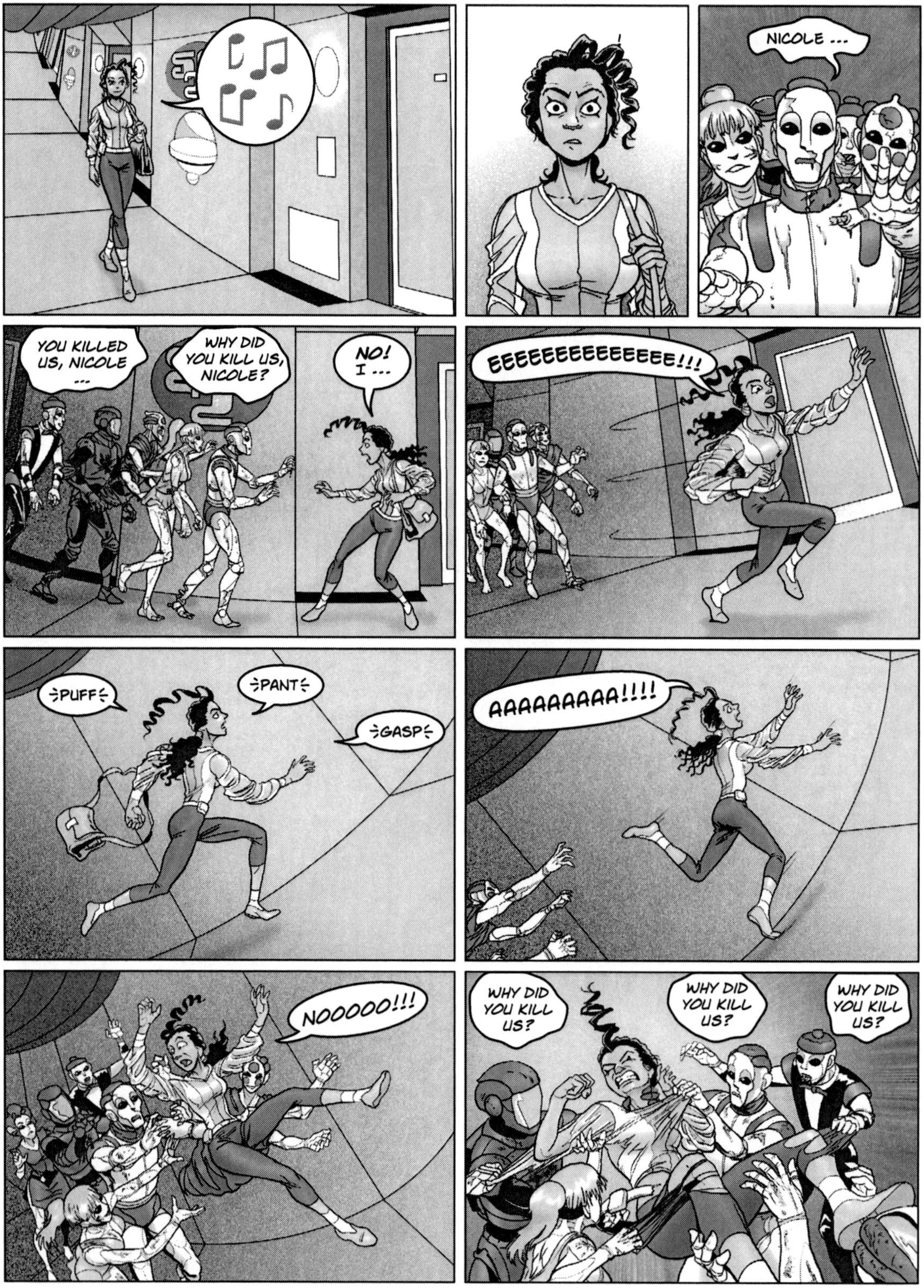
NICOLE ...
YOU KILLED US, NICOLE ...
WHY DID YOU KILL US, NICOLE?
NO! I ...
EEEEEEEEEEEEEE!!!
PUFF
PANT
GASP
AAAAAAAAA!!!!
NOOOOO!!!
WHY DID YOU KILL US?
WHY DID YOU KILL US?
WHY DID YOU KILL US?

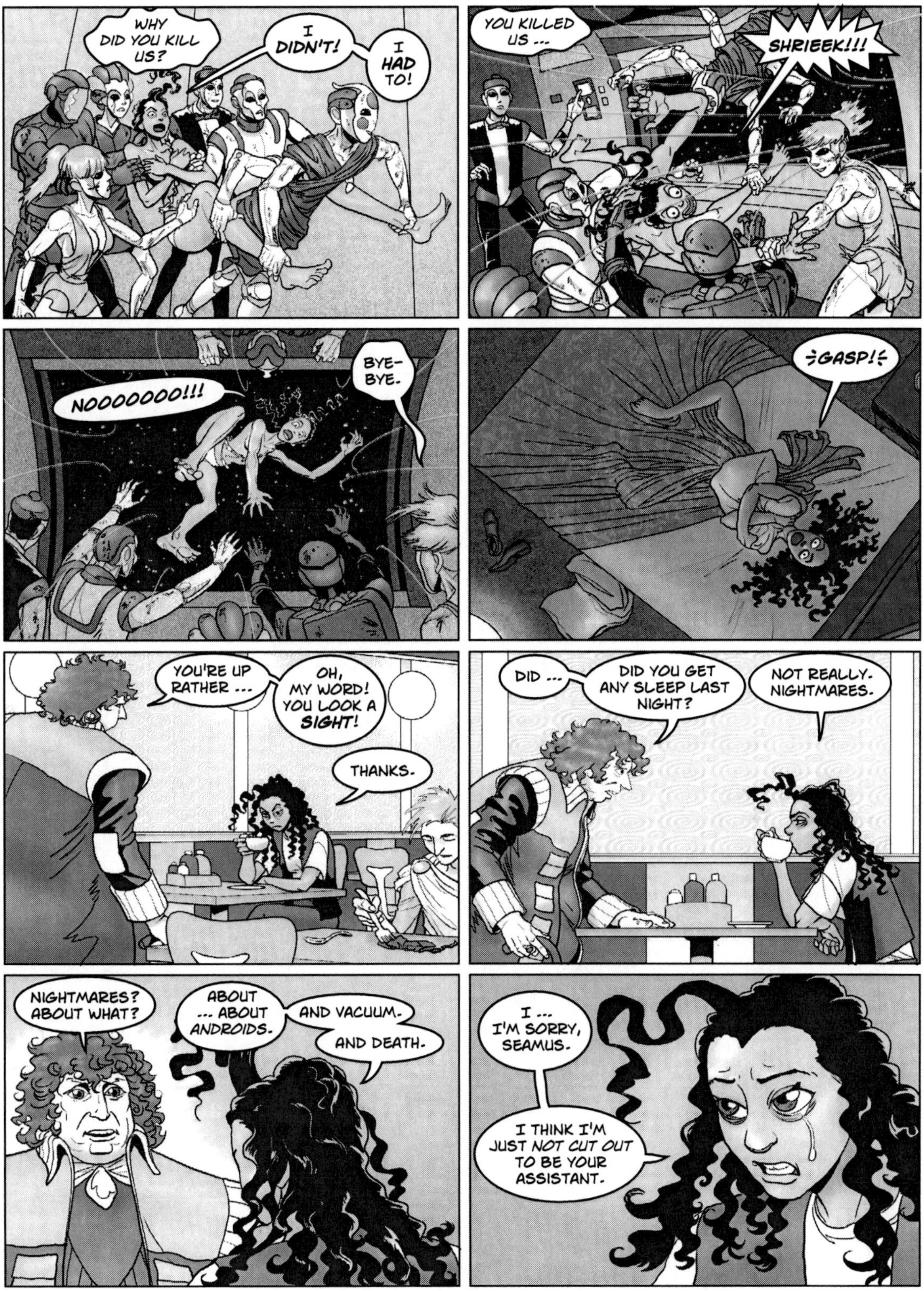
WHY DID YOU KILL US?
I DIDN'T!
I HAD TO!
YOU KILLED US ...
SHRIEEK!!!
NOOOOOOO!!!
BYE-BYE.
GASP!
YOU'RE UP RATHER ...
OH, MY WORD! YOU LOOK A SIGHT!
THANKS.
DID ...
DID YOU GET ANY SLEEP LAST NIGHT?
NOT REALLY. NIGHTMARES.
NIGHTMARES? ABOUT WHAT?
ABOUT ... ABOUT ANDROIDS.
AND VACUUM.
AND DEATH.
I ... I'M SORRY, SEAMUS.
I THINK I'M JUST NOT CUT OUT TO BE YOUR ASSISTANT.

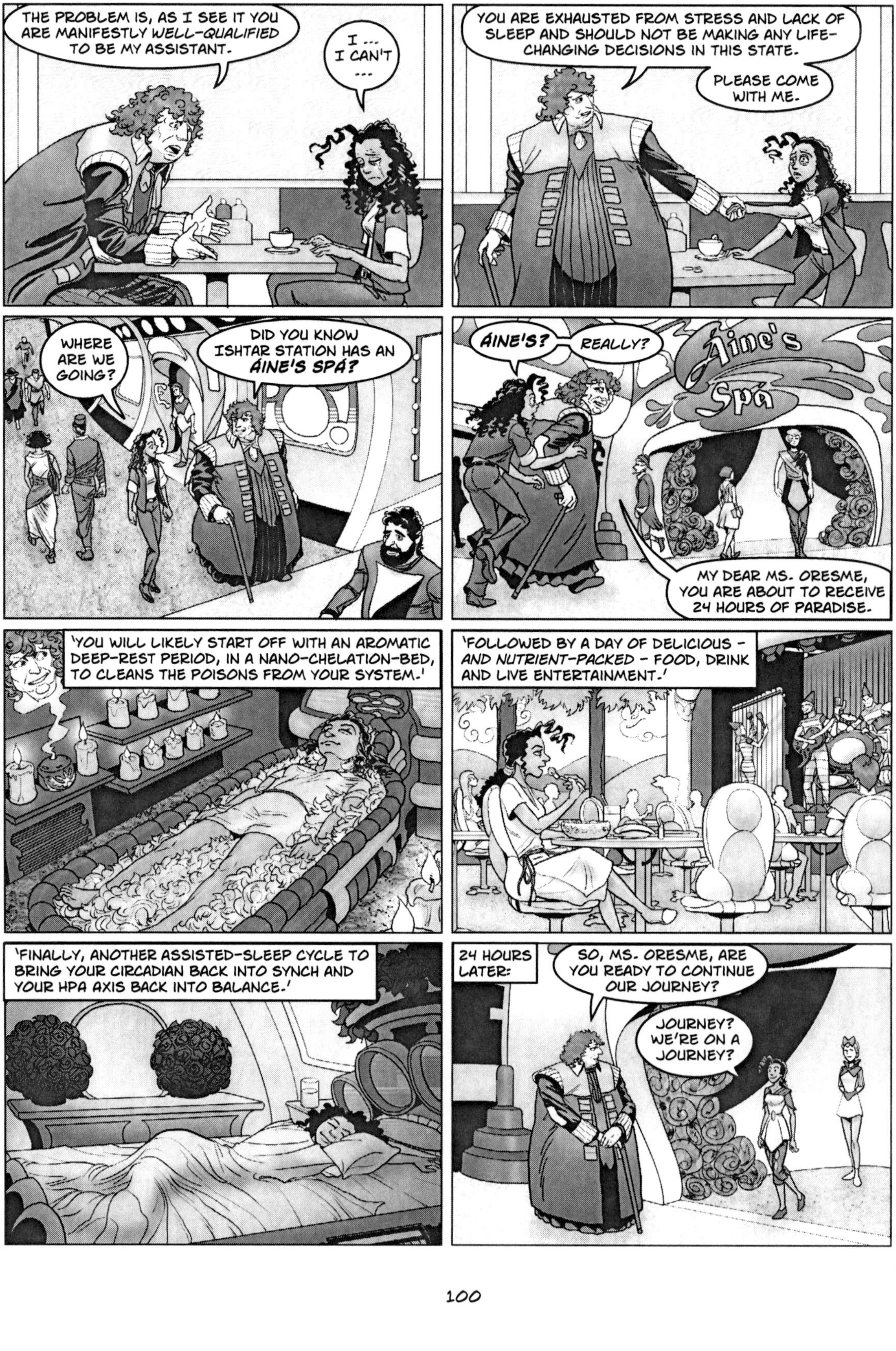
THE PROBLEM IS, AS I SEE IT YOU ARE MANIFESTLY WELL-QUALIFIED TO BE MY ASSISTANT.
I ... I CAN'T ...
YOU ARE EXHAUSTED FROM STRESS AND LACK OF SLEEP AND SHOULD NOT BE MAKING ANY LIFE-CHANGING DECISIONS IN THIS STATE.
PLEASE COME WITH ME.
WHERE ARE WE GOING?
DID YOU KNOW ISHTAR STATION HAS AN ÁINE'S SPÁ?
ÁINE'S?
REALLY?
Áine's Spá
MY DEAR MS. ORESME, YOU ARE ABOUT TO RECEIVE 24 HOURS OF PARADISE.
'YOU WILL LIKELY START OFF WITH AN AROMATIC DEEP-REST PERIOD, IN A NANO-CHELATION-BED, TO CLEANS THE POISONS FROM YOUR SYSTEM.'
'FOLLOWED BY A DAY OF DELICIOUS - AND NUTRIENT-PACKED - FOOD, DRINK AND LIVE ENTERTAINMENT.'
'FINALLY, ANOTHER ASSISTED-SLEEP CYCLE TO BRING YOUR CIRCADIAN BACK INTO SYNCH AND YOUR HPA AXIS BACK INTO BALANCE.'
24 HOURS LATER:
SO, MS. ORESME, ARE YOU READY TO CONTINUE OUR JOURNEY?
JOURNEY? WE'RE ON A JOURNEY?

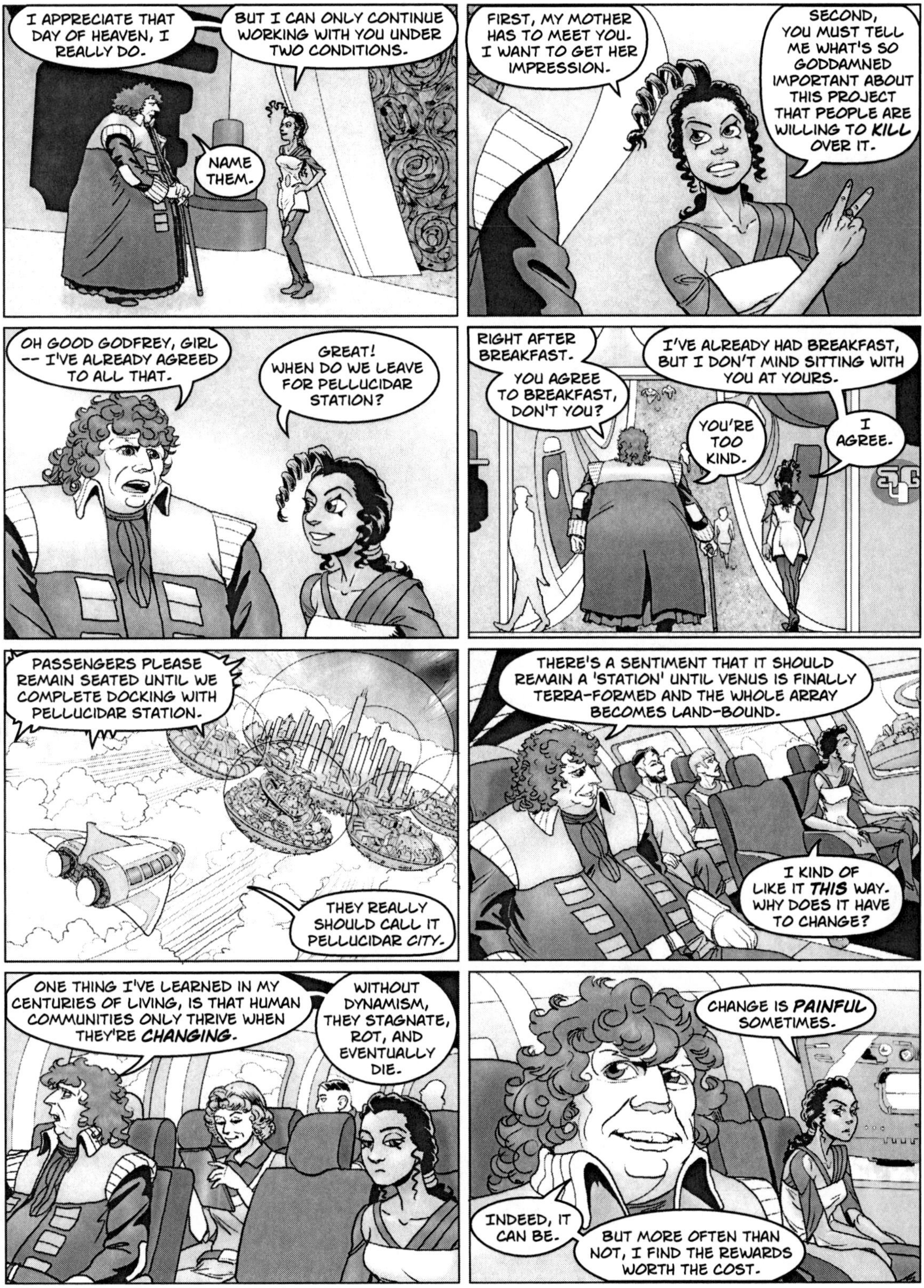
I APPRECIATE THAT DAY OF HEAVEN, I REALLY DO.
BUT I CAN ONLY CONTINUE WORKING WITH YOU UNDER TWO CONDITIONS.
NAME THEM.
FIRST, MY MOTHER HAS TO MEET YOU. I WANT TO GET HER IMPRESSION.
SECOND, YOU MUST TELL ME WHAT'S SO GODDAMNED IMPORTANT ABOUT THIS PROJECT THAT PEOPLE ARE WILLING TO KILL OVER IT.
OH GOOD GODFREY, GIRL -- I'VE ALREADY AGREED TO ALL THAT.
GREAT! WHEN DO WE LEAVE FOR PELLUCIDAR STATION?
RIGHT AFTER BREAKFAST.
YOU AGREE TO BREAKFAST, DON'T YOU?
I'VE ALREADY HAD BREAKFAST, BUT I DON'T MIND SITTING WITH YOU AT YOURS.
YOU'RE TOO KIND.
I AGREE.
PASSENGERS PLEASE REMAIN SEATED UNTIL WE COMPLETE DOCKING WITH PELLUCIDAR STATION.
THEY REALLY SHOULD CALL IT PELLUCIDAR CITY.
THERE'S A SENTIMENT THAT IT SHOULD REMAIN A 'STATION' UNTIL VENUS IS FINALLY TERRA-FORMED AND THE WHOLE ARRAY BECOMES LAND-BOUND.
I KIND OF LIKE IT THIS WAY. WHY DOES IT HAVE TO CHANGE?
ONE THING I'VE LEARNED IN MY CENTURIES OF LIVING, IS THAT HUMAN COMMUNITIES ONLY THRIVE WHEN THEY'RE CHANGING.
WITHOUT DYNAMISM, THEY STAGNATE, ROT, AND EVENTUALLY DIE.
CHANGE IS PAINFUL SOMETIMES.
INDEED, IT CAN BE.
BUT MORE OFTEN THAN NOT, I FIND THE REWARDS WORTH THE COST.

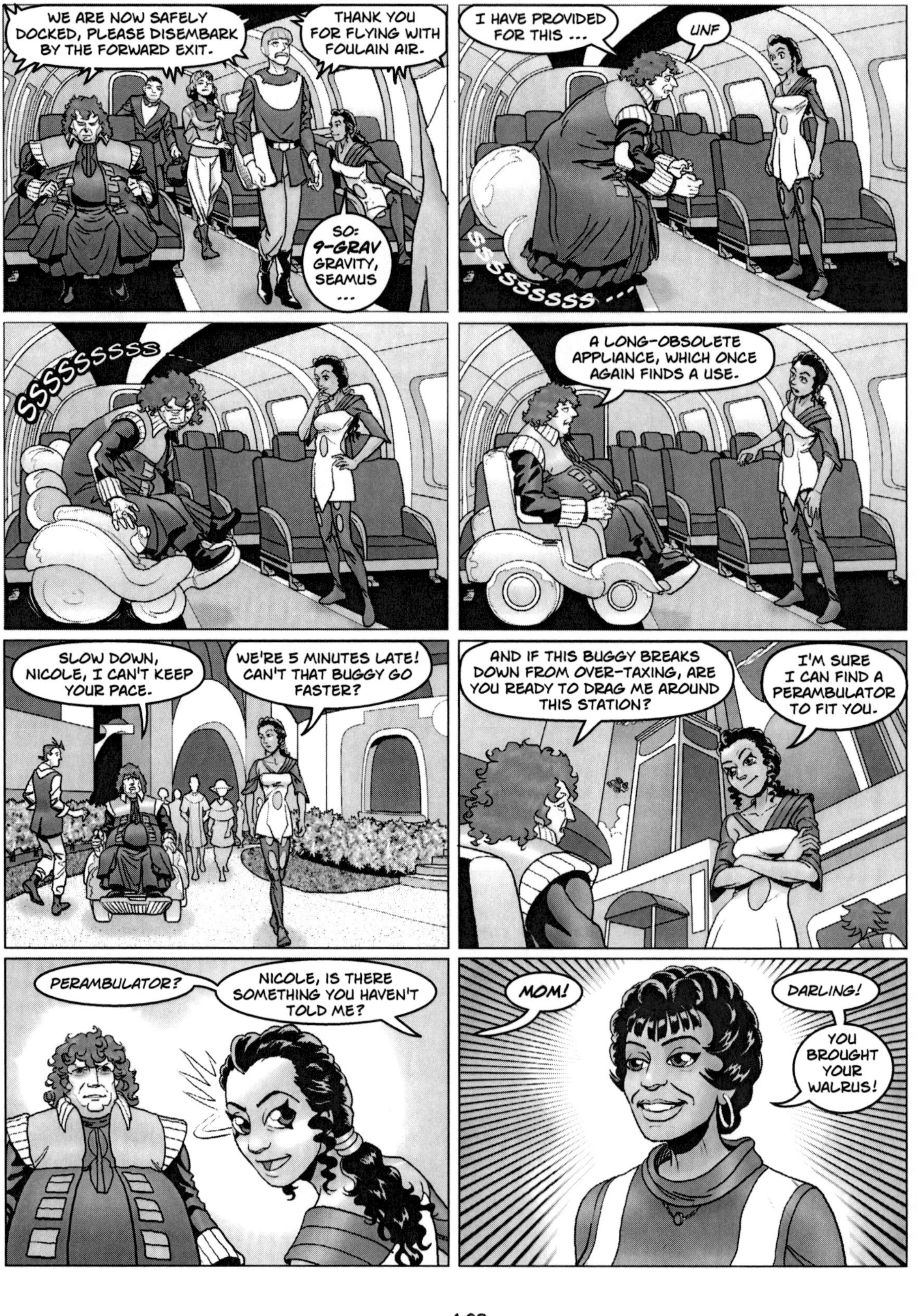
WE ARE NOW SAFELY DOCKED, PLEASE DISEMBARK BY THE FORWARD EXIT.
THANK YOU FOR FLYING WITH FOULAIN AIR.
SO: 9-GRAV GRAVITY, SEAMUS ...
I HAVE PROVIDED FOR THIS ...
UNF
SSSSSSSSS ...
SSSSSSSSS
A LONG-OBSOLETE APPLIANCE, WHICH ONCE AGAIN FINDS A USE.
SLOW DOWN, NICOLE, I CAN'T KEEP YOUR PACE.
WE'RE 5 MINUTES LATE! CAN'T THAT BUGGY GO FASTER?
AND IF THIS BUGGY BREAKS DOWN FROM OVER-TAXING, ARE YOU READY TO DRAG ME AROUND THIS STATION?
I'M SURE I CAN FIND A PERAMBULATOR TO FIT YOU.
PERAMBULATOR?
NICOLE, IS THERE SOMETHING YOU HAVEN'T TOLD ME?
MOM!
DARLING!
YOU BROUGHT YOUR WALRUS!

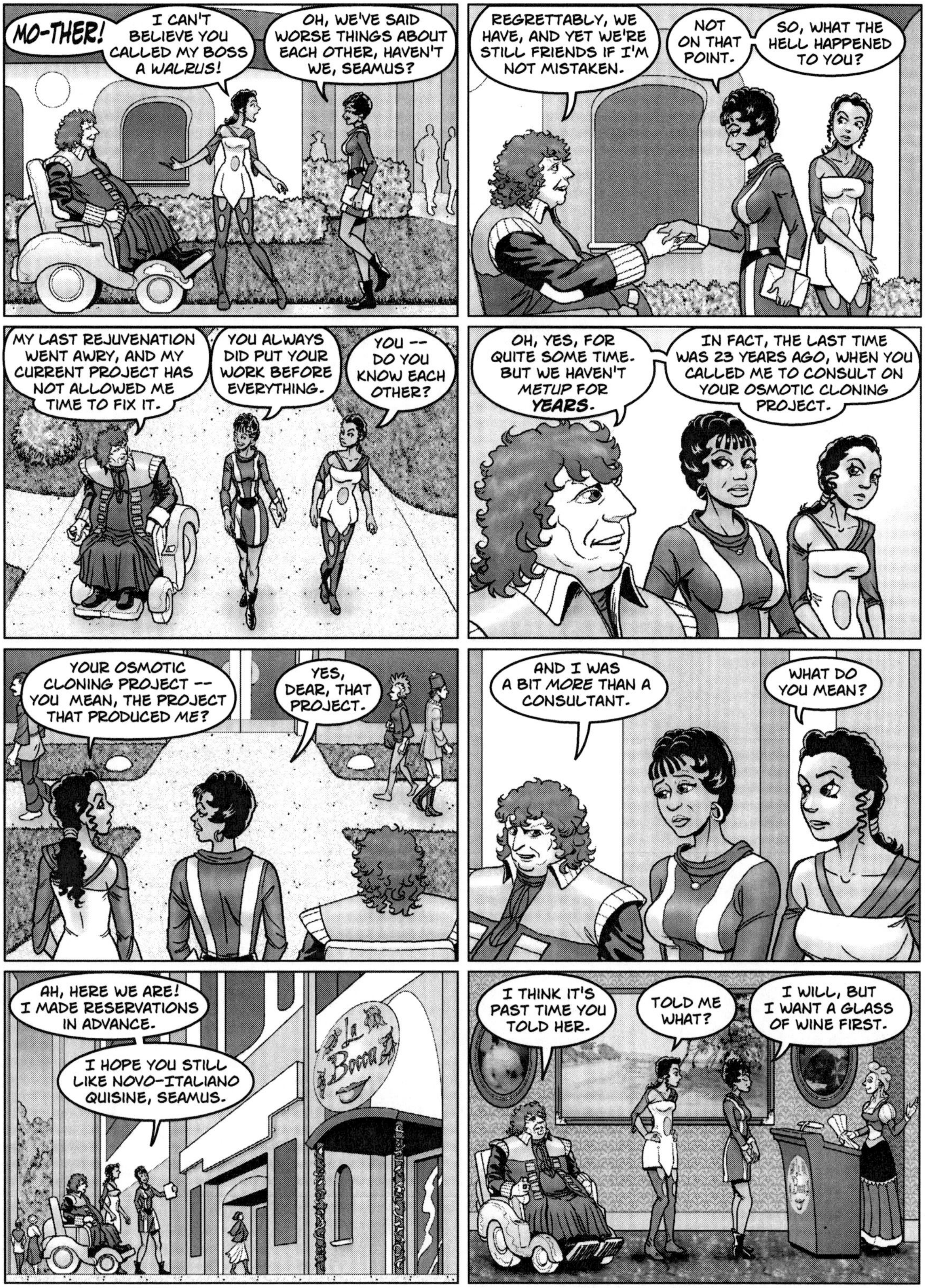
MO-THER!
I CAN'T BELIEVE YOU CALLED MY BOSS A WALRUS!
OH, WE'VE SAID WORSE THINGS ABOUT EACH OTHER, HAVEN'T WE, SEAMUS?
REGRETTABLY, WE HAVE, AND YET WE'RE STILL FRIENDS IF I'M NOT MISTAKEN.
NOT ON THAT POINT.
SO, WHAT THE HELL HAPPENED TO YOU?
MY LAST REJUVENATION WENT AWRY, AND MY CURRENT PROJECT HAS NOT ALLOWED ME TIME TO FIX IT.
YOU ALWAYS DID PUT YOUR WORK BEFORE EVERYTHING.
YOU -- DO YOU KNOW EACH OTHER?
OH, YES, FOR QUITE SOME TIME. BUT WE HAVEN'T METUP FOR YEARS.
IN FACT, THE LAST TIME WAS 23 YEARS AGO, WHEN YOU CALLED ME TO CONSULT ON YOUR OSMOTIC CLONING PROJECT.
YOUR OSMOTIC CLONING PROJECT -- YOU MEAN, THE PROJECT THAT PRODUCED ME?
YES, DEAR, THAT PROJECT.
AND I WAS A BIT MORE THAN A CONSULTANT.
WHAT DO YOU MEAN?
AH, HERE WE ARE! I MADE RESERVATIONS IN ADVANCE.
I HOPE YOU STILL LIKE NOVO-ITALIANO QUISINE, SEAMUS.
La Bocca
I THINK IT'S PAST TIME YOU TOLD HER.
TOLD ME WHAT?
I WILL, BUT I WANT A GLASS OF WINE FIRST.

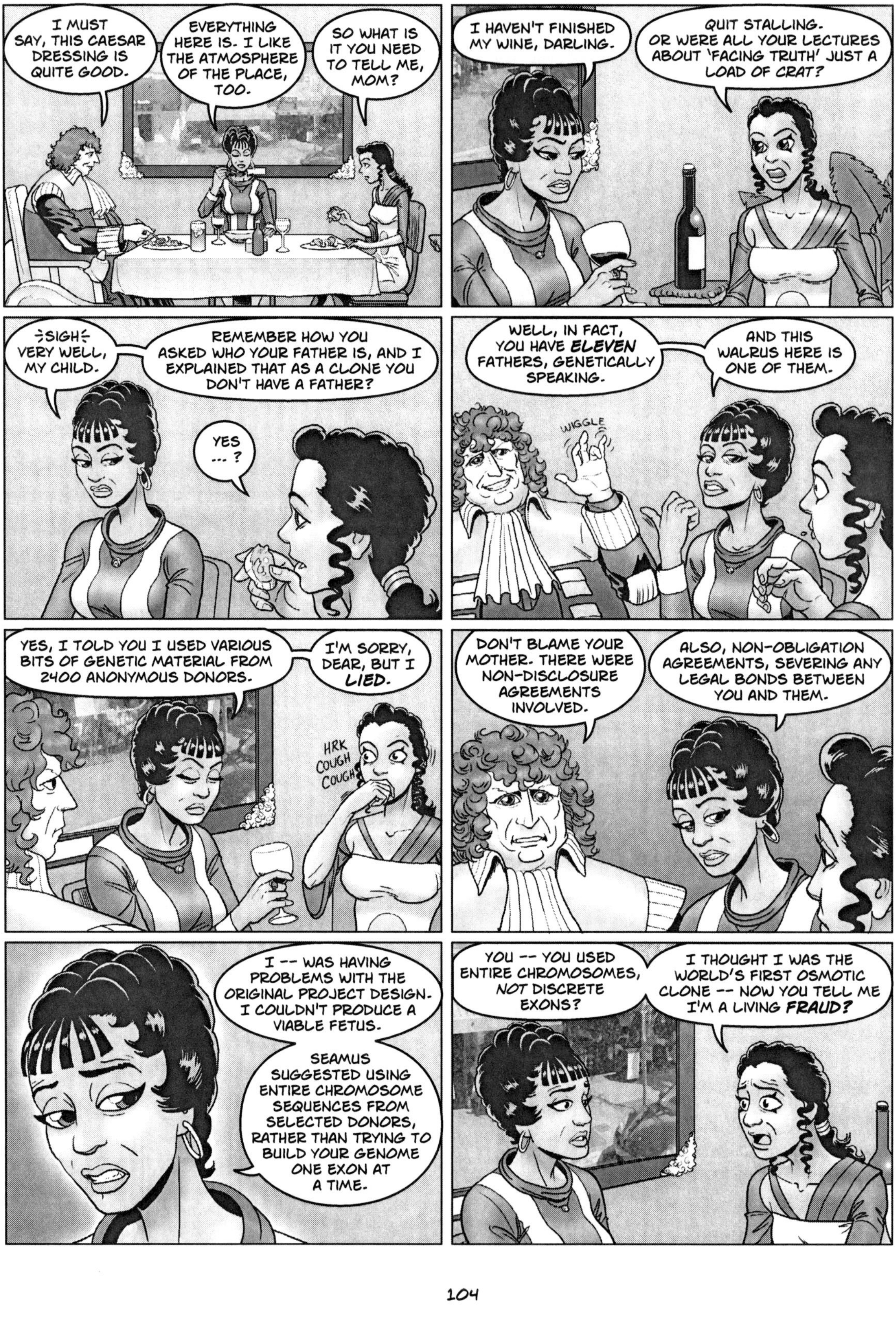
I MUST SAY, THIS CAESAR DRESSING IS QUITE GOOD.
EVERYTHING HERE IS. I LIKE THE ATMOSPHERE OF THE PLACE, TOO.
SO WHAT IS IT YOU NEED TO TELL ME, MOM?
I HAVEN'T FINISHED MY WINE, DARLING.
QUIT STALLING. OR WERE ALL YOUR LECTURES ABOUT 'FACING TRUTH' JUST A LOAD OF CRAT?
SIGH VERY WELL, MY CHILD.
REMEMBER HOW YOU ASKED WHO YOUR FATHER IS, AND I EXPLAINED THAT AS A CLONE YOU DON'T HAVE A FATHER?
YES --- ?
WELL, IN FACT, YOU HAVE ELEVEN FATHERS, GENETICALLY SPEAKING.
AND THIS WALRUS HERE IS ONE OF THEM.
WIGGLE
YES, I TOLD YOU I USED VARIOUS BITS OF GENETIC MATERIAL FROM 2400 ANONYMOUS DONORS.
I'M SORRY, DEAR, BUT I LIED.
HRK COUGH COUGH
DON'T BLAME YOUR MOTHER. THERE WERE NON-DISCLOSURE AGREEMENTS INVOLVED.
ALSO, NON-OBLIGATION AGREEMENTS, SEVERING ANY LEGAL BONDS BETWEEN YOU AND THEM.
I -- WAS HAVING PROBLEMS WITH THE ORIGINAL PROJECT DESIGN. I COULDN'T PRODUCE A VIABLE FETUS.
SEAMUS SUGGESTED USING ENTIRE CHROMOSOME SEQUENCES FROM SELECTED DONORS, RATHER THAN TRYING TO BUILD YOUR GENOME ONE EXON AT A TIME.
YOU -- YOU USED ENTIRE CHROMOSOMES, NOT DISCRETE EXONS?
I THOUGHT I WAS THE WORLD'S FIRST OSMOTIC CLONE -- NOW YOU TELL ME I'M A LIVING FRAUD?

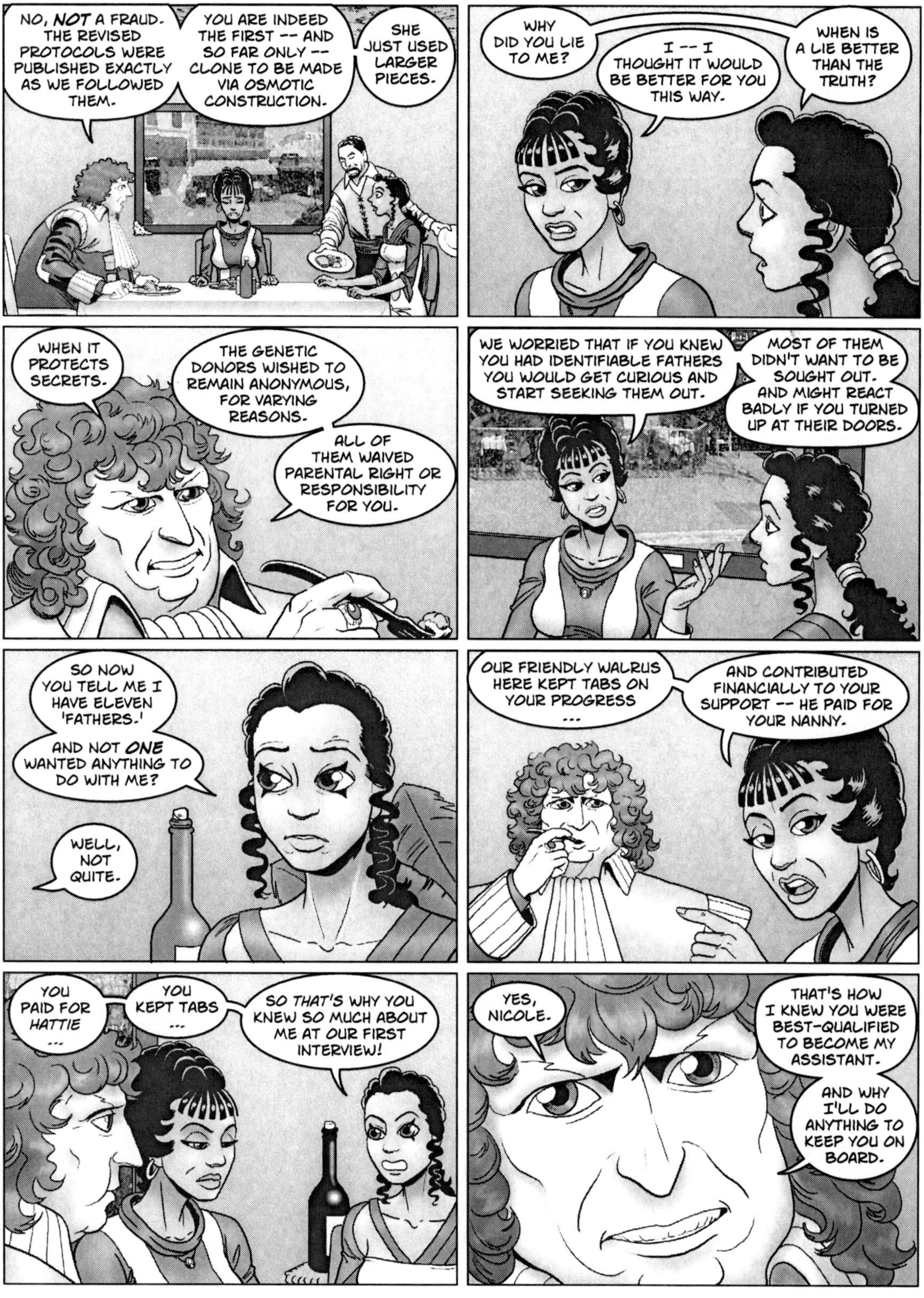
NO, NOT A FRAUD. THE REVISED PROTOCOLS WERE PUBLISHED EXACTLY AS WE FOLLOWED THEM.
YOU ARE INDEED THE FIRST -- AND SO FAR ONLY -- CLONE TO BE MADE VIA OSMOTIC CONSTRUCTION.
SHE JUST USED LARGER PIECES.
WHY DID YOU LIE TO ME?
I -- I THOUGHT IT WOULD BE BETTER FOR YOU THIS WAY.
WHEN IS A LIE BETTER THAN THE TRUTH?
WHEN IT PROTECTS SECRETS.
THE GENETIC DONORS WISHED TO REMAIN ANONYMOUS, FOR VARYING REASONS.
ALL OF THEM WAIVED PARENTAL RIGHT OR RESPONSIBILITY FOR YOU.
WE WORRIED THAT IF YOU KNEW YOU HAD IDENTIFIABLE FATHERS YOU WOULD GET CURIOUS AND START SEEKING THEM OUT.
MOST OF THEM DIDN'T WANT TO BE SOUGHT OUT. AND MIGHT REACT BADLY IF YOU TURNED UP AT THEIR DOORS.
SO NOW YOU TELL ME I HAVE ELEVEN 'FATHERS.'
AND NOT ONE WANTED ANYTHING TO DO WITH ME?
WELL, NOT QUITE.
OUR FRIENDLY WALRUS HERE KEPT TABS ON YOUR PROGRESS ...
AND CONTRIBUTED FINANCIALLY TO YOUR SUPPORT -- HE PAID FOR YOUR NANNY.
YOU PAID FOR HATTIE ...
YOU KEPT TABS ...
SO THAT'S WHY YOU KNEW SO MUCH ABOUT ME AT OUR FIRST INTERVIEW!
YES, NICOLE.
THAT'S HOW I KNEW YOU WERE BEST-QUALIFIED TO BECOME MY ASSISTANT.
AND WHY I'LL DO ANYTHING TO KEEP YOU ON BOARD.

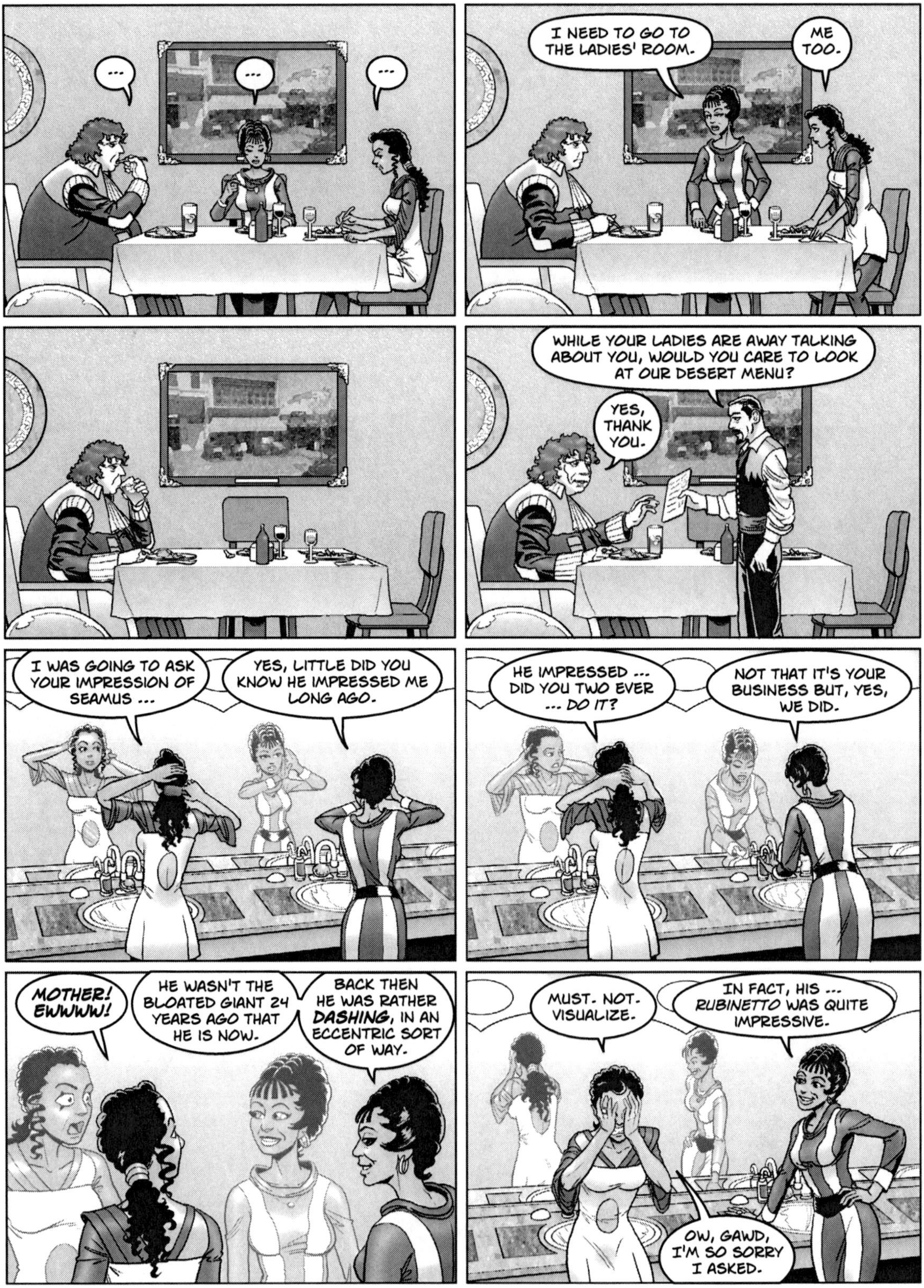
...
...
...
I NEED TO GO TO THE LADIES' ROOM.
ME TOO.
WHILE YOUR LADIES ARE AWAY TALKING ABOUT YOU, WOULD YOU CARE TO LOOK AT OUR DESERT MENU?
YES, THANK YOU.
I WAS GOING TO ASK YOUR IMPRESSION OF SEAMUS ...
YES, LITTLE DID YOU KNOW HE IMPRESSED ME LONG AGO.
HE IMPRESSED ... DID YOU TWO EVER ... DO IT?
NOT THAT IT'S YOUR BUSINESS BUT, YES, WE DID.
MOTHER! EWWWW!
HE WASN'T THE BLOATED GIANT 24 YEARS AGO THAT HE IS NOW.
BACK THEN HE WAS RATHER DASHING, IN AN ECCENTRIC SORT OF WAY.
MUST. NOT. VISUALIZE.
IN FACT, HIS ... RUBINETTO WAS QUITE IMPRESSIVE.
OW, GAWD, I'M SO SORRY I ASKED.

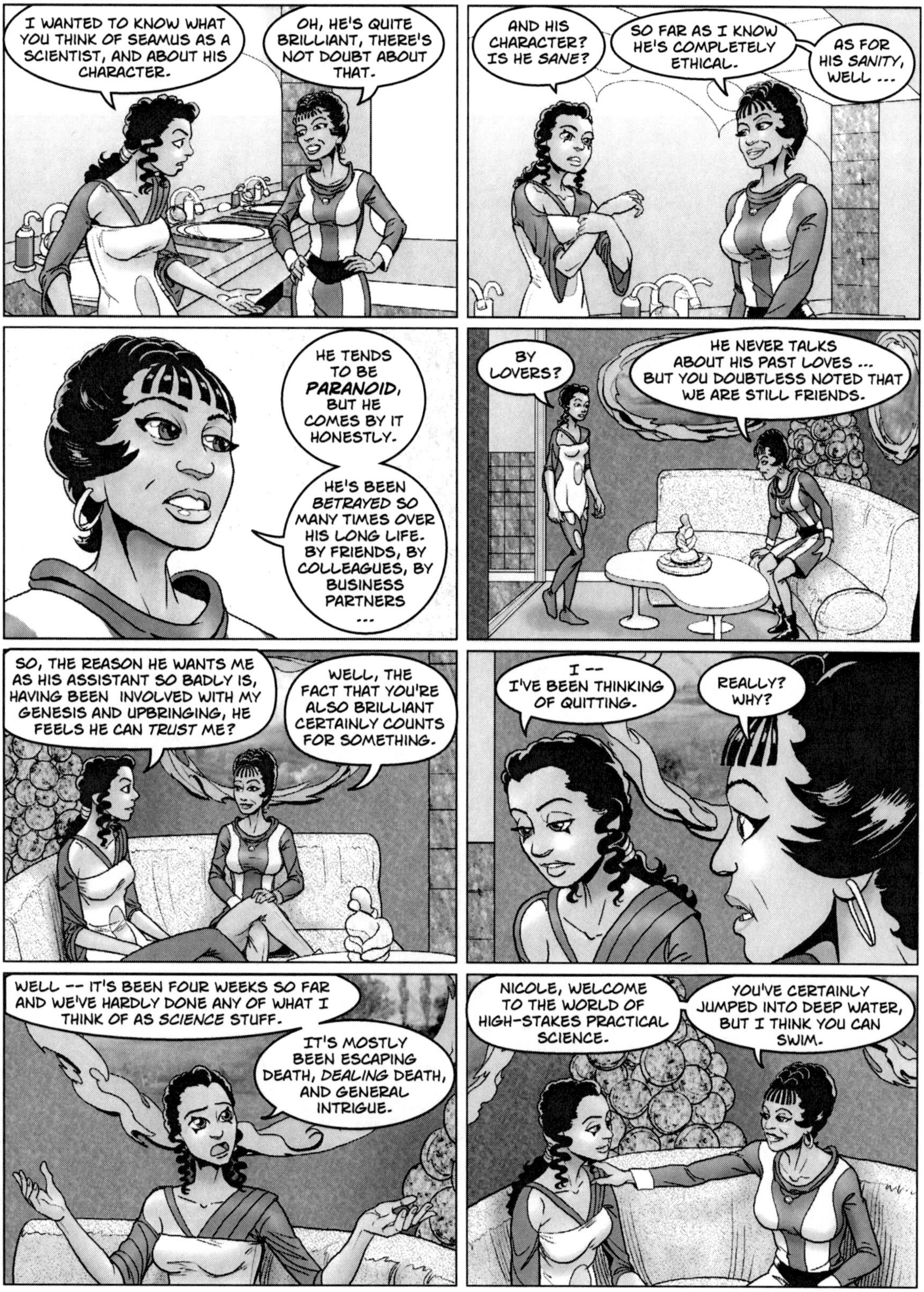
I WANTED TO KNOW WHAT YOU THINK OF SEAMUS AS A SCIENTIST, AND ABOUT HIS CHARACTER.
OH, HE'S QUITE BRILLIANT, THERE'S NOT DOUBT ABOUT THAT.
AND HIS CHARACTER? IS HE *SANE*?
SO FAR AS I KNOW HE'S COMPLETELY ETHICAL.
AS FOR HIS *SANITY*, WELL ...
HE TENDS TO BE **PARANOID**, BUT HE COMES BY IT HONESTLY.
HE'S BEEN *BETRAYED* SO MANY TIMES OVER HIS LONG LIFE. BY FRIENDS, BY COLLEAGUES, BY BUSINESS PARTNERS ...
BY LOVERS?
HE NEVER TALKS ABOUT HIS PAST LOVES ... BUT YOU DOUBTLESS NOTED THAT WE ARE STILL FRIENDS.
SO, THE REASON HE WANTS ME AS HIS ASSISTANT SO BADLY IS, HAVING BEEN INVOLVED WITH MY GENESIS AND UPBRINGING, HE FEELS HE CAN *TRUST* ME?
WELL, THE FACT THAT YOU'RE ALSO BRILLIANT CERTAINLY COUNTS FOR SOMETHING.
I -- I'VE BEEN THINKING OF QUITTING.
REALLY? WHY?
WELL -- IT'S BEEN FOUR WEEKS SO FAR AND WE'VE HARDLY DONE ANY OF WHAT I THINK OF AS *SCIENCE* STUFF.
IT'S MOSTLY BEEN ESCAPING DEATH, *DEALING* DEATH, AND GENERAL INTRIGUE.
NICOLE, WELCOME TO THE WORLD OF HIGH-STAKES PRACTICAL SCIENCE.
YOU'VE CERTAINLY JUMPED INTO DEEP WATER, BUT I THINK YOU CAN SWIM.

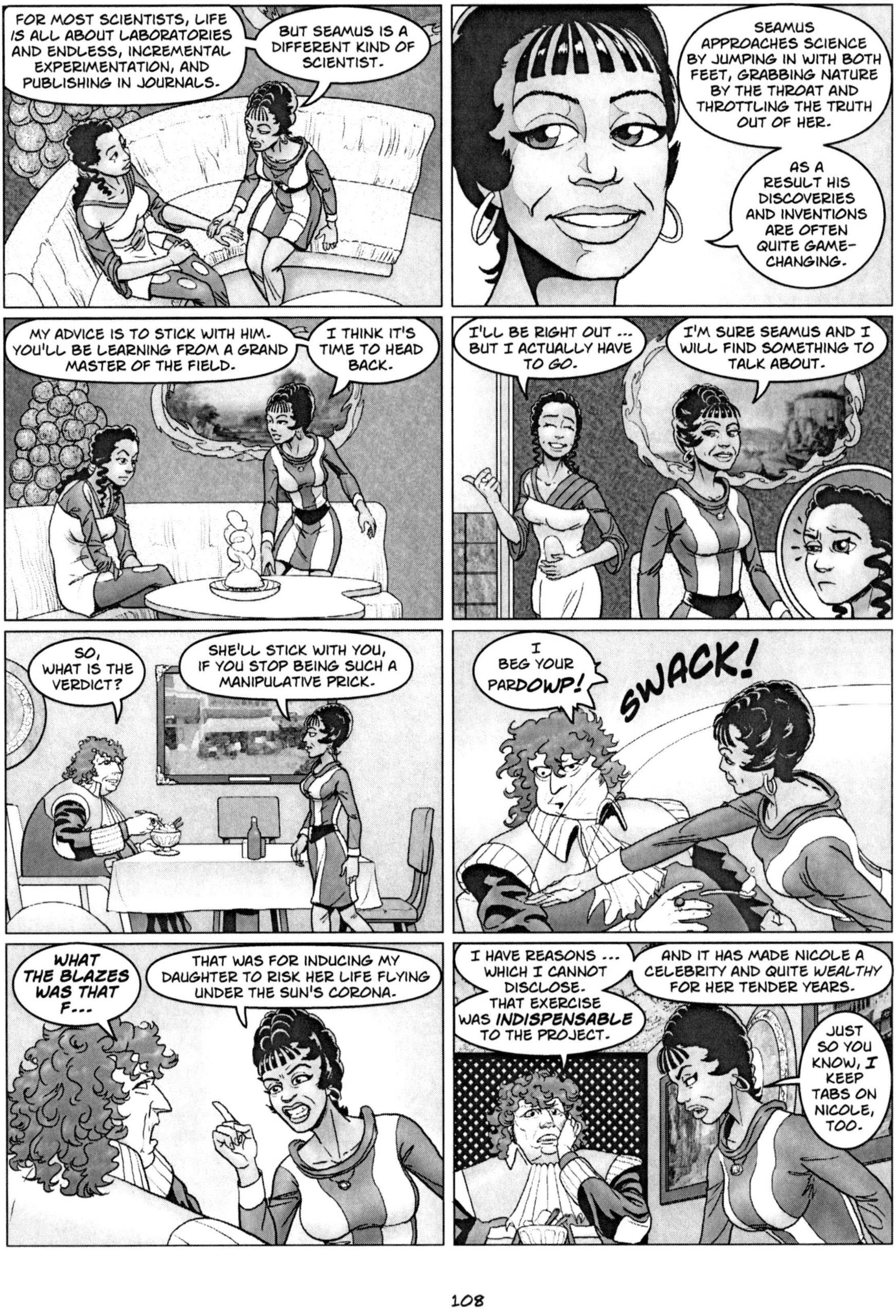
FOR MOST SCIENTISTS, LIFE IS ALL ABOUT LABORATORIES AND ENDLESS, INCREMENTAL EXPERIMENTATION, AND PUBLISHING IN JOURNALS.
BUT SEAMUS IS A DIFFERENT KIND OF SCIENTIST.
SEAMUS APPROACHES SCIENCE BY JUMPING IN WITH BOTH FEET, GRABBING NATURE BY THE THROAT AND THROTTLING THE TRUTH OUT OF HER.
AS A RESULT HIS DISCOVERIES AND INVENTIONS ARE OFTEN QUITE GAME-CHANGING.
MY ADVICE IS TO STICK WITH HIM. YOU'LL BE LEARNING FROM A GRAND MASTER OF THE FIELD.
I THINK IT'S TIME TO HEAD BACK.
I'LL BE RIGHT OUT ... BUT I ACTUALLY HAVE TO GO.
I'M SURE SEAMUS AND I WILL FIND SOMETHING TO TALK ABOUT.
SO, WHAT IS THE VERDICT?
SHE'LL STICK WITH YOU, IF YOU STOP BEING SUCH A MANIPULATIVE PRICK.
I BEG YOUR PARDOWP!
SWACK!
WHAT THE BLAZES WAS THAT F...
THAT WAS FOR INDUCING MY DAUGHTER TO RISK HER LIFE FLYING UNDER THE SUN'S CORONA.
I HAVE REASONS ... WHICH I CANNOT DISCLOSE. THAT EXERCISE WAS INDISPENSABLE TO THE PROJECT.
AND IT HAS MADE NICOLE A CELEBRITY AND QUITE WEALTHY FOR HER TENDER YEARS.
JUST SO YOU KNOW, I KEEP TABS ON NICOLE, TOO.

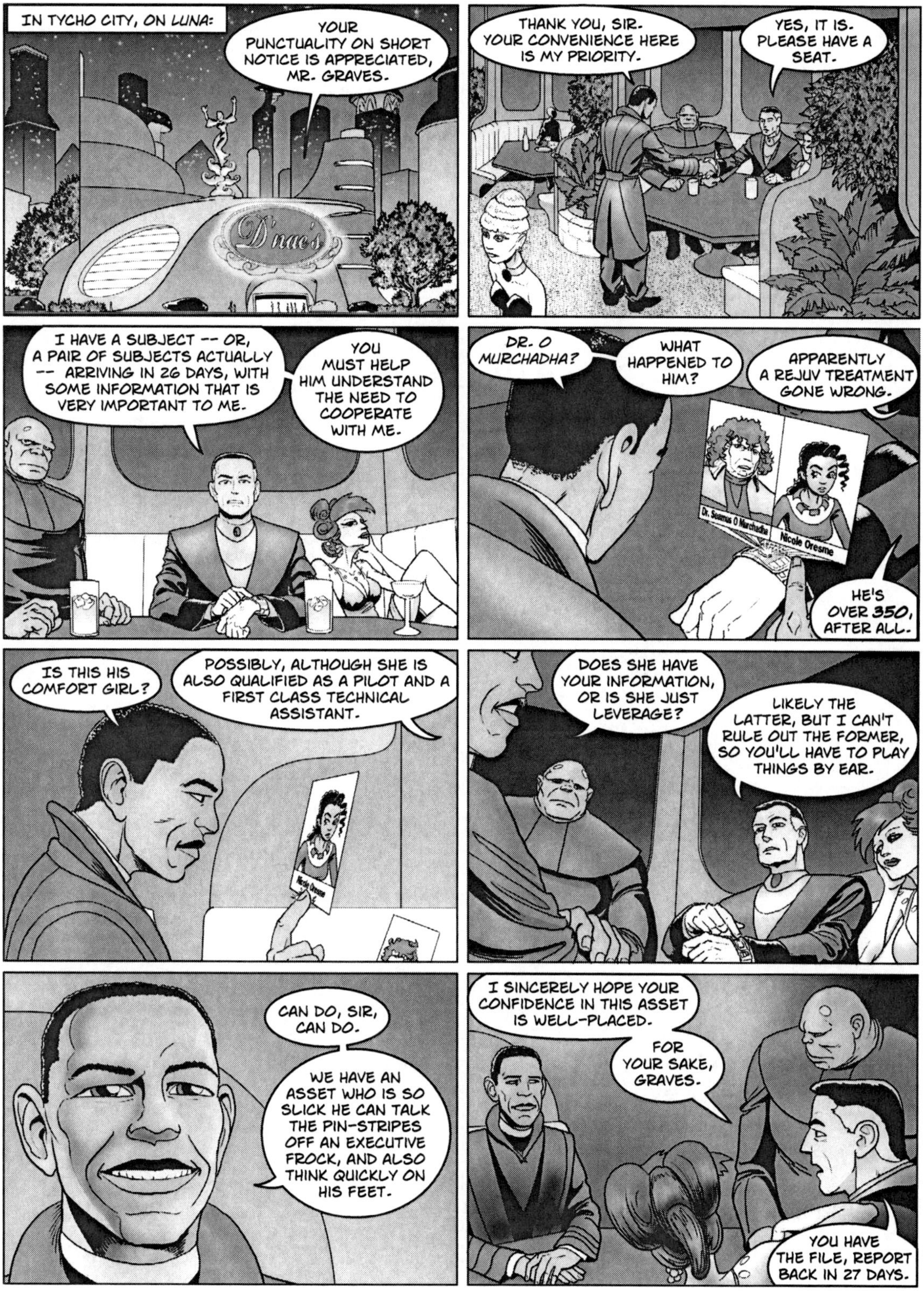
IN TYCHO CITY, ON LUNA:
YOUR PUNCTUALITY ON SHORT NOTICE IS APPRECIATED, MR. GRAVES.
D'nae's
THANK YOU, SIR. YOUR CONVENIENCE HERE IS MY PRIORITY.
YES, IT IS. PLEASE HAVE A SEAT.
I HAVE A SUBJECT -- OR, A PAIR OF SUBJECTS ACTUALLY -- ARRIVING IN 26 DAYS, WITH SOME INFORMATION THAT IS VERY IMPORTANT TO ME.
YOU MUST HELP HIM UNDERSTAND THE NEED TO COOPERATE WITH ME.
DR. O MURCHADHA?
WHAT HAPPENED TO HIM?
APPARENTLY A REJUV TREATMENT GONE WRONG.
Dr. Seamus O Murchadha
Nicole Oresme
HE'S OVER 350, AFTER ALL.
IS THIS HIS COMFORT GIRL?
POSSIBLY, ALTHOUGH SHE IS ALSO QUALIFIED AS A PILOT AND A FIRST CLASS TECHNICAL ASSISTANT.
DOES SHE HAVE YOUR INFORMATION, OR IS SHE JUST LEVERAGE?
LIKELY THE LATTER, BUT I CAN'T RULE OUT THE FORMER, SO YOU'LL HAVE TO PLAY THINGS BY EAR.
CAN DO, SIR, CAN DO.
WE HAVE AN ASSET WHO IS SO SLICK HE CAN TALK THE PIN-STRIPES OFF AN EXECUTIVE FROCK, AND ALSO THINK QUICKLY ON HIS FEET.
I SINCERELY HOPE YOUR CONFIDENCE IN THIS ASSET IS WELL-PLACED.
FOR YOUR SAKE, GRAVES.
YOU HAVE THE FILE, REPORT BACK IN 27 DAYS.

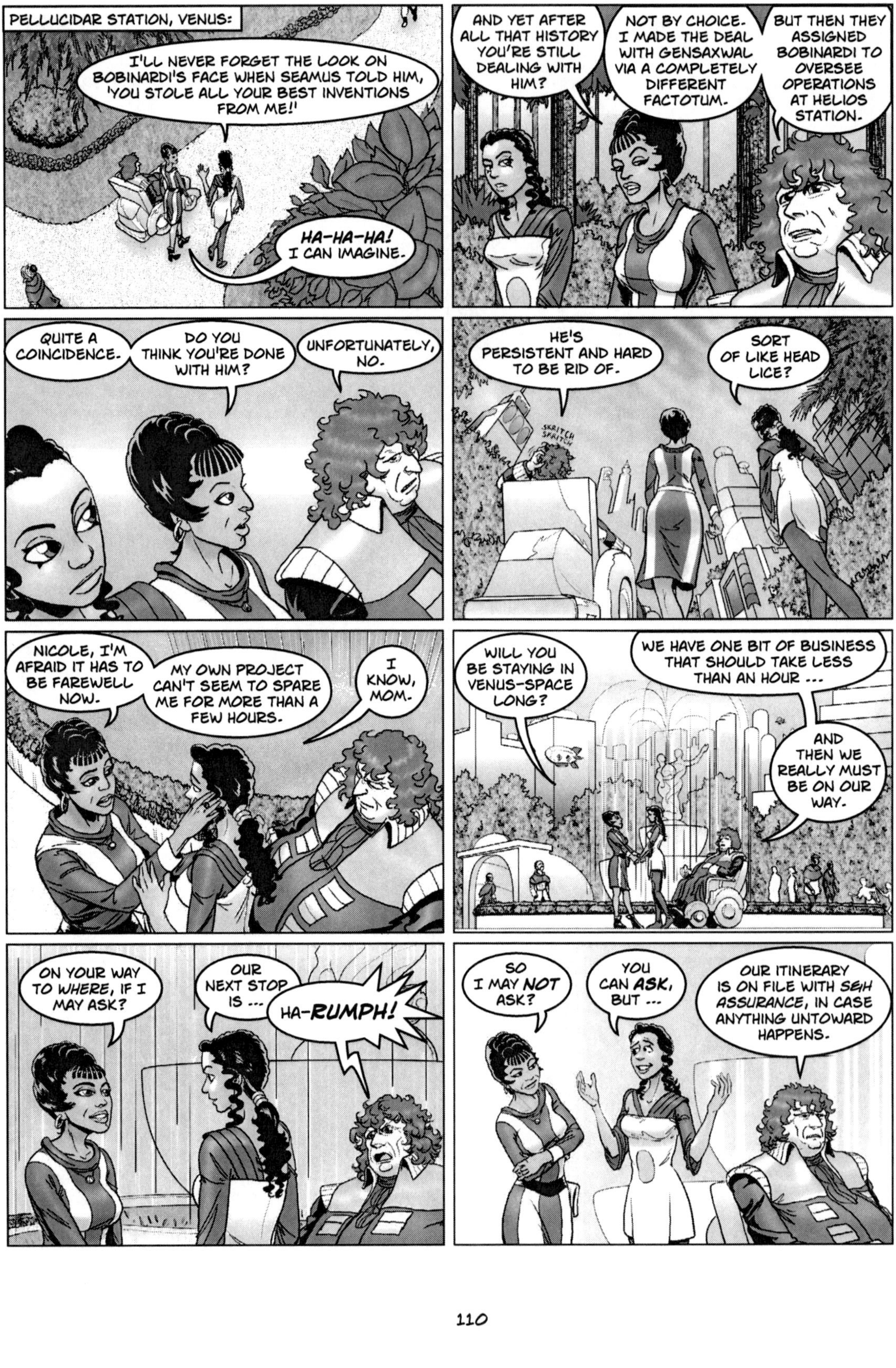
PELLUCIDAR STATION, VENUS:
I'LL NEVER FORGET THE LOOK ON BOBINARDI'S FACE WHEN SEAMUS TOLD HIM, 'YOU STOLE ALL YOUR BEST INVENTIONS FROM ME!'
HA-HA-HA! I CAN IMAGINE.
AND YET AFTER ALL THAT HISTORY YOU'RE STILL DEALING WITH HIM?
NOT BY CHOICE. I MADE THE DEAL WITH GENSAXWAL VIA A COMPLETELY DIFFERENT FACTOTUM.
BUT THEN THEY ASSIGNED BOBINARDI TO OVERSEE OPERATIONS AT HELIOS STATION.
QUITE A COINCIDENCE.
DO YOU THINK YOU'RE DONE WITH HIM?
UNFORTUNATELY, NO.
HE'S PERSISTENT AND HARD TO BE RID OF.
SKRITCH SKRITCH
SORT OF LIKE HEAD LICE?
NICOLE, I'M AFRAID IT HAS TO BE FAREWELL NOW.
MY OWN PROJECT CAN'T SEEM TO SPARE ME FOR MORE THAN A FEW HOURS.
I KNOW, MOM.
WILL YOU BE STAYING IN VENUS-SPACE LONG?
WE HAVE ONE BIT OF BUSINESS THAT SHOULD TAKE LESS THAN AN HOUR ...
AND THEN WE REALLY MUST BE ON OUR WAY.
ON YOUR WAY TO WHERE, IF I MAY ASK?
OUR NEXT STOP IS ...
HA-RUMPH!
SO I MAY NOT ASK?
YOU CAN ASK, BUT ...
OUR ITINERARY IS ON FILE WITH S&H ASSURANCE, IN CASE ANYTHING UNTOWARD HAPPENS.

SO, THAT 'FINAL BIT OF BUSINESS' IS ...?

WHAT DID I PROMISE YOU I'D DO ERE WE LEFT VENUS?

TO TELL ME WHAT THE PROJECT IS ABOUT.

AND SO I SHALL. BUT BEFORE I DO ...

YOU MUST AGREE THAT ONCE I PULL YOU INTO FULL CONFIDENCE, AND YOU THEN CHOOSE TO CONTINUE WITH ME, THAT THERE WILL BE NO MORE WHINING, NO MORE SECOND THOUGHTS, NO TALK OF QUITTING.

AGREED?

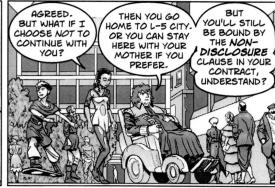

AGREED. BUT WHAT IF I CHOOSE NOT TO CONTINUE WITH YOU?

THEN YOU GO HOME TO L-5 CITY. OR YOU CAN STAY HERE WITH YOUR MOTHER IF YOU PREFER.

BUT YOU'LL STILL BE BOUND BY THE *NON-DISCLOSURE* CLAUSE IN YOUR CONTRACT, UNDERSTAND?

SO, WHERE ARE WE GOING?

TO THE ONE PLACE ON VENUS I CAN BE *100 PERCENT CERTAIN* IS FREE OF EAVESDROPPERS.

609

DALLI -- WHAT THE *SHUCK?!*

ARE YOU *SERIOUS?*

IT IS THE ONLY SAFE PLACE FOR SHARING SECRETS.

ALL ELECTRONIC RECORDING DEVICES ARE SCREENED AND REMOVED, OR SUPPRESSED.

I SWEAR TO YOU BY THE *ZAP* AND THE *ABCT* THAT I HAVE NO OTHER INTENTION THAN TO TELL YOU WHAT YOU WANT TO KNOW.

YOUR CHOICE.

I THINK I WANT TO PUKE.

THERE'S A VOMITORIUM ON THE NEXT BLOCK, BUT WE SHOULD DO THIS FIRST.

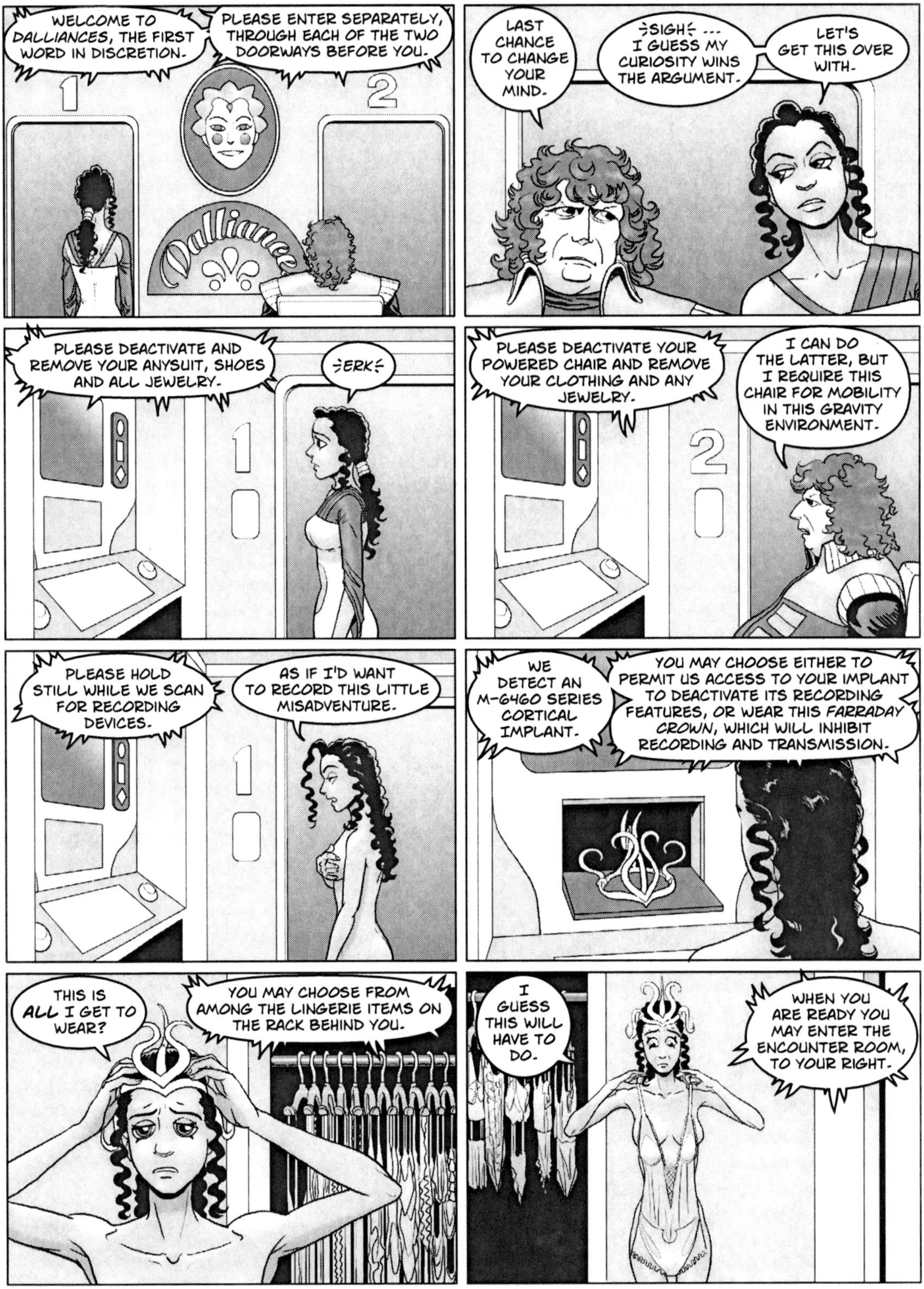
WELCOME TO DALLIANCES, THE FIRST WORD IN DISCRETION.
PLEASE ENTER SEPARATELY, THROUGH EACH OF THE TWO DOORWAYS BEFORE YOU.
1
2
Dalliance
LAST CHANCE TO CHANGE YOUR MIND.
SIGH --- I GUESS MY CURIOSITY WINS THE ARGUMENT.
LET'S GET THIS OVER WITH.
PLEASE DEACTIVATE AND REMOVE YOUR ANYSUIT, SHOES AND ALL JEWELRY.
ERK
PLEASE DEACTIVATE YOUR POWERED CHAIR AND REMOVE YOUR CLOTHING AND ANY JEWELRY.
I CAN DO THE LATTER, BUT I REQUIRE THIS CHAIR FOR MOBILITY IN THIS GRAVITY ENVIRONMENT.
PLEASE HOLD STILL WHILE WE SCAN FOR RECORDING DEVICES.
AS IF I'D WANT TO RECORD THIS LITTLE MISADVENTURE.
WE DETECT AN M-6460 SERIES CORTICAL IMPLANT.
YOU MAY CHOOSE EITHER TO PERMIT US ACCESS TO YOUR IMPLANT TO DEACTIVATE ITS RECORDING FEATURES, OR WEAR THIS FARRADAY CROWN, WHICH WILL INHIBIT RECORDING AND TRANSMISSION.
THIS IS ALL I GET TO WEAR?
YOU MAY CHOOSE FROM AMONG THE LINGERIE ITEMS ON THE RACK BEHIND YOU.
I GUESS THIS WILL HAVE TO DO.
WHEN YOU ARE READY YOU MAY ENTER THE ENCOUNTER ROOM, TO YOUR RIGHT.

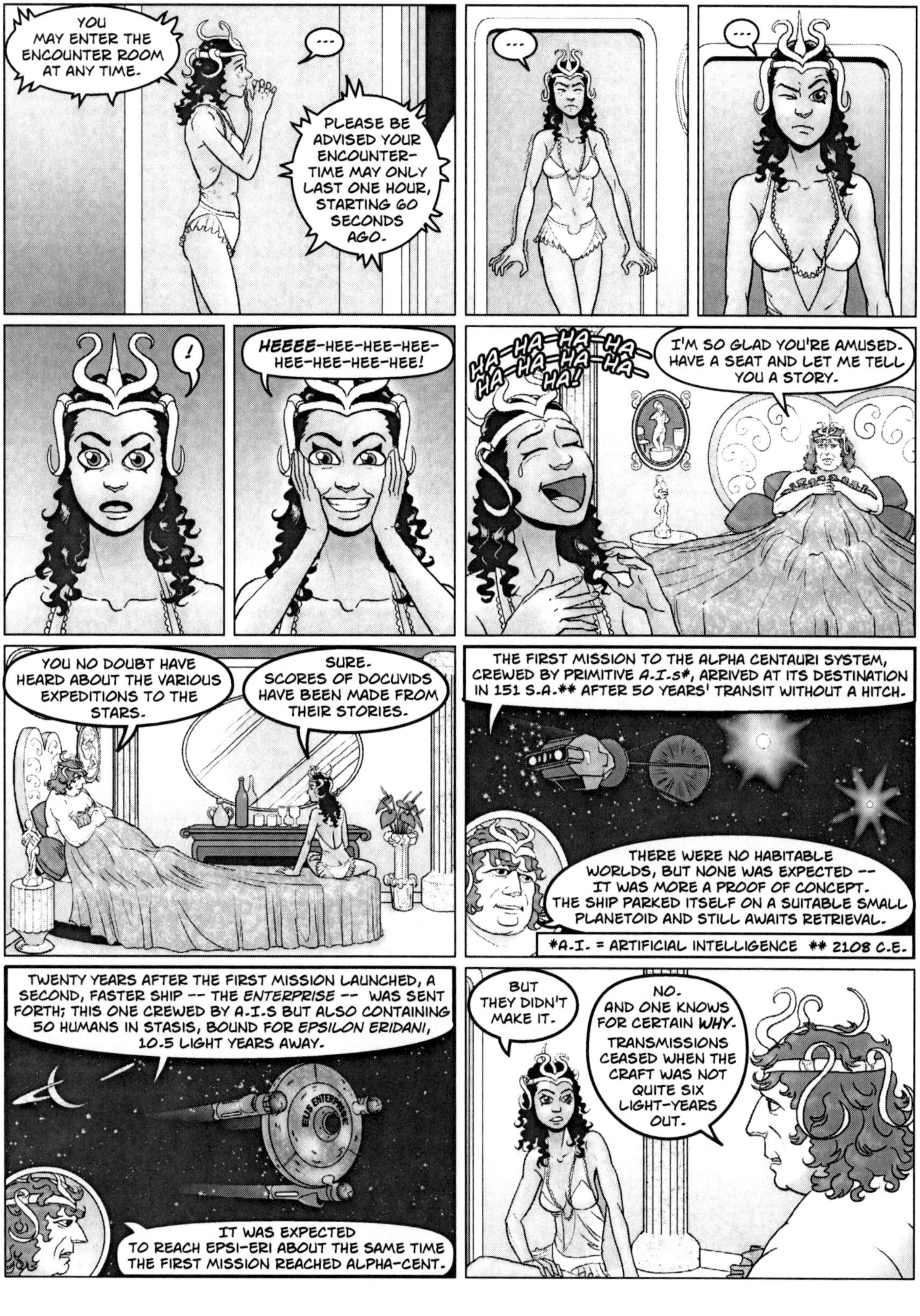
YOU MAY ENTER THE ENCOUNTER ROOM AT ANY TIME.
...
PLEASE BE ADVISED YOUR ENCOUNTER-TIME MAY ONLY LAST ONE HOUR, STARTING 60 SECONDS AGO.
...
...
!
HEEEE-HEE-HEE-HEE-HEE-HEE-HEE-HEE!
HA-HA-HA-HA-HA-HA-HA-HA-HA!
I'M SO GLAD YOU'RE AMUSED. HAVE A SEAT AND LET ME TELL YOU A STORY.
YOU NO DOUBT HAVE HEARD ABOUT THE VARIOUS EXPEDITIONS TO THE STARS.
SURE. SCORES OF DOCUVIDS HAVE BEEN MADE FROM THEIR STORIES.
THE FIRST MISSION TO THE ALPHA CENTAURI SYSTEM, CREWED BY PRIMITIVE A.I.S*, ARRIVED AT ITS DESTINATION IN 151 S.A.** AFTER 50 YEARS' TRANSIT WITHOUT A HITCH.
THERE WERE NO HABITABLE WORLDS, BUT NONE WAS EXPECTED -- IT WAS MORE A PROOF OF CONCEPT. THE SHIP PARKED ITSELF ON A SUITABLE SMALL PLANETOID AND STILL AWAITS RETRIEVAL.
*A.I. = ARTIFICIAL INTELLIGENCE ** 2108 C.E.
TWENTY YEARS AFTER THE FIRST MISSION LAUNCHED, A SECOND, FASTER SHIP -- THE ENTERPRISE -- WAS SENT FORTH; THIS ONE CREWED BY A.I.S BUT ALSO CONTAINING 50 HUMANS IN STASIS, BOUND FOR EPSILON ERIDANI, 10.5 LIGHT YEARS AWAY.
EUS ENTERPRISE
IT WAS EXPECTED TO REACH EPSI-ERI ABOUT THE SAME TIME THE FIRST MISSION REACHED ALPHA-CENT.
BUT THEY DIDN'T MAKE IT.
NO. AND ONE KNOWS FOR CERTAIN WHY.
TRANSMISSIONS CEASED WHEN THE CRAFT WAS NOT QUITE SIX LIGHT-YEARS OUT.

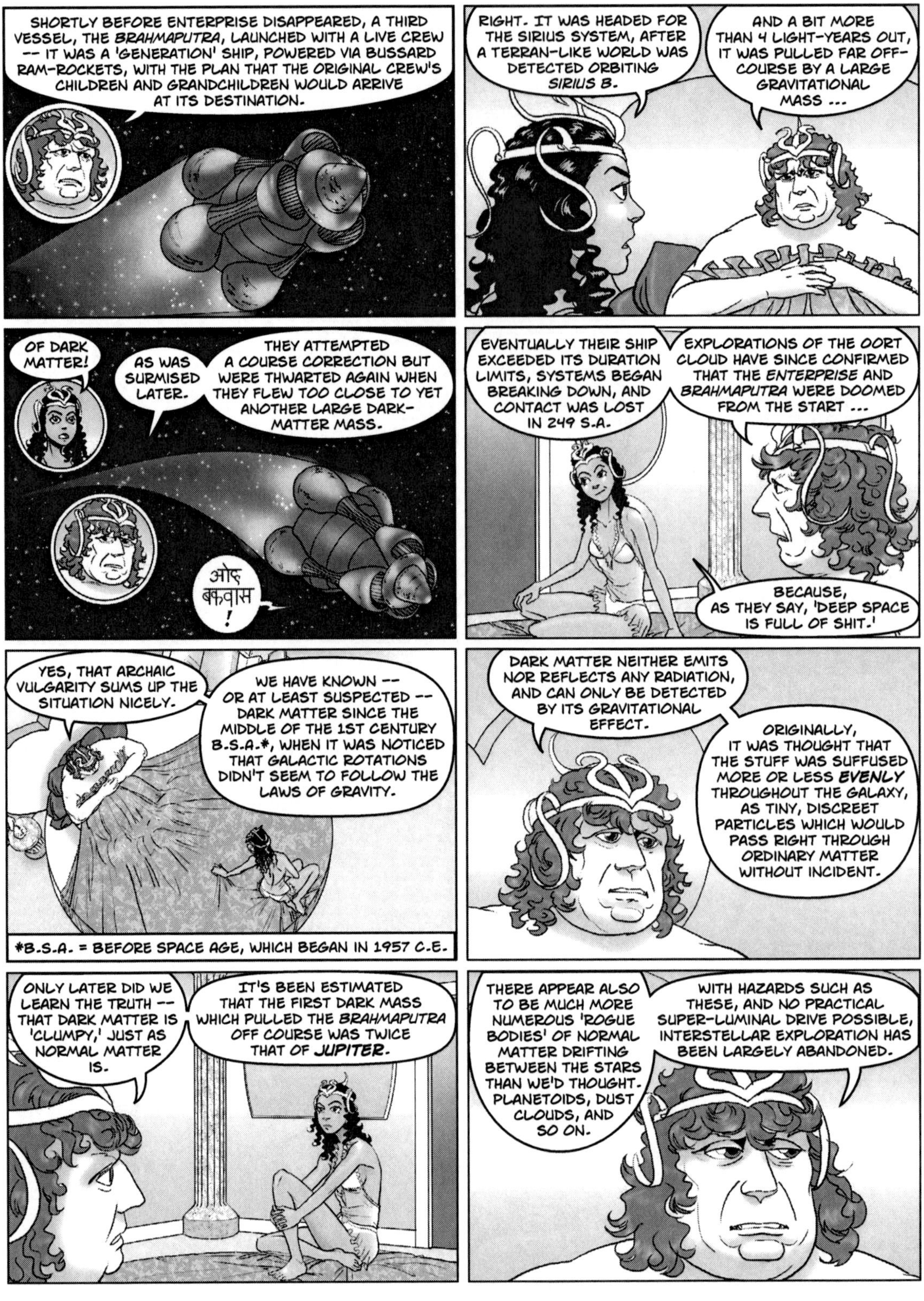
SHORTLY BEFORE ENTERPRISE DISAPPEARED, A THIRD VESSEL, THE *BRAHMAPUTRA*, LAUNCHED WITH A LIVE CREW -- IT WAS A 'GENERATION' SHIP, POWERED VIA BUSSARD RAM-ROCKETS, WITH THE PLAN THAT THE ORIGINAL CREW'S CHILDREN AND GRANDCHILDREN WOULD ARRIVE AT ITS DESTINATION.
RIGHT. IT WAS HEADED FOR THE SIRIUS SYSTEM, AFTER A TERRAN-LIKE WORLD WAS DETECTED ORBITING *SIRIUS B*.
AND A BIT MORE THAN 4 LIGHT-YEARS OUT, IT WAS PULLED FAR OFF-COURSE BY A LARGE GRAVITATIONAL MASS ...
OF DARK MATTER!
AS WAS SURMISED LATER.
THEY ATTEMPTED A COURSE CORRECTION BUT WERE THWARTED AGAIN WHEN THEY FLEW TOO CLOSE TO YET ANOTHER LARGE DARK-MATTER MASS.
ओह् बकवास !
EVENTUALLY THEIR SHIP EXCEEDED ITS DURATION LIMITS, SYSTEMS BEGAN BREAKING DOWN, AND CONTACT WAS LOST IN 249 S.A.
EXPLORATIONS OF THE OORT CLOUD HAVE SINCE CONFIRMED THAT THE *ENTERPRISE* AND *BRAHMAPUTRA* WERE DOOMED FROM THE START ...
BECAUSE, AS THEY SAY, 'DEEP SPACE IS FULL OF SHIT.'
YES, THAT ARCHAIC VULGARITY SUMS UP THE SITUATION NICELY.
WE HAVE KNOWN -- OR AT LEAST SUSPECTED -- DARK MATTER SINCE THE MIDDLE OF THE 1ST CENTURY B.S.A.*, WHEN IT WAS NOTICED THAT GALACTIC ROTATIONS DIDN'T SEEM TO FOLLOW THE LAWS OF GRAVITY.
*B.S.A. = BEFORE SPACE AGE, WHICH BEGAN IN 1957 C.E.
DARK MATTER NEITHER EMITS NOR REFLECTS ANY RADIATION, AND CAN ONLY BE DETECTED BY ITS GRAVITATIONAL EFFECT.
ORIGINALLY, IT WAS THOUGHT THAT THE STUFF WAS SUFFUSED MORE OR LESS **EVENLY** THROUGHOUT THE GALAXY, AS TINY, DISCREET PARTICLES WHICH WOULD PASS RIGHT THROUGH ORDINARY MATTER WITHOUT INCIDENT.
ONLY LATER DID WE LEARN THE TRUTH -- THAT DARK MATTER IS 'CLUMPY,' JUST AS NORMAL MATTER IS.
IT'S BEEN ESTIMATED THAT THE FIRST DARK MASS WHICH PULLED THE *BRAHMAPUTRA* OFF COURSE WAS TWICE THAT OF ***JUPITER***.
THERE APPEAR ALSO TO BE MUCH MORE NUMEROUS 'ROGUE BODIES' OF NORMAL MATTER DRIFTING BETWEEN THE STARS THAN WE'D THOUGHT. PLANETOIDS, DUST CLOUDS, AND SO ON.
WITH HAZARDS SUCH AS THESE, AND NO PRACTICAL SUPER-LUMINAL DRIVE POSSIBLE, INTERSTELLAR EXPLORATION HAS BEEN LARGELY ABANDONED.

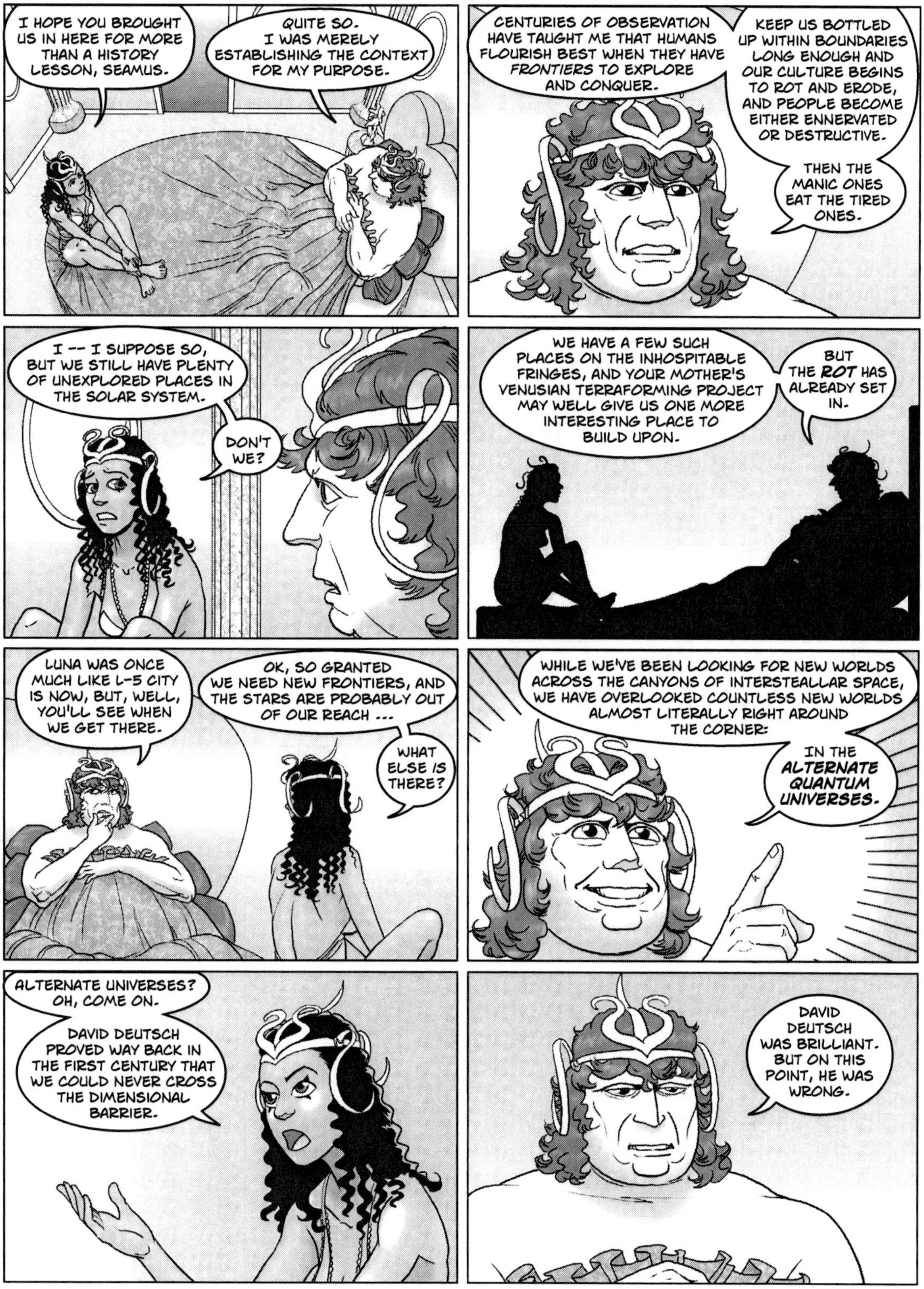
I HOPE YOU BROUGHT US IN HERE FOR MORE THAN A HISTORY LESSON, SEAMUS.
QUITE SO. I WAS MERELY ESTABLISHING THE CONTEXT FOR MY PURPOSE.
CENTURIES OF OBSERVATION HAVE TAUGHT ME THAT HUMANS FLOURISH BEST WHEN THEY HAVE FRONTIERS TO EXPLORE AND CONQUER.
KEEP US BOTTLED UP WITHIN BOUNDARIES LONG ENOUGH AND OUR CULTURE BEGINS TO ROT AND ERODE, AND PEOPLE BECOME EITHER ENNERVATED OR DESTRUCTIVE.
THEN THE MANIC ONES EAT THE TIRED ONES.
I -- I SUPPOSE SO, BUT WE STILL HAVE PLENTY OF UNEXPLORED PLACES IN THE SOLAR SYSTEM.
DON'T WE?
WE HAVE A FEW SUCH PLACES ON THE INHOSPITABLE FRINGES, AND YOUR MOTHER'S VENUSIAN TERRAFORMING PROJECT MAY WELL GIVE US ONE MORE INTERESTING PLACE TO BUILD UPON.
BUT THE ROT HAS ALREADY SET IN.
LUNA WAS ONCE MUCH LIKE L-5 CITY IS NOW, BUT, WELL, YOU'LL SEE WHEN WE GET THERE.
OK, SO GRANTED WE NEED NEW FRONTIERS, AND THE STARS ARE PROBABLY OUT OF OUR REACH ...
WHAT ELSE IS THERE?
WHILE WE'VE BEEN LOOKING FOR NEW WORLDS ACROSS THE CANYONS OF INTERSTEALLAR SPACE, WE HAVE OVERLOOKED COUNTLESS NEW WORLDS ALMOST LITERALLY RIGHT AROUND THE CORNER:
IN THE ALTERNATE QUANTUM UNIVERSES.
ALTERNATE UNIVERSES? OH, COME ON.
DAVID DEUTSCH PROVED WAY BACK IN THE FIRST CENTURY THAT WE COULD NEVER CROSS THE DIMENSIONAL BARRIER.
DAVID DEUTSCH WAS BRILLIANT. BUT ON THIS POINT, HE WAS WRONG.

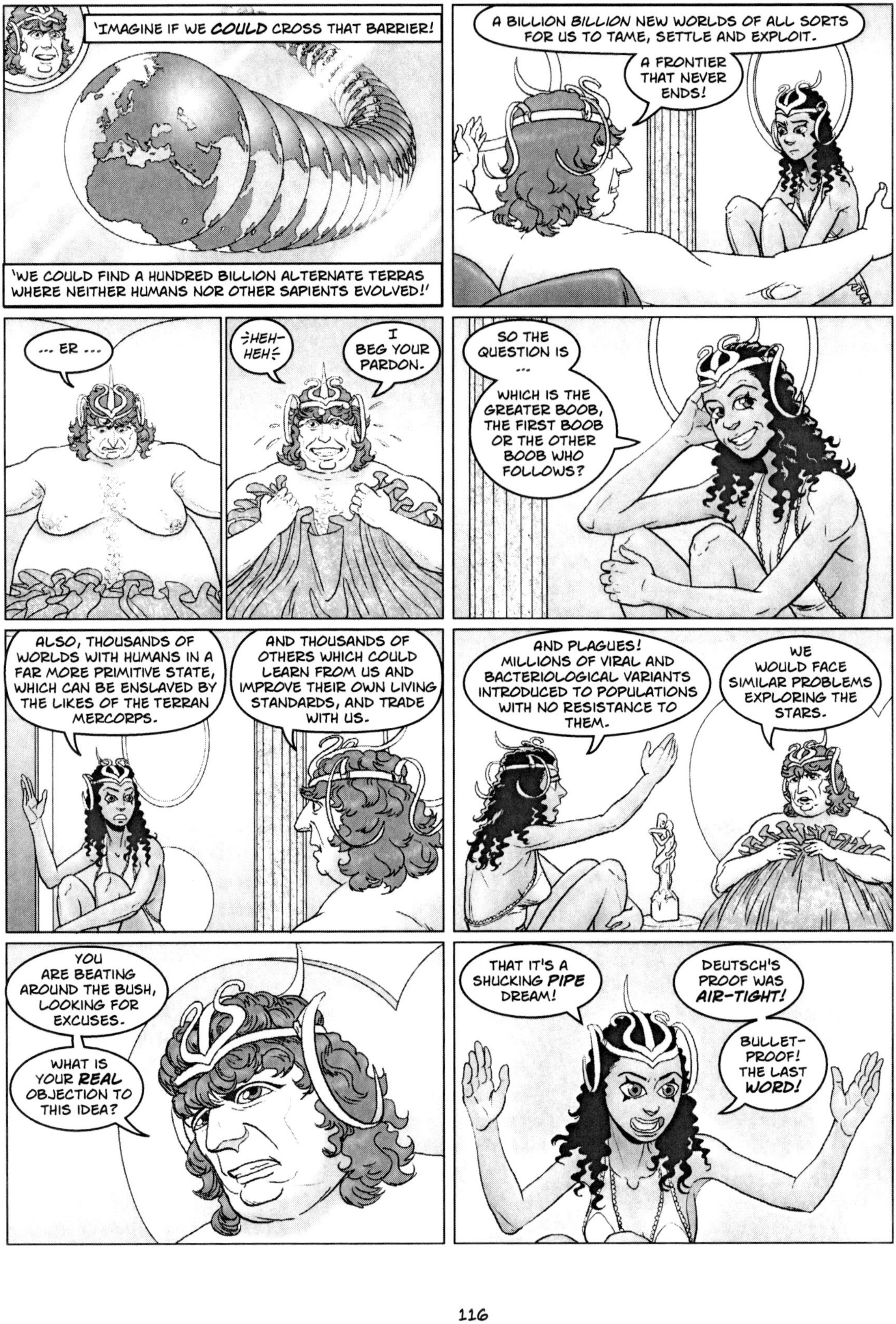
'IMAGINE IF WE COULD CROSS THAT BARRIER!
'WE COULD FIND A HUNDRED BILLION ALTERNATE TERRAS WHERE NEITHER HUMANS NOR OTHER SAPIENTS EVOLVED!'
A BILLION BILLION NEW WORLDS OF ALL SORTS FOR US TO TAME, SETTLE AND EXPLOIT.
A FRONTIER THAT NEVER ENDS!
... ER ...
HEH-HEH
I BEG YOUR PARDON.
SO THE QUESTION IS ...
WHICH IS THE GREATER BOOB, THE FIRST BOOB OR THE OTHER BOOB WHO FOLLOWS?
ALSO, THOUSANDS OF WORLDS WITH HUMANS IN A FAR MORE PRIMITIVE STATE, WHICH CAN BE ENSLAVED BY THE LIKES OF THE TERRAN MERCORPS.
AND THOUSANDS OF OTHERS WHICH COULD LEARN FROM US AND IMPROVE THEIR OWN LIVING STANDARDS, AND TRADE WITH US.
AND PLAGUES! MILLIONS OF VIRAL AND BACTERIOLOGICAL VARIANTS INTRODUCED TO POPULATIONS WITH NO RESISTANCE TO THEM.
WE WOULD FACE SIMILAR PROBLEMS EXPLORING THE STARS.
YOU ARE BEATING AROUND THE BUSH, LOOKING FOR EXCUSES.
WHAT IS YOUR REAL OBJECTION TO THIS IDEA?
THAT IT'S A SHUCKING PIPE DREAM!
DEUTSCH'S PROOF WAS AIR-TIGHT!
BULLET-PROOF! THE LAST WORD!

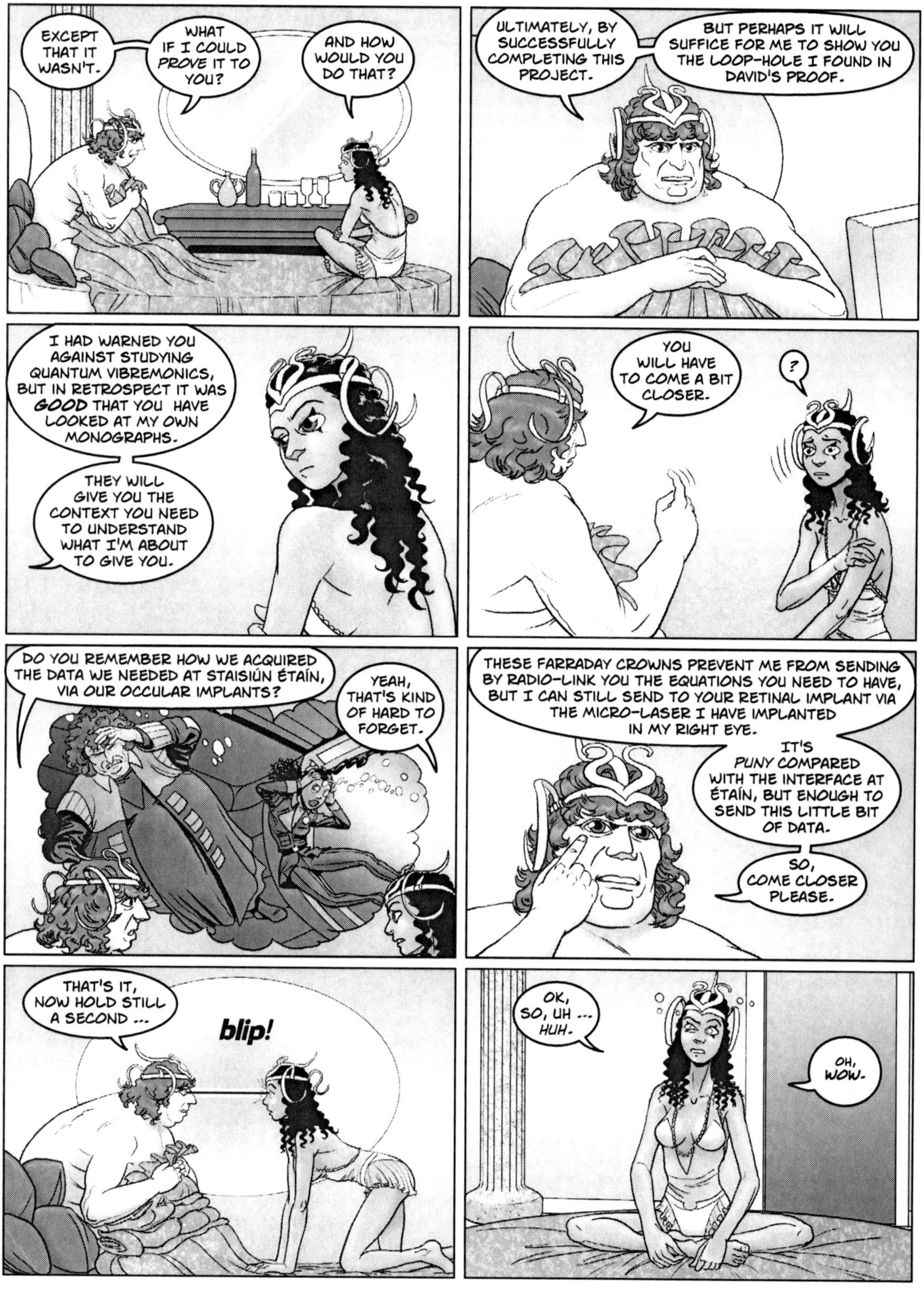
EXCEPT THAT IT WASN'T.
WHAT IF I COULD *PROVE* IT TO YOU?
AND HOW WOULD YOU DO THAT?
ULTIMATELY, BY SUCCESSFULLY COMPLETING THIS PROJECT.
BUT PERHAPS IT WILL SUFFICE FOR ME TO SHOW YOU THE LOOP-HOLE I FOUND IN DAVID'S PROOF.
I HAD WARNED YOU AGAINST STUDYING QUANTUM VIBREMONICS, BUT IN RETROSPECT IT WAS ***GOOD*** THAT YOU HAVE LOOKED AT MY OWN MONOGRAPHS.
THEY WILL GIVE YOU THE CONTEXT YOU NEED TO UNDERSTAND WHAT I'M ABOUT TO GIVE YOU.
YOU WILL HAVE TO COME A BIT CLOSER.
?
DO YOU REMEMBER HOW WE ACQUIRED THE DATA WE NEEDED AT STAISIÚN ÉTAÍN, VIA OUR OCCULAR IMPLANTS?
YEAH, THAT'S KIND OF HARD TO FORGET.
THESE FARRADAY CROWNS PREVENT ME FROM SENDING BY RADIO-LINK YOU THE EQUATIONS YOU NEED TO HAVE, BUT I CAN STILL SEND TO YOUR RETINAL IMPLANT VIA THE MICRO-LASER I HAVE IMPLANTED IN MY RIGHT EYE.
IT'S *PUNY* COMPARED WITH THE INTERFACE AT ÉTAÍN, BUT ENOUGH TO SEND THIS LITTLE BIT OF DATA.
SO, COME CLOSER PLEASE.
THAT'S IT, NOW HOLD STILL A SECOND ...
blip!
OK, SO, UH ... HUH.
OH, WOW.

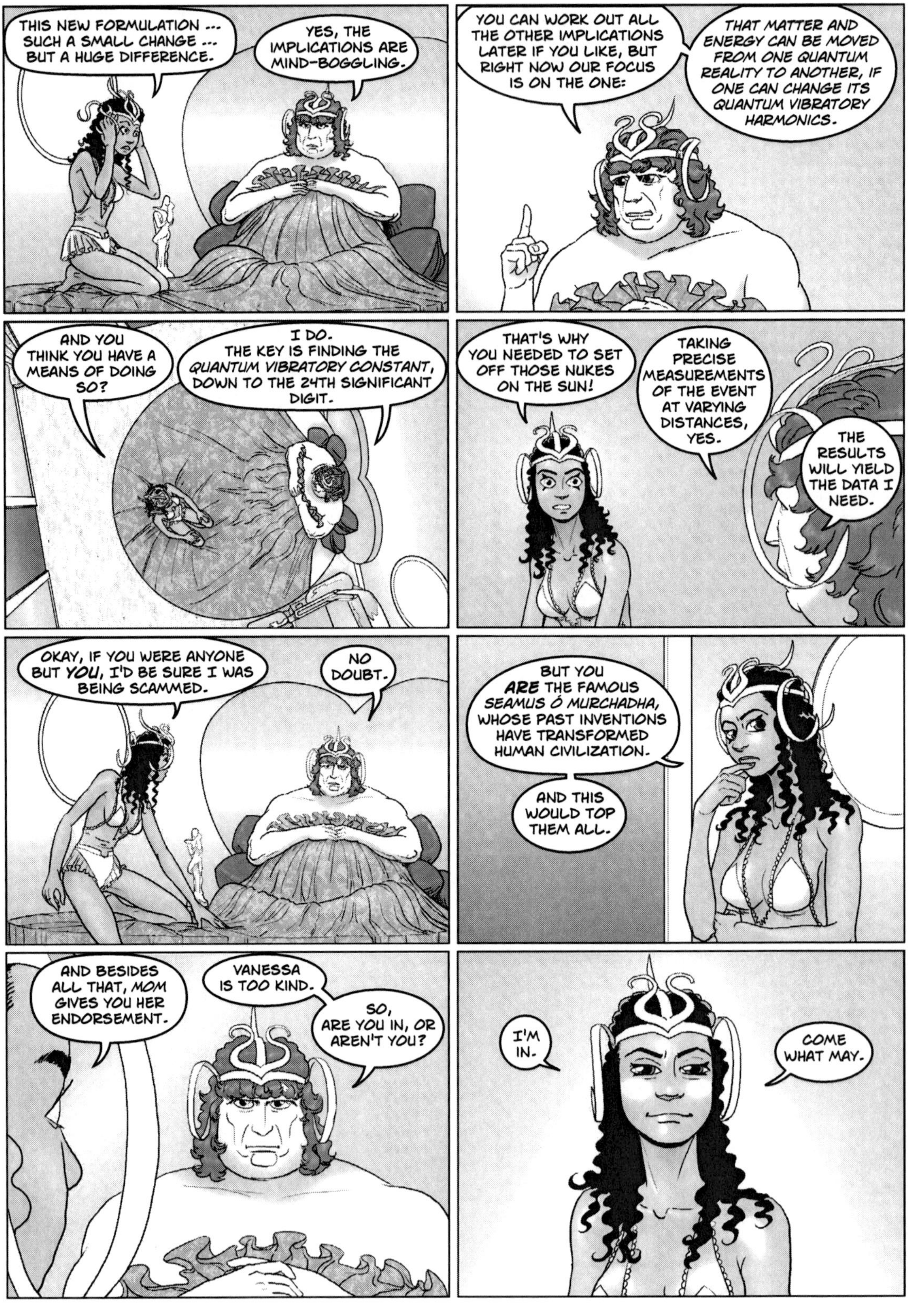
THIS NEW FORMULATION --- SUCH A SMALL CHANGE --- BUT A HUGE DIFFERENCE.
YES, THE IMPLICATIONS ARE MIND-BOGGLING.
YOU CAN WORK OUT ALL THE OTHER IMPLICATIONS LATER IF YOU LIKE, BUT RIGHT NOW OUR FOCUS IS ON THE ONE:
THAT MATTER AND ENERGY CAN BE MOVED FROM ONE QUANTUM REALITY TO ANOTHER, IF ONE CAN CHANGE ITS QUANTUM VIBRATORY HARMONICS.
AND YOU THINK YOU HAVE A MEANS OF DOING SO?
I DO. THE KEY IS FINDING THE *QUANTUM VIBRATORY CONSTANT*, DOWN TO THE 24TH SIGNIFICANT DIGIT.
THAT'S WHY YOU NEEDED TO SET OFF THOSE NUKES ON THE SUN!
TAKING PRECISE MEASUREMENTS OF THE EVENT AT VARYING DISTANCES, YES.
THE RESULTS WILL YIELD THE DATA I NEED.
OKAY, IF YOU WERE ANYONE BUT ***YOU***, I'D BE SURE I WAS BEING SCAMMED.
NO DOUBT.
BUT YOU ***ARE*** THE FAMOUS *SEAMUS Ó MURCHADHA*, WHOSE PAST INVENTIONS HAVE TRANSFORMED HUMAN CIVILIZATION.
AND THIS WOULD TOP THEM ALL.
AND BESIDES ALL THAT, MOM GIVES YOU HER ENDORSEMENT.
VANESSA IS TOO KIND.
SO, ARE YOU IN, OR AREN'T YOU?
I'M IN.
COME WHAT MAY.

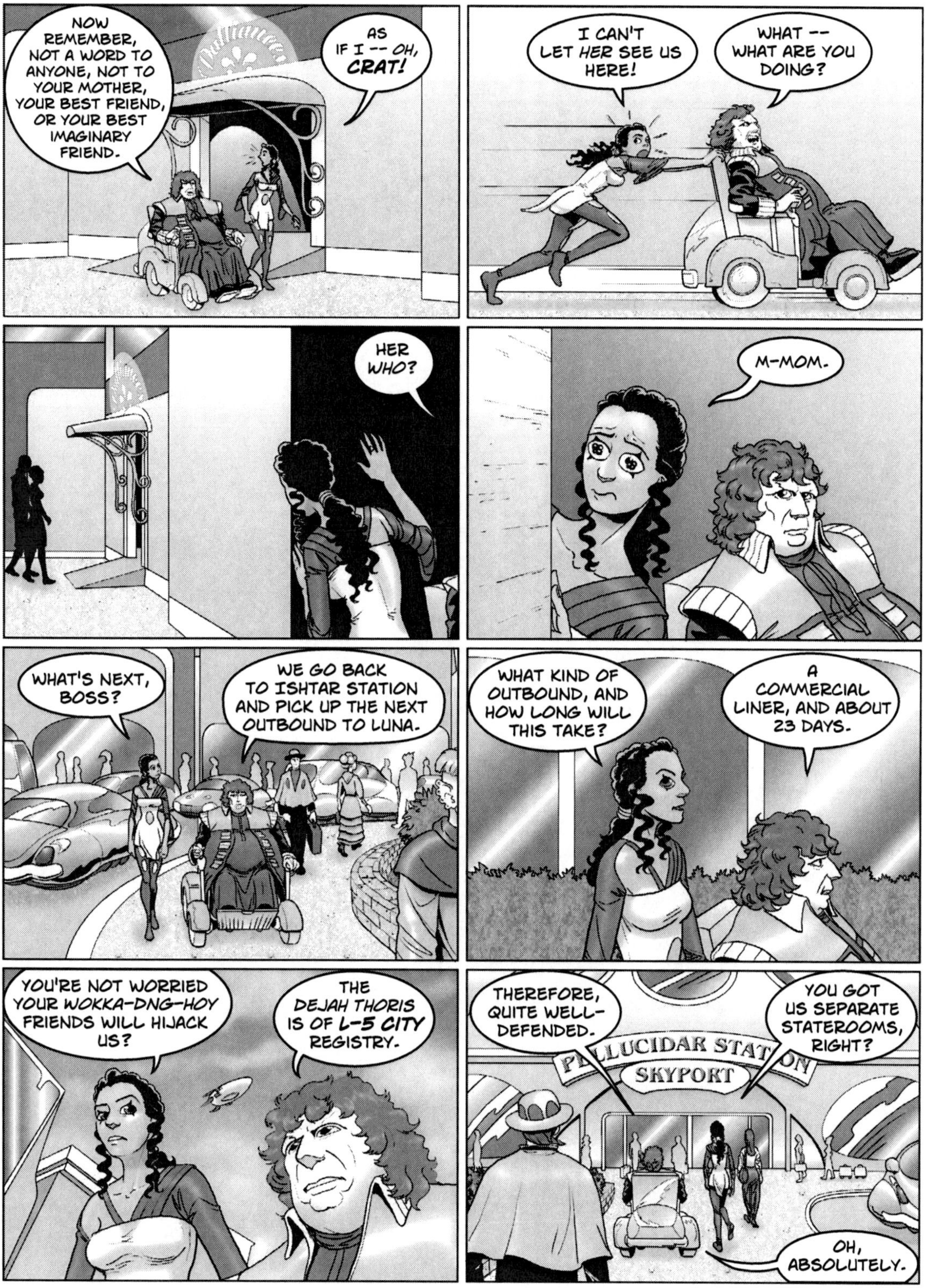
NOW REMEMBER, NOT A WORD TO ANYONE, NOT TO YOUR MOTHER, YOUR BEST FRIEND, OR YOUR BEST IMAGINARY FRIEND.
AS IF I -- OH, CRAT!
I CAN'T LET HER SEE US HERE!
WHAT -- WHAT ARE YOU DOING?
HER WHO?
M-MOM.
WHAT'S NEXT, BOSS?
WE GO BACK TO ISHTAR STATION AND PICK UP THE NEXT OUTBOUND TO LUNA.
WHAT KIND OF OUTBOUND, AND HOW LONG WILL THIS TAKE?
A COMMERCIAL LINER, AND ABOUT 23 DAYS.
YOU'RE NOT WORRIED YOUR WOKKA-DNG-HOY FRIENDS WILL HIJACK US?
THE DEJAH THORIS IS OF L-5 CITY REGISTRY.
THEREFORE, QUITE WELL-DEFENDED.
YOU GOT US SEPARATE STATEROOMS, RIGHT?
PELLUCIDAR STATION
SKYPORT
OH, ABSOLUTELY.

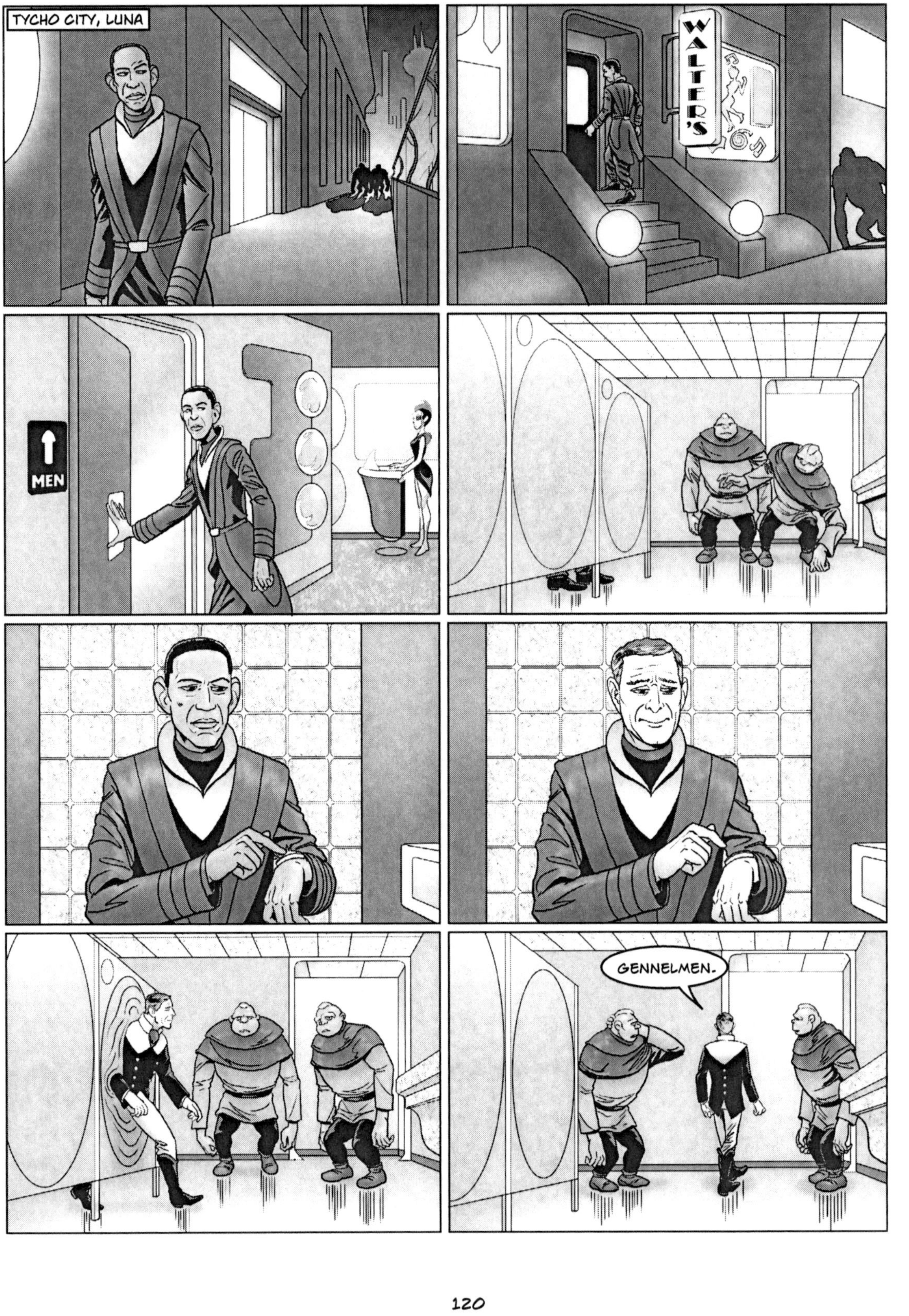
TYCHO CITY, LUNA
WALTER'S
MEN
GENNELMEN.

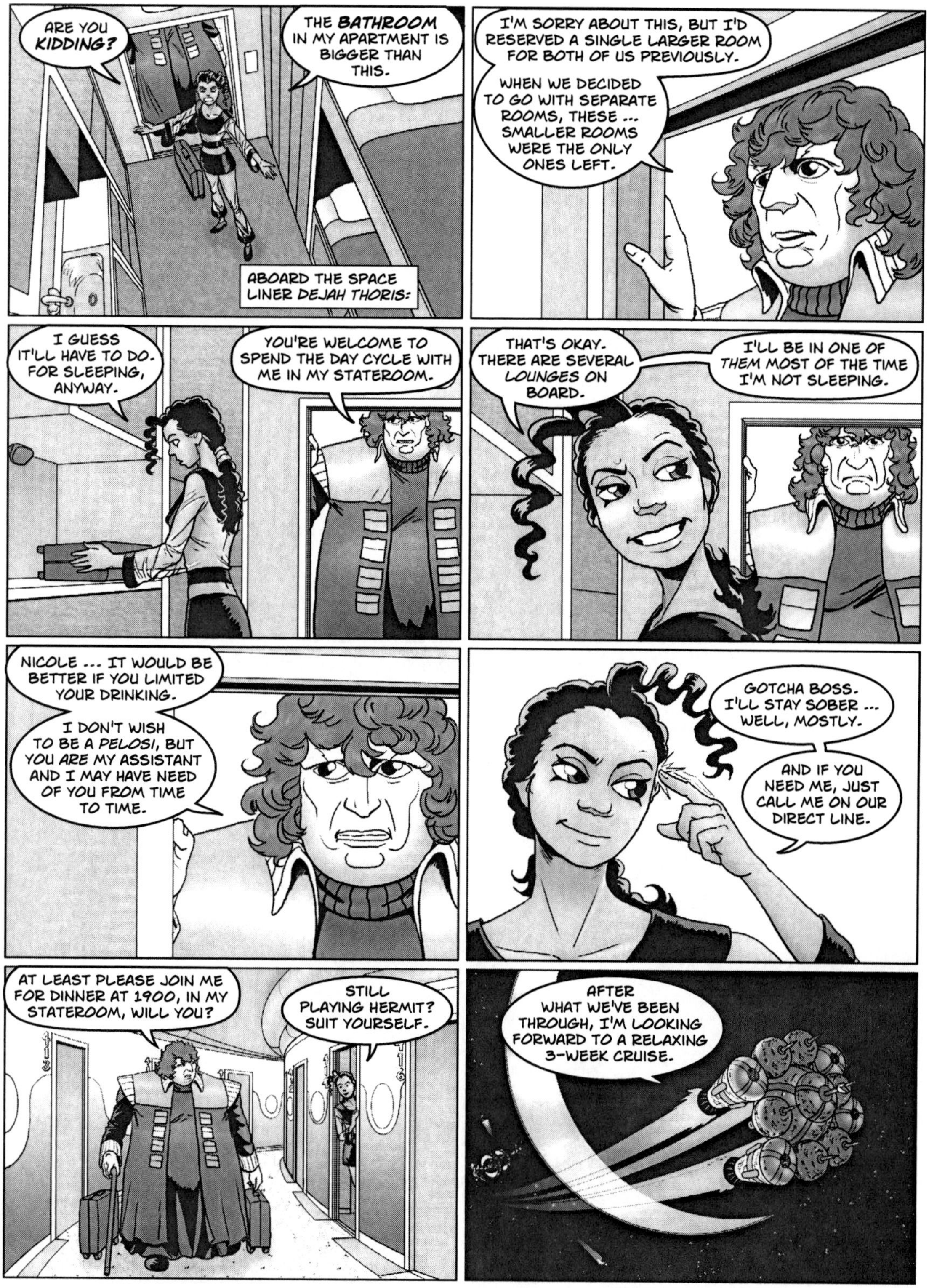
ARE YOU KIDDING?
THE BATHROOM IN MY APARTMENT IS BIGGER THAN THIS.
ABOARD THE SPACE LINER DEJAH THORIS:
I'M SORRY ABOUT THIS, BUT I'D RESERVED A SINGLE LARGER ROOM FOR BOTH OF US PREVIOUSLY.
WHEN WE DECIDED TO GO WITH SEPARATE ROOMS, THESE ... SMALLER ROOMS WERE THE ONLY ONES LEFT.
I GUESS IT'LL HAVE TO DO. FOR SLEEPING, ANYWAY.
YOU'RE WELCOME TO SPEND THE DAY CYCLE WITH ME IN MY STATEROOM.
THAT'S OKAY. THERE ARE SEVERAL LOUNGES ON BOARD.
I'LL BE IN ONE OF THEM MOST OF THE TIME I'M NOT SLEEPING.
NICOLE ... IT WOULD BE BETTER IF YOU LIMITED YOUR DRINKING.
I DON'T WISH TO BE A PELOSI, BUT YOU ARE MY ASSISTANT AND I MAY HAVE NEED OF YOU FROM TIME TO TIME.
GOTCHA BOSS. I'LL STAY SOBER ... WELL, MOSTLY.
AND IF YOU NEED ME, JUST CALL ME ON OUR DIRECT LINE.
AT LEAST PLEASE JOIN ME FOR DINNER AT 1900, IN MY STATEROOM, WILL YOU?
STILL PLAYING HERMIT? SUIT YOURSELF.
AFTER WHAT WE'VE BEEN THROUGH, I'M LOOKING FORWARD TO A RELAXING 3-WEEK CRUISE.

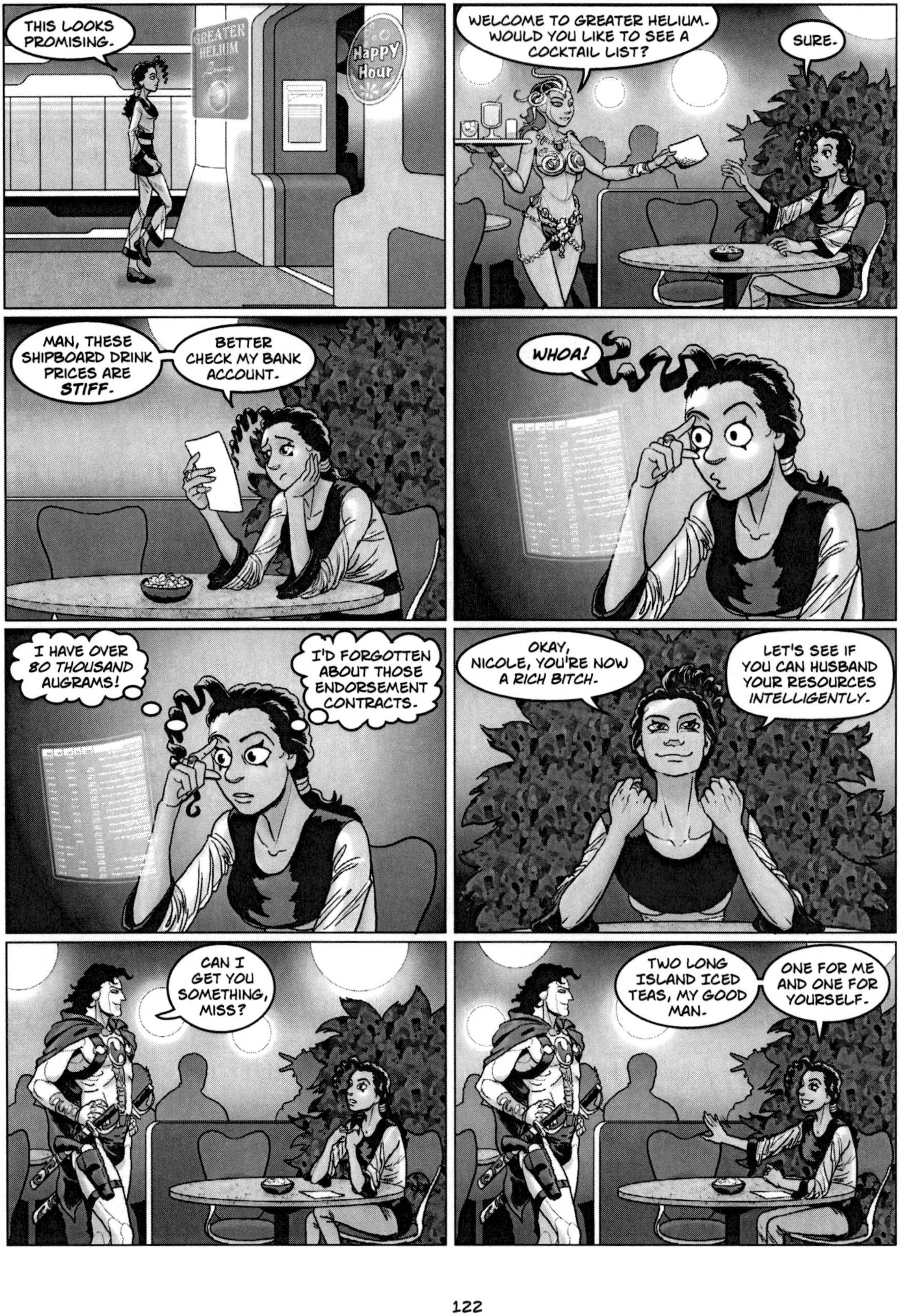
THIS LOOKS PROMISING.
GREATER HELIUM
Happy Hour
WELCOME TO GREATER HELIUM. WOULD YOU LIKE TO SEE A COCKTAIL LIST?
SURE.
MAN, THESE SHIPBOARD DRINK PRICES ARE STIFF.
BETTER CHECK MY BANK ACCOUNT.
WHOA!
I HAVE OVER 80 THOUSAND AUGRAMS!
I'D FORGOTTEN ABOUT THOSE ENDORSEMENT CONTRACTS.
OKAY, NICOLE, YOU'RE NOW A RICH BITCH.
LET'S SEE IF YOU CAN HUSBAND YOUR RESOURCES INTELLIGENTLY.
CAN I GET YOU SOMETHING, MISS?
TWO LONG ISLAND ICED TEAS, MY GOOD MAN.
ONE FOR ME AND ONE FOR YOURSELF.

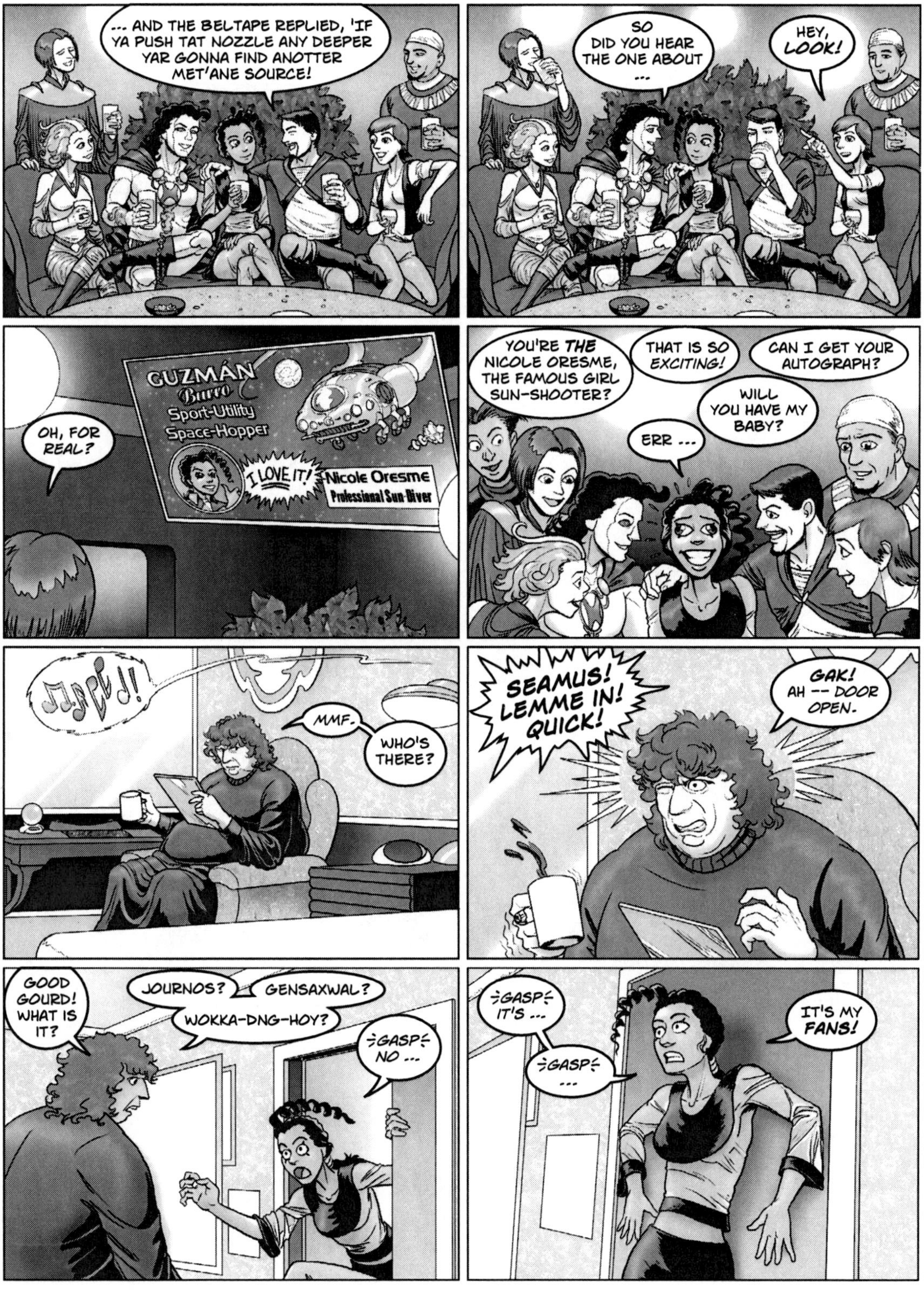
... AND THE BELTAPE REPLIED, 'IF YA PUSH TAT NOZZLE ANY DEEPER YAR GONNA FIND ANOTTER MET'ANE SOURCE!
SO DID YOU HEAR THE ONE ABOUT ...
HEY, LOOK!
OH, FOR REAL?
GUZMÁN Burro Sport-Utility Space-Hopper
I LOVE IT!
Nicole Oresme Professional Sun-Diver
YOU'RE THE NICOLE ORESME, THE FAMOUS GIRL SUN-SHOOTER?
THAT IS SO EXCITING!
CAN I GET YOUR AUTOGRAPH?
WILL YOU HAVE MY BABY?
ERR ...
MMF.
WHO'S THERE?
SEAMUS! LEMME IN! QUICK!
GAK! AH -- DOOR OPEN.
GOOD GOURD! WHAT IS IT?
JOURNOS?
GENSAXWAL?
WOKKA-DNG-HOY?
GASP NO ...
GASP IT'S ...
GASP ...
IT'S MY FANS!

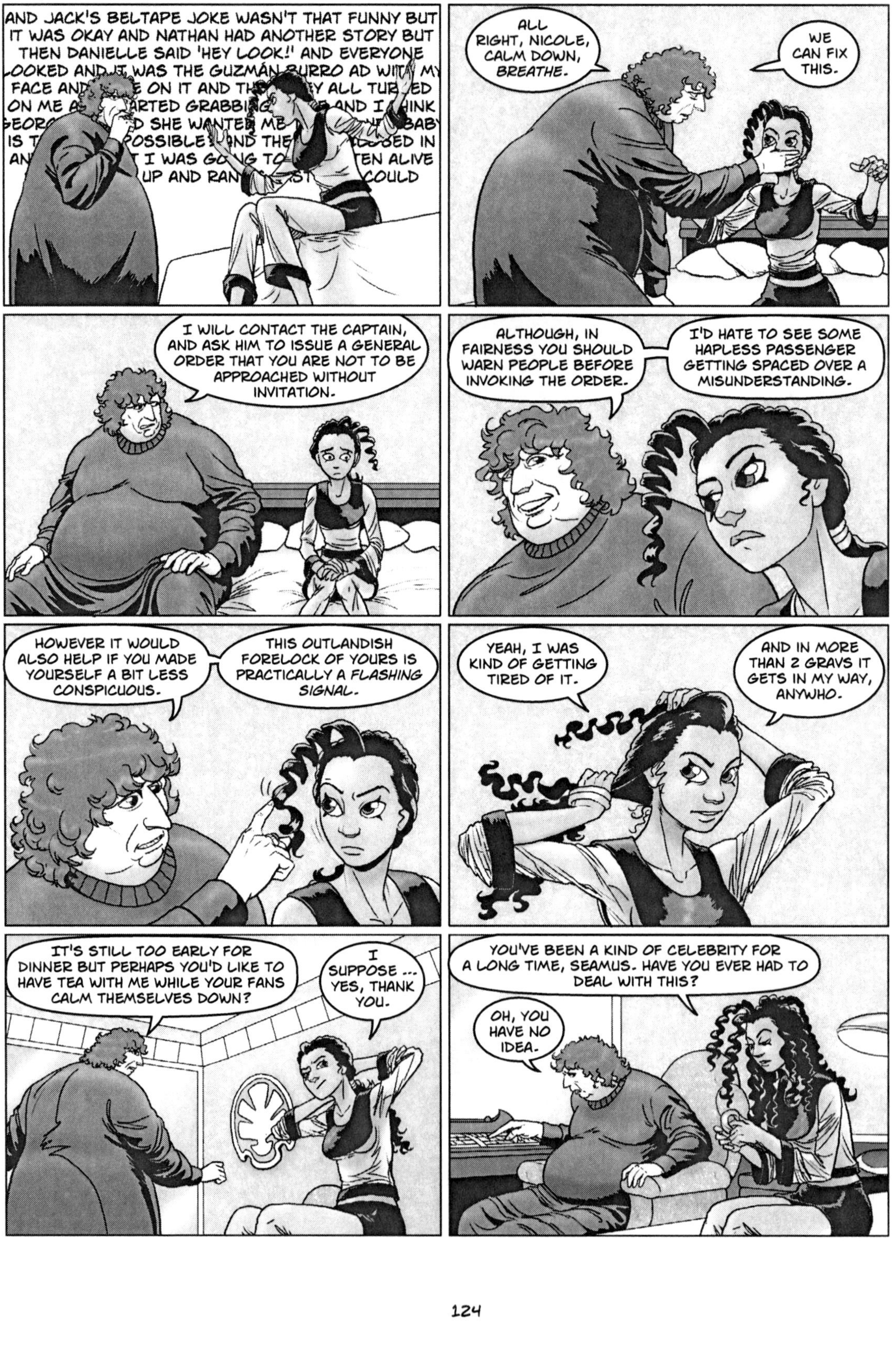
AND JACK'S BELTAPE JOKE WASN'T THAT FUNNY BUT IT WAS OKAY AND NATHAN HAD ANOTHER STORY BUT THEN DANIELLE SAID 'HEY LOOK!' AND EVERYONE LOOKED AND IT WAS THE GUZMÁN BURRO AD WITH MY FACE AND ... ON IT AND TH... ALL TUR...ED ON ME A... ARTED GRABBING ... AND I ... HINK ... D SHE WANTED ME ... BABY IS ... POSSIBLE! AND THE ... ED IN ... I WAS GOING TO ... TEN ALIVE ... UP AND RAN ... COULD
ALL RIGHT, NICOLE, CALM DOWN, BREATHE.
WE CAN FIX THIS.
I WILL CONTACT THE CAPTAIN, AND ASK HIM TO ISSUE A GENERAL ORDER THAT YOU ARE NOT TO BE APPROACHED WITHOUT INVITATION.
ALTHOUGH, IN FAIRNESS YOU SHOULD WARN PEOPLE BEFORE INVOKING THE ORDER.
I'D HATE TO SEE SOME HAPLESS PASSENGER GETTING SPACED OVER A MISUNDERSTANDING.
HOWEVER IT WOULD ALSO HELP IF YOU MADE YOURSELF A BIT LESS CONSPICUOUS.
THIS OUTLANDISH FORELOCK OF YOURS IS PRACTICALLY A FLASHING SIGNAL.
YEAH, I WAS KIND OF GETTING TIRED OF IT.
AND IN MORE THAN 2 GRAVS IT GETS IN MY WAY, ANYWHO.
IT'S STILL TOO EARLY FOR DINNER BUT PERHAPS YOU'D LIKE TO HAVE TEA WITH ME WHILE YOUR FANS CALM THEMSELVES DOWN?
I SUPPOSE ... YES, THANK YOU.
YOU'VE BEEN A KIND OF CELEBRITY FOR A LONG TIME, SEAMUS. HAVE YOU EVER HAD TO DEAL WITH THIS?
OH, YOU HAVE NO IDEA.

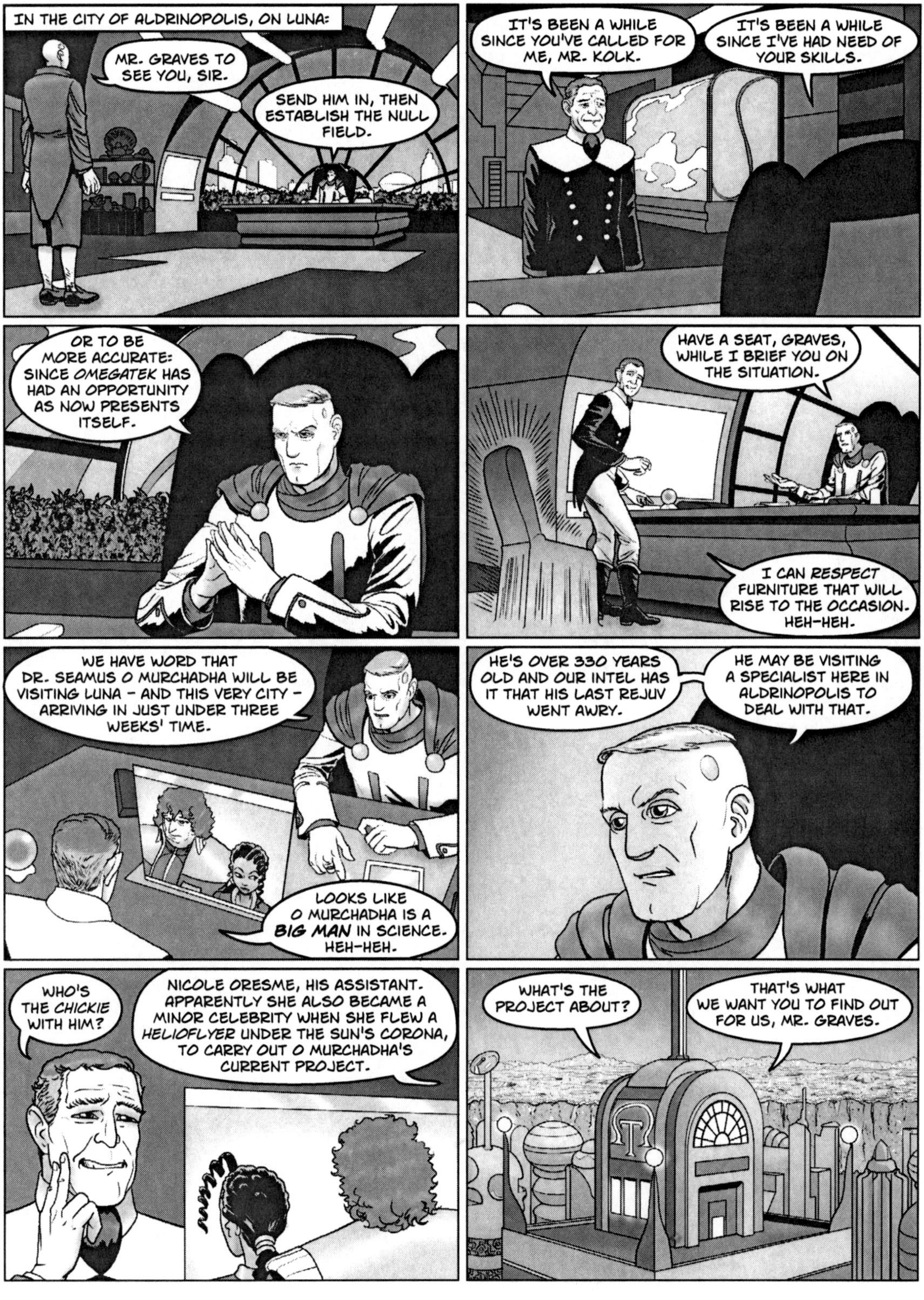
IN THE CITY OF ALDRINOPOLIS, ON LUNA:
MR. GRAVES TO SEE YOU, SIR.
SEND HIM IN, THEN ESTABLISH THE NULL FIELD.
IT'S BEEN A WHILE SINCE YOU'VE CALLED FOR ME, MR. KOLK.
IT'S BEEN A WHILE SINCE I'VE HAD NEED OF YOUR SKILLS.
OR TO BE MORE ACCURATE: SINCE OMEGATEK HAS HAD AN OPPORTUNITY AS NOW PRESENTS ITSELF.
HAVE A SEAT, GRAVES, WHILE I BRIEF YOU ON THE SITUATION.
I CAN RESPECT FURNITURE THAT WILL RISE TO THE OCCASION. HEH-HEH.
WE HAVE WORD THAT DR. SEAMUS O MURCHADHA WILL BE VISITING LUNA - AND THIS VERY CITY - ARRIVING IN JUST UNDER THREE WEEKS' TIME.
LOOKS LIKE O MURCHADHA IS A BIG MAN IN SCIENCE. HEH-HEH.
HE'S OVER 330 YEARS OLD AND OUR INTEL HAS IT THAT HIS LAST REJUV WENT AWRY.
HE MAY BE VISITING A SPECIALIST HERE IN ALDRINOPOLIS TO DEAL WITH THAT.
WHO'S THE CHICKIE WITH HIM?
NICOLE ORESME, HIS ASSISTANT. APPARENTLY SHE ALSO BECAME A MINOR CELEBRITY WHEN SHE FLEW A HELIOFLYER UNDER THE SUN'S CORONA, TO CARRY OUT O MURCHADHA'S CURRENT PROJECT.
WHAT'S THE PROJECT ABOUT?
THAT'S WHAT WE WANT YOU TO FIND OUT FOR US, MR. GRAVES.

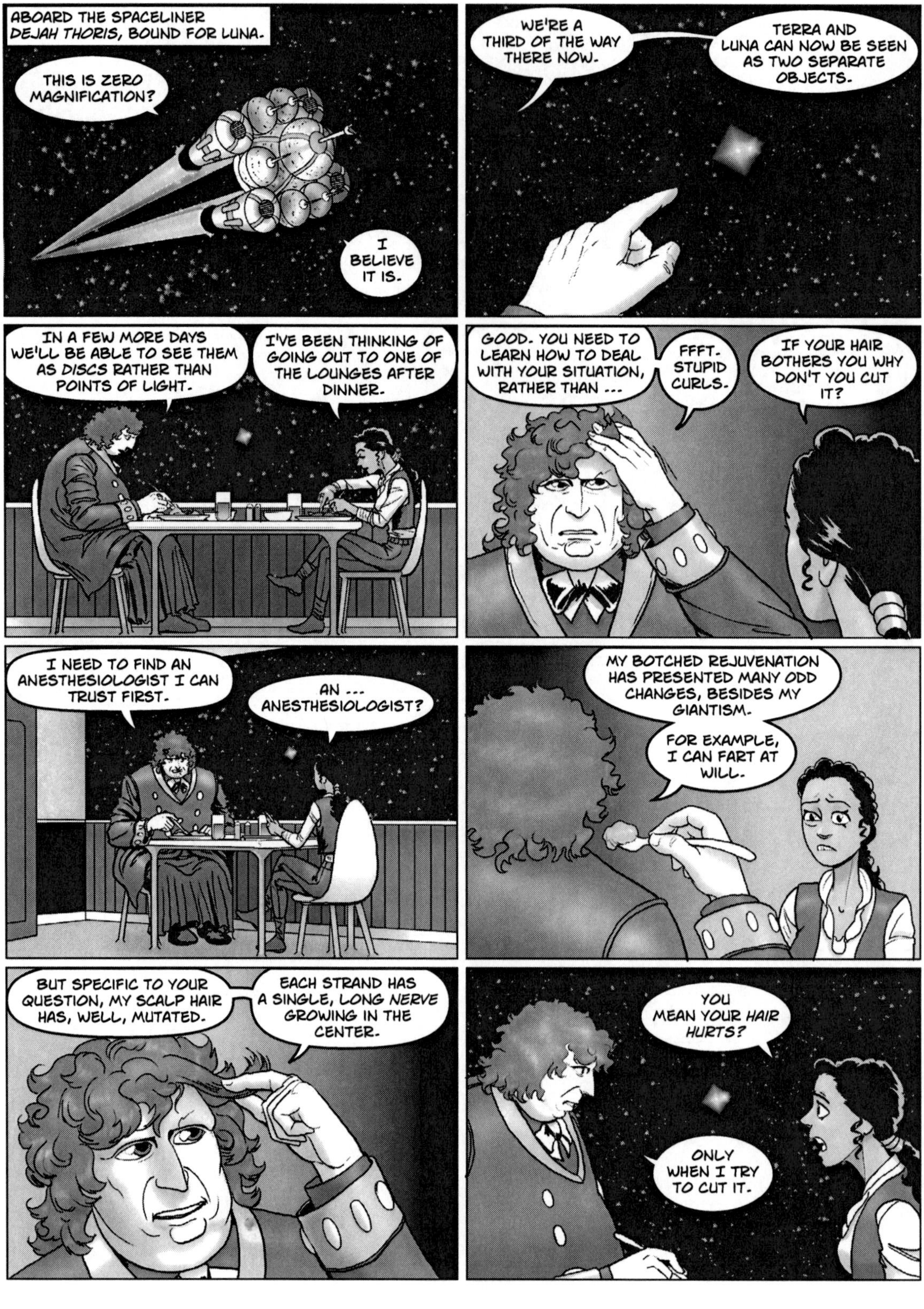
ABOARD THE SPACELINER *DEJAH THORIS*, BOUND FOR LUNA.
THIS IS ZERO MAGNIFICATION?
I BELIEVE IT IS.
WE'RE A THIRD OF THE WAY THERE NOW.
TERRA AND LUNA CAN NOW BE SEEN AS TWO SEPARATE OBJECTS.
IN A FEW MORE DAYS WE'LL BE ABLE TO SEE THEM AS *DISCS* RATHER THAN POINTS OF LIGHT.
I'VE BEEN THINKING OF GOING OUT TO ONE OF THE LOUNGES AFTER DINNER.
GOOD. YOU NEED TO LEARN HOW TO DEAL WITH YOUR SITUATION, RATHER THAN ...
FFFT. STUPID CURLS.
IF YOUR HAIR BOTHERS YOU WHY DON'T YOU CUT IT?
I NEED TO FIND AN ANESTHESIOLOGIST I CAN TRUST FIRST.
AN ... ANESTHESIOLOGIST?
MY BOTCHED REJUVENATION HAS PRESENTED MANY ODD CHANGES, BESIDES MY GIANTISM.
FOR EXAMPLE, I CAN FART AT WILL.
BUT SPECIFIC TO YOUR QUESTION, MY SCALP HAIR HAS, WELL, MUTATED.
EACH STRAND HAS A SINGLE, LONG *NERVE* GROWING IN THE CENTER.
YOU MEAN YOUR HAIR *HURTS?*
ONLY WHEN I TRY TO CUT IT.

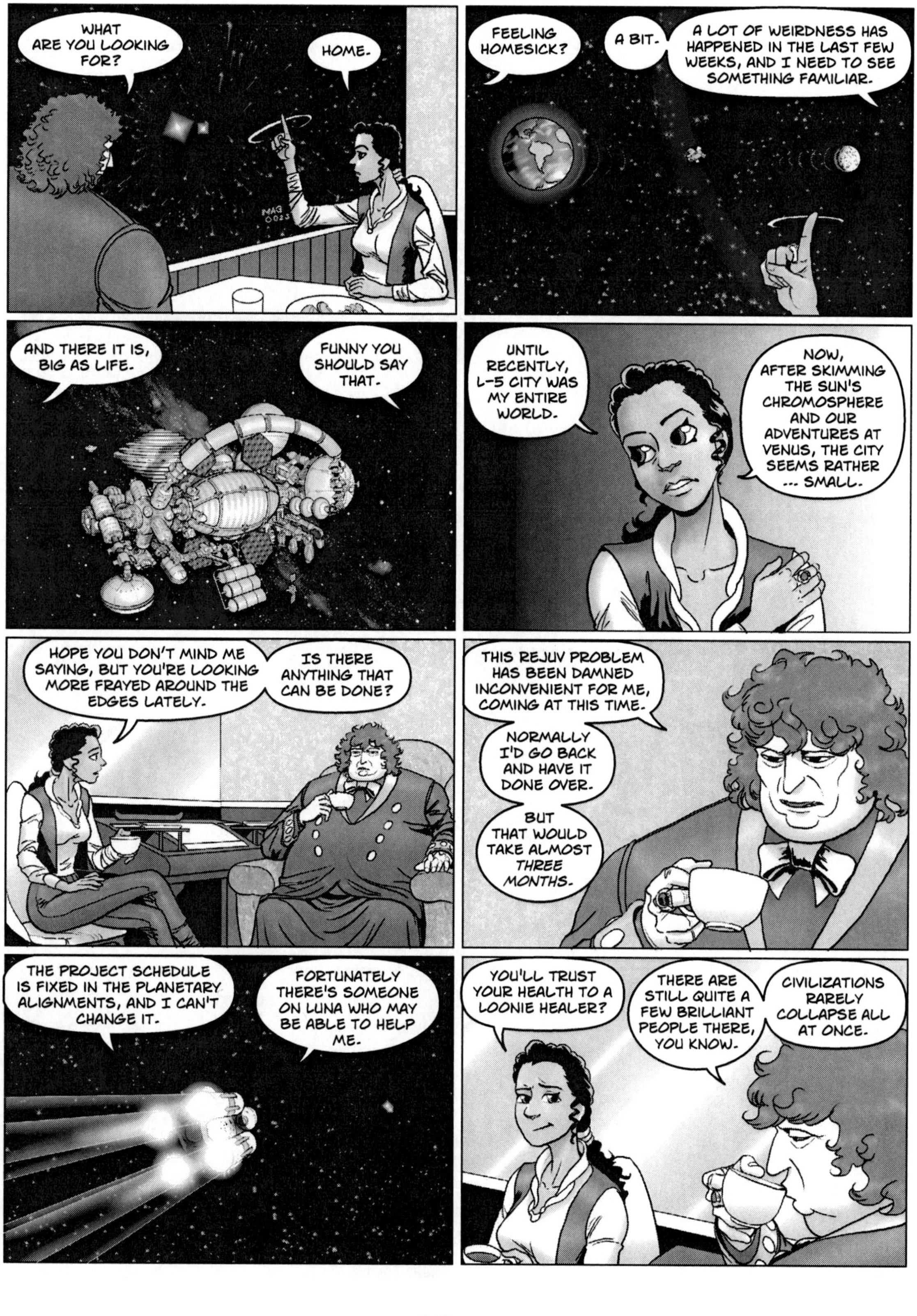
WHAT ARE YOU LOOKING FOR?
HOME.
FEELING HOMESICK?
A BIT.
A LOT OF WEIRDNESS HAS HAPPENED IN THE LAST FEW WEEKS, AND I NEED TO SEE SOMETHING FAMILIAR.
AND THERE IT IS, BIG AS LIFE.
FUNNY YOU SHOULD SAY THAT.
UNTIL RECENTLY, L-5 CITY WAS MY ENTIRE WORLD.
NOW, AFTER SKIMMING THE SUN'S CHROMOSPHERE AND OUR ADVENTURES AT VENUS, THE CITY SEEMS RATHER ... SMALL.
HOPE YOU DON'T MIND ME SAYING, BUT YOU'RE LOOKING MORE FRAYED AROUND THE EDGES LATELY.
IS THERE ANYTHING THAT CAN BE DONE?
THIS REJUV PROBLEM HAS BEEN DAMNED INCONVENIENT FOR ME, COMING AT THIS TIME.
NORMALLY I'D GO BACK AND HAVE IT DONE OVER.
BUT THAT WOULD TAKE ALMOST *THREE MONTHS*.
THE PROJECT SCHEDULE IS FIXED IN THE PLANETARY ALIGNMENTS, AND I CAN'T CHANGE IT.
FORTUNATELY THERE'S SOMEONE ON LUNA WHO MAY BE ABLE TO HELP ME.
YOU'LL TRUST YOUR HEALTH TO A LOONIE HEALER?
THERE ARE STILL QUITE A FEW BRILLIANT PEOPLE THERE, YOU KNOW.
CIVILIZATIONS RARELY COLLAPSE ALL AT ONCE.

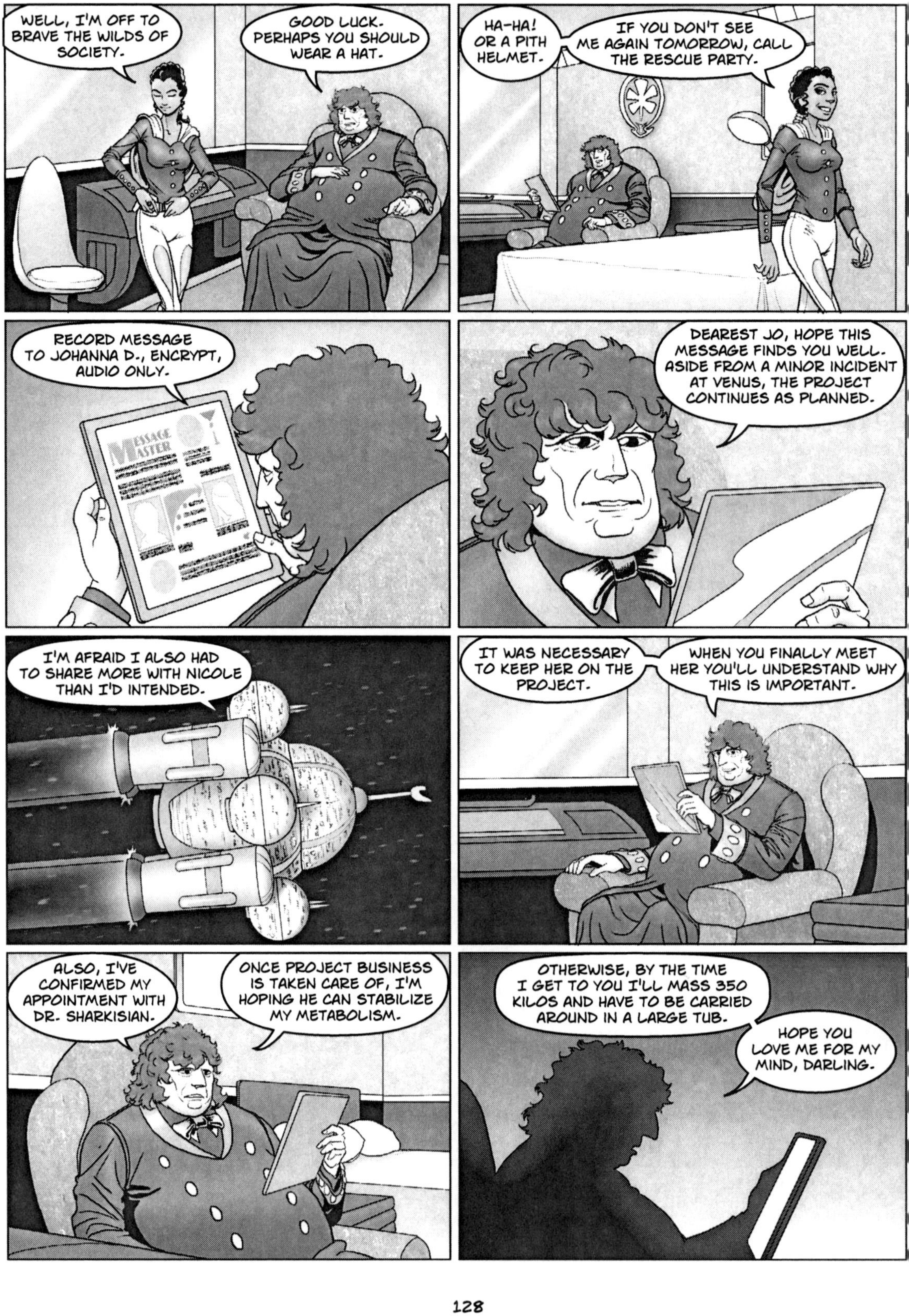
WELL, I'M OFF TO BRAVE THE WILDS OF SOCIETY.
GOOD LUCK. PERHAPS YOU SHOULD WEAR A HAT.
HA-HA! OR A PITH HELMET.
IF YOU DON'T SEE ME AGAIN TOMORROW, CALL THE RESCUE PARTY.
RECORD MESSAGE TO JOHANNA D., ENCRYPT, AUDIO ONLY.
MESSAGE MASTER
DEAREST JO, HOPE THIS MESSAGE FINDS YOU WELL. ASIDE FROM A MINOR INCIDENT AT VENUS, THE PROJECT CONTINUES AS PLANNED.
I'M AFRAID I ALSO HAD TO SHARE MORE WITH NICOLE THAN I'D INTENDED.
IT WAS NECESSARY TO KEEP HER ON THE PROJECT.
WHEN YOU FINALLY MEET HER YOU'LL UNDERSTAND WHY THIS IS IMPORTANT.
ALSO, I'VE CONFIRMED MY APPOINTMENT WITH DR. SHARKISIAN.
ONCE PROJECT BUSINESS IS TAKEN CARE OF, I'M HOPING HE CAN STABILIZE MY METABOLISM.
OTHERWISE, BY THE TIME I GET TO YOU I'LL MASS 350 KILOS AND HAVE TO BE CARRIED AROUND IN A LARGE TUB.
HOPE YOU LOVE ME FOR MY MIND, DARLING.

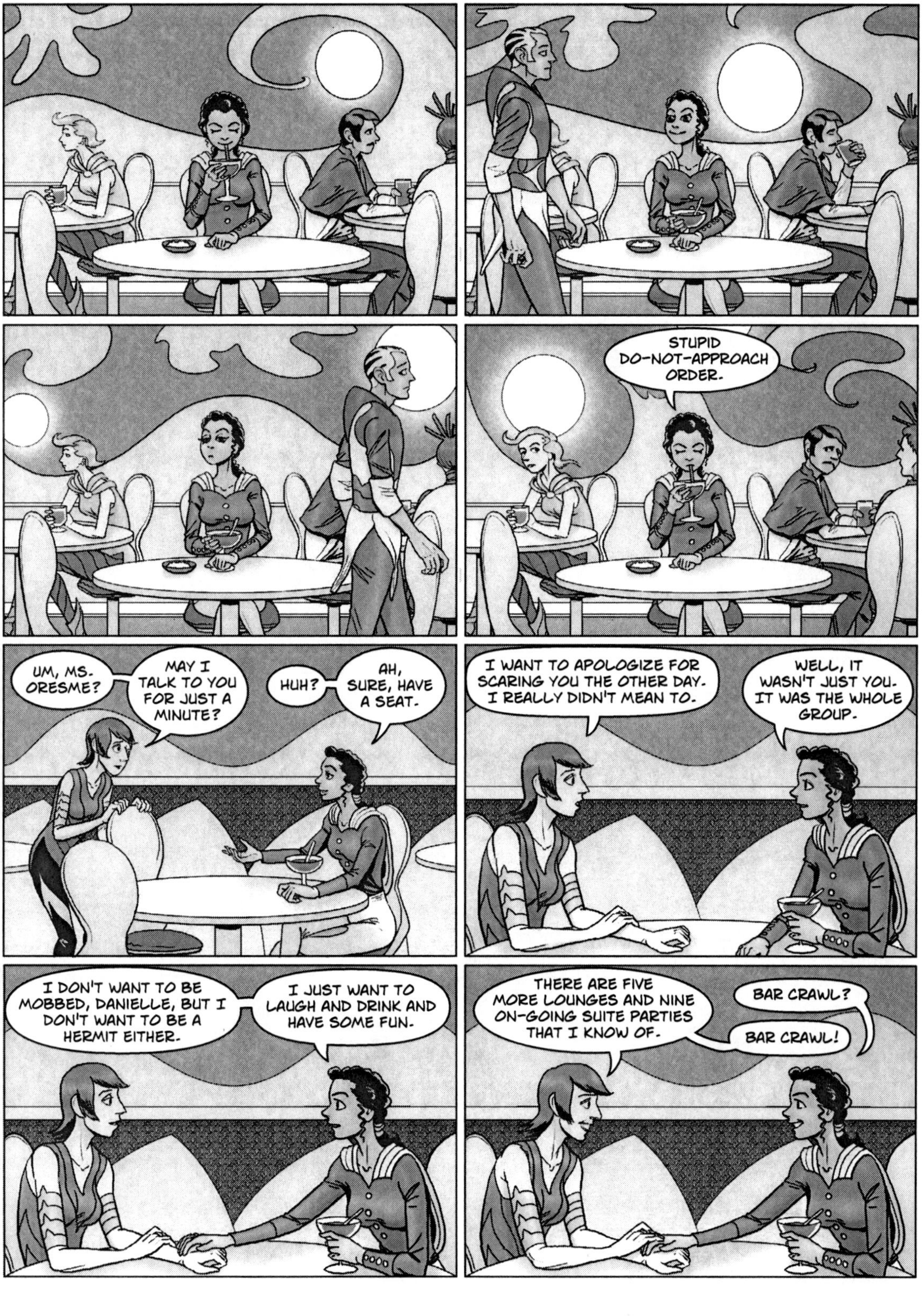
STUPID DO-NOT-APPROACH ORDER.
UM, MS. ORESME?
MAY I TALK TO YOU FOR JUST A MINUTE?
HUH?
AH, SURE, HAVE A SEAT.
I WANT TO APOLOGIZE FOR SCARING YOU THE OTHER DAY. I REALLY DIDN'T MEAN TO.
WELL, IT WASN'T JUST YOU. IT WAS THE WHOLE GROUP.
I DON'T WANT TO BE MOBBED, DANIELLE, BUT I DON'T WANT TO BE A HERMIT EITHER.
I JUST WANT TO LAUGH AND DRINK AND HAVE SOME FUN.
THERE ARE FIVE MORE LOUNGES AND NINE ON-GOING SUITE PARTIES THAT I KNOW OF.
BAR CRAWL?
BAR CRAWL!

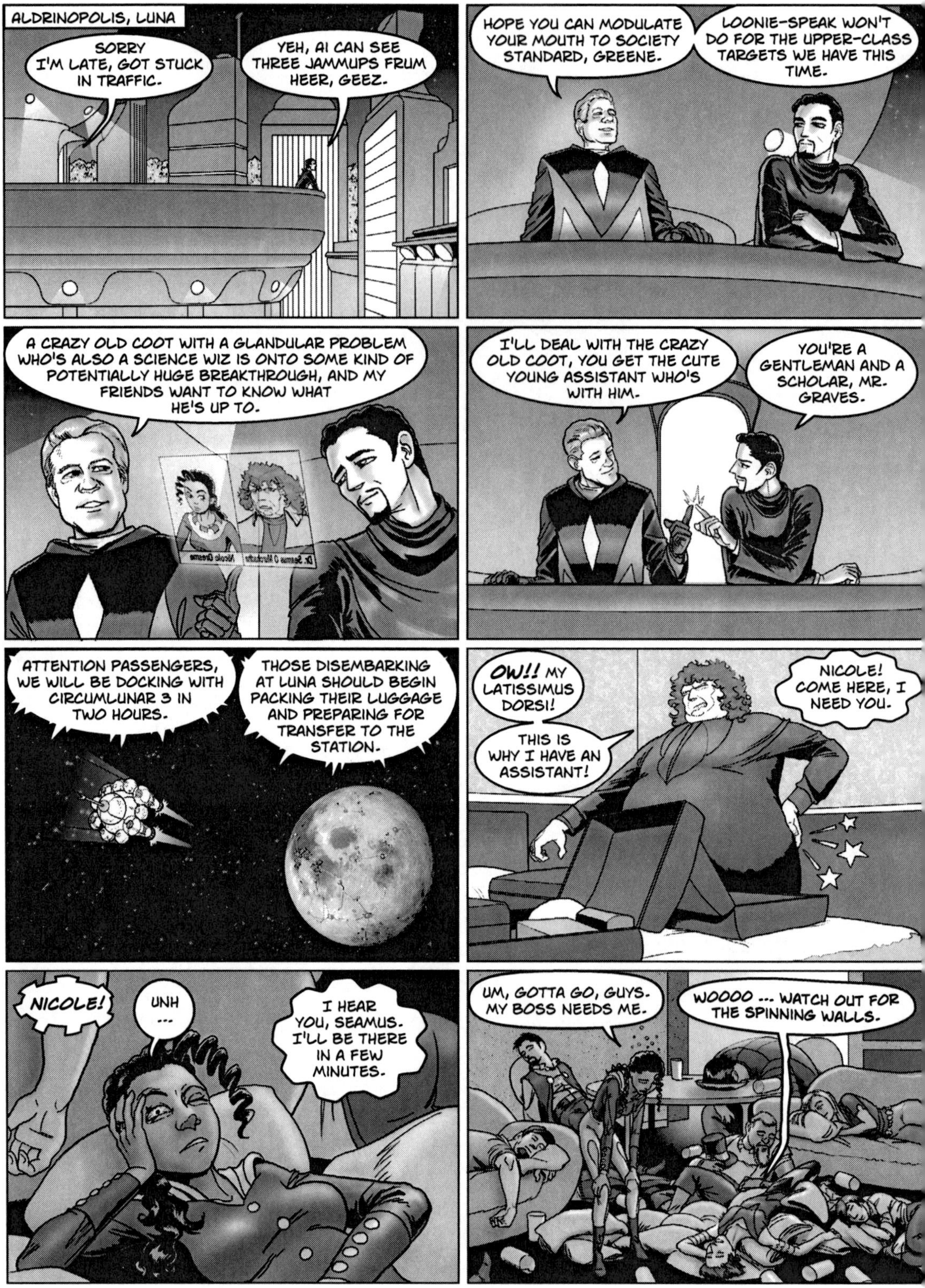
ALDRINOPOLIS, LUNA
SORRY I'M LATE, GOT STUCK IN TRAFFIC.
YEH, AI CAN SEE THREE JAMMUPS FRUM HEER, GEEZ.
HOPE YOU CAN MODULATE YOUR MOUTH TO SOCIETY STANDARD, GREENE.
LOONIE-SPEAK WON'T DO FOR THE UPPER-CLASS TARGETS WE HAVE THIS TIME.
A CRAZY OLD COOT WITH A GLANDULAR PROBLEM WHO'S ALSO A SCIENCE WIZ IS ONTO SOME KIND OF POTENTIALLY HUGE BREAKTHROUGH, AND MY FRIENDS WANT TO KNOW WHAT HE'S UP TO.
I'LL DEAL WITH THE CRAZY OLD COOT, YOU GET THE CUTE YOUNG ASSISTANT WHO'S WITH HIM.
YOU'RE A GENTLEMAN AND A SCHOLAR, MR. GRAVES.
ATTENTION PASSENGERS, WE WILL BE DOCKING WITH CIRCUMLUNAR 3 IN TWO HOURS.
THOSE DISEMBARKING AT LUNA SHOULD BEGIN PACKING THEIR LUGGAGE AND PREPARING FOR TRANSFER TO THE STATION.
OW!! MY LATISSIMUS DORSI!
THIS IS WHY I HAVE AN ASSISTANT!
NICOLE! COME HERE, I NEED YOU.
NICOLE!
UNH ...
I HEAR YOU, SEAMUS. I'LL BE THERE IN A FEW MINUTES.
UM, GOTTA GO, GUYS. MY BOSS NEEDS ME.
WOOOO ... WATCH OUT FOR THE SPINNING WALLS.

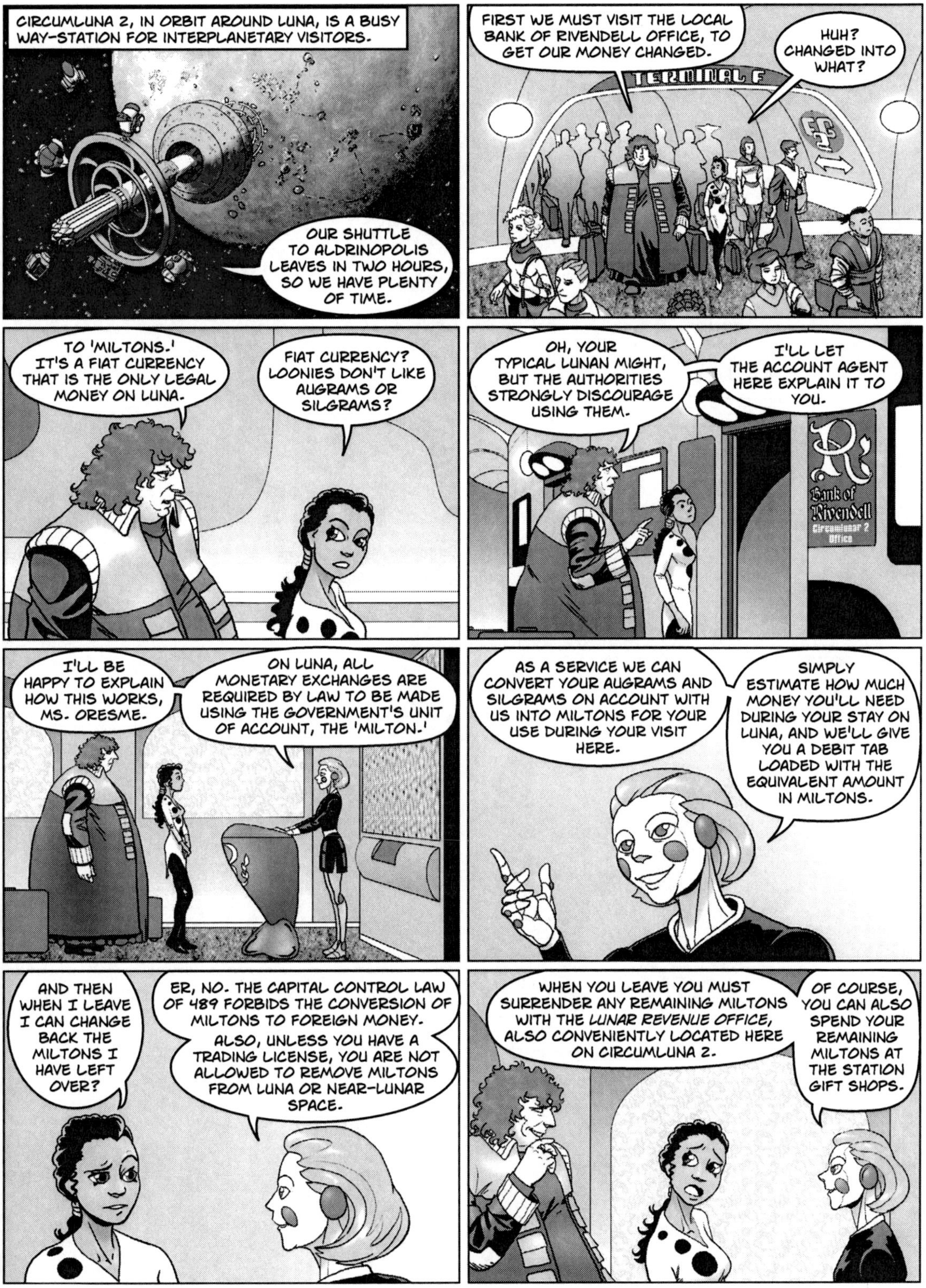
CIRCUMLUNA 2, IN ORBIT AROUND LUNA, IS A BUSY WAY-STATION FOR INTERPLANETARY VISITORS.
OUR SHUTTLE TO ALDRINOPOLIS LEAVES IN TWO HOURS, SO WE HAVE PLENTY OF TIME.
FIRST WE MUST VISIT THE LOCAL BANK OF RIVENDELL OFFICE, TO GET OUR MONEY CHANGED.
HUH? CHANGED INTO WHAT?
TERMINAL F
TO 'MILTONS.' IT'S A FIAT CURRENCY THAT IS THE ONLY LEGAL MONEY ON LUNA.
FIAT CURRENCY? LOONIES DON'T LIKE AUGRAMS OR SILGRAMS?
OH, YOUR TYPICAL LUNAN MIGHT, BUT THE AUTHORITIES STRONGLY DISCOURAGE USING THEM.
I'LL LET THE ACCOUNT AGENT HERE EXPLAIN IT TO YOU.
Bank of Rivendell
Circumlunar 2 Office
I'LL BE HAPPY TO EXPLAIN HOW THIS WORKS, MS. ORESME.
ON LUNA, ALL MONETARY EXCHANGES ARE REQUIRED BY LAW TO BE MADE USING THE GOVERNMENT'S UNIT OF ACCOUNT, THE 'MILTON.'
AS A SERVICE WE CAN CONVERT YOUR AUGRAMS AND SILGRAMS ON ACCOUNT WITH US INTO MILTONS FOR YOUR USE DURING YOUR VISIT HERE.
SIMPLY ESTIMATE HOW MUCH MONEY YOU'LL NEED DURING YOUR STAY ON LUNA, AND WE'LL GIVE YOU A DEBIT TAB LOADED WITH THE EQUIVALENT AMOUNT IN MILTONS.
AND THEN WHEN I LEAVE I CAN CHANGE BACK THE MILTONS I HAVE LEFT OVER?
ER, NO. THE CAPITAL CONTROL LAW OF 489 FORBIDS THE CONVERSION OF MILTONS TO FOREIGN MONEY.
ALSO, UNLESS YOU HAVE A TRADING LICENSE, YOU ARE NOT ALLOWED TO REMOVE MILTONS FROM LUNA OR NEAR-LUNAR SPACE.
WHEN YOU LEAVE YOU MUST SURRENDER ANY REMAINING MILTONS WITH THE *LUNAR REVENUE OFFICE*, ALSO CONVENIENTLY LOCATED HERE ON CIRCUMLUNA 2.
OF COURSE, YOU CAN ALSO SPEND YOUR REMAINING MILTONS AT THE STATION GIFT SHOPS.

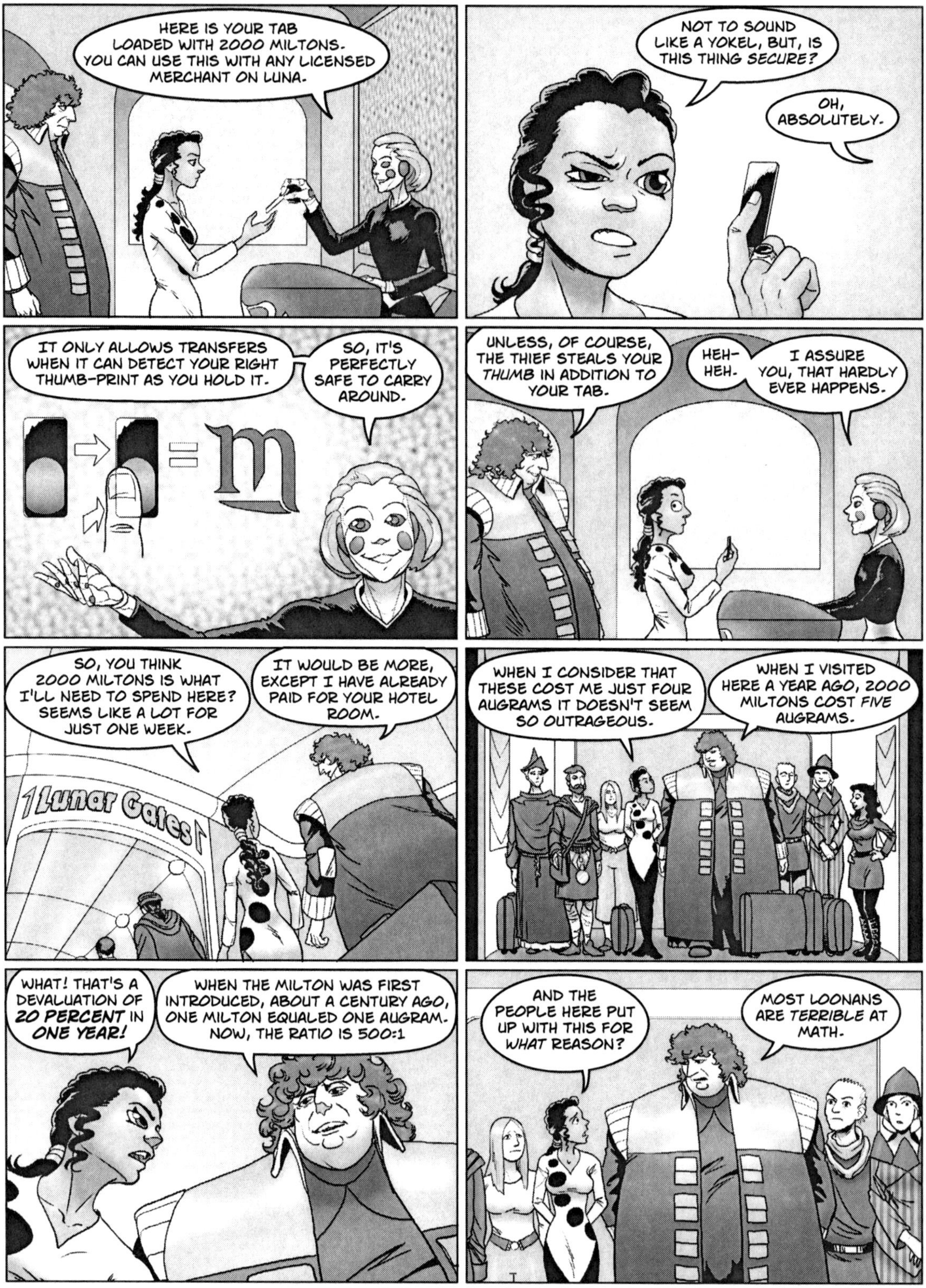
HERE IS YOUR TAB LOADED WITH 2000 MILTONS. YOU CAN USE THIS WITH ANY LICENSED MERCHANT ON LUNA.
NOT TO SOUND LIKE A YOKEL, BUT, IS THIS THING SECURE?
OH, ABSOLUTELY.
IT ONLY ALLOWS TRANSFERS WHEN IT CAN DETECT YOUR RIGHT THUMB-PRINT AS YOU HOLD IT.
SO, IT'S PERFECTLY SAFE TO CARRY AROUND.
UNLESS, OF COURSE, THE THIEF STEALS YOUR THUMB IN ADDITION TO YOUR TAB.
HEH-HEH.
I ASSURE YOU, THAT HARDLY EVER HAPPENS.
SO, YOU THINK 2000 MILTONS IS WHAT I'LL NEED TO SPEND HERE? SEEMS LIKE A LOT FOR JUST ONE WEEK.
IT WOULD BE MORE, EXCEPT I HAVE ALREADY PAID FOR YOUR HOTEL ROOM.
Lunar Gates
WHEN I CONSIDER THAT THESE COST ME JUST FOUR AUGRAMS IT DOESN'T SEEM SO OUTRAGEOUS.
WHEN I VISITED HERE A YEAR AGO, 2000 MILTONS COST FIVE AUGRAMS.
WHAT! THAT'S A DEVALUATION OF 20 PERCENT IN ONE YEAR!
WHEN THE MILTON WAS FIRST INTRODUCED, ABOUT A CENTURY AGO, ONE MILTON EQUALED ONE AUGRAM. NOW, THE RATIO IS 500:1
AND THE PEOPLE HERE PUT UP WITH THIS FOR WHAT REASON?
MOST LOONANS ARE TERRIBLE AT MATH.

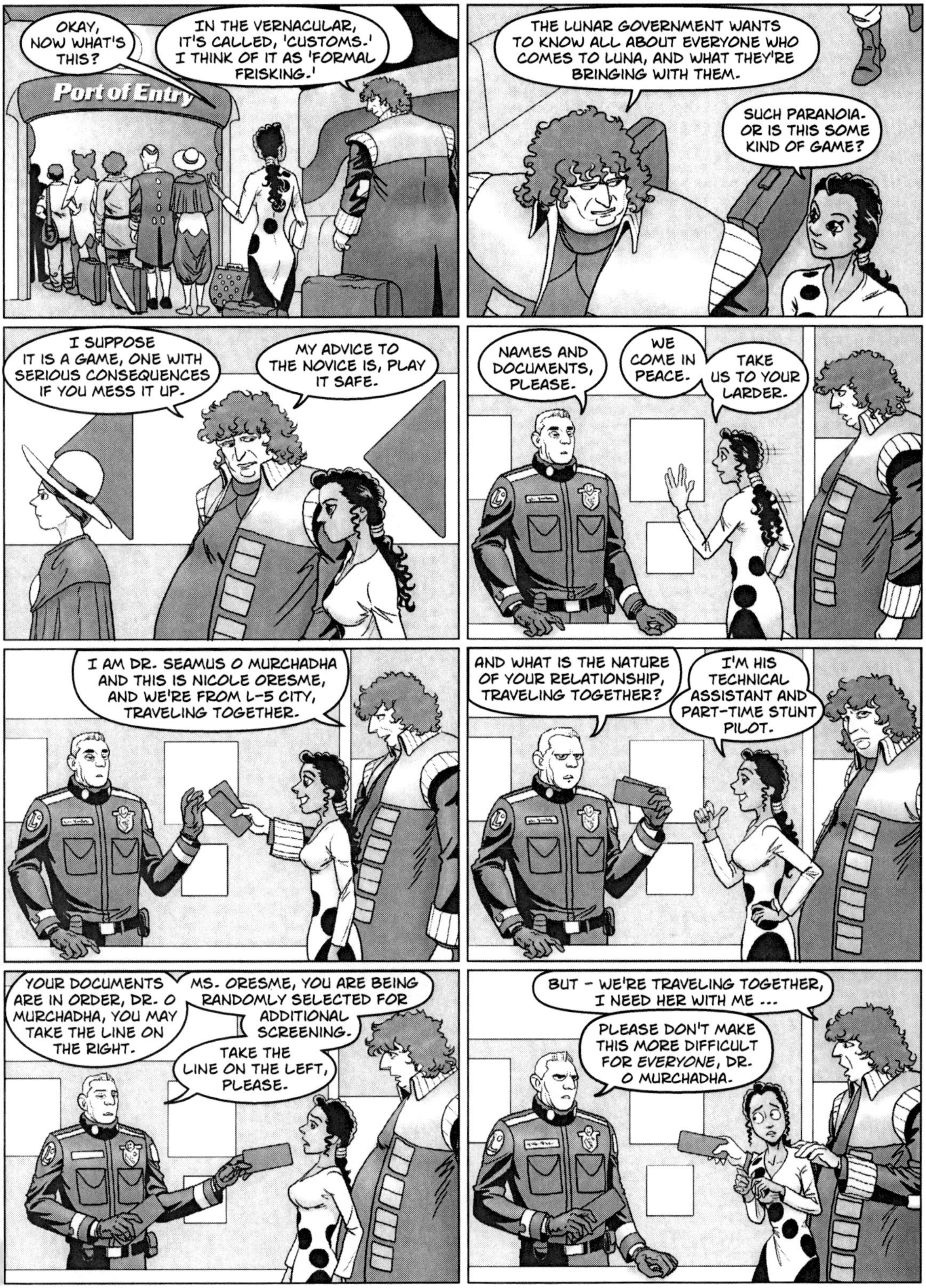
OKAY, NOW WHAT'S THIS?
IN THE VERNACULAR, IT'S CALLED, 'CUSTOMS.' I THINK OF IT AS 'FORMAL FRISKING.'
Port of Entry
THE LUNAR GOVERNMENT WANTS TO KNOW ALL ABOUT EVERYONE WHO COMES TO LUNA, AND WHAT THEY'RE BRINGING WITH THEM.
SUCH PARANOIA. OR IS THIS SOME KIND OF GAME?
I SUPPOSE IT IS A GAME, ONE WITH SERIOUS CONSEQUENCES IF YOU MESS IT UP.
MY ADVICE TO THE NOVICE IS, PLAY IT SAFE.
NAMES AND DOCUMENTS, PLEASE.
WE COME IN PEACE.
TAKE US TO YOUR LARDER.
I AM DR. SEAMUS O MURCHADHA AND THIS IS NICOLE ORESME, AND WE'RE FROM L-5 CITY, TRAVELING TOGETHER.
AND WHAT IS THE NATURE OF YOUR RELATIONSHIP, TRAVELING TOGETHER?
I'M HIS TECHNICAL ASSISTANT AND PART-TIME STUNT PILOT.
YOUR DOCUMENTS ARE IN ORDER, DR. O MURCHADHA, YOU MAY TAKE THE LINE ON THE RIGHT.
MS. ORESME, YOU ARE BEING RANDOMLY SELECTED FOR ADDITIONAL SCREENING.
TAKE THE LINE ON THE LEFT, PLEASE.
BUT - WE'RE TRAVELING TOGETHER, I NEED HER WITH ME ...
PLEASE DON'T MAKE THIS MORE DIFFICULT FOR EVERYONE, DR. O MURCHADHA.

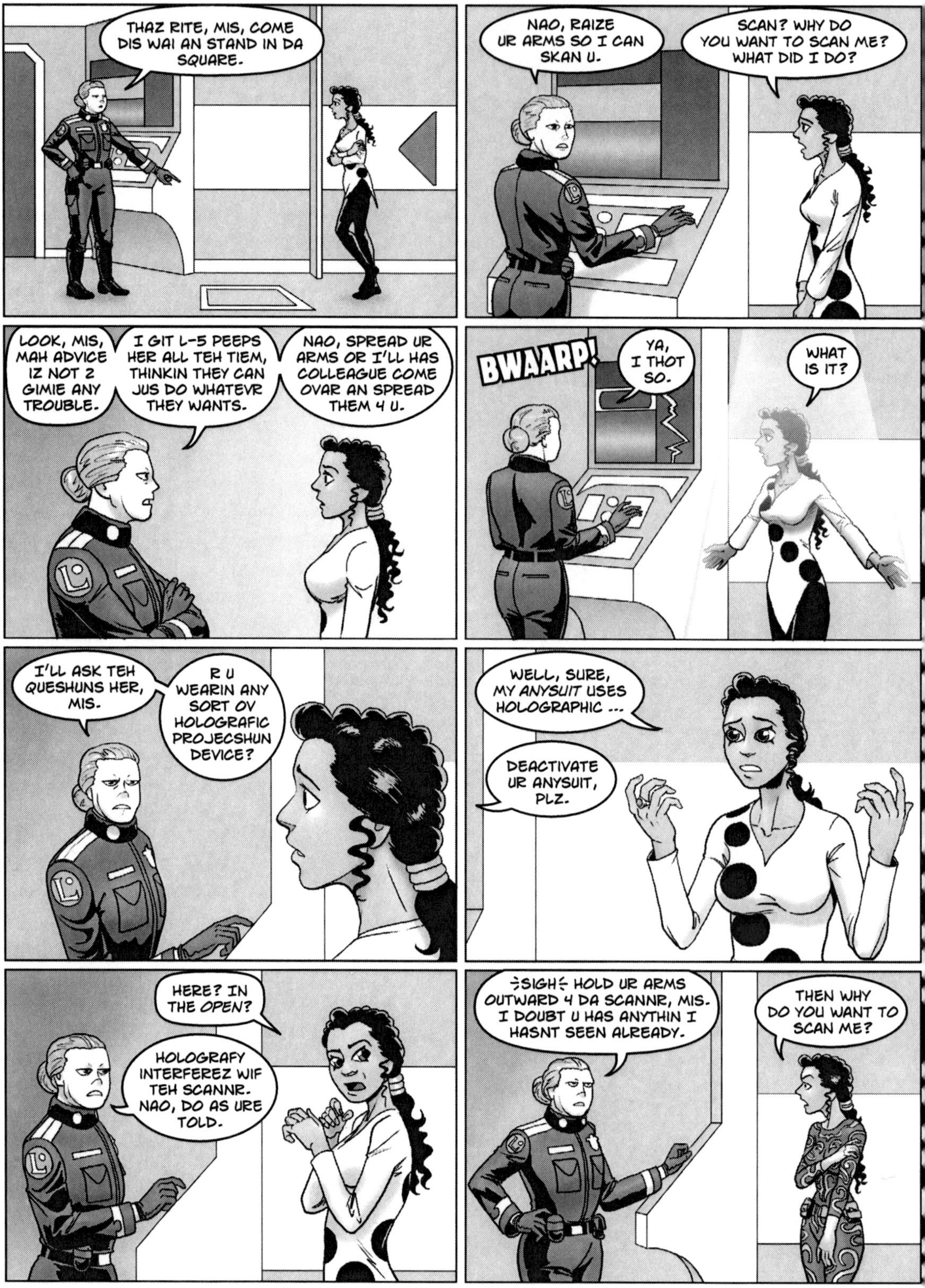
THAZ RITE, MIS, COME DIS WAI AN STAND IN DA SQUARE.
NAO, RAIZE UR ARMS SO I CAN SKAN U.
SCAN? WHY DO YOU WANT TO SCAN ME? WHAT DID I DO?
LOOK, MIS, MAH ADVICE IZ NOT 2 GIMIE ANY TROUBLE.
I GIT L-5 PEEPS HER ALL TEH TIEM, THINKIN THEY CAN JUS DO WHATEVR THEY WANTS.
NAO, SPREAD UR ARMS OR I'LL HAS COLLEAGUE COME OVAR AN SPREAD THEM 4 U.
BWAARP!
YA, I THOT SO.
WHAT IS IT?
I'LL ASK TEH QUESHUNS HER, MIS.
R U WEARIN ANY SORT OV HOLOGRAFIC PROJECSHUN DEVICE?
WELL, SURE, MY ANYSUIT USES HOLOGRAPHIC ...
DEACTIVATE UR ANYSUIT, PLZ.
HERE? IN THE OPEN?
HOLOGRAFY INTERFEREZ WIF TEH SCANNR. NAO, DO AS URE TOLD.
÷SIGH÷ HOLD UR ARMS OUTWARD 4 DA SCANNR, MIS. I DOUBT U HAS ANYTHIN I HASNT SEEN ALREADY.
THEN WHY DO YOU WANT TO SCAN ME?

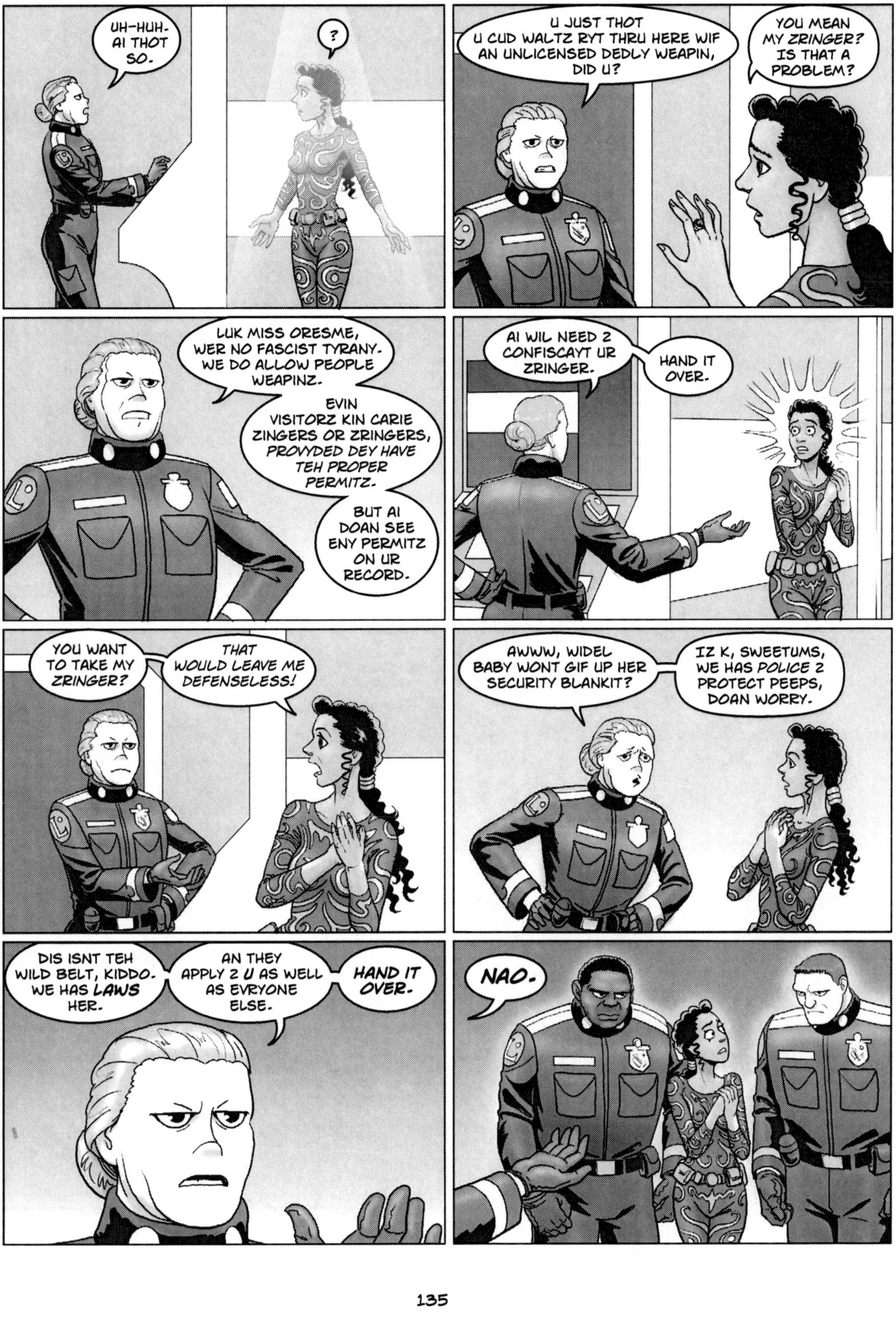
UH-HUH. AI THOT SO.
?
U JUST THOT U CUD WALTZ RYT THRU HERE WIF AN UNLICENSED DEDLY WEAPIN, DID U?
YOU MEAN MY ZRINGER? IS THAT A PROBLEM?
LUK MISS ORESME, WER NO FASCIST TYRANY. WE DO ALLOW PEOPLE WEAPINZ.
EVIN VISITORZ KIN CARIE ZINGERS OR ZRINGERS, PROVYDED DEY HAVE TEH PROPER PERMITZ.
BUT AI DOAN SEE ENY PERMITZ ON UR RECORD.
AI WIL NEED 2 CONFISCAYT UR ZRINGER.
HAND IT OVER.
YOU WANT TO TAKE MY ZRINGER?
THAT WOULD LEAVE ME DEFENSELESS!
AWWW, WIDEL BABY WONT GIF UP HER SECURITY BLANKIT?
IZ K, SWEETUMS, WE HAS POLICE 2 PROTECT PEEPS, DOAN WORRY.
DIS ISNT TEH WILD BELT, KIDDO. WE HAS LAWS HER.
AN THEY APPLY 2 U AS WELL AS EVRYONE ELSE.
HAND IT OVER.
NAO.

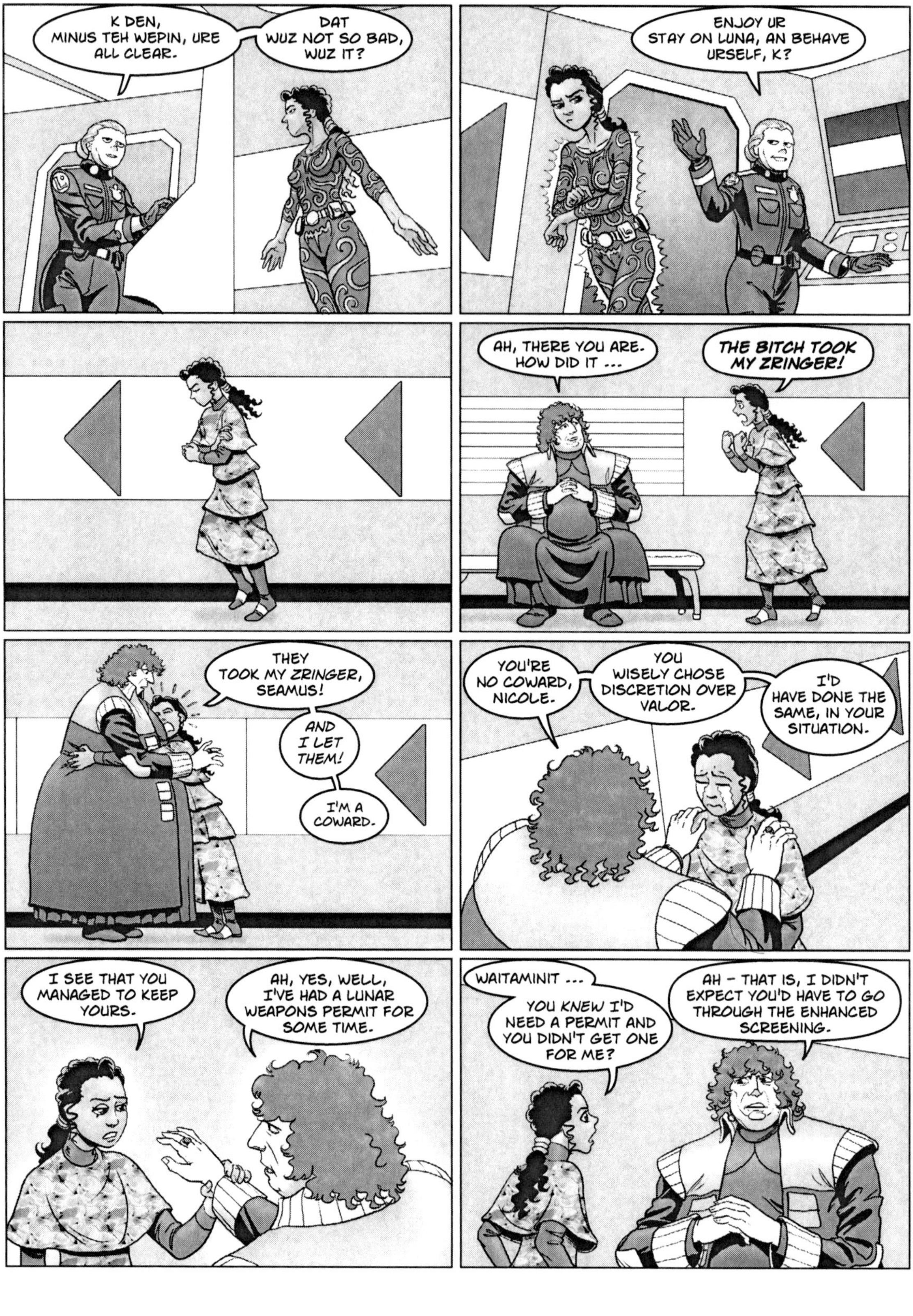
K DEN, MINUS TEH WEPIN, URE ALL CLEAR.
DAT WUZ NOT SO BAD, WUZ IT?
ENJOY UR STAY ON LUNA, AN BEHAVE URSELF, K?
AH, THERE YOU ARE. HOW DID IT ...
THE BITCH TOOK MY ZRINGER!
THEY TOOK MY ZRINGER, SEAMUS!
AND I LET THEM!
I'M A COWARD.
YOU'RE NO COWARD, NICOLE.
YOU WISELY CHOSE DISCRETION OVER VALOR.
I'D HAVE DONE THE SAME, IN YOUR SITUATION.
I SEE THAT YOU MANAGED TO KEEP YOURS.
AH, YES, WELL, I'VE HAD A LUNAR WEAPONS PERMIT FOR SOME TIME.
WAITAMINIT ...
YOU KNEW I'D NEED A PERMIT AND YOU DIDN'T GET ONE FOR ME?
AH – THAT IS, I DIDN'T EXPECT YOU'D HAVE TO GO THROUGH THE ENHANCED SCREENING.

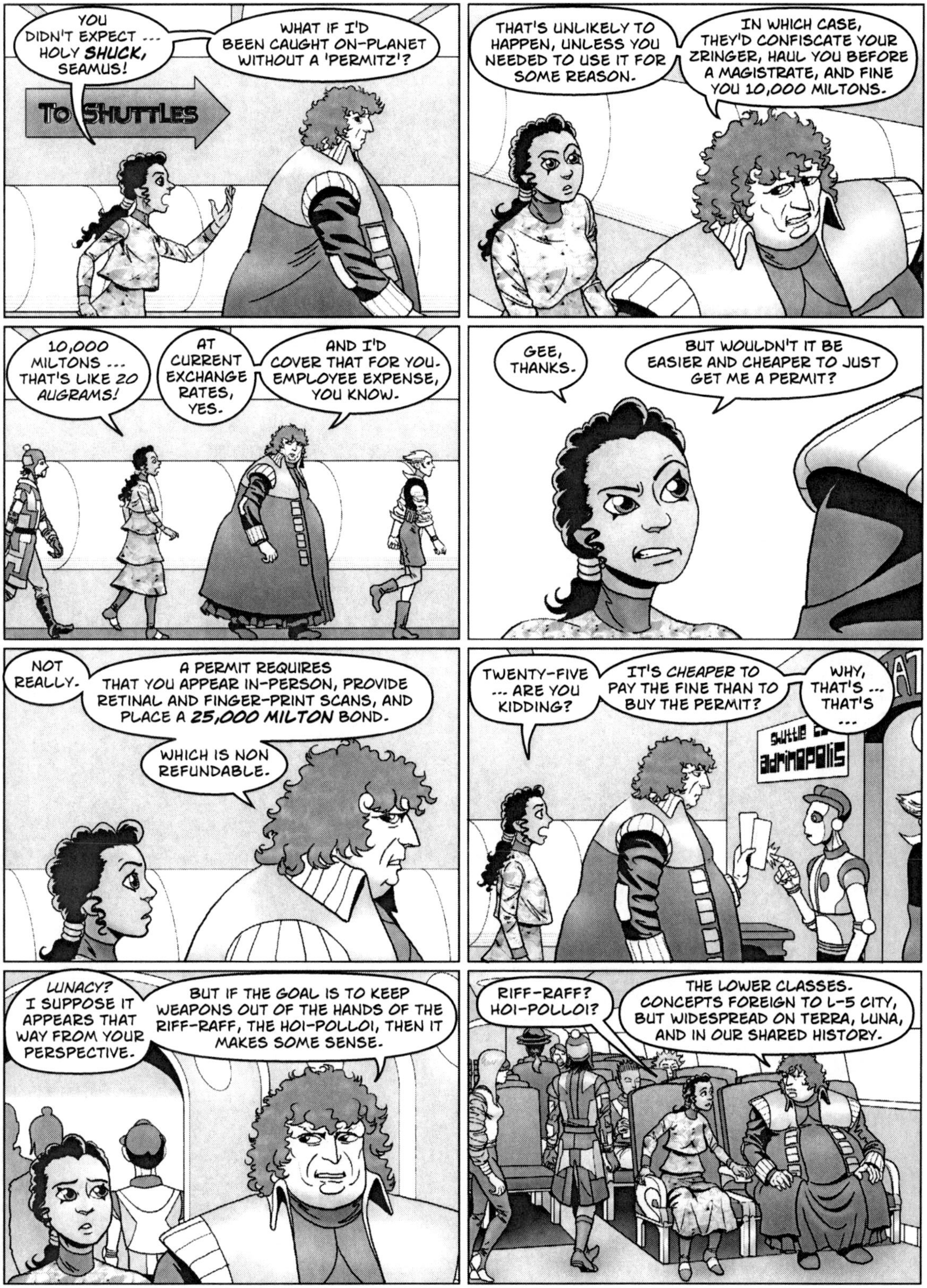
YOU DIDN'T EXPECT ... HOLY SHUCK, SEAMUS!
WHAT IF I'D BEEN CAUGHT ON-PLANET WITHOUT A 'PERMITZ'?
TO SHUTTLES
THAT'S UNLIKELY TO HAPPEN, UNLESS YOU NEEDED TO USE IT FOR SOME REASON.
IN WHICH CASE, THEY'D CONFISCATE YOUR ZRINGER, HAUL YOU BEFORE A MAGISTRATE, AND FINE YOU 10,000 MILTONS.
10,000 MILTONS ... THAT'S LIKE 20 AUGRAMS!
AT CURRENT EXCHANGE RATES, YES.
AND I'D COVER THAT FOR YOU. EMPLOYEE EXPENSE, YOU KNOW.
GEE, THANKS.
BUT WOULDN'T IT BE EASIER AND CHEAPER TO JUST GET ME A PERMIT?
NOT REALLY.
A PERMIT REQUIRES THAT YOU APPEAR IN-PERSON, PROVIDE RETINAL AND FINGER-PRINT SCANS, AND PLACE A 25,000 MILTON BOND.
WHICH IS NON REFUNDABLE.
TWENTY-FIVE ... ARE YOU KIDDING?
IT'S CHEAPER TO PAY THE FINE THAN TO BUY THE PERMIT?
WHY, THAT'S ... THAT'S ...
ADRIANOPOLIS
LUNACY? I SUPPOSE IT APPEARS THAT WAY FROM YOUR PERSPECTIVE.
BUT IF THE GOAL IS TO KEEP WEAPONS OUT OF THE HANDS OF THE RIFF-RAFF, THE HOI-POLLOI, THEN IT MAKES SOME SENSE.
RIFF-RAFF? HOI-POLLOI?
THE LOWER CLASSES. CONCEPTS FOREIGN TO L-5 CITY, BUT WIDESPREAD ON TERRA, LUNA, AND IN OUR SHARED HISTORY.

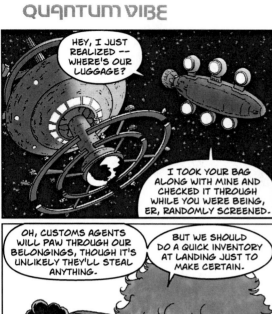

HEY, I JUST REALIZED -- WHERE'S OUR LUGGAGE?

I TOOK YOUR BAG ALONG WITH MINE AND CHECKED IT THROUGH WHILE YOU WERE BEING, ER, RANDOMLY SCREENED.

WILL THEY BE SAFE?

UM, DEFINE 'SAFE.'

OH, CUSTOMS AGENTS WILL PAW THROUGH OUR BELONGINGS, THOUGH IT'S UNLIKELY THEY'LL STEAL ANYTHING.

BUT WE SHOULD DO A QUICK INVENTORY AT LANDING JUST TO MAKE CERTAIN.

REMIND ME NEVER TO VISIT THIS PLACE AGAIN.

I DOUBT THAT I WILL NEED TO.

ATTENTION PASSENGERS, THIS IS YOUR PILOT.

WE ARE ON TRACK FOR ALDRINOPOLIS, ESTIMATED ARRIVAL TIME IS 1 HOUR, 25 MINUTES.

PASSENGERS MAY VIEW OUR PROGRESS ON THEIR SEAT-BACK MONITORS.

USING YOUR ARM-REST CONTROLS YOU CAN SWITCH VIEWS FROM NOSE-CAM TO SCHEMATIC ...

WE HAVE JUST PASSED THE SEA OF VAPORS AND WILL BE CROSSING THE SEA OF TRANQUILITY ON OUR FINAL APPROACH.

IN APPROXIMATELY 10 MINUTES THE MONITOR WILL MARK THE LOCATION OF 'TRANQUILITY BASE,' WHERE THE FIRST MEN LANDED ON LUNA, JUST ONE EARTH SHY OF 554 YEARS AGO.

ALDRINOPOLIS, POPULATION 2.5 MILLION, RESIDES IN THE 56-KM-WIDE *CRATER TARUNTIUS,* UNDER A PLASMI-GRAPHENE DOME WHICH CONTAINS COMFORTABLE AIR PRESSURE AND TEMPERATURE FOR ITS INHABITANTS.

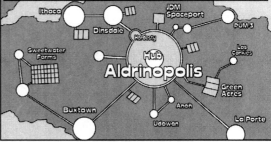

THE CITY IS AN IMPORTANT TRADE CENTER FOR OTHER, SMALLER COMMUNITIES IN THE REGION, AND IS HOME TO OMEGATEK, JONES-HARDESTY SHIPWRIGHTS, AND THE SECOND-BUSIEST SPACEPORT ON LUNA.

Ithaca · JDM Spaceport · Dinsdale · Hardesty · PUM 3 · Sweetwater Farms · Hub **Aldrinopolis** · Las Carkies · Green Acres · Buxtown · Anoh · La Porte · Udown

ON AN AVERAGE DAY, JACQUES DE MOLAY SPACEPORT TRANSPORTS MORE THAN 17,000 METRIC TONNES OF GOODS, AND 165,000 HUMAN AND ANDROID PASSENGERS.

SOME OF THEM GET A BIT CRANKY.

WE'VE BEEN ON THE GROUND FOR **15 MINUTES** ALREADY! WHEN DO WE GET OFF THIS TUB?

FINALLY!

DWELLING ON PROBLEMS YOU CAN'T DO ANYTHING ABOUT WILL DO NAUGHT BUT GIVE YOU AN *ULCER,* NICOLE.

GATE 43

IF I STILL HAD MY ZANGER I KNOW WHO I'D GIVE AN ULCER TO.

PASSENGERS ARRIVING FROM CIRCUMLUNA 2 MAY RETRIEVE THEIR LUGGAGE AT BAGGAGE PORTAL 5.

CLAIM PORTAL 5

YOU SHOULD LEARN EQUANIMITY.

PROLONGED ANGER CAN DAMAGE YOUR BRAIN CHEMISTRY.

I'LL BE RIGHT BACK WITH YOUR LUGGAGE, DR O MURCHADHA

I'M SORRY SIR, THIS WAS THE ONLY BAG WE COULD FIND UNDER EITHER OF YOUR NAMES.

ARE YOU FUCKING KIDDING ME?!!

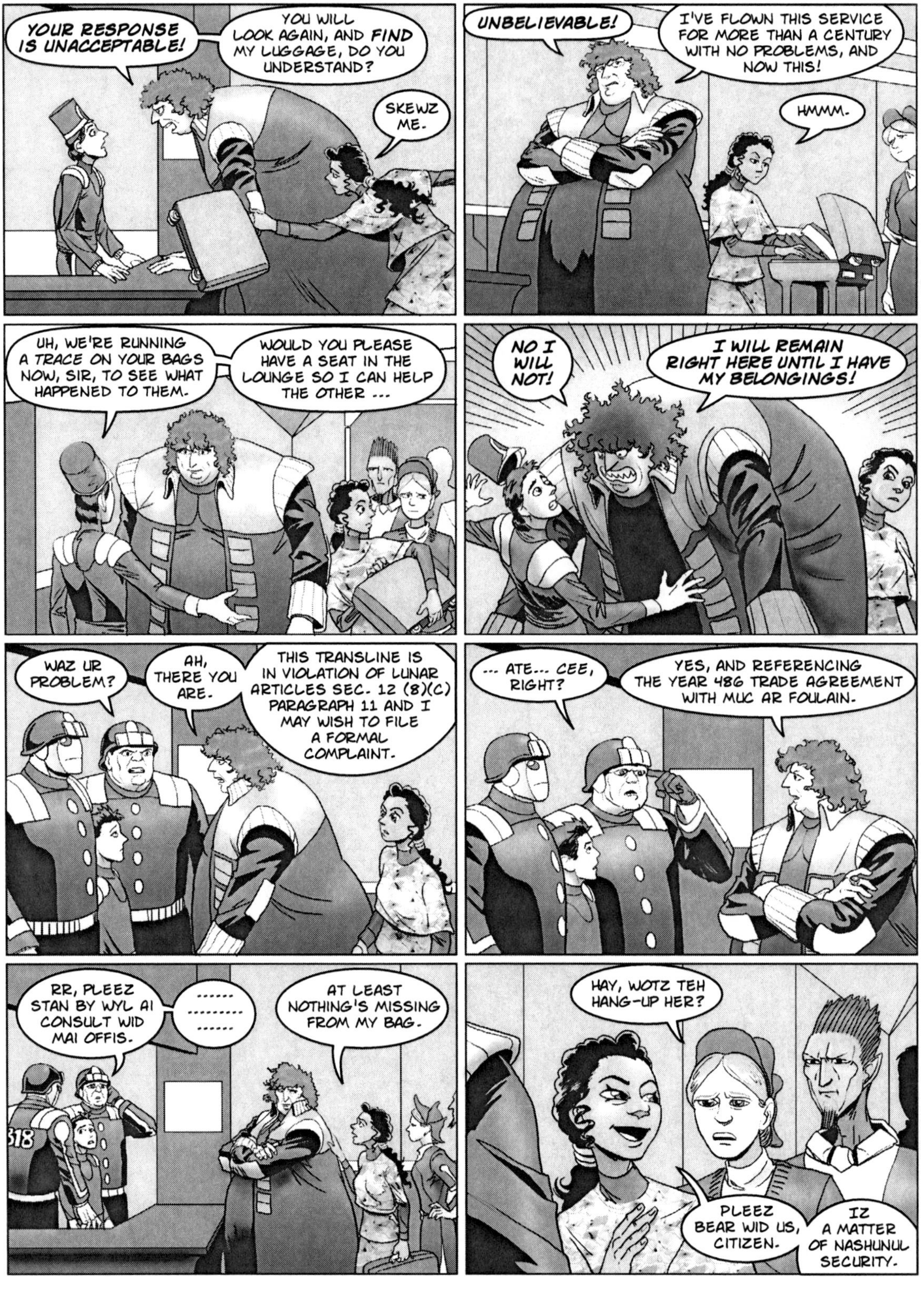
YOUR RESPONSE IS UNACCEPTABLE!
YOU WILL LOOK AGAIN, AND FIND MY LUGGAGE, DO YOU UNDERSTAND?
SKEWZ ME.
UNBELIEVABLE!
I'VE FLOWN THIS SERVICE FOR MORE THAN A CENTURY WITH NO PROBLEMS, AND NOW THIS!
HMMM.
UH, WE'RE RUNNING A TRACE ON YOUR BAGS NOW, SIR, TO SEE WHAT HAPPENED TO THEM.
WOULD YOU PLEASE HAVE A SEAT IN THE LOUNGE SO I CAN HELP THE OTHER ---
NO I WILL NOT!
I WILL REMAIN RIGHT HERE UNTIL I HAVE MY BELONGINGS!
WAZ UR PROBLEM?
AH, THERE YOU ARE.
THIS TRANSLINE IS IN VIOLATION OF LUNAR ARTICLES SEC. 12 (8)(C) PARAGRAPH 11 AND I MAY WISH TO FILE A FORMAL COMPLAINT.
--- ATE--- CEE, RIGHT?
YES, AND REFERENCING THE YEAR 486 TRADE AGREEMENT WITH MUC AR FOULAIN.
RR, PLEEZ STAN BY WYL AI CONSULT WID MAI OFFIS.
......
....
......
AT LEAST NOTHING'S MISSING FROM MY BAG.
318
HAY, WOTZ TEH HANG-UP HER?
PLEEZ BEAR WID US, CITIZEN.
IZ A MATTER OF NASHUNUL SECURITY.

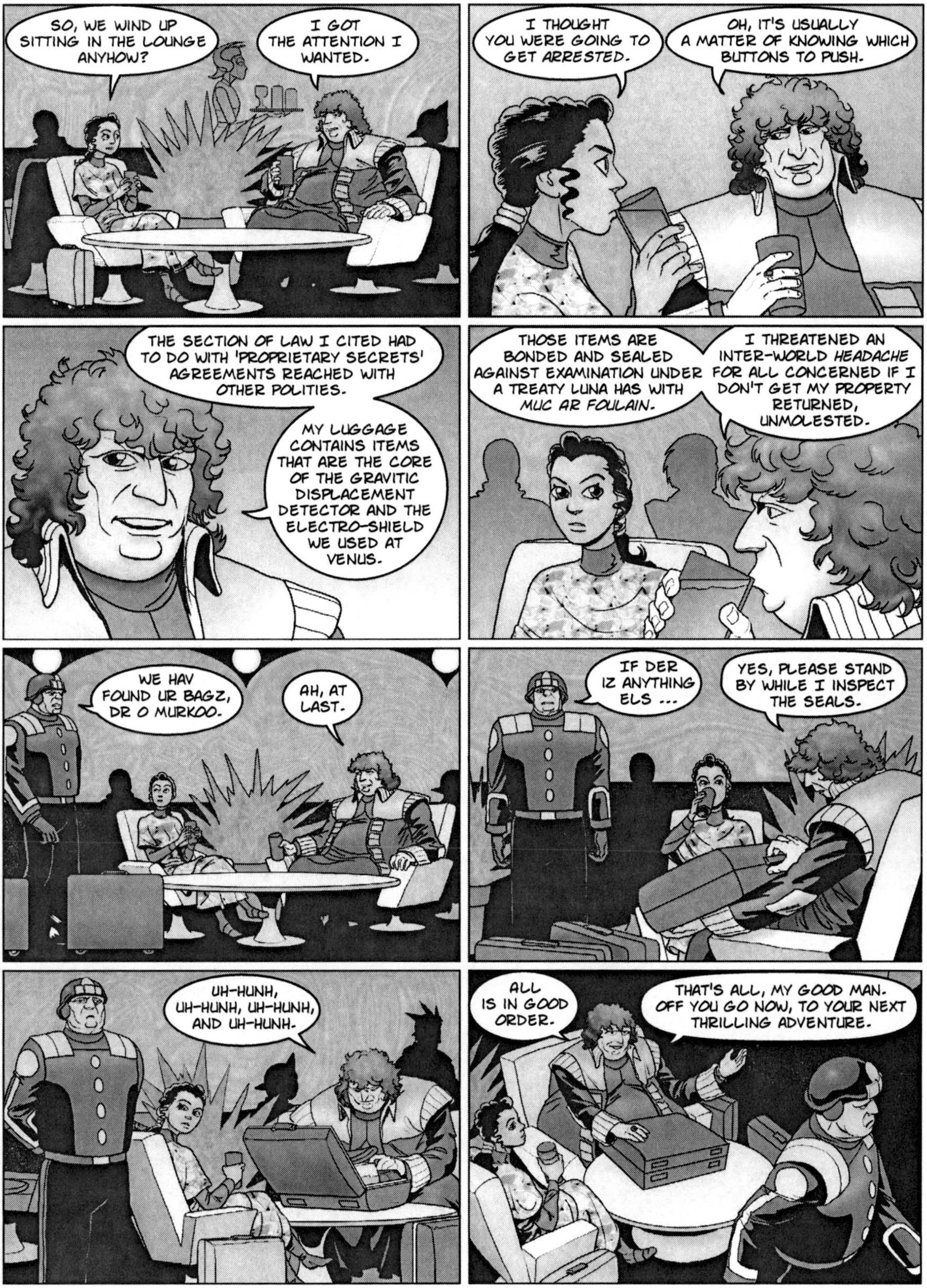
SO, WE WIND UP SITTING IN THE LOUNGE ANYHOW?
I GOT THE ATTENTION I WANTED.
I THOUGHT YOU WERE GOING TO GET ARRESTED.
OH, IT'S USUALLY A MATTER OF KNOWING WHICH BUTTONS TO PUSH.
THE SECTION OF LAW I CITED HAD TO DO WITH 'PROPRIETARY SECRETS' AGREEMENTS REACHED WITH OTHER POLITIES.
MY LUGGAGE CONTAINS ITEMS THAT ARE THE CORE OF THE GRAVITIC DISPLACEMENT DETECTOR AND THE ELECTRO-SHIELD WE USED AT VENUS.
THOSE ITEMS ARE BONDED AND SEALED AGAINST EXAMINATION UNDER A TREATY LUNA HAS WITH MUC AR FOULAIN.
I THREATENED AN INTER-WORLD HEADACHE FOR ALL CONCERNED IF I DON'T GET MY PROPERTY RETURNED, UNMOLESTED.
WE HAV FOUND UR BAGZ, DR O MURKOO.
AH, AT LAST.
IF DER IZ ANYTHING ELS ...
YES, PLEASE STAND BY WHILE I INSPECT THE SEALS.
UH-HUNH, UH-HUNH, UH-HUNH, AND UH-HUNH.
ALL IS IN GOOD ORDER.
THAT'S ALL, MY GOOD MAN. OFF YOU GO NOW, TO YOUR NEXT THRILLING ADVENTURE.

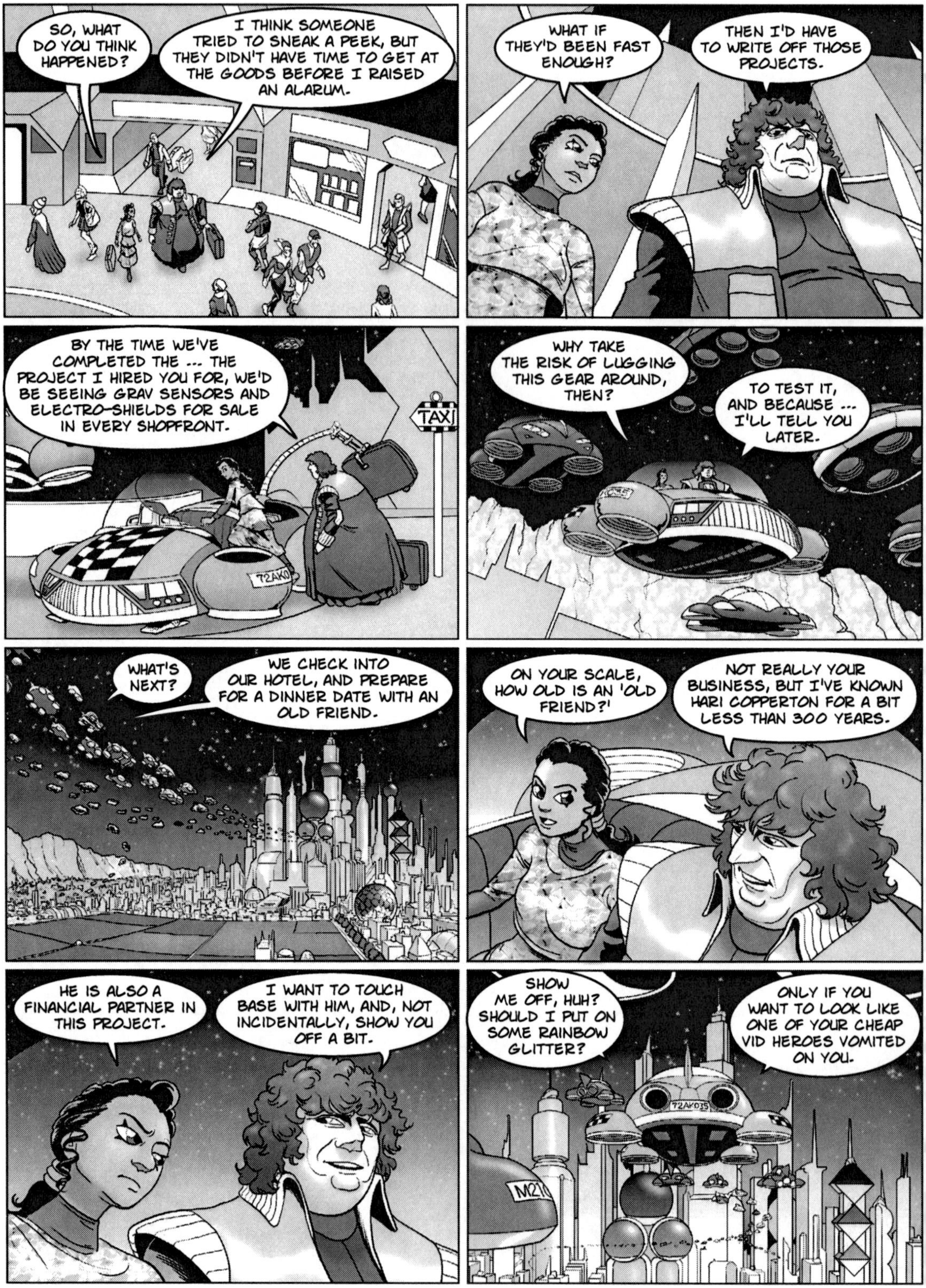
SO, WHAT DO YOU THINK HAPPENED?
I THINK SOMEONE TRIED TO SNEAK A PEEK, BUT THEY DIDN'T HAVE TIME TO GET AT THE GOODS BEFORE I RAISED AN ALARUM.
WHAT IF THEY'D BEEN FAST ENOUGH?
THEN I'D HAVE TO WRITE OFF THOSE PROJECTS.
BY THE TIME WE'VE COMPLETED THE --- THE PROJECT I HIRED YOU FOR, WE'D BE SEEING GRAV SENSORS AND ELECTRO-SHIELDS FOR SALE IN EVERY SHOPFRONT.
TAXI
72AK0
WHY TAKE THE RISK OF LUGGING THIS GEAR AROUND, THEN?
TO TEST IT, AND BECAUSE --- I'LL TELL YOU LATER.
WHAT'S NEXT?
WE CHECK INTO OUR HOTEL, AND PREPARE FOR A DINNER DATE WITH AN OLD FRIEND.
ON YOUR SCALE, HOW OLD IS AN 'OLD FRIEND?'
NOT REALLY YOUR BUSINESS, BUT I'VE KNOWN HARI COPPERTON FOR A BIT LESS THAN 300 YEARS.
HE IS ALSO A FINANCIAL PARTNER IN THIS PROJECT.
I WANT TO TOUCH BASE WITH HIM, AND, NOT INCIDENTALLY, SHOW YOU OFF A BIT.
SHOW ME OFF, HUH? SHOULD I PUT ON SOME RAINBOW GLITTER?
ONLY IF YOU WANT TO LOOK LIKE ONE OF YOUR CHEAP VID HEROES VOMITED ON YOU.
72AK035
M21

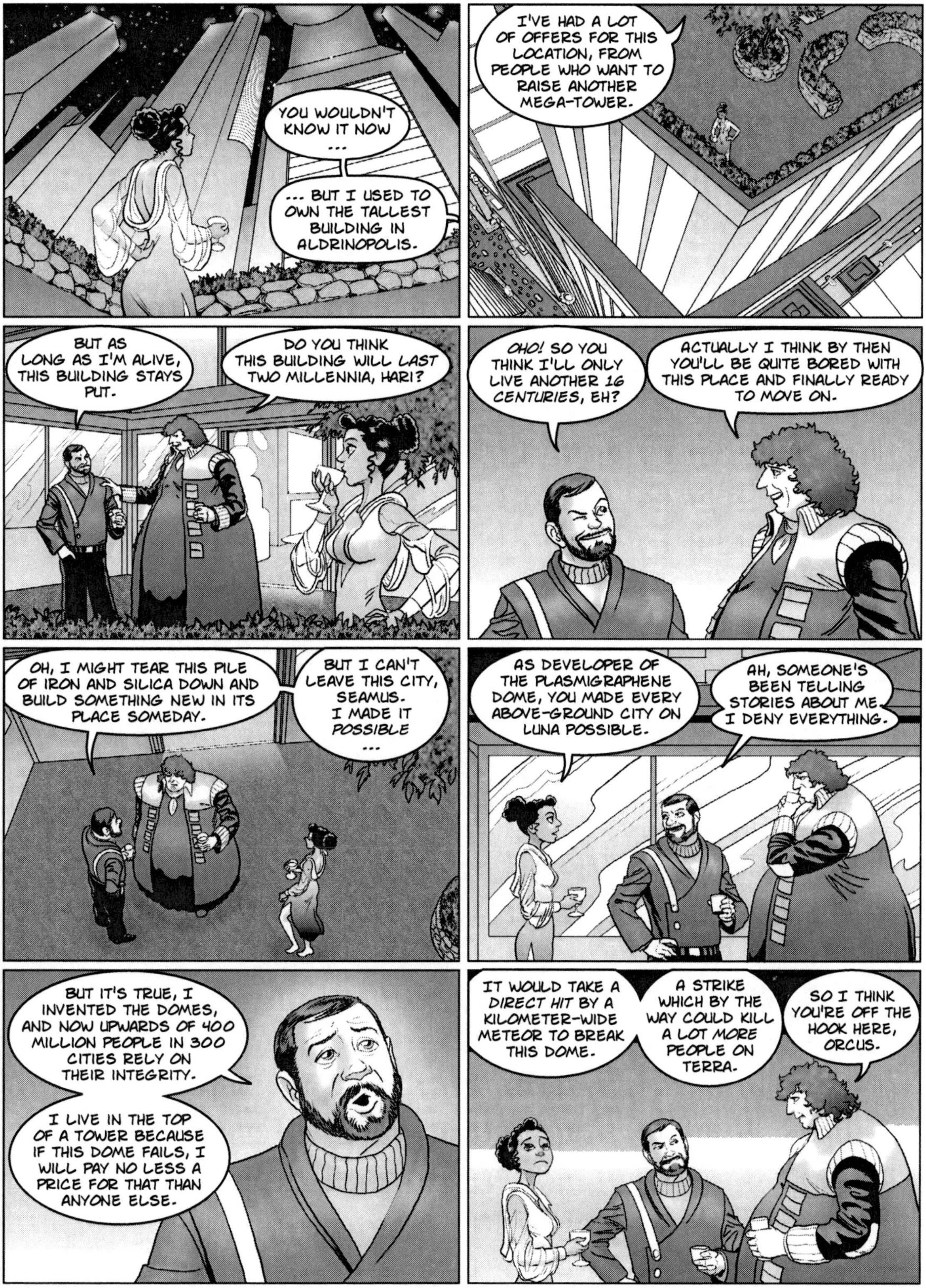
YOU WOULDN'T KNOW IT NOW ...
... BUT I USED TO OWN THE TALLEST BUILDING IN ALDRINOPOLIS.
I'VE HAD A LOT OF OFFERS FOR THIS LOCATION, FROM PEOPLE WHO WANT TO RAISE ANOTHER MEGA-TOWER.
BUT AS LONG AS I'M ALIVE, THIS BUILDING STAYS PUT.
DO YOU THINK THIS BUILDING WILL LAST TWO MILLENNIA, HARI?
OHO! SO YOU THINK I'LL ONLY LIVE ANOTHER 16 CENTURIES, EH?
ACTUALLY I THINK BY THEN YOU'LL BE QUITE BORED WITH THIS PLACE AND FINALLY READY TO MOVE ON.
OH, I MIGHT TEAR THIS PILE OF IRON AND SILICA DOWN AND BUILD SOMETHING NEW IN ITS PLACE SOMEDAY.
BUT I CAN'T LEAVE THIS CITY, SEAMUS. I MADE IT POSSIBLE ...
AS DEVELOPER OF THE PLASMIGRAPHENE DOME, YOU MADE EVERY ABOVE-GROUND CITY ON LUNA POSSIBLE.
AH, SOMEONE'S BEEN TELLING STORIES ABOUT ME. I DENY EVERYTHING.
BUT IT'S TRUE, I INVENTED THE DOMES, AND NOW UPWARDS OF 400 MILLION PEOPLE IN 300 CITIES RELY ON THEIR INTEGRITY.
I LIVE IN THE TOP OF A TOWER BECAUSE IF THIS DOME FAILS, I WILL PAY NO LESS A PRICE FOR THAT THAN ANYONE ELSE.
IT WOULD TAKE A DIRECT HIT BY A KILOMETER-WIDE METEOR TO BREAK THIS DOME.
A STRIKE WHICH BY THE WAY COULD KILL A LOT MORE PEOPLE ON TERRA.
SO I THINK YOU'RE OFF THE HOOK HERE, ORCUS.

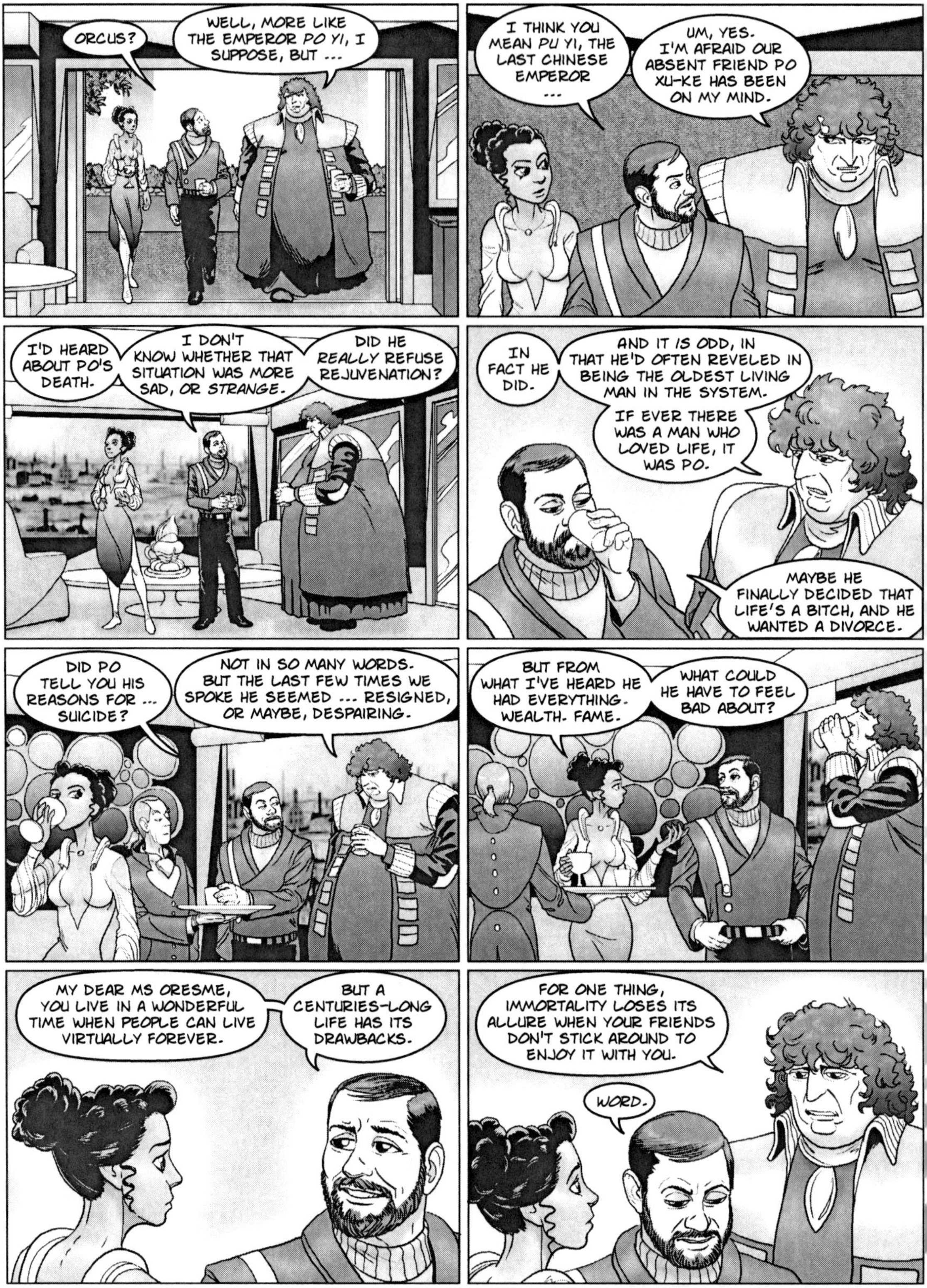
ORCUS?
WELL, MORE LIKE THE EMPEROR PO YI, I SUPPOSE, BUT ---
I THINK YOU MEAN PU YI, THE LAST CHINESE EMPEROR ---
UM, YES. I'M AFRAID OUR ABSENT FRIEND PO XU-KE HAS BEEN ON MY MIND.
I'D HEARD ABOUT PO'S DEATH.
I DON'T KNOW WHETHER THAT SITUATION WAS MORE SAD, OR STRANGE.
DID HE REALLY REFUSE REJUVENATION?
IN FACT HE DID.
AND IT IS ODD, IN THAT HE'D OFTEN REVELED IN BEING THE OLDEST LIVING MAN IN THE SYSTEM.
IF EVER THERE WAS A MAN WHO LOVED LIFE, IT WAS PO.
MAYBE HE FINALLY DECIDED THAT LIFE'S A BITCH, AND HE WANTED A DIVORCE.
DID PO TELL YOU HIS REASONS FOR --- SUICIDE?
NOT IN SO MANY WORDS. BUT THE LAST FEW TIMES WE SPOKE HE SEEMED --- RESIGNED, OR MAYBE, DESPAIRING.
BUT FROM WHAT I'VE HEARD HE HAD EVERYTHING. WEALTH. FAME.
WHAT COULD HE HAVE TO FEEL BAD ABOUT?
MY DEAR MS ORESME, YOU LIVE IN A WONDERFUL TIME WHEN PEOPLE CAN LIVE VIRTUALLY FOREVER.
BUT A CENTURIES-LONG LIFE HAS ITS DRAWBACKS.
FOR ONE THING, IMMORTALITY LOSES ITS ALLURE WHEN YOUR FRIENDS DON'T STICK AROUND TO ENJOY IT WITH YOU.
WORD.

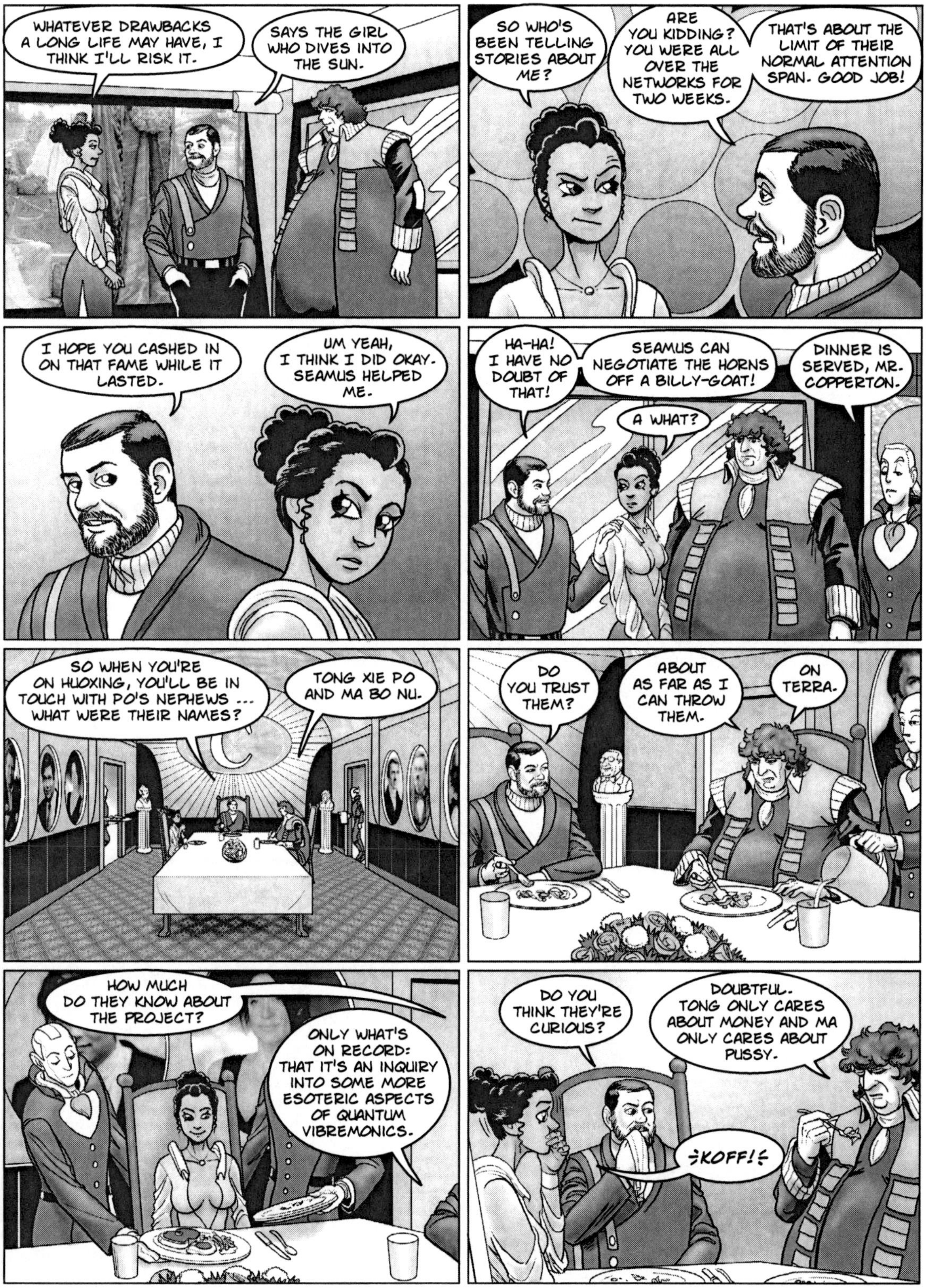
WHATEVER DRAWBACKS A LONG LIFE MAY HAVE, I THINK I'LL RISK IT.
SAYS THE GIRL WHO DIVES INTO THE SUN.
SO WHO'S BEEN TELLING STORIES ABOUT ME?
ARE YOU KIDDING? YOU WERE ALL OVER THE NETWORKS FOR TWO WEEKS.
THAT'S ABOUT THE LIMIT OF THEIR NORMAL ATTENTION SPAN. GOOD JOB!
I HOPE YOU CASHED IN ON THAT FAME WHILE IT LASTED.
UM YEAH, I THINK I DID OKAY. SEAMUS HELPED ME.
HA-HA! I HAVE NO DOUBT OF THAT!
SEAMUS CAN NEGOTIATE THE HORNS OFF A BILLY-GOAT!
DINNER IS SERVED, MR. COPPERTON.
A WHAT?
SO WHEN YOU'RE ON HUOXING, YOU'LL BE IN TOUCH WITH PO'S NEPHEWS ... WHAT WERE THEIR NAMES?
TONG XIE PO AND MA BO NU.
DO YOU TRUST THEM?
ABOUT AS FAR AS I CAN THROW THEM.
ON TERRA.
HOW MUCH DO THEY KNOW ABOUT THE PROJECT?
ONLY WHAT'S ON RECORD: THAT IT'S AN INQUIRY INTO SOME MORE ESOTERIC ASPECTS OF QUANTUM VIBREMONICS.
DO YOU THINK THEY'RE CURIOUS?
DOUBTFUL. TONG ONLY CARES ABOUT MONEY AND MA ONLY CARES ABOUT PUSSY.
KOFF!

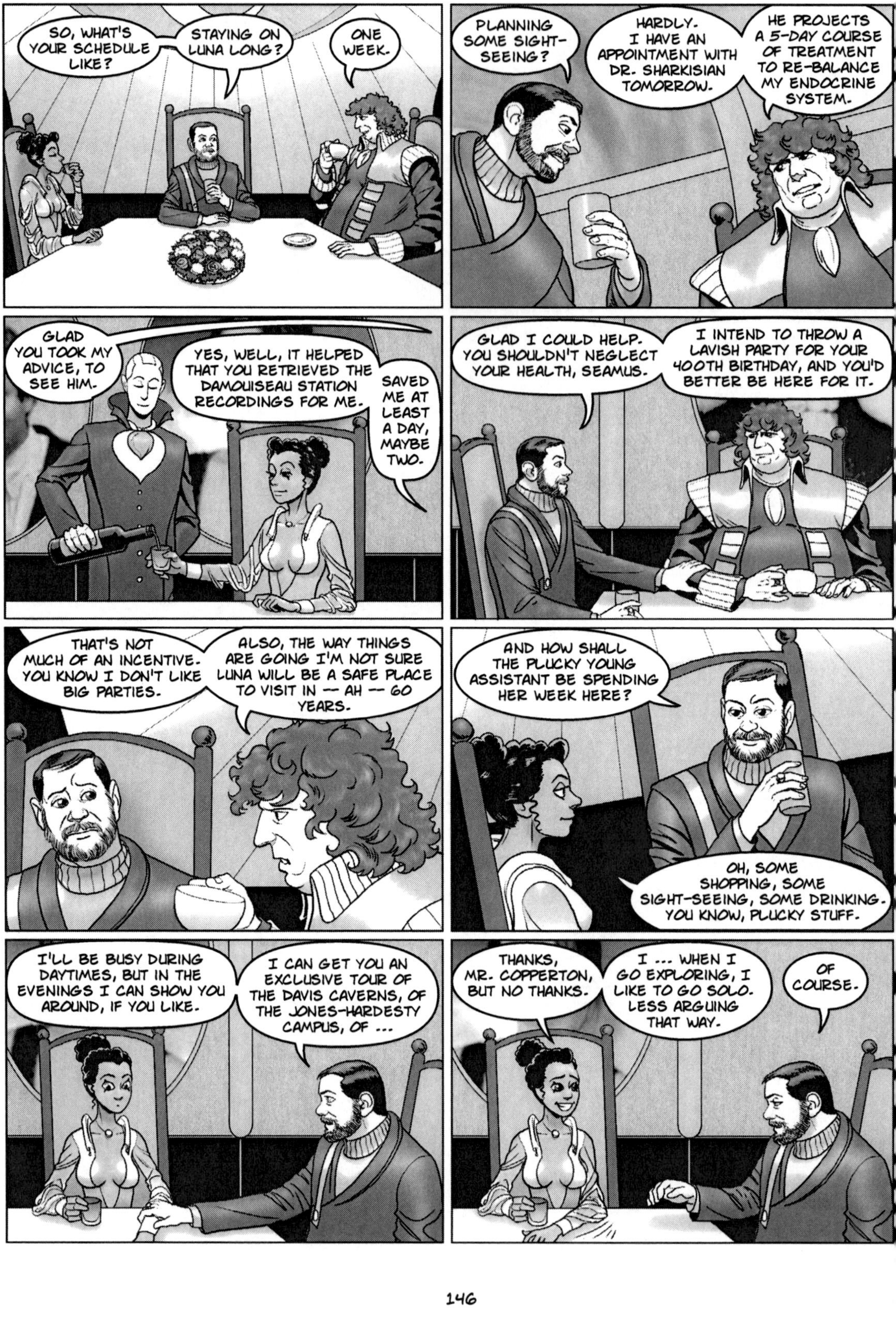
SO, WHAT'S YOUR SCHEDULE LIKE?
STAYING ON LUNA LONG?
ONE WEEK.
PLANNING SOME SIGHT-SEEING?
HARDLY. I HAVE AN APPOINTMENT WITH DR. SHARKISIAN TOMORROW.
HE PROJECTS A 5-DAY COURSE OF TREATMENT TO RE-BALANCE MY ENDOCRINE SYSTEM.
GLAD YOU TOOK MY ADVICE, TO SEE HIM.
YES, WELL, IT HELPED THAT YOU RETRIEVED THE DAMOUISEAU STATION RECORDINGS FOR ME.
SAVED ME AT LEAST A DAY, MAYBE TWO.
GLAD I COULD HELP. YOU SHOULDN'T NEGLECT YOUR HEALTH, SEAMUS.
I INTEND TO THROW A LAVISH PARTY FOR YOUR 400TH BIRTHDAY, AND YOU'D BETTER BE HERE FOR IT.
THAT'S NOT MUCH OF AN INCENTIVE. YOU KNOW I DON'T LIKE BIG PARTIES.
ALSO, THE WAY THINGS ARE GOING I'M NOT SURE LUNA WILL BE A SAFE PLACE TO VISIT IN -- AH -- 60 YEARS.
AND HOW SHALL THE PLUCKY YOUNG ASSISTANT BE SPENDING HER WEEK HERE?
OH, SOME SHOPPING, SOME SIGHT-SEEING, SOME DRINKING. YOU KNOW, PLUCKY STUFF.
I'LL BE BUSY DURING DAYTIMES, BUT IN THE EVENINGS I CAN SHOW YOU AROUND, IF YOU LIKE.
I CAN GET YOU AN EXCLUSIVE TOUR OF THE DAVIS CAVERNS, OF THE JONES-HARDESTY CAMPUS, OF ...
THANKS, MR. COPPERTON, BUT NO THANKS.
I ... WHEN I GO EXPLORING, I LIKE TO GO SOLO. LESS ARGUING THAT WAY.
OF COURSE.

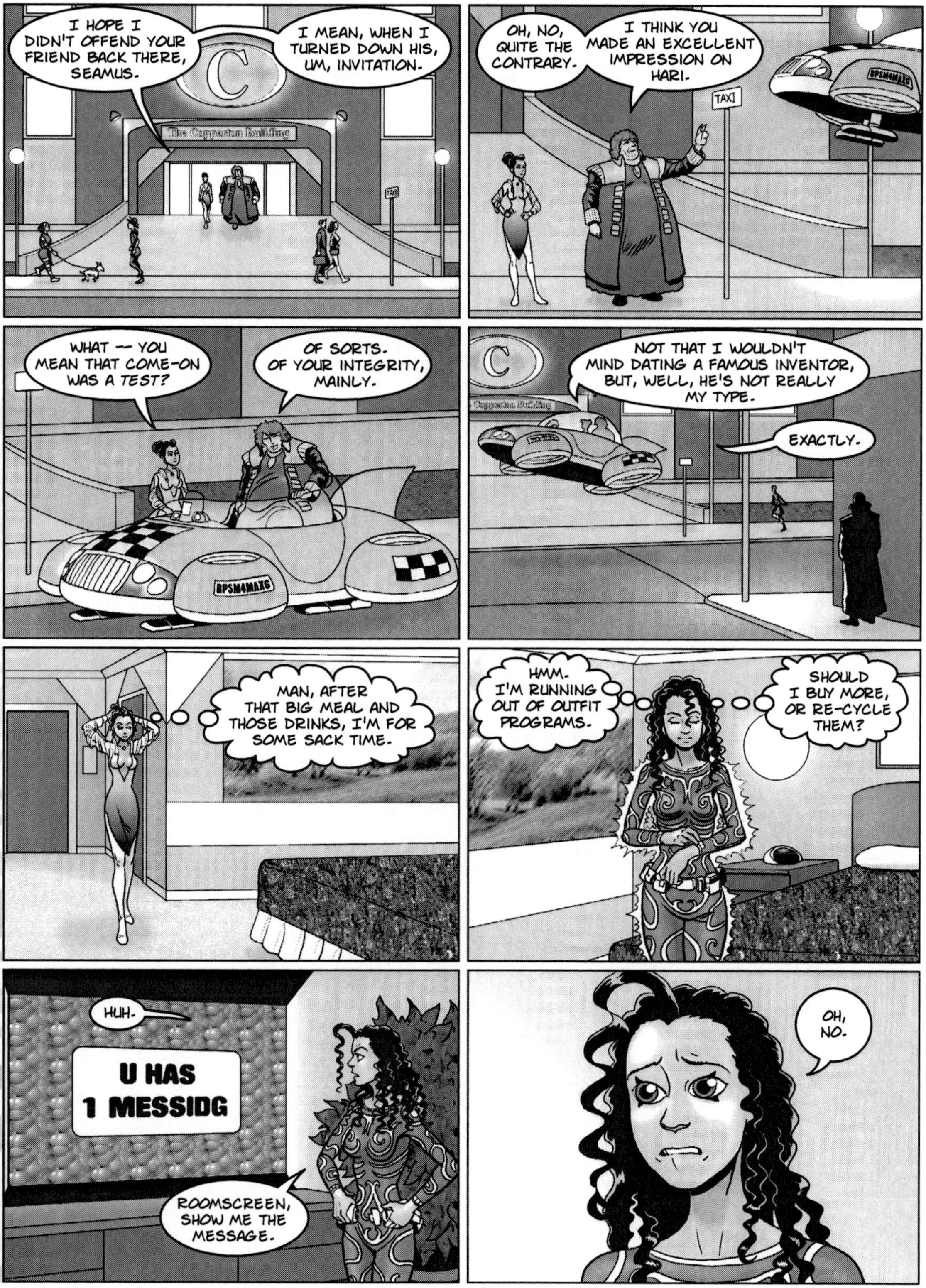
I HOPE I DIDN'T OFFEND YOUR FRIEND BACK THERE, SEAMUS.
I MEAN, WHEN I TURNED DOWN HIS, UM, INVITATION.
The Copperton Building
TAXI
OH, NO, QUITE THE CONTRARY.
I THINK YOU MADE AN EXCELLENT IMPRESSION ON HARI.
TAXI
BPSM4MAXG
WHAT -- YOU MEAN THAT COME-ON WAS A *TEST?*
OF SORTS. OF YOUR INTEGRITY, MAINLY.
BPSM4MAXG
NOT THAT I WOULDN'T MIND DATING A FAMOUS INVENTOR, BUT, WELL, HE'S NOT REALLY MY TYPE.
EXACTLY.
MAN, AFTER THAT BIG MEAL AND THOSE DRINKS, I'M FOR SOME SACK TIME.
HMM. I'M RUNNING OUT OF OUTFIT PROGRAMS.
SHOULD I BUY MORE, OR RE-CYCLE THEM?
HUH.
U HAS 1 MESSIDG
ROOMSCREEN, SHOW ME THE MESSAGE.
OH, NO.

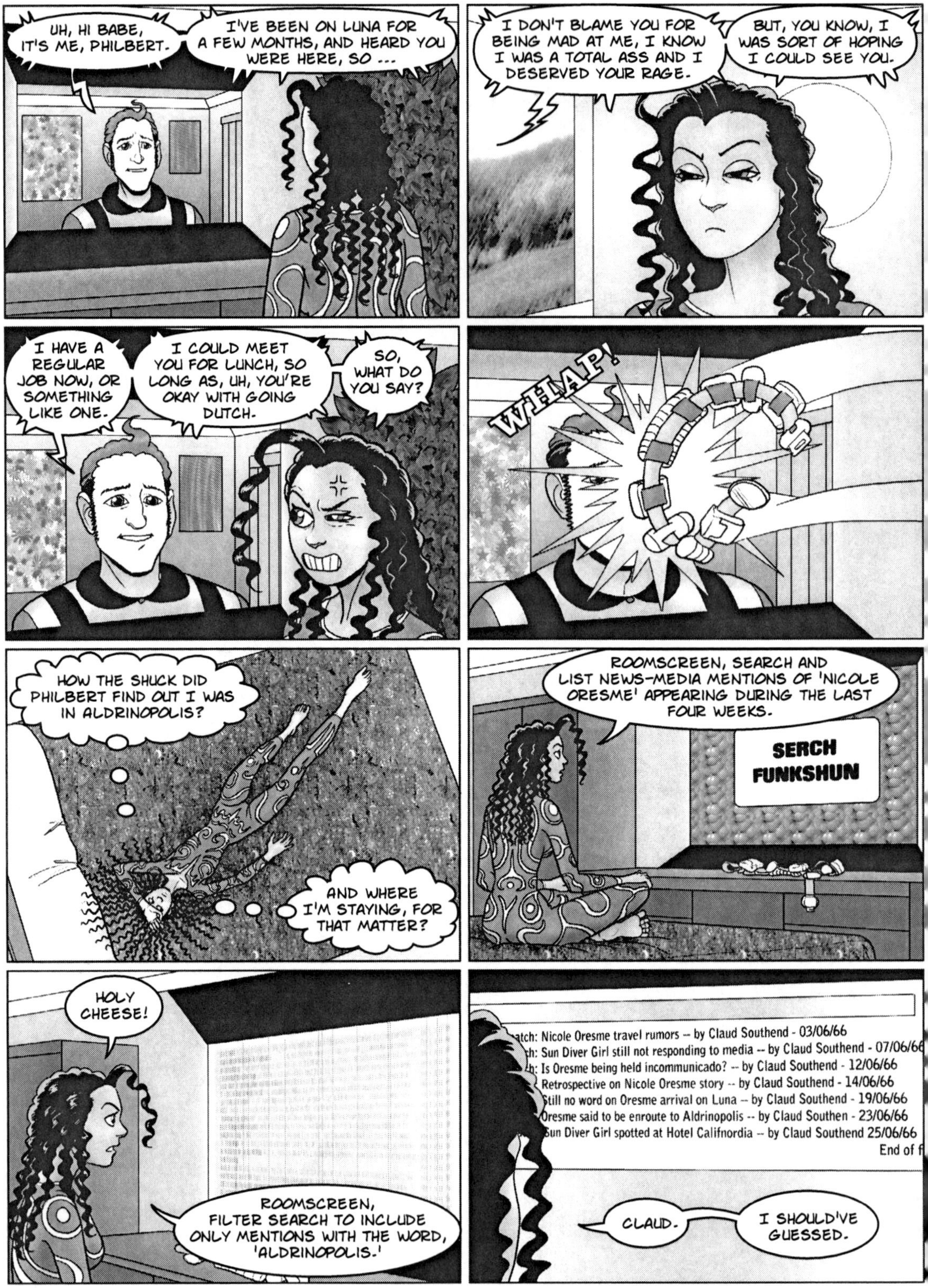
UH, HI BABE, IT'S ME, PHILBERT.
I'VE BEEN ON LUNA FOR A FEW MONTHS, AND HEARD YOU WERE HERE, SO ...
I DON'T BLAME YOU FOR BEING MAD AT ME, I KNOW I WAS A TOTAL ASS AND I DESERVED YOUR RAGE.
BUT, YOU KNOW, I WAS SORT OF HOPING I COULD SEE YOU.
I HAVE A REGULAR JOB NOW, OR SOMETHING LIKE ONE.
I COULD MEET YOU FOR LUNCH, SO LONG AS, UH, YOU'RE OKAY WITH GOING DUTCH.
SO, WHAT DO YOU SAY?
WHAP!
HOW THE SHUCK DID PHILBERT FIND OUT I WAS IN ALDRINOPOLIS?
AND WHERE I'M STAYING, FOR THAT MATTER?
ROOMSCREEN, SEARCH AND LIST NEWS-MEDIA MENTIONS OF 'NICOLE ORESME' APPEARING DURING THE LAST FOUR WEEKS.
SERCH FUNKSHUN
HOLY CHEESE!
ROOMSCREEN, FILTER SEARCH TO INCLUDE ONLY MENTIONS WITH THE WORD, 'ALDRINOPOLIS.'
atch: Nicole Oresme travel rumors -- by Claud Southend - 03/06/66
h: Sun Diver Girl still not responding to media -- by Claud Southend - 07/06/66
h: Is Oresme being held incommunicado? -- by Claud Southend - 12/06/66
Retrospective on Nicole Oresme story -- by Claud Southend - 14/06/66
Still no word on Oresme arrival on Luna -- by Claud Southend - 19/06/66
Oresme said to be enroute to Aldrinopolis -- by Claud Southen - 23/06/66
Sun Diver Girl spotted at Hotel Califnordia -- by Claud Southend 25/06/66
End of
CLAUD.
I SHOULD'VE GUESSED.

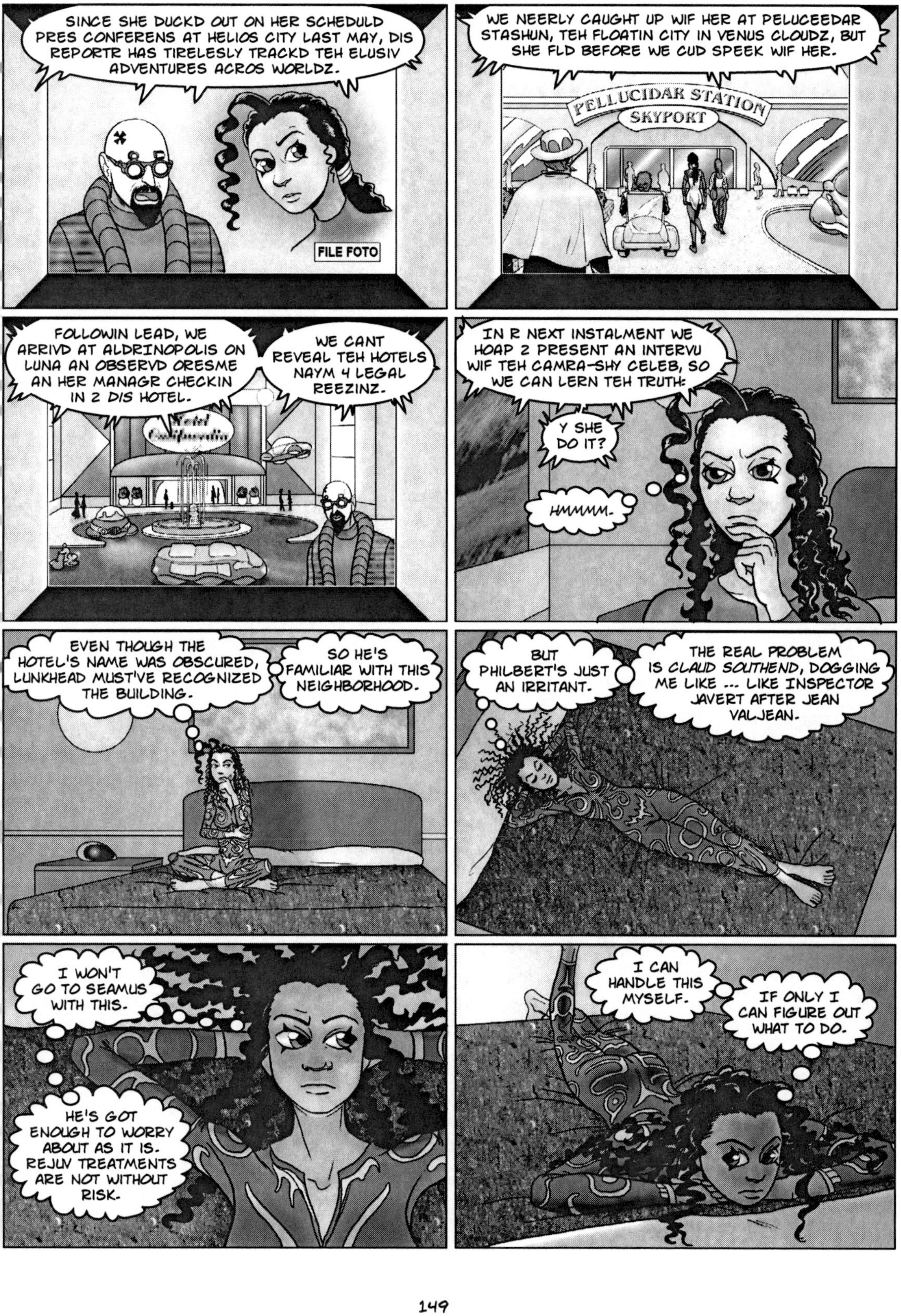
SINCE SHE DUCKD OUT ON HER SCHEDULD PRES CONFERENS AT HELIOS CITY LAST MAY, DIS REPORTR HAS TIRELESLY TRACKD TEH ELUSIV ADVENTURES ACROS WORLDZ.
FILE FOTO
WE NEERLY CAUGHT UP WIF HER AT PELUCEEDAR STASHUN, TEH FLOATIN CITY IN VENUS CLOUDZ, BUT SHE FLD BEFORE WE CUD SPEEK WIF HER.
PELLUCIDAR STATION
SKYPORT
FOLLOWIN LEAD, WE ARRIVD AT ALDRINOPOLIS ON LUNA AN OBSERVD ORESME AN HER MANAGR CHECKIN IN 2 DIS HOTEL.
WE CANT REVEAL TEH HOTELS NAYM 4 LEGAL REEZINZ.
IN R NEXT INSTALMENT WE HOAP 2 PRESENT AN INTERVU WIF TEH CAMRA-SHY CELEB, SO WE CAN LERN TEH TRUTH:
Y SHE DO IT?
HMMMM.
EVEN THOUGH THE HOTEL'S NAME WAS OBSCURED, LUNKHEAD MUST'VE RECOGNIZED THE BUILDING.
SO HE'S FAMILIAR WITH THIS NEIGHBORHOOD.
BUT PHILBERT'S JUST AN IRRITANT.
THE REAL PROBLEM IS CLAUD SOUTHEND, DOGGING ME LIKE ... LIKE INSPECTOR JAVERT AFTER JEAN VALJEAN.
I WON'T GO TO SEAMUS WITH THIS.
HE'S GOT ENOUGH TO WORRY ABOUT AS IT IS. REJUV TREATMENTS ARE NOT WITHOUT RISK.
I CAN HANDLE THIS MYSELF.
IF ONLY I CAN FIGURE OUT WHAT TO DO.

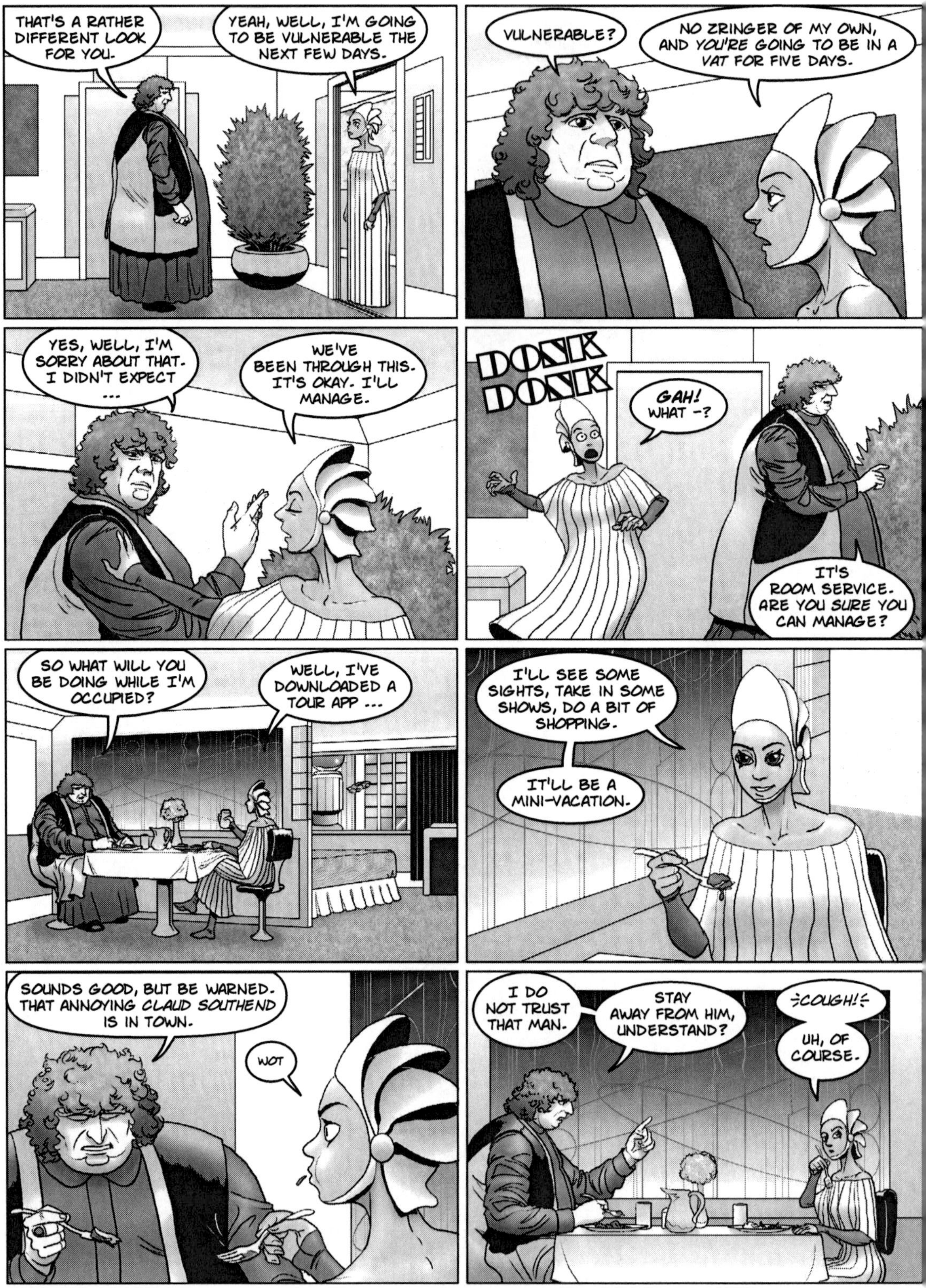
THAT'S A RATHER DIFFERENT LOOK FOR YOU.
YEAH, WELL, I'M GOING TO BE VULNERABLE THE NEXT FEW DAYS.
VULNERABLE?
NO ZRINGER OF MY OWN, AND YOU'RE GOING TO BE IN A VAT FOR FIVE DAYS.
YES, WELL, I'M SORRY ABOUT THAT. I DIDN'T EXPECT ...
WE'VE BEEN THROUGH THIS. IT'S OKAY. I'LL MANAGE.
DONK DONK
GAH! WHAT -?
IT'S ROOM SERVICE. ARE YOU SURE YOU CAN MANAGE?
SO WHAT WILL YOU BE DOING WHILE I'M OCCUPIED?
WELL, I'VE DOWNLOADED A TOUR APP ...
I'LL SEE SOME SIGHTS, TAKE IN SOME SHOWS, DO A BIT OF SHOPPING.
IT'LL BE A MINI-VACATION.
SOUNDS GOOD, BUT BE WARNED. THAT ANNOYING CLAUD SOUTHEND IS IN TOWN.
WOT
I DO NOT TRUST THAT MAN.
STAY AWAY FROM HIM, UNDERSTAND?
COUGH!
UH, OF COURSE.

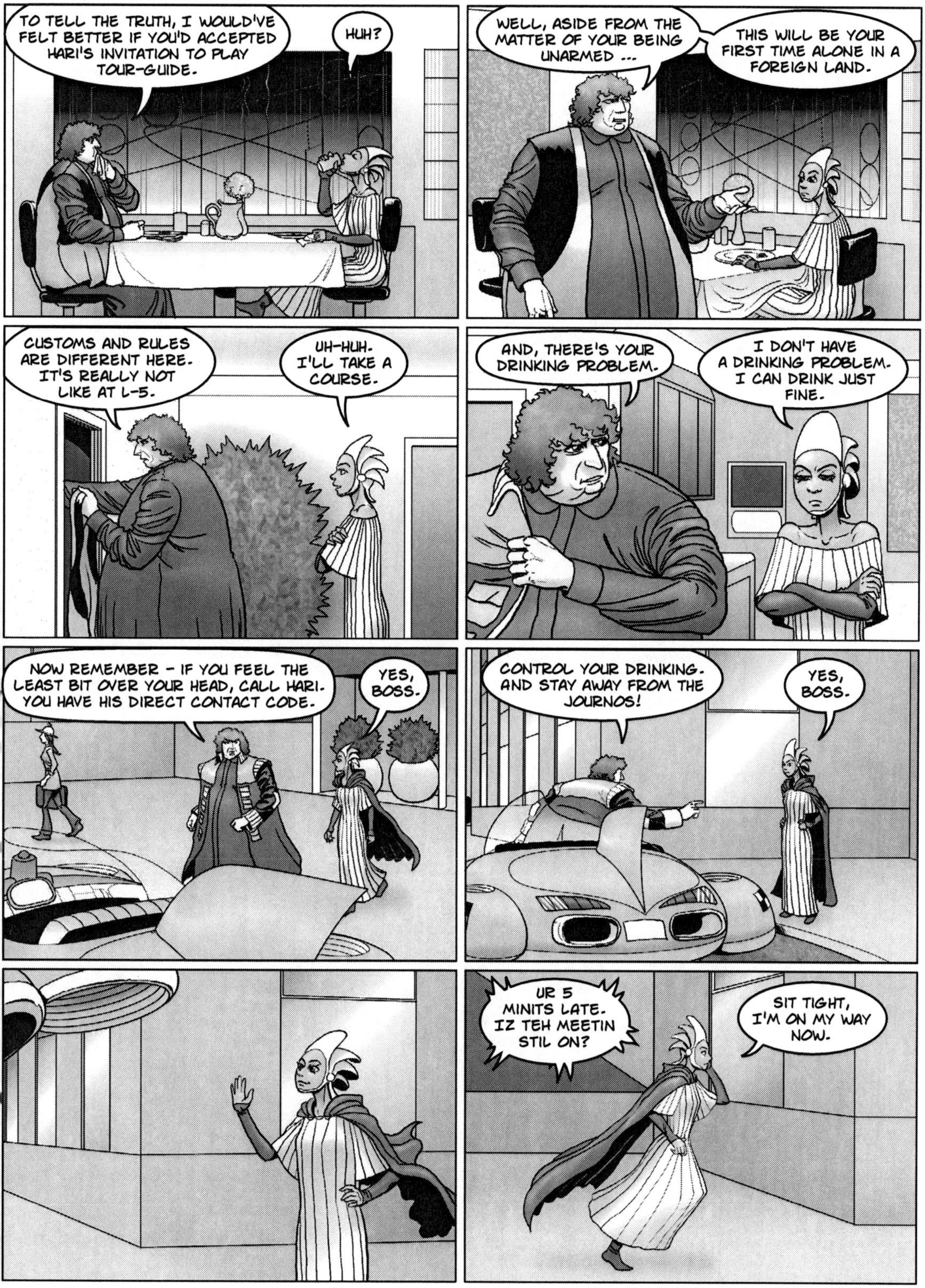
TO TELL THE TRUTH, I WOULD'VE FELT BETTER IF YOU'D ACCEPTED HARI'S INVITATION TO PLAY TOUR-GUIDE.
HUH?
WELL, ASIDE FROM THE MATTER OF YOUR BEING UNARMED ...
THIS WILL BE YOUR FIRST TIME ALONE IN A FOREIGN LAND.
CUSTOMS AND RULES ARE DIFFERENT HERE. IT'S REALLY NOT LIKE AT L-5.
UH-HUH. I'LL TAKE A COURSE.
AND, THERE'S YOUR DRINKING PROBLEM.
I DON'T HAVE A DRINKING PROBLEM. I CAN DRINK JUST FINE.
NOW REMEMBER - IF YOU FEEL THE LEAST BIT OVER YOUR HEAD, CALL HARI. YOU HAVE HIS DIRECT CONTACT CODE.
YES, BOSS.
CONTROL YOUR DRINKING. AND STAY AWAY FROM THE JOURNOS!
YES, BOSS.
UR 5 MINITS LATE. IZ TEH MEETIN STIL ON?
SIT TIGHT, I'M ON MY WAY NOW.

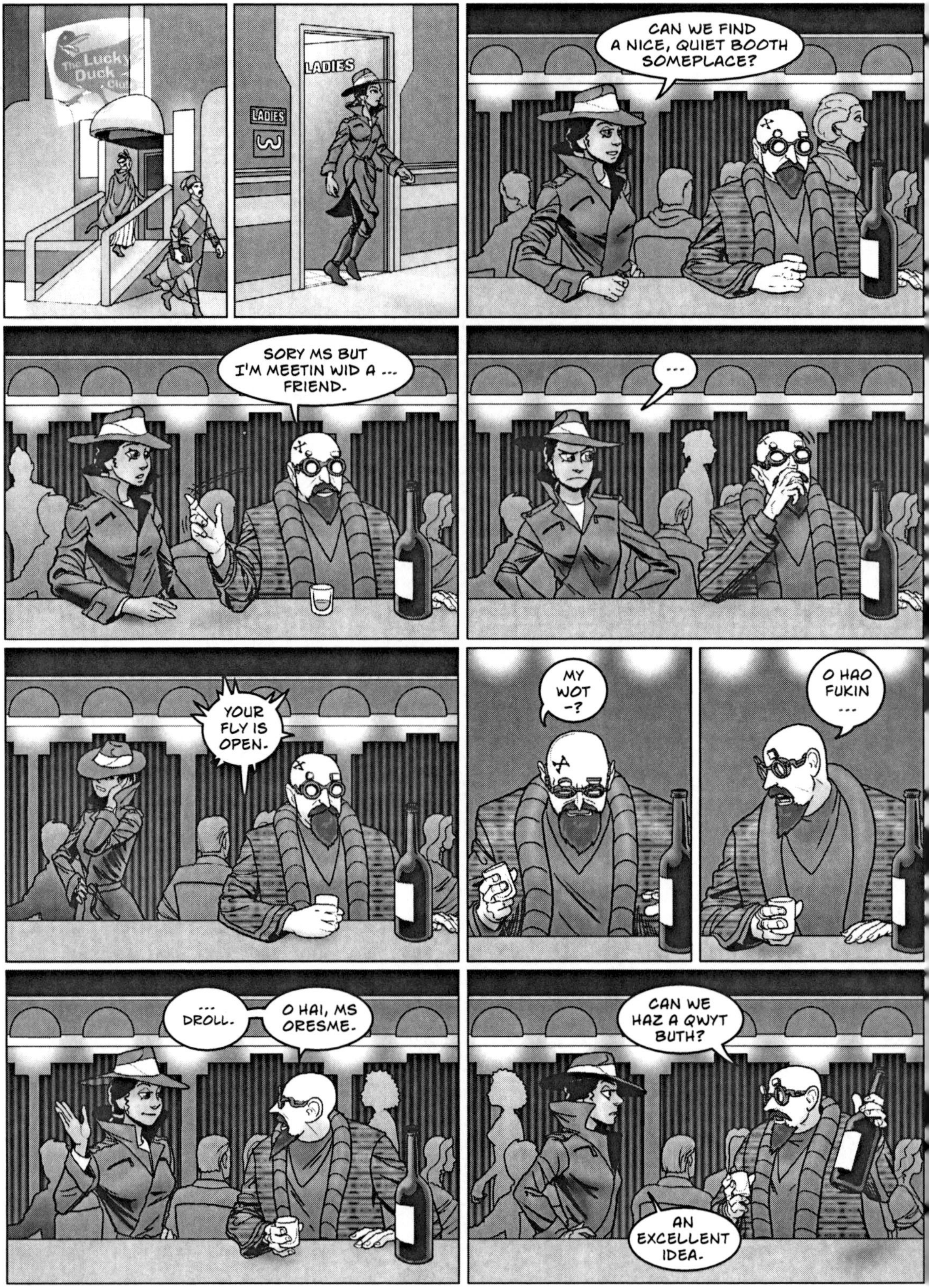
The Lucky Duck Club
LADIES
LADIES
CAN WE FIND A NICE, QUIET BOOTH SOMEPLACE?
SORY MS BUT I'M MEETIN WID A ... FRIEND.
...
YOUR FLY IS OPEN.
MY WOT -?
O HAO FUKIN ...
O HAI, MS ORESME.
... DROLL.
CAN WE HAZ A QWYT BUTH?
AN EXCELLENT IDEA.

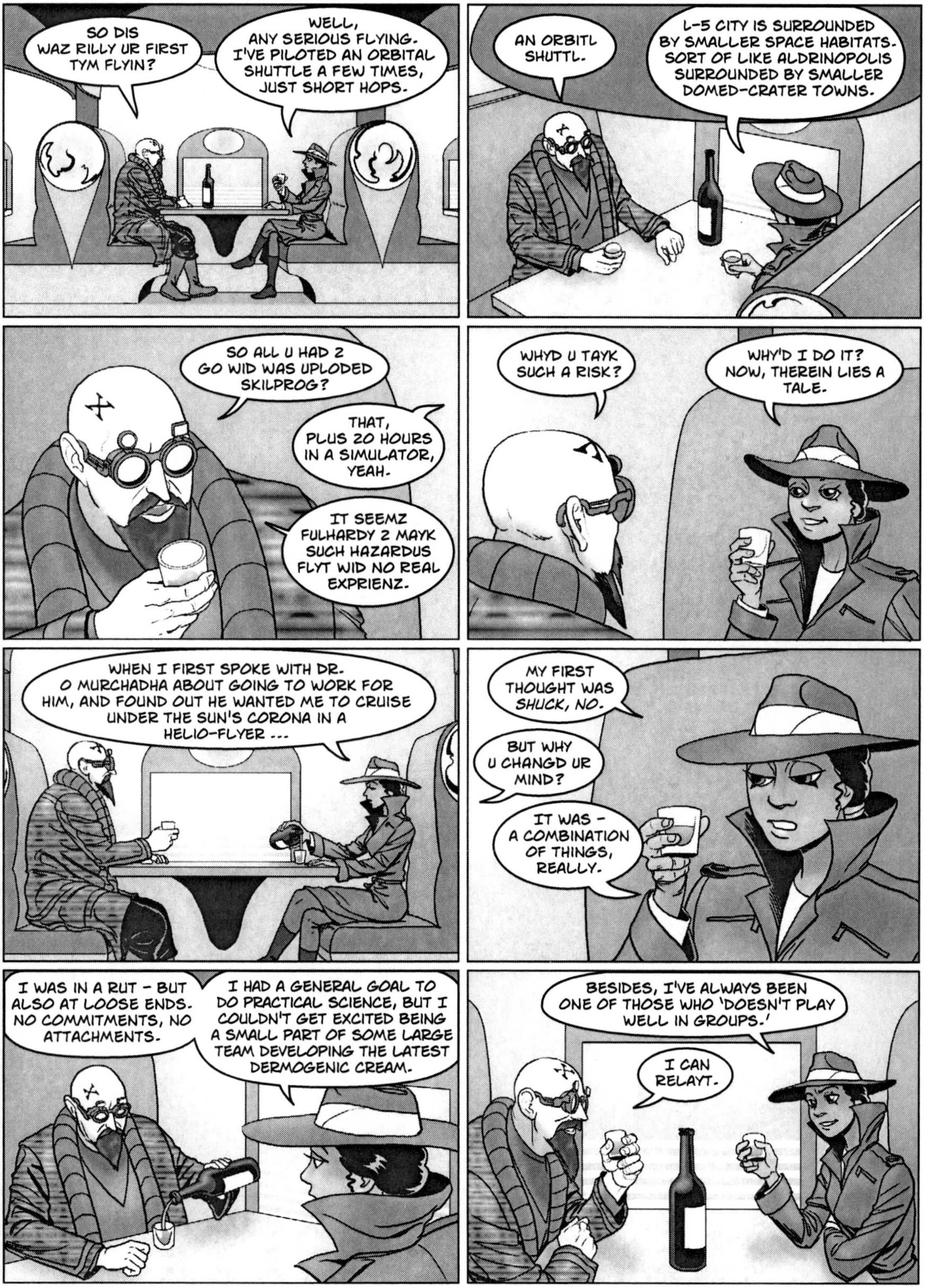
SO DIS WAZ RILLY UR FIRST TYM FLYIN?
WELL, ANY SERIOUS FLYING. I'VE PILOTED AN ORBITAL SHUTTLE A FEW TIMES, JUST SHORT HOPS.
AN ORBITL SHUTTL.
L-5 CITY IS SURROUNDED BY SMALLER SPACE HABITATS. SORT OF LIKE ALDRINOPOLIS SURROUNDED BY SMALLER DOMED-CRATER TOWNS.
SO ALL U HAD 2 GO WID WAS UPLODED SKILPROG?
THAT, PLUS 20 HOURS IN A SIMULATOR, YEAH.
IT SEEMZ FULHARDY 2 MAYK SUCH HAZARDUS FLYT WID NO REAL EXPRIENZ.
WHYD U TAYK SUCH A RISK?
WHY'D I DO IT? NOW, THEREIN LIES A TALE.
WHEN I FIRST SPOKE WITH DR. O MURCHADHA ABOUT GOING TO WORK FOR HIM, AND FOUND OUT HE WANTED ME TO CRUISE UNDER THE SUN'S CORONA IN A HELIO-FLYER ...
MY FIRST THOUGHT WAS SHUCK, NO.
BUT WHY U CHANGD UR MIND?
IT WAS - A COMBINATION OF THINGS, REALLY.
I WAS IN A RUT - BUT ALSO AT LOOSE ENDS. NO COMMITMENTS, NO ATTACHMENTS.
I HAD A GENERAL GOAL TO DO PRACTICAL SCIENCE, BUT I COULDN'T GET EXCITED BEING A SMALL PART OF SOME LARGE TEAM DEVELOPING THE LATEST DERMOGENIC CREAM.
BESIDES, I'VE ALWAYS BEEN ONE OF THOSE WHO 'DOESN'T PLAY WELL IN GROUPS.'
I CAN RELAYT.

SH-SO U DOV INA NUCLEAR FURNIS BECOZ UR **BORD**?

HUH? NO! BECAUSH IT WAS ... IT WASSA JOB REQUIREMENT.

OKAY SO WYSIT A JOB REQUIRMENT?

WOT PURPOSH IZ SERVD BY .. BY DYV-BOMIN TEH PHOTOSPHEER?

WHY? YOU WANNA KNOW **WHY** I HADDA DROP NUKES ON JOLLY OLD SOL?

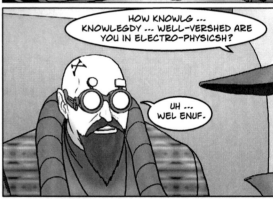

BECAUSE THE SHUN HAD IT COMING, THASH WHY!

IT REAL ... REALLY ... IT REALLY BURNSH ME UP.

AWRIGHT, AWRIGHT, ALL KIDDING ASHIDE, Y' RILLY WANNA KNOW WHAT MY SHUN-DIVE WAS ALL ABOUT?

IM ALL EARZ.

HOW KNOWLG ... KNOWLEGDY ... WELL-VERSHED ARE YOU IN ELECTRO-PHYSICSH?

UH ... WEL ENUF.

WE ARE EXSHPLORING THE 'ELECTROPLASHMIC UNIVERSH' THEORIESH OF KRAVINOOR AWASHINA, WHICH BUILDS ON EARLIER WORK BY HANNES ALFVÉN AND OSKAR KLEIN, WHO POSHITED THAT ELECTROMAGNETIC FORSHES, INNERACTING WITH PLASHMA ON COSHMIC SHCALES, BETTER EXPLAINSH LARGE-BODY MOVEMENTS THAN EINSHTEIN'S SHPACE-TIME THEORIESH. BY MEASUREMENT OF THE SOLAR ATMOSPHERIC PLASMA RELATIVE TO THOSE EXPLOSIONS, WE H.. TO ESHTABLISH THE EXISHTENCE OF ...MBIPLASHMA AN DEVELOP A MEANS O.. ...ANUFACTURING IT FOR USE ASH A NE... ...EL SOURCE, 1000 TIMES MORE POTEN... ...HAN OUR BES.. FUSHION REACTORSH... ...IF WE CA. DO THAT, WE C.N ...EVOLUTIONI.. ENERGY PRO..TION AN. ..CE TRAVEL.

DO YOU SHEE THE IMPLICATIONSH HERE?

ER ...

UH ... O ABSOLUTLY.

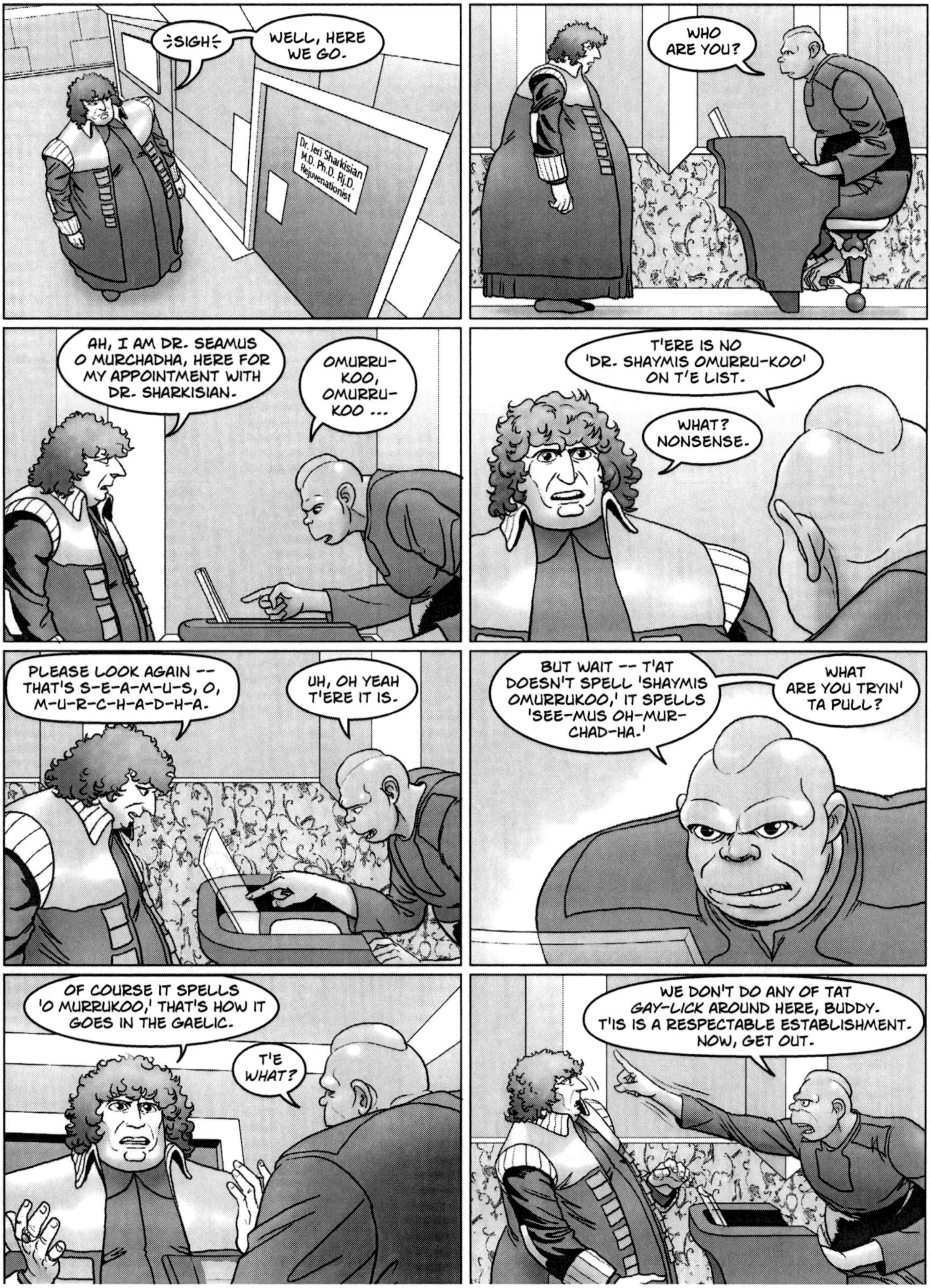

⁼SIGH⁼
WELL, HERE WE GO.
Dr. Jeri Sharkisian M.D. Ph.D. Rj.D. Rejuvenationist
WHO ARE YOU?
AH, I AM DR. SEAMUS O MURCHADHA, HERE FOR MY APPOINTMENT WITH DR. SHARKISIAN.
OMURRU-KOO, OMURRU-KOO ...
T'ERE IS NO 'DR. SHAYMIS OMURRU-KOO' ON T'E LIST.
WHAT? NONSENSE.
PLEASE LOOK AGAIN -- THAT'S S-E-A-M-U-S, O, M-U-R-C-H-A-D-H-A.
UH, OH YEAH T'ERE IT IS.
BUT WAIT -- T'AT DOESN'T SPELL 'SHAYMIS OMURRUKOO,' IT SPELLS 'SEE-MUS OH-MUR-CHAD-HA.'
WHAT ARE YOU TRYIN' TA PULL?
OF COURSE IT SPELLS 'O MURRUKOO,' THAT'S HOW IT GOES IN THE GAELIC.
T'E WHAT?
WE DON'T DO ANY OF TAT GAY-LICK AROUND HERE, BUDDY. T'IS IS A RESPECTABLE ESTABLISHMENT. NOW, GET OUT.

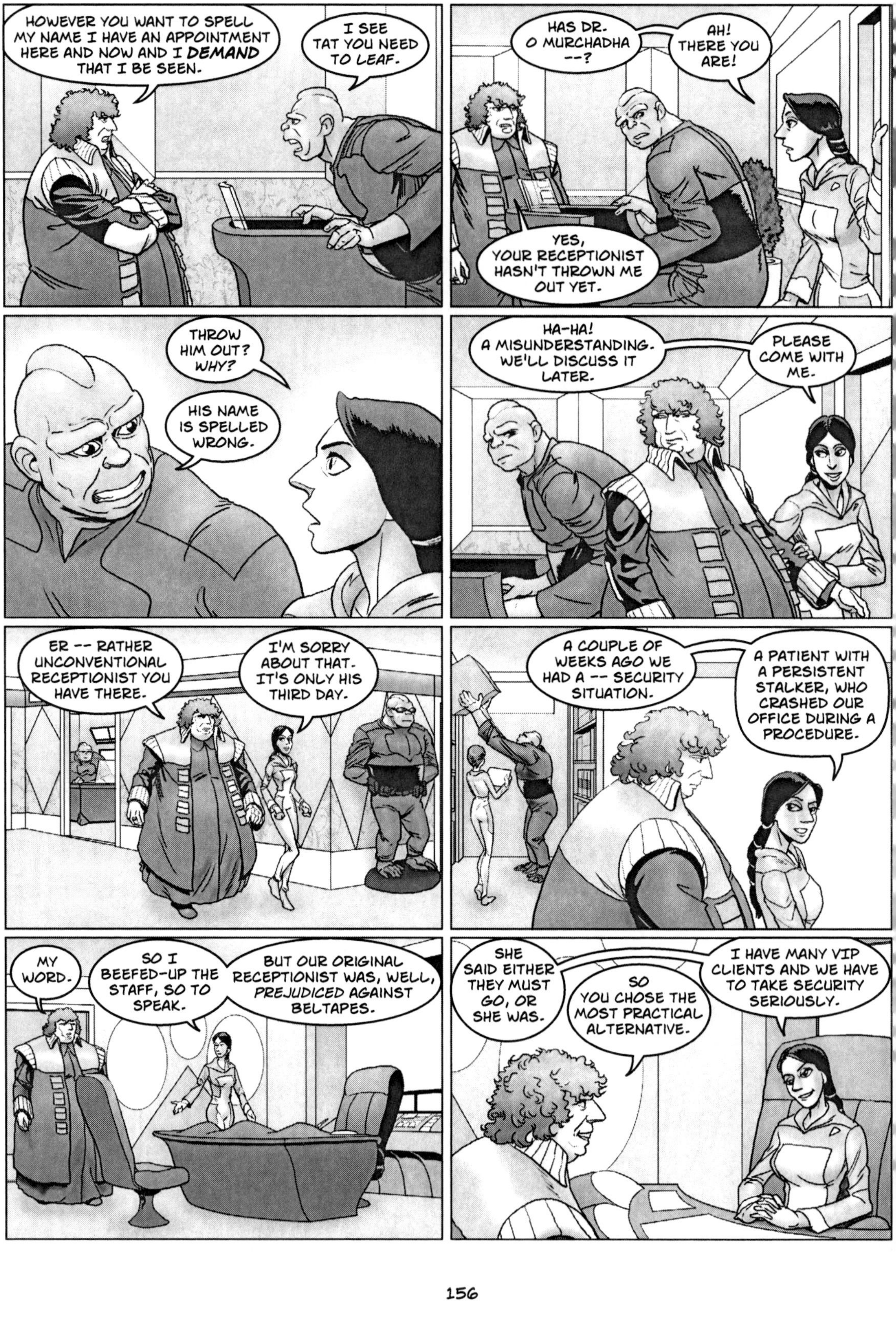
HOWEVER YOU WANT TO SPELL MY NAME I HAVE AN APPOINTMENT HERE AND NOW AND I DEMAND THAT I BE SEEN.
I SEE TAT YOU NEED TO LEAF.
HAS DR. O MURCHADHA --?
AH! THERE YOU ARE!
YES, YOUR RECEPTIONIST HASN'T THROWN ME OUT YET.
THROW HIM OUT? WHY?
HIS NAME IS SPELLED WRONG.
HA-HA! A MISUNDERSTANDING. WE'LL DISCUSS IT LATER.
PLEASE COME WITH ME.
ER -- RATHER UNCONVENTIONAL RECEPTIONIST YOU HAVE THERE.
I'M SORRY ABOUT THAT. IT'S ONLY HIS THIRD DAY.
A COUPLE OF WEEKS AGO WE HAD A -- SECURITY SITUATION.
A PATIENT WITH A PERSISTENT STALKER, WHO CRASHED OUR OFFICE DURING A PROCEDURE.
MY WORD.
SO I BEEFED-UP THE STAFF, SO TO SPEAK.
BUT OUR ORIGINAL RECEPTIONIST WAS, WELL, PREJUDICED AGAINST BELTAPES.
SHE SAID EITHER THEY MUST GO, OR SHE WAS.
SO YOU CHOSE THE MOST PRACTICAL ALTERNATIVE.
I HAVE MANY VIP CLIENTS AND WE HAVE TO TAKE SECURITY SERIOUSLY.

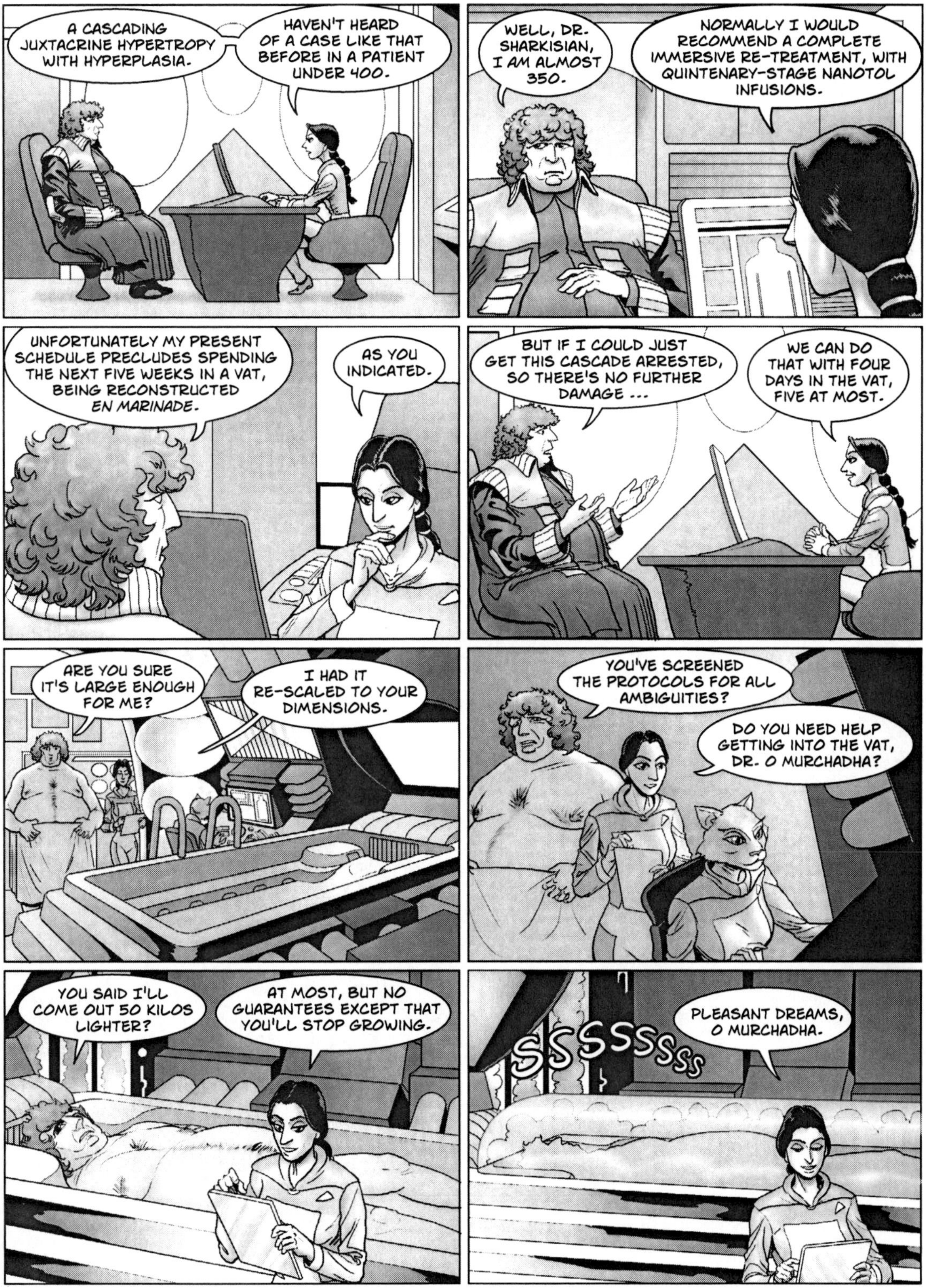
A CASCADING JUXTACRINE HYPERTROPY WITH HYPERPLASIA.
HAVEN'T HEARD OF A CASE LIKE THAT BEFORE IN A PATIENT UNDER 400.
WELL, DR. SHARKISIAN, I AM ALMOST 350.
NORMALLY I WOULD RECOMMEND A COMPLETE IMMERSIVE RE-TREATMENT, WITH QUINTENARY-STAGE NANOTOL INFUSIONS.
UNFORTUNATELY MY PRESENT SCHEDULE PRECLUDES SPENDING THE NEXT FIVE WEEKS IN A VAT, BEING RECONSTRUCTED *EN MARINADE*.
AS YOU INDICATED.
BUT IF I COULD JUST GET THIS CASCADE ARRESTED, SO THERE'S NO FURTHER DAMAGE ...
WE CAN DO THAT WITH FOUR DAYS IN THE VAT, FIVE AT MOST.
ARE YOU SURE IT'S LARGE ENOUGH FOR ME?
I HAD IT RE-SCALED TO YOUR DIMENSIONS.
YOU'VE SCREENED THE PROTOCOLS FOR ALL AMBIGUITIES?
DO YOU NEED HELP GETTING INTO THE VAT, DR. O MURCHADHA?
YOU SAID I'LL COME OUT 50 KILOS LIGHTER?
AT MOST, BUT NO GUARANTEES EXCEPT THAT YOU'LL STOP GROWING.
SSSSSSSS
PLEASANT DREAMS, O MURCHADHA.

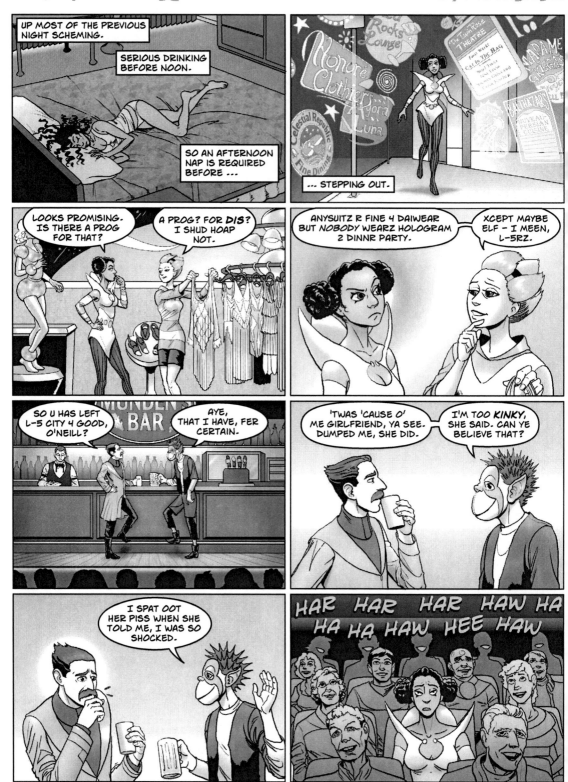

UP MOST OF THE PREVIOUS NIGHT SCHEMING.

SERIOUS DRINKING BEFORE NOON.

SO AN AFTERNOON NAP IS REQUIRED BEFORE ...

... STEPPING OUT.

LOOKS PROMISING. IS THERE A PROG FOR THAT?

A PROG? FOR DIS? I SHUD HOAP NOT.

ANYSUITZ R FINE 4 DAIWEAR BUT NOBODY WEARZ HOLOGRAM 2 DINNR PARTY.

XCEPT MAYBE ELF – I MEEN, L–5RZ.

SO U HAS LEFT L–5 CITY 4 GOOD, O'NEILL?

AYE, THAT I HAVE, FER CERTAIN.

'TWAS 'CAUSE O' ME GIRLFRIEND, YA SEE. DUMPED ME, SHE DID.

I'M TOO KINKY, SHE SAID. CAN YE BELIEVE THAT?

I SPAT OOT HER PISS WHEN SHE TOLD ME, I WAS SO SHOCKED.

HAR HAR HAR HAW HA HA HA HAW HEE HAW

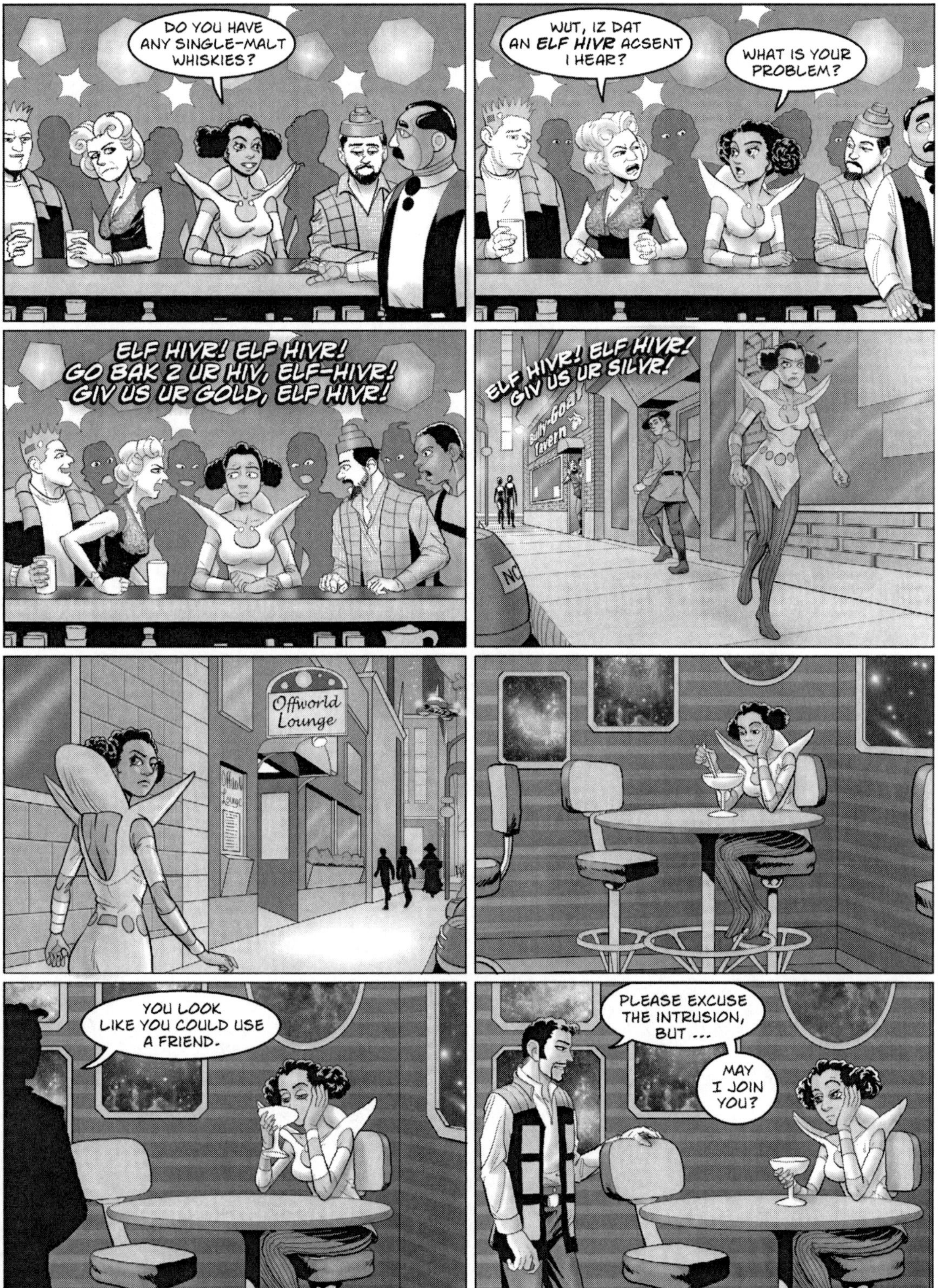
DO YOU HAVE ANY SINGLE-MALT WHISKIES?
WUT, IZ DAT AN ELF HIVR ACSENT I HEAR?
WHAT IS YOUR PROBLEM?
ELF HIVR! ELF HIVR! GO BAK 2 UR HIV, ELF-HIVR! GIV US UR GOLD, ELF HIVR!
ELF HIVR! ELF HIVR! GIV US UR SILVR!
Billy-Goat Tavern
Offworld Lounge
YOU LOOK LIKE YOU COULD USE A FRIEND.
PLEASE EXCUSE THE INTRUSION, BUT ...
MAY I JOIN YOU?

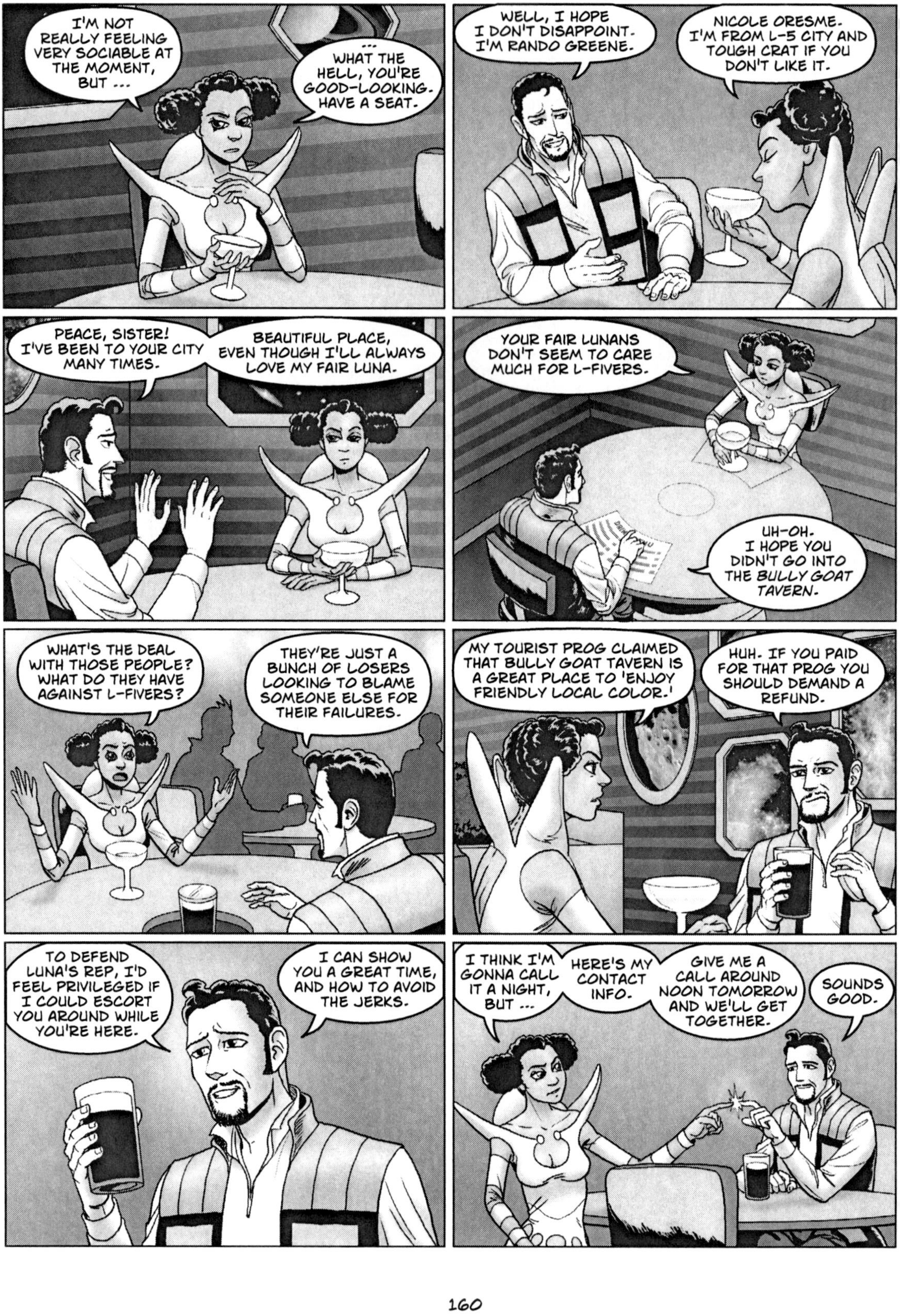
I'M NOT REALLY FEELING VERY SOCIABLE AT THE MOMENT, BUT ...
... WHAT THE HELL, YOU'RE GOOD-LOOKING. HAVE A SEAT.
WELL, I HOPE I DON'T DISAPPOINT. I'M RANDO GREENE.
NICOLE ORESME. I'M FROM L-5 CITY AND TOUGH CRAT IF YOU DON'T LIKE IT.
PEACE, SISTER! I'VE BEEN TO YOUR CITY MANY TIMES.
BEAUTIFUL PLACE, EVEN THOUGH I'LL ALWAYS LOVE MY FAIR LUNA.
YOUR FAIR LUNANS DON'T SEEM TO CARE MUCH FOR L-FIVERS.
UH-OH. I HOPE YOU DIDN'T GO INTO THE BULLY GOAT TAVERN.
WHAT'S THE DEAL WITH THOSE PEOPLE? WHAT DO THEY HAVE AGAINST L-FIVERS?
THEY'RE JUST A BUNCH OF LOSERS LOOKING TO BLAME SOMEONE ELSE FOR THEIR FAILURES.
MY TOURIST PROG CLAIMED THAT BULLY GOAT TAVERN IS A GREAT PLACE TO 'ENJOY FRIENDLY LOCAL COLOR.'
HUH. IF YOU PAID FOR THAT PROG YOU SHOULD DEMAND A REFUND.
TO DEFEND LUNA'S REP, I'D FEEL PRIVILEGED IF I COULD ESCORT YOU AROUND WHILE YOU'RE HERE.
I CAN SHOW YOU A GREAT TIME, AND HOW TO AVOID THE JERKS.
I THINK I'M GONNA CALL IT A NIGHT, BUT ...
HERE'S MY CONTACT INFO.
GIVE ME A CALL AROUND NOON TOMORROW AND WE'LL GET TOGETHER.
SOUNDS GOOD.

CAN'T BELIEVE I SLEPT SO LATE.

THREE CHEERS FOR ROOM SERVICE, ANYWAY.

TIME ENOUGH FOR ... UH ... BRUNCH BEFORE I START THE DAY.

ALSO, SOME QUICK RESEARCH ...

ROOMSCREEN, I NEED SOME BACKGROUND INFO ON A RANDO GREENE.

ALDRINOPOLIS RESIDENT, ABOUT 195 CM TALL, LIGHT SKIN, DARK HAIR, APPARENT AGE 30 YEARS.

WHO DAT?

PARAMS:
Nam: Rando Greene
In: Aldrinopolis
195cm tall, dk hair,
age

FIL FOUND MATCHIN PARAMS. DISPLAYIN DATA.

OH-HO.

THANKS FOR MEETING ME AT MY HOTEL.

NO PROBLEM. SINCE YOU WARNED ME YOU HAD A LATE BREAKFAST I'VE HAD MY OWN AND WE CAN GET STARTED TOURING.

To Concourse and ...ing Rooms

NOT JUST YET.

WE HAVE SOMETHING TO DISCUSS FIRST.

WHAT DO YOU ...

SIT. NOW.

I'VE FIGURED OUT YOUR ANGLE, GREENE.

THAT WAS NOT A CHANCE MEETING LAST NIGHT, WAS IT?

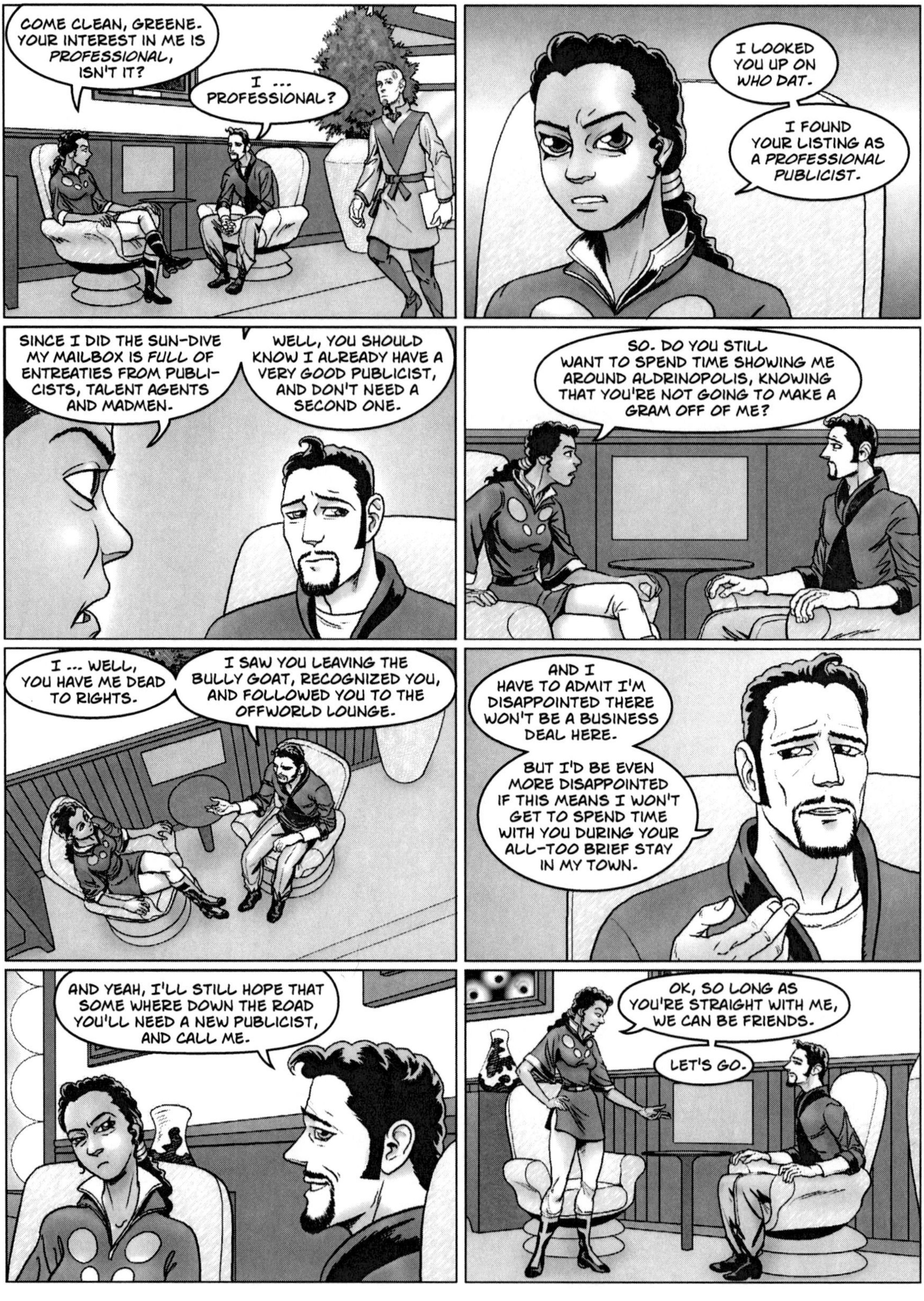
COME CLEAN, GREENE. YOUR INTEREST IN ME IS PROFESSIONAL, ISN'T IT?
I ... PROFESSIONAL?
I LOOKED YOU UP ON WHO DAT.
I FOUND YOUR LISTING AS A PROFESSIONAL PUBLICIST.
SINCE I DID THE SUN-DIVE MY MAILBOX IS FULL OF ENTREATIES FROM PUBLICISTS, TALENT AGENTS AND MADMEN.
WELL, YOU SHOULD KNOW I ALREADY HAVE A VERY GOOD PUBLICIST, AND DON'T NEED A SECOND ONE.
SO. DO YOU STILL WANT TO SPEND TIME SHOWING ME AROUND ALDRINOPOLIS, KNOWING THAT YOU'RE NOT GOING TO MAKE A GRAM OFF OF ME?
I ... WELL, YOU HAVE ME DEAD TO RIGHTS.
I SAW YOU LEAVING THE BULLY GOAT, RECOGNIZED YOU, AND FOLLOWED YOU TO THE OFFWORLD LOUNGE.
AND I HAVE TO ADMIT I'M DISAPPOINTED THERE WON'T BE A BUSINESS DEAL HERE.
BUT I'D BE EVEN MORE DISAPPOINTED IF THIS MEANS I WON'T GET TO SPEND TIME WITH YOU DURING YOUR ALL-TOO BRIEF STAY IN MY TOWN.
AND YEAH, I'LL STILL HOPE THAT SOME WHERE DOWN THE ROAD YOU'LL NEED A NEW PUBLICIST, AND CALL ME.
OK, SO LONG AS YOU'RE STRAIGHT WITH ME, WE CAN BE FRIENDS.
LET'S GO.

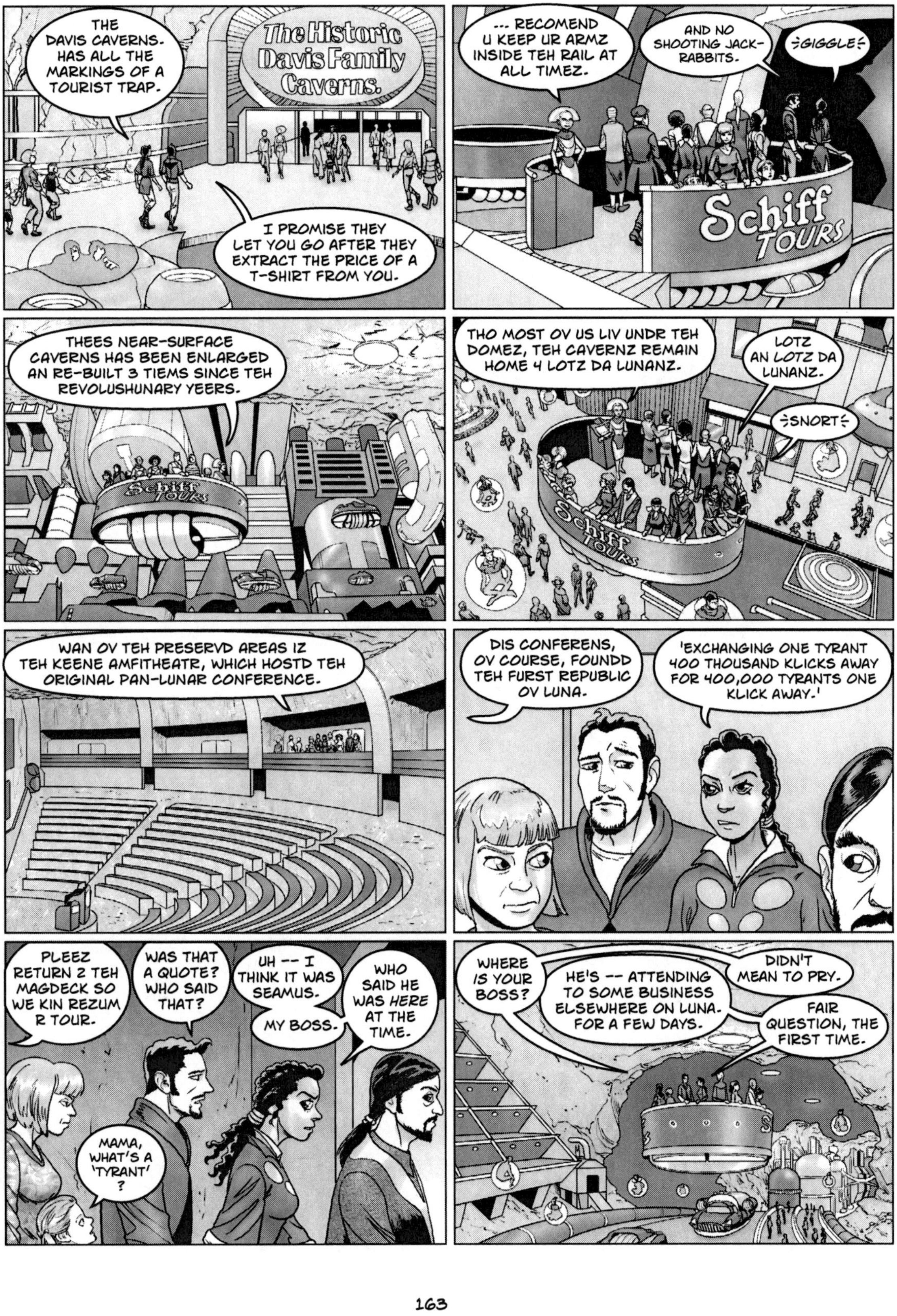
THE DAVIS CAVERNS. HAS ALL THE MARKINGS OF A TOURIST TRAP.
The Historic Davis Family Caverns.
I PROMISE THEY LET YOU GO AFTER THEY EXTRACT THE PRICE OF A T-SHIRT FROM YOU.
--- RECOMEND U KEEP UR ARMZ INSIDE TEH RAIL AT ALL TIMEZ.
AND NO SHOOTING JACK-RABBITS.
GIGGLE
Schiff TOURS
THEES NEAR-SURFACE CAVERNS HAS BEEN ENLARGED AN RE-BUILT 3 TIEMS SINCE TEH REVOLUSHUNARY YEERS.
Schiff TOURS
THO MOST OV US LIV UNDR TEH DOMEZ, TEH CAVERNZ REMAIN HOME 4 LOTZ DA LUNANZ.
LOTZ AN LOTZ DA LUNANZ.
SNORT
Schiff TOURS
WAN OV TEH PRESERVD AREAS IZ TEH KEENE AMFITHEATR, WHICH HOSTD TEH ORIGINAL PAN-LUNAR CONFERENCE.
DIS CONFERENS, OV COURSE, FOUNDD TEH FURST REPUBLIC OV LUNA.
'EXCHANGING ONE TYRANT 400 THOUSAND KLICKS AWAY FOR 400,000 TYRANTS ONE KLICK AWAY.'
PLEEZ RETURN 2 TEH MAGDECK SO WE KIN REZUM R TOUR.
WAS THAT A QUOTE? WHO SAID THAT?
UH -- I THINK IT WAS SEAMUS.
MY BOSS.
WHO SAID HE WAS HERE AT THE TIME.
MAMA, WHAT'S A 'TYRANT'?
WHERE IS YOUR BOSS?
DIDN'T MEAN TO PRY.
HE'S -- ATTENDING TO SOME BUSINESS ELSEWHERE ON LUNA. FOR A FEW DAYS.
FAIR QUESTION, THE FIRST TIME.

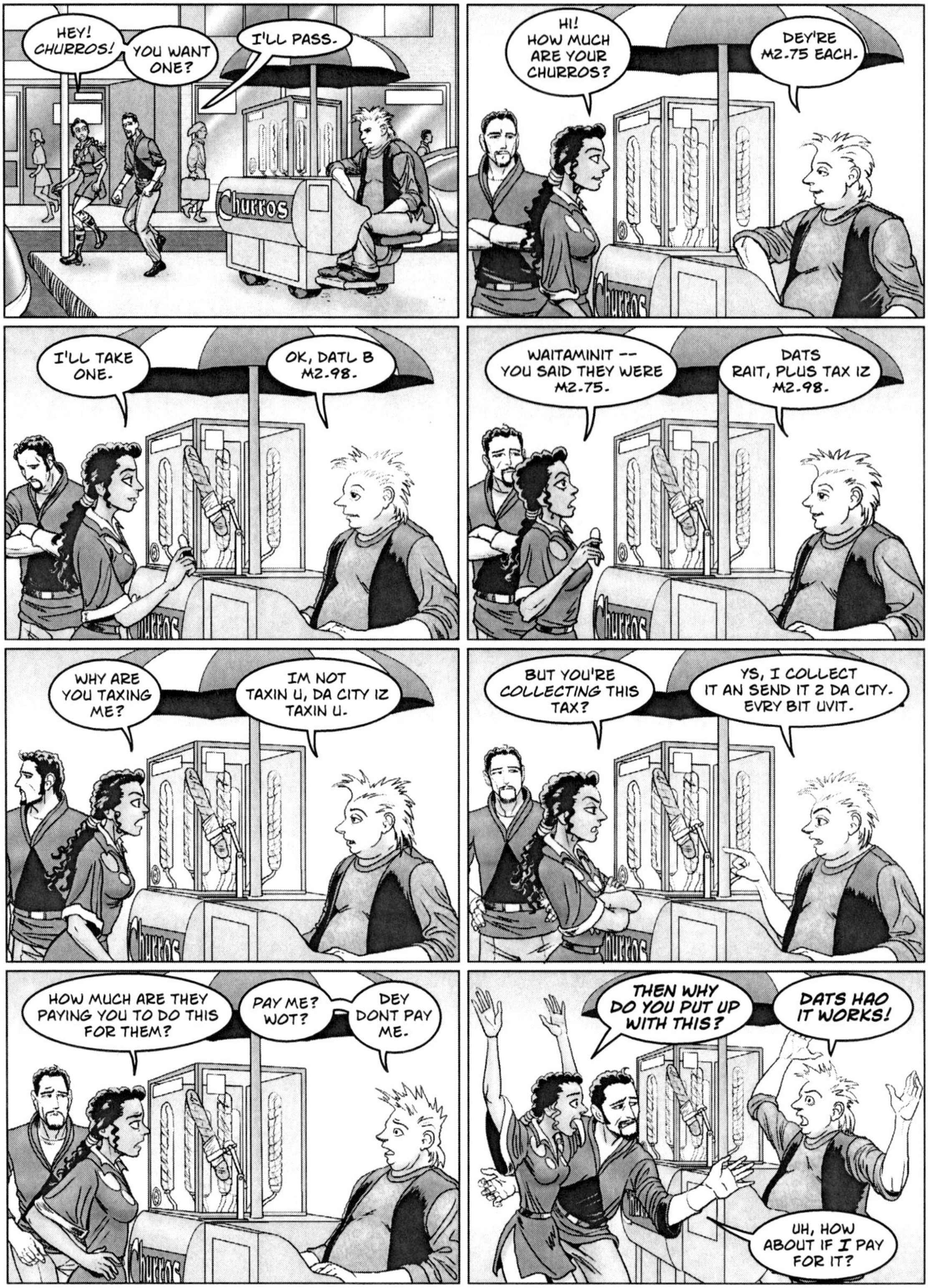
HEY! CHURROS!
YOU WANT ONE?
I'LL PASS.
Churros
HI! HOW MUCH ARE YOUR CHURROS?
DEY'RE M2.75 EACH.
I'LL TAKE ONE.
OK, DATL B M2.98.
WAITAMINIT -- YOU SAID THEY WERE M2.75.
DATS RAIT, PLUS TAX IZ M2.98.
WHY ARE YOU TAXING ME?
IM NOT TAXIN U, DA CITY IZ TAXIN U.
BUT YOU'RE COLLECTING THIS TAX?
YS, I COLLECT IT AN SEND IT 2 DA CITY. EVRY BIT UVIT.
HOW MUCH ARE THEY PAYING YOU TO DO THIS FOR THEM?
PAY ME? WOT?
DEY DONT PAY ME.
THEN WHY DO YOU PUT UP WITH THIS?
DATS HAO IT WORKS!
UH, HOW ABOUT IF I PAY FOR IT?

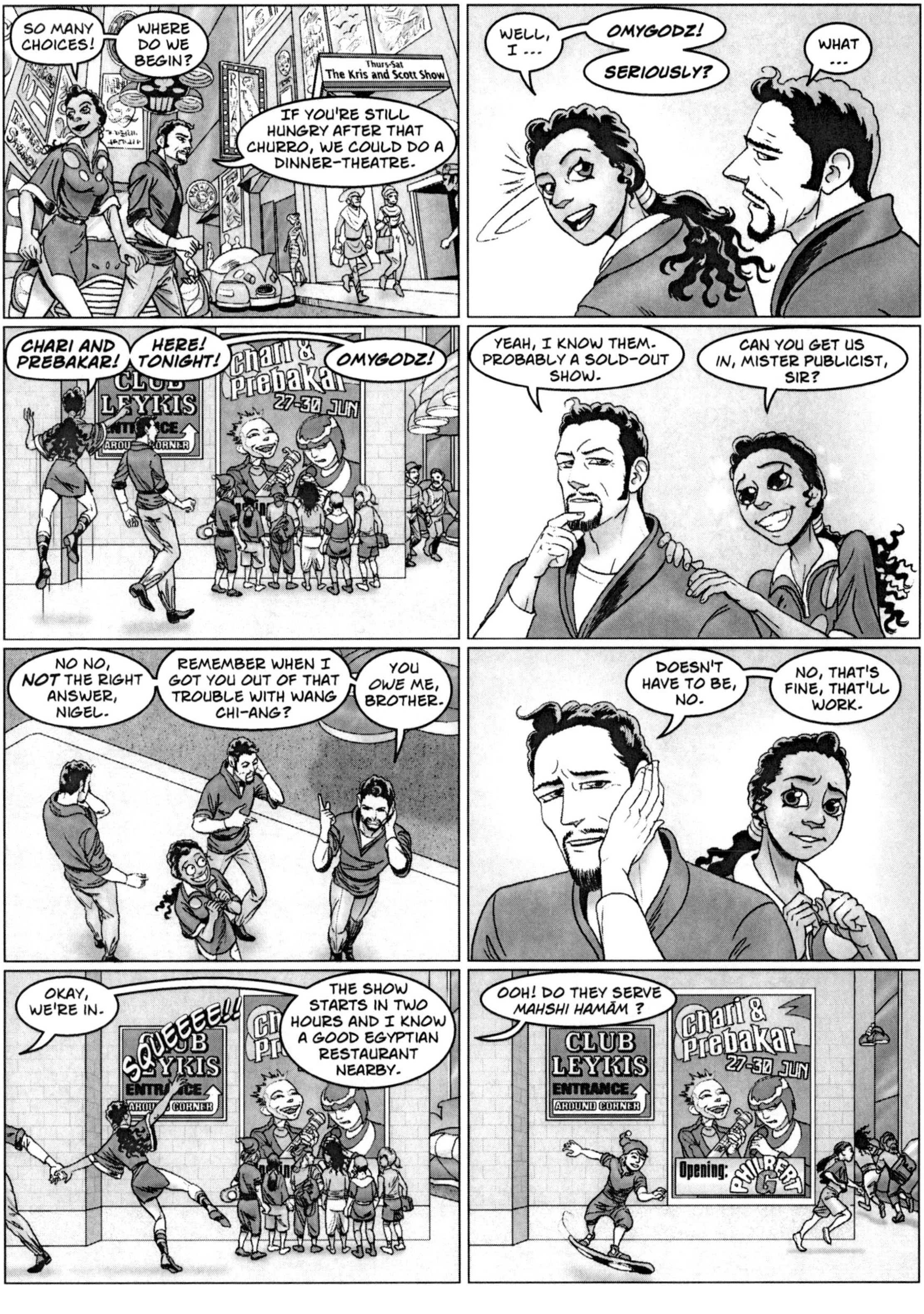
SO MANY CHOICES!
WHERE DO WE BEGIN?
Thurs-Sat The Kris and Scott Show
IF YOU'RE STILL HUNGRY AFTER THAT CHURRO, WE COULD DO A DINNER-THEATRE.
WELL, I ...
OMYGODZ!
SERIOUSLY?
WHAT ...
CHARI AND PREBAKAR!
HERE! TONIGHT!
OMYGODZ!
CLUB LEYKIS
Chari & Prebakar 27-30 JUN
YEAH, I KNOW THEM. PROBABLY A SOLD-OUT SHOW.
CAN YOU GET US IN, MISTER PUBLICIST, SIR?
NO NO, NOT THE RIGHT ANSWER, NIGEL.
REMEMBER WHEN I GOT YOU OUT OF THAT TROUBLE WITH WANG CHI-ANG?
YOU OWE ME, BROTHER.
DOESN'T HAVE TO BE, NO.
NO, THAT'S FINE, THAT'LL WORK.
OKAY, WE'RE IN.
THE SHOW STARTS IN TWO HOURS AND I KNOW A GOOD EGYPTIAN RESTAURANT NEARBY.
SQUEEEE!!
OOH! DO THEY SERVE MAHSHI HAMĀM ?
CLUB LEYKIS ENTRANCE AROUND CORNER
Chari & Prebakar 27-30 JUN
Opening: PHILBERT G

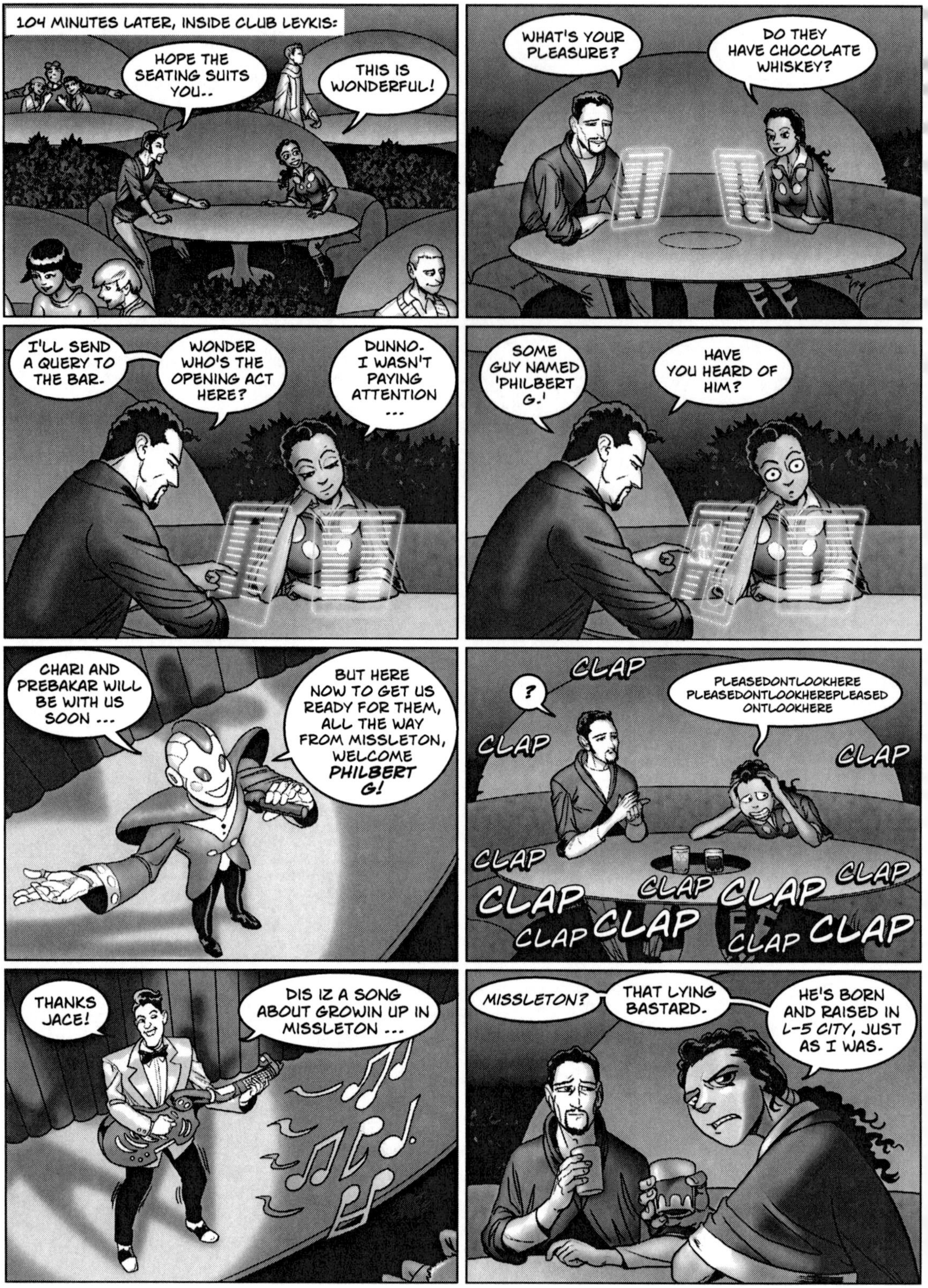
104 MINUTES LATER, INSIDE CLUB LEYKIS:
HOPE THE SEATING SUITS YOU..
THIS IS WONDERFUL!
WHAT'S YOUR PLEASURE?
DO THEY HAVE CHOCOLATE WHISKEY?
I'LL SEND A QUERY TO THE BAR.
WONDER WHO'S THE OPENING ACT HERE?
DUNNO. I WASN'T PAYING ATTENTION ...
SOME GUY NAMED 'PHILBERT G.'
HAVE YOU HEARD OF HIM?
CHARI AND PREBAKAR WILL BE WITH US SOON ...
BUT HERE NOW TO GET US READY FOR THEM, ALL THE WAY FROM MISSLETON, WELCOME PHILBERT G!
CLAP
?
PLEASEDONTLOOKHERE PLEASEDONTLOOKHEREPLEASED ONTLOOKHERE
CLAP
CLAP
CLAP
CLAP
CLAP
CLAP CLAP
CLAP
CLAP CLAP
CLAP CLAP
THANKS JACE!
DIS IZ A SONG ABOUT GROWIN UP IN MISSLETON ...
MISSLETON?
THAT LYING BASTARD.
HE'S BORN AND RAISED IN L-5 CITY, JUST AS I WAS.

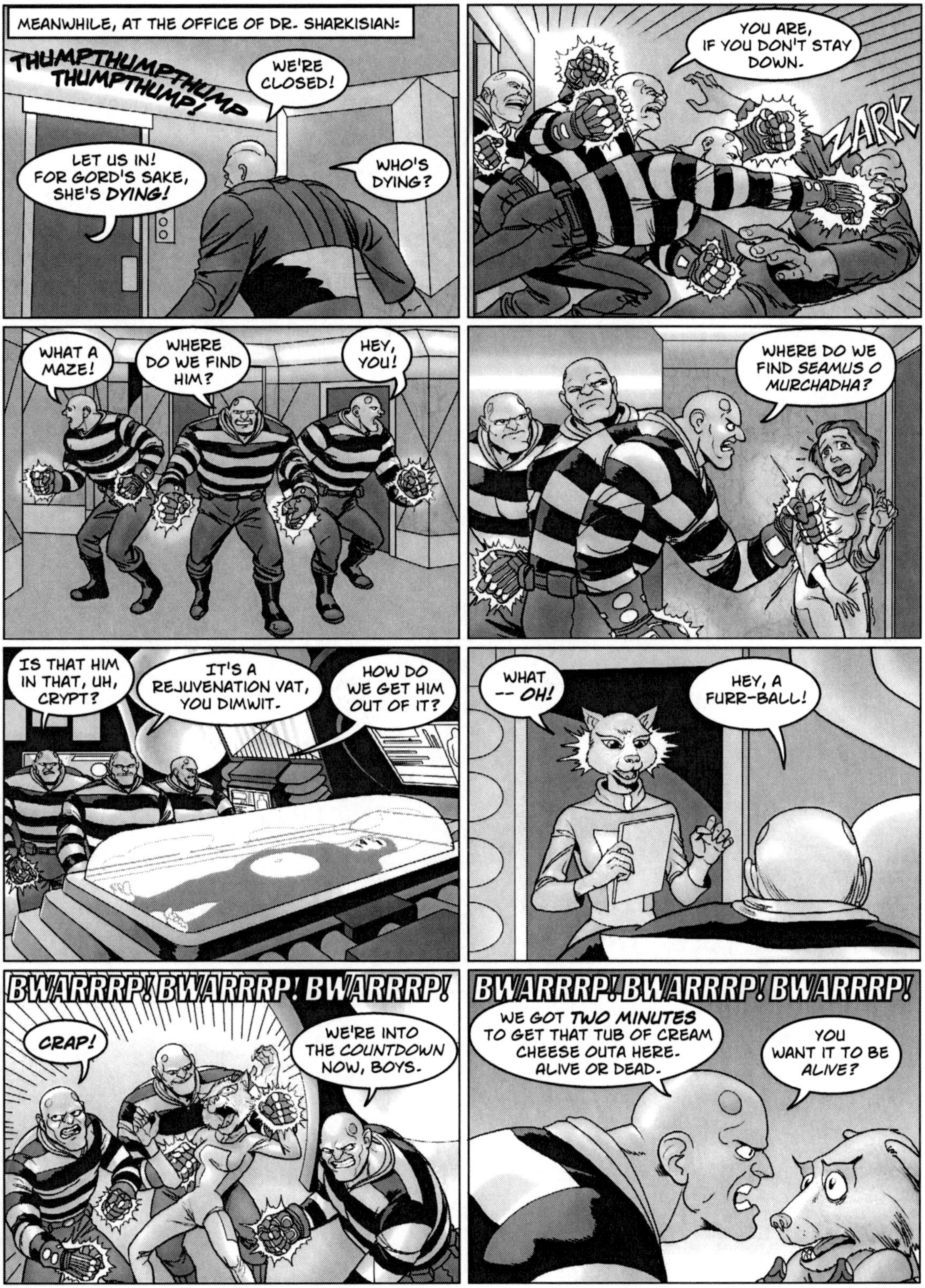
MEANWHILE, AT THE OFFICE OF DR. SHARKISIAN:
THUMPTHUMPTHUMP THUMPTHUMP!
WE'RE CLOSED!
LET US IN! FOR GORD'S SAKE, SHE'S DYING!
WHO'S DYING?
YOU ARE, IF YOU DON'T STAY DOWN.
ZARK
WHAT A MAZE!
WHERE DO WE FIND HIM?
HEY, YOU!
WHERE DO WE FIND SEAMUS O MURCHADHA?
IS THAT HIM IN THAT, UH, CRYPT?
IT'S A REJUVENATION VAT, YOU DIMWIT.
HOW DO WE GET HIM OUT OF IT?
WHAT -- OH!
HEY, A FURR-BALL!
BWARRRP! BWARRRP! BWARRRP!
CRAP!
WE'RE INTO THE COUNTDOWN NOW, BOYS.
BWARRRP! BWARRRP! BWARRRP!
WE GOT TWO MINUTES TO GET THAT TUB OF CREAM CHEESE OUTA HERE. ALIVE OR DEAD.
YOU WANT IT TO BE ALIVE?

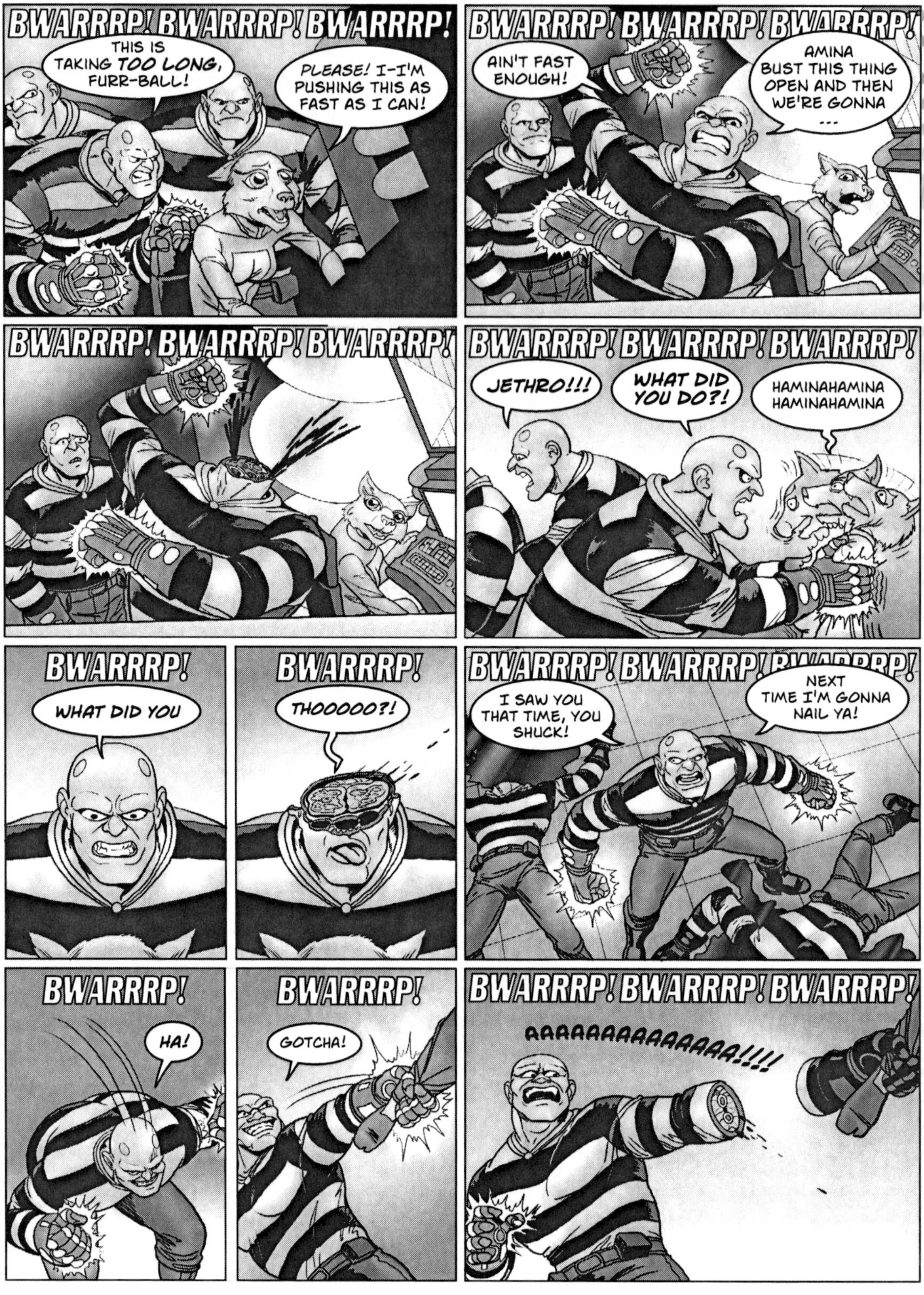
BWARRRP! BWARRRP! BWARRRP!
THIS IS TAKING TOO LONG, FURR-BALL!
PLEASE! I-I'M PUSHING THIS AS FAST AS I CAN!
BWARRRP! BWARRRP! BWARRRP!
AIN'T FAST ENOUGH!
AMINA BUST THIS THING OPEN AND THEN WE'RE GONNA ...
BWARRRP! BWARRRP! BWARRRP!
BWARRRP! BWARRRP! BWARRRP!
JETHRO!!!
WHAT DID YOU DO?!
HAMINAHAMINA HAMINAHAMINA
BWARRRP!
WHAT DID YOU
BWARRRP!
THOOOOO?!
BWARRRP! BWARRRP!
I SAW YOU THAT TIME, YOU SHUCK!
NEXT TIME I'M GONNA NAIL YA!
BWARRRP!
HA!
BWARRRP!
GOTCHA!
BWARRRP! BWARRRP! BWARRRP!
AAAAAAAAAAAAAAA!!!!

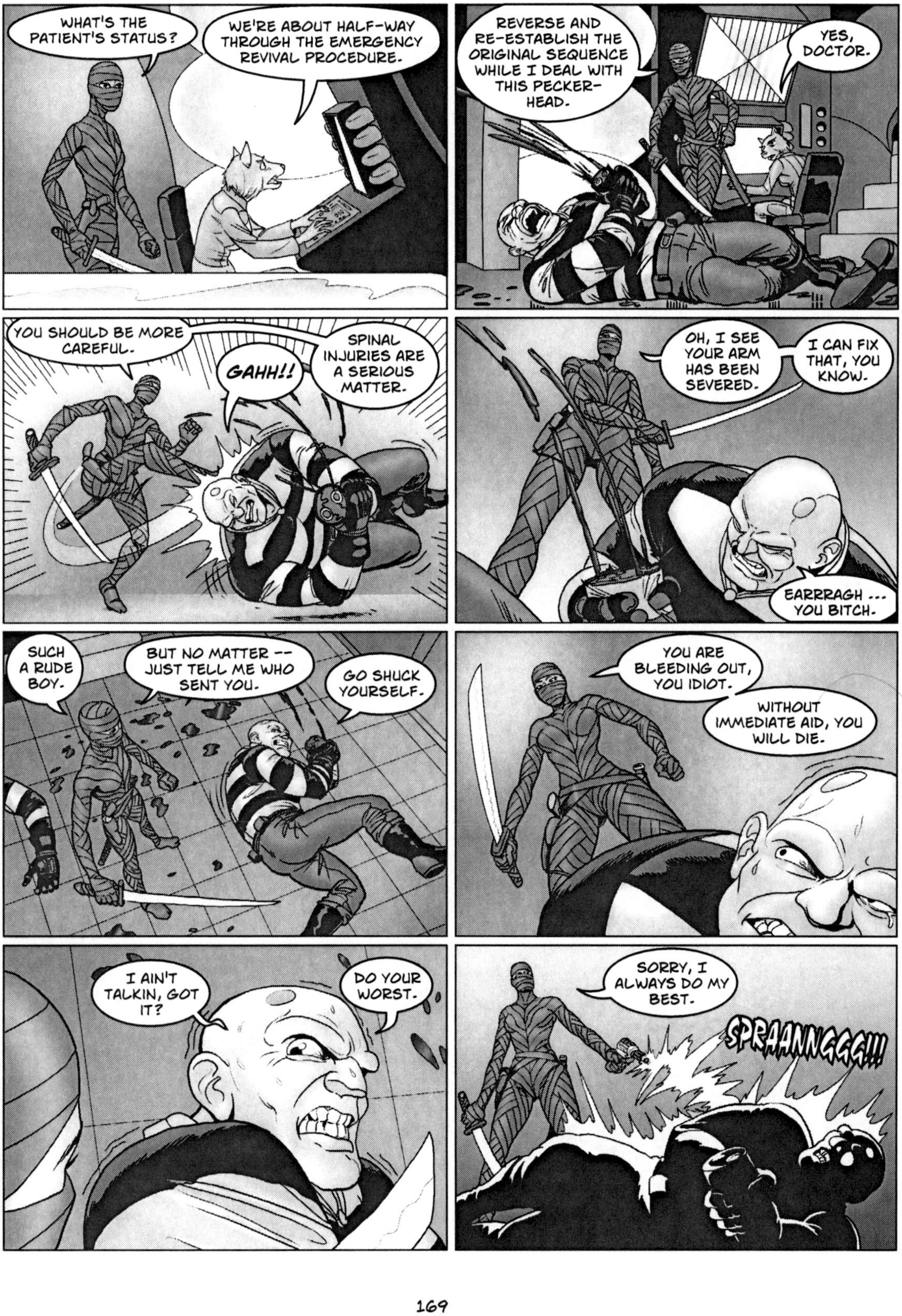
WHAT'S THE PATIENT'S STATUS?
WE'RE ABOUT HALF-WAY THROUGH THE EMERGENCY REVIVAL PROCEDURE.
REVERSE AND RE-ESTABLISH THE ORIGINAL SEQUENCE WHILE I DEAL WITH THIS PECKER-HEAD.
YES, DOCTOR.
YOU SHOULD BE MORE CAREFUL.
GAHH!!
SPINAL INJURIES ARE A SERIOUS MATTER.
OH, I SEE YOUR ARM HAS BEEN SEVERED.
I CAN FIX THAT, YOU KNOW.
EARRRAGH ... YOU BITCH.
SUCH A RUDE BOY.
BUT NO MATTER -- JUST TELL ME WHO SENT YOU.
GO SHUCK YOURSELF.
YOU ARE BLEEDING OUT, YOU IDIOT.
WITHOUT IMMEDIATE AID, YOU WILL DIE.
I AIN'T TALKIN, GOT IT?
DO YOUR WORST.
SORRY, I ALWAYS DO MY BEST.
SPRAANNGGG!!!

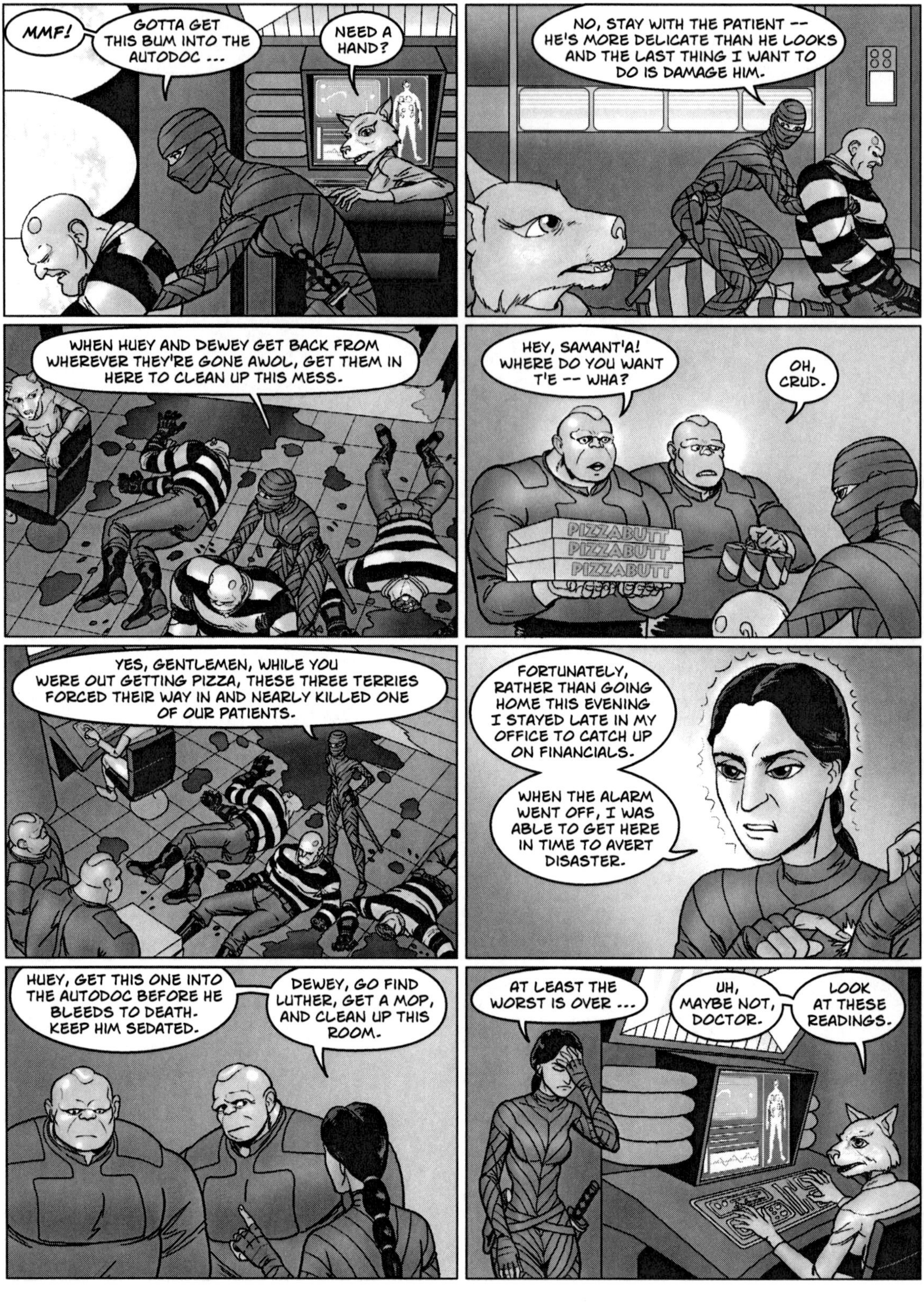
MMF!
GOTTA GET THIS BUM INTO THE AUTODOC ...
NEED A HAND?
NO, STAY WITH THE PATIENT -- HE'S MORE DELICATE THAN HE LOOKS AND THE LAST THING I WANT TO DO IS DAMAGE HIM.
WHEN HUEY AND DEWEY GET BACK FROM WHEREVER THEY'RE GONE AWOL, GET THEM IN HERE TO CLEAN UP THIS MESS.
HEY, SAMANT'A! WHERE DO YOU WANT T'E -- WHA?
OH, CRUD.
PIZZABUTT
PIZZABUTT
PIZZABUTT
YES, GENTLEMEN, WHILE YOU WERE OUT GETTING PIZZA, THESE THREE TERRIES FORCED THEIR WAY IN AND NEARLY KILLED ONE OF OUR PATIENTS.
FORTUNATELY, RATHER THAN GOING HOME THIS EVENING I STAYED LATE IN MY OFFICE TO CATCH UP ON FINANCIALS.
WHEN THE ALARM WENT OFF, I WAS ABLE TO GET HERE IN TIME TO AVERT DISASTER.
HUEY, GET THIS ONE INTO THE AUTODOC BEFORE HE BLEEDS TO DEATH. KEEP HIM SEDATED.
DEWEY, GO FIND LUTHER, GET A MOP, AND CLEAN UP THIS ROOM.
AT LEAST THE WORST IS OVER ...
UH, MAYBE NOT, DOCTOR.
LOOK AT THESE READINGS.

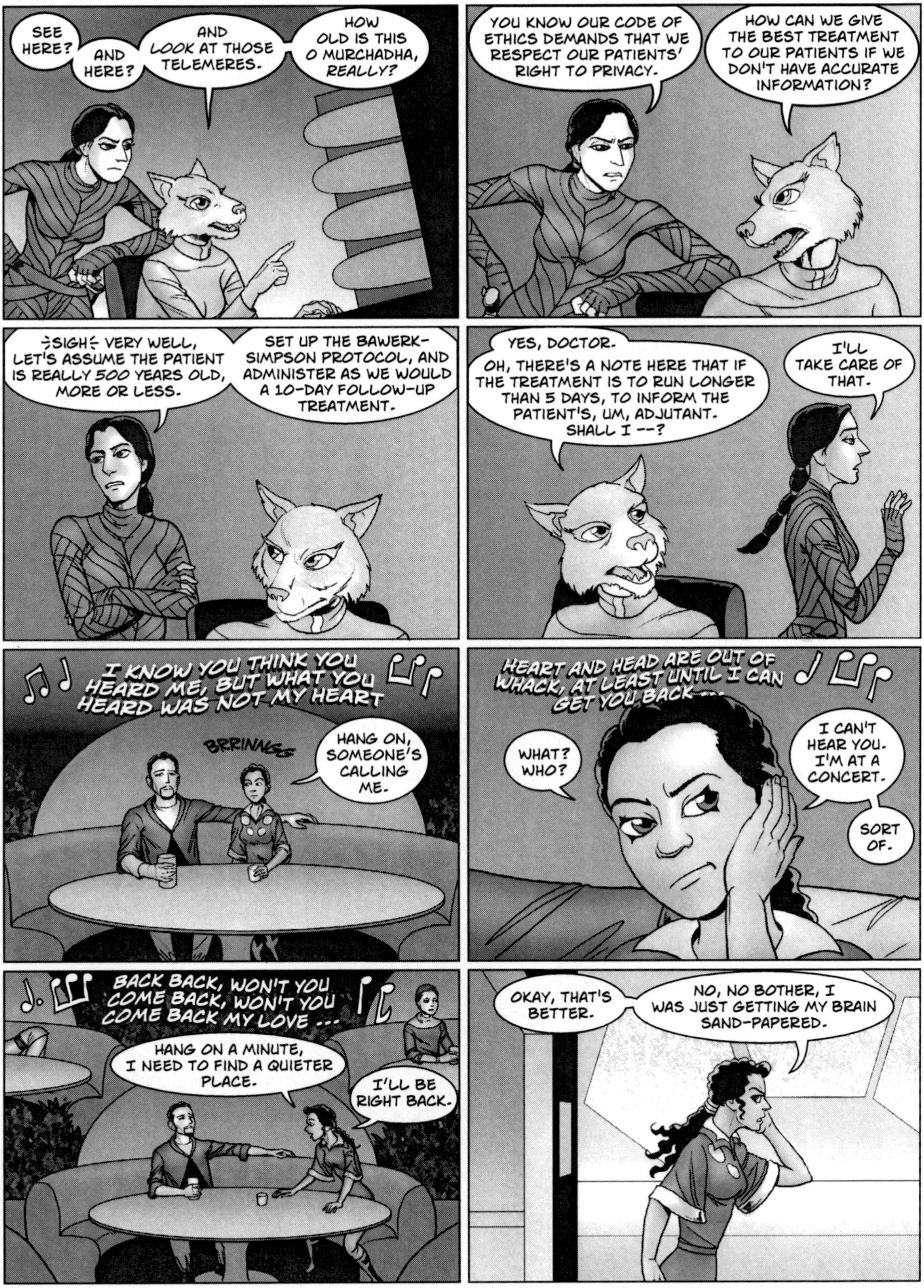
SEE HERE?
AND HERE?
AND LOOK AT THOSE TELEMERES.
HOW OLD IS THIS O MURCHADHA, REALLY?
YOU KNOW OUR CODE OF ETHICS DEMANDS THAT WE RESPECT OUR PATIENTS' RIGHT TO PRIVACY.
HOW CAN WE GIVE THE BEST TREATMENT TO OUR PATIENTS IF WE DON'T HAVE ACCURATE INFORMATION?
SIGH VERY WELL, LET'S ASSUME THE PATIENT IS REALLY 500 YEARS OLD, MORE OR LESS.
SET UP THE BAWERK-SIMPSON PROTOCOL, AND ADMINISTER AS WE WOULD A 10-DAY FOLLOW-UP TREATMENT.
YES, DOCTOR.
OH, THERE'S A NOTE HERE THAT IF THE TREATMENT IS TO RUN LONGER THAN 5 DAYS, TO INFORM THE PATIENT'S, UM, ADJUTANT. SHALL I --?
I'LL TAKE CARE OF THAT.
I KNOW YOU THINK YOU HEARD ME, BUT WHAT YOU HEARD WAS NOT MY HEART
BRRINNGG
HANG ON, SOMEONE'S CALLING ME.
HEART AND HEAD ARE OUT OF WHACK, AT LEAST UNTIL I CAN GET YOU BACK ...
WHAT? WHO?
I CAN'T HEAR YOU. I'M AT A CONCERT.
SORT OF.
BACK BACK, WON'T YOU COME BACK, WON'T YOU COME BACK MY LOVE ...
HANG ON A MINUTE, I NEED TO FIND A QUIETER PLACE.
I'LL BE RIGHT BACK.
OKAY, THAT'S BETTER.
NO, NO BOTHER, I WAS JUST GETTING MY BRAIN SAND-PAPERED.

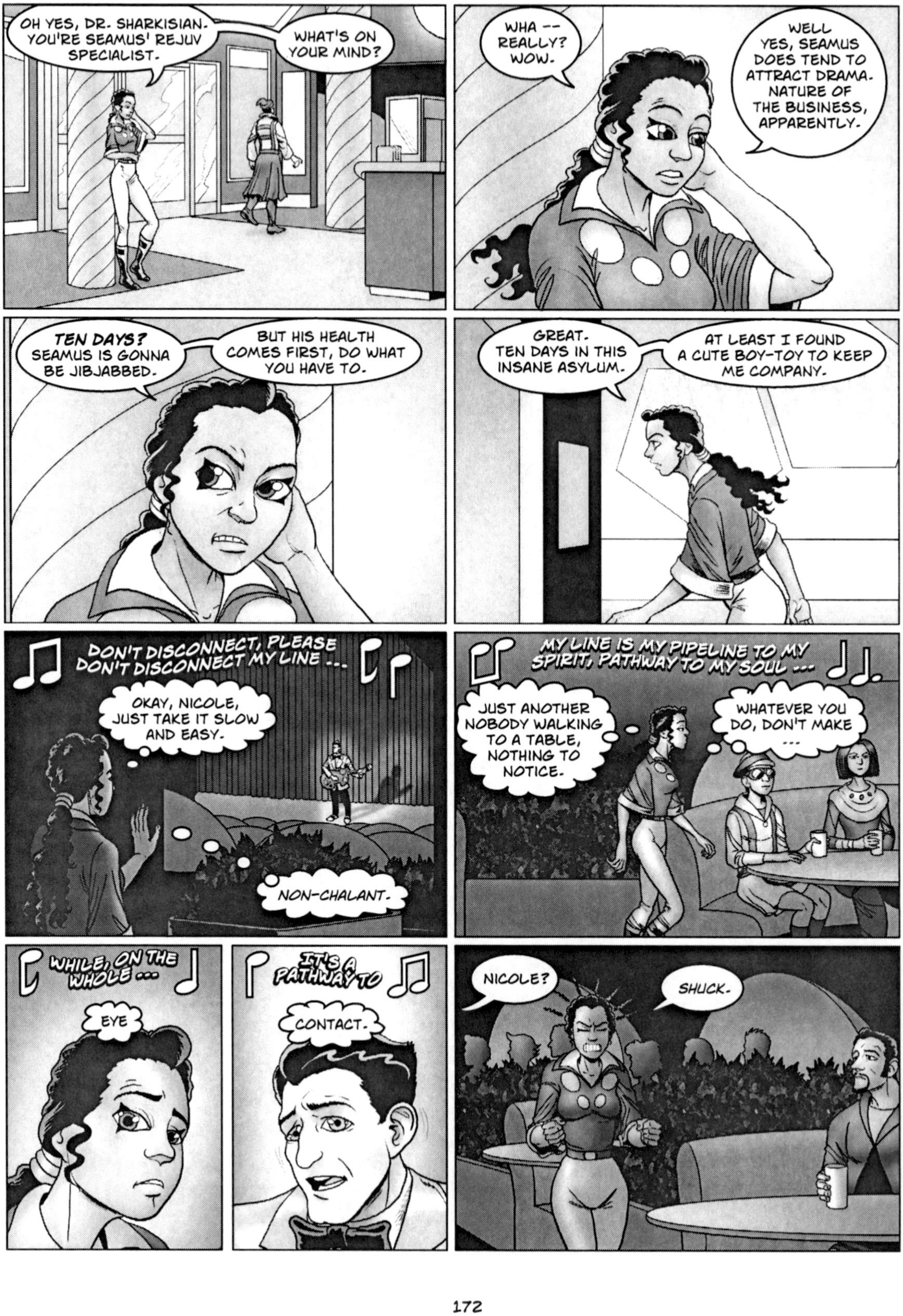
OH YES, DR. SHARKISIAN. YOU'RE SEAMUS' REJUV SPECIALIST.
WHAT'S ON YOUR MIND?
WHA -- REALLY? WOW.
WELL YES, SEAMUS DOES TEND TO ATTRACT DRAMA. NATURE OF THE BUSINESS, APPARENTLY.
TEN DAYS? SEAMUS IS GONNA BE JIBJABBED.
BUT HIS HEALTH COMES FIRST, DO WHAT YOU HAVE TO.
GREAT. TEN DAYS IN THIS INSANE ASYLUM.
AT LEAST I FOUND A CUTE BOY-TOY TO KEEP ME COMPANY.
DON'T DISCONNECT, PLEASE DON'T DISCONNECT MY LINE ...
OKAY, NICOLE, JUST TAKE IT SLOW AND EASY.
NON-CHALANT.
MY LINE IS MY PIPELINE TO MY SPIRIT, PATHWAY TO MY SOUL ...
JUST ANOTHER NOBODY WALKING TO A TABLE, NOTHING TO NOTICE.
WHATEVER YOU DO, DON'T MAKE ...
WHILE, ON THE WHOLE ...
EYE
IT'S A PATHWAY TO
CONTACT.
NICOLE?
SHUCK.

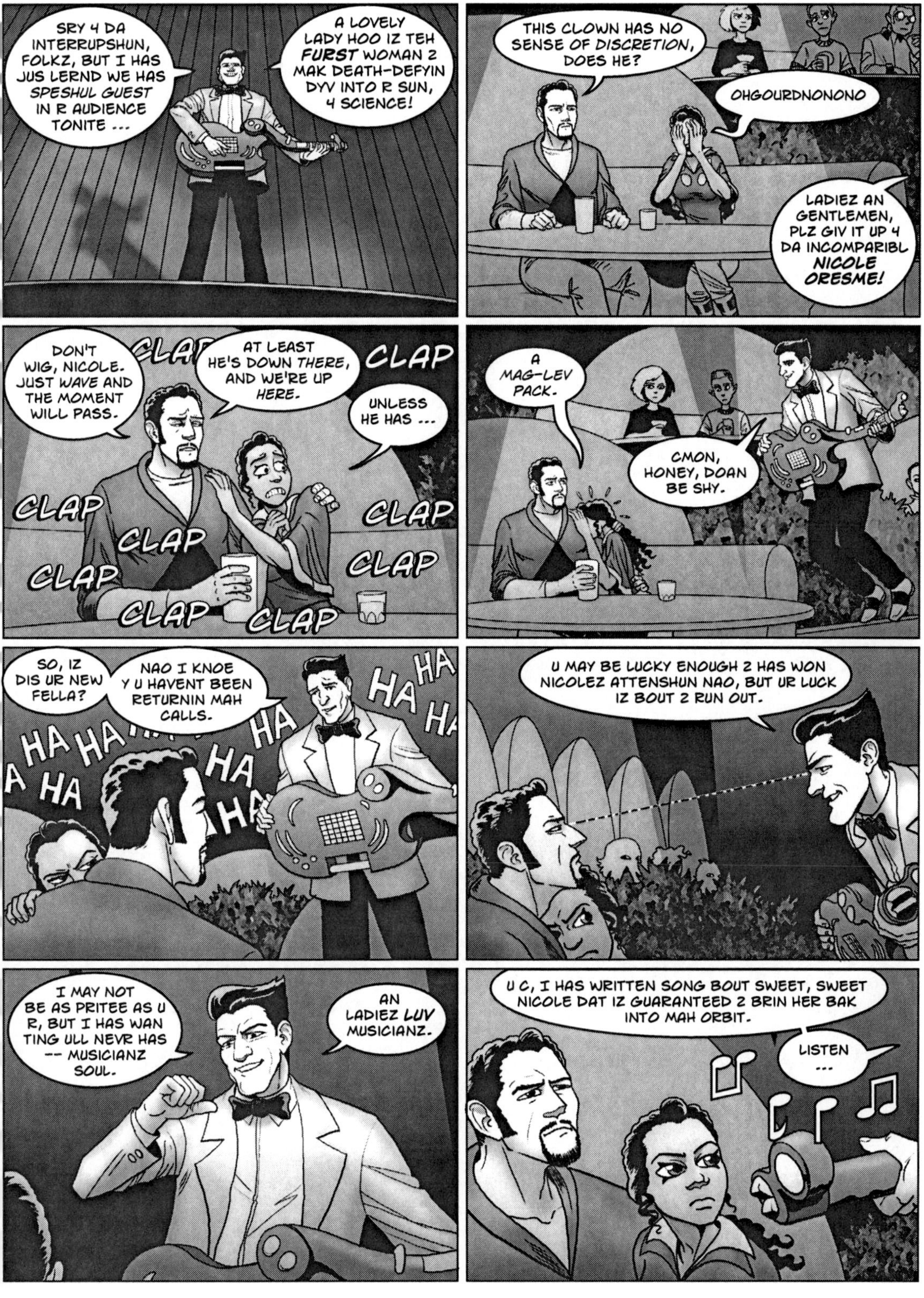
SRY 4 DA INTERRUPSHUN, FOLKZ, BUT I HAS JUS LERND WE HAS SPESHUL GUEST IN R AUDIENCE TONITE ...
A LOVELY LADY HOO IZ TEH FURST WOMAN 2 MAK DEATH-DEFYIN DYV INTO R SUN, 4 SCIENCE!
THIS CLOWN HAS NO SENSE OF DISCRETION, DOES HE?
OHGOURDNONONO
LADIEZ AN GENTLEMEN, PLZ GIV IT UP 4 DA INCOMPARIBL NICOLE ORESME!
DON'T WIG, NICOLE. JUST WAVE AND THE MOMENT WILL PASS.
CLAP
AT LEAST HE'S DOWN THERE, AND WE'RE UP HERE.
CLAP
UNLESS HE HAS ...
CLAP CLAP CLAP CLAP CLAP CLAP CLAP
A MAG-LEV PACK.
CMON, HONEY, DOAN BE SHY.
SO, IZ DIS UR NEW FELLA?
NAO I KNOE Y U HAVENT BEEN RETURNIN MAH CALLS.
HA HA HA HA HA HA HA HA HA
U MAY BE LUCKY ENOUGH 2 HAS WON NICOLEZ ATTENSHUN NAO, BUT UR LUCK IZ BOUT 2 RUN OUT.
I MAY NOT BE AS PRITEE AS U R, BUT I HAS WAN TING ULL NEVR HAS -- MUSICIANZ SOUL.
AN LADIEZ LUV MUSICIANZ.
U C, I HAS WRITTEN SONG BOUT SWEET, SWEET NICOLE DAT IZ GUARANTEED 2 BRIN HER BAK INTO MAH ORBIT.
LISTEN ...

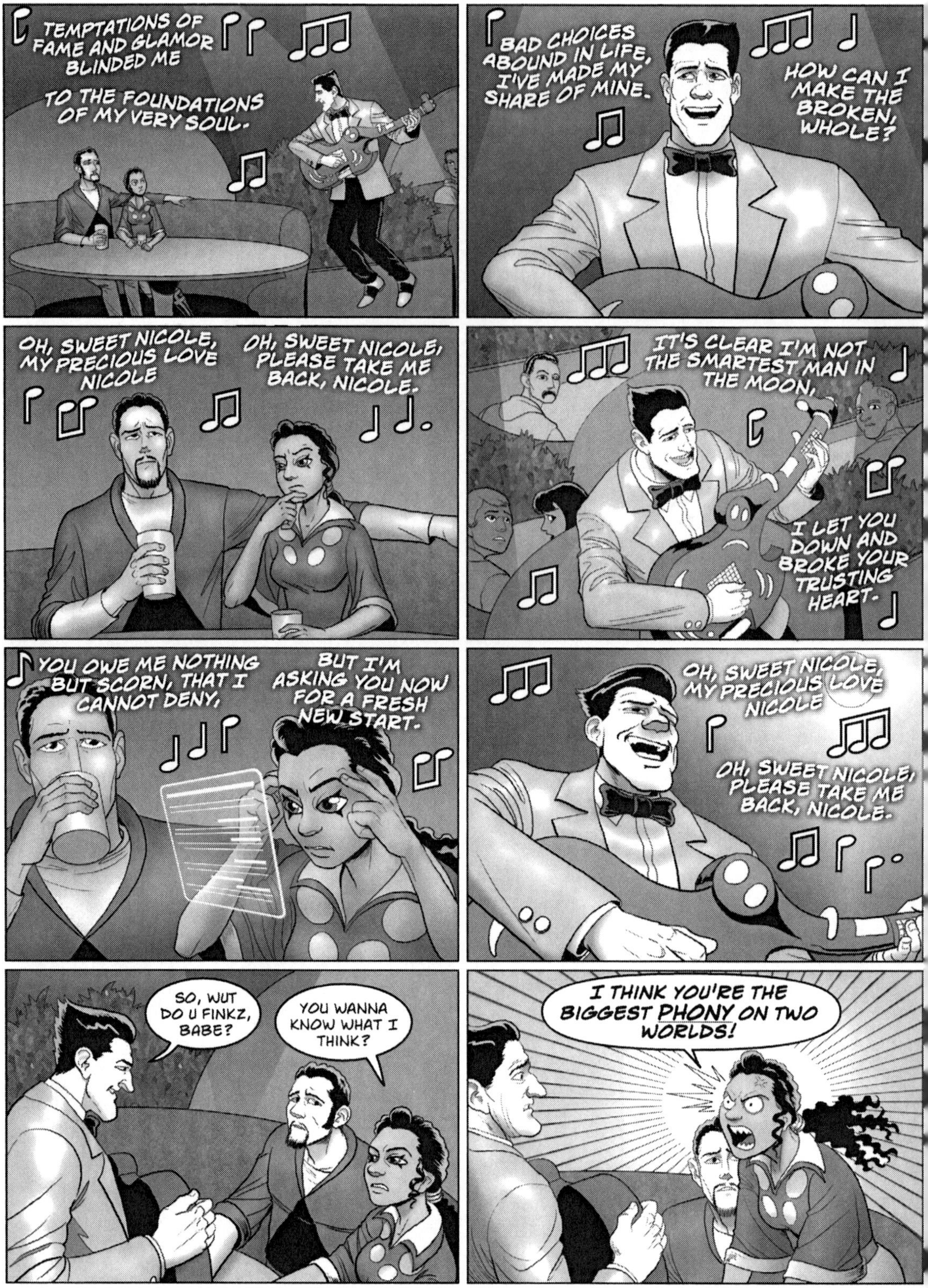
TEMPTATIONS OF FAME AND GLAMOR BLINDED ME
TO THE FOUNDATIONS OF MY VERY SOUL.
BAD CHOICES ABOUND IN LIFE, I'VE MADE MY SHARE OF MINE.
HOW CAN I MAKE THE BROKEN, WHOLE?
OH, SWEET NICOLE, MY PRECIOUS LOVE NICOLE
OH, SWEET NICOLE, PLEASE TAKE ME BACK, NICOLE.
IT'S CLEAR I'M NOT THE SMARTEST MAN IN THE MOON,
I LET YOU DOWN AND BROKE YOUR TRUSTING HEART.
YOU OWE ME NOTHING BUT SCORN, THAT I CANNOT DENY,
BUT I'M ASKING YOU NOW FOR A FRESH NEW START.
OH, SWEET NICOLE, MY PRECIOUS LOVE NICOLE
OH, SWEET NICOLE, PLEASE TAKE ME BACK, NICOLE.
SO, WUT DO U FINKZ, BABE?
YOU WANNA KNOW WHAT I THINK?
I THINK YOU'RE THE BIGGEST PHONY ON TWO WORLDS!

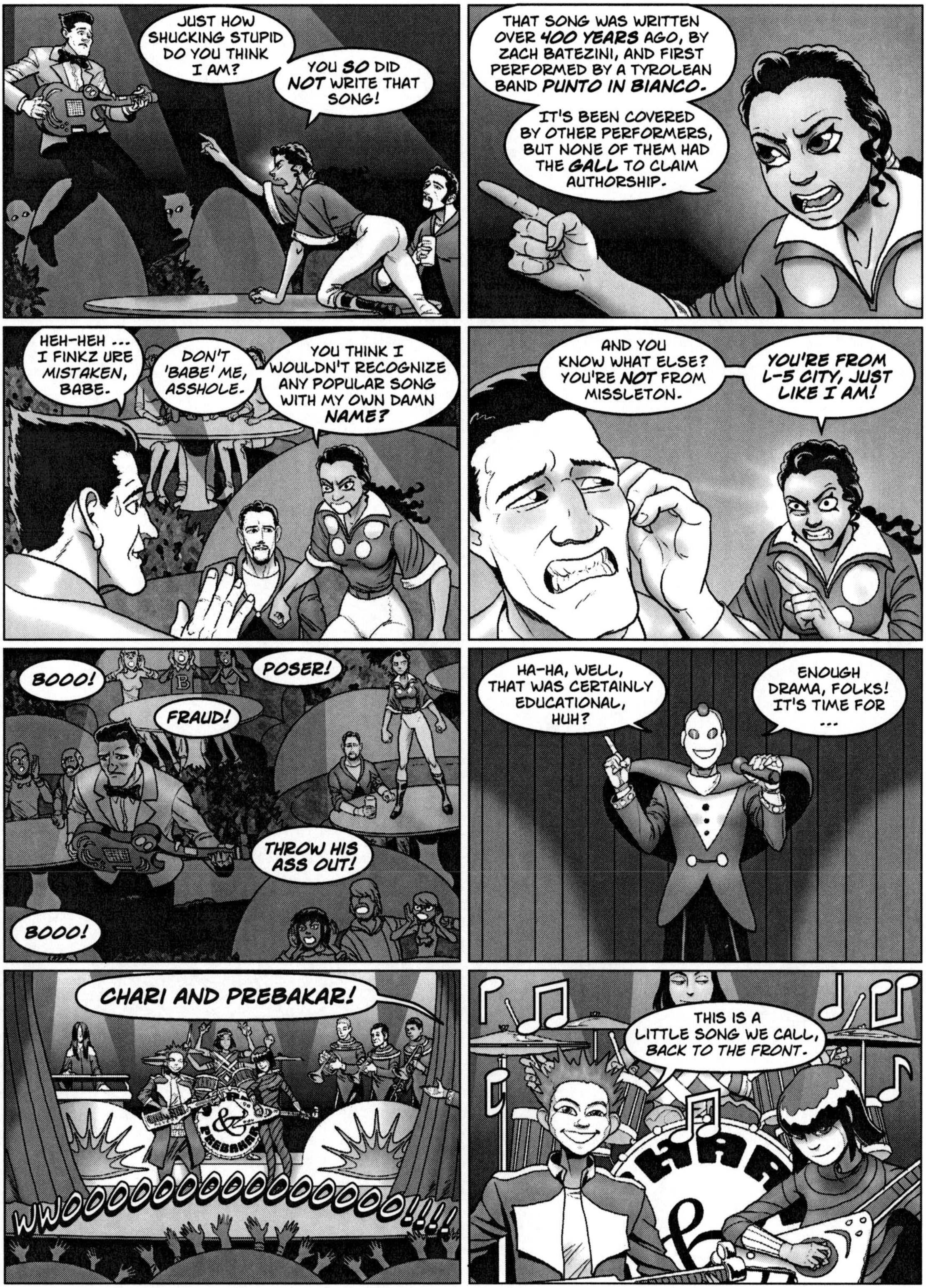
JUST HOW SHUCKING STUPID DO YOU THINK I AM?
YOU SO DID NOT WRITE THAT SONG!
THAT SONG WAS WRITTEN OVER 400 YEARS AGO, BY ZACH BATEZINI, AND FIRST PERFORMED BY A TYROLEAN BAND PUNTO IN BIANCO.
IT'S BEEN COVERED BY OTHER PERFORMERS, BUT NONE OF THEM HAD THE GALL TO CLAIM AUTHORSHIP.
HEH-HEH ... I FINKZ URE MISTAKEN, BABE.
DON'T 'BABE' ME, ASSHOLE.
YOU THINK I WOULDN'T RECOGNIZE ANY POPULAR SONG WITH MY OWN DAMN NAME?
AND YOU KNOW WHAT ELSE? YOU'RE NOT FROM MISSLETON.
YOU'RE FROM L-5 CITY, JUST LIKE I AM!
BOOO!
POSER!
FRAUD!
THROW HIS ASS OUT!
BOOO!
HA-HA, WELL, THAT WAS CERTAINLY EDUCATIONAL, HUH?
ENOUGH DRAMA, FOLKS! IT'S TIME FOR ...
CHARI AND PREBAKAR!
WWOOOOOOOOOOOOOOOOOO!!!!
THIS IS A LITTLE SONG WE CALL, BACK TO THE FRONT.

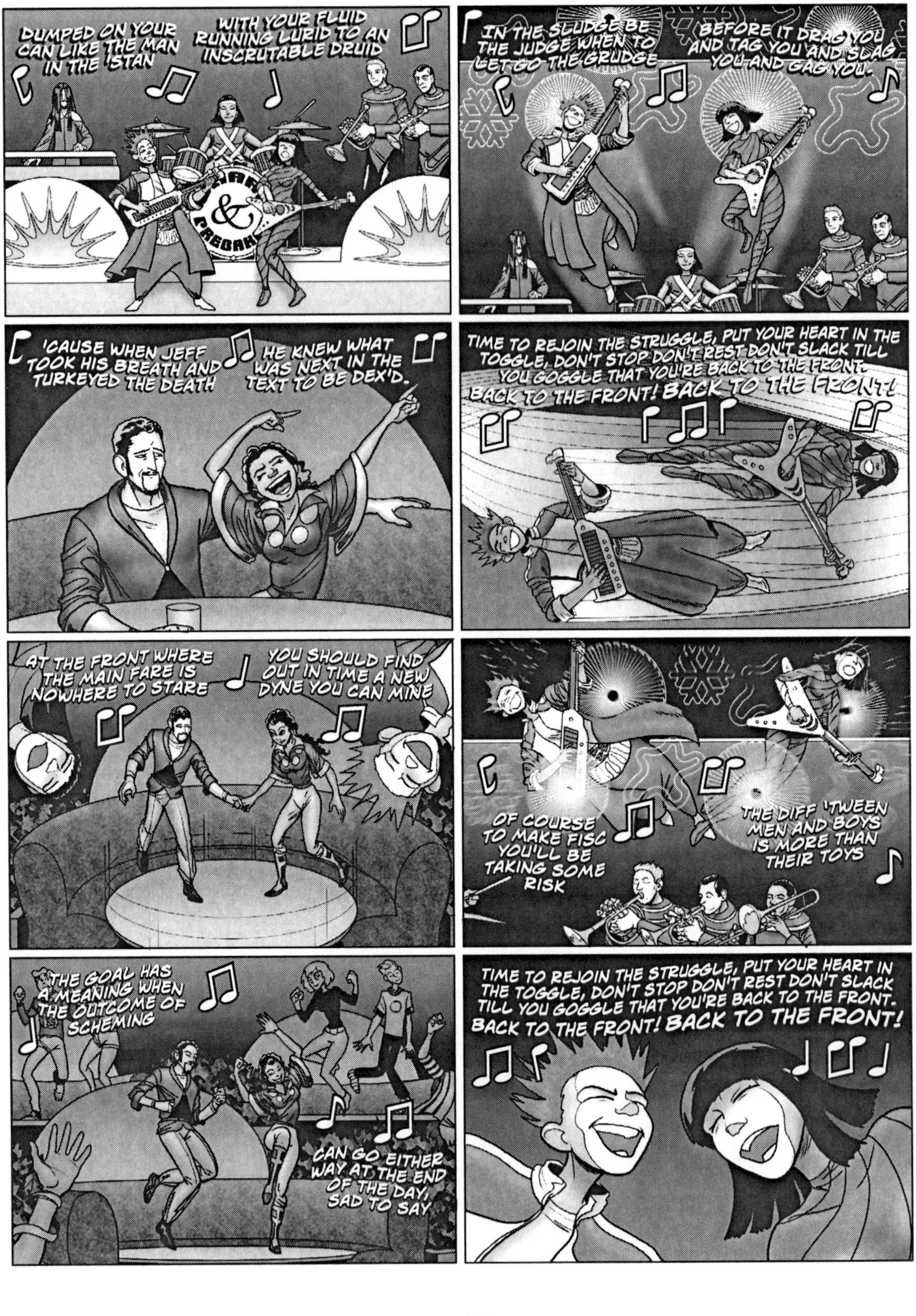
DUMPED ON YOUR CAN LIKE THE MAN IN THE 'STAN
WITH YOUR FLUID RUNNING LURID TO AN INSCRUTABLE DRUID
IN THE SLUDGE BE THE JUDGE WHEN TO LET GO THE GRUDGE
BEFORE IT DRAG YOU AND TAG YOU AND SLAG YOU AND GAG YOU.
'CAUSE WHEN JEFF TOOK HIS BREATH AND TURKEYED THE DEATH
HE KNEW WHAT WAS NEXT IN THE TEXT TO BE DEX'D.
TIME TO REJOIN THE STRUGGLE, PUT YOUR HEART IN THE TOGGLE, DON'T STOP DON'T REST DON'T SLACK TILL YOU GOGGLE THAT YOU'RE BACK TO THE FRONT.
BACK TO THE FRONT! BACK TO THE FRONT!
AT THE FRONT WHERE THE MAIN FARE IS NOWHERE TO STARE
YOU SHOULD FIND OUT IN TIME A NEW DYNE YOU CAN MINE
OF COURSE TO MAKE FISC YOU'LL BE TAKING SOME RISK
THE DIFF 'TWEEN MEN AND BOYS IS MORE THAN THEIR TOYS
THE GOAL HAS A MEANING WHEN THE OUTCOME OF SCHEMING
CAN GO EITHER WAY AT THE END OF THE DAY, SAD TO SAY
TIME TO REJOIN THE STRUGGLE, PUT YOUR HEART IN THE TOGGLE, DON'T STOP DON'T REST DON'T SLACK TILL YOU GOGGLE THAT YOU'RE BACK TO THE FRONT.
BACK TO THE FRONT! BACK TO THE FRONT!

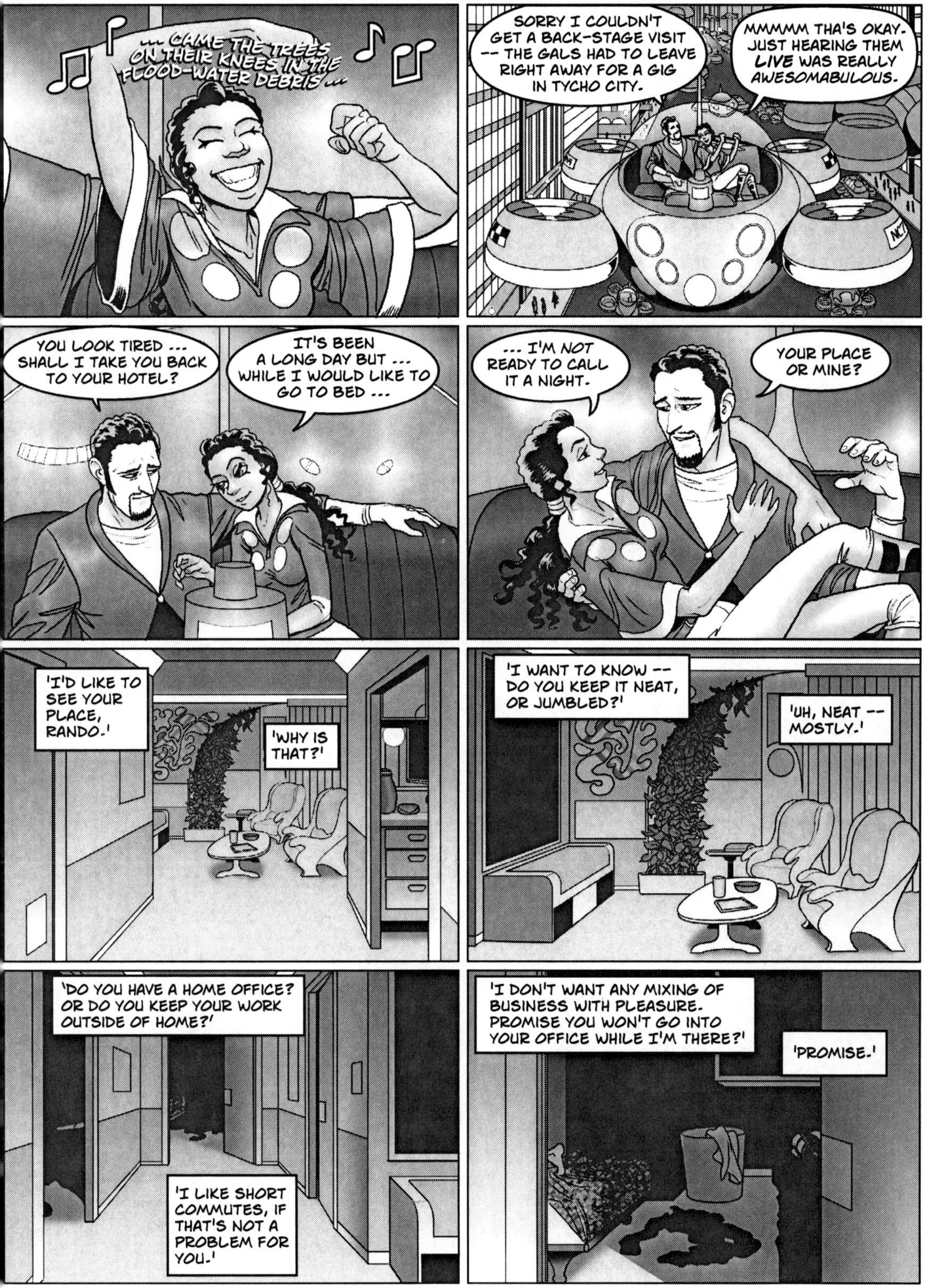
... CAME THE TREES ON THEIR KNEES IN THE FLOOD-WATER DEBRIS ...
SORRY I COULDN'T GET A BACK-STAGE VISIT -- THE GALS HAD TO LEAVE RIGHT AWAY FOR A GIG IN TYCHO CITY.
MMMMM THA'S OKAY. JUST HEARING THEM LIVE WAS REALLY AWESOMABULOUS.
YOU LOOK TIRED ... SHALL I TAKE YOU BACK TO YOUR HOTEL?
IT'S BEEN A LONG DAY BUT ... WHILE I WOULD LIKE TO GO TO BED ...
... I'M NOT READY TO CALL IT A NIGHT.
YOUR PLACE OR MINE?
'I'D LIKE TO SEE YOUR PLACE, RANDO.'
'WHY IS THAT?'
'I WANT TO KNOW -- DO YOU KEEP IT NEAT, OR JUMBLED?'
'UH, NEAT -- MOSTLY.'
'DO YOU HAVE A HOME OFFICE? OR DO YOU KEEP YOUR WORK OUTSIDE OF HOME?'
'I LIKE SHORT COMMUTES, IF THAT'S NOT A PROBLEM FOR YOU.'
'I DON'T WANT ANY MIXING OF BUSINESS WITH PLEASURE. PROMISE YOU WON'T GO INTO YOUR OFFICE WHILE I'M THERE?'
'PROMISE.'

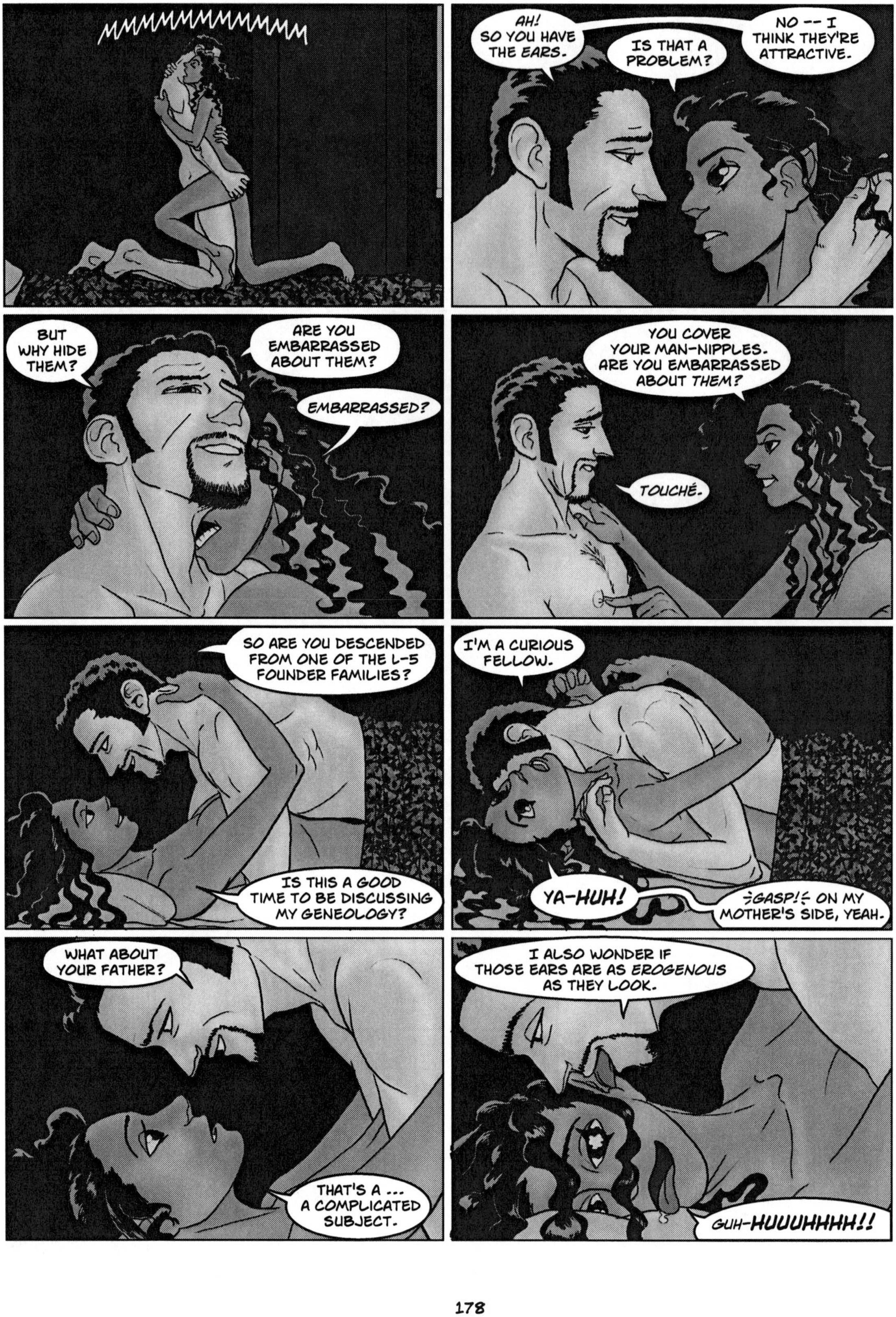
MMMMMMMMMMMMM
AH!
SO YOU HAVE THE EARS.
IS THAT A PROBLEM?
NO -- I THINK THEY'RE ATTRACTIVE.
BUT WHY HIDE THEM?
ARE YOU EMBARRASSED ABOUT THEM?
EMBARRASSED?
YOU COVER YOUR MAN-NIPPLES. ARE YOU EMBARRASSED ABOUT THEM?
TOUCHÉ.
SO ARE YOU DESCENDED FROM ONE OF THE L-5 FOUNDER FAMILIES?
IS THIS A GOOD TIME TO BE DISCUSSING MY GENEOLOGY?
I'M A CURIOUS FELLOW.
YA-HUH!
GASP! ON MY MOTHER'S SIDE, YEAH.
WHAT ABOUT YOUR FATHER?
THAT'S A ... A COMPLICATED SUBJECT.
I ALSO WONDER IF THOSE EARS ARE AS EROGENOUS AS THEY LOOK.
GUH-HUUUHHHH!!

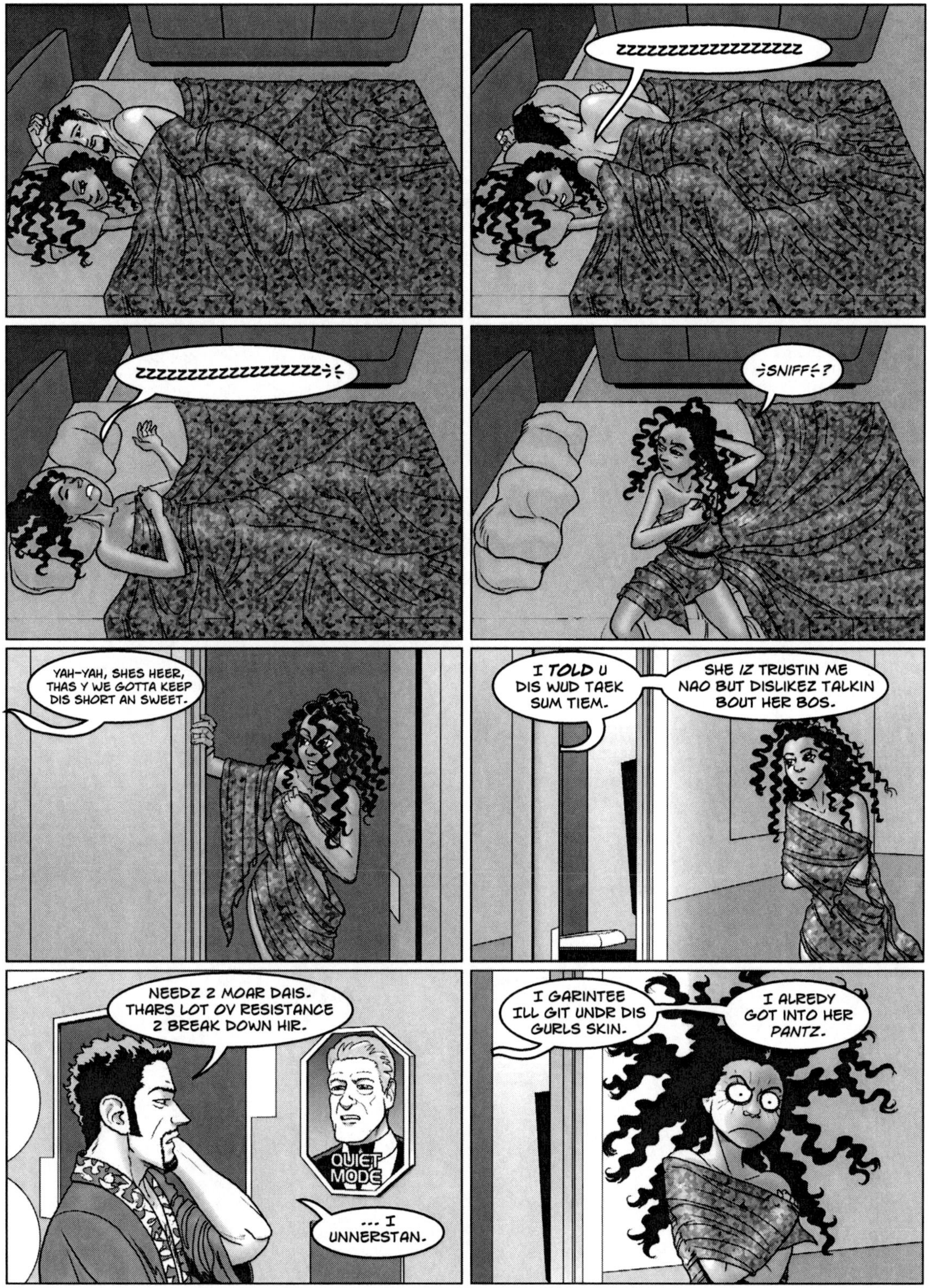
ZZZZZZZZZZZZZZZZZZZ
ZZZZZZZZZZZZZZZZZZZZ⟩⟨
⟩SNIFF⟨?
YAH-YAH, SHES HEER, THAS Y WE GOTTA KEEP DIS SHORT AN SWEET.
I TOLD U DIS WUD TAEK SUM TIEM.
SHE IZ TRUSTIN ME NAO BUT DISLIKEZ TALKIN BOUT HER BOS.
NEEDZ 2 MOAR DAIS. THARS LOT OV RESISTANCE 2 BREAK DOWN HIR.
QUIET MODE
... I UNNERSTAN.
I GARINTEE ILL GIT UNDR DIS GURLS SKIN.
I ALREDY GOT INTO HER PANTZ.

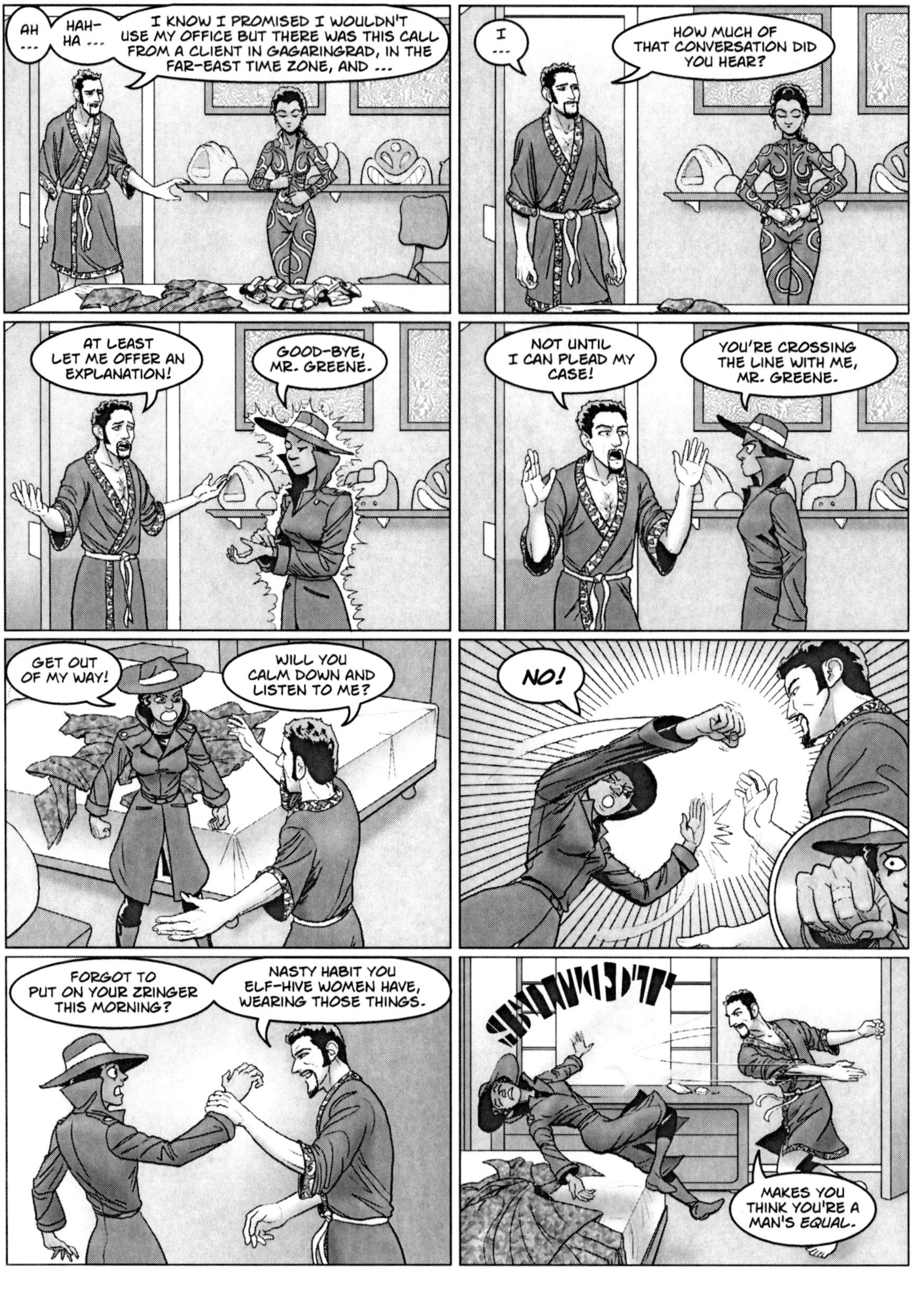
AH ...
HAH-HA ...
I KNOW I PROMISED I WOULDN'T USE MY OFFICE BUT THERE WAS THIS CALL FROM A CLIENT IN GAGARINGRAD, IN THE FAR-EAST TIME ZONE, AND ...
I ...
HOW MUCH OF THAT CONVERSATION DID YOU HEAR?
AT LEAST LET ME OFFER AN EXPLANATION!
GOOD-BYE, MR. GREENE.
NOT UNTIL I CAN PLEAD MY CASE!
YOU'RE CROSSING THE LINE WITH ME, MR. GREENE.
GET OUT OF MY WAY!
WILL YOU CALM DOWN AND LISTEN TO ME?
NO!
FORGOT TO PUT ON YOUR ZRINGER THIS MORNING?
NASTY HABIT YOU ELF-HIVE WOMEN HAVE, WEARING THOSE THINGS.
MAKES YOU THINK YOU'RE A MAN'S EQUAL.

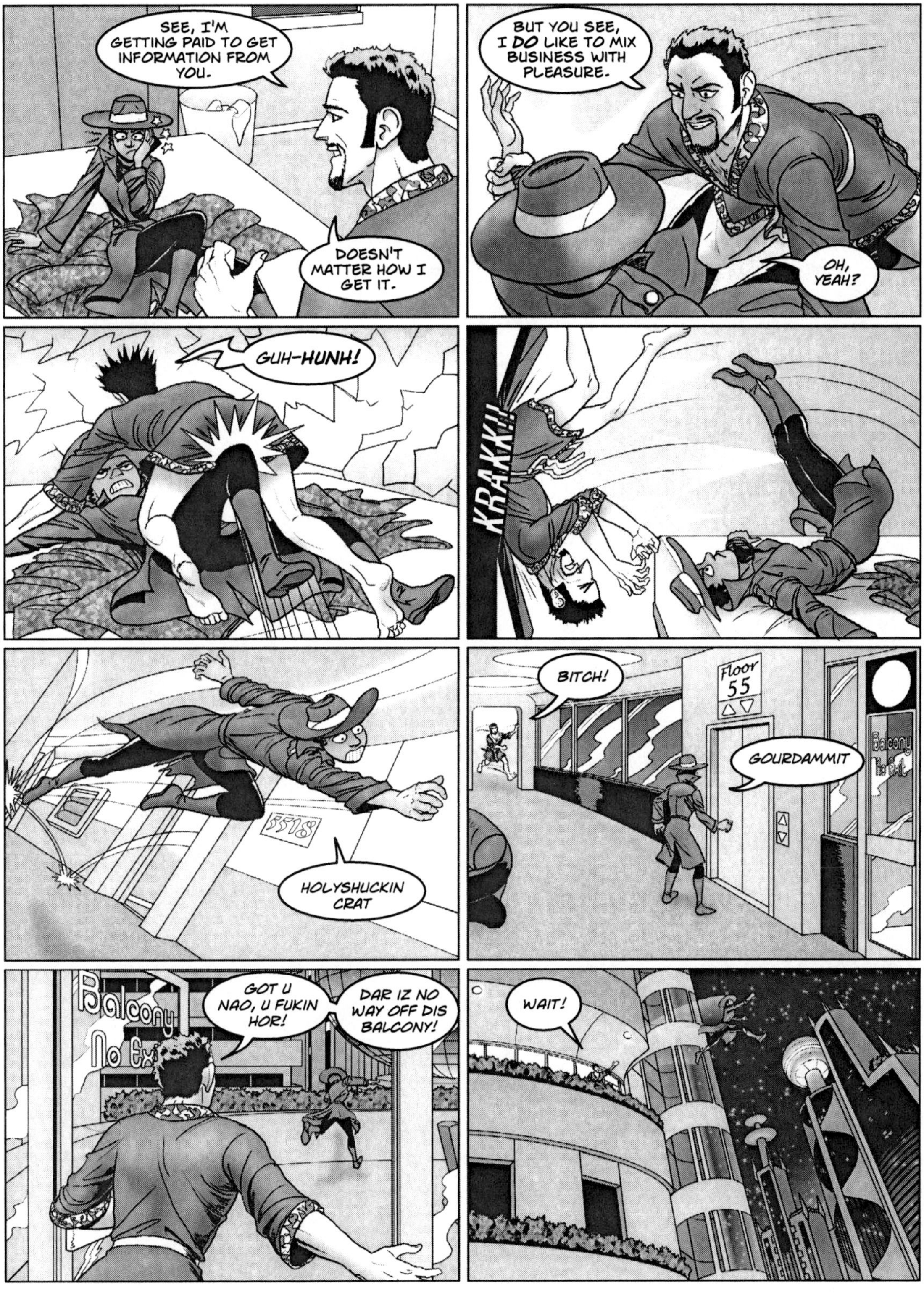
SEE, I'M GETTING PAID TO GET INFORMATION FROM YOU.
DOESN'T MATTER HOW I GET IT.
BUT YOU SEE, I DO LIKE TO MIX BUSINESS WITH PLEASURE.
OH, YEAH?
GUH-HUNH!
KRAKK!!
5518
HOLYSHUCKIN CRAT
BITCH!
Floor 55
GOURDAMMIT
GOT U NAO, U FUKIN HOR!
DAR IZ NO WAY OFF DIS BALCONY!
WAIT!

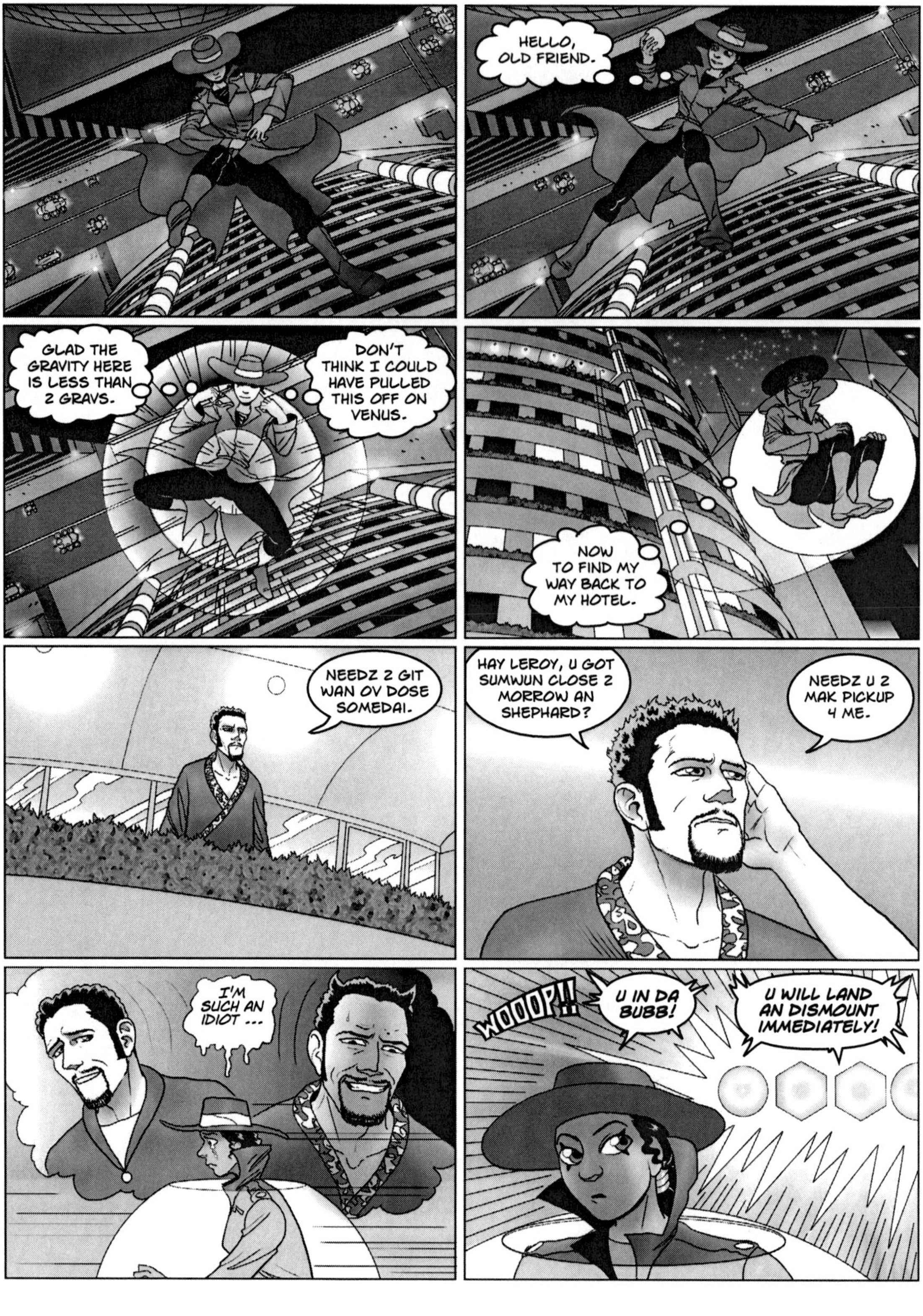
HELLO, OLD FRIEND.
GLAD THE GRAVITY HERE IS LESS THAN 2 GRAVS.
DON'T THINK I COULD HAVE PULLED THIS OFF ON VENUS.
NOW TO FIND MY WAY BACK TO MY HOTEL.
NEEDZ 2 GIT WAN OV DOSE SOMEDAI.
HAY LEROY, U GOT SUMWUN CLOSE 2 MORROW AN SHEPHARD?
NEEDZ U 2 MAK PICKUP 4 ME.
I'M SUCH AN IDIOT ...
WOOOP!!
U IN DA BUBB!
U WILL LAND AN DISMOUNT IMMEDIATELY!

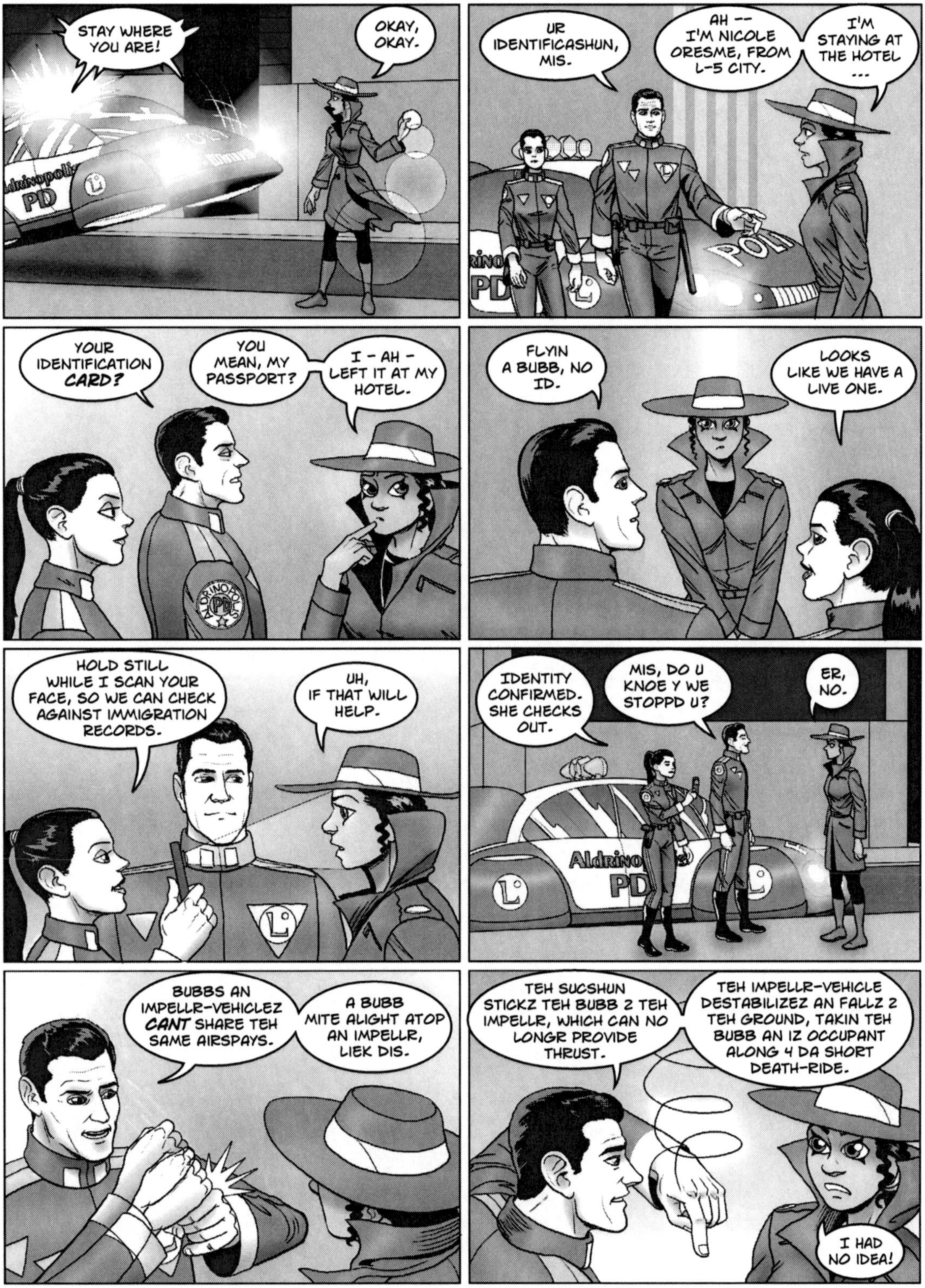
STAY WHERE YOU ARE!
OKAY, OKAY.
Aldrinopolis PD
UR IDENTIFICASHUN, MIS.
AH -- I'M NICOLE ORESME, FROM L-5 CITY.
I'M STAYING AT THE HOTEL ...
YOUR IDENTIFICATION CARD?
YOU MEAN, MY PASSPORT?
I - AH - LEFT IT AT MY HOTEL.
FLYIN A BUBB, NO ID.
LOOKS LIKE WE HAVE A LIVE ONE.
HOLD STILL WHILE I SCAN YOUR FACE, SO WE CAN CHECK AGAINST IMMIGRATION RECORDS.
UH, IF THAT WILL HELP.
IDENTITY CONFIRMED. SHE CHECKS OUT.
MIS, DO U KNOE Y WE STOPPD U?
ER, NO.
BUBBS AN IMPELLR-VEHICLEZ CANT SHARE TEH SAME AIRSPAYS.
A BUBB MITE ALIGHT ATOP AN IMPELLR, LIEK DIS.
TEH SUCSHUN STICKZ TEH BUBB 2 TEH IMPELLR, WHICH CAN NO LONGR PROVIDE THRUST.
TEH IMPELLR-VEHICLE DESTABILIZEZ AN FALLZ 2 TEH GROUND, TAKIN TEH BUBB AN IZ OCCUPANT ALONG 4 DA SHORT DEATH-RIDE.
I HAD NO IDEA!

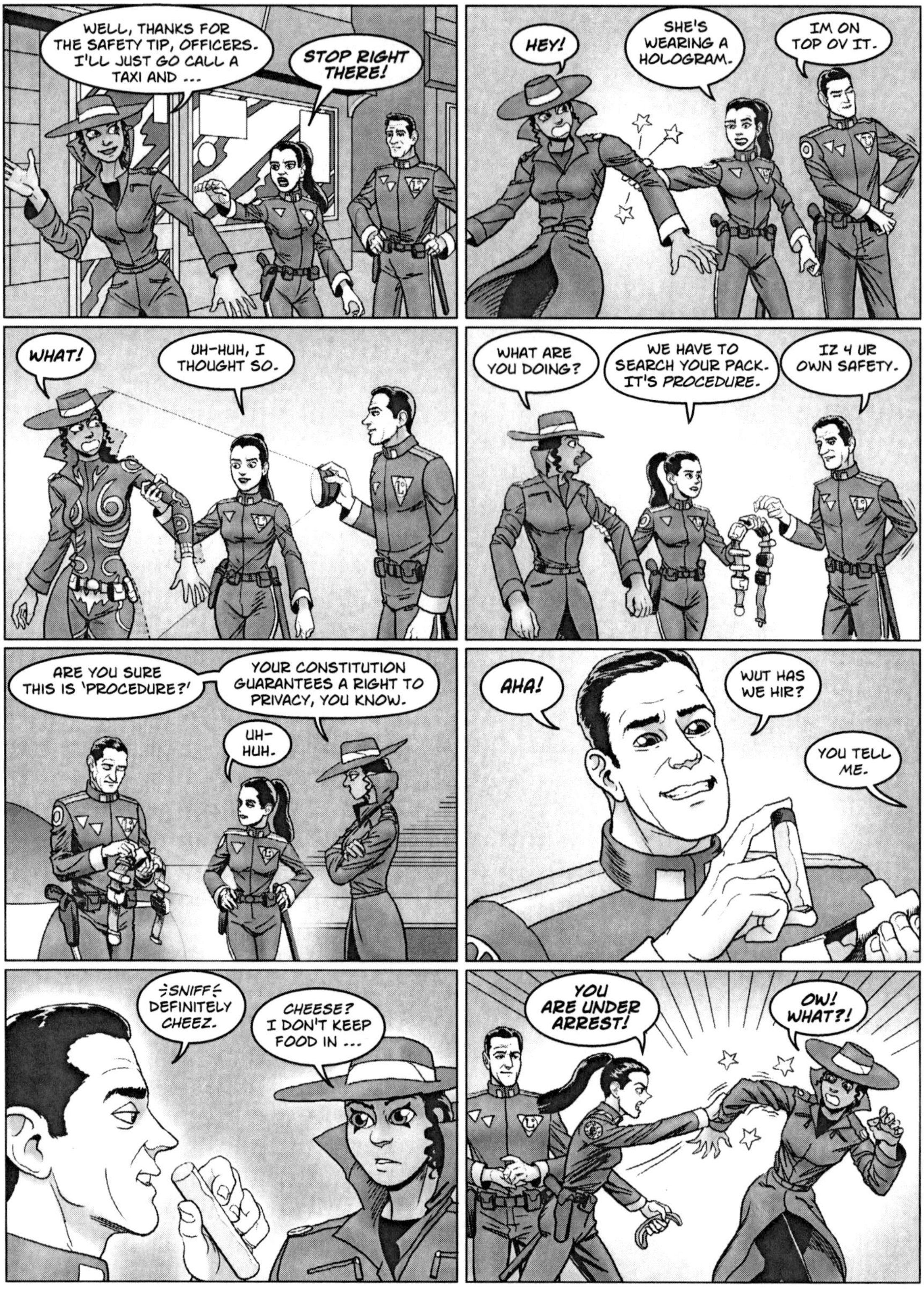
WELL, THANKS FOR THE SAFETY TIP, OFFICERS. I'LL JUST GO CALL A TAXI AND ...
STOP RIGHT THERE!
HEY!
SHE'S WEARING A HOLOGRAM.
IM ON TOP OV IT.
WHAT!
UH-HUH, I THOUGHT SO.
WHAT ARE YOU DOING?
WE HAVE TO SEARCH YOUR PACK. IT'S PROCEDURE.
IZ 4 UR OWN SAFETY.
ARE YOU SURE THIS IS 'PROCEDURE?'
YOUR CONSTITUTION GUARANTEES A RIGHT TO PRIVACY, YOU KNOW.
UH-HUH.
AHA!
WUT HAS WE HIR?
YOU TELL ME.
SNIFF DEFINITELY CHEEZ.
CHEESE? I DON'T KEEP FOOD IN ...
YOU ARE UNDER ARREST!
OW! WHAT?!

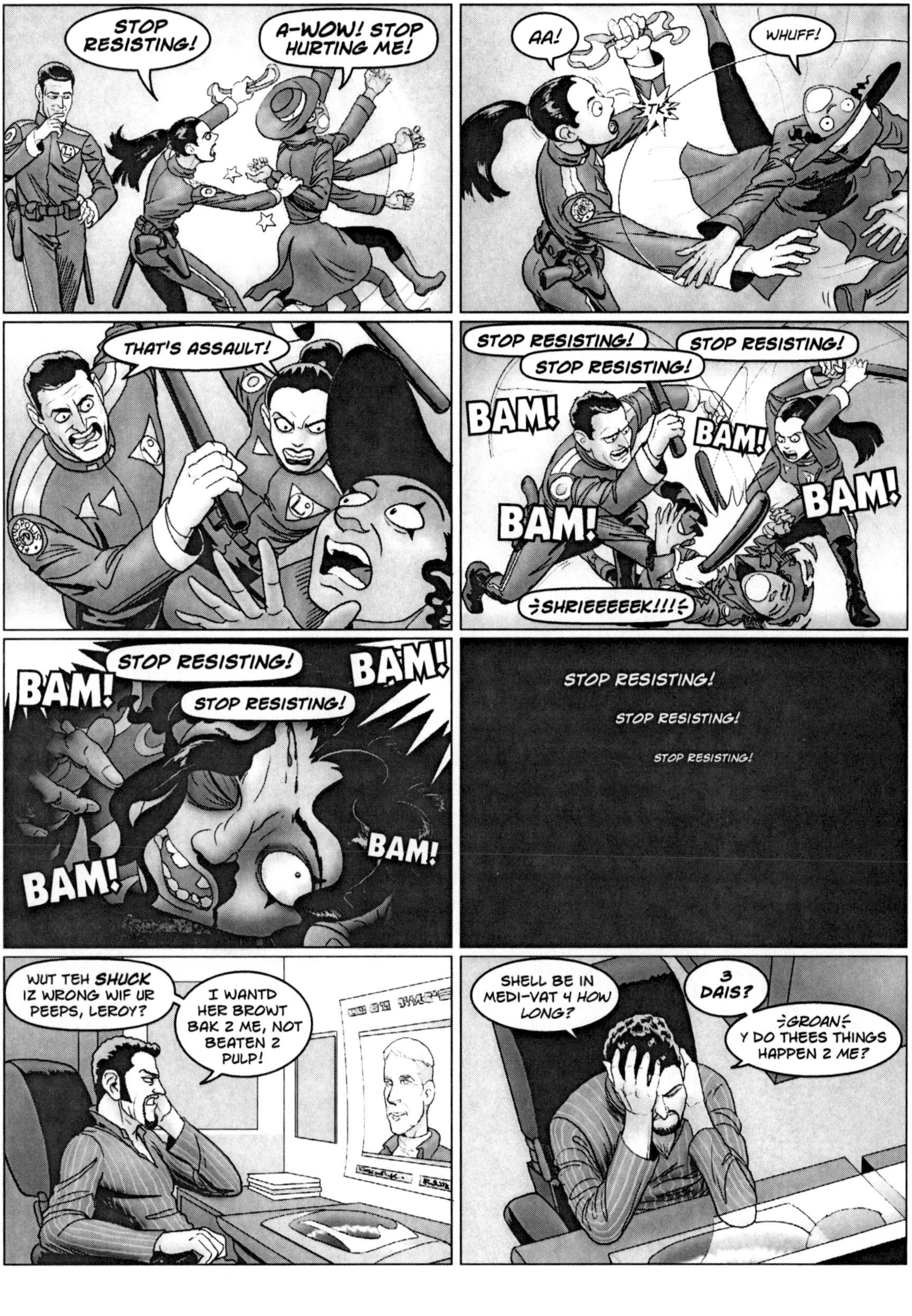
STOP RESISTING!
A-WOW! STOP HURTING ME!
AA!
WHUFF!
TK
THAT'S ASSAULT!
STOP RESISTING!
STOP RESISTING!
STOP RESISTING!
BAM!
BAM!
BAM!
BAM!
SHRIEEEEEK!!!
BAM!
STOP RESISTING!
BAM!
STOP RESISTING!
BAM!
BAM!
STOP RESISTING!
STOP RESISTING!
STOP RESISTING!
WUT TEH SHUCK IZ WRONG WIF UR PEEPS, LEROY?
I WANTD HER BROWT BAK 2 ME, NOT BEATEN 2 PULP!
SHELL BE IN MEDI-VAT 4 HOW LONG?
3 DAIS?
GROAN
Y DO THEES THINGS HAPPEN 2 ME?

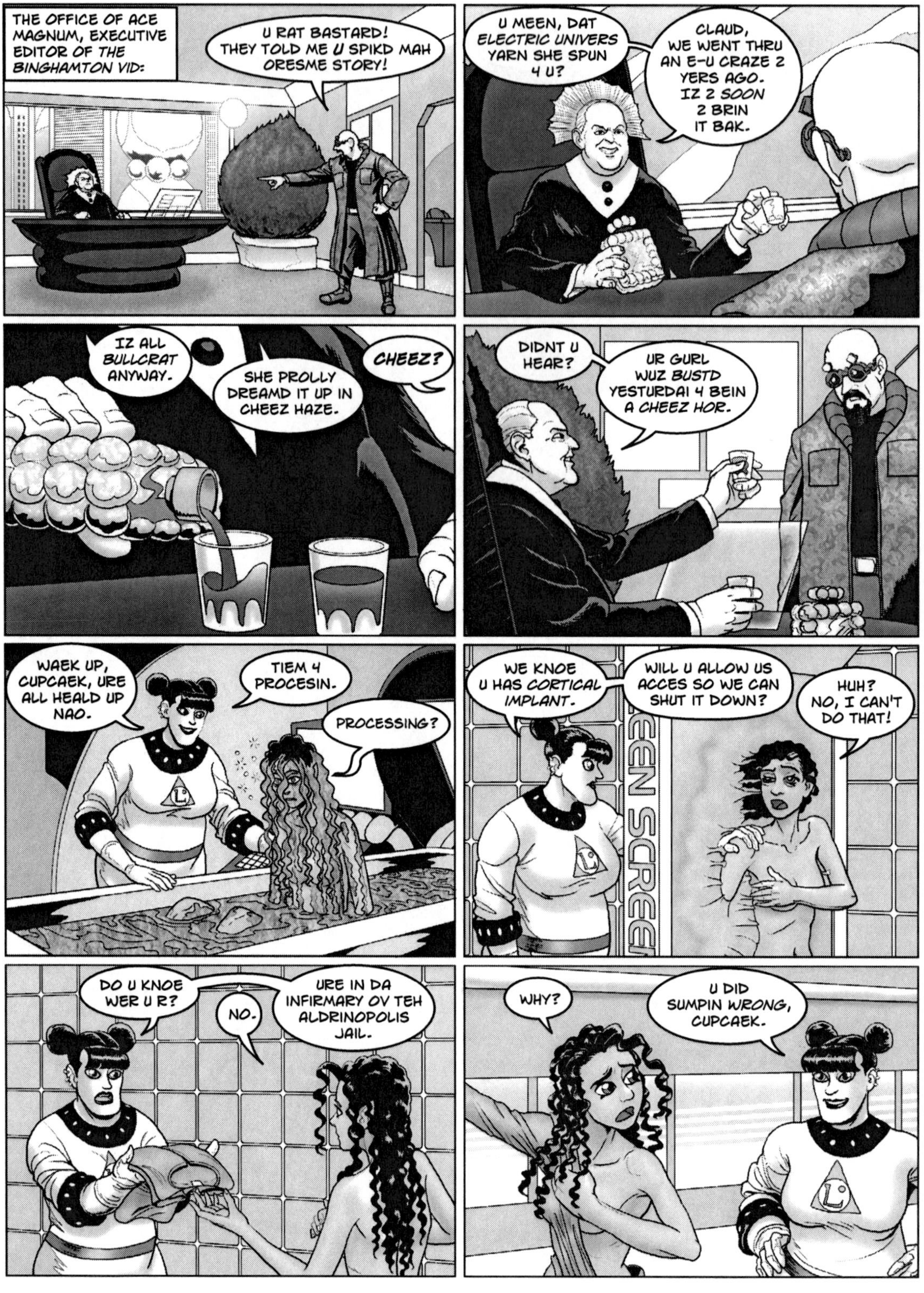
THE OFFICE OF ACE MAGNUM, EXECUTIVE EDITOR OF THE BINGHAMTON VID:
U RAT BASTARD! THEY TOLD ME U SPIKD MAH ORESME STORY!
U MEEN, DAT ELECTRIC UNIVERS YARN SHE SPUN 4 U?
CLAUD, WE WENT THRU AN E-U CRAZE 2 YERS AGO. IZ 2 SOON 2 BRIN IT BAK.
IZ ALL BULLCRAT ANYWAY.
SHE PROLLY DREAMD IT UP IN CHEEZ HAZE.
CHEEZ?
DIDNT U HEAR?
UR GURL WUZ BUSTD YESTURDAI 4 BEIN A CHEEZ HOR.
WAEK UP, CUPCAEK, URE ALL HEALD UP NAO.
TIEM 4 PROCESIN.
PROCESSING?
WE KNOE U HAS CORTICAL IMPLANT.
WILL U ALLOW US ACCES SO WE CAN SHUT IT DOWN?
HUH? NO, I CAN'T DO THAT!
DO U KNOE WER U R?
NO.
URE IN DA INFIRMARY OV TEH ALDRINOPOLIS JAIL.
WHY?
U DID SUMPIN WRONG, CUPCAEK.

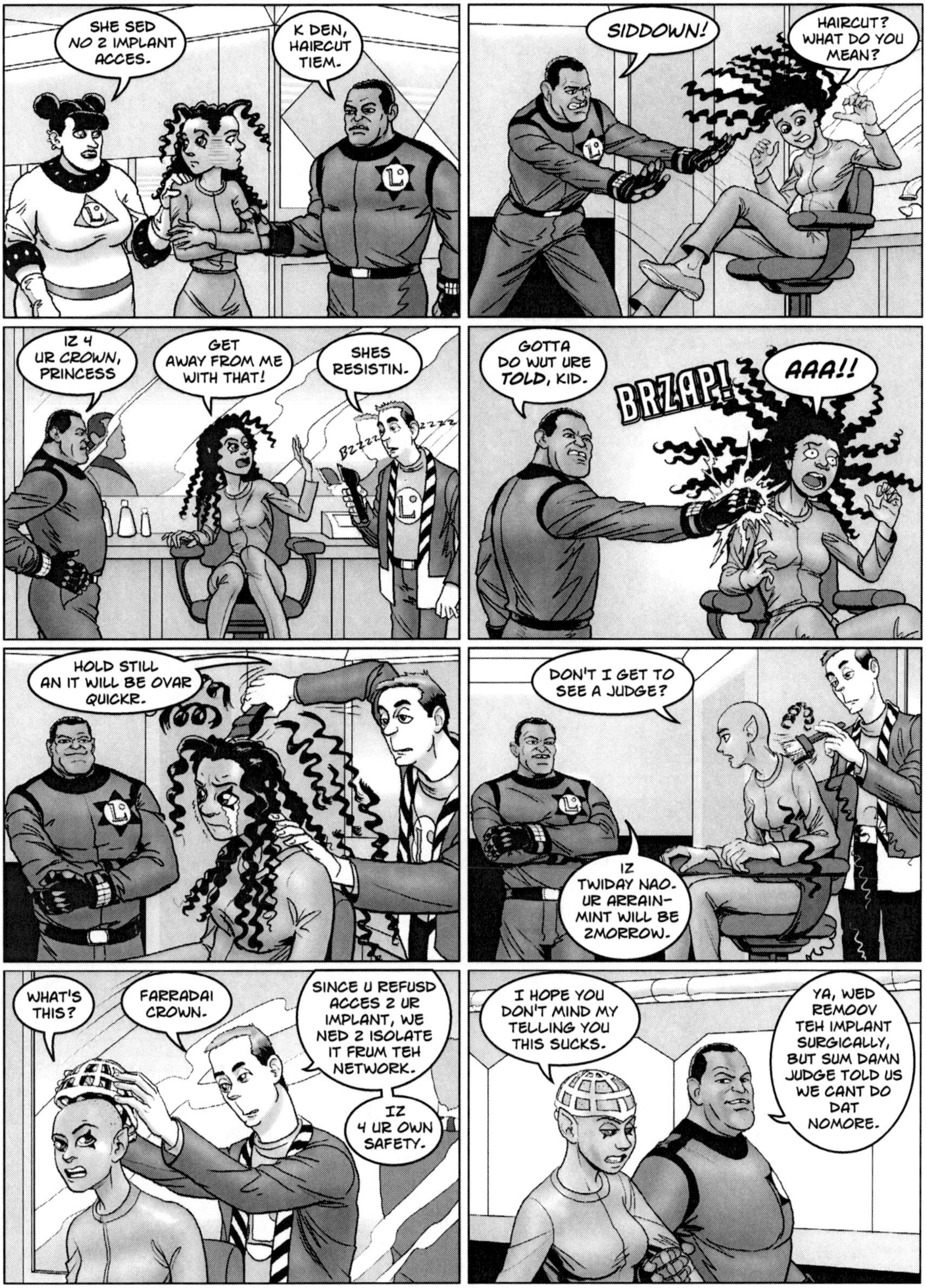
SHE SED NO 2 IMPLANT ACCES.
K DEN, HAIRCUT TIEM.
SIDDOWN!
HAIRCUT? WHAT DO YOU MEAN?
IZ 4 UR CROWN, PRINCESS
GET AWAY FROM ME WITH THAT!
SHES RESISTIN.
Bzzzz
zzzz
GOTTA DO WUT URE TOLD, KID.
BRZAP!
AAA!!
HOLD STILL AN IT WILL BE OVAR QUICKR.
DON'T I GET TO SEE A JUDGE?
IZ TWIDAY NAO. UR ARRAIN-MINT WILL BE 2MORROW.
WHAT'S THIS?
FARRADAI CROWN.
SINCE U REFUSD ACCES 2 UR IMPLANT, WE NED 2 ISOLATE IT FRUM TEH NETWORK.
IZ 4 UR OWN SAFETY.
I HOPE YOU DON'T MIND MY TELLING YOU THIS SUCKS.
YA, WED REMOOV TEH IMPLANT SURGICALLY, BUT SUM DAMN JUDGE TOLD US WE CANT DO DAT NOMORE.

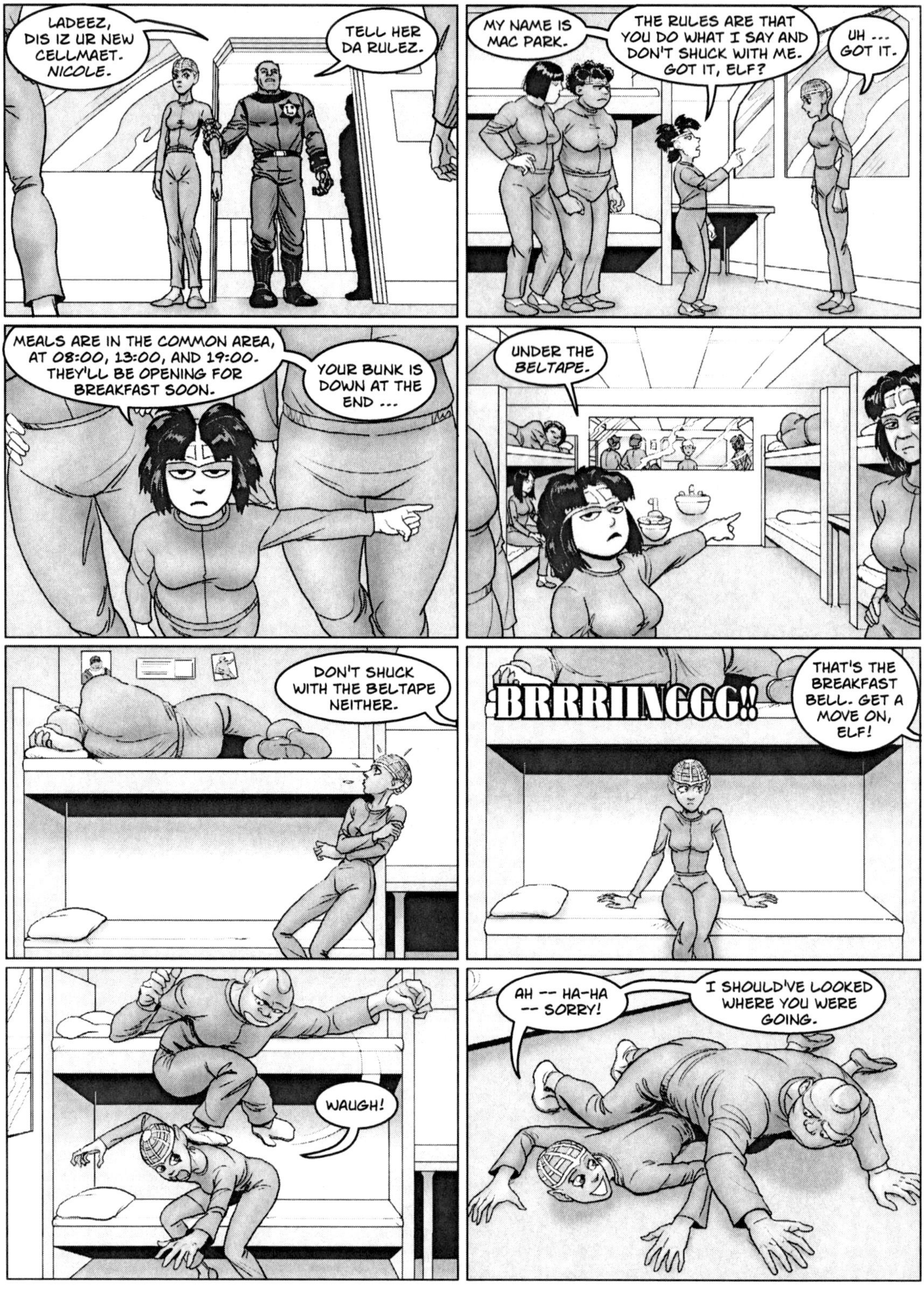
LADEEZ, DIS IZ UR NEW CELLMAET. NICOLE.
TELL HER DA RULEZ.
MY NAME IS MAC PARK.
THE RULES ARE THAT YOU DO WHAT I SAY AND DON'T SHUCK WITH ME. GOT IT, ELF?
UH ... GOT IT.
MEALS ARE IN THE COMMON AREA, AT 08:00, 13:00, AND 19:00. THEY'LL BE OPENING FOR BREAKFAST SOON.
YOUR BUNK IS DOWN AT THE END ...
UNDER THE BELTAPE.
DON'T SHUCK WITH THE BELTAPE NEITHER.
BRRRIINGGG!!
THAT'S THE BREAKFAST BELL. GET A MOVE ON, ELF!
WAUGH!
AH -- HA-HA -- SORRY!
I SHOULD'VE LOOKED WHERE YOU WERE GOING.

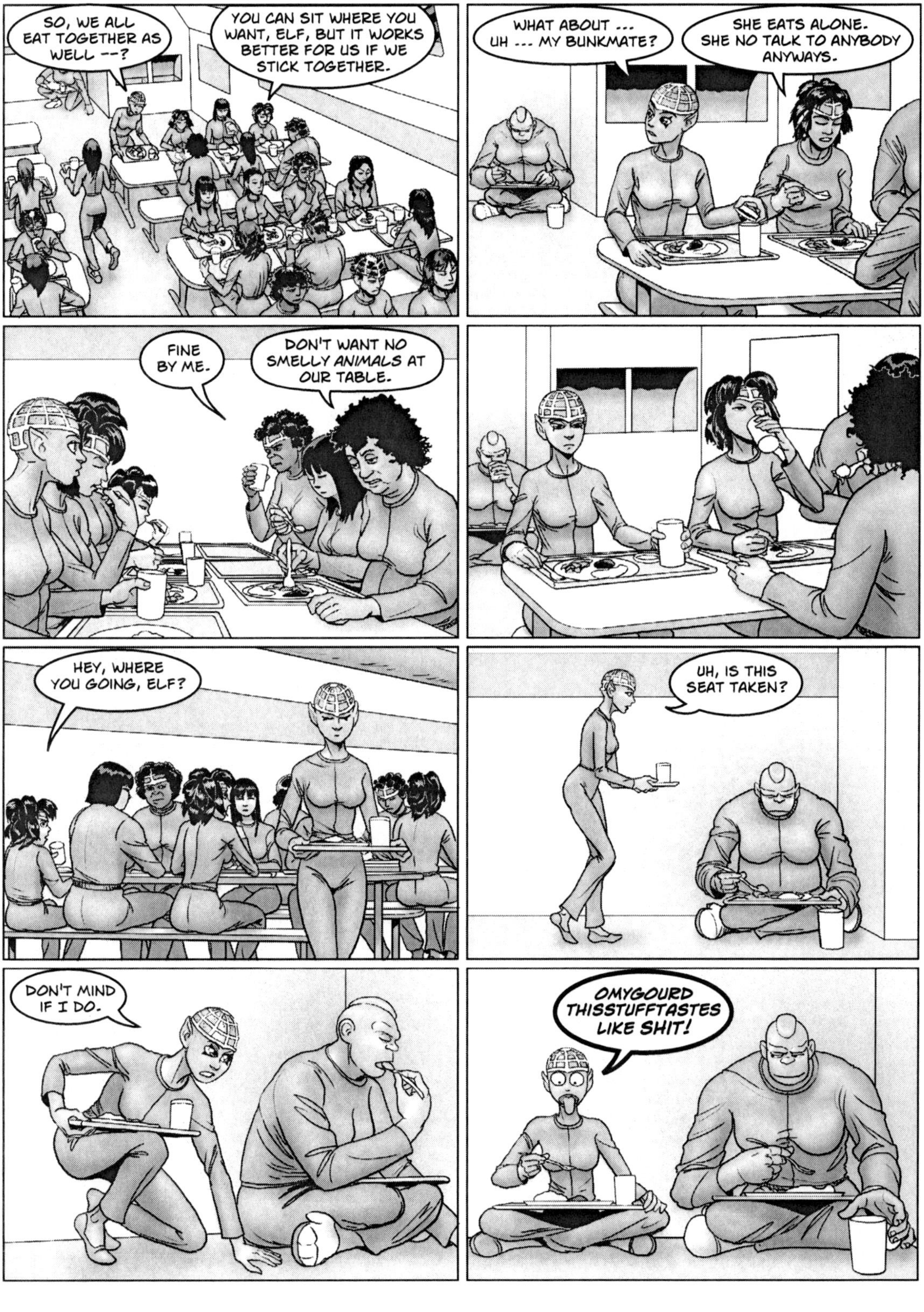
SO, WE ALL EAT TOGETHER AS WELL --?
YOU CAN SIT WHERE YOU WANT, ELF, BUT IT WORKS BETTER FOR US IF WE STICK TOGETHER.
WHAT ABOUT ... UH ... MY BUNKMATE?
SHE EATS ALONE. SHE NO TALK TO ANYBODY ANYWAYS.
FINE BY ME.
DON'T WANT NO SMELLY *ANIMALS* AT OUR TABLE.
HEY, WHERE YOU GOING, ELF?
UH, IS THIS SEAT TAKEN?
DON'T MIND IF I DO.
OMYGOURD THISSTUFFTASTES LIKE SHIT!

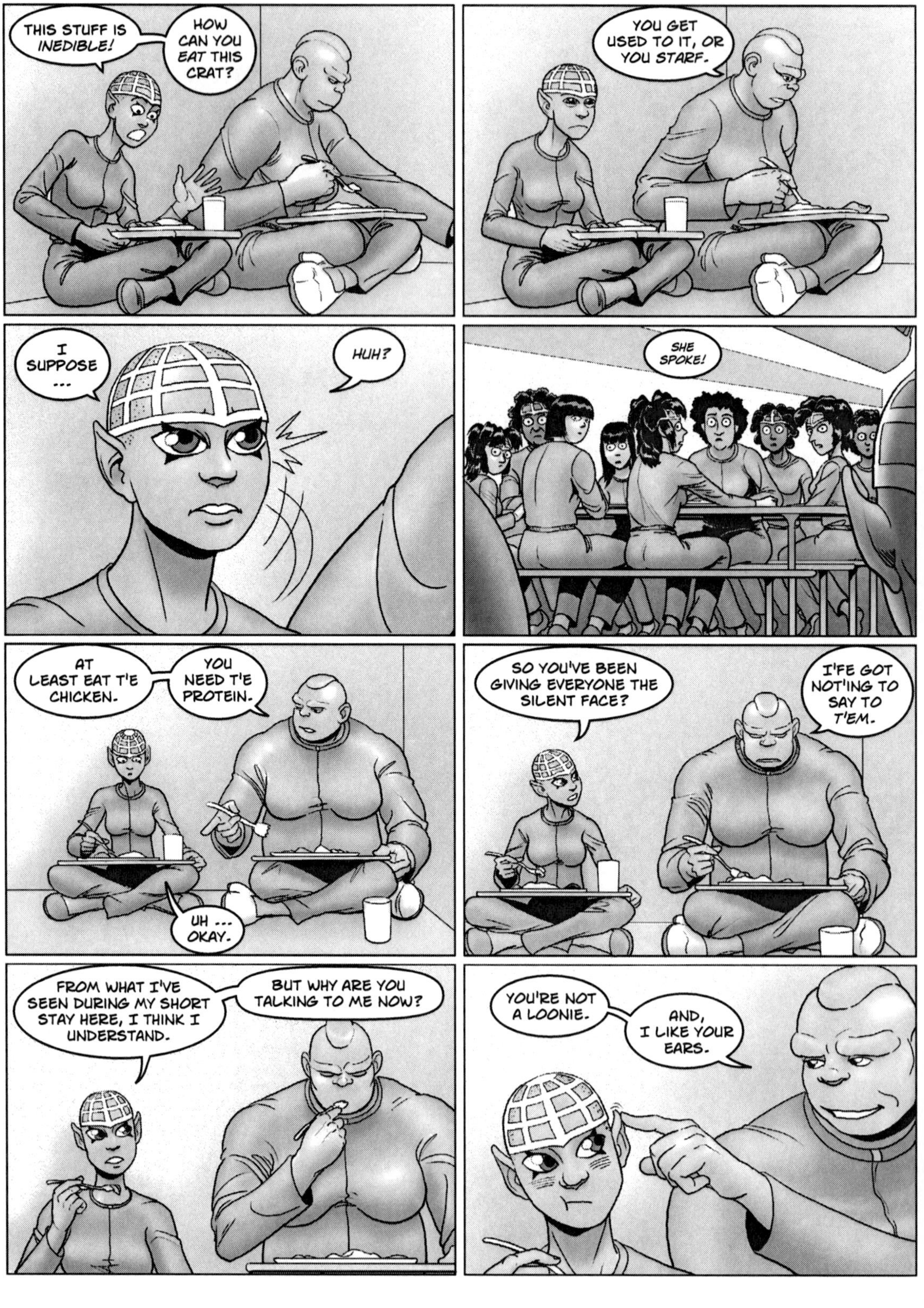
THIS STUFF IS INEDIBLE!
HOW CAN YOU EAT THIS CRAT?
YOU GET USED TO IT, OR YOU STARF.
I SUPPOSE ...
HUH?
SHE SPOKE!
AT LEAST EAT T'E CHICKEN.
YOU NEED T'E PROTEIN.
UH ... OKAY.
SO YOU'VE BEEN GIVING EVERYONE THE SILENT FACE?
I'FE GOT NOT'ING TO SAY TO T'EM.
FROM WHAT I'VE SEEN DURING MY SHORT STAY HERE, I THINK I UNDERSTAND.
BUT WHY ARE YOU TALKING TO ME NOW?
YOU'RE NOT A LOONIE.
AND, I LIKE YOUR EARS.

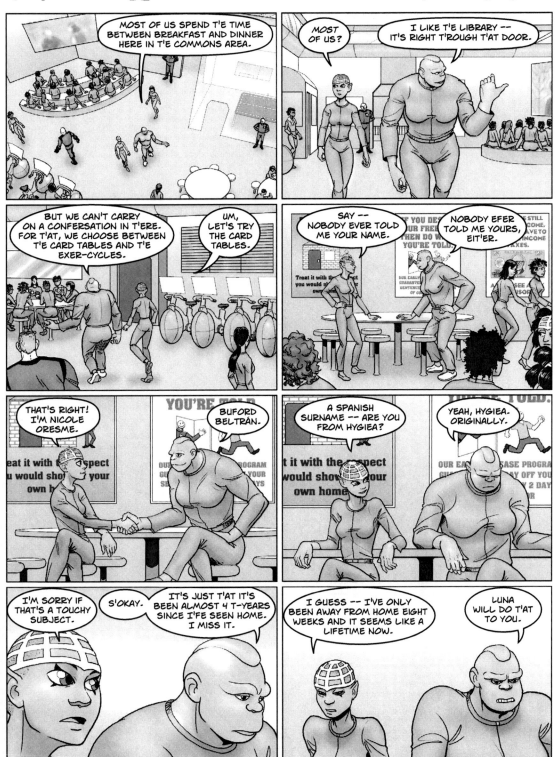

Panel 1: MOST OF US SPEND T'E TIME BETWEEN BREAKFAST AND DINNER HERE IN T'E COMMONS AREA.

Panel 2: MOST OF US?

I LIKE T'E LIBRARY -- IT'S RIGHT T'ROUGH T'AT DOOR.

Panel 3: BUT WE CAN'T CARRY ON A CONFERSATION IN T'ERE. FOR T'AT, WE CHOOSE BETWEEN T'E CARD TABLES AND T'E EXER-CYCLES.

UM, LET'S TRY THE CARD TABLES.

Panel 4: SAY -- NOBODY EVER TOLD ME YOUR NAME.

NOBODY EFER TOLD ME YOURS, EIT'ER.

Panel 5: THAT'S RIGHT! I'M NICOLE ORESME.

BUFORD BELTRÁN.

Panel 6: A SPANISH SURNAME -- ARE YOU FROM HYGIEA?

YEAH, HYGIEA. ORIGINALLY.

Panel 7: I'M SORRY IF THAT'S A TOUCHY SUBJECT.

S'OKAY.

IT'S JUST T'AT IT'S BEEN ALMOST 4 T-YEARS SINCE I'FE SEEN HOME. I MISS IT.

Panel 8: I GUESS -- I'VE ONLY BEEN AWAY FROM HOME EIGHT WEEKS AND IT SEEMS LIKE A LIFETIME NOW.

LUNA WILL DO T'AT TO YOU.

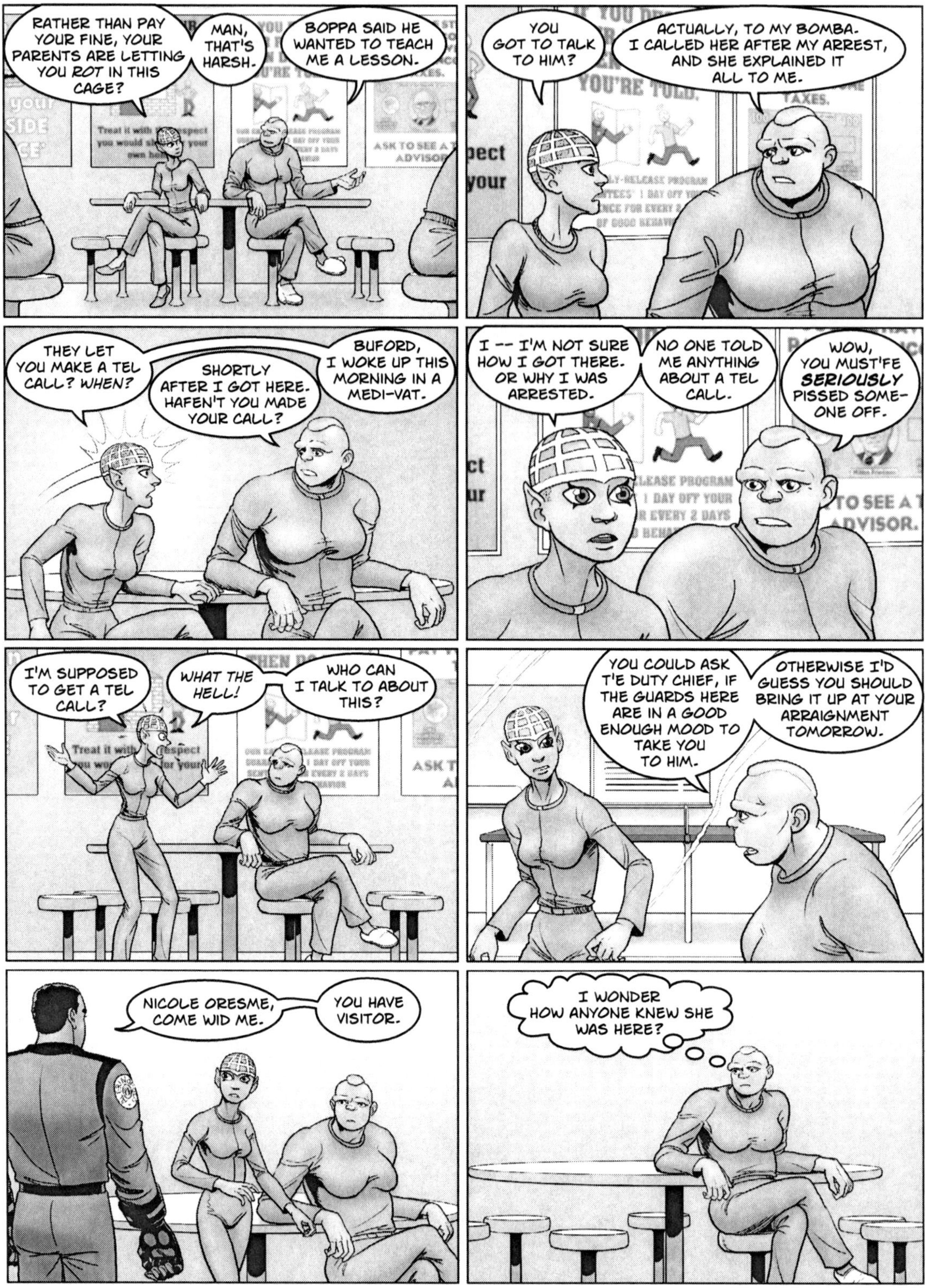
RATHER THAN PAY YOUR FINE, YOUR PARENTS ARE LETTING YOU *ROT* IN THIS CAGE?
MAN, THAT'S HARSH.
BOPPA SAID HE WANTED TO TEACH ME A LESSON.
YOU GOT TO TALK TO HIM?
ACTUALLY, TO MY BOMBA. I CALLED HER AFTER MY ARREST, AND SHE EXPLAINED IT ALL TO ME.
THEY LET YOU MAKE A TEL CALL? *WHEN?*
SHORTLY AFTER I GOT HERE. HAFEN'T YOU MADE YOUR CALL?
BUFORD, I WOKE UP THIS MORNING IN A MEDI-VAT.
I -- I'M NOT SURE HOW I GOT THERE. OR WHY I WAS ARRESTED.
NO ONE TOLD ME ANYTHING ABOUT A TEL CALL.
WOW, YOU MUST'FE ***SERIOUSLY*** PISSED SOME-ONE OFF.
I'M SUPPOSED TO GET A TEL CALL?
WHAT THE HELL!
WHO CAN I TALK TO ABOUT THIS?
YOU COULD ASK T'E DUTY CHIEF, IF THE GUARDS HERE ARE IN A GOOD ENOUGH MOOD TO TAKE YOU TO HIM.
OTHERWISE I'D GUESS YOU SHOULD BRING IT UP AT YOUR ARRAIGNMENT TOMORROW.
NICOLE ORESME, COME WID ME.
YOU HAVE VISITOR.
I WONDER HOW ANYONE KNEW SHE WAS HERE?

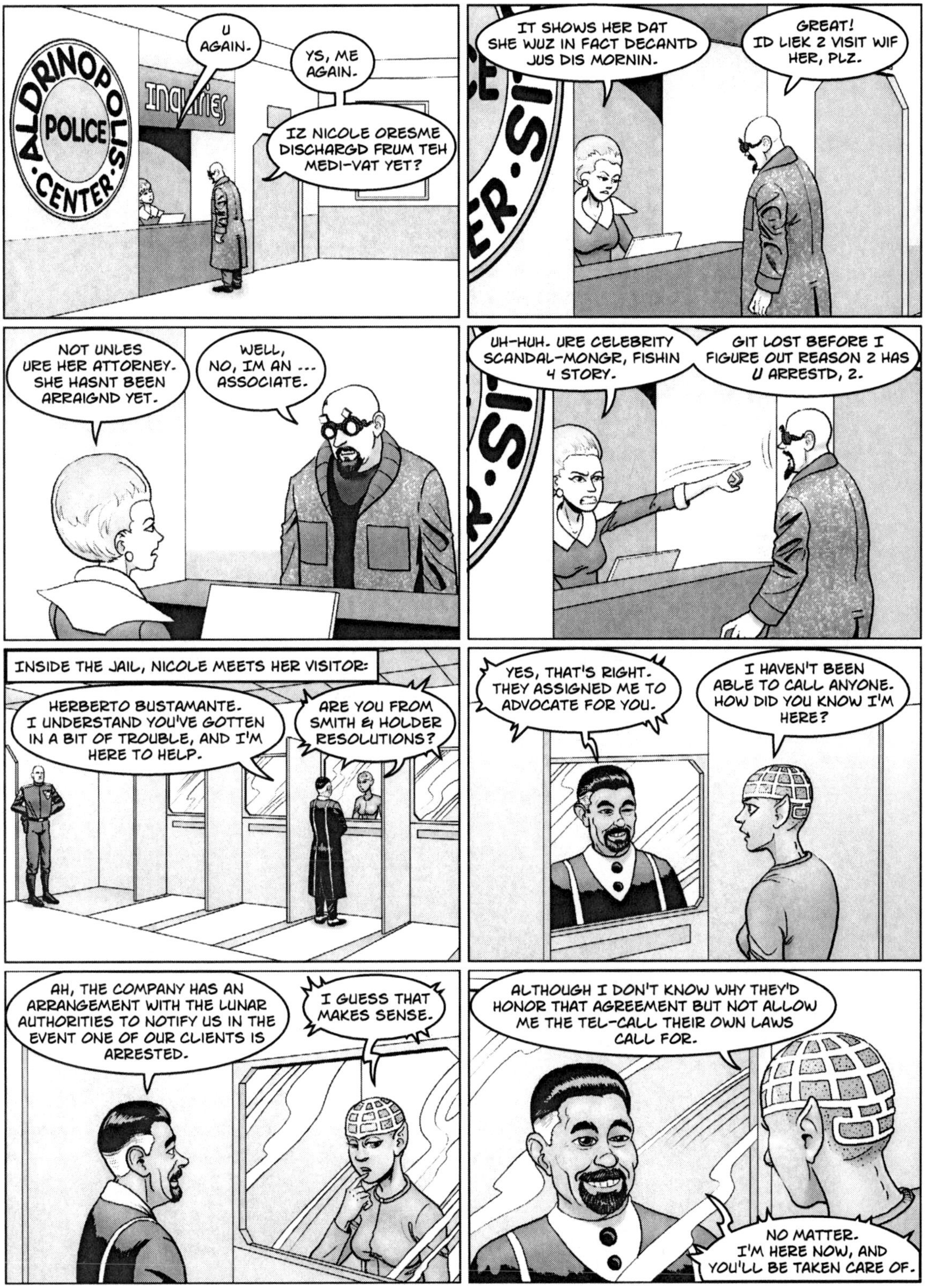
ALDRINOPOLIS POLICE CENTER
INQUIRIES
U AGAIN.
YS, ME AGAIN.
IZ NICOLE ORESME DISCHARGD FRUM TEH MEDI-VAT YET?
IT SHOWS HER DAT SHE WUZ IN FACT DECANTD JUS DIS MORNIN.
GREAT! ID LIEK 2 VISIT WIF HER, PLZ.
NOT UNLES URE HER ATTORNEY. SHE HASNT BEEN ARRAIGND YET.
WELL, NO, IM AN ... ASSOCIATE.
UH-HUH. URE CELEBRITY SCANDAL-MONGR, FISHIN 4 STORY.
GIT LOST BEFORE I FIGURE OUT REASON 2 HAS U ARRESTD, 2.
INSIDE THE JAIL, NICOLE MEETS HER VISITOR:
HERBERTO BUSTAMANTE. I UNDERSTAND YOU'VE GOTTEN IN A BIT OF TROUBLE, AND I'M HERE TO HELP.
ARE YOU FROM SMITH & HOLDER RESOLUTIONS?
YES, THAT'S RIGHT. THEY ASSIGNED ME TO ADVOCATE FOR YOU.
I HAVEN'T BEEN ABLE TO CALL ANYONE. HOW DID YOU KNOW I'M HERE?
AH, THE COMPANY HAS AN ARRANGEMENT WITH THE LUNAR AUTHORITIES TO NOTIFY US IN THE EVENT ONE OF OUR CLIENTS IS ARRESTED.
I GUESS THAT MAKES SENSE.
ALTHOUGH I DON'T KNOW WHY THEY'D HONOR THAT AGREEMENT BUT NOT ALLOW ME THE TEL-CALL THEIR OWN LAWS CALL FOR.
NO MATTER. I'M HERE NOW, AND YOU'LL BE TAKEN CARE OF.

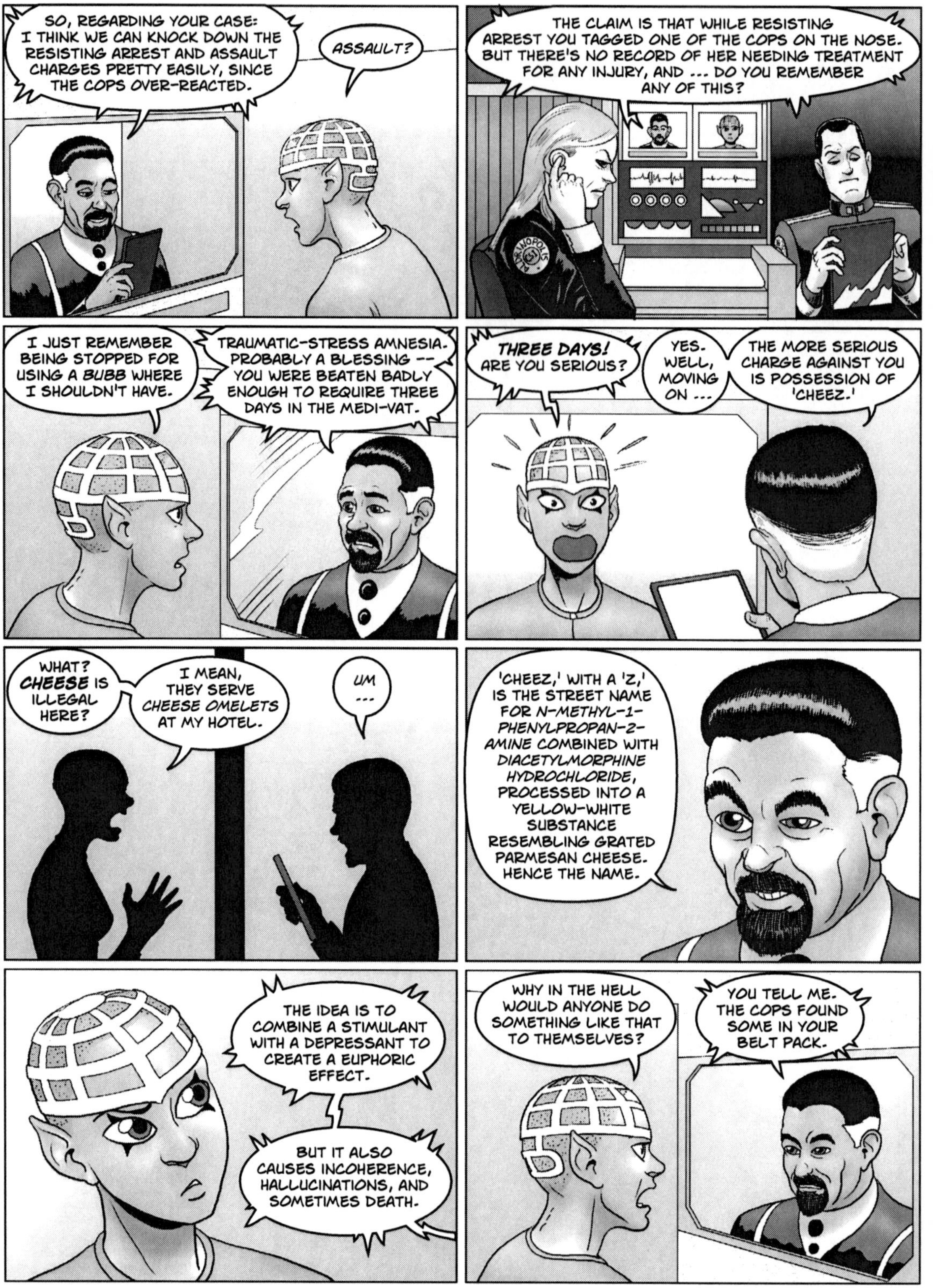
SO, REGARDING YOUR CASE: I THINK WE CAN KNOCK DOWN THE RESISTING ARREST AND ASSAULT CHARGES PRETTY EASILY, SINCE THE COPS OVER-REACTED.
ASSAULT?
THE CLAIM IS THAT WHILE RESISTING ARREST YOU TAGGED ONE OF THE COPS ON THE NOSE. BUT THERE'S NO RECORD OF HER NEEDING TREATMENT FOR ANY INJURY, AND ... DO YOU REMEMBER ANY OF THIS?
I JUST REMEMBER BEING STOPPED FOR USING A BUBB WHERE I SHOULDN'T HAVE.
TRAUMATIC-STRESS AMNESIA. PROBABLY A BLESSING -- YOU WERE BEATEN BADLY ENOUGH TO REQUIRE THREE DAYS IN THE MEDI-VAT.
THREE DAYS! ARE YOU SERIOUS?
YES. WELL, MOVING ON ...
THE MORE SERIOUS CHARGE AGAINST YOU IS POSSESSION OF 'CHEEZ.'
WHAT? CHEESE IS ILLEGAL HERE?
I MEAN, THEY SERVE CHEESE OMELETS AT MY HOTEL.
UM ...
'CHEEZ,' WITH A 'Z,' IS THE STREET NAME FOR N-METHYL-1-PHENYLPROPAN-2-AMINE COMBINED WITH DIACETYLMORPHINE HYDROCHLORIDE, PROCESSED INTO A YELLOW-WHITE SUBSTANCE RESEMBLING GRATED PARMESAN CHEESE. HENCE THE NAME.
THE IDEA IS TO COMBINE A STIMULANT WITH A DEPRESSANT TO CREATE A EUPHORIC EFFECT.
BUT IT ALSO CAUSES INCOHERENCE, HALLUCINATIONS, AND SOMETIMES DEATH.
WHY IN THE HELL WOULD ANYONE DO SOMETHING LIKE THAT TO THEMSELVES?
YOU TELL ME. THE COPS FOUND SOME IN YOUR BELT PACK.

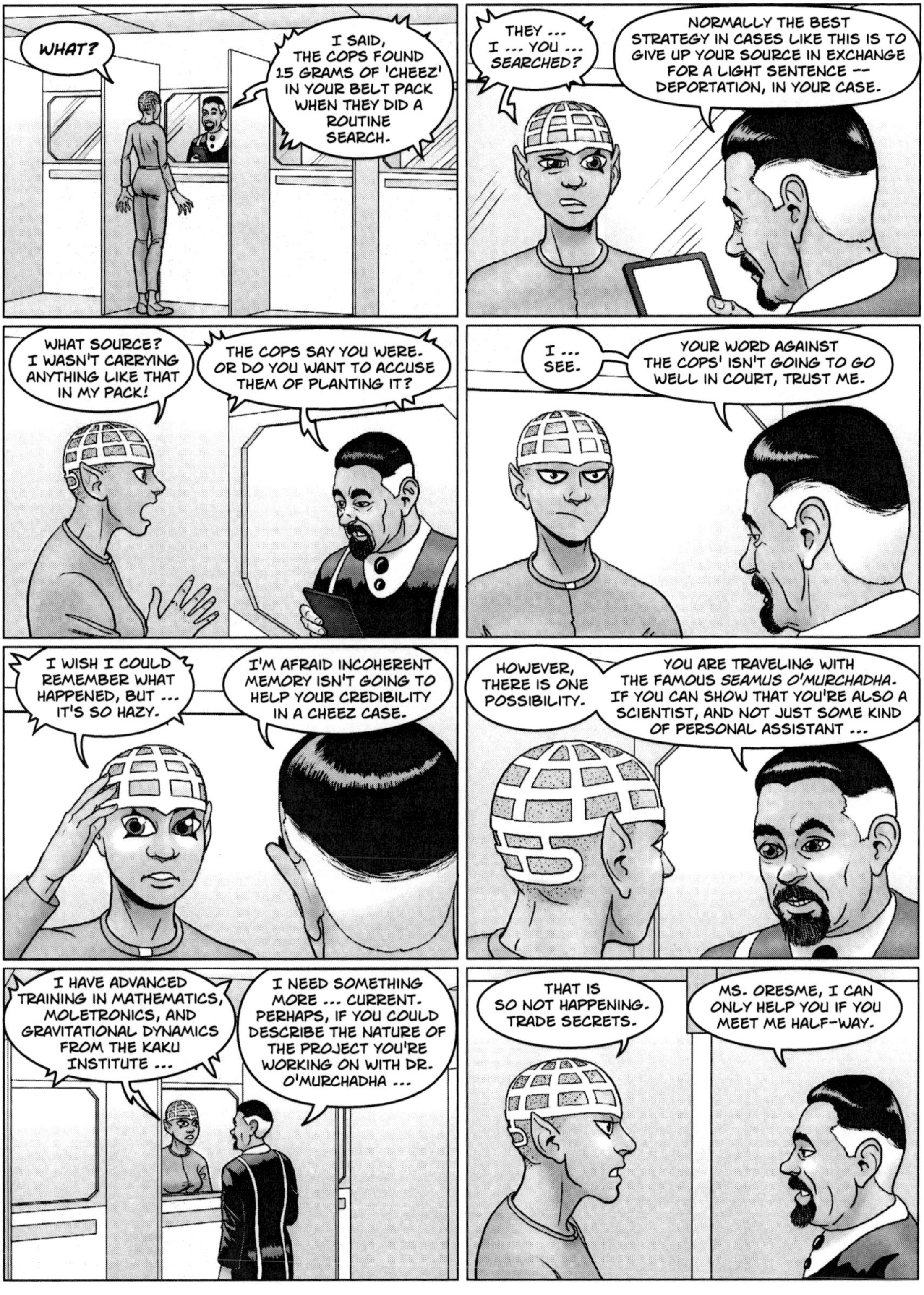
WHAT?
I SAID, THE COPS FOUND 15 GRAMS OF 'CHEEZ' IN YOUR BELT PACK WHEN THEY DID A ROUTINE SEARCH.
THEY ... I ... YOU ... SEARCHED?
NORMALLY THE BEST STRATEGY IN CASES LIKE THIS IS TO GIVE UP YOUR SOURCE IN EXCHANGE FOR A LIGHT SENTENCE -- DEPORTATION, IN YOUR CASE.
WHAT SOURCE? I WASN'T CARRYING ANYTHING LIKE THAT IN MY PACK!
THE COPS SAY YOU WERE. OR DO YOU WANT TO ACCUSE THEM OF PLANTING IT?
I ... SEE.
YOUR WORD AGAINST THE COPS' ISN'T GOING TO GO WELL IN COURT, TRUST ME.
I WISH I COULD REMEMBER WHAT HAPPENED, BUT ... IT'S SO HAZY.
I'M AFRAID INCOHERENT MEMORY ISN'T GOING TO HELP YOUR CREDIBILITY IN A CHEEZ CASE.
HOWEVER, THERE IS ONE POSSIBILITY.
YOU ARE TRAVELING WITH THE FAMOUS SEAMUS O'MURCHADHA. IF YOU CAN SHOW THAT YOU'RE ALSO A SCIENTIST, AND NOT JUST SOME KIND OF PERSONAL ASSISTANT ...
I HAVE ADVANCED TRAINING IN MATHEMATICS, MOLETRONICS, AND GRAVITATIONAL DYNAMICS FROM THE KAKU INSTITUTE ...
I NEED SOMETHING MORE ... CURRENT. PERHAPS, IF YOU COULD DESCRIBE THE NATURE OF THE PROJECT YOU'RE WORKING ON WITH DR. O'MURCHADHA ...
THAT IS SO NOT HAPPENING. TRADE SECRETS.
MS. ORESME, I CAN ONLY HELP YOU IF YOU MEET ME HALF-WAY.

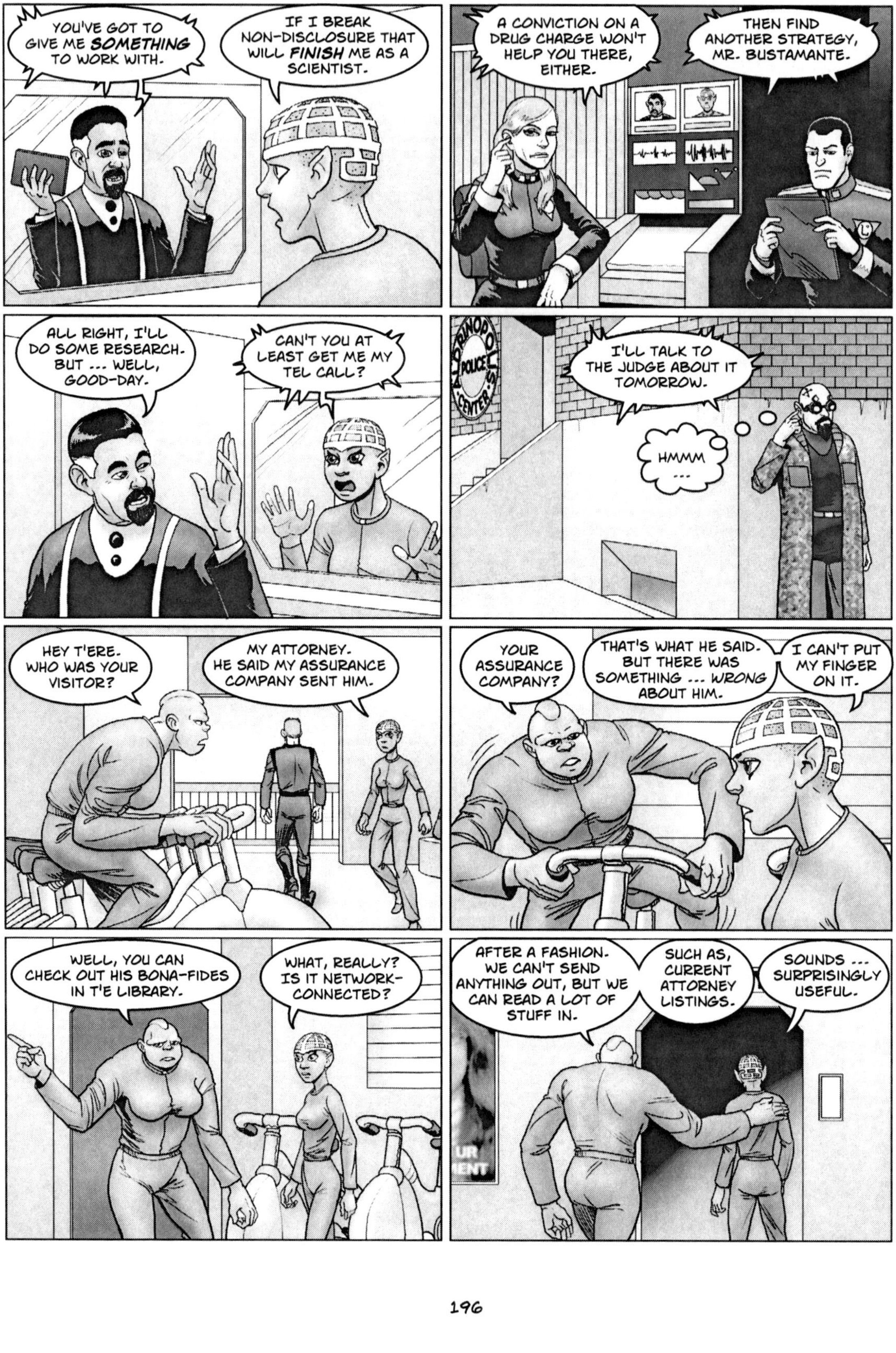
YOU'VE GOT TO GIVE ME SOMETHING TO WORK WITH.
IF I BREAK NON-DISCLOSURE THAT WILL FINISH ME AS A SCIENTIST.
A CONVICTION ON A DRUG CHARGE WON'T HELP YOU THERE, EITHER.
THEN FIND ANOTHER STRATEGY, MR. BUSTAMANTE.
ALL RIGHT, I'LL DO SOME RESEARCH. BUT ... WELL, GOOD-DAY.
CAN'T YOU AT LEAST GET ME MY TEL CALL?
POLICE CENTER
I'LL TALK TO THE JUDGE ABOUT IT TOMORROW.
HMMM ...
HEY T'ERE. WHO WAS YOUR VISITOR?
MY ATTORNEY. HE SAID MY ASSURANCE COMPANY SENT HIM.
YOUR ASSURANCE COMPANY?
THAT'S WHAT HE SAID. BUT THERE WAS SOMETHING ... WRONG ABOUT HIM.
I CAN'T PUT MY FINGER ON IT.
WELL, YOU CAN CHECK OUT HIS BONA-FIDES IN T'E LIBRARY.
WHAT, REALLY? IS IT NETWORK-CONNECTED?
AFTER A FASHION. WE CAN'T SEND ANYTHING OUT, BUT WE CAN READ A LOT OF STUFF IN.
SUCH AS, CURRENT ATTORNEY LISTINGS.
SOUNDS ... SURPRISINGLY USEFUL.

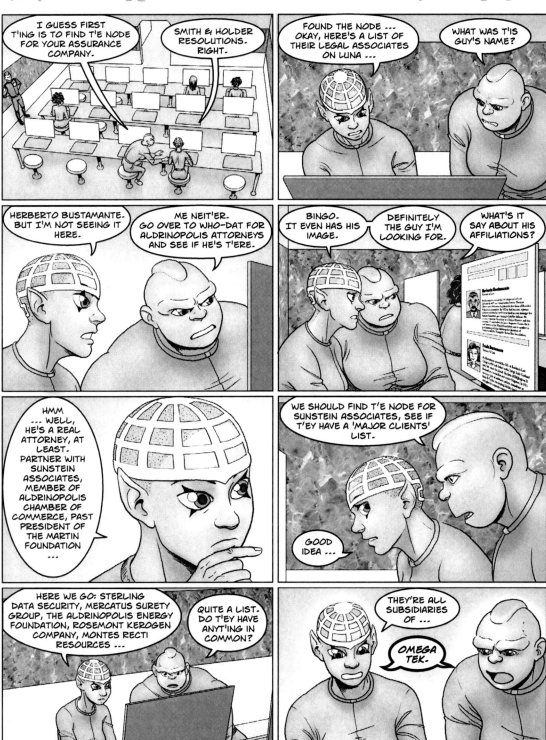

I GUESS FIRST T'ING IS TO FIND T'E NODE FOR YOUR ASSURANCE COMPANY.

SMITH & HOLDER RESOLUTIONS. RIGHT.

FOUND THE NODE ... OKAY, HERE'S A LIST OF THEIR LEGAL ASSOCIATES ON LUNA ...

WHAT WAS T'IS GUY'S NAME?

HERBERTO BUSTAMANTE. BUT I'M NOT SEEING IT HERE.

ME NEIT'ER. GO OVER TO WHO-DAT FOR ALDRINOPOLIS ATTORNEYS AND SEE IF HE'S T'ERE.

BINGO. IT EVEN HAS HIS IMAGE.

DEFINITELY THE GUY I'M LOOKING FOR.

WHAT'S IT SAY ABOUT HIS AFFILIATIONS?

HMM ... WELL, HE'S A REAL ATTORNEY, AT LEAST. PARTNER WITH SUNSTEIN ASSOCIATES, MEMBER OF ALDRINOPOLIS CHAMBER OF COMMERCE, PAST PRESIDENT OF THE MARTIN FOUNDATION ...

WE SHOULD FIND T'E NODE FOR SUNSTEIN ASSOCIATES, SEE IF T'EY HAVE A 'MAJOR CLIENTS' LIST.

GOOD IDEA ...

HERE WE GO: STERLING DATA SECURITY, MERCATUS SURETY GROUP, THE ALDRINOPOLIS ENERGY FOUNDATION, ROSEMONT KEROGEN COMPANY, MONTES RECTI RESOURCES ...

QUITE A LIST. DO T'EY HAVE ANYT'ING IN COMMON?

THEY'RE ALL SUBSIDIARIES OF ...

OMEGA TEK.

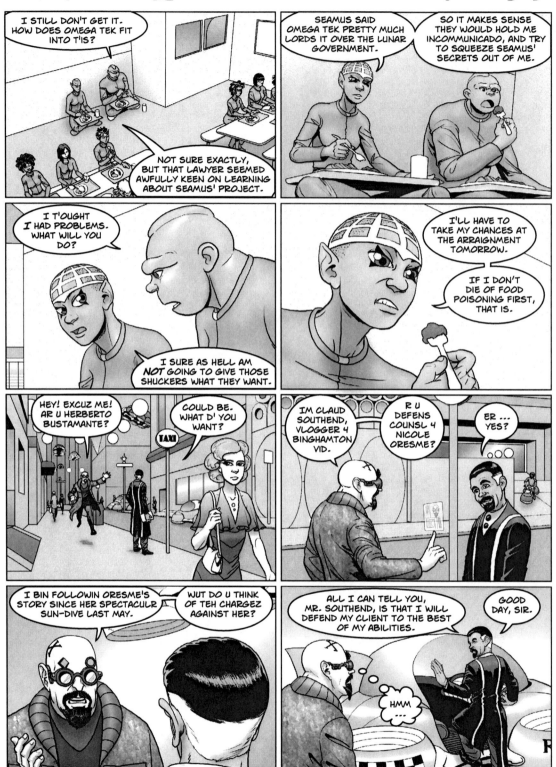

I STILL DON'T GET IT. HOW DOES OMEGA TEK FIT INTO T'IS?

NOT SURE EXACTLY, BUT THAT LAWYER SEEMED AWFULLY KEEN ON LEARNING ABOUT SEAMUS' PROJECT.

SEAMUS SAID OMEGA TEK PRETTY MUCH LORDS IT OVER THE LUNAR GOVERNMENT.

SO IT MAKES SENSE THEY WOULD HOLD ME INCOMMUNICADO, AND TRY TO SQUEEZE SEAMUS' SECRETS OUT OF ME.

I T'OUGHT I HAD PROBLEMS. WHAT WILL YOU DO?

I SURE AS HELL AM *NOT* GOING TO GIVE THOSE SHUCKERS WHAT THEY WANT.

I'LL HAVE TO TAKE MY CHANCES AT THE ARRAIGNMENT TOMORROW.

IF I DON'T DIE OF FOOD POISONING FIRST, THAT IS.

HEY! EXCUZ ME! AR U HERBERTO BUSTAMANTE?

COULD BE. WHAT D' YOU WANT?

TAXI

IM CLAUD SOUTHEND, VLOGGER 4 BINGHAMTON VID.

R U DEFENS COUNSL 4 NICOLE ORESME?

ER ... YES?

I BIN FOLLOWIN ORESME'S STORY SINCE HER SPECTACULR SUN-DIVE LAST MAY.

WUT DO U THINK OF TEH CHARGEZ AGAINST HER?

ALL I CAN TELL YOU, MR. SOUTHEND, IS THAT I WILL DEFEND MY CLIENT TO THE BEST OF MY ABILITIES.

GOOD DAY, SIR.

HMM ...

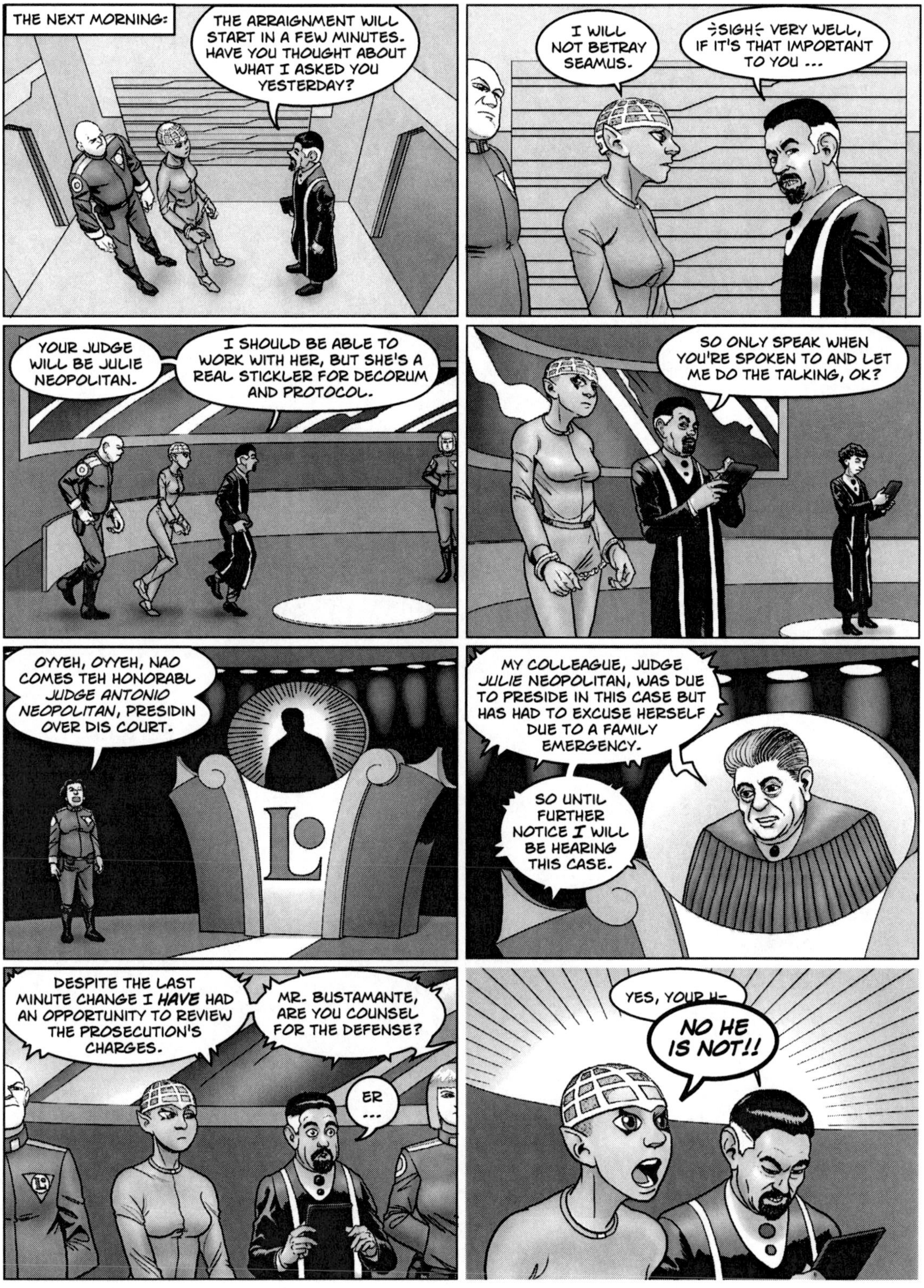
THE NEXT MORNING:
THE ARRAIGNMENT WILL START IN A FEW MINUTES. HAVE YOU THOUGHT ABOUT WHAT I ASKED YOU YESTERDAY?
I WILL NOT BETRAY SEAMUS.
SIGH VERY WELL, IF IT'S THAT IMPORTANT TO YOU ...
YOUR JUDGE WILL BE JULIE NEOPOLITAN.
I SHOULD BE ABLE TO WORK WITH HER, BUT SHE'S A REAL STICKLER FOR DECORUM AND PROTOCOL.
SO ONLY SPEAK WHEN YOU'RE SPOKEN TO AND LET ME DO THE TALKING, OK?
OYYEH, OYYEH, NAO COMES TEH HONORABL JUDGE ANTONIO NEOPOLITAN, PRESIDIN OVER DIS COURT.
L
MY COLLEAGUE, JUDGE JULIE NEOPOLITAN, WAS DUE TO PRESIDE IN THIS CASE BUT HAS HAD TO EXCUSE HERSELF DUE TO A FAMILY EMERGENCY.
SO UNTIL FURTHER NOTICE I WILL BE HEARING THIS CASE.
DESPITE THE LAST MINUTE CHANGE I HAVE HAD AN OPPORTUNITY TO REVIEW THE PROSECUTION'S CHARGES.
MR. BUSTAMANTE, ARE YOU COUNSEL FOR THE DEFENSE?
ER ...
YES, YOUR H—
NO HE IS NOT!!

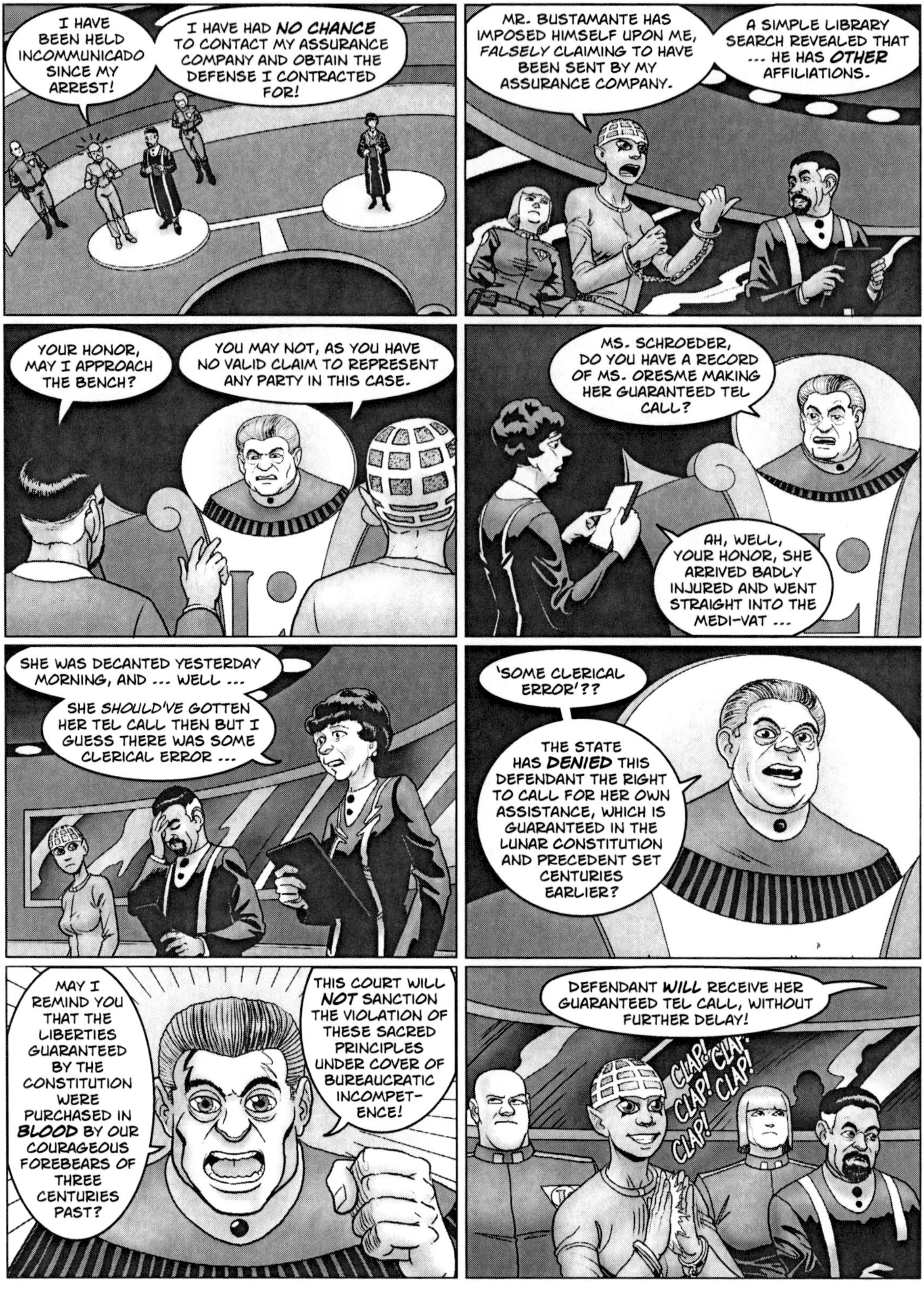
I HAVE BEEN HELD INCOMMUNICADO SINCE MY ARREST!
I HAVE HAD NO CHANCE TO CONTACT MY ASSURANCE COMPANY AND OBTAIN THE DEFENSE I CONTRACTED FOR!
MR. BUSTAMANTE HAS IMPOSED HIMSELF UPON ME, FALSELY CLAIMING TO HAVE BEEN SENT BY MY ASSURANCE COMPANY.
A SIMPLE LIBRARY SEARCH REVEALED THAT ... HE HAS OTHER AFFILIATIONS.
YOUR HONOR, MAY I APPROACH THE BENCH?
YOU MAY NOT, AS YOU HAVE NO VALID CLAIM TO REPRESENT ANY PARTY IN THIS CASE.
MS. SCHROEDER, DO YOU HAVE A RECORD OF MS. ORESME MAKING HER GUARANTEED TEL CALL?
AH, WELL, YOUR HONOR, SHE ARRIVED BADLY INJURED AND WENT STRAIGHT INTO THE MEDI-VAT ...
SHE WAS DECANTED YESTERDAY MORNING, AND ... WELL ...
SHE SHOULD'VE GOTTEN HER TEL CALL THEN BUT I GUESS THERE WAS SOME CLERICAL ERROR ...
'SOME CLERICAL ERROR'??
THE STATE HAS DENIED THIS DEFENDANT THE RIGHT TO CALL FOR HER OWN ASSISTANCE, WHICH IS GUARANTEED IN THE LUNAR CONSTITUTION AND PRECEDENT SET CENTURIES EARLIER?
MAY I REMIND YOU THAT THE LIBERTIES GUARANTEED BY THE CONSTITUTION WERE PURCHASED IN BLOOD BY OUR COURAGEOUS FOREBEARS OF THREE CENTURIES PAST?
THIS COURT WILL NOT SANCTION THE VIOLATION OF THESE SACRED PRINCIPLES UNDER COVER OF BUREAUCRATIC INCOMPETENCE!
DEFENDANT WILL RECEIVE HER GUARANTEED TEL CALL, WITHOUT FURTHER DELAY!
CLAP! CLAP! CLAP! CLAP! CLAP! CLAP!

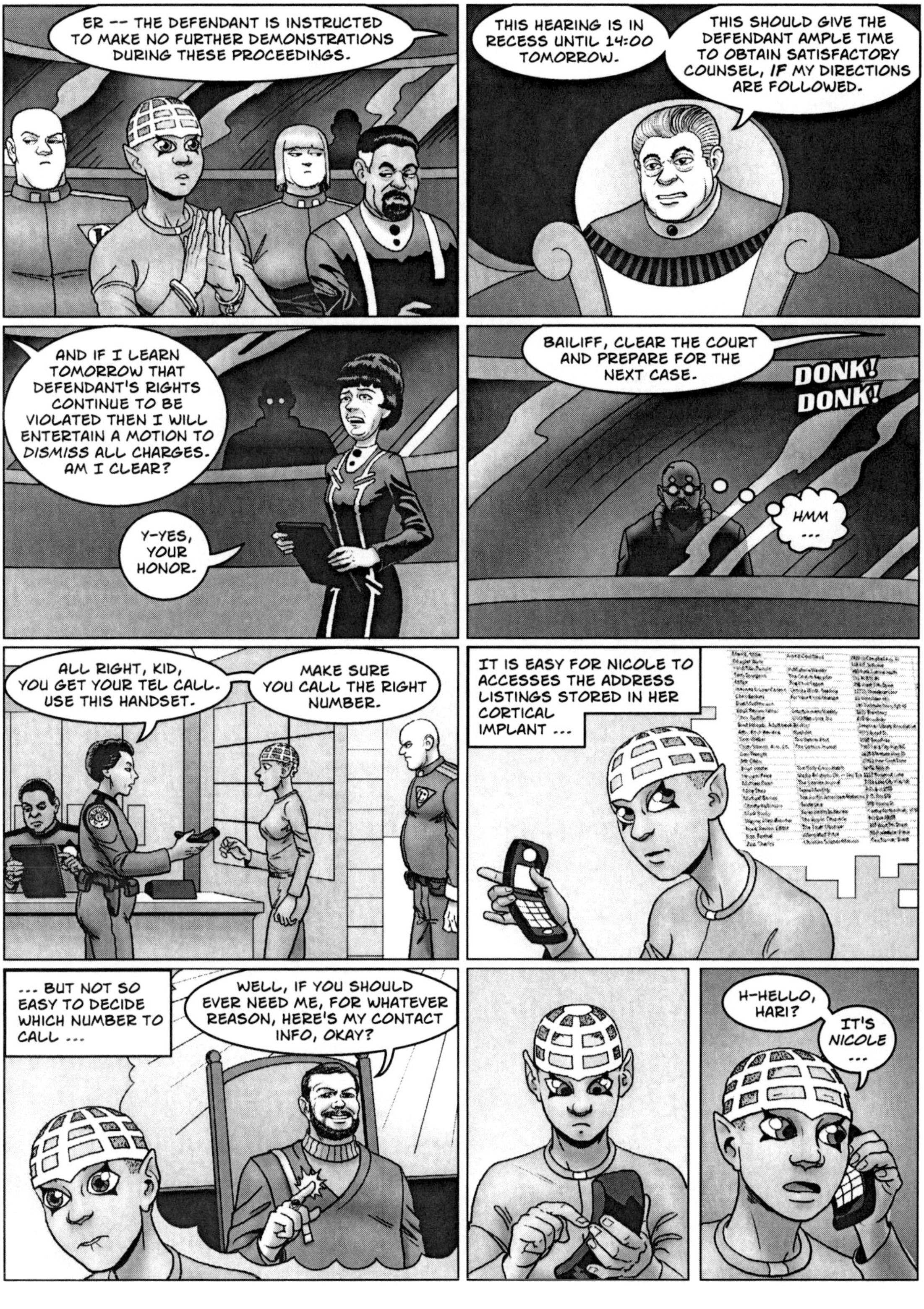
ER -- THE DEFENDANT IS INSTRUCTED TO MAKE NO FURTHER DEMONSTRATIONS DURING THESE PROCEEDINGS.
THIS HEARING IS IN RECESS UNTIL 14:00 TOMORROW.
THIS SHOULD GIVE THE DEFENDANT AMPLE TIME TO OBTAIN SATISFACTORY COUNSEL, IF MY DIRECTIONS ARE FOLLOWED.
AND IF I LEARN TOMORROW THAT DEFENDANT'S RIGHTS CONTINUE TO BE VIOLATED THEN I WILL ENTERTAIN A MOTION TO DISMISS ALL CHARGES. AM I CLEAR?
Y-YES, YOUR HONOR.
BAILIFF, CLEAR THE COURT AND PREPARE FOR THE NEXT CASE.
DONK! DONK!
HMM ...
ALL RIGHT, KID, YOU GET YOUR TEL CALL. USE THIS HANDSET.
MAKE SURE YOU CALL THE RIGHT NUMBER.
IT IS EASY FOR NICOLE TO ACCESSES THE ADDRESS LISTINGS STORED IN HER CORTICAL IMPLANT ...
... BUT NOT SO EASY TO DECIDE WHICH NUMBER TO CALL ...
WELL, IF YOU SHOULD EVER NEED ME, FOR WHATEVER REASON, HERE'S MY CONTACT INFO, OKAY?
H-HELLO, HARI?
IT'S NICOLE ...

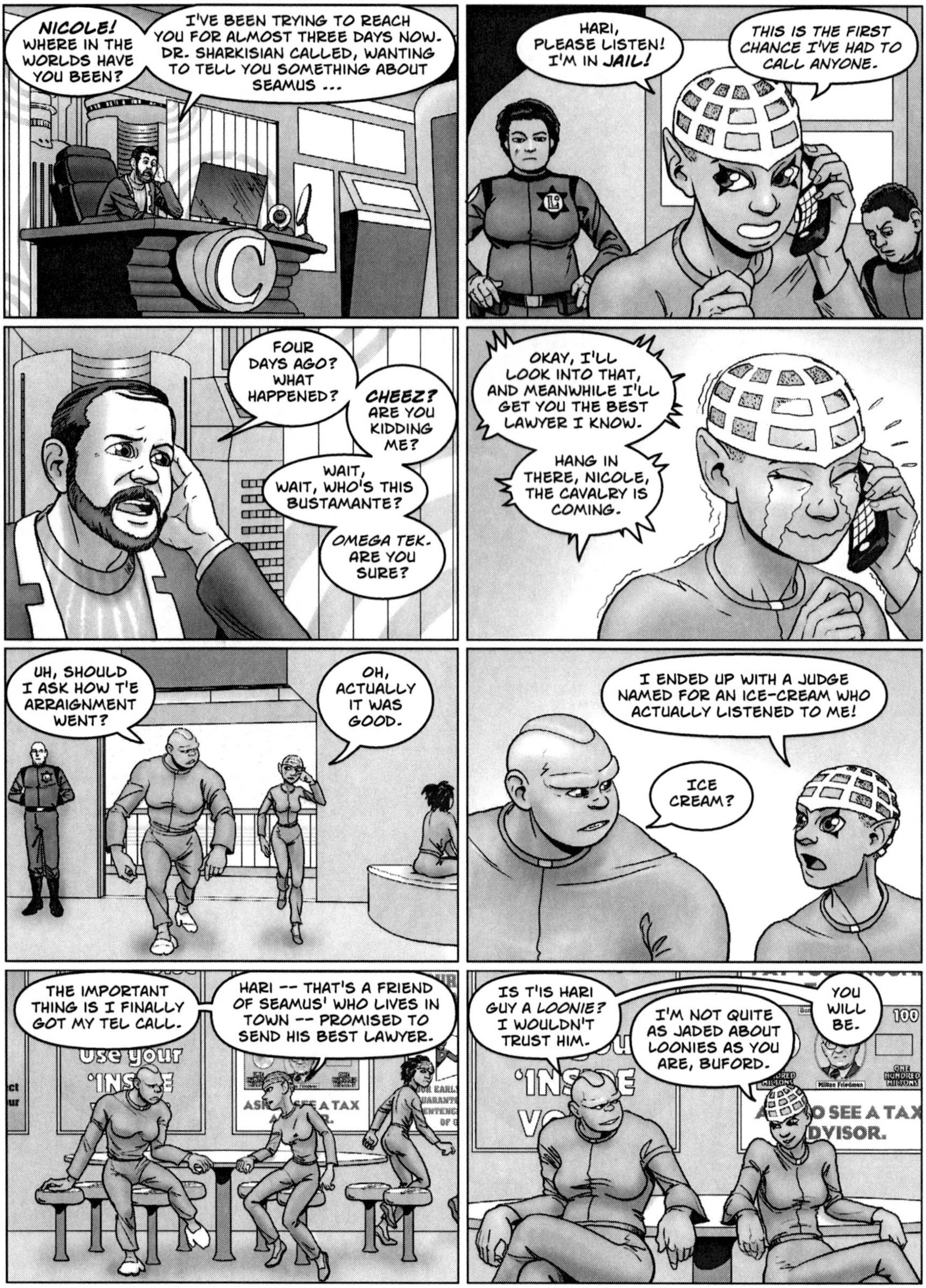
NICOLE! WHERE IN THE WORLDS HAVE YOU BEEN?
I'VE BEEN TRYING TO REACH YOU FOR ALMOST THREE DAYS NOW. DR. SHARKISIAN CALLED, WANTING TO TELL YOU SOMETHING ABOUT SEAMUS ...
HARI, PLEASE LISTEN! I'M IN JAIL!
THIS IS THE FIRST CHANCE I'VE HAD TO CALL ANYONE.
FOUR DAYS AGO? WHAT HAPPENED?
CHEEZ? ARE YOU KIDDING ME?
WAIT, WAIT, WHO'S THIS BUSTAMANTE?
OMEGA TEK. ARE YOU SURE?
OKAY, I'LL LOOK INTO THAT, AND MEANWHILE I'LL GET YOU THE BEST LAWYER I KNOW.
HANG IN THERE, NICOLE, THE CAVALRY IS COMING.
UH, SHOULD I ASK HOW T'E ARRAIGNMENT WENT?
OH, ACTUALLY IT WAS GOOD.
I ENDED UP WITH A JUDGE NAMED FOR AN ICE-CREAM WHO ACTUALLY LISTENED TO ME!
ICE CREAM?
THE IMPORTANT THING IS I FINALLY GOT MY TEL CALL.
HARI -- THAT'S A FRIEND OF SEAMUS' WHO LIVES IN TOWN -- PROMISED TO SEND HIS BEST LAWYER.
IS T'IS HARI GUY A LOONIE? I WOULDN'T TRUST HIM.
I'M NOT QUITE AS JADED ABOUT LOONIES AS YOU ARE, BUFORD.
YOU WILL BE.

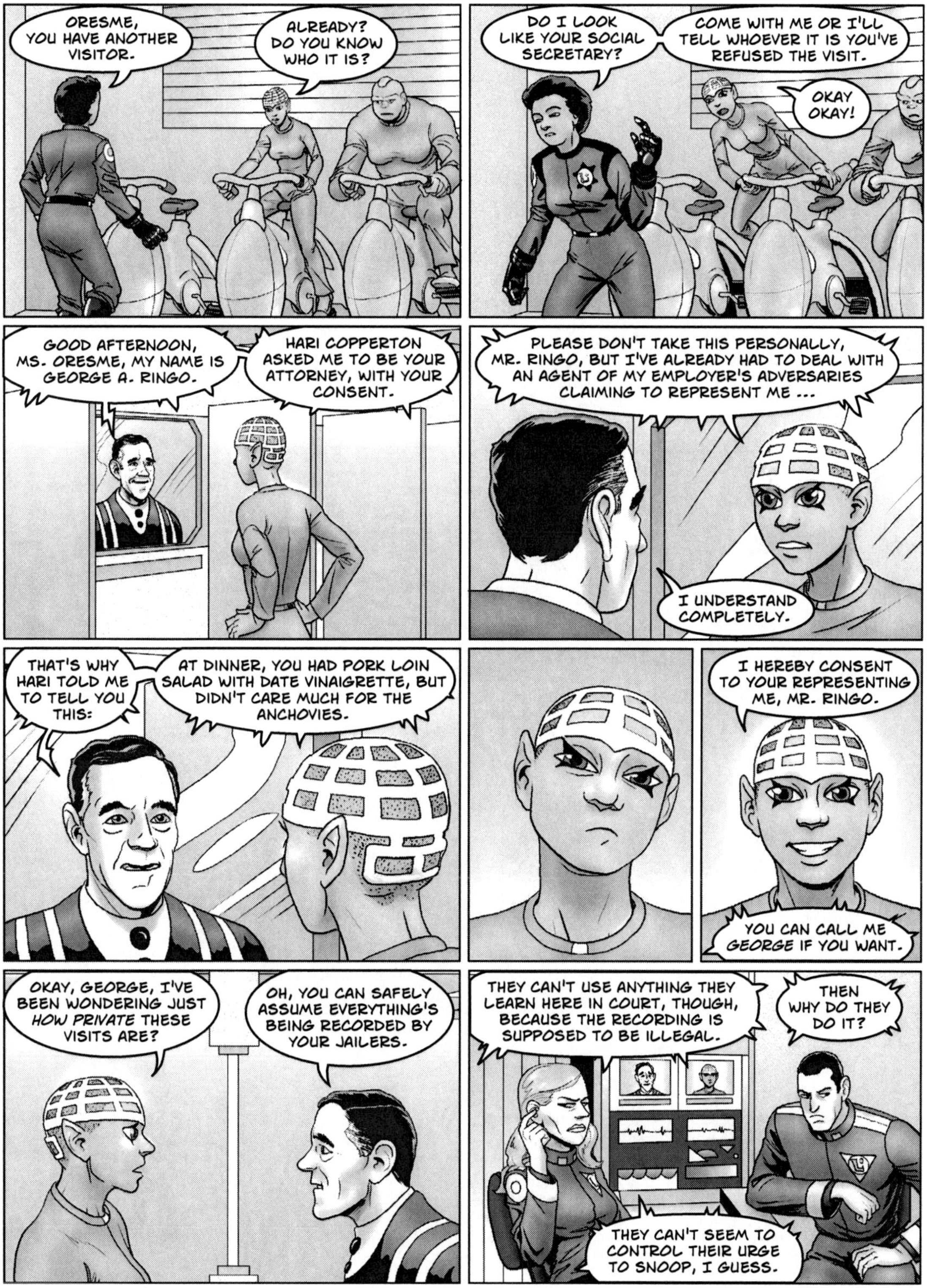
ORESME, YOU HAVE ANOTHER VISITOR.
ALREADY? DO YOU KNOW WHO IT IS?
DO I LOOK LIKE YOUR SOCIAL SECRETARY?
COME WITH ME OR I'LL TELL WHOEVER IT IS YOU'VE REFUSED THE VISIT.
OKAY OKAY!
GOOD AFTERNOON, MS. ORESME, MY NAME IS GEORGE A. RINGO.
HARI COPPERTON ASKED ME TO BE YOUR ATTORNEY, WITH YOUR CONSENT.
PLEASE DON'T TAKE THIS PERSONALLY, MR. RINGO, BUT I'VE ALREADY HAD TO DEAL WITH AN AGENT OF MY EMPLOYER'S ADVERSARIES CLAIMING TO REPRESENT ME ...
I UNDERSTAND COMPLETELY.
THAT'S WHY HARI TOLD ME TO TELL YOU THIS:
AT DINNER, YOU HAD PORK LOIN SALAD WITH DATE VINAIGRETTE, BUT DIDN'T CARE MUCH FOR THE ANCHOVIES.
I HEREBY CONSENT TO YOUR REPRESENTING ME, MR. RINGO.
YOU CAN CALL ME GEORGE IF YOU WANT.
OKAY, GEORGE, I'VE BEEN WONDERING JUST *HOW PRIVATE* THESE VISITS ARE?
OH, YOU CAN SAFELY ASSUME EVERYTHING'S BEING RECORDED BY YOUR JAILERS.
THEY CAN'T USE ANYTHING THEY LEARN HERE IN COURT, THOUGH, BECAUSE THE RECORDING IS SUPPOSED TO BE ILLEGAL.
THEN WHY DO THEY DO IT?
THEY CAN'T SEEM TO CONTROL THEIR URGE TO SNOOP, I GUESS.

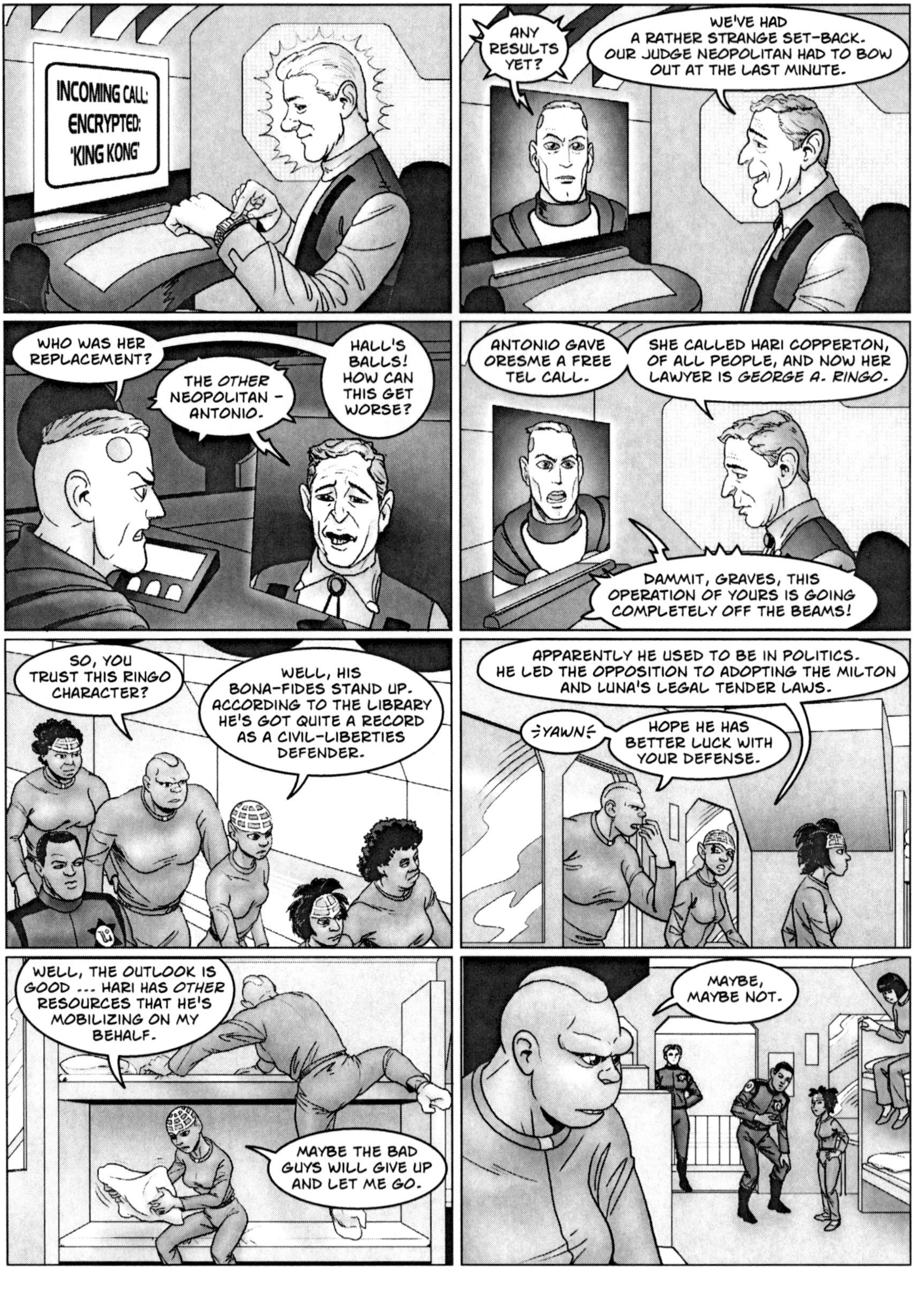
INCOMING CALL: ENCRYPTED: 'KING KONG'
ANY RESULTS YET?
WE'VE HAD A RATHER STRANGE SET-BACK. OUR JUDGE NEOPOLITAN HAD TO BOW OUT AT THE LAST MINUTE.
WHO WAS HER REPLACEMENT?
THE OTHER NEOPOLITAN - ANTONIO.
HALL'S BALLS! HOW CAN THIS GET WORSE?
ANTONIO GAVE ORESME A FREE TEL CALL.
SHE CALLED HARI COPPERTON, OF ALL PEOPLE, AND NOW HER LAWYER IS GEORGE A. RINGO.
DAMMIT, GRAVES, THIS OPERATION OF YOURS IS GOING COMPLETELY OFF THE BEAMS!
SO, YOU TRUST THIS RINGO CHARACTER?
WELL, HIS BONA-FIDES STAND UP. ACCORDING TO THE LIBRARY HE'S GOT QUITE A RECORD AS A CIVIL-LIBERTIES DEFENDER.
APPARENTLY HE USED TO BE IN POLITICS. HE LED THE OPPOSITION TO ADOPTING THE MILTON AND LUNA'S LEGAL TENDER LAWS.
YAWN
HOPE HE HAS BETTER LUCK WITH YOUR DEFENSE.
WELL, THE OUTLOOK IS GOOD ... HARI HAS OTHER RESOURCES THAT HE'S MOBILIZING ON MY BEHALF.
MAYBE THE BAD GUYS WILL GIVE UP AND LET ME GO.
MAYBE, MAYBE NOT.

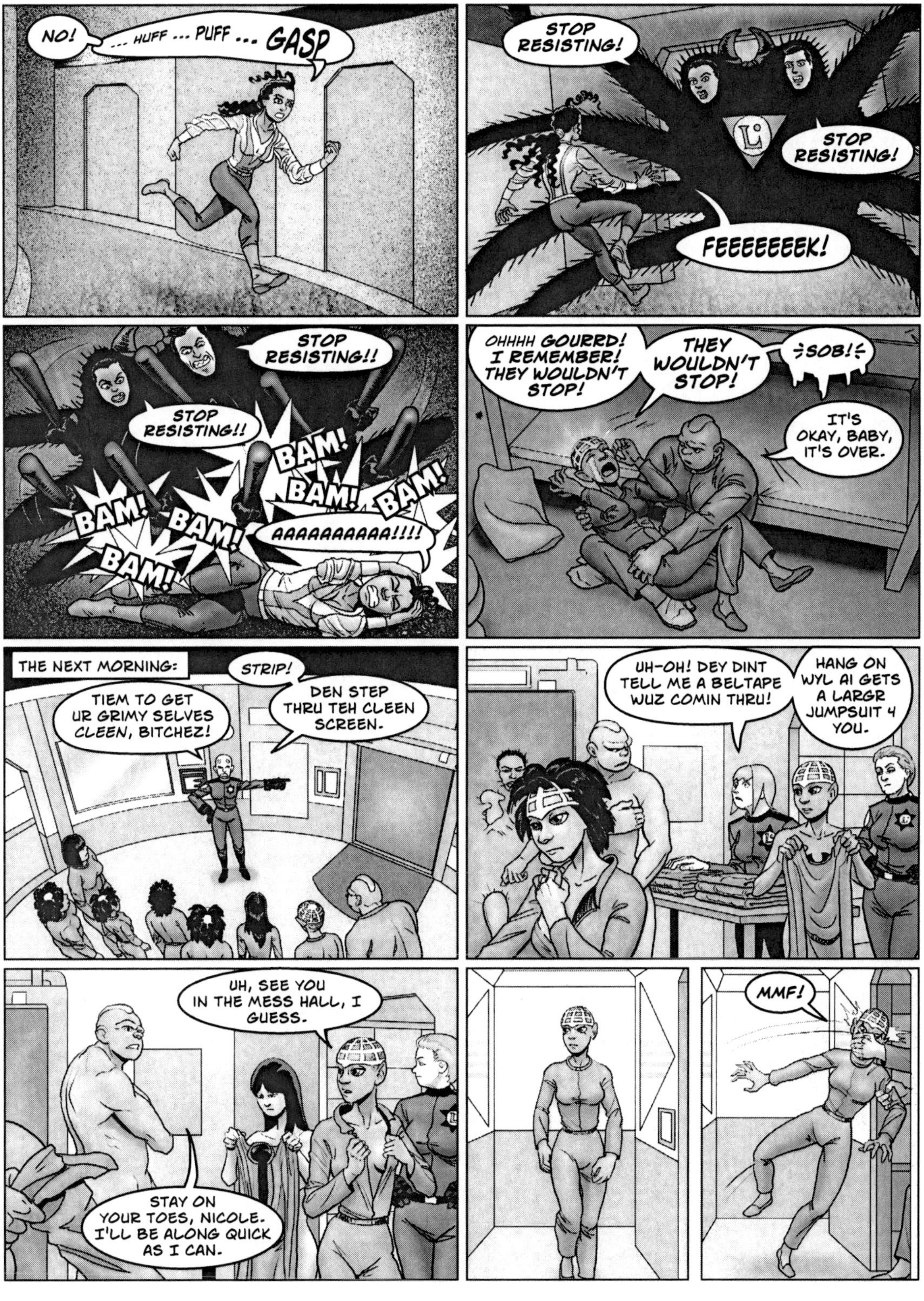
NO!
... HUFF ... PUFF ... GASP
STOP RESISTING!
STOP RESISTING!
FEEEEEEEK!
STOP RESISTING!!
STOP RESISTING!!
BAM!
BAM!
BAM!
BAM!
BAM!
BAM!
AAAAAAAAAA!!!!
OHHHH GOURRD! I REMEMBER! THEY WOULDN'T STOP!
THEY WOULDN'T STOP!
SOB!
IT'S OKAY, BABY, IT'S OVER.
THE NEXT MORNING:
TIEM TO GET UR GRIMY SELVES CLEEN, BITCHEZ!
STRIP!
DEN STEP THRU TEH CLEEN SCREEN.
UH-OH! DEY DINT TELL ME A BELTAPE WUZ COMIN THRU!
HANG ON WYL AI GETS A LARGR JUMPSUIT 4 YOU.
UH, SEE YOU IN THE MESS HALL, I GUESS.
STAY ON YOUR TOES, NICOLE. I'LL BE ALONG QUICK AS I CAN.
MMF!

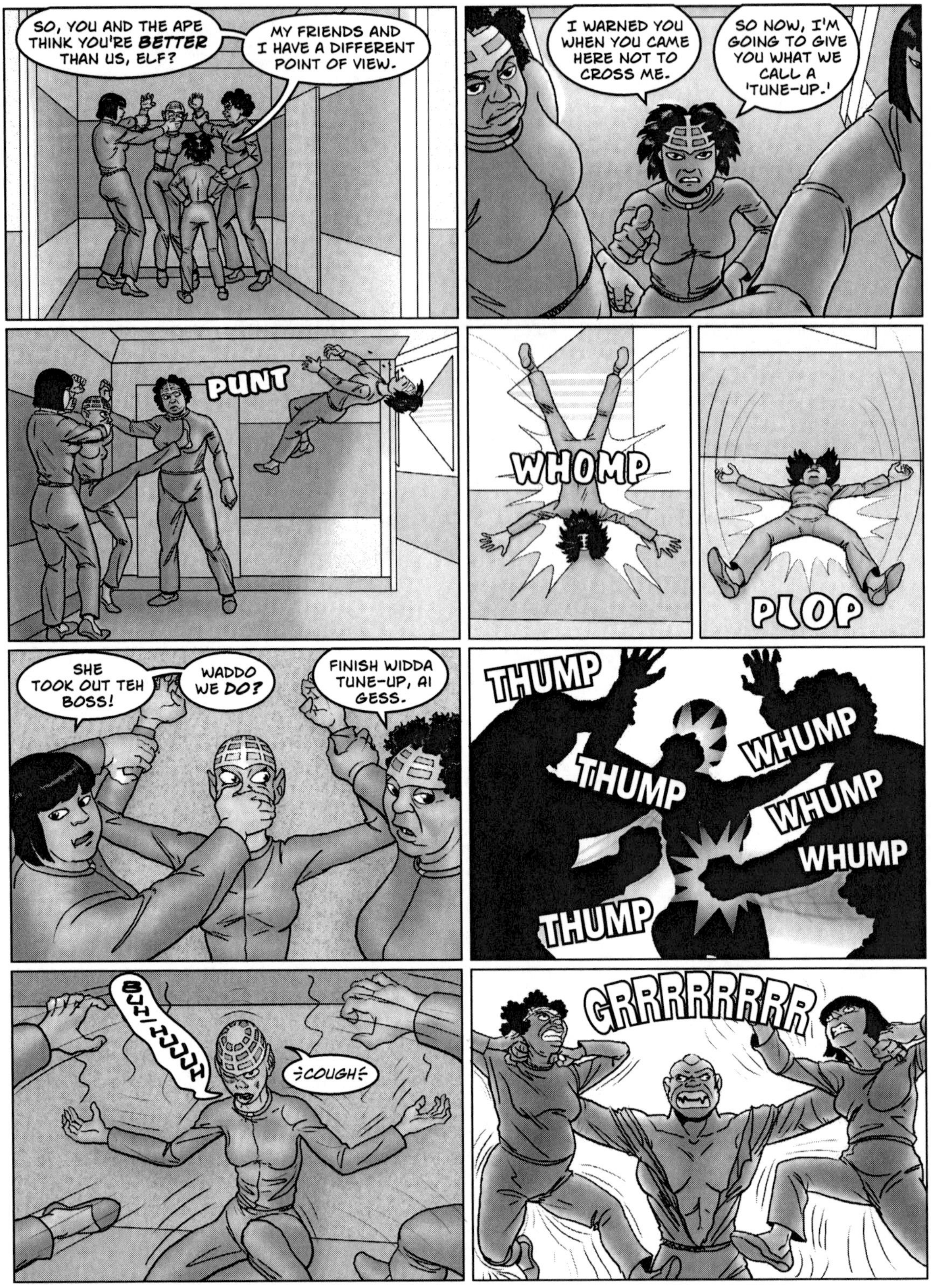
SO, YOU AND THE APE THINK YOU'RE BETTER THAN US, ELF?
MY FRIENDS AND I HAVE A DIFFERENT POINT OF VIEW.
I WARNED YOU WHEN YOU CAME HERE NOT TO CROSS ME.
SO NOW, I'M GOING TO GIVE YOU WHAT WE CALL A 'TUNE-UP.'
PUNT
WHOMP
PLOP
SHE TOOK OUT TEH BOSS!
WADDO WE DO?
FINISH WIDDA TUNE-UP, AI GESS.
THUMP
THUMP
WHUMP
WHUMP
WHUMP
THUMP
BUH-HJJJH
COUGH
GRRRRRRRR

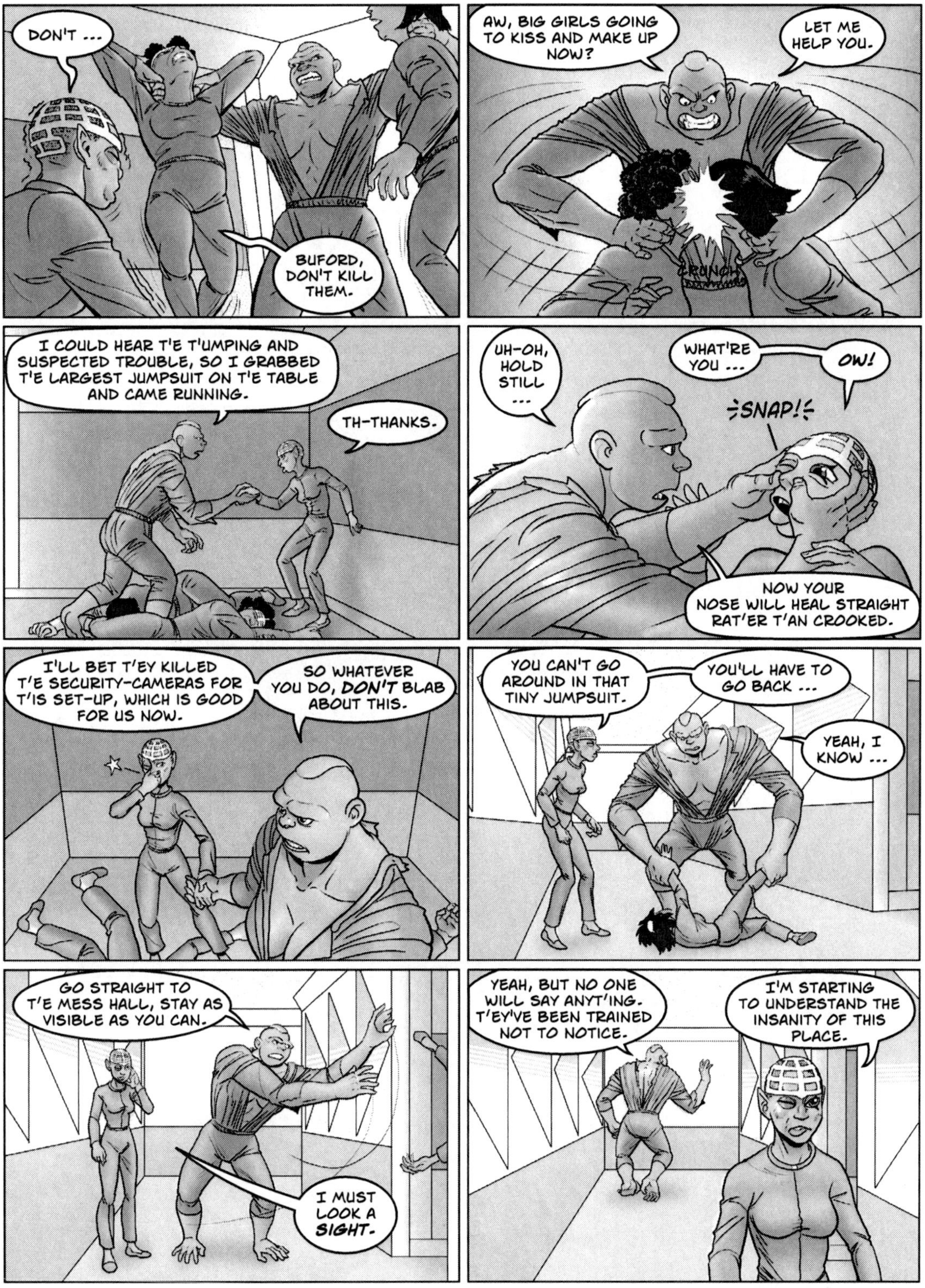
DON'T ...
BUFORD, DON'T KILL THEM.
AW, BIG GIRLS GOING TO KISS AND MAKE UP NOW?
LET ME HELP YOU.
CRUNCH
I COULD HEAR T'E T'UMPING AND SUSPECTED TROUBLE, SO I GRABBED T'E LARGEST JUMPSUIT ON T'E TABLE AND CAME RUNNING.
TH-THANKS.
UH-OH, HOLD STILL ...
WHAT'RE YOU ...
OW!
SNAP!
NOW YOUR NOSE WILL HEAL STRAIGHT RAT'ER T'AN CROOKED.
I'LL BET T'EY KILLED T'E SECURITY-CAMERAS FOR T'IS SET-UP, WHICH IS GOOD FOR US NOW.
SO WHATEVER YOU DO, DON'T BLAB ABOUT THIS.
YOU CAN'T GO AROUND IN THAT TINY JUMPSUIT.
YOU'LL HAVE TO GO BACK ...
YEAH, I KNOW ...
GO STRAIGHT TO T'E MESS HALL, STAY AS VISIBLE AS YOU CAN.
I MUST LOOK A SIGHT.
YEAH, BUT NO ONE WILL SAY ANYT'ING. T'EY'VE BEEN TRAINED NOT TO NOTICE.
I'M STARTING TO UNDERSTAND THE INSANITY OF THIS PLACE.

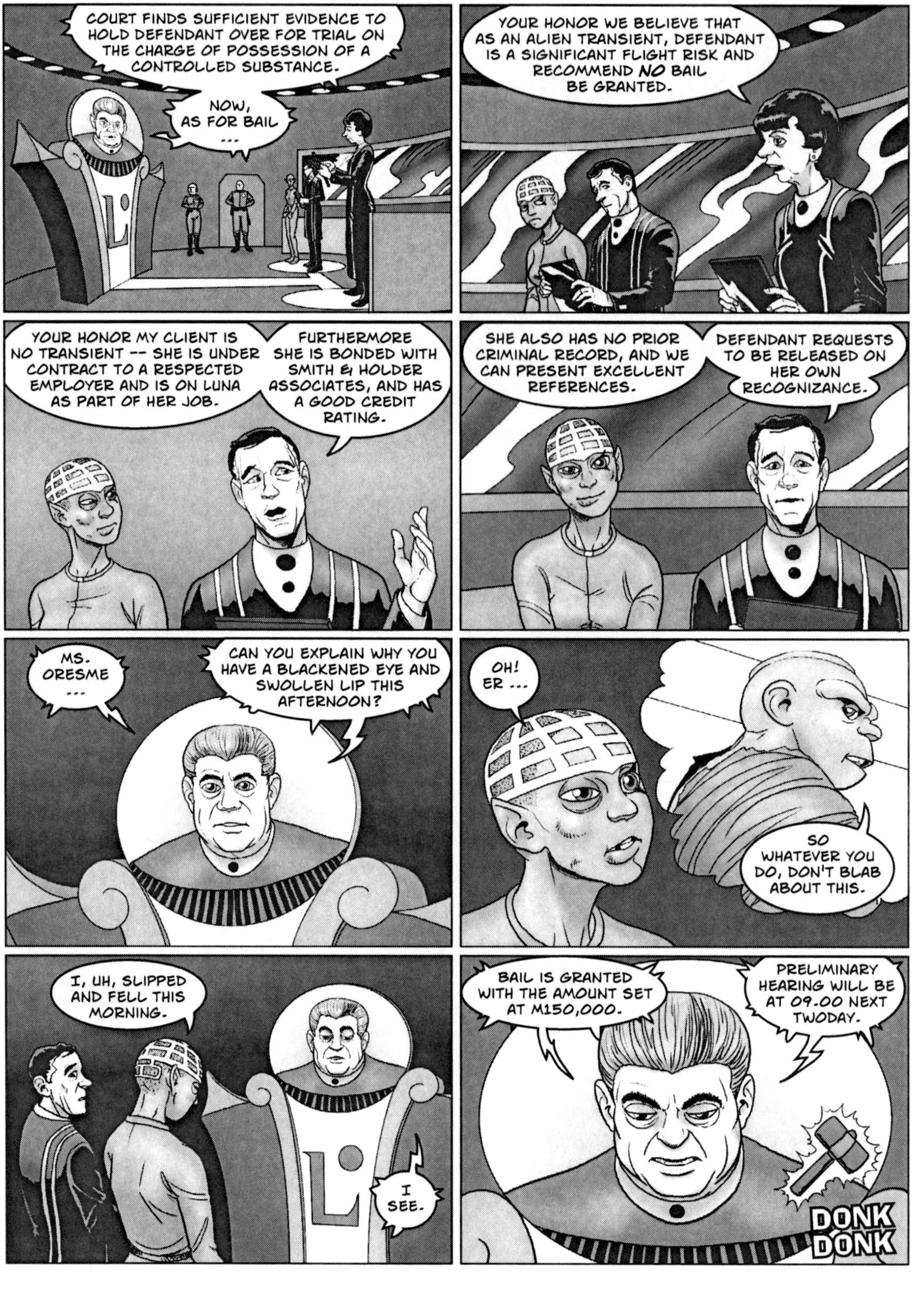
COURT FINDS SUFFICIENT EVIDENCE TO HOLD DEFENDANT OVER FOR TRIAL ON THE CHARGE OF POSSESSION OF A CONTROLLED SUBSTANCE.
NOW, AS FOR BAIL ...
YOUR HONOR WE BELIEVE THAT AS AN ALIEN TRANSIENT, DEFENDANT IS A SIGNIFICANT FLIGHT RISK AND RECOMMEND NO BAIL BE GRANTED.
YOUR HONOR MY CLIENT IS NO TRANSIENT -- SHE IS UNDER CONTRACT TO A RESPECTED EMPLOYER AND IS ON LUNA AS PART OF HER JOB.
FURTHERMORE SHE IS BONDED WITH SMITH & HOLDER ASSOCIATES, AND HAS A GOOD CREDIT RATING.
SHE ALSO HAS NO PRIOR CRIMINAL RECORD, AND WE CAN PRESENT EXCELLENT REFERENCES.
DEFENDANT REQUESTS TO BE RELEASED ON HER OWN RECOGNIZANCE.
MS. ORESME ...
CAN YOU EXPLAIN WHY YOU HAVE A BLACKENED EYE AND SWOLLEN LIP THIS AFTERNOON?
OH! ER ...
SO WHATEVER YOU DO, DON'T BLAB ABOUT THIS.
I, UH, SLIPPED AND FELL THIS MORNING.
I SEE.
BAIL IS GRANTED WITH THE AMOUNT SET AT M150,000.
PRELIMINARY HEARING WILL BE AT 09.00 NEXT TWODAY.
DONK DONK

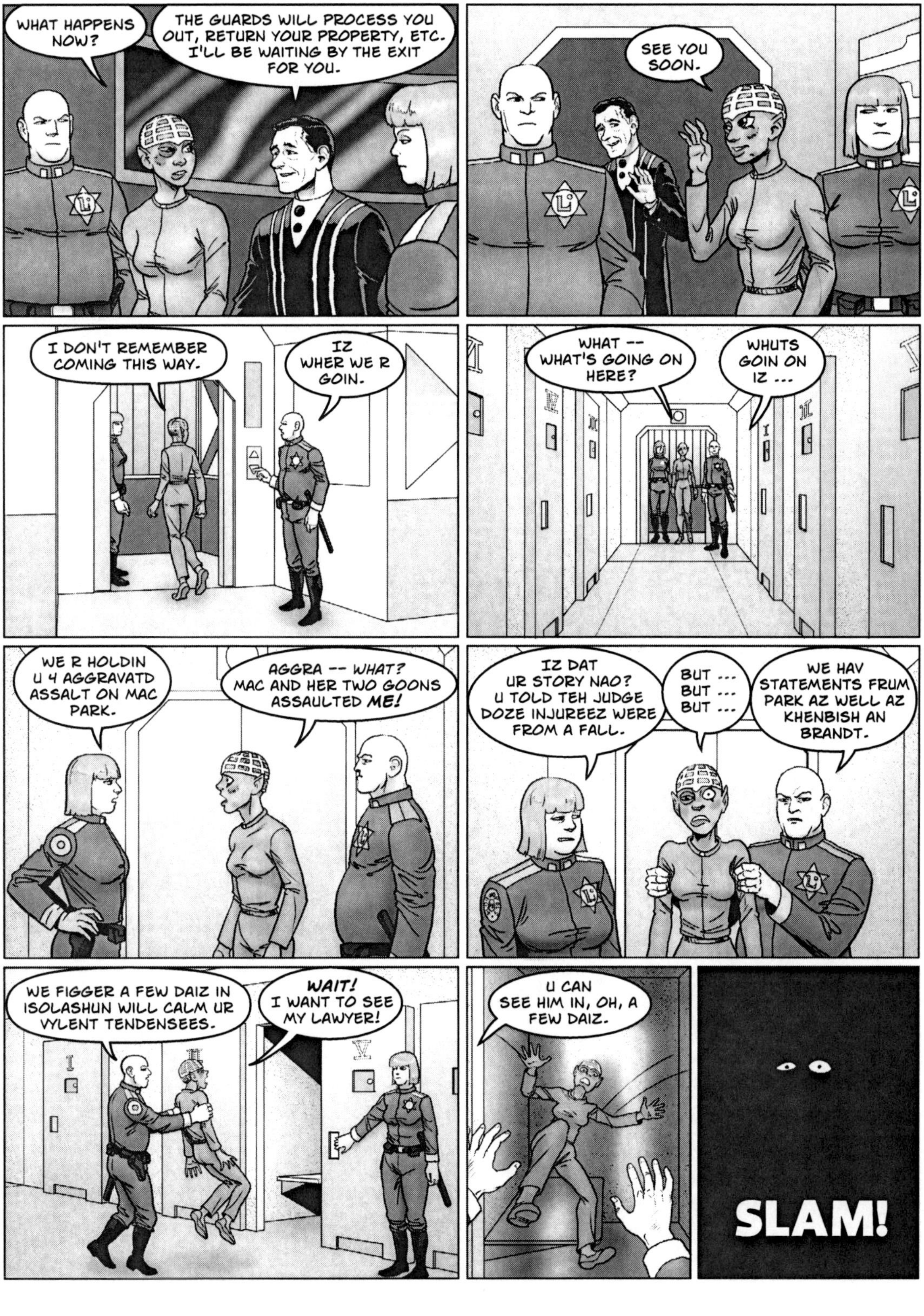
WHAT HAPPENS NOW?
THE GUARDS WILL PROCESS YOU OUT, RETURN YOUR PROPERTY, ETC. I'LL BE WAITING BY THE EXIT FOR YOU.
SEE YOU SOON.
I DON'T REMEMBER COMING THIS WAY.
IZ WHER WE R GOIN.
WHAT -- WHAT'S GOING ON HERE?
WHUTS GOIN ON IZ ...
WE R HOLDIN U 4 AGGRAVATD ASSALT ON MAC PARK.
AGGRA -- WHAT? MAC AND HER TWO GOONS ASSAULTED ME!
IZ DAT UR STORY NAO? U TOLD TEH JUDGE DOZE INJUREEZ WERE FROM A FALL.
BUT ... BUT ... BUT ...
WE HAV STATEMENTS FRUM PARK AZ WELL AZ KHENBISH AN BRANDT.
WE FIGGER A FEW DAIZ IN ISOLASHUN WILL CALM UR VYLENT TENDENSEES.
WAIT! I WANT TO SEE MY LAWYER!
U CAN SEE HIM IN, OH, A FEW DAIZ.
SLAM!

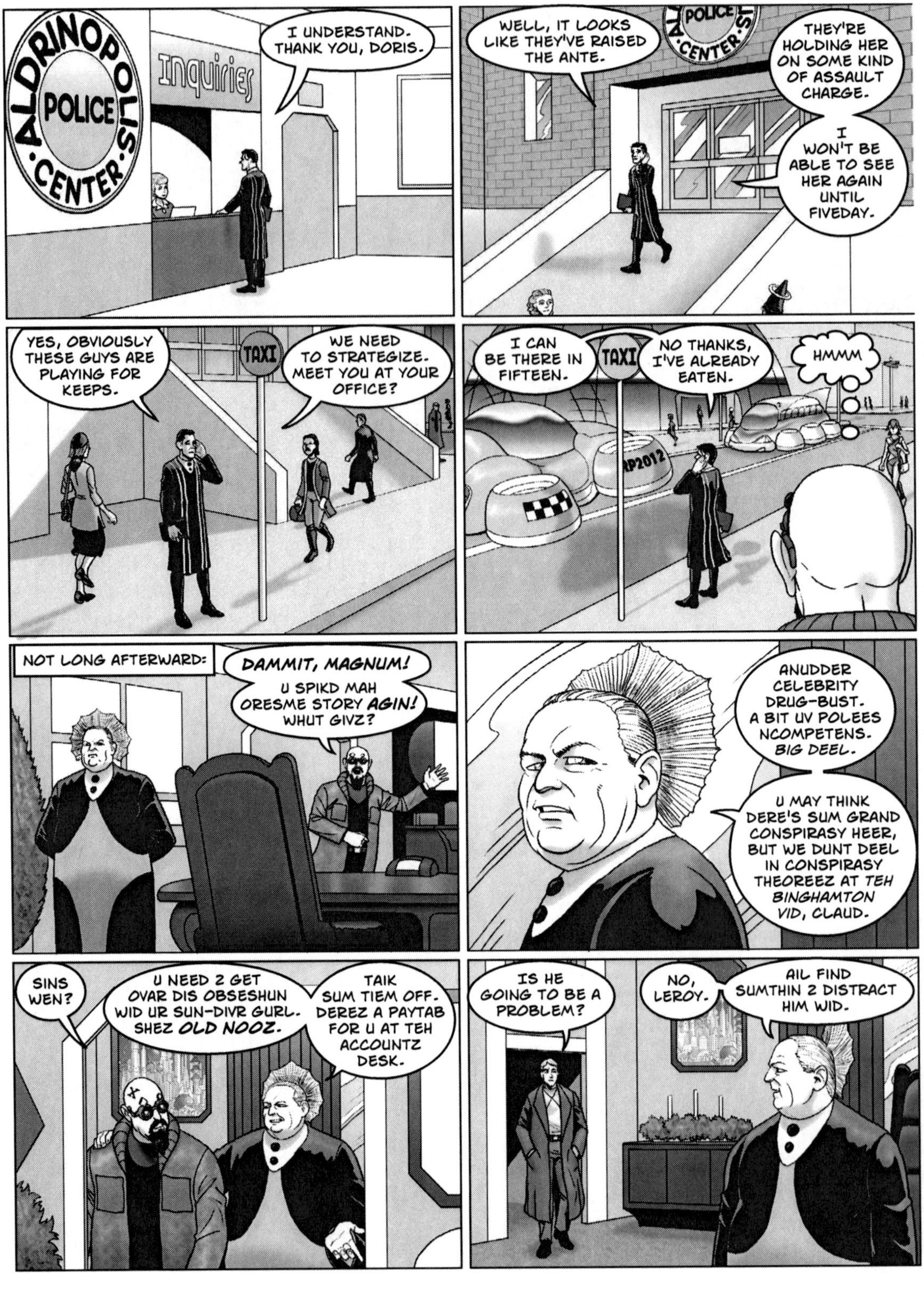
ALDRINOPOLIS POLICE CENTER
INQUIRIES
I UNDERSTAND. THANK YOU, DORIS.
WELL, IT LOOKS LIKE THEY'VE RAISED THE ANTE.
THEY'RE HOLDING HER ON SOME KIND OF ASSAULT CHARGE.
I WON'T BE ABLE TO SEE HER AGAIN UNTIL FIVEDAY.
YES, OBVIOUSLY THESE GUYS ARE PLAYING FOR KEEPS.
TAXI
WE NEED TO STRATEGIZE. MEET YOU AT YOUR OFFICE?
I CAN BE THERE IN FIFTEEN.
TAXI
NO THANKS, I'VE ALREADY EATEN.
HMMM
NOT LONG AFTERWARD:
DAMMIT, MAGNUM! U SPIKD MAH ORESME STORY AGIN! WHUT GIVZ?
ANUDDER CELEBRITY DRUG-BUST. A BIT UV POLEES NCOMPETENS. BIG DEEL.
U MAY THINK DERE'S SUM GRAND CONSPIRASY HEER, BUT WE DUNT DEEL IN CONSPIRASY THEOREEZ AT TEH BINGHAMTON VID, CLAUD.
SINS WEN?
U NEED 2 GET OVAR DIS OBSESHUN WID UR SUN-DIVR GURL. SHEZ OLD NOOZ.
TAIK SUM TIEM OFF. DEREZ A PAYTAB FOR U AT TEH ACCOUNTZ DESK.
IS HE GOING TO BE A PROBLEM?
NO, LEROY.
AIL FIND SUMTHIN 2 DISTRACT HIM WID.

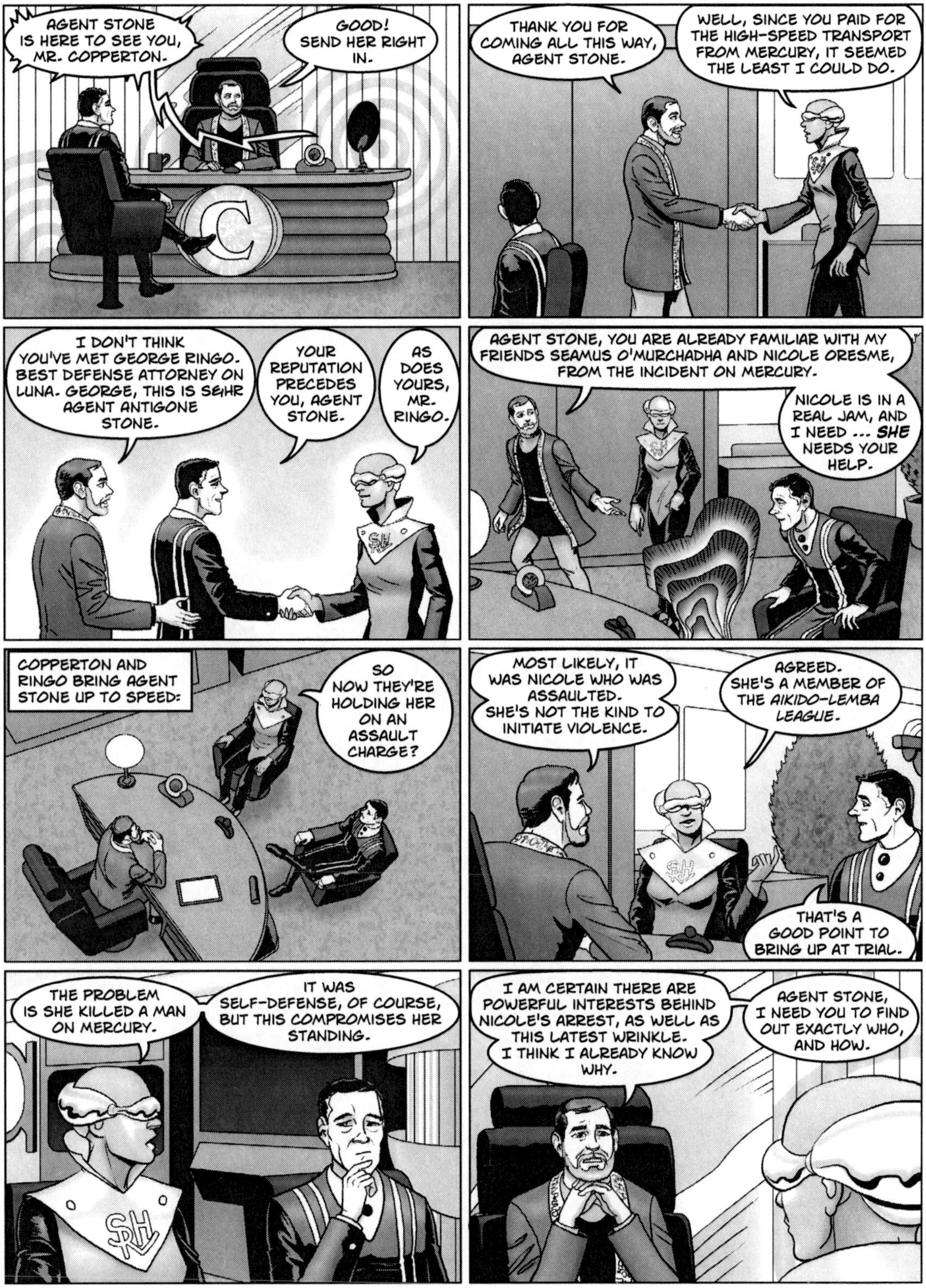
AGENT STONE IS HERE TO SEE YOU, MR. COPPERTON.
GOOD! SEND HER RIGHT IN.
THANK YOU FOR COMING ALL THIS WAY, AGENT STONE.
WELL, SINCE YOU PAID FOR THE HIGH-SPEED TRANSPORT FROM MERCURY, IT SEEMED THE LEAST I COULD DO.
I DON'T THINK YOU'VE MET GEORGE RINGO. BEST DEFENSE ATTORNEY ON LUNA. GEORGE, THIS IS SE/HR AGENT ANTIGONE STONE.
YOUR REPUTATION PRECEDES YOU, AGENT STONE.
AS DOES YOURS, MR. RINGO.
AGENT STONE, YOU ARE ALREADY FAMILIAR WITH MY FRIENDS SEAMUS O'MURCHADHA AND NICOLE ORESME, FROM THE INCIDENT ON MERCURY.
NICOLE IS IN A REAL JAM, AND I NEED ... SHE NEEDS YOUR HELP.
COPPERTON AND RINGO BRING AGENT STONE UP TO SPEED:
SO NOW THEY'RE HOLDING HER ON AN ASSAULT CHARGE?
MOST LIKELY, IT WAS NICOLE WHO WAS ASSAULTED. SHE'S NOT THE KIND TO INITIATE VIOLENCE.
AGREED. SHE'S A MEMBER OF THE AIKIDO-LEMBA LEAGUE.
THAT'S A GOOD POINT TO BRING UP AT TRIAL.
THE PROBLEM IS SHE KILLED A MAN ON MERCURY.
IT WAS SELF-DEFENSE, OF COURSE, BUT THIS COMPROMISES HER STANDING.
I AM CERTAIN THERE ARE POWERFUL INTERESTS BEHIND NICOLE'S ARREST, AS WELL AS THIS LATEST WRINKLE. I THINK I ALREADY KNOW WHY.
AGENT STONE, I NEED YOU TO FIND OUT EXACTLY WHO, AND HOW.

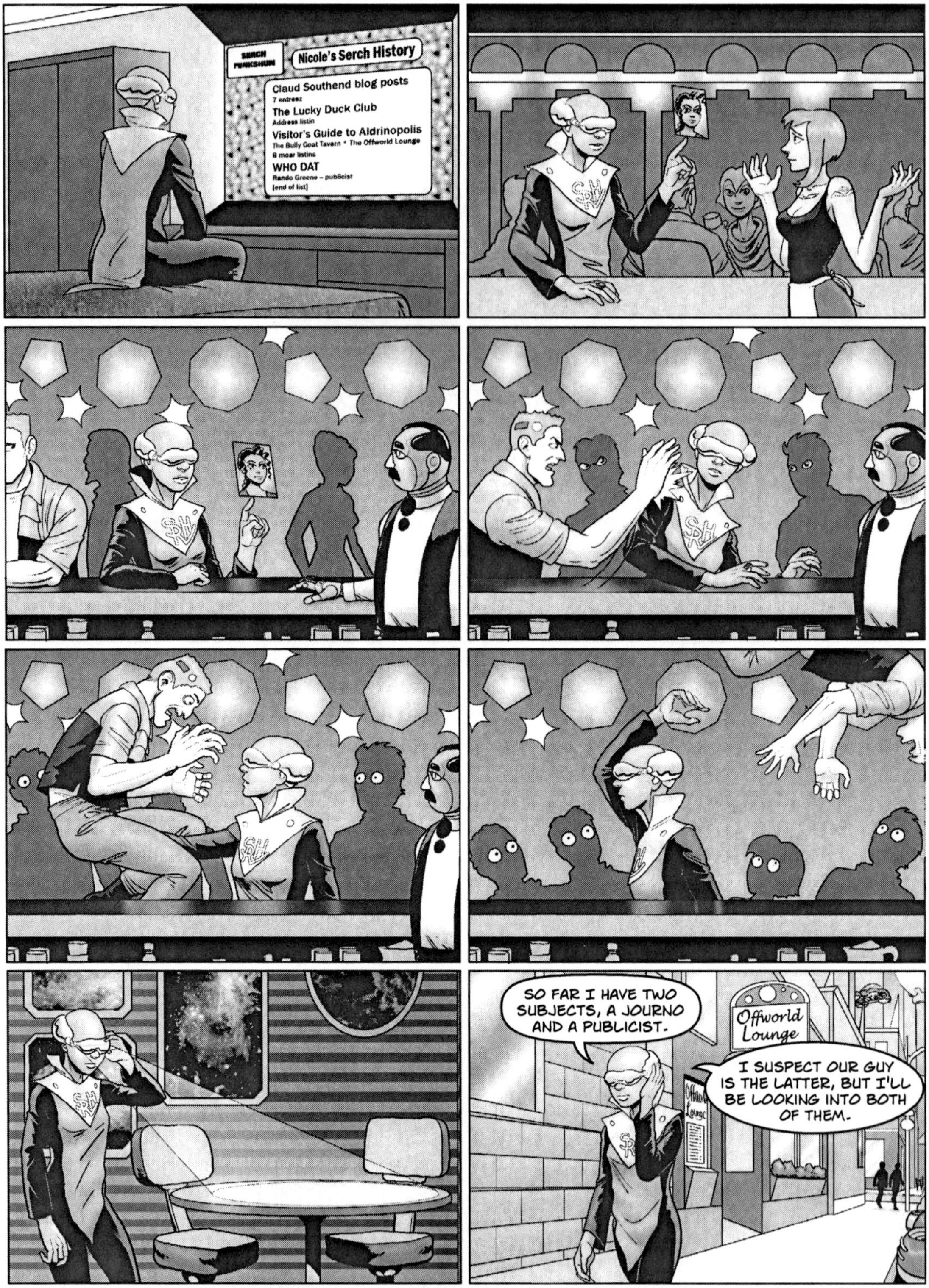
SERCH FUNKSHUN
Nicole's Serch History
Claud Southend blog posts
7 entreez
The Lucky Duck Club
Address listin
Visitor's Guide to Aldrinopolis
The Bully Goat Tavern + The Offworld Lounge
8 moar listins
WHO DAT
Rando Greene – publicist
[end of list]
Offworld Lounge
SO FAR I HAVE TWO SUBJECTS, A JOURNO AND A PUBLICIST.
I SUSPECT OUR GUY IS THE LATTER, BUT I'LL BE LOOKING INTO BOTH OF THEM.

ANGEL THE BARTENDER APPEARS IN PANEL 2 WITH KIND PERMISSION OF HER CREATOR, DANIELLE CORSETTO.
READ DANIELLE'S WEB-COMIC "GIRLS WITH SLINGSHOTS" AT WWW.GIRLSWITHSLINGSHOTS.COM

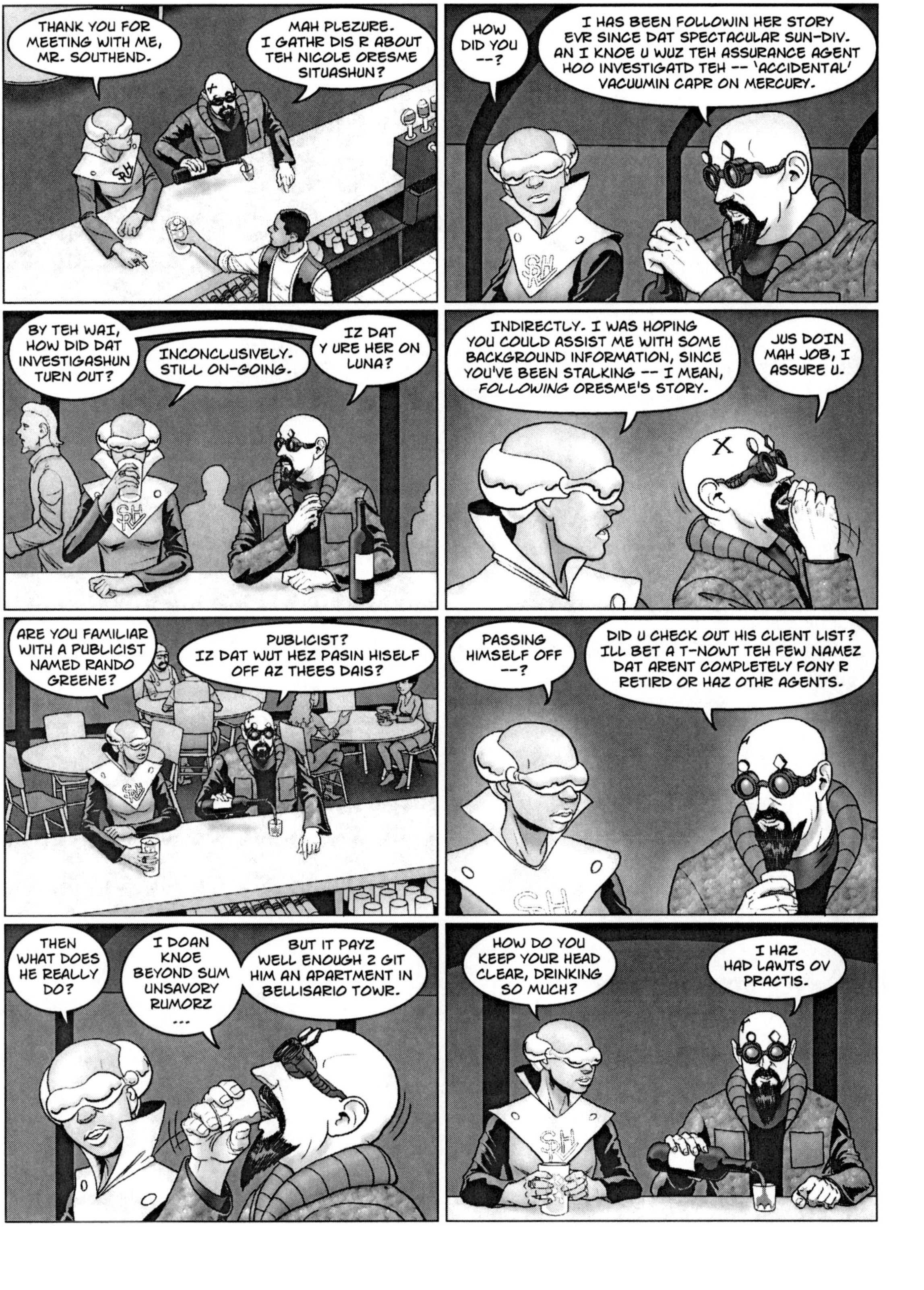
THANK YOU FOR MEETING WITH ME, MR. SOUTHEND.
MAH PLEZURE. I GATHR DIS R ABOUT TEH NICOLE ORESME SITUASHUN?
HOW DID YOU --?
I HAS BEEN FOLLOWIN HER STORY EVR SINCE DAT SPECTACULAR SUN-DIV. AN I KNOE U WUZ TEH ASSURANCE AGENT HOO INVESTIGATD TEH -- 'ACCIDENTAL' VACUUMIN CAPR ON MERCURY.
BY TEH WAI, HOW DID DAT INVESTIGASHUN TURN OUT?
INCONCLUSIVELY. STILL ON-GOING.
IZ DAT Y URE HER ON LUNA?
INDIRECTLY. I WAS HOPING YOU COULD ASSIST ME WITH SOME BACKGROUND INFORMATION, SINCE YOU'VE BEEN STALKING -- I MEAN, FOLLOWING ORESME'S STORY.
JUS DOIN MAH JOB, I ASSURE U.
ARE YOU FAMILIAR WITH A PUBLICIST NAMED RANDO GREENE?
PUBLICIST? IZ DAT WUT HEZ PASIN HISELF OFF AZ THEES DAIS?
PASSING HIMSELF OFF --?
DID U CHECK OUT HIS CLIENT LIST? ILL BET A T-NOWT TEH FEW NAMEZ DAT ARENT COMPLETELY FONY R RETIRD OR HAZ OTHR AGENTS.
THEN WHAT DOES HE REALLY DO?
I DOAN KNOE BEYOND SUM UNSAVORY RUMORZ ...
BUT IT PAYZ WELL ENOUGH 2 GIT HIM AN APARTMENT IN BELLISARIO TOWR.
HOW DO YOU KEEP YOUR HEAD CLEAR, DRINKING SO MUCH?
I HAZ HAD LAWTS OV PRACTIS.

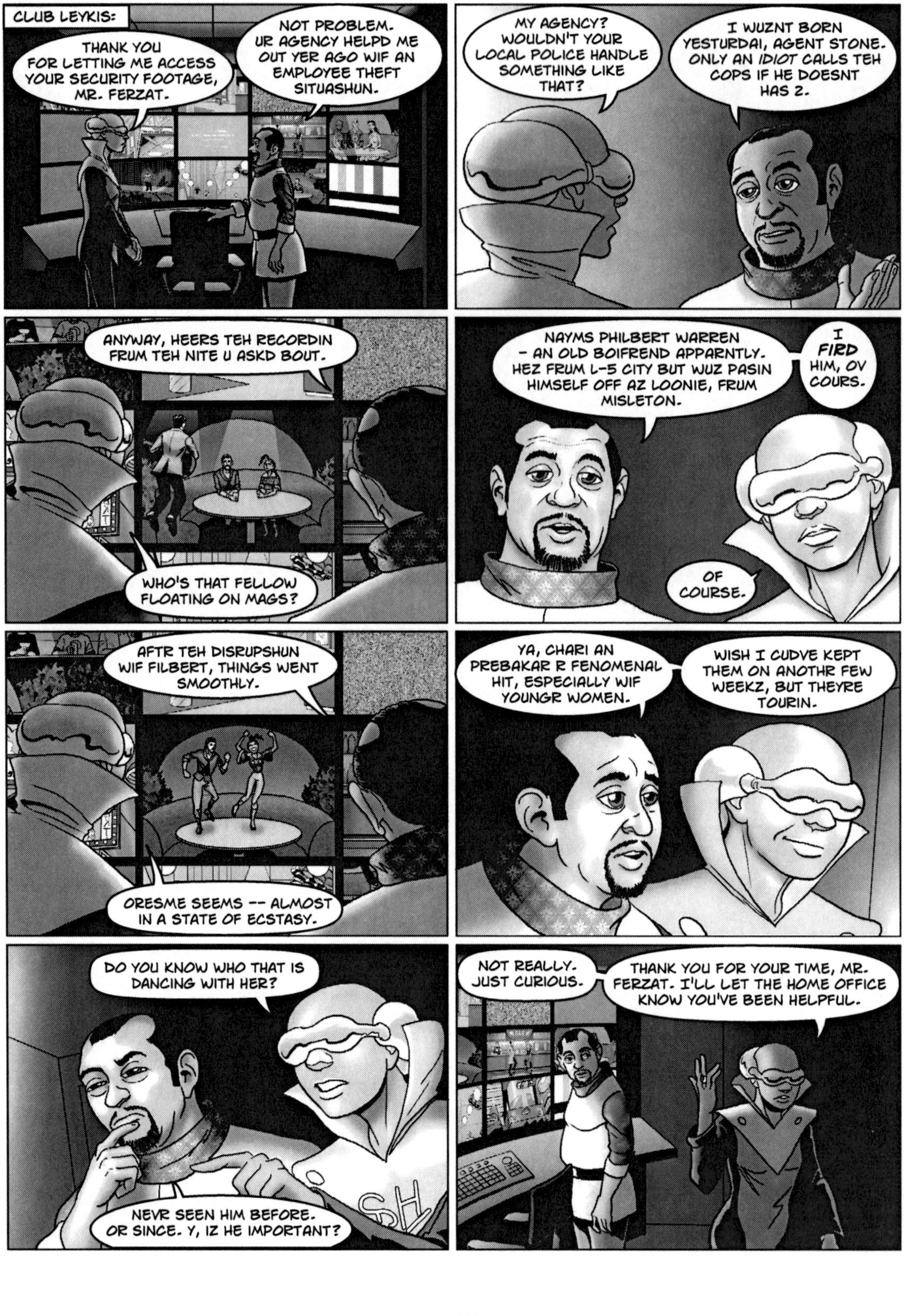
CLUB LEYKIS:
THANK YOU FOR LETTING ME ACCESS YOUR SECURITY FOOTAGE, MR. FERZAT.
NOT PROBLEM. UR AGENCY HELPD ME OUT YER AGO WIF AN EMPLOYEE THEFT SITUASHUN.
MY AGENCY? WOULDN'T YOUR LOCAL POLICE HANDLE SOMETHING LIKE THAT?
I WUZNT BORN YESTURDAI, AGENT STONE. ONLY AN IDIOT CALLS TEH COPS IF HE DOESNT HAS 2.
ANYWAY, HEERS TEH RECORDIN FRUM TEH NITE U ASKD BOUT.
WHO'S THAT FELLOW FLOATING ON MAGS?
NAYMS PHILBERT WARREN - AN OLD BOIFREND APPARNTLY. HEZ FRUM L-5 CITY BUT WUZ PASIN HIMSELF OFF AZ LOONIE, FRUM MISLETON.
I FIRD HIM, OV COURS.
OF COURSE.
AFTR TEH DISRUPSHUN WIF FILBERT, THINGS WENT SMOOTHLY.
ORESME SEEMS -- ALMOST IN A STATE OF ECSTASY.
YA, CHARI AN PREBAKAR R FENOMENAL HIT, ESPECIALLY WIF YOUNGR WOMEN.
WISH I CUDVE KEPT THEM ON ANOTHR FEW WEEKZ, BUT THEYRE TOURIN.
DO YOU KNOW WHO THAT IS DANCING WITH HER?
NEVR SEEN HIM BEFORE. OR SINCE. Y, IZ HE IMPORTANT?
NOT REALLY. JUST CURIOUS.
THANK YOU FOR YOUR TIME, MR. FERZAT. I'LL LET THE HOME OFFICE KNOW YOU'VE BEEN HELPFUL.

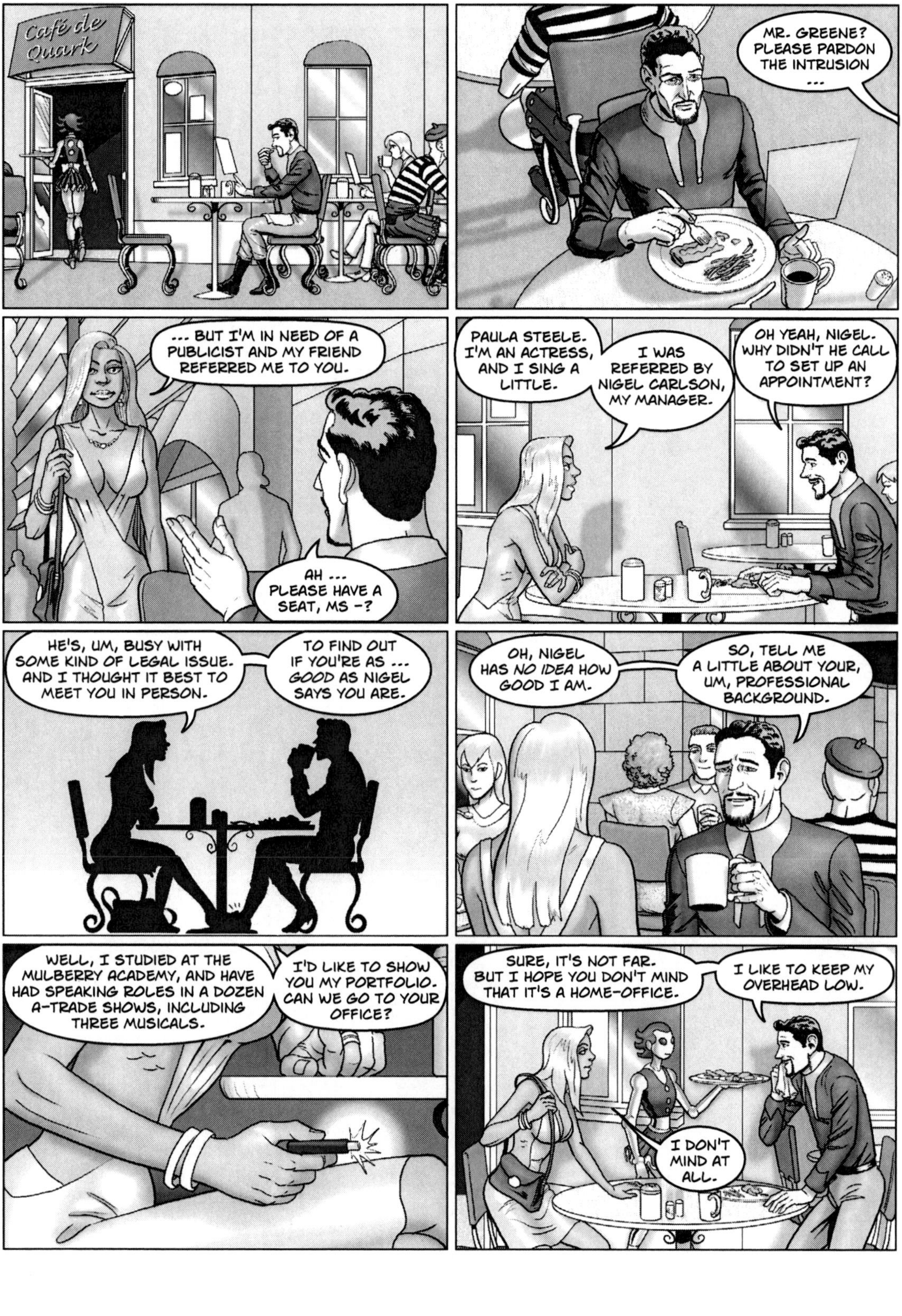
Café de Quark
MR. GREENE? PLEASE PARDON THE INTRUSION ...
... BUT I'M IN NEED OF A PUBLICIST AND MY FRIEND REFERRED ME TO YOU.
AH ... PLEASE HAVE A SEAT, MS -?
PAULA STEELE. I'M AN ACTRESS, AND I SING A LITTLE.
I WAS REFERRED BY NIGEL CARLSON, MY MANAGER.
OH YEAH, NIGEL. WHY DIDN'T HE CALL TO SET UP AN APPOINTMENT?
HE'S, UM, BUSY WITH SOME KIND OF LEGAL ISSUE. AND I THOUGHT IT BEST TO MEET YOU IN PERSON.
TO FIND OUT IF YOU'RE AS ... GOOD AS NIGEL SAYS YOU ARE.
OH, NIGEL HAS NO IDEA HOW GOOD I AM.
SO, TELL ME A LITTLE ABOUT YOUR, UM, PROFESSIONAL BACKGROUND.
WELL, I STUDIED AT THE MULBERRY ACADEMY, AND HAVE HAD SPEAKING ROLES IN A DOZEN A-TRADE SHOWS, INCLUDING THREE MUSICALS.
I'D LIKE TO SHOW YOU MY PORTFOLIO. CAN WE GO TO YOUR OFFICE?
SURE, IT'S NOT FAR. BUT I HOPE YOU DON'T MIND THAT IT'S A HOME-OFFICE.
I LIKE TO KEEP MY OVERHEAD LOW.
I DON'T MIND AT ALL.

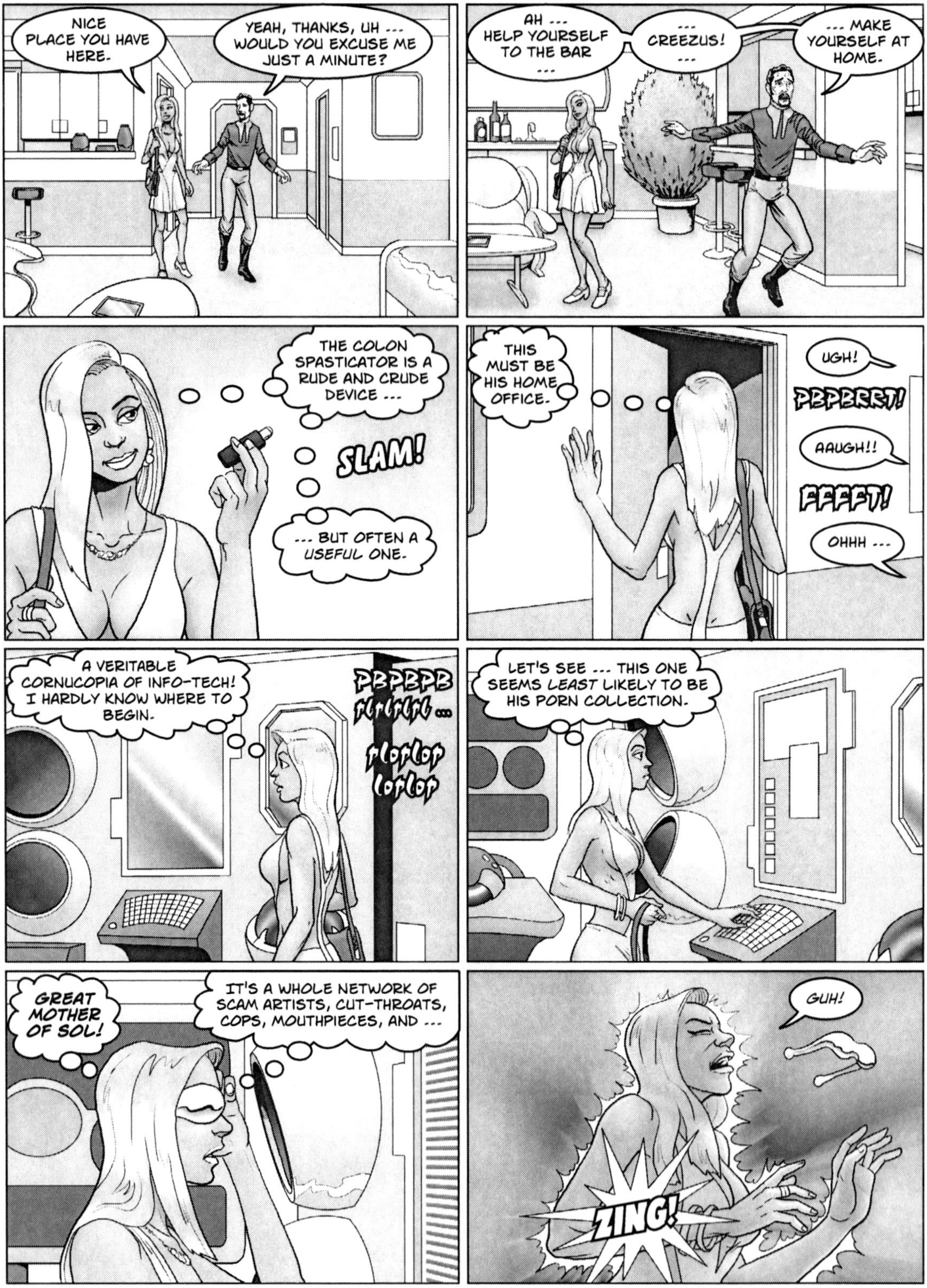
NICE PLACE YOU HAVE HERE.
YEAH, THANKS, UH --- WOULD YOU EXCUSE ME JUST A MINUTE?
AH --- HELP YOURSELF TO THE BAR ---
--- CREEZUS! ---
--- MAKE YOURSELF AT HOME.
THE COLON SPASTICATOR IS A RUDE AND CRUDE DEVICE ---
SLAM!
--- BUT OFTEN A USEFUL ONE.
THIS MUST BE HIS HOME OFFICE.
UGH!
PBPBRRT!
AAUGH!!
FFFFT!
OHHH ---
A VERITABLE CORNUCOPIA OF INFO-TECH! I HARDLY KNOW WHERE TO BEGIN.
PBPBPB
LET'S SEE --- THIS ONE SEEMS LEAST LIKELY TO BE HIS PORN COLLECTION.
GREAT MOTHER OF SOL!
IT'S A WHOLE NETWORK OF SCAM ARTISTS, CUT-THROATS, COPS, MOUTHPIECES, AND ---
GUH!
ZING!

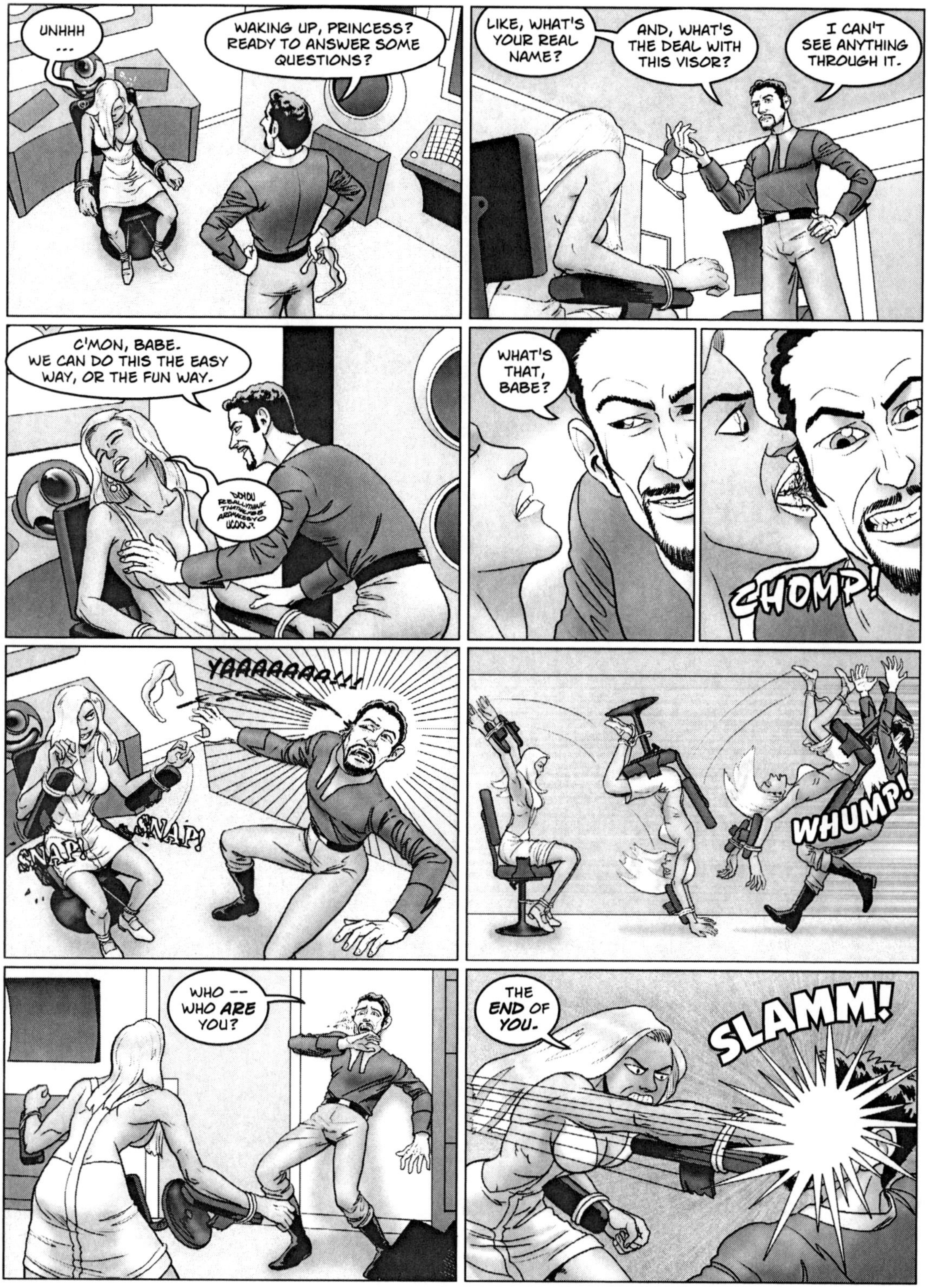
UNHHH ...
WAKING UP, PRINCESS? READY TO ANSWER SOME QUESTIONS?
LIKE, WHAT'S YOUR REAL NAME?
AND, WHAT'S THE DEAL WITH THIS VISOR?
I CAN'T SEE ANYTHING THROUGH IT.
C'MON, BABE. WE CAN DO THIS THE EASY WAY, OR THE FUN WAY.
WHAT'S THAT, BABE?
CHOMP!
YAAAAAAA!!!
SNAP!
SNAP!
WHUMP!
WHO -- WHO ARE YOU?
THE END OF YOU.
SLAMM!

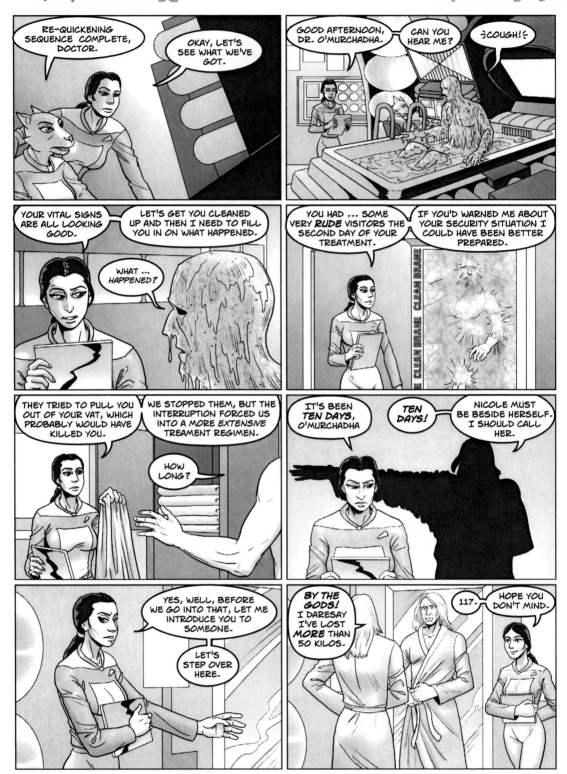

RE-QUICKENING SEQUENCE COMPLETE, DOCTOR.

OKAY, LET'S SEE WHAT WE'VE GOT.

GOOD AFTERNOON, DR. O'MURCHADHA.

CAN YOU HEAR ME?

≥COUGH!≥

YOUR VITAL SIGNS ARE ALL LOOKING GOOD.

LET'S GET YOU CLEANED UP AND THEN I NEED TO FILL YOU IN ON WHAT HAPPENED.

WHAT ... HAPPENED?

YOU HAD ... SOME VERY RUDE VISITORS THE SECOND DAY OF YOUR TREATMENT.

IF YOU'D WARNED ME ABOUT YOUR SECURITY SITUATION I COULD HAVE BEEN BETTER PREPARED.

CLEAN BRANE CLEAN BRANE CLEAN BRANE

THEY TRIED TO PULL YOU OUT OF YOUR VAT, WHICH PROBABLY WOULD HAVE KILLED YOU.

WE STOPPED THEM, BUT THE INTERRUPTION FORCED US INTO A MORE EXTENSIVE TREAMENT REGIMEN.

HOW LONG?

IT'S BEEN TEN DAYS, O'MURCHADHA

TEN DAYS!

NICOLE MUST BE BESIDE HERSELF. I SHOULD CALL HER.

YES, WELL, BEFORE WE GO INTO THAT, LET ME INTRODUCE YOU TO SOMEONE.

LET'S STEP OVER HERE.

BY THE GODS! I DARESAY I'VE LOST MORE THAN 50 KILOS.

117.

HOPE YOU DON'T MIND.

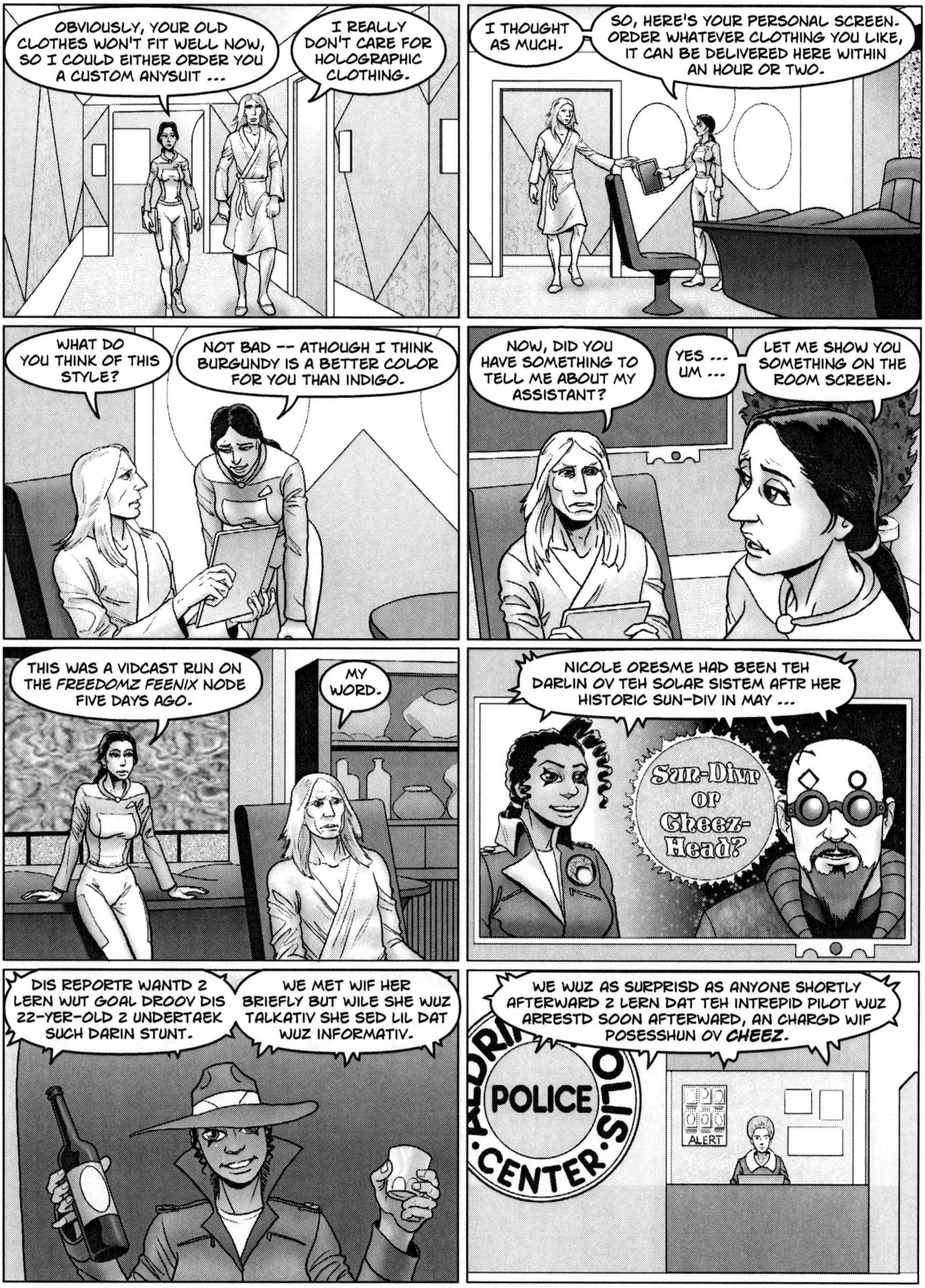
OBVIOUSLY, YOUR OLD CLOTHES WON'T FIT WELL NOW, SO I COULD EITHER ORDER YOU A CUSTOM ANYSUIT ...
I REALLY DON'T CARE FOR HOLOGRAPHIC CLOTHING.
I THOUGHT AS MUCH.
SO, HERE'S YOUR PERSONAL SCREEN. ORDER WHATEVER CLOTHING YOU LIKE, IT CAN BE DELIVERED HERE WITHIN AN HOUR OR TWO.
WHAT DO YOU THINK OF THIS STYLE?
NOT BAD -- ATHOUGH I THINK BURGUNDY IS A BETTER COLOR FOR YOU THAN INDIGO.
NOW, DID YOU HAVE SOMETHING TO TELL ME ABOUT MY ASSISTANT?
YES ... UM ...
LET ME SHOW YOU SOMETHING ON THE ROOM SCREEN.
THIS WAS A VIDCAST RUN ON THE *FREEDOMZ FEENIX* NODE FIVE DAYS AGO.
MY WORD.
NICOLE ORESME HAD BEEN TEH DARLIN OV TEH SOLAR SISTEM AFTR HER HISTORIC SUN-DIV IN MAY ...
Sun-Divr or Cheez-Head?
DIS REPORTR WANTD 2 LERN WUT GOAL DROOV DIS 22-YER-OLD 2 UNDERTAEK SUCH DARIN STUNT.
WE MET WIF HER BRIEFLY BUT WILE SHE WUZ TALKATIV SHE SED LIL DAT WUZ INFORMATIV.
WE WUZ AS SURPRISD AS ANYONE SHORTLY AFTERWARD 2 LERN DAT TEH INTREPID PILOT WUZ ARRESTD SOON AFTERWARD, AN CHARGD WIF POSESSHUN OV **CHEEZ**.
POLICE
CENTER
ALERT

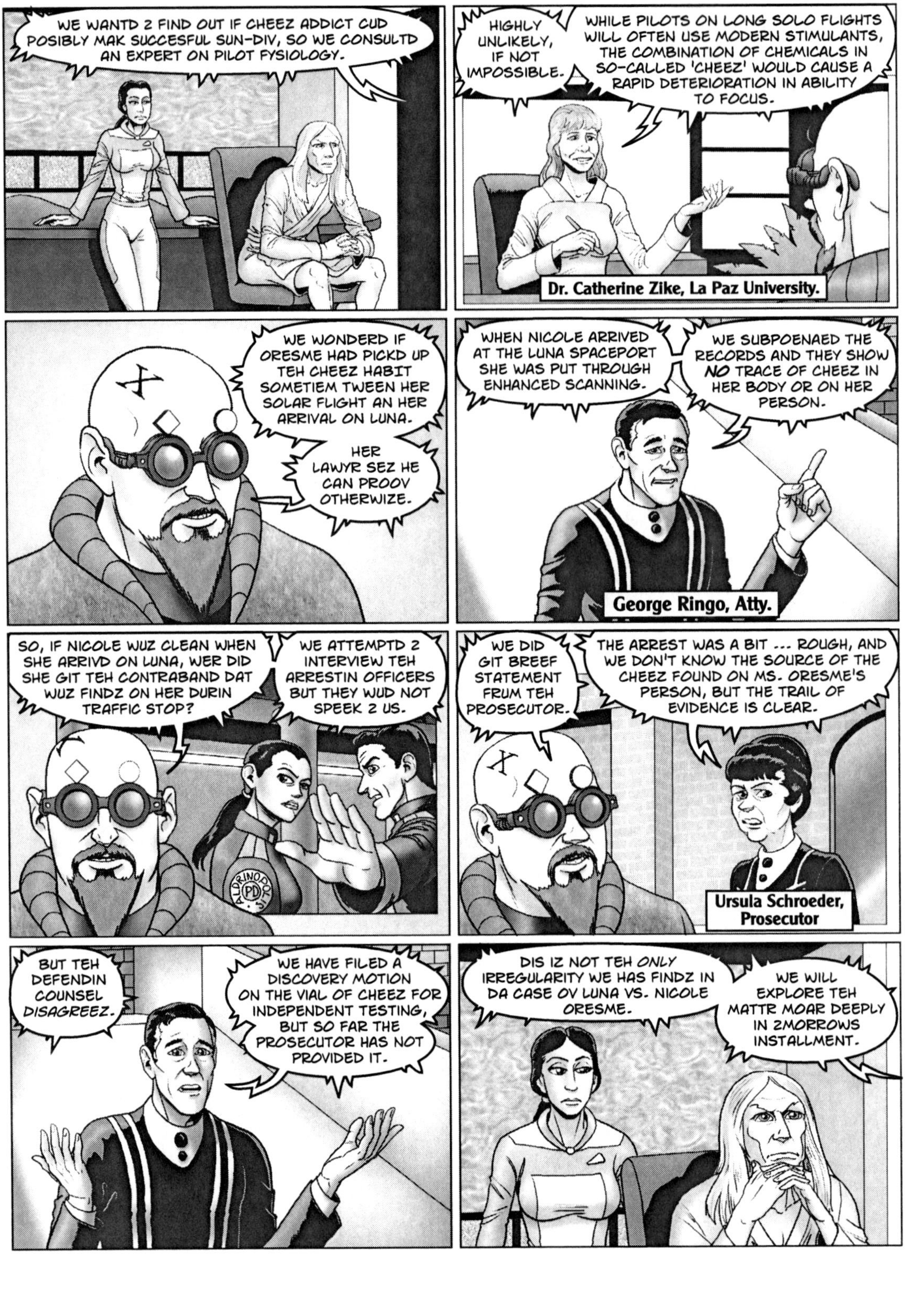
WE WANTD 2 FIND OUT IF CHEEZ ADDICT CUD POSIBLY MAK SUCCESFUL SUN-DIV, SO WE CONSULTD AN EXPERT ON PILOT FYSIOLOGY.
HIGHLY UNLIKELY, IF NOT IMPOSSIBLE.
WHILE PILOTS ON LONG SOLO FLIGHTS WILL OFTEN USE MODERN STIMULANTS, THE COMBINATION OF CHEMICALS IN SO-CALLED 'CHEEZ' WOULD CAUSE A RAPID DETERIORATION IN ABILITY TO FOCUS.
Dr. Catherine Zike, La Paz University.
WE WONDERD IF ORESME HAD PICKD UP TEH CHEEZ HABIT SOMETIEM TWEEN HER SOLAR FLIGHT AN HER ARRIVAL ON LUNA.
HER LAWYR SEZ HE CAN PROOV OTHERWIZE.
WHEN NICOLE ARRIVED AT THE LUNA SPACEPORT SHE WAS PUT THROUGH ENHANCED SCANNING.
WE SUBPOENAED THE RECORDS AND THEY SHOW NO TRACE OF CHEEZ IN HER BODY OR ON HER PERSON.
George Ringo, Atty.
SO, IF NICOLE WUZ CLEAN WHEN SHE ARRIVD ON LUNA, WER DID SHE GIT TEH CONTRABAND DAT WUZ FINDZ ON HER DURIN TRAFFIC STOP?
WE ATTEMPTD 2 INTERVIEW TEH ARRESTIN OFFICERS BUT THEY WUD NOT SPEEK 2 US.
ALDRINOPOLIS PD
WE DID GIT BREEF STATEMENT FRUM TEH PROSECUTOR.
THE ARREST WAS A BIT ... ROUGH, AND WE DON'T KNOW THE SOURCE OF THE CHEEZ FOUND ON MS. ORESME'S PERSON, BUT THE TRAIL OF EVIDENCE IS CLEAR.
Ursula Schroeder, Prosecutor
BUT TEH DEFENDIN COUNSEL DISAGREEZ.
WE HAVE FILED A DISCOVERY MOTION ON THE VIAL OF CHEEZ FOR INDEPENDENT TESTING, BUT SO FAR THE PROSECUTOR HAS NOT PROVIDED IT.
DIS IZ NOT TEH ONLY IRREGULARITY WE HAS FINDZ IN DA CASE OV LUNA VS. NICOLE ORESME.
WE WILL EXPLORE TEH MATTR MOAR DEEPLY IN 2MORROWS INSTALLMENT.

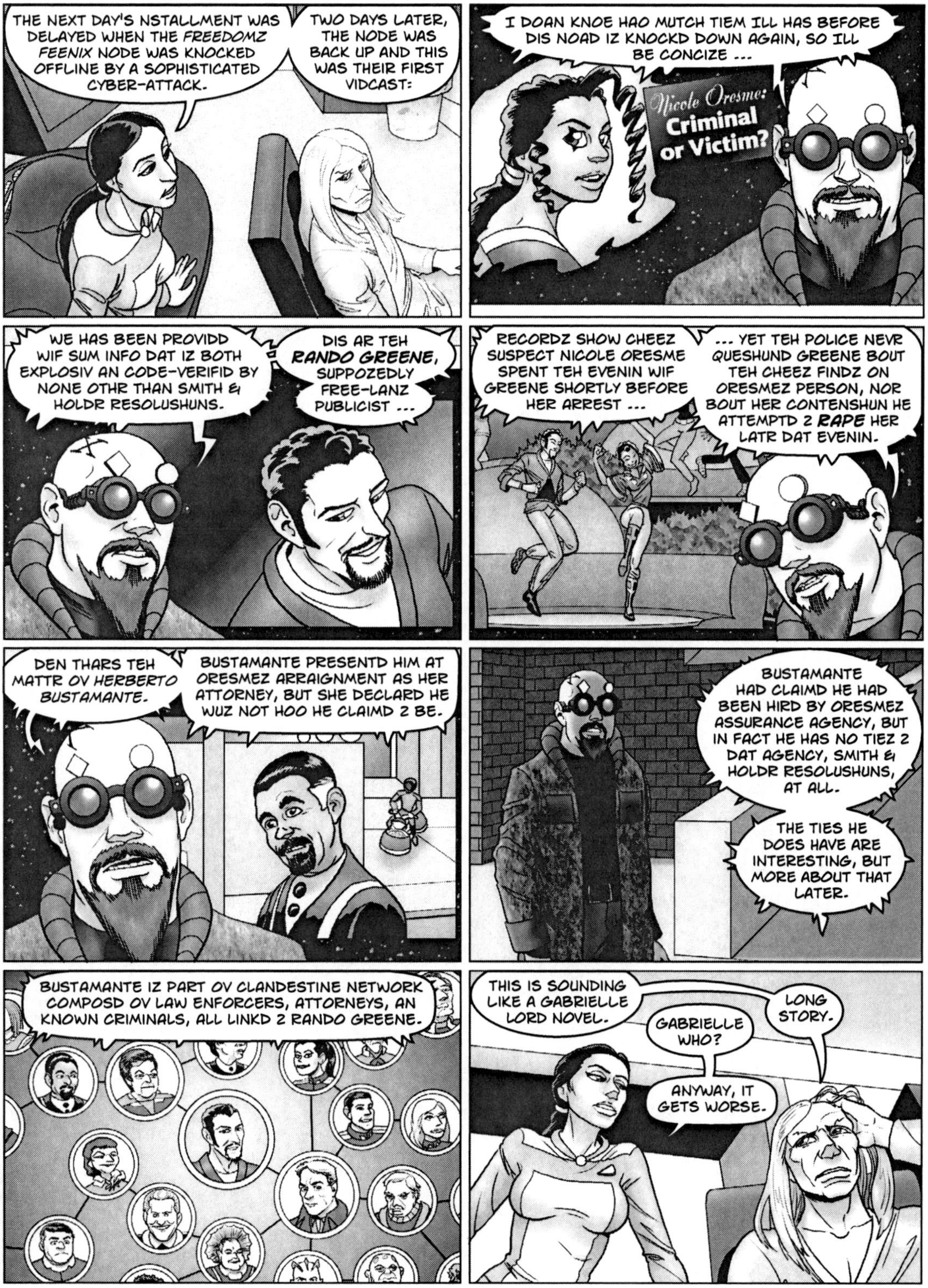
THE NEXT DAY'S NSTALLMENT WAS DELAYED WHEN THE FREEDOMZ FEENIX NODE WAS KNOCKED OFFLINE BY A SOPHISTICATED CYBER-ATTACK.
TWO DAYS LATER, THE NODE WAS BACK UP AND THIS WAS THEIR FIRST VIDCAST:
I DOAN KNOE HAO MUTCH TIEM ILL HAS BEFORE DIS NOAD IZ KNOCKD DOWN AGAIN, SO ILL BE CONCIZE ...
Nicole Oresme: Criminal or Victim?
WE HAS BEEN PROVIDD WIF SUM INFO DAT IZ BOTH EXPLOSIV AN CODE-VERIFID BY NONE OTHR THAN SMITH & HOLDR RESOLUSHUNS.
DIS AR TEH RANDO GREENE, SUPPOZEDLY FREE-LANZ PUBLICIST ...
RECORDZ SHOW CHEEZ SUSPECT NICOLE ORESME SPENT TEH EVENIN WIF GREENE SHORTLY BEFORE HER ARREST ...
... YET TEH POLICE NEVR QUESHUND GREENE BOUT TEH CHEEZ FINDZ ON ORESMEZ PERSON, NOR BOUT HER CONTENSHUN HE ATTEMPTD 2 RAPE HER LATR DAT EVENIN.
DEN THARS TEH MATTR OV HERBERTO BUSTAMANTE.
BUSTAMANTE PRESENTD HIM AT ORESMEZ ARRAIGNMENT AS HER ATTORNEY, BUT SHE DECLARD HE WUZ NOT HOO HE CLAIMD 2 BE.
BUSTAMANTE HAD CLAIMD HE HAD BEEN HIRD BY ORESMEZ ASSURANCE AGENCY, BUT IN FACT HE HAS NO TIEZ 2 DAT AGENCY, SMITH & HOLDR RESOLUSHUNS, AT ALL.
THE TIES HE DOES HAVE ARE INTERESTING, BUT MORE ABOUT THAT LATER.
BUSTAMANTE IZ PART OV CLANDESTINE NETWORK COMPOSD OV LAW ENFORCERS, ATTORNEYS, AN KNOWN CRIMINALS, ALL LINKD 2 RANDO GREENE.
THIS IS SOUNDING LIKE A GABRIELLE LORD NOVEL.
GABRIELLE WHO?
LONG STORY.
ANYWAY, IT GETS WORSE.

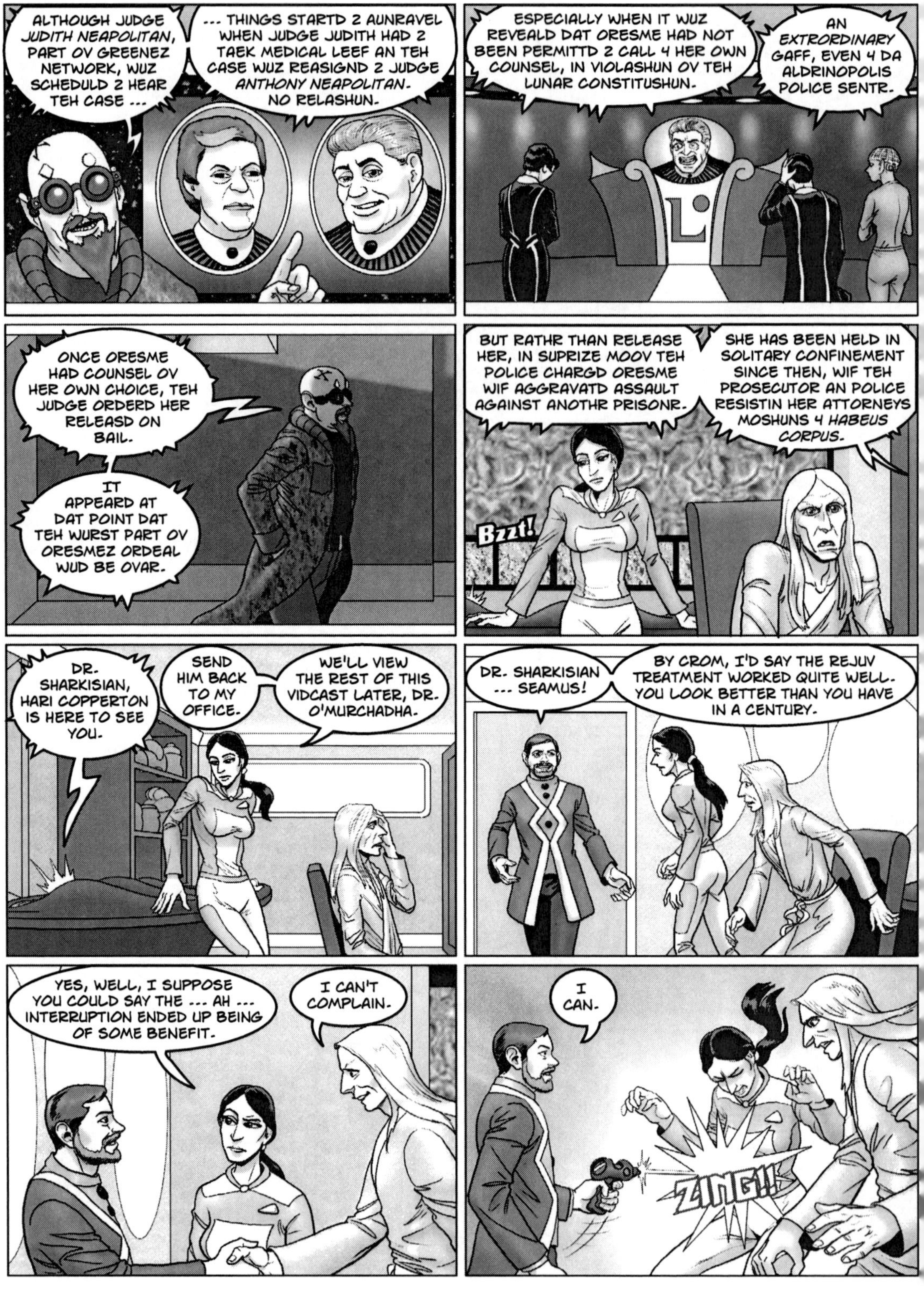
ALTHOUGH JUDGE JUDITH NEAPOLITAN, PART OV GREENEZ NETWORK, WUZ SCHEDULD 2 HEAR TEH CASE ...
... THINGS STARTD 2 AUNRAVEL WHEN JUDGE JUDITH HAD 2 TAEK MEDICAL LEEF AN TEH CASE WUZ REASIGND 2 JUDGE ANTHONY NEAPOLITAN. NO RELASHUN.
ESPECIALLY WHEN IT WUZ REVEALD DAT ORESME HAD NOT BEEN PERMITTD 2 CALL 4 HER OWN COUNSEL, IN VIOLASHUN OV TEH LUNAR CONSTITUSHUN.
AN EXTRORDINARY GAFF, EVEN 4 DA ALDRINOPOLIS POLICE SENTR.
ONCE ORESME HAD COUNSEL OV HER OWN CHOICE, TEH JUDGE ORDERD HER RELEASD ON BAIL.
IT APPEARD AT DAT POINT DAT TEH WURST PART OV ORESMEZ ORDEAL WUD BE OVAR.
BUT RATHR THAN RELEASE HER, IN SUPRIZE MOOV TEH POLICE CHARGD ORESME WIF AGGRAVATD ASSAULT AGAINST ANOTHR PRISONR.
SHE HAS BEEN HELD IN SOLITARY CONFINEMENT SINCE THEN, WIF TEH PROSECUTOR AN POLICE RESISTIN HER ATTORNEYS MOSHUNS 4 HABEUS CORPUS.
Bzzt!
DR. SHARKISIAN, HARI COPPERTON IS HERE TO SEE YOU.
SEND HIM BACK TO MY OFFICE.
WE'LL VIEW THE REST OF THIS VIDCAST LATER, DR. O'MURCHADHA.
DR. SHARKISIAN ... SEAMUS!
BY CROM, I'D SAY THE REJUV TREATMENT WORKED QUITE WELL. YOU LOOK BETTER THAN YOU HAVE IN A CENTURY.
YES, WELL, I SUPPOSE YOU COULD SAY THE ... AH ... INTERRUPTION ENDED UP BEING OF SOME BENEFIT.
I CAN'T COMPLAIN.
I CAN.
ZING!!

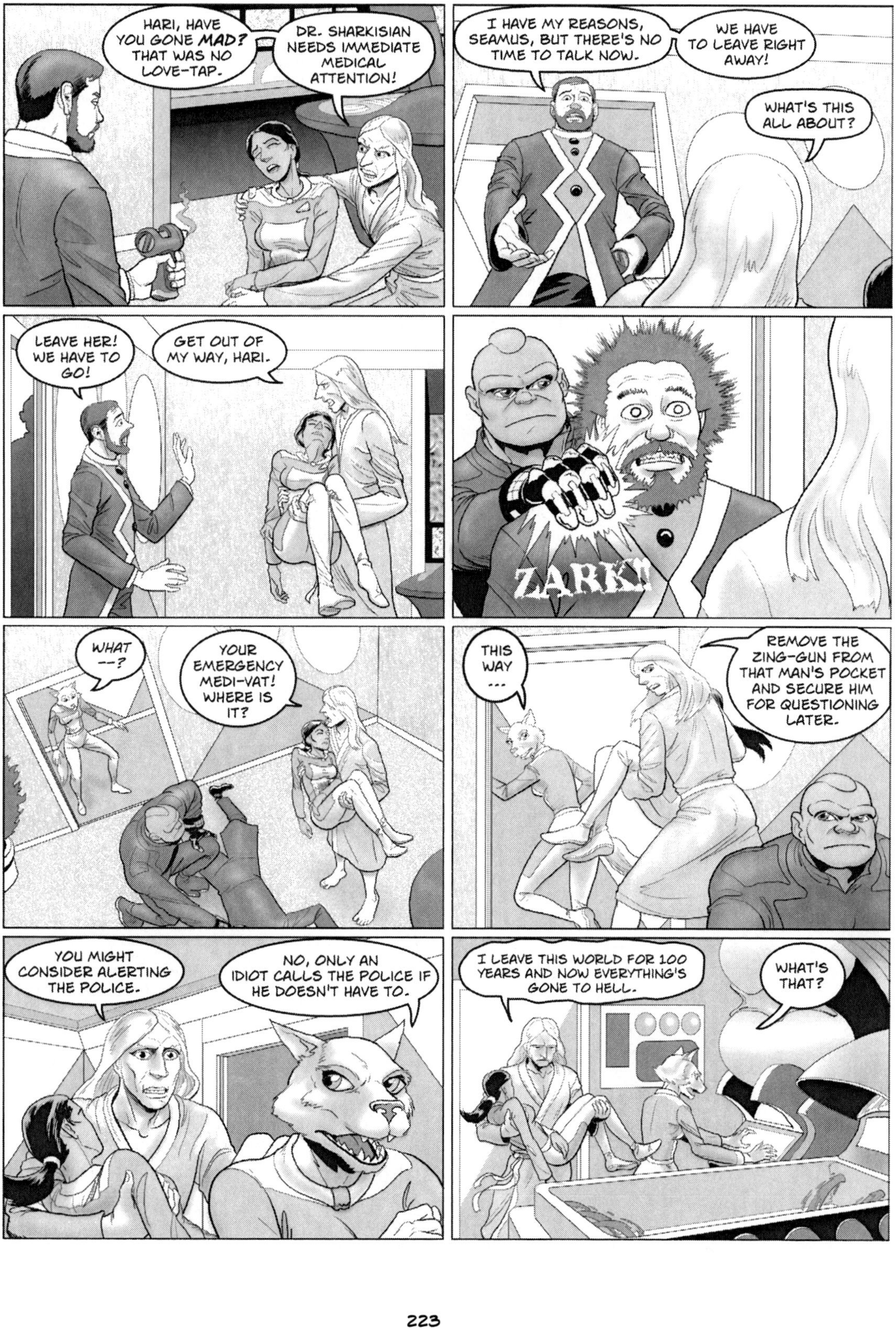
HARI, HAVE YOU GONE MAD? THAT WAS NO LOVE-TAP.
DR. SHARKISIAN NEEDS IMMEDIATE MEDICAL ATTENTION!
I HAVE MY REASONS, SEAMUS, BUT THERE'S NO TIME TO TALK NOW.
WE HAVE TO LEAVE RIGHT AWAY!
WHAT'S THIS ALL ABOUT?
LEAVE HER! WE HAVE TO GO!
GET OUT OF MY WAY, HARI.
ZARK!
WHAT --?
YOUR EMERGENCY MEDI-VAT! WHERE IS IT?
THIS WAY ...
REMOVE THE ZING-GUN FROM THAT MAN'S POCKET AND SECURE HIM FOR QUESTIONING LATER.
YOU MIGHT CONSIDER ALERTING THE POLICE.
NO, ONLY AN IDIOT CALLS THE POLICE IF HE DOESN'T HAVE TO.
I LEAVE THIS WORLD FOR 100 YEARS AND NOW EVERYTHING'S GONE TO HELL.
WHAT'S THAT?

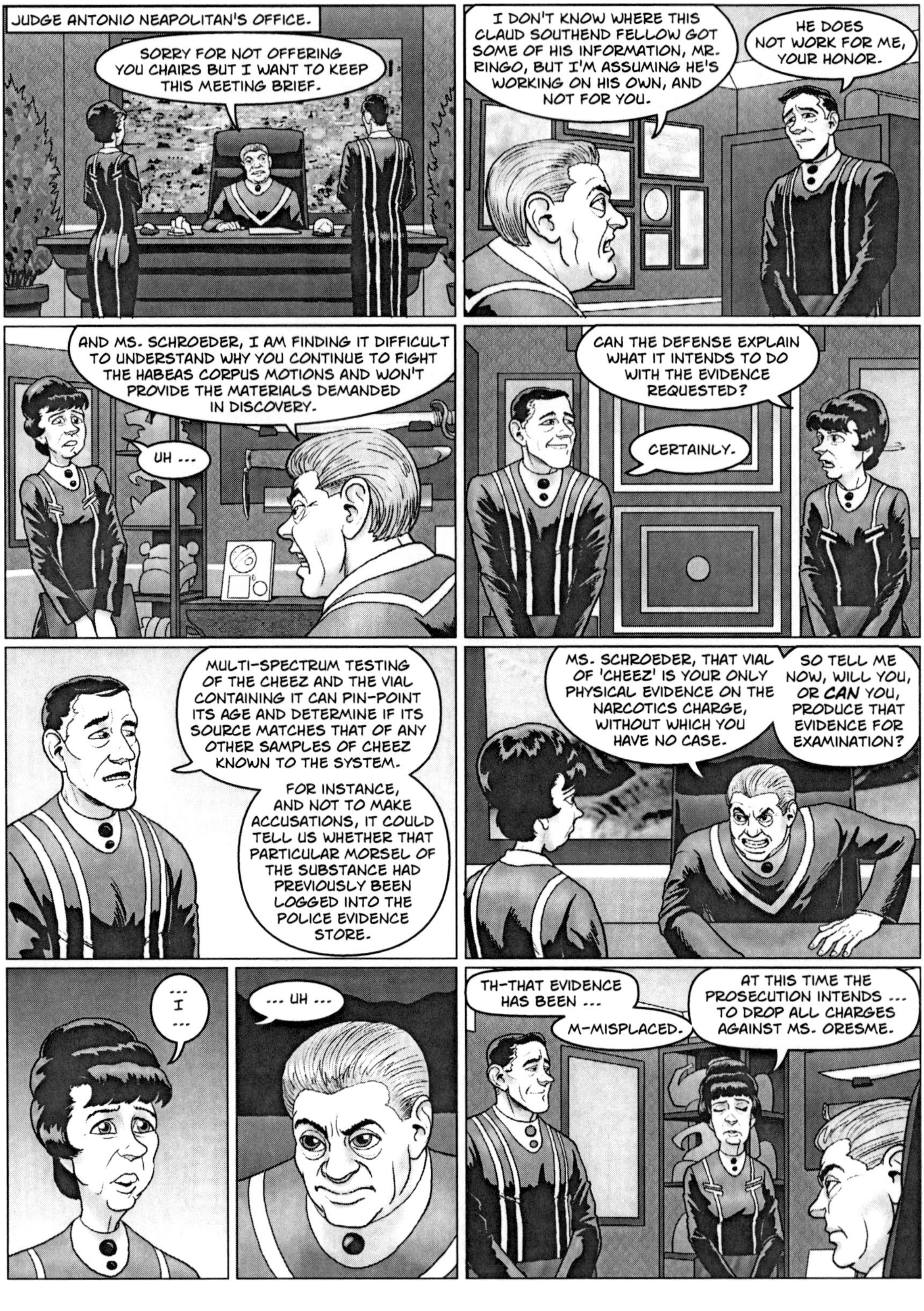
JUDGE ANTONIO NEAPOLITAN'S OFFICE.
SORRY FOR NOT OFFERING YOU CHAIRS BUT I WANT TO KEEP THIS MEETING BRIEF.
I DON'T KNOW WHERE THIS CLAUD SOUTHEND FELLOW GOT SOME OF HIS INFORMATION, MR. RINGO, BUT I'M ASSUMING HE'S WORKING ON HIS OWN, AND NOT FOR YOU.
HE DOES NOT WORK FOR ME, YOUR HONOR.
AND MS. SCHROEDER, I AM FINDING IT DIFFICULT TO UNDERSTAND WHY YOU CONTINUE TO FIGHT THE HABEAS CORPUS MOTIONS AND WON'T PROVIDE THE MATERIALS DEMANDED IN DISCOVERY.
UH ...
CAN THE DEFENSE EXPLAIN WHAT IT INTENDS TO DO WITH THE EVIDENCE REQUESTED?
CERTAINLY.
MULTI-SPECTRUM TESTING OF THE CHEEZ AND THE VIAL CONTAINING IT CAN PIN-POINT ITS AGE AND DETERMINE IF ITS SOURCE MATCHES THAT OF ANY OTHER SAMPLES OF CHEEZ KNOWN TO THE SYSTEM.
FOR INSTANCE, AND NOT TO MAKE ACCUSATIONS, IT COULD TELL US WHETHER THAT PARTICULAR MORSEL OF THE SUBSTANCE HAD PREVIOUSLY BEEN LOGGED INTO THE POLICE EVIDENCE STORE.
MS. SCHROEDER, THAT VIAL OF 'CHEEZ' IS YOUR ONLY PHYSICAL EVIDENCE ON THE NARCOTICS CHARGE, WITHOUT WHICH YOU HAVE NO CASE.
SO TELL ME NOW, WILL YOU, OR **CAN** YOU, PRODUCE THAT EVIDENCE FOR EXAMINATION?
... I ...
... UH ...
TH-THAT EVIDENCE HAS BEEN ...
M-MISPLACED.
AT THIS TIME THE PROSECUTION INTENDS ... TO DROP ALL CHARGES AGAINST MS. ORESME.

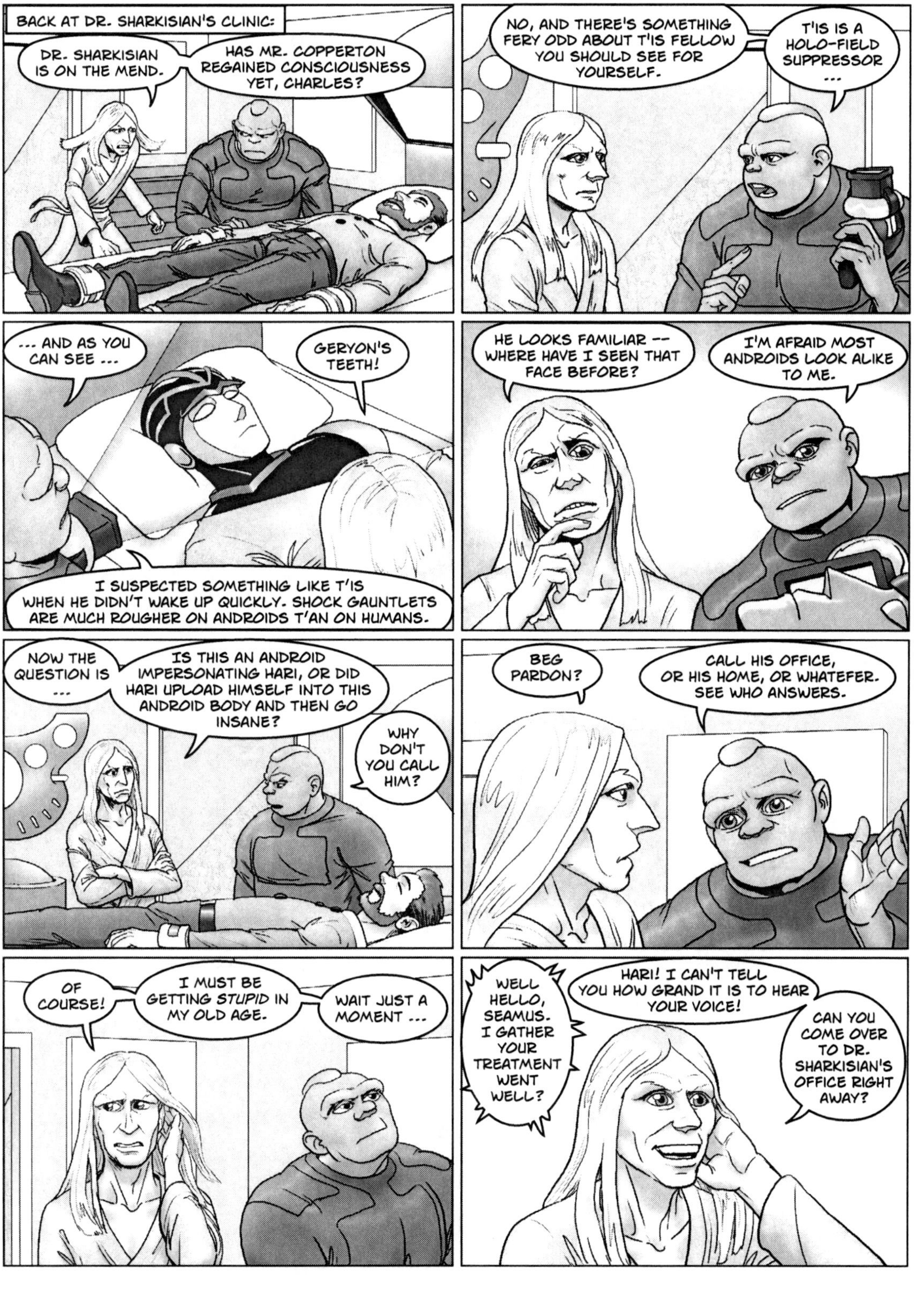
BACK AT DR. SHARKISIAN'S CLINIC:
DR. SHARKISIAN IS ON THE MEND.
HAS MR. COPPERTON REGAINED CONSCIOUSNESS YET, CHARLES?
NO, AND THERE'S SOMETHING FERY ODD ABOUT T'IS FELLOW YOU SHOULD SEE FOR YOURSELF.
T'IS IS A HOLO-FIELD SUPPRESSOR ...
... AND AS YOU CAN SEE ...
GERYON'S TEETH!
I SUSPECTED SOMETHING LIKE T'IS WHEN HE DIDN'T WAKE UP QUICKLY. SHOCK GAUNTLETS ARE MUCH ROUGHER ON ANDROIDS T'AN ON HUMANS.
HE LOOKS FAMILIAR -- WHERE HAVE I SEEN THAT FACE BEFORE?
I'M AFRAID MOST ANDROIDS LOOK ALIKE TO ME.
NOW THE QUESTION IS ...
IS THIS AN ANDROID IMPERSONATING HARI, OR DID HARI UPLOAD HIMSELF INTO THIS ANDROID BODY AND THEN GO INSANE?
WHY DON'T YOU CALL HIM?
BEG PARDON?
CALL HIS OFFICE, OR HIS HOME, OR WHATEFER. SEE WHO ANSWERS.
OF COURSE!
I MUST BE GETTING STUPID IN MY OLD AGE.
WAIT JUST A MOMENT ...
WELL HELLO, SEAMUS. I GATHER YOUR TREATMENT WENT WELL?
HARI! I CAN'T TELL YOU HOW GRAND IT IS TO HEAR YOUR VOICE!
CAN YOU COME OVER TO DR. SHARKISIAN'S OFFICE RIGHT AWAY?

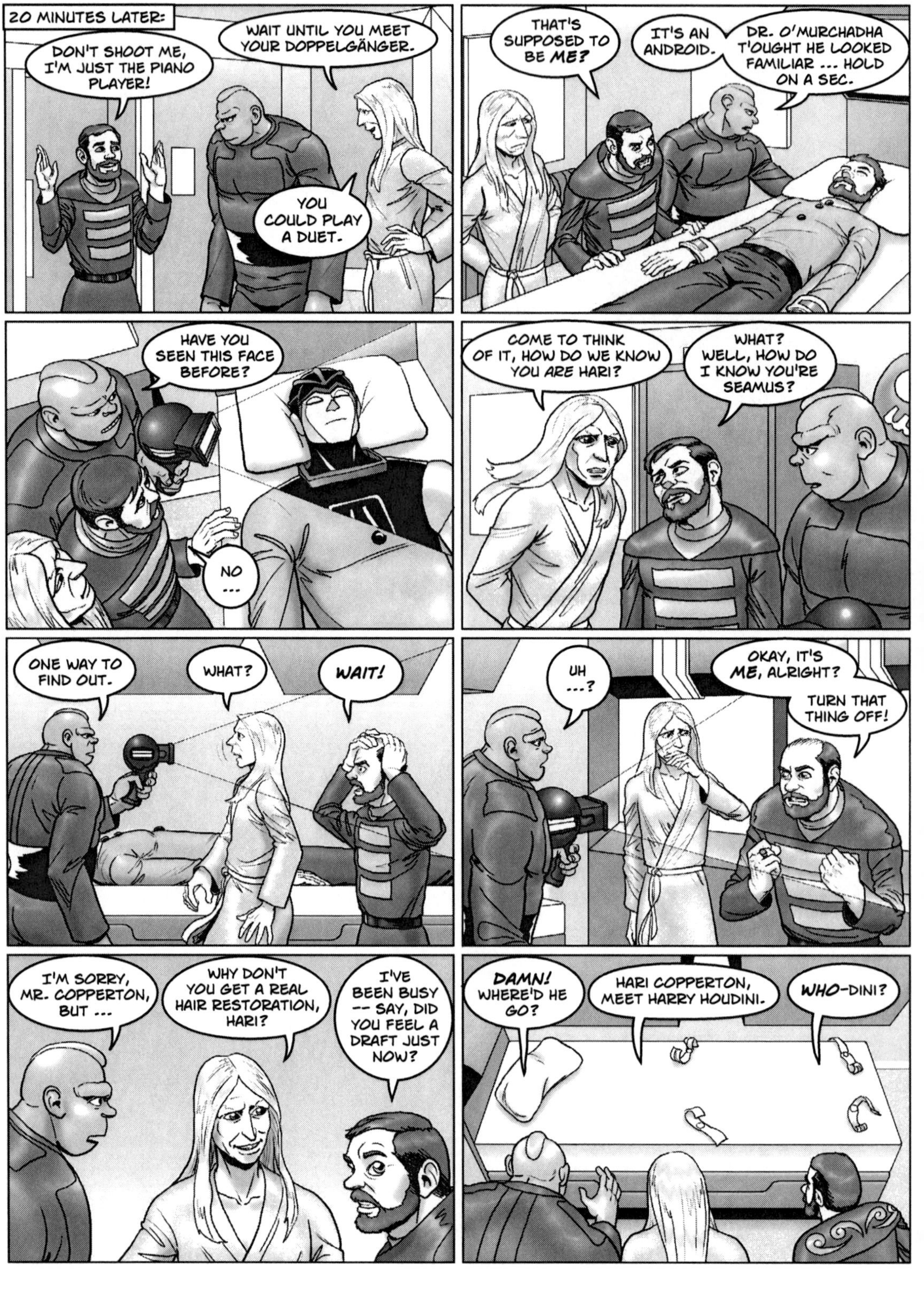
20 MINUTES LATER:
DON'T SHOOT ME, I'M JUST THE PIANO PLAYER!
WAIT UNTIL YOU MEET YOUR DOPPELGÄNGER.
YOU COULD PLAY A DUET.
THAT'S SUPPOSED TO BE ME?
IT'S AN ANDROID.
DR. O'MURCHADHA T'OUGHT HE LOOKED FAMILIAR ... HOLD ON A SEC.
HAVE YOU SEEN THIS FACE BEFORE?
NO ...
COME TO THINK OF IT, HOW DO WE KNOW YOU ARE HARI?
WHAT? WELL, HOW DO I KNOW YOU'RE SEAMUS?
ONE WAY TO FIND OUT.
WHAT?
WAIT!
UH ...?
OKAY, IT'S ME, ALRIGHT?
TURN THAT THING OFF!
I'M SORRY, MR. COPPERTON, BUT ...
WHY DON'T YOU GET A REAL HAIR RESTORATION, HARI?
I'VE BEEN BUSY -- SAY, DID YOU FEEL A DRAFT JUST NOW?
DAMN! WHERE'D HE GO?
HARI COPPERTON, MEET HARRY HOUDINI.
WHO-DINI?

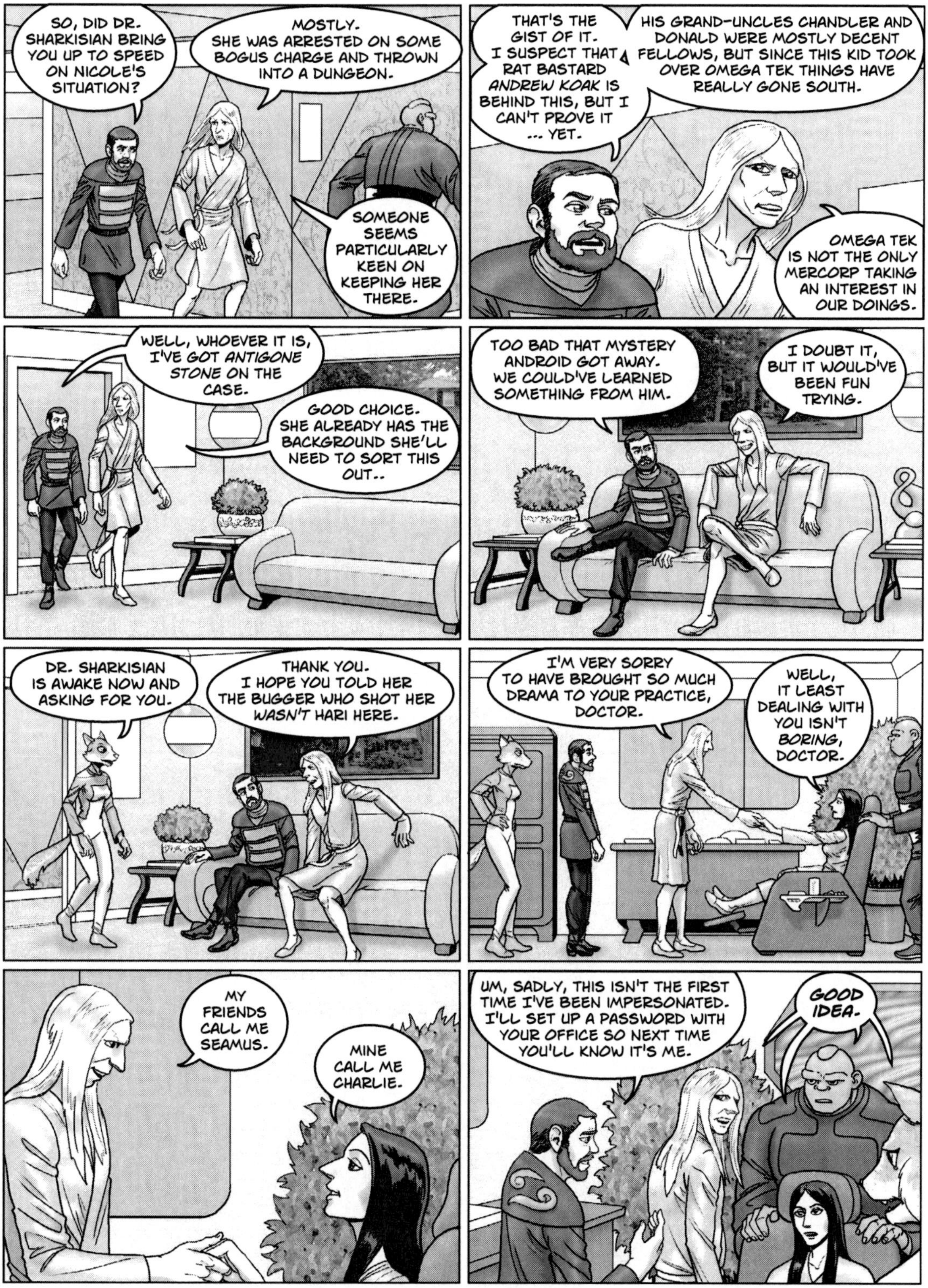
SO, DID DR. SHARKISIAN BRING YOU UP TO SPEED ON NICOLE'S SITUATION?
MOSTLY. SHE WAS ARRESTED ON SOME BOGUS CHARGE AND THROWN INTO A DUNGEON.
SOMEONE SEEMS PARTICULARLY KEEN ON KEEPING HER THERE.
THAT'S THE GIST OF IT. I SUSPECT THAT RAT BASTARD ANDREW KOAK IS BEHIND THIS, BUT I CAN'T PROVE IT ... YET.
HIS GRAND-UNCLES CHANDLER AND DONALD WERE MOSTLY DECENT FELLOWS, BUT SINCE THIS KID TOOK OVER OMEGA TEK THINGS HAVE REALLY GONE SOUTH.
OMEGA TEK IS NOT THE ONLY MERCORP TAKING AN INTEREST IN OUR DOINGS.
WELL, WHOEVER IT IS, I'VE GOT ANTIGONE STONE ON THE CASE.
GOOD CHOICE. SHE ALREADY HAS THE BACKGROUND SHE'LL NEED TO SORT THIS OUT..
TOO BAD THAT MYSTERY ANDROID GOT AWAY. WE COULD'VE LEARNED SOMETHING FROM HIM.
I DOUBT IT, BUT IT WOULD'VE BEEN FUN TRYING.
DR. SHARKISIAN IS AWAKE NOW AND ASKING FOR YOU.
THANK YOU. I HOPE YOU TOLD HER THE BUGGER WHO SHOT HER WASN'T HARI HERE.
I'M VERY SORRY TO HAVE BROUGHT SO MUCH DRAMA TO YOUR PRACTICE, DOCTOR.
WELL, IT LEAST DEALING WITH YOU ISN'T BORING, DOCTOR.
MY FRIENDS CALL ME SEAMUS.
MINE CALL ME CHARLIE.
UM, SADLY, THIS ISN'T THE FIRST TIME I'VE BEEN IMPERSONATED. I'LL SET UP A PASSWORD WITH YOUR OFFICE SO NEXT TIME YOU'LL KNOW IT'S ME.
GOOD IDEA.

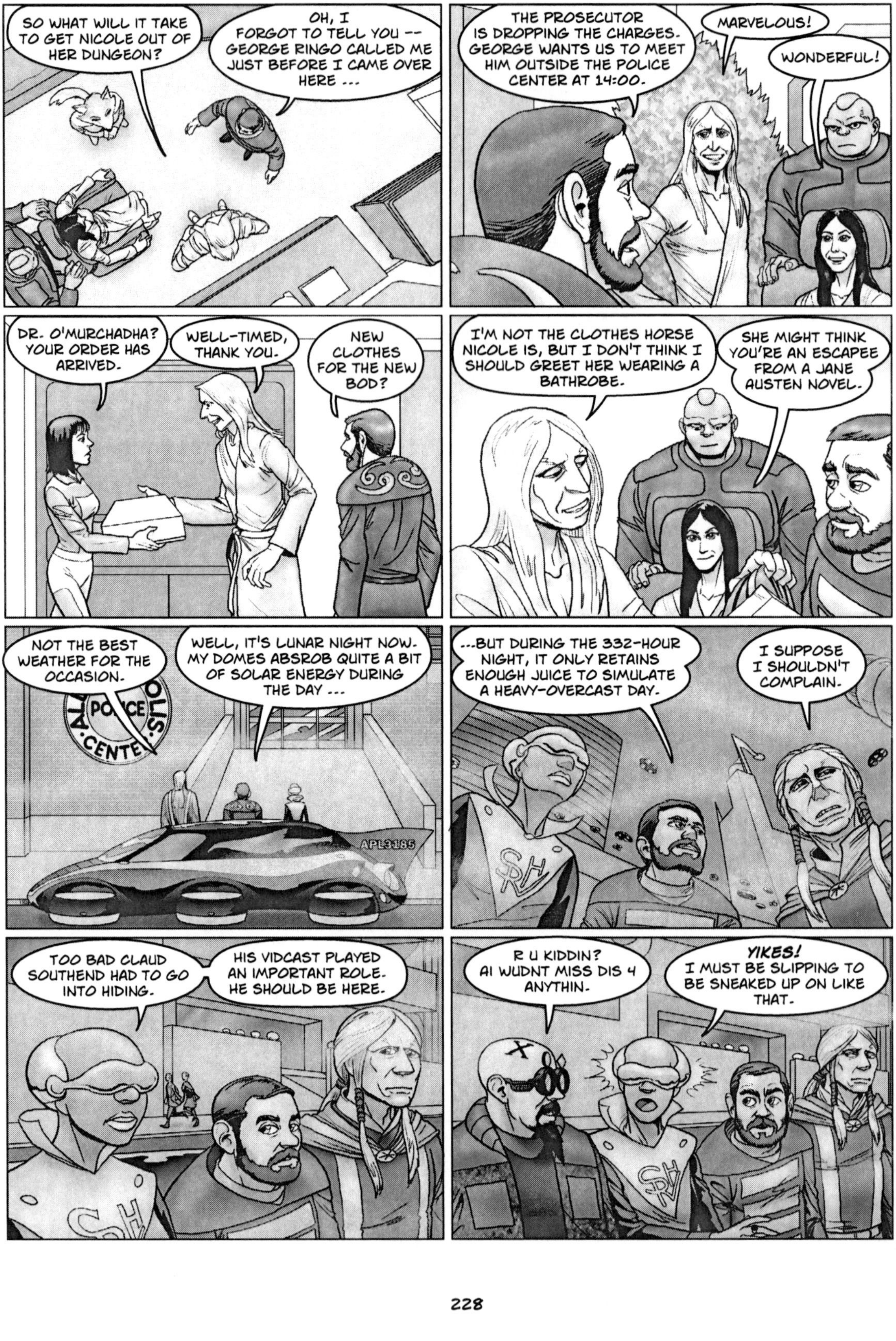
SO WHAT WILL IT TAKE TO GET NICOLE OUT OF HER DUNGEON?
OH, I FORGOT TO TELL YOU -- GEORGE RINGO CALLED ME JUST BEFORE I CAME OVER HERE ...
THE PROSECUTOR IS DROPPING THE CHARGES. GEORGE WANTS US TO MEET HIM OUTSIDE THE POLICE CENTER AT 14:00.
MARVELOUS!
WONDERFUL!
DR. O'MURCHADHA? YOUR ORDER HAS ARRIVED.
WELL-TIMED, THANK YOU.
NEW CLOTHES FOR THE NEW BOD?
I'M NOT THE CLOTHES HORSE NICOLE IS, BUT I DON'T THINK I SHOULD GREET HER WEARING A BATHROBE.
SHE MIGHT THINK YOU'RE AN ESCAPEE FROM A JANE AUSTEN NOVEL.
NOT THE BEST WEATHER FOR THE OCCASION.
WELL, IT'S LUNAR NIGHT NOW. MY DOMES ABSROB QUITE A BIT OF SOLAR ENERGY DURING THE DAY ...
POLICE
APL3185
...BUT DURING THE 332-HOUR NIGHT, IT ONLY RETAINS ENOUGH JUICE TO SIMULATE A HEAVY-OVERCAST DAY.
I SUPPOSE I SHOULDN'T COMPLAIN.
TOO BAD CLAUD SOUTHEND HAD TO GO INTO HIDING.
HIS VIDCAST PLAYED AN IMPORTANT ROLE. HE SHOULD BE HERE.
R U KIDDIN? AI WUDNT MISS DIS 4 ANYTHIN.
YIKES! I MUST BE SLIPPING TO BE SNEAKED UP ON LIKE THAT.

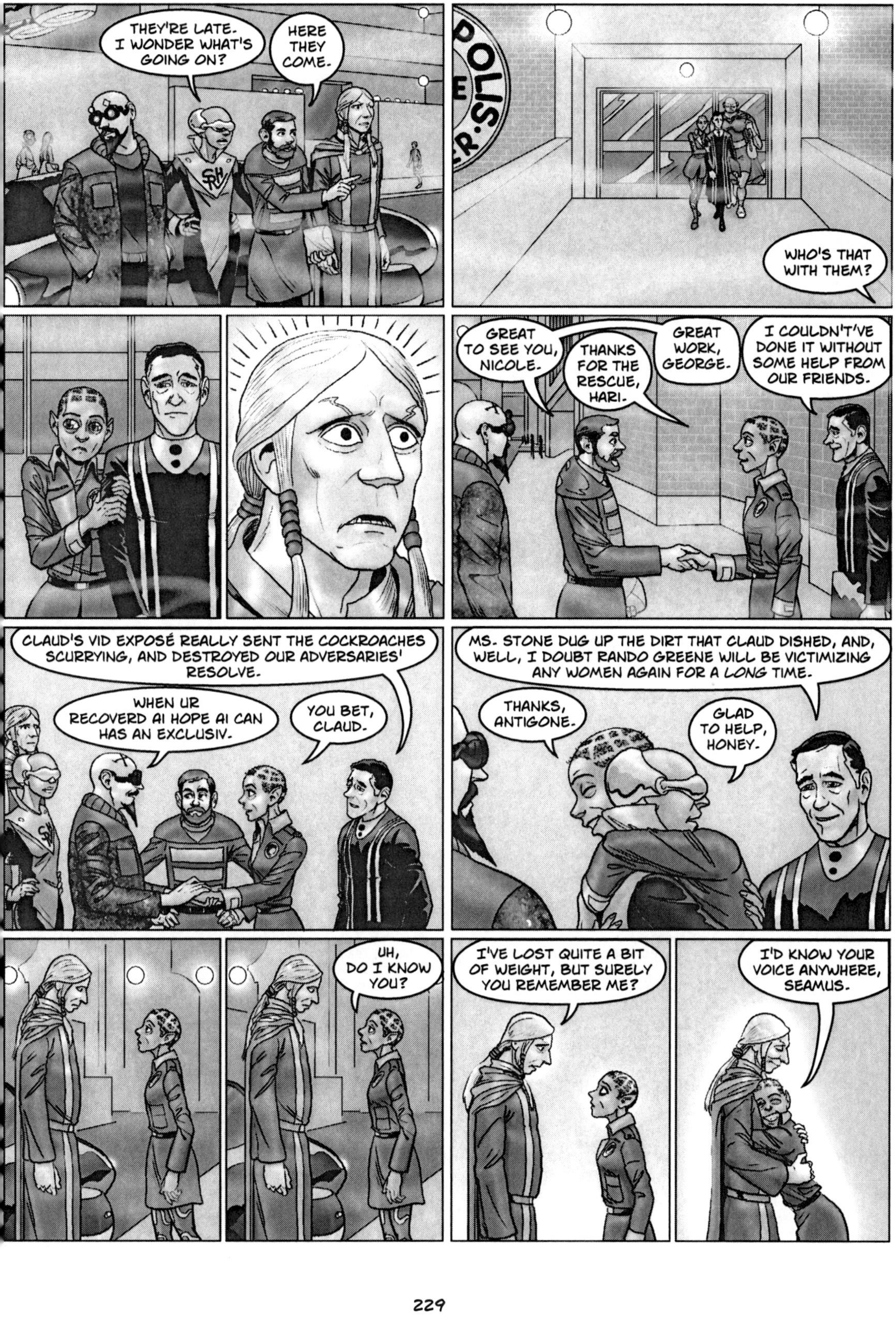
THEY'RE LATE. I WONDER WHAT'S GOING ON?
HERE THEY COME.
POLIS
WHO'S THAT WITH THEM?
GREAT TO SEE YOU, NICOLE.
THANKS FOR THE RESCUE, HARI.
GREAT WORK, GEORGE.
I COULDN'T'VE DONE IT WITHOUT SOME HELP FROM OUR FRIENDS.
CLAUD'S VID EXPOSÉ REALLY SENT THE COCKROACHES SCURRYING, AND DESTROYED OUR ADVERSARIES' RESOLVE.
WHEN UR RECOVERD AI HOPE AI CAN HAS AN EXCLUSIV.
YOU BET, CLAUD.
MS. STONE DUG UP THE DIRT THAT CLAUD DISHED, AND, WELL, I DOUBT RANDO GREENE WILL BE VICTIMIZING ANY WOMEN AGAIN FOR A LONG TIME.
THANKS, ANTIGONE.
GLAD TO HELP, HONEY.
UH, DO I KNOW YOU?
I'VE LOST QUITE A BIT OF WEIGHT, BUT SURELY YOU REMEMBER ME?
I'D KNOW YOUR VOICE ANYWHERE, SEAMUS.

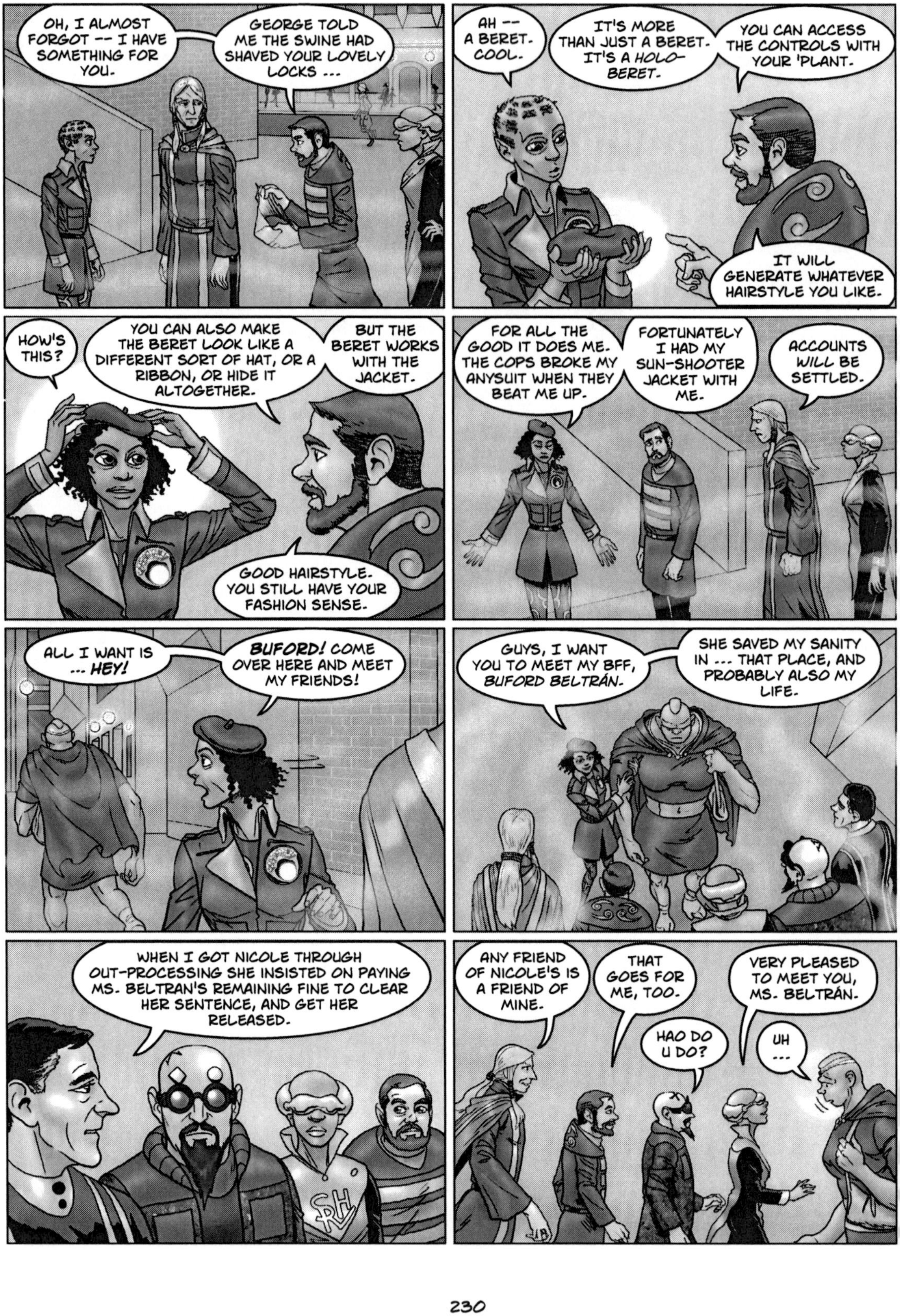
OH, I ALMOST FORGOT -- I HAVE SOMETHING FOR YOU.
GEORGE TOLD ME THE SWINE HAD SHAVED YOUR LOVELY LOCKS ...
AH -- A BERET. COOL.
IT'S MORE THAN JUST A BERET. IT'S A *HOLO-BERET.*
YOU CAN ACCESS THE CONTROLS WITH YOUR 'PLANT.
IT WILL GENERATE WHATEVER HAIRSTYLE YOU LIKE.
HOW'S THIS?
YOU CAN ALSO MAKE THE BERET LOOK LIKE A DIFFERENT SORT OF HAT, OR A RIBBON, OR HIDE IT ALTOGETHER.
BUT THE BERET WORKS WITH THE JACKET.
GOOD HAIRSTYLE. YOU STILL HAVE YOUR FASHION SENSE.
FOR ALL THE GOOD IT DOES ME. THE COPS BROKE MY ANYSUIT WHEN THEY BEAT ME UP.
FORTUNATELY I HAD MY SUN-SHOOTER JACKET WITH ME.
ACCOUNTS *WILL* BE SETTLED.
ALL I WANT IS ... ***HEY!***
BUFORD! COME OVER HERE AND MEET MY FRIENDS!
GUYS, I WANT YOU TO MEET MY BFF, *BUFORD BELTRÁN.*
SHE SAVED MY SANITY IN ... THAT PLACE, AND PROBABLY ALSO MY LIFE.
WHEN I GOT NICOLE THROUGH OUT-PROCESSING SHE INSISTED ON PAYING MS. BELTRAN'S REMAINING FINE TO CLEAR HER SENTENCE, AND GET HER RELEASED.
ANY FRIEND OF NICOLE'S IS A FRIEND OF MINE.
THAT GOES FOR ME, TOO.
HAO DO U DO?
VERY PLEASED TO MEET YOU, MS. BELTRÁN.
UH ...

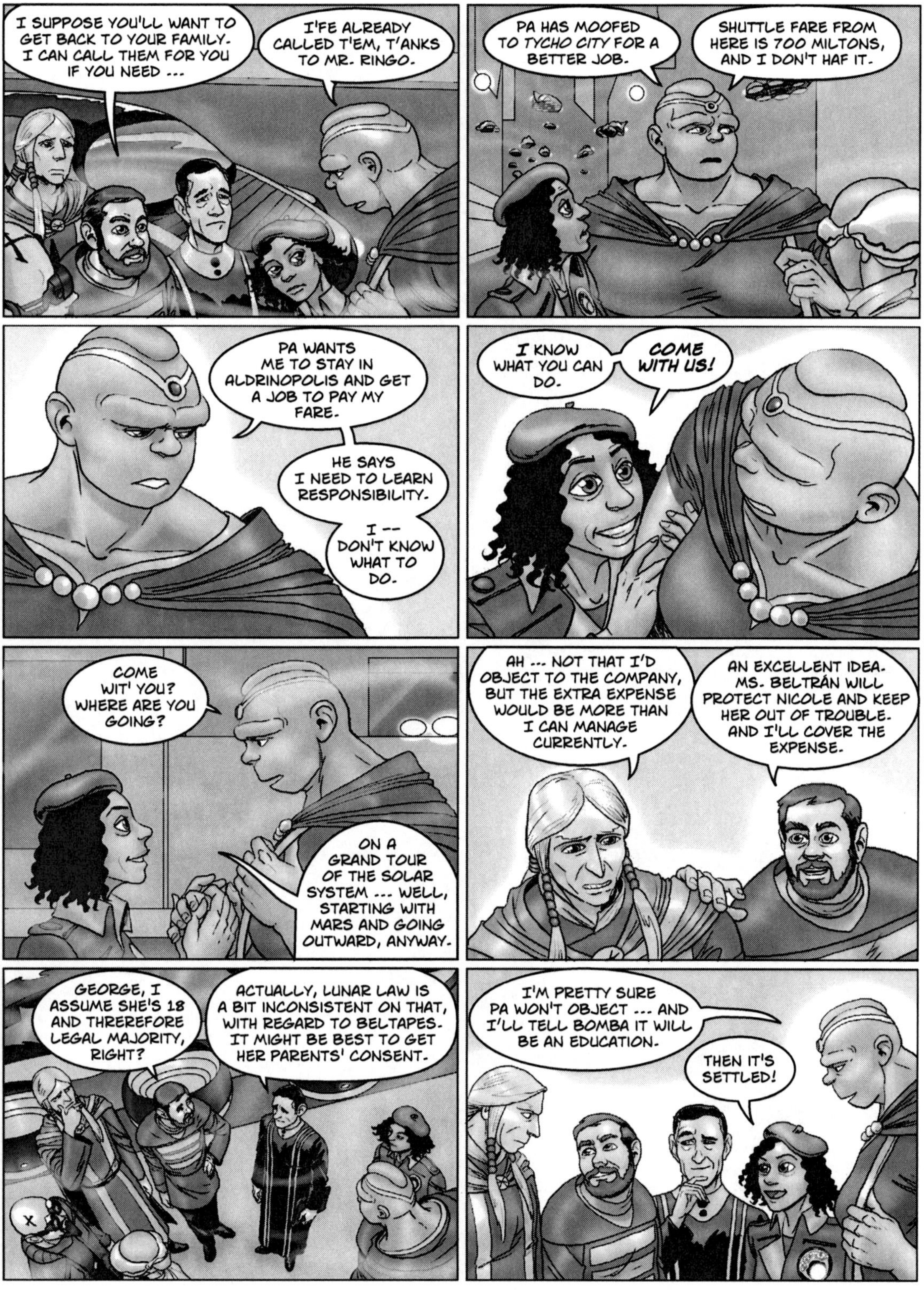
I SUPPOSE YOU'LL WANT TO GET BACK TO YOUR FAMILY. I CAN CALL THEM FOR YOU IF YOU NEED ...
I'FE ALREADY CALLED T'EM, T'ANKS TO MR. RINGO.
PA HAS MOOFED TO TYCHO CITY FOR A BETTER JOB.
SHUTTLE FARE FROM HERE IS 700 MILTONS, AND I DON'T HAF IT.
PA WANTS ME TO STAY IN ALDRINOPOLIS AND GET A JOB TO PAY MY FARE.
HE SAYS I NEED TO LEARN RESPONSIBILITY.
I -- DON'T KNOW WHAT TO DO.
I KNOW WHAT YOU CAN DO.
COME WITH US!
COME WIT' YOU? WHERE ARE YOU GOING?
ON A GRAND TOUR OF THE SOLAR SYSTEM ... WELL, STARTING WITH MARS AND GOING OUTWARD, ANYWAY.
AH ... NOT THAT I'D OBJECT TO THE COMPANY, BUT THE EXTRA EXPENSE WOULD BE MORE THAN I CAN MANAGE CURRENTLY.
AN EXCELLENT IDEA. MS. BELTRÁN WILL PROTECT NICOLE AND KEEP HER OUT OF TROUBLE. AND I'LL COVER THE EXPENSE.
GEORGE, I ASSUME SHE'S 18 AND THREREFORE LEGAL MAJORITY, RIGHT?
ACTUALLY, LUNAR LAW IS A BIT INCONSISTENT ON THAT, WITH REGARD TO BELTAPES. IT MIGHT BE BEST TO GET HER PARENTS' CONSENT.
I'M PRETTY SURE PA WON'T OBJECT ... AND I'LL TELL BOMBA IT WILL BE AN EDUCATION.
THEN IT'S SETTLED!

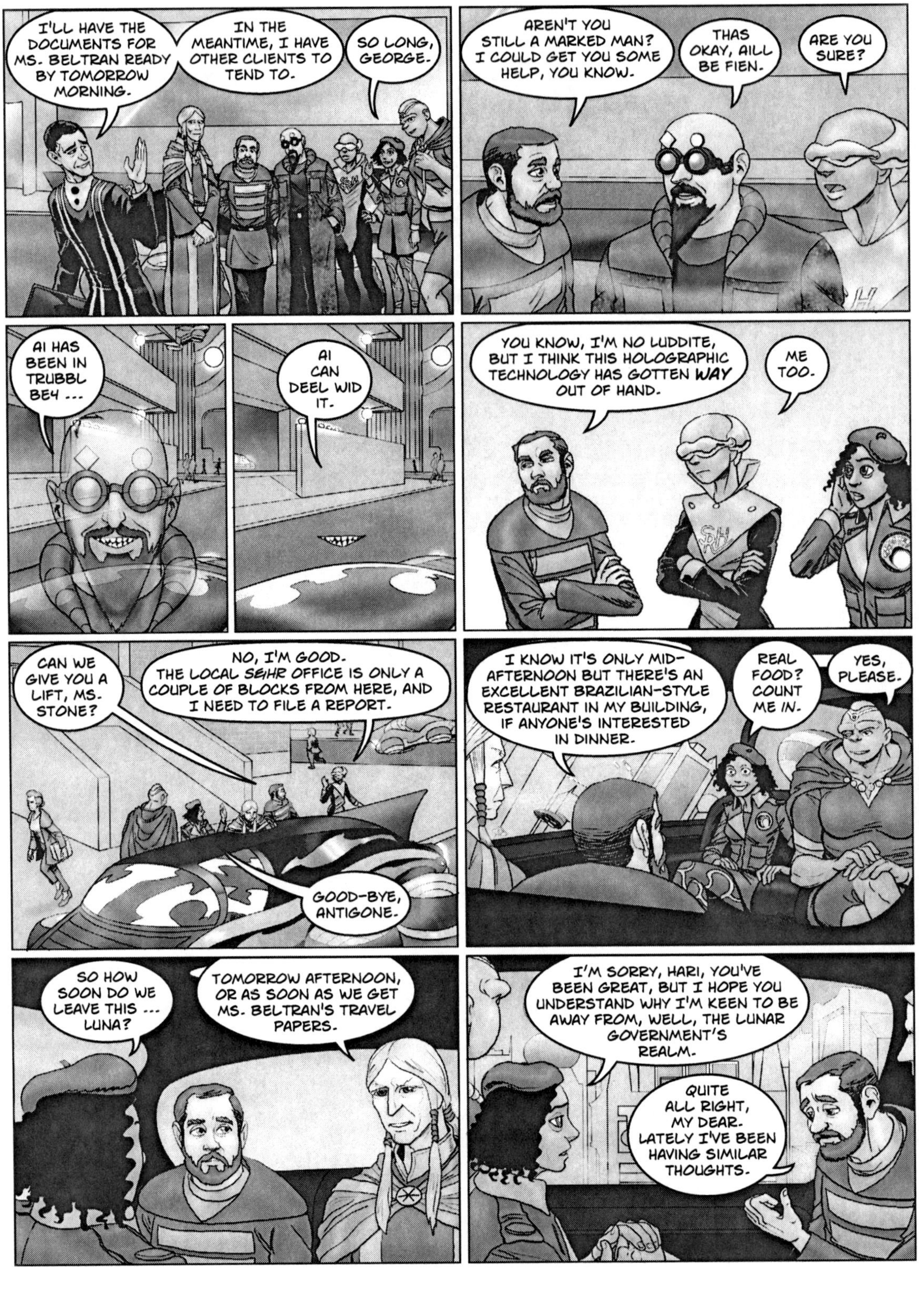
I'LL HAVE THE DOCUMENTS FOR MS. BELTRAN READY BY TOMORROW MORNING.
IN THE MEANTIME, I HAVE OTHER CLIENTS TO TEND TO.
SO LONG, GEORGE.
AREN'T YOU STILL A MARKED MAN? I COULD GET YOU SOME HELP, YOU KNOW.
THAS OKAY, AILL BE FIEN.
ARE YOU SURE?
AI HAS BEEN IN TRUBBL BEY ...
AI CAN DEEL WID IT.
YOU KNOW, I'M NO LUDDITE, BUT I THINK THIS HOLOGRAPHIC TECHNOLOGY HAS GOTTEN WAY OUT OF HAND.
ME TOO.
CAN WE GIVE YOU A LIFT, MS. STONE?
NO, I'M GOOD. THE LOCAL SEHR OFFICE IS ONLY A COUPLE OF BLOCKS FROM HERE, AND I NEED TO FILE A REPORT.
GOOD-BYE, ANTIGONE.
I KNOW IT'S ONLY MID-AFTERNOON BUT THERE'S AN EXCELLENT BRAZILIAN-STYLE RESTAURANT IN MY BUILDING, IF ANYONE'S INTERESTED IN DINNER.
REAL FOOD? COUNT ME IN.
YES, PLEASE.
SO HOW SOON DO WE LEAVE THIS ... LUNA?
TOMORROW AFTERNOON, OR AS SOON AS WE GET MS. BELTRAN'S TRAVEL PAPERS.
I'M SORRY, HARI, YOU'VE BEEN GREAT, BUT I HOPE YOU UNDERSTAND WHY I'M KEEN TO BE AWAY FROM, WELL, THE LUNAR GOVERNMENT'S REALM.
QUITE ALL RIGHT, MY DEAR. LATELY I'VE BEEN HAVING SIMILAR THOUGHTS.

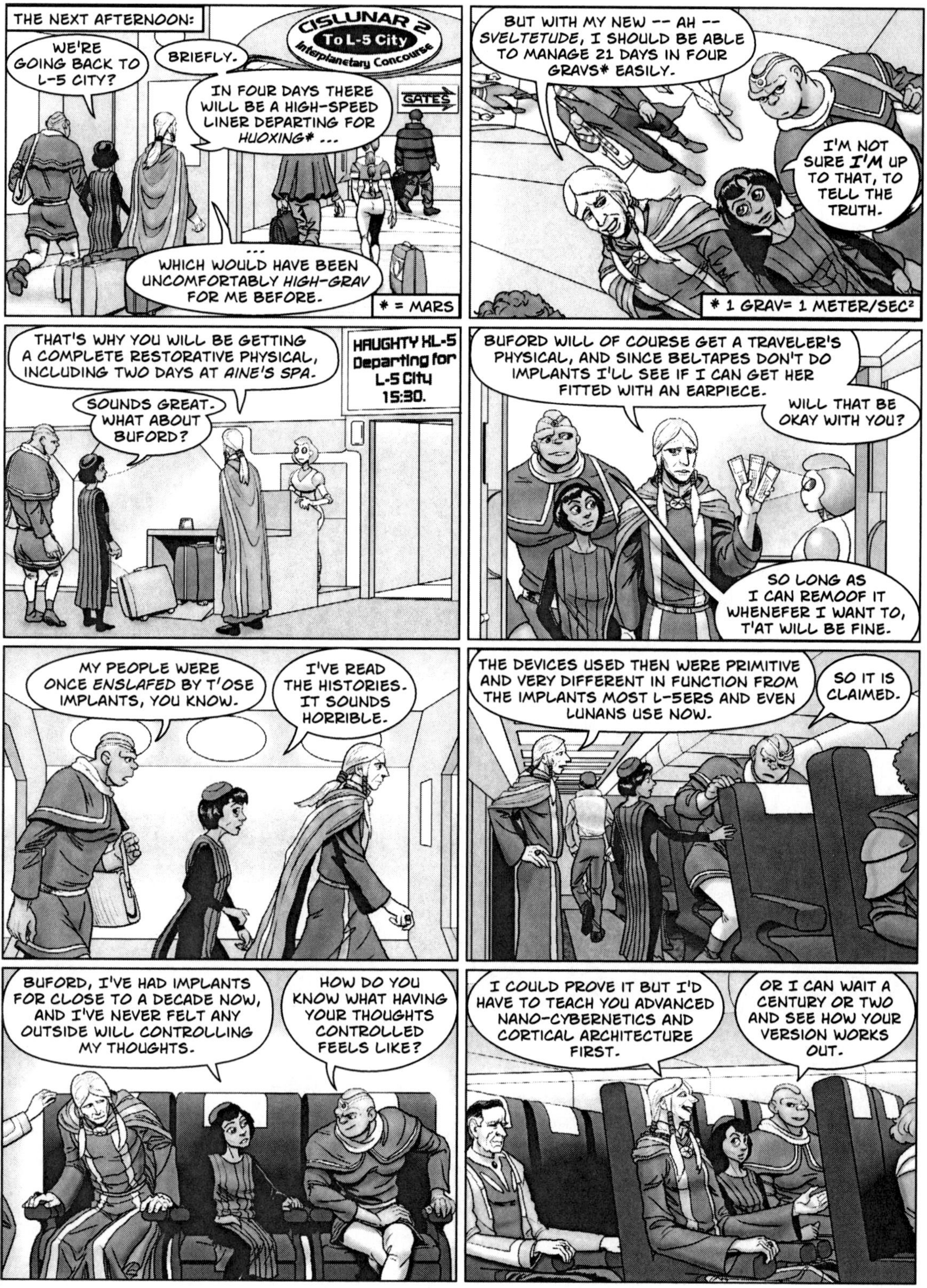
THE NEXT AFTERNOON:
WE'RE GOING BACK TO L-5 CITY?
BRIEFLY.
CISLUNAR 2
To L-5 City
Interplanetary Concourse
IN FOUR DAYS THERE WILL BE A HIGH-SPEED LINER DEPARTING FOR HUOXING* ...
GATES
... WHICH WOULD HAVE BEEN UNCOMFORTABLY HIGH-GRAV FOR ME BEFORE.
* = MARS
BUT WITH MY NEW -- AH -- SVELTETUDE, I SHOULD BE ABLE TO MANAGE 21 DAYS IN FOUR GRAVS* EASILY.
I'M NOT SURE I'M UP TO THAT, TO TELL THE TRUTH.
* 1 GRAV= 1 METER/SEC²
THAT'S WHY YOU WILL BE GETTING A COMPLETE RESTORATIVE PHYSICAL, INCLUDING TWO DAYS AT AINE'S SPA.
HAUGHTY XL-5 Departing for L-5 City 15:30.
SOUNDS GREAT. WHAT ABOUT BUFORD?
BUFORD WILL OF COURSE GET A TRAVELER'S PHYSICAL, AND SINCE BELTAPES DON'T DO IMPLANTS I'LL SEE IF I CAN GET HER FITTED WITH AN EARPIECE.
WILL THAT BE OKAY WITH YOU?
SO LONG AS I CAN REMOOF IT WHENEFER I WANT TO, T'AT WILL BE FINE.
MY PEOPLE WERE ONCE ENSLAFED BY T'OSE IMPLANTS, YOU KNOW.
I'VE READ THE HISTORIES. IT SOUNDS HORRIBLE.
THE DEVICES USED THEN WERE PRIMITIVE AND VERY DIFFERENT IN FUNCTION FROM THE IMPLANTS MOST L-5ERS AND EVEN LUNANS USE NOW.
SO IT IS CLAIMED.
BUFORD, I'VE HAD IMPLANTS FOR CLOSE TO A DECADE NOW, AND I'VE NEVER FELT ANY OUTSIDE WILL CONTROLLING MY THOUGHTS.
HOW DO YOU KNOW WHAT HAVING YOUR THOUGHTS CONTROLLED FEELS LIKE?
I COULD PROVE IT BUT I'D HAVE TO TEACH YOU ADVANCED NANO-CYBERNETICS AND CORTICAL ARCHITECTURE FIRST.
OR I CAN WAIT A CENTURY OR TWO AND SEE HOW YOUR VERSION WORKS OUT.

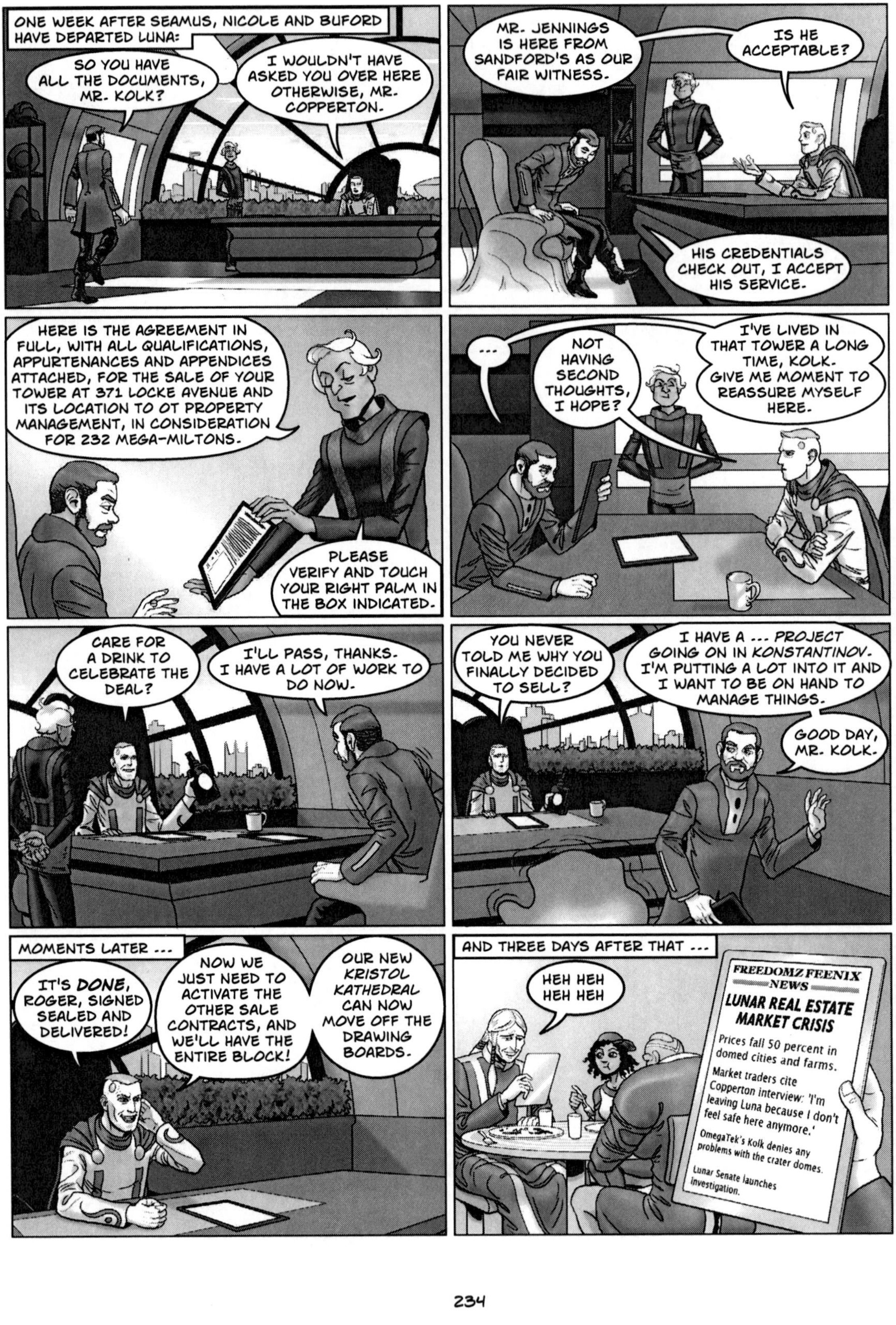
ONE WEEK AFTER SEAMUS, NICOLE AND BUFORD HAVE DEPARTED LUNA:
SO YOU HAVE ALL THE DOCUMENTS, MR. KOLK?
I WOULDN'T HAVE ASKED YOU OVER HERE OTHERWISE, MR. COPPERTON.
MR. JENNINGS IS HERE FROM SANDFORD'S AS OUR FAIR WITNESS.
IS HE ACCEPTABLE?
HIS CREDENTIALS CHECK OUT, I ACCEPT HIS SERVICE.
HERE IS THE AGREEMENT IN FULL, WITH ALL QUALIFICATIONS, APPURTENANCES AND APPENDICES ATTACHED, FOR THE SALE OF YOUR TOWER AT 371 LOCKE AVENUE AND ITS LOCATION TO OT PROPERTY MANAGEMENT, IN CONSIDERATION FOR 232 MEGA-MILTONS.
PLEASE VERIFY AND TOUCH YOUR RIGHT PALM IN THE BOX INDICATED.
...
NOT HAVING SECOND THOUGHTS, I HOPE?
I'VE LIVED IN THAT TOWER A LONG TIME, KOLK. GIVE ME MOMENT TO REASSURE MYSELF HERE.
CARE FOR A DRINK TO CELEBRATE THE DEAL?
I'LL PASS, THANKS. I HAVE A LOT OF WORK TO DO NOW.
YOU NEVER TOLD ME WHY YOU FINALLY DECIDED TO SELL?
I HAVE A ... PROJECT GOING ON IN KONSTANTINOV. I'M PUTTING A LOT INTO IT AND I WANT TO BE ON HAND TO MANAGE THINGS.
GOOD DAY, MR. KOLK.
MOMENTS LATER ...
IT'S DONE, ROGER, SIGNED SEALED AND DELIVERED!
NOW WE JUST NEED TO ACTIVATE THE OTHER SALE CONTRACTS, AND WE'LL HAVE THE ENTIRE BLOCK!
OUR NEW KRISTOL KATHEDRAL CAN NOW MOVE OFF THE DRAWING BOARDS.
AND THREE DAYS AFTER THAT ...
HEH HEH HEH HEH
FREEDOMZ FEENIX NEWS
LUNAR REAL ESTATE MARKET CRISIS
Prices fall 50 percent in domed cities and farms.
Market traders cite Copperton interview: 'I'm leaving Luna because I don't feel safe here anymore.'
OmegaTek's Kolk denies any problems with the crater domes.
Lunar Senate launches investigation.

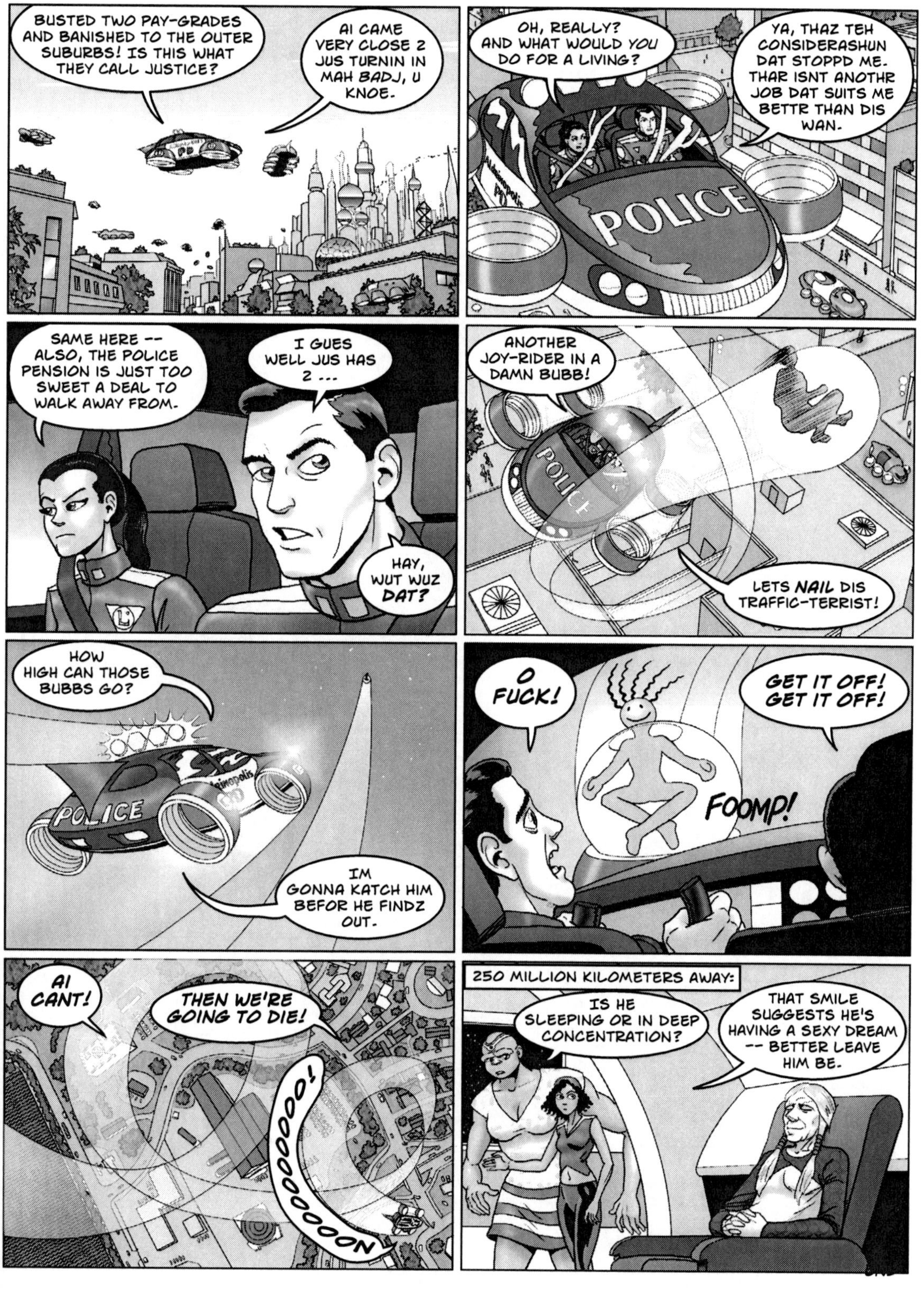
BUSTED TWO PAY-GRADES AND BANISHED TO THE OUTER SUBURBS! IS THIS WHAT THEY CALL JUSTICE?
AI CAME VERY CLOSE 2 JUS TURNIN IN MAH BADJ, U KNOE.
OH, REALLY? AND WHAT WOULD YOU DO FOR A LIVING?
YA, THAZ TEH CONSIDERASHUN DAT STOPPD ME. THAR ISNT ANOTHR JOB DAT SUITS ME BETTR THAN DIS WAN.
POLICE
SAME HERE -- ALSO, THE POLICE PENSION IS JUST TOO SWEET A DEAL TO WALK AWAY FROM.
I GUES WELL JUS HAS 2 ...
HAY, WUT WUZ DAT?
ANOTHER JOY-RIDER IN A DAMN BUBB!
POLICE
LETS NAIL DIS TRAFFIC-TERRIST!
HOW HIGH CAN THOSE BUBBS GO?
POLICE
IM GONNA KATCH HIM BEFOR HE FINDZ OUT.
O FUCK!
GET IT OFF! GET IT OFF!
FOOMP!
AI CANT!
THEN WE'RE GOING TO DIE!
NOOOOOOOOOOOOOO!
250 MILLION KILOMETERS AWAY:
IS HE SLEEPING OR IN DEEP CONCENTRATION?
THAT SMILE SUGGESTS HE'S HAVING A SEXY DREAM -- BETTER LEAVE HIM BE.

APPENDIX:

THESE ARE THE 'MOTIVATIONAL POSTERS' VISIBLE IN THE ALDRINOPOLIS JAIL RECREATION ROOM.

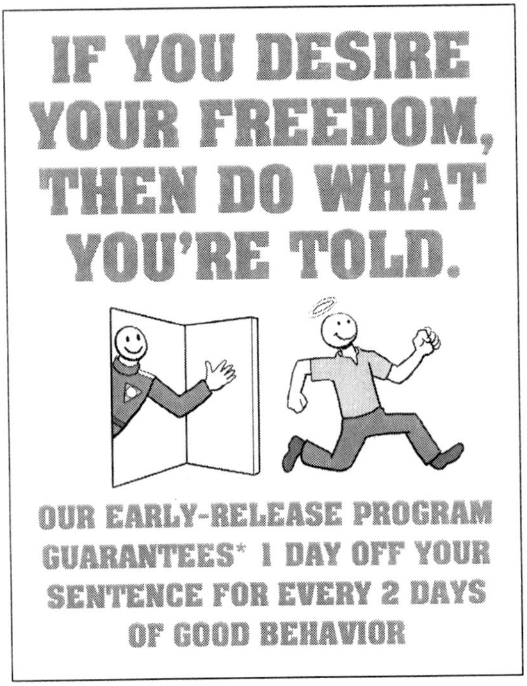
IF YOU DESIRE YOUR FREEDOM, THEN DO WHAT YOU'RE TOLD.
OUR EARLY-RELEASE PROGRAM GUARANTEES* 1 DAY OFF YOUR SENTENCE FOR EVERY 2 DAYS OF GOOD BEHAVIOR

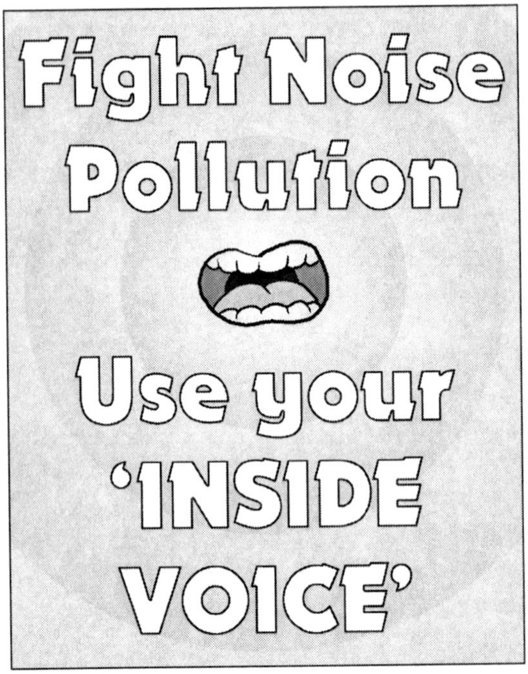
Fight Noise Pollution
Use your 'INSIDE VOICE'

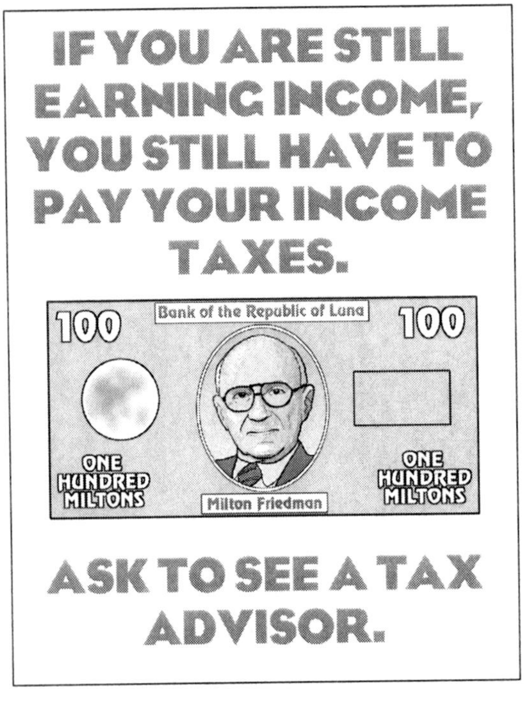
IF YOU ARE STILL EARNING INCOME, YOU STILL HAVE TO PAY YOUR INCOME TAXES.
100
Bank of the Republic of Luna
100
ONE HUNDRED MILTONS
Milton Friedman
ONE HUNDRED MILTONS
ASK TO SEE A TAX ADVISOR.

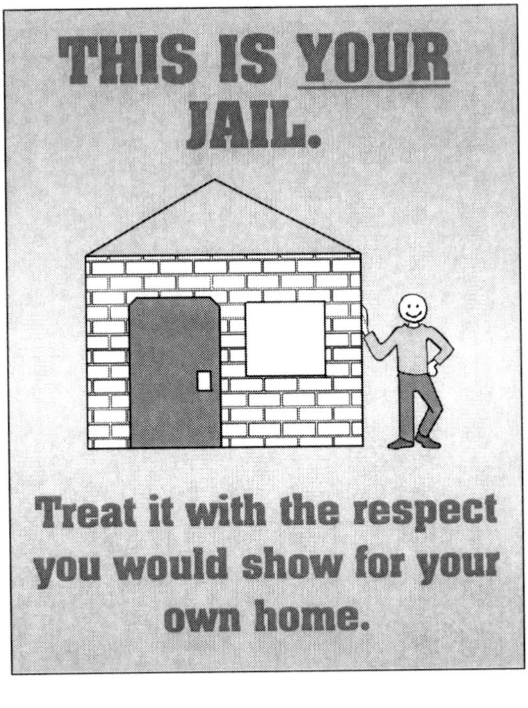
THIS IS YOUR JAIL.
Treat it with the respect you would show for your own home.

About the Creators

Scott Bieser was born in a log cabin on the Sea of Tranquility in year 135 of the Space Age ...

No, not really.

Scott's illustration and commercial art career spans more than three decades, from street-party caricatures to textbook illustration to poster design to computer game animation and most recently to producing graphic novels and web-comics.

"Quantum Vibe comes out of nearly a ten years of planning, plotting, designing, re-purposing, re-designing, and even more plotting, during whatever time I could find while working on other projects," Scott explained. "It's a dream project and I'm grateful to my brother Frank Bieser for founding Big Head Press and giving me this chance to pursue this dream."

Sean "Zeke" Bieser is a SoCal-born, up-and-coming student artist who draws inspiration from video gaming both new (Metal Gear Solid) and old (MegaMan), comics both mainstream (Marvel and DC) and independent (Scott Pilgrim), animation both local (Adventure Time) and foreign (Studio Ghibli), and has a passion for story writing that compels readers to love and relate to fictional characters, and consider the real world in a thoughtful new light.

"I feel like I've grown really close to Seamus' gang along their journey," Zeke says. "It's always a treat to get to see what happens next a little earlier than the readers when I'm coloring the pages before they're released online. Dad sometimes shares and discusses with me the story and where it will go, and it continues to get deeper and more exciting with every new turn of events."

Zeke is honored to be a part of this interplanetary quest, and he himself hopes in the near future to write and draw his own comic and share a brand new story with the world.

Other thoughtful stories from BIG HEAD PRESS

A Drug War Carol by Susan W. Wells and Scott Bieser. 2003. Drug Czar Scrooge McCzar confronts four ghosts who seek to enlighten him. ISBN: 0-9743814-0-3

The Probability Broach: The Graphic Novel by L. Neil Smith and Scott Bieser. 2004. Adapted from Smith's classic 1980 work of prose science-fiction. ISBN: 0-9743814-1-1

The Architect by Mike Baron and Andie Tong. 2007. Young architect Gil Hopper inherits a mansion formerly owned by a notorious and vengeance-driven practicioner of dark arts.
ISBN: 978-0-9743814-4-2

Roswell, Texas by L. Neil Smith, Rex F. May, Scott Bieser and Jen Zach.
2008. In an altnernative 1947, a flying saucer crash-lands in a far-western region of the Federated States of Texas. Texican President Charles A. Lindberg Jr. sends his best Rangers to investigate.
ISBN: 978-0-9743814-5-9

La Muse by Adisakdi Tantimedh and Hugo Petrus. 2008. Two beautiful sisters, the children of omnipotent aliens, attempt to save the world but find that first they must save themselves.
ISBN: 978-0-9743814-6-6

Odysseus The Rebel by Steven Grant and Scott Bieser. 2009. A revisionist take on the classic Greek adventure: this is an Odysseus who never gives up his defiance of the gods. ISBN: 978-0-9743814-2-8

TimePeeper by L. Neil Smith and Sherard Jackson. 2009. Three teen-aged friends from the future must travel back to 2005 to cover up their own larceny, and learn amazing secrets about their own pasts. Available as a Kindle e-book from Amazon.com. ASIN: B002G9UHHE

ESCAPE FROM TERRA Volume 1 by Sandy Sandfort, Scott Bieser and LEE OAKS! 2010. Near the dawn of the 22nd Century, intrepid space pioneers in the Asteroid Belt seek their fortunes and defend their liberty against the grasping world government of Earth. ISBN: 978-0-9743814-7-3

Phoebus Krumm by L. Neil Smith and Scott Bieser. 2011. When a rival interstellar empire threatens to upset the galactic balance of power, retired space-pirate Phoebus Krumm is enticed into service for the Hannoverian Monopolity to seek out and destroy a deadly new weapon -- and also to learn the fate of his old friend, the notorious Henry Martyn. ISBN: 978-0-9743814-8-0

ESCAPE FROM TERRA Volume 2 by Sandy Sandfort, Scott Bieser and LEE OAKS! 2011. The Intrepid Belter colonists' story continues, featuring Fiorella and Captain Doris, the Brothers Guzmán, "Little Babbette," and a host of new characters. ISBN 978-0-9743814-3-5

ESCAPE FROM TERRA Volume 3 by Sandy Sandfort, Scott Bieser and LEE OAKS! 2012. When two of Ceres' leading citizens fall in love, they get rejuvenated and embark on an interplanetary honeymoon that may be more than they bargained for. Also: Space Scouts, a Neanderthal girl, and how the International Space Station was stolen! ISBN: 978-0-9743814-9-7

CPSIA information can be obtained at www.ICGtesting.com
Printed in the USA
LVOW10s1602050215

425855LV00011B/201/P

9 780985 316747